Where Pademelons Play

Where Pademelons Play

A presentation

TERRY DEAGUE

Cover design by Andrea Ucini

Typeset by BookPOD

Cataloguing-in-Publication entry is available
from the National Library of Australia
http://catalogue.nla.gov.au

ISBN: 978-0-6484287-0-1 (paperback)

eISBN: 978-0-6484287-1-8 (ebook)

Contents

pademelon *noun.*
[ORIGIN Prob. alt. of Dharuk *badimaliyan* wallaby or
badagarang eastern grey kangaroo.]
Any of several small brush wallabies, *esp.* one of the genus
Thylogale.

I

Proscenium Arch

It's absurd, says Sticks, to include your own birth in an autobiography.

Why? asks Harry.

Because nobody I know actually remembers the moment of their birth.

Irrelevant, says Harry.

Subjectively, your life starts with your first memory, says Sticks, and that is *never* your birth moment.

I know one of a set of triplets, says Sonia. He says his first memory is of being in a very crowded place.

Matt touches her hand gently, and flashes her an ironic smile.

Why be subjective? asks Harry. I believe if you do your own life story it should start at its objective beginning and finish at its objective end.

Are you going to do your own death, boyo? asks Matt.

Yes, says Harry.

Nyevozmózhna![1] says Elena. Death must choose its *own* moment.

II

Cut. Cut. Cut. For the sake of my gormless granny's galloping goitre, cut.

Scotty, what sort of fool technical support do I have here? This segment's not due to make an appearance till the cows come home.

… shall no one rid me of this troublesome crew? …

Scotty. I know, by general consent and through no fault of your own, you are a shingle short of a roof. But do you think you can possibly contrive to put things into reverse?

You've got it! Rewind. That's the ticket. Back. Back. Back. Back. Back. When you get to the big bang, you'll

---

1   *nyevozmózhna!*: impossible!

know you've gone too far.

OK you say?

Fine. Then beam me up Scotty.

Yes. Me live. Me alone. I'm doing this segment live and solo. That's the freaking plan, the whole freaking plan, and nothing but the freaking plan.

Cue me in. One, two, three …

… oops! …

<< 1st Unit

Listen up, pademelons.

Open your eyes. Engage all your senses. All. Because mine is to be an omni-sensual presentation, in conformity with the received house-style. The subject of my presentation is: the life and many deaths of Harry McMinn, nerd. Obsessed he may have been with the theatrical realization of *his* many deaths, but it was *my* life – my one and only *earthly* life – that was lost through his agency. Perhaps you can understand then why I might have a special interest – both intense and abiding – in the subject of this presentation.

What is to be my methodology? Will it be simply to start with Harry's birth and keep on chugging like a dogged freight train along the tracks of a more-or-less undeviating time line? Yes, up to a point, but with one important modification. You see, pademelons, Harry – having only recently turned forty – decided that he – in his vanity – would very much like to tell his *own* story, in the medium of *his* choice. Specifically: in the medium of live theatre, a medium to which Harry was to bring his own inimitable style.

So who am I – lazy by inclination – to disregard such a valuable and ready-made resource? I shall retain Harry and his team as my unwitting second unit. We – that's you and I, paddies – shall then make frequent excursions forward in time to those most fruitful moments, moments of raw creativity, moments catching Harry in the thrall of presenting the story of his very own life and many deaths. In between such excursions, I promise to fall back to that (more-or-less) undeviating time line and, having once regained it, to continue chugging doggedly along it. My role in these episodes of dogged chuggery will be to maintain continuity, to clarify where I feel clarification is necessary, and to fill in the gaps – of which there *are* a few – as gaps arise. Rest assured, paddies, I shall maintain a grip on the role of director of the *first* unit akin to that of an attack-dog with attitude.

It will not have escaped your attention that – albeit in a rhetorical context – I asked the question, Who am I?, and I suspect you might want to know my answer to this question. The answer is pending and shall be revealed. Preserve yourselves in patience.

You will also have noticed I refer to you as 'pademelons'. This is not meant to be anything more nor less than a term of endearment, and I trust it shall be accepted by you in such spirit. I certainly do *not* mean to imply any kind of shape-shift on your part. It would be perfectly ridiculous, of course, for anybody – me included – to seriously suggest – or even to allow the thought to graze the threshold of their mind – that any of you show any real likeness – anatomically or cognitively – to a pademelon. No more likeness, anyway, than has any other representative of our exalted species, past or present.

Let me say – in defence, should defence be necessary – these cute and furry ground-hoppers and grass-eaters were part of my daily life when I once trod my little patch of earth overlooking the beautiful d'Entrecasteaux Channel. The little darlings were endemic there, and I grew to love them. It's not hard to grow to love them and – in similar fashion – I have grown to love you, my latter-day pademelons.

The land of my tender years is not altogether God's own country, as some would have it. Its essence has been encapsulated vividly in song by a former acquaintance of mine in the sublunary world, one Ronald Dash by name, whom you shall have the privilege to meet face to face later in my presentation. I offer you his rendition:

Oh, give me a home[2]
where the thylacene roam,
and the dear little p-melons play,
where devils sport sores
on their cancerous jaws,
and blackfellers push up the hay.

As it turns out, I left this dubious Eden, aged in my late teens, drawn by the big smoke like so many others before and after me. I forded the ditch and found the smoke, and plenty of fire too.

But this is a digression.

Re my presentation: there are partners in an exercise of this kind, and they can be classified as first, second, and third persons. Let's take them in reverse order. In third person, we have Harry and his various friends and associates, both with and without benefits. In second person, we have you, pademelons, my indispensable audience. And first person is the mysterious one-and-only and yet-to-be-revealed 'I', beloved of storytellers since the dawn of Neolithic times.

Let's proceed.

>

Harry was born Henry Athol McMinn, sired by the seldom-seen Michael Conaught McMinn out of the lovely Brenda Rose McMinn, nee Bailey. It was the early 70s, and the Vietnam War

---

2 'Home' is Tasmania. 'Thylacene' is the (almost certainly extinct) Tasmanian tiger. 'Devil' is the Tasmanian Devil, an indigenous species of mammal under threat because of a transmissible (species-specific) cancer affecting its jaw. 'Blackfellers push up the hay' is a reference to the genocidal colonization of Tasmania by white settlers.

was entering its more apocalyptic phase when the young couple – coming down with a serious case of brick-veneerial disease – settled for a mortgage on a dream home whose façade consisted of identical cuboids of cream-coloured baked clay, a.k.a. house bricks. Their dwelling was in an unremarkable bayside suburb. Specifically, it was in the character-deprived Bee Street: a long, straight, flat thoroughfare boasting predatory speed bumps and mangy oleanders. A street where the houses were – as if the macro must imitate the micro – identical cream-coloured cuboids.

Harry was the firstborn, heir to the benefits supposedly attached to such temporal pre-eminence in the family tree. The birth went smoothly enough. The accidents of Harry's birth included a mother, a father (when present), a dream home, and a neighbourhood. Nurtured haphazardly by these humble beginnings, and helped along by a modicum of natural luck, Harry was able – against the odds – to collar his future and wrestle it to the ground.

The process did not work out so well for those in Harry's immediate orbit. He failed for the most part to take these people with him on his propitious journey. You may ask why, and I shall be glad to tell you. It was not – in my opinion – through any malice on Harry's part that he happened to let his friends fall by the wayside like so much unwanted baggage. Rather – I am inclined to believe – it was the upshot of his innocent predilection to narcissism combined with a congenital inability to adequately empathize. Or, to use that single simple word so beloved of all chiding mothers of children: he was 'thoughtless'.

For some, the consequences of Harry's unfortunate disposition were benign, for others, they were dire, and for most they fell somewhere in between. My case belonged without question in the 'dire' category. Being disabused of one's mortal coil must certainly be at the pointy end of dire, the very worst of it all being one's collateral severance from people and things one once loved, and loved moreover with such brief bright intensity.

This I regret.

I fear I am getting way ahead of myself. Harry, forty years or so down the track – in a future decade, a future century, a future millennium – is willing and able to tell his *own* story of his birth and beyond, and – in accordance with the methodology I myself have proposed – I should let him do so forthwith. Consequently, I shall pass the baton. I'm sure Harry will gladly accept it. Pademelons, are you ready to make your inaugural excursion into the future?

There has been change. Harry has developed from homunculus to fully-grown hulk of human protoplasm. The cream brick suburb where Harry was raised – but no longer lives – has gone upmarket. The brick veneerial disease has run its course, and has been replaced by an epidemic of security-alarmed pre-stressed concrete fortresses. Bee Street itself is under consideration for massive condo development. Vietnam is a tourist destination.

Don't fret, dearest pademelons. While Harry is doing his thespian bit, I shall be right there by your side to pass both sympathetic and critical comment on proceedings, and to threadneedle you through the bright footlights, the tawdry tinsel, the declamations, and the melodrama. Harry may be calling the shots but I shall be available at all times, my paddies, to hold your little furry paws whenever we make these forays into 21st century amateur dramatics.

Over to you, Harry. Your turn. Put your best foot forward. And – threat or promise? – be assured, bane of my life though you may once have been, my unseen and unheard presence shall at all times be within spitting distance of you.

… but, Harry, why do I bother addressing myself to you? As I had remarked in the very same breath, you are unable to hear me …

2nd Unit >>

Here he is.

Focus your attention on him, pademelons. What is it you see?

Is it the large brown eyes like olive slices? Is it the dense dark eyebrows resembling frowns in hairy guise? Is it his undulating mouse-brown locks he (clearly) is in the habit of attacking neurotically in a vain attempt to smooth out those unwanted kinks? Is it the thin solemn face which, south of the prominent equatorial ears, narrows to an abrupt pointy peninsula? Is it the plumpish cheeks beneath which lies the faint suggestion he was at one time a drawn and callow stripling with prominent facial bones?

Given his more than average height, it is easy to imagine he was indeed a beanpole in his youth, and that prosperity has fleshed him out. Yet he has retained some of his youthful gawkiness and the ungainly gait deriving from uncoordinated motor responses. Competitive athletics and team sports – we can imagine – would be a foreign country to him. But if the call were to go out for someone to stand still and plug the leaking dyke with a finger, Harry would be the ticket.

Watch him, pademelons, as – carrying his skin with him as all mortals must – he enters the Sleek Street amateur theatrical precincts and penetrates its *sanctum sanctorum*, i.e. its performance arena. Here he is both protagonist in and presenter of the theatrical events we are about to enjoy.

The stall seats are empty and house lights are full up, so Harry has lots of choice and the illumination by which to find it. He chooses a row near the back of the stalls and then seeks out seat number seventeen. He has his reasons for preferring this seat number. His crew are very familiar with his 'seventeen' fetish.

His seat is comfortable. Like all seats in the theatre, it is in the old-fashioned style whereby the seat cushion swivels back with a hefty clunk when vacated. It is deep royal green in colour, and nicely plumped out.

Three aisles lead down steps from the back of the stalls to stage. They are carpeted – as is indeed the entire house and front-of-house floor – in a cheap and well-worn synthetic fabric, whose background colour is an anaemic blood-red. Superimposed on this unremarkable background is a repeating motif of river pebbles: flat, stone-grey, and water-worn. Consequently, the steps have the appearance of cascades in a busy downhill stream, though what could be bleeding upstream is anybody's guess. Harry has often felt uncomfortable on these steps, not so much because of the suggestion of blood, but because of the illusion invariably invading his mind of the stones slipping and moving beneath his untutored feet.

Seated, at leisure, and free from this illusion for the moment, he nevertheless has an issue with the stage curtains. Every time he sees them, as he is doing right now, he finds himself thoroughly bemused by them. They are in shades, principally, of a bland beige and a plummy red. They accommodate an absurd repeating pattern consisting of what could pass for a Middle Eastern man – though Harry would contend he is South East Asian – in a black songkok and long loose-fitting white kaftan, leading by rope an animal that to all appearances is a cross between a leopard and a giraffe.

Harry's bemused state has nothing to do with the hybrid animal, although the capacity of such a creature to bemuse could hardly be denied. The problem is the man in the songkok. The very first time Harry saw that vignette on the curtain, a deep sense of *déjà vu* welled up inside him, and it has welled up inside him every time he has set eyes on it since. Regrettably for Harry, I've no doubt it will continue to well up inside him every time henceforth he chances to see it. For Harry, these sightings are flashbacks to experiences of the not so distant past and a reminder of his worst premonitions for the not so distant future. A rolled-gold link between yesterday, today, and tomorrow. Harry is certain the man is … well, to be absolutely precise, Malaysian.

The curtains have been drawn back to reveal a well trod proscenium-arch stage. All of you will know the function of such a stage according to classical tradition. Harry has made some significant modifications that some of you may regard as a capricious subjugation of this function. He has enclosed almost the entire stage-front view in a large silver rectangular border approximately in the ratio 16:9 which, as all savvy citizens of the world would know, happens to be the ratio of most modern television screens. Writ large, that is what the precinct of the main stage looks like and is intended to look like.

There is, as you might expect, a drop of about one metre from stage to stalls. The top fifteen to twenty centimetres – say – of this drop, located just over the lip of the stage, has been excised by the large silver border and painted black. This black strip, as a consequence, lies in reserve as part of the putative television viewing area. Reserved for what? you might ask. Pademelons, you have two choices at this juncture: you can either engage the imaginings of your macropod minds or hang about nibbling wet grass while you wait and see.

Positioned in each corner of the silver border are *actual* CCTV flat screens. They are large: of sufficient size that any person seated right at the back of the stalls would nevertheless be able to see adequate detail on them. Currently, all four of these screens are blank. Nor is there anything on stage except for bare boards and cockroaches.

Beyond the folds of drawn curtain on each side of the stage are – as is common in older theatres like this one – small exposed wings. Each of these wings has its own silver border. They too are intended to look like television screens, albeit smaller than the main one. They are suggestive of two islands that have drifted away tectonically from their parent land mass.

Have you been counting, pademelons? I make that seven TV

screens in all, both the real ones and the pretend ones. What – I find myself wondering – is the collective noun for TV screens: a school, a pride, a gaggle? More seriously, why is Harry so determined to make everything appear as if it is happening on screen? Why take a perfectly adequate theatrical stage and subvert its purpose with mock idiot boxes?

I shall endeavour to give you my personal take on this matter. Doubtless, you have heard the proud boast, 'as seen on TV'. In line with this, Harry has become enamoured of the view that events are invariably ennobled by television. It follows – in *his* mind – that any event worth enacting should be afforded due respect by edging it in an essential oblong. How did Harry come to form this extraordinary view? Pademelons, can I ask you once again to take a rain check on that? For the moment, will you please defer to Harry's determination to have things this way?

I would like to introduce you to Isadore Fauntleroy Gillespie. Izzie, as he is mostly known, is seated behind his music synthesizer, installed more-or-less permanently on the left hand wing. He is hunched over its keyboard, his nuggetty frame heaving sympathetically, doing what he loves doing: improvising. He is playing about with a bass melody: repetitive, with a steady boogie rhythm, in 4/4 time and a minor key. The visible parts of Izzie are his amber cravat and his bright lemon-green jacket. That's the other thing Izzie loves doing: dressing to fit the bill. In recent years he has become – to some degree – an image person, a fashion tramp.

I almost forgot to mention it. Izzie's other notable feature is his shaved head which inevitably accentuates his impressible moon face. What do you think, pademelons? Is a shaved head really consistent with the image a committed muso might feel compelled to project? Peter Garrett[3], I hear you say? A single example proves nothing.

---

3   Peter Garrett: former leader of a popular Australian rock group ('Midnight Oil'), turned federal politician for a time.

I should perhaps tell you that Harry and Izzie were contemporaries at secondary school and, at the time, had had a significant influence on each other. In fact, they found religion together. When that miserable affliction had run its rabid course, as it was always destined to do, they were – each of them respectively – too embarrassed to admit the fact of their backsliding to the other, so instead they chose to drift apart. Harry distinguished himself by drifting – *sans* compass and rudder – into university, where he flunked ingloriously. Izzie drifted into almost everywhere else, even – to his ultimate regret – into the United States marines. Eventually, with the skill of a blind man finding his way in the dark, Izzie found Harry again. Or was it the other way round? In any case, they launched this theatrical project together. Izzie had found his niche. Music for him was always a great love and consolation.

From the depths of the stalls, Harry catches Izzie's eye and gives him an impromptu wave. In recognition, and without allowing slack in the melody line for as much as a fraction of a demisemiquaver, Izzie dips his shaven head ever so slightly in Harry's direction.

At which moment Sticks bursts on to the front of stage.

Her overall appearance, in both effect and intention, is neat and businesslike, decidedly 'sleeves-rolled-up'. She is of medium height only, but her erect posture has the capacity to startle. Whether seen full on or caught in profile, her figure is exquisitely proportioned, with essential features relating to each other in precisely those ratios that have – down the ages – been deemed ideal by consensus where-ever men have been known to show their appreciation of women. Or women of women.

Only the profile of her face fails to meet these sublime specifications. It is a shade too concave, which unduly brings to notice the jut of her strong wide jaw.

Loose lavender blouse and flowing rainbow skirt down to the calves are unable, despite their apparent artlessness, to disguise a most up-front female presence. Anybody asked half an hour later how she had been dressed would have been hard pressed to give details, yet would remember they had met a most attractive and assertive operator.

You should dress with more chic, Matt had once told her. I remember the arch look he had flashed in her direction as he said this. It was his professional opinion and, as such, carried weight. But *she* knew what would work for *her*.

Behind Sticks, right at the back of stage, a group of half a dozen or so pretend doctors and theatre nurses assemble, dressed in surgical gowns, caps, masks, and gloves. These are actors, ready to strut. Sticks gives them a quick glance of acknowledgement. She has shanghaied them from among her friends and associates for this purpose. This is both her duty and her prerogative as stage manager.

Timmy, aged twelve, bursts on stage and runs to his mother. He is dressed in school uniform, including his first ever pair of long grey trousers, but excluding the tedious bits like necktie and cap. Sticks bends her knees, and cradles his head between armpit and breast. Can I go and sit with Poppa? he asks. Good idea, darling, she replies. Timmy leaps down into the stalls, runs to Harry, and takes a seat next to him. When's it gonna start? he asks, then settles back with his Nintendo box.

Harry glances across at the Nintendo screen. Ugh, he thinks. 'Casino Cataclysmo'. He has seen this game before, courtesy of his dubious son and of his dubious son's dubious peers. Gangland rivalry over gambling turf. Bursts of automatic fire across gaming tables, with rocket launchers and grenades as optional extras. Punters and croupiers, finally singing from the same song sheet, as they lie dying together in a slurry of blood, gore, playing cards, and gambling chips. What *is* the younger generation coming to?

Sticks looks in Harry's direction. Ready to start, *Herr Direktor*? she asks. Her raised voice is alloyed with irony. Harry nods.

OK, crew. Let's move, she shouts. She extracts a cell phone

from the depths of a pocket in the front of her allegedly un-chic skirt, looks up in the direction of the lighting box, stabs a button, and speaks into the phone.

Elena, she says.

There is a pause.

Elena. The 'off' switch, please.

The theatre is plunged into total darkness, or so it seems to Harry, acclimatized, as are his eyes, to everyday light. Izzie's inexorable boogie rhythm is Harry's universe, a universe with neither time nor space. To put an appropriately poetic spin on matters:

> The account in *Singspiel*
> of events in the real
> life of Harry McMinn
> is about to begin.

Choose a seat, won't you? It may involve a bit of a stumble in the dark, but your marsupial eyes are – I understand – equipped for such a purpose, and the worst that can happen anyway is you will fall into a comfortable lap. You, my pademelons, are the audience. Please join *Herr Direktor* in the moment of his illustrious birth.

>

Singspielstück #1: The Birth of Harry McMinn

The first thing of which we become aware is this cryptic caption, back projected in white lettering onto that excised black strip below the lip of the stage. It hangs there – for a few seconds only – before being subsumed into nothingness.

Boogie prevails, swinging back and forth between tonic and dominant. Darkness prevails, feeding the eye with nothing it might possibly resolve. Boogie darkness.

A chorus of whispers begins, in time and in tune with the boogie beat. The whispers seem to say to us: Sh, Sh, Sh, Sh. When they get louder and more distinct, it becomes clear what they are *really* saying: Push, Push, Push, Push.

Do we see the tiniest point of light? Is it real? We peer. We squint. We drill the darkness with our eyes. Nothing is clear, because something resembling mucous seems to be obscuring our vision.

YES. *Bórzhe moy!*[4], as Elena might have said. It is real.

The point of light now has an extent, a diameter. Then it becomes more than a mere circle of light. It has, courtesy of Elena's wizardry, become a tube of light. The tube of light extends towards the trusty hands of the midwife, positioned in readiness to grasp the emergent boy child, as yet un-named, but who is soon to be known as Harry.

You, pademelons, peering and squinting through amniotic fluid, are proxy for the yet-to-be-born Harry. We, the audience, are seeing everything through eyes yet to be exposed to the light of day.

Did you notice that the four CCTV screens have come on? They display alternative views to enable us better to grapple with this momentous event. Clockwise from top left we see the modern and coldly clinical hospital from outside, the bustling maternity ward desk complete with bullying matron, the grimace on the face of the soon-to-be mother decidedly in the custody of mother nature, and a close view of that part of the soon-to-be mother where business is happening.

The tube of light is wide enough across now for us to see the delivery team, bunched shoulder to shoulder as in a rugby scrum, positively salivating at the thought of that ball dropping into their hands. This is a view such as you might see through a fisheye lens. It is clear they are delivering more than just a boy child. They are delivering – in robust soprano, alto, tenor, and baritone – the Push, Push, Push, Push line.

---

4 *Bórzhe moy!*: My God!

The boogie remains. Nothing can stop that boogie.

Izzie – as it turns out – has more than the boogie card up his sleeve. A triumphant treble line – like a reveille, and indeed drenched in the colour of bugle tones – bursts forth to accompany the boogie and the Push. This treble line is in a minor key, and because it uses only five notes of the diatonic scale, succeeds in sounding starkly primitive. Like the events – one might say – in which we are being invited to participate.

The midwife and the chief attendant doctor separate themselves from the scrum and proceed, with choreographed physicality, to support the treble line, in duo soprano and tenor. Their little dance routine, if I may be permitted to push the word 'dance' to the limits of its intended meaning, was designed by Sonia, and has them prancing around each other, legs and arms flaying, brandishing accessories such as forceps, steaming towels, and surgical masks. Strobe lights, synchronized to the beat of the music, accentuate the vigour of the action, and this effect is Elena's work.

The lyrics? They're by Harry. Who else would produce such dubious doggerel?

Delivery Team:

Harry McMinn,
with umbilical thing,
has a mind to quit the comfortable womb.
See his poor mummy
with her bloated tummy
brave the push of the delivery room.

Between verses, the tube of light expands and contracts violently, the Push, Push, Push, Push increases in intensity, and the delivery team thrash about desperately.

This wee mite
's in a headlong flight,
determined to alight upon our land.
He pops out

then there'll be singin' and shoutin'
from Coonabarabran to Samarkand.

What a stroke of luck
that an innocent fuck
should deliver him to our fey shores.
Without his arrival
we'd be fightin' for survival,
right up the creek with insufficient oars.

What more could we want
than this young *savant*
with sagacity to lick us into shape?
We'll show him the ropes
and the buggered up hopes
of all of us descended from the ape.

So give him three cheers
and the same amount of beers
with a vigorous hip hip hip hip hooray.
From the 'burbs to the bush,
let's kiss his little tush
'cause every dog has gotta have his day.

Izzie stabs the keyboard with multi-fingered determination, bringing the music to a halt with a chord unequivocally minor in its modality. His shoulders relax.

According to all the clichés, this is the moment when the mother is about due to give out a piercing shriek. Right on cue, this is precisely what we hear. The shriek electrifies the air and, simultaneously, the stage lights come up full and blinding, so it's almost whiteout there on the bare boards where the actors – frozen in tableau – mix it with the terrified cockroaches.

We all know the cliché doesn't end there. The baby must emit its first cry now. So he does. We all know that unique mix of howl, splutter, and gurgle. We can see the accompanying action in digital view if we wish because, as the stage lights dim obligingly, the four CCTV screens show baby (yet to be named) Harry in a variety of poses. One of them has him dangling upside down, his tiny feet in the proud grip of the midwife.

II

As the house lights come up, the curtains close, our excitement subsides, and a natural pause takes effect, I believe the moment is ripe for a brief explanatory message. Pademelons, if you please, allow your attention to drift in my general direction for a brief moment. I feel the addressing of this matter is not at all untimely, even perhaps a tad overdue. It concerns that ungainly word '*Singspielstück*', whose appearance – I'm sure you must have noticed – announced the start of Harry's theatrical creation.

We have none other than Sticks – who prides herself on her linguistic ability – to blame for this piece of verbal frippery. For some time, she and Harry had been looking around for a suitable word to describe one in the sequence of theatrical events Harry intends to launch on his bastardized proscenium-arch stage.

'Song' is inadequate, because it gives no promise of unsung dialogue. 'Scene' is inadequate because it gives no promise of song. There is a host of other possibilities, each of which – I think you must agree – falls short for one reason or another: aria, oratorio, item, spectacle, ensemble, tableau, canto, &etc. Elena suggested the Russian '*vyeshch*', but this was deemed by all in the crew to sound more like the swish of a balmy breeze than like any actual word. After much communal soul-searching, Sticks hit upon the idea of using to advantage the unique facility of the German language to stack nouns end-to-end in order to achieve more-or-less precisely the meaning required. *Sing-Spiel-Stück*. Ugh! Irredeemably ugly – even Sticks admits this – but I put it to you that perhaps the ends may in this case justify the means.

>

Harry is on the defensive against friendly fire.

You're a bloody egomaniac, says Matt.

Everyone will get their turn, says Harry.

Matt and Sonia both talk at once. Matt says, Good, we can all be egomaniacs. Sonia says, That's what worries me.

Matt apologizes to Sonia for interrupting.

Sheba, says Sticks, that's not like any birth *I've* ever known.

You want naturalism? asks Harry.

What is the context of this conversation? Harry and his crew are taking refreshments around a collapsible card table on the right hand wing of the stage. Izzie is the only defector from this putative debriefing, having decided to stay at his post behind the synthesizer. None of the actors have appeared yet. Presumably they are removing their grease paint, &etc.

Clockwise round the table – each member of the self-appointed circle having assumed possession of one edge of it – there is Harry (against the curtain), then Sticks, then Matt, then Elena. Each sits in a collapsible director's chair. Harry and Matt are contemporaries, both having recently celebrated their fortieth year, as indeed had Izzie. Sticks is about three years younger than them. Elena is about five years younger again. Collectively, they look a pleasant enough crew, all in robust health, with nothing about their respective physical appearances that could be deemed especially gross. They range from pop-star beautiful (Elena) to marginally acceptable in decent society (Harry).

Wait. Who is the woman, maybe a year or so younger than Harry, etched in starkest tones against the ferocity of the house lighting, squeezed awkwardly onto a corner of the table between Sticks and Matt, and sitting not in a director's chair but on a small collapsible camp stool? She looks for all the world as if she doesn't really belong in the circle. Can she not – equally with the others – lay claim to good health and decorous appearance?

This person is Sonia, who – a breath or two back – was heard to voice her concerns about rampant egomania.

Her fine hair, black and lustrous as a Shiraz grape, offsets to great effect the smooth pallid texture of her skin. Her alert eyes, dark and brooding, are suggestive of an intelligence within bearing the same attributes. Her upper lip folds almost imperceptibly over the lower, imparting to her expression a permanent (and not unbecoming) pout, like that of a platypus one might be half inclined to say. The upper portion of her light-framed body is graced by a pair of exquisitely delicate arms always seeming to be poised on the point of telling the world a story.

Yet, pademelons, do you perhaps notice she manages to effect an ever-so-subtle – and doubtless insensate – feint of neck and shoulder – suggestive of a tendency to reticence perhaps – the consequence of which is to ensure her destiny more often than not will be to inhabit the periphery only of any group of people gathered together for social purposes? And what exactly is the provenance of this 'tendency to reticence'? Does Sonia own it or does she incite the group to assume its ownership? Should we describe it as Sonia's reticence to join the group or as the group's reticence to accept Sonia?

Even for supernal folk like us, this is a devilishly difficult matter to resolve with any certainty. What we *can* assert with confidence is that these considerations make no difference to the result at the end of the day, which is that not infrequently – in social situations – Sonia is fated to take on the role of an isolate.

Let's deal with the dress of our second unit crew in a little more detail, because many people believe dress to be a window opening onto the worldview of the person who dresses. Certainly Matt could be expected to spruik that view with vigour.

Harry and Sonia are dressed carelessly in scruffy jeans and T-shirt, and Harry has accidental odd socks. It could be said they are making a minimal attempt to advertise what natural attributes they may or may not have.

By contrast, Matt and Elena are casually but consummately dressed. All their gear is top of the range, or close to it. But – b'Jesus! – I can swear by the galloping goitre of my gormless granny, their styles are poles apart.

For Matt, a tall dark man eager to be seen as having impeccable taste according to the dictates of high fashion, it is pale slacks and pale open-neck shirt, so the focus of all attention is directed to his sky-blue cravat and matching sky-blue eyes. I know his habits well, and can reveal that the cravat is his choice for leisure moments with a bow tie his preference when engaged in business. Always blue. I should add that he puts himself to considerable trouble and expense to look after his external appearance and – to no less an extent – his physical condition.

For Elena, naturally blonde, long legged, and with taste more peccable, it is red stiletto heels, and short skirt skating round the tops of her thighs. Her cotton blouse is adorned with peasant motifs, colourful, handcrafted, and Slavic. She has left its top buttons undone, the purpose being – one must assume – to affect an enticing décolletage. Her overall presentation understates nothing. Colours are bright, tending towards gaudy, and her make-up draws the attention like, by reputation, free beer does.

I believe I have previously given you a sufficient description of what Izzie and Sticks are wearing. We need not go there again.

Izzie, bent low over his keyboard, starts probing the possibilities of the next song on the programme, a peaceful melody, a lullaby. This – or so the timing would indicate – prompts a remark from Elena.

Shouldn't we be going back to walk? she asks.

Walk? asks Sonia.

Sticks, the linguist, sorts things out.

You mean work, she says. Not walk. *Rabóta* not *progúlka*.

Elena laughs. OK. Should we be getting back to *work*?

No rush. Drink your *chai*, says Harry.

To bring you up to speed, it might help if I tell you Elena

migrated from Russia when she was still in her teens. Until then, she had lived in Petrozavodsk in the northwest, city of short white summer nights and long black winter nights. If this conjures up thoughts of coffee, let me assure you – as I'm sure Matt would testify – it's very hard to get a decent cup in Petrozavodsk. As it transpires, Elena has few fond memories of Petrozavodsk, and since she is doing her best to forget about it, so shall we. For the moment.

I think, however, you should learn to pronounce her name. (If *I* don't insist on this, I'm sure Sticks soon will.)

Few people actually get it right. Harry is one of the worst offenders, but Elena is cool about this. Stress is on the second syllable, and that means the second 'e' is pronounced as 'ye'. El-*YE*-na. It actually sounds pretty that way, wouldn't you say?

Harry is still under attack.

It's absurd, says Sticks, to include your own birth in an autobiography.

Why? asks Harry.

Because nobody I know actually remembers the moment of their birth.

Irrelevant, says Harry.

Subjectively, your life starts with your first memory, says Sticks, and that is *never* your birth moment.

I know one of a set of triplets, says Sonia. He says his first memory is of being in a very crowded place.

Matt touches her hand gently, and flashes her an ironic smile.

Why be subjective? asks Harry. I believe if you do your own life story it should start at its objective beginning and finish at its objective end.

Are you going to do your own death, boyo? asks Matt.

Yes, says Harry.

Nyevozmózhna! says Elena. Death must choose its *own* moment.

Pademelons! Did you see that? DID YOU? Or is my

imagination out of control? At the moment Harry made that decisive affirmation, I swear his eyes were drawn for an instant to the folds of curtain hanging beside him. Or, more specifically, to that South East Asian man in the songkok leading that strange animal.

Elena and Sonia make a move to get up from the table. Their action triggers a similar movement – though tentative – by the others. Harry lingers as if staring at the pattern of tealeaves in the bottom of his cup. The tealeaves are not an issue. He is counting up to seventeen, slowly, in his head.

Sonia – who has been observing Harry – shrugs, and joins Matt who is ambling in the direction of backstage. Since they are in charge, respectively, of choreography and costuming, it might be expected they would work together to an extent. Elena heads up the left-hand aisle, away from the stage and towards the lighting box. Harry, having finished his count, gets up and hastens to join Sticks as she moves more or less across stage.

You get so stroppy when I play loose with the facts, says Harry.

You want me to give you a medal?

My mother taught me how to lie. And *that* is my first memory.

I'm not sure if Harry's mother actually hears that remark. She, in white apron, with undisguised sexagenarian wrinkles and blemishes, is at that moment clearing away the card table of its Coke bottles, cups of tea, &etc. She has appeared – apparently – from nowhere, unnoticed by anyone, which is what she likes to do. Invisibility is her impossible but most ardent desire.

Timmy has seen her. He runs to her from backstage.

Grammy, he says, was it really awful?

What, dear?

Giving birth.

I'd do it every morning before breakfast. Look what I got? My lovely boy, Harry, and my even lovelier little Tim Tam[5]. Scrumptious, he is.

---

5 Tim Tam: an iconic Australian chocolate biscuit.

Brenda McMinn bends down, draws Timmy to her breast, and nibbles his neck, an oft-repeated ritual whose design and effect is to draw a hearty cackle up from the depths of her grandson's lungs.

||

I have mentioned Harry's accidents of birth. Before proceeding further, I wish to make one further observation – of a metaphysical nature – on the subject of another accident of birth, one that afflicts or has afflicted all of us. Please bear with me.

From the moment a person – any person – enters the world of earthly life, they find themselves trapped in an ephemeral sliver of time known as 'the present' which almost instantly melds to the solid immutable past and is replaced by a sliver shaved off from the enigmatic unknowable future. I am deeply moved by the predicament of those trapped in this manner, but at the same time I am endlessly fascinated by the phenomenon itself. Sometimes I have difficulty holding the thought steady in my head. The mere fact of thinking about it – I find – is enough to have it wobble back and forth between the ordinary and the extraordinary, like light strobing through a white picket fence.

Living persons are slaves to this inexorable process, from which only death can free them. Or storytelling. For when a person tells a story, it's usually the *solid immutable past* they shave into slivers, and *those* slivers – each in its turn – become an ephemeral proxy-present. Of course, there is almost always a substantial injection of imagination, exaggeration, forgetfulness, wishful thinking, misrepresentation, bias, revisionism, and/or blatant falsehood advising the process. The storyteller may even feel inclined on occasion to cut – or even shuffle – the deck. But people enjoy being part of storytelling nevertheless, because it gives them a sense of control the process of life itself so often *fails* to give them.

So much for these philosophical musings. Let's give the nod

to earthbound realities and to the bottom line. The bottom line is that Harry and I are the storytellers in question here. We, already a proven team, are eager to build on our initial success and, in the process, show ourselves capable of even greater things. With you, pademelons, as our rapt audience.

An aside to you Harry. Apropos of what I have said, I believe a pledge is in order. I intend to give this presentation my very best shot. I trust you intend to return the favour. Will you give me a high five on that?

… Harry, this is *so* silly of me. I apologize. A high five is out of the question. I cannot cross the bridge to your world, and you – I fancy – have no inclination to cross the bridge to mine …

<< 1ˢᵗ Unit

The young Brenda, the Brenda McMinn of the early Bee Street days, and especially the Brenda Bailey of the days before Mick McMinn confounded her with his blarney, had her feet planted firmly on the earth. Educated only to year 11, she was nevertheless able to exercise a degree of pragmatism in her daily life and display a breadth of understanding of the workings of the world that many people with serious paper qualifications could only envy or else belittle gratuitously.

Her problem was she was beautiful. Hair, eyelashes, and eyebrows in glossy black on an 'English rose' face. Hazel eyes, seemingly molten. Fair skin. Breasts to magnetize male eyes. A figure whose contours not even a potato sack would have been able to disguise. Slender legs in classical proportions. Yet most of what defined her beauty was unknown and unknowable.

Men hung round. The good ones hung back. Perhaps they did this out of consideration for her, in the realization that what she needed most was space. More likely they did it through timidity, and the fear their power of speech would desert them if they got any closer to this beautiful apparition. She wouldn't want somebody like me, they argued to themselves as they gawked from a distance. Doubtless they settled, in later life, for plainer women, and learnt to love them ferociously and gained their ferocious love in return.

Brenda was left with the Neanderthals. Neanderthals, gross by nature and by number. They had no qualms of the above kind, no qualms of *any* kind. Brenda's relationships with men amounted to fending off importunate Neanderthals. She managed this well, but the price she paid was the slow attrition of her self esteem.

Then the dashing Mick McMinn came on the scene. He was no Neanderthal. He was something far more dangerous. By his own account, he was an Irishman, the Oz in his voice and the Mc in his name notwithstanding. There was little doubting he played the part of the mercurial Celt to the peak of perfection and sometimes to the point of parody.

He cajoled her, wooed her, flashed his pale blue eyes at her, smothered her in flowers, pranced circles round her with his wiry body, top-dressed her bosom with his curly brown locks, smooched her with his clean-shaven and deodorized face, kissed her, showed her the ring, and bedded her. Then he went out drinking with the Neanderthals, and told them she was his.

They married. Brenda and Mick. Mick and Brenda.

Mick was a plasterer by trade, and very, very good at it. He *always* had work. Some of the work was close by, some even in Bee Street. What Mick was *not* good at was the management of anything other than his trowel. The business side of his operations was like sorcery to him.

Brenda stepped up to the breech. She took over all the finances, banked his cheques, did the tax, paid his apprentices, negotiated with builders and developers, and doled out a weekly allowance to Mick. She was canny enough to be generous with Mick's allowance, so he never complained. They prospered.

In due course, Brenda – by now pregnant – became aware of

what, according to her best judgment in these early days, was a *minor* failing on Mick's part. He could never resist a shady deal. It *had* to be shady. Let me try to explain.

If a builder with a deadline were to approach him and offer him doubletime to do a job, Mick would typically accept the offer without any particular enthusiasm and – through apathy – might easily overlook the obvious opportunity to drive home his competitive advantage, e.g. to hold out for triple-time. But if a regular drinking buddy were to tell him on the sly that such-and-such a horse in race number so-and-so was expected to be pulled by the jockey, he would slap his betting money down on the table before you could say 'don't you worry 'bout that'[6]. It had to be shady.

Shady was spicy. Shady was sexy. Shady was also to prove Mick McMinn's undoing.

To indulge his addiction to the thrill and buzz of the shady deal, to get his 'fix' so to speak, Mick found himself frequenting Delaney's pub, an establishment – pademelons – of notoriety, conveniently located in his immediate precincts. Here a person – known popularly as Hefty – presided over a den of shady deals the likes of which Mick had formerly only dreamt about. When in proximity to Hefty, Mick was like a little lap dog with tongue hanging loose.

<

I feel obliged at this stage – before we proceed any further with the tragi-comedy of Brenda's and Mick's marital enterprise – to give you a brief historical run-down on the nature of the beast

---

6 'Don't you worry 'bout that.' This was the notorious catchcry of Sir Joh Bjelke-Petersen, a former premier of the Australian State of Queensland, when responding (for example) to questions about rampant corruption within the ranks of his administration.

we are dealing with here. Convenience dictates we pick up said beast's story at some time in the 60s, a decade or so before Harry was born. Around then, a party known as Sal ('Hefty') Heffernan was in the process of emerging from the obscurity of the criminal subculture into the full glare and stare of public voyeurism.

Yes, indeed. That's *the* Sal ('Hefty') Heffernan. For the benefit of those of you who have been living on Mars, I introduce him forthwith.

As the name would suggest, Hefty was tall and broad, his frame solid, his presence imposing. He was young, bullet proof, with the indelible brashness that often accompanies youth. He had a chisel jaw, a large mouth with perfect teeth, eyes no more than slits (but which could change from sparkle to steel in an instant), and a full head of dark straight hair parted meticulously and precisely in the centre.

In those early days, Hefty's name was inevitably associated with that of Delaney's rubbity[7]. This popular watering hole was situated – information of which you have been apprised – in one of the less salubrious pockets of the bayside sprawl enveloping Bee Street, the soon-to-be birthplace of Harry McMinn.

Hefty would always, and by a country mile, be the best-dressed person at Delaney's. His suits were tailored from pure wool, in a conservative deep-grey, imported from Milan. His shoes, of calf leather and slim-of-line, were (likewise) Italian. His shirts were pressed, white, cotton, of top quality. Even when – by way of whim – he wore a necktie, silk of course, his shirt would be unbuttoned at the neck. If some brave pedant had approached Hefty with the effrontery to ask him why he didn't do up his neck buttons, and if Hefty had responded with other than just a blunt expletive, then the answer might have gone along the lines of, The only fucker whose rules I follow is yours truly.

When not on operational duty, Hefty could almost invariably be found within cooee of the public bar at Delaney's. Some

---

7   rubbity: Australian (rhyming) slang, meaning 'pub'.

wondered if this was where he crashed at night. Certainly it was here Hefty planned his operations and did his deals. Usually his trusted lieutenant, Snow, would be hovering close at hand. Snow was slim, drawn, wiry, with protruding ears and fair hair slicked back, an elf-of-a-man about the same age as Hefty. Physically they were chalk and cheese. Or – more appositely – Abbott and Costello. Snow, wise elf that he was, always deferred to Hefty.

So did all Hefty's other troops, or 'amigos' as he liked to call them collectively. It was the sort of strategy that, around Hefty's camp, was an adjunct necessary (though by no means sufficient) for survival.

Knowing if Hefty was in session at Delaney's was simple. The late-model white Ferrari, parked directly outside the main entrance to the bar, was the signal. As if the white Ferrari weren't signal enough, its personalized number plate announced '**HEFTY**' in blood-red lettering on a bright white background. Hefty replaced his vehicle annually, and always with the newest model. The parking spot was never occupied by any vehicle other than his Ferrari. It was a brave man who – on finding the spot vacant – would try to park his Kingswood there.

There were a variety of theories – none proved or provable – as to exactly how Hefty came by his stripes. Did he earn them by dint of corporate embezzlement in the big end of town or by dint of connecting punters with hookers (and vice versa) in the inner suburban fleshpots? Did he earn them in the amphetamine labs of the far flung suburbs or in the headquarters of the bikie gangs closer in? Did he earn them pulling heists on freshly stocked warehouses or making illegal book behind sleazy streetscapes?

Nobody knew. It might be all of the above or none of the above. Nor could anyone actually remember how and when it was Hefty turned up at Delaney's one day and summarily took charge of all business other than the retail supply of beverages and victuals.

And prior to that auspicious but unremembered day?

According to a rumour doing the rounds, the juvenile Hefty had come fresh from the seclusion of a Christian Brothers orphanage, located somewhere out back of beyond, to slide seamlessly into a city-centric life of crime.

In those early days at Delaney's, a handful of his amigos – showing scant regard for their own welfare – had dared to suggest Hefty was too young to take on the role of godfather. Nobody can recollect what happened subsequently to these recalcitrant compadres. Indeed, Hefty gave out a most convincing impression of somebody who had clawed his fingernails to shreds in order to reach the top of the high wall, and – having reached it – was ready to stomp on the fingernails of anybody bringing up the rear. He didn't abide competition. He would nip its incipiency in the bud and, if anything *did* make it through to fruit or flowers, he would crush it brutally, like a grape beneath the heel.

Of what were his operations comprised during his stint – which might better be called a reign because it was to last for decades – at Delaney's? In a nutshell: any viable form of bent activity you might care to name. Give me a list, I hear you say. Well for starters (or so the stories go): trafficking in drugs, money laundering, grand larceny, fencing of stolen goods, forgery, financial scams, false identities, bribery, blackmail, extortion, … and – believe me – he was always looking to expand his portfolio.

What was his *modus operandi*? I hear you ask. I shall tackle this question in some detail.

Please envisage – if you will oblige me – a Manual of Criminality. You heard me. A Manual of Criminality. Sal Heffernan himself, had he been inclined towards scholarship of this kind – of any kind! – might well have been its author.

We can surmise such a Manual, if it existed, would contain prudent advice for the benefit of those with determined criminal intent. Some aspects of this advice would doubtless be crucial to the point of being axiomatic. Any criminal ignoring such axioms would incur forthwith a significant encumbrance to his/her ability to exercise his/her chosen profession, it being difficult (though not impossible) for such person to operate effectively from within the slammer.

Some of these axioms might – we can imagine – have been:

Keep the Action at a Distance. The grubby hands doing the dirty work should be several echelons removed from the squeaky clean hands directing operations. If and when the law has a mind to descend, no connection – direct or otherwise – shall at such time be found between the two sets of hands.

Never Repeat Successful Methodology. Predictability is the Achilles' heel of every criminal operator. In order to prevail, such an operator should strive at all times for maximum variability. The law must always be kept guessing. In practical terms, this means tracks once trodden should not be re-trodden. Not ever.

Take Insurance. For any service under the sun, there shall always be found a payment somebody somewhere – given careful grooming – can be induced to accept. It follows that whichever agency of the law is poised at any given time to crack down on any scam, heist, or other illegal activity approaching the serious planning stage, should be distracted at the opportune moment by the lure of cold hard and untraceable cash in brown-paper envelopes.

&etc in similar vein.

We cannot be sure if Hefty had read any such Manual belonging to this exclusive genre. What we *can* know is that his endurance while others stumbled was proof he adhered – in the practice of his profession – to the maxims supposedly contained therein. Adhered to them absolutely, though perhaps not advertently.

By way of illustration, consider 'insurance' of the type mentioned above. Hefty played this game with consummate artistry, having developed in almost no time at all an infallible (and olfactory?) instinct re the who, how, when, where, and why of payola. By way of partial clarification, and in case there is the slightest smidgeon of a doubt, I should mention that the 'who' invariably included personnel at the highest levels of law enforcement.

One incident, which has become legendary, should serve to illustrate the supreme confidence of the maestro in this regard. Seated at the bar one evening – with his amigos gathered close around him, giving him their rapt attention – Hefty placed his right elbow on said bar and extended the fingers of his right hand skywards, as if he were inviting an arm wrestle. The gold of cuff link and Rolex gleamed, adding an opulent feel to the comradely ambience of the moment. The facets of chunky topaz and ruby on his fourth and fifth fingers generated sharply chromatic refractions that became messages slicing the air, messages without obvious content but whose directions were determined with precision and with the strictest adherence to the requirements of geometry.

His gleaming eye-slits swivelled round the assembled as he regarded his amigos with what passed in his tight orbit for familial kindness, plucked casually from the limited domain of his natural feelings. With his left hand he proceeded to tweak each of the digits of his right hand, one by one. As he did so, he recited:

> This little piggy's in my pocket.
> This little piggy stayed mum.
> This little piggy's got two blind eyes.
> This little piggy's struck dumb.
> And this little piggy squealed gimmee dollar,
> gimmee dollar, gimmee dollar, gimmee dollar
> all the way home.

With this, he set the table on a roar. Few if any of the amigos understood the laugh was as much on them as it was on shonky law enforcers.

>

Pademelons, let us return to our story of Brenda and Mick before we lose track of this cautionary tale altogether. After all, at this point in my presentation, I intend the main thread of our narrative should be the fate of the unlucky couple. So I apologize to you for leaving this thread dangling as I did. I am hopeful we shall have minimal trouble picking it up again. Let me cue you in: when we left off, Mick was discovering Hefty's den of shady deals and was enamoured of what he saw. Whenever he happened at Delaney's, which in those days was more often than was good for his wellbeing, he was like a little boy in short pants and freckles, encountering a penny arcade for the first time.

The moment most thrilling to Mick was when Hefty signalled to Snow with the merest flick of his head. Snow would then do the rounds of the bar, tapping various of the amigos on the shoulder. Hefty, Snow, and the amigos thus selected would adjourn to an upstairs room, staying there behind closed doors for an hour or so. Mick's imagination went into overdrive trying to fathom what went on up there. An adrenalin rush jolted his neurons when they all galumphed down the stairs again, and the distribution of jobs began.

Eventually, to his immense delight, he found himself selected for certain minor jobs: launching small amounts of counterfeit banknotes into circulation, or helping to break down a van-load of hot TVs into marketable parcels. The pay was good, but Mick was not in it for money. He was in it for the chance to win honour and to confer adulation. For the sheer romance of it. Sometimes he actually refused jobs: for example, perhaps on the basis of irrational preconceptions, anything to do with illegal drugs. Once he was asked to be 'driver', but this seemed a little too close to the coal face for his comfort. He was like your typical carnivore: happy to eat meat, but eager to keep his distance from the kill.

In most instances, though, he accepted the job and swelled with pride. On the job, he was like a little kid running errands for the big boys. Soon the police were regular callers at Mick's home, asking him what he knew about X or Y, to which Mick's predictable response was, Nothing.

There were nosy neighbours over every back fence in this suburban environment, and they noticed everything. Some of the stories that began to circulate were over-the-top, e.g. that Mick had Brenda tied up in the back room as a sex slave. Brenda was mortified. She made a point of parading up and down Bee Street in full-on maternity wear. The neighbours would look at her sideways. The women might nod brusquely to her. The men might wink lewdly at her. But nobody spoke to her.

She tried to have it out with Mick. She would typically say to him, There's something going on here and I've a right to know what it is. But the genial rogue kept saying, Storm in a teacup, my lovely, that's what it is.

Fury. Fury rose up inside her as insistent as vomit. Sad to say, in the end it's power, not fury, that is needed.

As if to drive this point home, nature – at this juncture – decided she, Brenda, should give birth. Baby Harry came into their lives. Brenda was tired but happy. Mick was ecstatic. His fascination with shady dealings was off his agenda for the time being, and it was most certainly off hers.

But, soon after this happy event, there was a sudden new development down at Delaney's. Sal Heffernan needed a fall guy and Mick McMinn fitted the bill.

The immediate upshot for Mick was the police changed their tactic with respect to him. Instead of calling on him at Bee Street, they 'invited' him to their station. Here, they asked him the usual questions about X or Y, except this time when he replied, Nothing, they hit him about the head with telephone books. It was looking bad for Mick. The crims and the cops were in the collaborative mode they do so well. Both were determined to clear their books.

Mick was dumbfounded. The choicest sweetbreads in the larder of his inner man had turned rancid. He mustered the reserves of his intellectual capability, but still couldn't figure out what he had done to offend Hefty. The lap dog was looking leprous, with slinking gait and tail between legs. At Delaney's, he sat at the bar, cold-shouldered by everyone. Thinking: I did what I was asked, I was loyal, I didn't cheat, I didn't grass. How come Hefty's cut me off at the knees?

The truth was worse than he knew. He didn't even *register* on Hefty's radar. At one of the upstairs meetings, Hefty had tabled his need for a fall guy, and some amigo or other had come up with a name he, Hefty, hadn't heard before, or more likely hadn't remembered. Mick's name. Mick McMinn, one of Hefty's lesser minions, a sub- sub- sub- operative. Perfect. Just the ticket. No sentiment entered into it. No malice entered into it. The fall guy. A hard-headed business decision.

Snow sidled up to Mick at the bar and through lips barely moving said, Do a runner, mate. That's *my* advice.

There was nothing for it. Mick took Snow's advice. He skedaddled. Over the next few frantic months, stretching into frantic years, the dashing Mick McMinn became adept at staying one quick dash ahead of the posse. His photo was on posters in cop shops all over the country.

In a textbook case of aversion therapy, his bowels loosened whenever he came close to a shady deal. Even TV crime shows would do it. Even some of the ads on TV.

He stayed clear of the Bee Street house, at least for a couple of years, until he figured the risk was sufficiently low and/or until compelled by a need that was correspondingly great. Then, sporting a beard of tangled curls, he would creep in at the dead of night – like a criminal, one might say – and stay for several days, never leaving the house. In the dead of night, he would leave again. Harry's younger sister, Madeleine, was conceived during one of these clandestine visits.

Mick sent money, frequently and in generous amounts, for which Brenda was grateful. It was always in cash. No paper trail. It came from every corner of the country where plasterers were in demand. There was a different postmark on the envelope each time.

Brenda? For a time, she had to fend off the police almost on a daily basis. The nosy neighbours would have loved to have known her business but didn't want to know *her*. Mick's money was very useful but hardly consolation for such bitter and barren circumstances. The loneliness was a heavy black shroud wrapping itself around her by waking day and by sleepless night. She sobbed into the bedclothes to prevent the neighbours hearing. It seems, pademelons, to be the lot of the majority of living humanity that their chance of connubial bliss in this world is cruelly curtailed by situations over which they have no control. Being beautiful provides no immunity from this.

Harry, who hardly realized what had happened, became – overnight – the little man of the house.

Pademelons. You ask, Did Brenda remain faithful to Mick? and, Did Mick remain faithful to Brenda? I'll leave that to your imaginings, because it really is beyond the brief of my presentation. There's another potential presentation here in its own right. Perhaps one of you would like to run with it.

2ⁿᵈ **Unit** >>

Beautiful, says Penny.

Harry, in seat 17N, is passing around a photo: a close shot of his mother as she was forty odd years ago. In seat 16N on his left is the youngish woman, Penny, who is about to play Brenda as she was at that time. Penny Galatano is one of Matt's closest associates in the fashion industry. She is beautiful in her own way, but lacks the 'English rose' face. *Her* face is slender, angular, with high cheek bones. More European, one might say.

To his right, in seat 18N, is Matt. Others of the crew – Sticks, Elena, and Sonia – are hanging over the backs of their seats in row

M. Izzie, hunched behind his synthesizer on the left wing of the stage, is playing around with the devil only knows what melodies. Concocting. Composing. Improvising. Oblivious. Enjoying himself.

The photo travels from hand to hand invoking a variety of appreciative vowel-laden responses from each person in turn. Eventually it is back in Harry's possession. Harry feels vaguely embarrassed by the proceedings, as if his privacy is being artfully breached. He looks down at the photo. There is the woman in the prime of whose life, and at whose cherished hearth and home, he had been for the most part and for so long the one and only man.

One and only?

Yes, essentially, thinks Harry, quickly dispelling his own doubts.

Essentially *also*, thinks Harry, he had been the exclusive object of those loving liquescent eyes, and had often had the pleasure of experiencing in that exclusive way the meld of his gaze with hers.

Exclusive?

Yes, essentially, thinks Harry, assuring himself.

Those loving eyes are shining their lights on him from out of that browning photograph, reproaching him and at the same time offering him forgiveness in advance as, for example, they once did when he carelessly allowed her cakes to burn or when he uprooted her tomato plants by mistake or when he killed her favourite kitten under his clumsy feet. He, her accidental helpmate, had in no way presaged the end of all accidents for her. A chapter, a book, whole volumes of accidents had befallen this woman since his birth, and he had been the author of so many of them. Yet the only thing she had known how to do was to love him with her eyes.

Well, says Sticks, shall we play?

The show must go on, says Elena.

Lines off pat? asks Sticks of Penny.

Sure, says Penny.

Yours too? asks Sticks of Harry.

Of course, says Harry.

He shakes off the hovering ghost of Oedipus. They all move to their respective stations. We should too.

>

Singspielstück #2: The Lie at the Eye of the Lullaby

House lights are down. On the black strip below the lip of the stage is projected briefly in white lettering the title of this next theatrical presentation. As above.

The scene on stage is of a nursery, with cot at centre stage and colourful décor on all sides, suitable – according to popular convention – for a baby boy. There is a window with heavy drapes at backstage. The drapes are open. Bright sunlight streams in through the window, and the shadows of fluttering leaves are active on the nursery walls. These effects confirm Elena's skill.

Penny, playing Brenda as she was in the mid 70s, enters from stage left. Pademelons, I ask your indulgence. For simplicity, I suggest we – for the purposes of this particular *Stück* – call this person Brenda, even though we all know she is really Penny.

So 'Brenda' smooths the bunny rug inside the cot, plumps up the small pillow, and draws the drapes closed. The light in the nursery is now dim and the leaf shadows have ceased their eager dance.

Brenda exits at stage right.

Have you noticed the two CCTV screens at top-front-left and top-front-right of stage? An outdoor scene and an indoor scene? The left screen shows, in bright sunlight, the nursery window from outside, with eucalypts showcasing their leafy fandango nearby. The right screen shows baby Harry, in nappies, wriggling on the floor of the room – shall we suppose it to be the living room? – to which Brenda has made her exit. Brenda's hands can be seen reaching for baby and scooping him up together with a cuddly toy.

Then baby, cuddly toy, and hands disappear from the screen. All the screen shows is the bare floor of the living room.

As Brenda re-appears from stage right with baby Harry and the cuddly toy in her arms, a ghostly face appears on the left hand wing. It is Izzie's moon face, its lunar placidity illuminated – unintentionally and unavoidably – by his music light. We hear Izzie's introductory phrase. This is the melody he had been playing around with some time earlier, the lullaby, in a major key and in languorous 6/8 time. The tones of bowed strings predominate, but somewhere behind the strings I believe I can detect a note of hushed serenity from – can it really be? – a French horn. Izzie *is* a whiz with that synthesizer.

When Brenda reaches the cot with her infant, she stops, and begins to sing to Izzie's accompaniment in a mellow alto voice. Look at her. Look at the way she so gently and skilfully interpolates the cuddly toy into baby Harry's close proximity. Please give me leave to contend – if it's not too much of a cliché for you – that what we are privileged to see here is nothing less than Motherhood itself in fabulous human guise.

Brenda:

Child of my dreaming,
precious bundle dear to me:
moonlight is streaming
all about our hemisphere.
This truth I'll show
so then you'll know
to chase your dreams without a fear. So
close your eyes. Go sleepy byes.
Socialize with pies in skies.
Bide your time for shine and rise.
Go byezee sleepy byes.

A spot comes up on the right hand wing. The adult Harry is standing there to challenge his mother in baritone, on behalf of his infant self who hasn't had singing lessons yet. Directed with assurance by Izzie, the music changes from tonic to dominant and from languid 6/8 to a more up-beat 3/4 time. The baby Harry, at centre stage with his mother, appears to push the cuddly toy aside angrily.

Harry:

Mother, my treasure,
source of power and font of love:
sunlight for my pleasure
is beaming on our hemisphere,
and I feel it.
Don't conceal it!
or I'll stay awake for half a year. With
open eyes like big pork pies,
I'll realize the shine and rise,
and serenade the wide blue skies
and no more sleepy byes.

The spot on Harry, the adult, goes off. Brenda answers Harry's challenge, walking baby over to the drapes as she sings.

Brenda:

Love, you can be certain
you are the apple of my eye.
Over there's the curtain.
Outside of it the moonbeams play,
and I'll draw it.

Brenda pretends to draw the drapes back a fraction, at the same time holding baby Harry so he can't possibly see anything that is germane to the case. It's different for us, isn't it? We can see clearly on that left hand screen a bright sunny day outside.

There. You saw it.
You saw darkness, so pray get your sleep underway, and so please be wise and zip up your eyes.

Forget about singing to wide blue skies.
Postpone the occasion of shine and rise.
Go byezee sleepy byes.

Now: the *denouement*. Checkmate to Brenda is imminent.

The spot on the adult Harry returns. The music slips back to tonic key and 6/8 time, and the languid feel of the lullaby returns.

As Harry sings, Brenda walks baby back to the cot, puts him down gently, places the cuddly toy beside him, tucks them in together, bends low, and kisses him.

Harry:

O awesome master
of sleight of hand and fork of tongue:
You're a disaster
for youthful kin and truth alike,
but I would pick
as your best trick
the love you spark at every strike.
I know you lie but I'll comply
with your request for my shut-eye,
to dream about the pie in sky,
So I'll go sleepy bye.

Izzie finishes things off with a repeat of the introductory phrase.

>

House lights are up. The crew, pleased with themselves, are standing round the collapsible table on the right hand wing. Izzie, by preference, has remained slouched over his keyboard, improvising with busy fingers.

Matt has cracked a bottle of champagne. He shouts as he pours the spume into glasses:

Get that woman out here. She has no right to remain invisible.

Sticks heads off, in the direction of backstage, to find the invisible woman. As she does so, she shouts across to Izzie:

You too, Isadore. Stop playing with your instrument.

And leave the keyboard alone, says Harry.

Soon there are three extra people standing round the table: Izzie, Brenda, and Penny. Penny, moved to tears, is dabbing her eyes with a tissue. Brenda is looking round for an escape route. Matt raises his glass.

To Brenda, he says. Both of them.

They drink the toast.

Na zdoróvya! says Elena and they all have to drink the toast again.

I wouldn't call it lying, would you Brenda? says Sticks. I'd call it tactics.

It's what a mother would do, says Sonia.

Mother love, says Elena.

Regardless of what you want to call it, says Harry, it taught *me* how to *lie*. A valuable lesson.

You're so ungrateful to your mother, Harry, says Sticks.

On the contrary, says Harry. I'm *very* grateful.

<< 1ˢᵗ Unit

When the adult Harry had looked at that browning photograph of his mother and drifted off into the land of fond reminiscence, the word 'essentially' had sprung to his mind as a modifier for his perception of the role he had played back then as a child. He was right. Essentially, he *was* – back then in Bee Street – the only man about the house. He even slept in the queen-size bed with his mother, leaving his own little bed in his own little room unoccupied most of the time.

But Mick, as I have informed you, pademelons, was wont to pay occasional clandestine visits, and at these times Harry was relegated to the position of – in Mick's words – 'little tyke'. 'Essentially' was right on the money and, when Mick was on deck, the other side of this equivocal coinage was plain for all to see.

Typically, on these rare days when Mick was about, Harry would wake in the morning in his *own* bed and room. His first impressions – barely realized through his dreamy languor – would be of the shadows on the bare wall opposite his window, shadows of the big eucalypt flexing its branches and fluttering its leaves in the faint breeze. This little fragment of reality and reassurance would, however, be brushed aside promptly and brutally, as he realized the implications of this fluttery pantomime: he was in his own room, alone. A pastiche of some of his worst fears, would now invade his mind, unannounced and uninvited, supplemented by the aftershocks from his barely subsided dreams.

There were poisonous things out there – especially snakes and spiders – that could wriggle or – if they had legs – crawl through the minutest cracks in the doors or windows. He had seen them near Mr Sheridan's greenhouse and in other places he was inclined to avoid, so he knew they were on the prowl, looking for those cracks. Once he had seen a huntsman spider – its hairy mandibles menacing all takers – fall, plop, from his bedroom ceiling onto the carpeted floor near his discarded clothes. It might have been onto his head. Or into a shoe. Worst of all were the falling dominoes and the oozing yellow peril. He had seen the grim faces and heard the solemn voices of the newsreaders and anchors on TV talking about these horrors. He was constantly haunted by the fear of being drowned in a sea of yellow vomit or of being crushed under a toppling monolith.

Mick had proudly installed a cornice and ornamental rose on the ceiling of the master bedroom some years back before Harry was born. It was to this room and to his parents' bed Harry would flee on mornings such as this. He would lift the bedclothes at the end of the bed, crawl in, and make a tent? cave? for himself out of the covers, amidst bare feet and knees. It might have been a womb, except that it couldn't match a womb for darkness, a remnant of the soft morning light always contriving somehow to seep through the weave of the bedclothes. But here he felt safe.

He would hear the mild scold in his mother's voice, querulous and sleepy. She would say, with downwards inflexion, Ha-rry! Mick's tone would be more forceful. He would say, Get out a there, son.

Harry enjoyed the humidity of his cloth cave. He loved the encounter with limbs – lithe and familiar – warmly enmeshing each other. He relished the unique and inexplicable animal smell of fresh lovemaking he encountered, without having the slightest clue what was behind either the piquant odour or the sticky sheets that went with it. He would stay there even when he felt Mick lashing out with rolled-up newspaper at the bulge he was making under the bedclothes.

He would know the game was up, though, when he heard Mick's bare feet go clomp on the floor. Rough tradesman's hands would grip his ankles and pull him out from under the covers like a doctor effecting a recalcitrant breech birth. As he laid squealing and cackling on the floor, he would see Mick fling his threadbare dressing gown over his naked frame, and tie the tasselled cord in a bow.

OK, little tyke, Mick would say, me and you are requisitioned for kitchen duty. The menu says pancakes. Breakfast in bed for your mum.

These were happy, happy mornings for all three of them. But, for the adults, the flip side (no pun intended, pademelons) was the long periods of unremitting loneliness from which this was the briefest of respites.

2nd Unit >>

The performances have gone well so far, says Sticks.

Harry nods perfunctorily. We have seen he is prone to dreamy moments. This is one such moment. It is as if the thinking/feeling part of him has hunkered down in some remote corner at universe's end, while only his physical presence is impacting here in his earthly environs.

It is evening. They are alone together in a modish cafe, *La Spag*, to which they have walked from Sleek Street. Sticks likes this place. She likes the steaming metallic monster up front terrorizing the squealing jug of milk. She likes the smell of authentic coffee – roasted and ground on the premises – seeming to get into every grain, pore, weft, and warp of the accoutrements. She likes the pretend laminate tables that always wobble no matter how they are placed. She likes the wall posters with their eclectic juxtaposition of Venice Carnival, Dali Museum, Pamplona Bull Running, and World Cup at *Stade de France*. She likes the amiable lessee, Bruno, whose Mediterranean credentials are generations old. She tolerates his *faux* fashion-plate customers.

Matt is another person who likes this place. Its style screams out an invitation for the likes of him to haunt it. He and Bruno always manage to bounce jibes, japes, and jokes off each other, often with less than exquisite timing, but always with undiminished mutual pleasure. Matt, however, is not present on this occasion. Perhaps we can look forward on some future occasion to entertainment by this pair of illustrious impresarios.

Bruno, full faced with olive skin and glossy dark hair, sits at the cash register near the door. One of Bruno's sons – Roberto – stands behind the aforementioned metallic monster, pulling its levers, playing *barista*. Bruno's wife and daughter – serving table – are forever scooting back and forth between the tables and the kitchen, tributes to motion and energy in an otherwise sedentary precinct.

Sticks is sipping a long macchiato. She has a laptop with her. It is open, and the white glare of a blank document can be seen on the screen. The page a pallid virgin awaiting violation by grubby black verbiage.

Harry is spooning froth from his cappuccino into his mouth. He is savouring this froth and his distant, dreamy moment.

You're the boss, says Sticks. What happens next?

Um? says Harry

With your production.

That could be a problem.

Why?

I know what *should* come next, but I'm not sure it can be done.

The staging is a problem?

Yes. The staging would be difficult.

Tell me about it.

OK. If you're ready.

I am.

Harry settles back, pauses for thought. When he begins to talk, it is as if from some cosmic distance, and as if primarily to himself. He directs his gaze variously across the room, up at the recessed ceiling lights, and down at his empty pasta bowl on which the remains are slowly congealing. On the occasions when he appears to be looking at Sticks, he is in fact looking right through her. He is vaguely aware she knows he is doing this and is less than impressed.

It involves Sonia and me, when I was six years old, says Harry. She was five.

Cool.

Sticks records something – presumably their ages – on the laptop.

We lived in the south-eastern suburbs, near the beach. In Bee Street. The McMinns and the Sheridans lived a few doors from each other.

You were at school together?

I went to the State School and Sonia went to the Catholic

School. Otherwise we were inseparable. Every afternoon and weekend, except for the times when Sonia had ballet lessons.

We played well together. *Very* well. It was innocent play. Effervescent. Not a trace of selfconsciousness. No competition. In those days, we were *so close*.

Different now, says Sticks.

Sadly.

He pauses, as if in an effort to capture his six-year-old memories.

We were like dual suns in a double star, he says. In revolutionary motion around each other. Synergistic motion. Driving each other constantly with a force not unlike gravity ...

The force be with you, says Sticks.

... but lacking any grave quality. Happy. We loved to run. Loved to feel our muscles working so effortlessly. Free as birds and every bit as chirpy. We'd run the length of Bee Street, then cut through to the beach or the shops. We'd churn up the sand with our feet and throw broken bits of jellyfish at each other.

We *loved* to run. Loved to feel the slipstream in our hair. We'd run through vacant lots, through half-built houses, through hedges. We'd splash through little creeks, shinny up and down trees, vault over neighbourhood fences ...

Did your parents ever worry about you? asks Sticks.

Paedophilia? asks Harry.

Among other things.

This was the 70s.

There is a pause. Harry seems stuck for words.

Go on. I'm interested, says Sticks.

When he *does* resume speaking, his gaze actually meets hers for a moment or two, as if he has become aware for the first time she is listening.

I have this odd feeling, he says.

Tell me about your odd feeling.

I feel this happening all over again as I'm telling it.

Cool.

That's not all.

Go on.

You and me. We've known each other a long time.

We have.

It seems odd that, after all this time, it's only now I'm telling you this stuff.

You find that odd?

Yes.

Perhaps that's the reason we still have a relationship.

Uh?

Because there's still stuff left to tell.

Fair point.

Or stuff to feel.

This stops Harry in his tracks. He looks up at Sticks, who is biting her lower lip, a sign of her affective vulnerability. Simultaneously, they reach across the table for each other's hand.

On with the story, she says.

But Harry, his gaze vacant again, is stuck for words. The unsticking process is slow. His eyes wander in the general direction of the poster of the Dali museum on the far side of the room. The thought occurs to him there might be some connection between Dali-esque art and the story he is telling, but the thought won't properly crystallize. He is aware on another plane that Sticks is uncomfortable with him, believing her presence to be irrelevant, even unwanted.

Then the unsticking is complete. Conversation resumes. Threads are picked up. They let go of hands.

OK. We ran. I tell you, with all this running we were never more than a few metres away from each other. Sometimes I would lead and sometimes Sonia would. We used to startle old men in their walking frames and babies in prams. Jesus, it was bliss to move that way. It was joy to feel such power. Mutual elemental power.

Twin souls, says Sticks.

Uh?

Twin souls. Zig and Zag. Bonnie and Clyde. Chico and Harpo.

Right.

Another pause. Harry is the first to speak.

We did this every day even when it rained. We came back wet together and caught simultaneous colds. At night I relived and rehearsed events over and over in my dreams. I'm sure Sonia did too, in *her* dreams. We didn't stop running even in our dreams.

Another pause. Harry changes his tone. Around the perimeter of his mouth, the facial muscles tighten visibly. His bottom lip quivers.

All this came to an end. Forever. With a vengeance. I remember the exact day.

Sticks pushes her laptop aside, as if to better concentrate on what she is hearing. She takes a sip of her coffee, but it seems to have developed an unpleasant sour taste. She pushes this unpalatable beverage aside also.

Feller, she says, look at me while you're talking. It's spooky when you look right past me.

Sorry, says Harry.

He continues to look right past her. If it was difficult for him to fix his gaze on her before, it is impossible now.

That day, he says.

That day, she says.

At first it was just like always, he says. The magic of motion, the litheness of limbs, the air in our hair, the shared ecstasy, the creeks, the trees, half-built houses, babies in prams …

We turned into the shopping street, hurtled past the newsagent. I was leading Sonia. Then when we flashed past the hardware store, Sonia was leading *me*. Just beyond the hardware store, Sonia veered sharply into an alleyway we'd never explored before, and I followed.

He has Sticks' rapt attention.

It was a dingy alley, says Harry. I can picture it now, feel it, smell it. Only two metres or so across. The paving underfoot was rough, and it was coated with a slurry of slimy earth, muddy water, dead leaves, and soggy cardboard. And it was blind.

Sonia reached the brick wall at the end, stopped, and turned to face me. I was hot on her heels, and I skidded to a halt not a metre from her. She was panting. Her chest was heaving. Our school shoes – both soles and uppers – were caked with mud. Then I read her eyes, and she read mine, and I'm sure both pairs of eyes told the same story.

What story? asks Sticks.

That we were no longer interchangeable twins, says Harry. Not Zig and Zag, not Zag and Zig. Our roles were differentiated now. I was predator and she was prey. *I* was the predator who had trapped *her*, my prey, and I could proceed to have my will with her. This we both knew. We saw it in the fixed stare of each other's eyeballs. I remember feeling the horror crawling over my skin like centipedes. The shame like monkeys sitting on my shoulder blades. The fear like bolt cutters about to grip my vital organs. We were in the presence of some primeval throwback that, in turn, was inside ourselves. A monster from the timeless abyss had taken over the room of our minds – young emerging minds – and it was rampaging. I can't tell you how dreadful that moment was. Our innocence was over. It was a Garden-of-Eden moment, but without anything as concrete as a serpent or an apple.

Sonia's back was against the wall, her shoulders were heaving, and she was in tears. She must have felt her every single vertebra catch on every single rough brick in the wall as her spine slithered slowly down, her terror-stricken eyes never leaving mine. Eventually I guess she would have felt the back of her heels touch her haunches. Then she bent her head fully forward in a submissive attitude, exposing the hairline on the back of her neck to me. I could see the individual roots from which her fine dark hairs sprung. She was sobbing. Jesus, did she sob! Uncontrollably, into her hands.

I turned on my heels and ran back down the alley faster than I had ever run in any of our glory days. My shoes were throwing up great clods of wet earth. From the Sheridans, I heard Sonia was rescued an hour or so later, by the kindly proprietor of the hardware store as he was locking up.

My God, says Sticks.

Her face, usually full and ruddy, has become pinched and pallid. The snap as she shuts her laptop is loud enough to make many in the café turn their heads. For a few moments all that is heard is the low buzz of conversation and the tinkle of spoons from the *latte* crowd at the neighbouring tables. Harry gets up abruptly.

I'll pay, he says.

With Sticks following, he moves to the cash register and speaks to Bruno.

How much? he asks.

Bruno winks slyly at Sticks.

Quanta costa? Cinque euro, signore, says Bruno to Harry.

Euros?

Double it, you goose, says Sticks.

Harry hands over a ten-dollar note.

Grazie, signore.

Prego, says Sticks.

Out in the cool night air, stepping through the shimmering reflections of the urban streetscape on the damp pavement, Sticks extracts her cell phone from her handbag, punches a button, and speaks into it.

Matt?

There is a pause.

Matt? Oh Matt, we're on our way back.

She folds up the phone, puts it back in her handbag, and turns to Harry. She places her hand on his shoulder, tilts her head, and allows her lips to brush ever so lightly over Harry's lips.

You're right. It can't be staged, she says.

>

Something had to be staged next and, having done the necessary paperwork, Harry and Sticks are bustling around, handing out photocopies of their outline to the crew. The document, word processed by Brenda, looks like a battleground – the protagonists being Brenda's untutored neurones and Bill Gates' castigatory software – with fonts changing willy nilly, tabs and indents attacking from both flanks, and enhancements like cannons on the loose. Harry reflects that the over-large and over-bolded heading

S1NGSPeeLST*U*CK N^{u}m: 3

could probably be deciphered by spy satellites, and is expecting ASIO[8] or the Federal Police to land on the doorstep at any time, perhaps to lay a charge of unlawful disposal of an umlaut.

Perusing her copy with curiosity as she walks, Elena makes her way back towards the lighting box to dream up some illuminating effects. Matt, no less curious, heads backstage to select sets and to conjure up costumes.

Pademelons! Is some of this curiosity rubbing off on you? This theatre business can be exciting stuff when it gets under your skin. But, *merde*, nobody seems to have set aside copies for you. I can hardly be blamed for this oversight, but I apologize nonetheless. I must say I feel let down by my second unit.

Sticks hands a copy to Sonia and, together, they requisition a couple of seats for themselves in the back stalls to flesh?/flush? things out. Sticks, laptop at the ready, sits herself down properly on her seat. Sonia, however, chooses to kneel on hers and hang over the back of it to face Sticks.

---

8   ASIO: Australian Security Intelligence Organisation, the Australian equivalent (roughly) of MI5 or the CIA.

Harry meanwhile puts a copy on Izzie's music stand, level with Izzie's busy eyeballs. Then, as if snap frozen, he stands stiffly upright behind Izzie, with his eyes closed. Izzie, conscious of his presence, turns. When he sees Harry, he looks faintly exasperated. This has obviously happened before.

Counting to seventeen? Izzie asks.

Harry finishes his count, opens his eyes, relaxes his body.

Your point being … ? he asks.

Why the fascination with seventeen? Izzie asks.

Harry smiles. Izzie rises, his pudgy torso taking in air.

The time has come, man, for you to go public with this dirty little secret of yours, says Izzie. It's not as if I haven't shared *my* personal stuff with you. You're seriously giving me the shits. Do you tell me, or do I get physical?

It's not important really. Or interesting.

Want me to show you a little something I learnt from the marines in Basra? I'll give you a count of seventeen.

You really don't want to know.

Izzie butts Harry with his puffed-up chest.

Let me decide that.

It's strictly private.

Izzie twists Harry's arm up the middle of his back. Harry steps backwards sharply, sending Izzie staggering into his piano seat, which topples over, spilling out copious quantities of print music. The agile Izzie finds his feet quickly and, wrestling Harry to the ground, turns him face down applying a deadly-looking hold to head and neck. C2 and C3 are definitely under threat. Sticks and Sonia – earnestly think-tanking in the stalls – have paused in their conclave, afraid the main issue for their director may soon be quadriplegia.

OK, OK, says Harry.

Spit it out.

Seventeen is a lonely number. For that reason, I've taken pity on seventeen.

Izzie releases his grip.

How can a number be lonely, you loony? he asks.

Seventeen has no relationship with any other numbers. It's a prime.

Izzie looks blank.

Prime number, says Harry. A number without factors.

Don't patronize me. I know my maths. The primes are …

He counts them off on his fingers.

… two, three, five, seven, … ah … eleven, thirteen. Yes, thirteen's a prime too, for sure. So's seventeen. So's nineteen. Jesus, there's a shitload of them.

Of course.

So what makes seventeen so special?

It's got no social advantages.

Run that past me again.

It's got no social advantages.

Thirteen has?

Sure. It's the first of the numbers we know as the teens. You know. Thir*teen*, four*teen*, fif*teen*, six*teen*, etcetera. That gives it some importance in the scheme of things. And it's got well known associations with luck. And with bakers.

Bakers?

Bakers.

Not butchers?

Bakers. Think about it.

Fuck all bakers. What about nineteen?

I *do* feel sorry for nineteen. But at least it's got one thing going for it seventeen hasn't got.

What?

It's the *last* in the sequence.

What sequence?

Of teens.

Izzie begins to pick up his print music and return it to his piano seat.

You mad bastard, he says.

Sticks' voice carries from the back stalls. She is waving.

Harry. Get up here. There's something we need to resolve.

So Harry moves to the back stalls and – yes, you guessed it
– takes seat number seventeen, so the two women are forced to
relocate in order to consult with him.

>

Izzie's head is down. He is bringing his legendary powers of
concentration to bear. His fingers, like fitful ferrets, are determined
to nosey out the elusive essence of the next song. The manner of
this eccentric instrumentalist – rooted as it is in the here and now
– conveys no skerrick of evidence to suggest the recent happening
– the physical contretemps – had in fact happened at all.

We shift our attention to the back stalls. Sonia hovers over
the back of her seat, with the happy result that the three members
of the impromptu sub-committee – Sticks, Sonia, and Harry –
are able to talk eyeball to eyeball. Izzie inadvertently provides
background music – bright, breezy, and jazzy – to grease the
weighty wheels of their discourse.

Bit of a problem there with Izzie? asks Sticks.

Nothing, says Harry.

Sticks, doubtful, changes the subject.

I understand, says Sticks, these events took place when the two
of you were nine years old.

That's right, says Sonia.

That's three years after …

Yes, says Harry quickly.

Sticks takes the hint. Neither Harry nor Sticks is especially
willing, while Sonia is present, to allude to the traumatic events
having allegedly occurred in the alleyway.

This little bit, says Sticks, of home-grown juvenilia you call Main Street. Explain it to me.

It's a game we used to play ... , says Sonia.

Who's we?

Mainly the girls in Bee Street, says Sonia. But Harry played too.

When you deigned to let me, says Harry.

Sticks turns to Sonia.

OK, says Sticks. As I understand it, Harry was the only boy of your age group living in Bee Street. Such were the demographics. If he was going to play at all, he had to play with you girls. You were the only game going.

We *did* let him play, says Sonia.

Harry is scornful.

Well, shit, he says. I joined in ...

That's right, says Sonia. Admit it.

... and ten seconds later I was sent packing 'with extreme prejudice'. How fucking fair is that, you giddy bitch?

Sonia, un-nerved, strives visibly to remain in control.

Your tone, your language, and your suggestion are uncalled for, she says.

Girls and boys! No fisticuffs, says Sticks. I'm not trying to pass judgment. I'm trying to figure out how we're going to stage this bloody thing.

Conversation has ground to a halt. Daggers are drawn. The silence is like solid stone. Sticks is eager to extract from it the embedded figurine of fruitful discussion.

I gather this game is some sort of role play? she asks.

Harry takes control of the explanation.

You've got it, he says. The girls' club set up Main Street in a patch of dirt behind Mr Sheridan's greenhouse. It had cruddy little homes, cruddy little streets, cruddy little cars, and lots of cruddy little people.

Who were these people?

Whatever. Tinkers, tailors, soldiers, sailors. They owned the houses and the cars, they gave birth, they took their children to school, drank booze, spat the dummy, got thrown in the slammer. In short, they lived, consumed, and died.

Then, as an afterthought, Harry adds a provocative codicil.

Died. Especially me.

Bor-ing, says Sonia.

You didn't find it so fucking boring at the time, says Harry.

Children! Control yourselves, says Sticks. I really need to get a handle on the details here. How were these people represented on the ground?

Tokens, says Sonia. There was a gumnut painted with pink nail polish, known as Red Bum.

She gives a vapid chuckle.

That was me. There was a bottle-top known as Vic Bitter[9]. There was a big blue-glass Tom Bowler known as Chop Suey. Oh, and yes, how could I forget …

Sonia, laughing timidly, gives a placatory glance in Harry's direction.

… Holey Cow, you remember Holey Cow?

Harry mutters a grudging affirmation. He is not to be placated so easily. Sonia turns her attention to Sticks.

Holey Cow, she says, was a button, with four holes in the middle to take the threads. It was shaped like a cow and had typical Friesian colours.

Black and white? asks Sticks.

Yes, says Sonia.

Pretty cows, says Sticks.

Milk factories, says Sonia.

Sticks spends some time writing on her laptop. Harry fumes with impatience.

Don't you want to know about *my* token? asks Harry.

---

9 Vic Bitter: contraction of 'Victoria Bitter', a popular brand of Australian beer.

Tell us, says Sticks.

A lapel badge with a picture of an aviator on it. I called him Rasputin, because of the many and various deaths he endured.

Sonia and Sticks respond simultaneously and with indignation. Not true, ... says Sonia. Rasputin was no aviator, says Sticks. Sticks defers to Sonia. Sonia continues.

... liar, pants on fire. Own up or I'll shove your shitty words down your throat. You called him *Biggles*. Don't dare deny it.

Children! says Sticks.

Should I tell her the truth, Sonia? says Harry. Should I let her know how you made me run naked the whole length of Bee Street and back on the promise I'd get a game? Isn't that the truth Sonia?

Sonia is silent.

Should I say how you stationed all the little girls on their bicycles the whole length of Bee Street to make sure I didn't take a short cut? And all those respectable Bee Street families, back from church saying, There goes that weirdo McMinn boy again.

Sonia is silent.

Then when you *did* give me a game as promised, you made sure I was killed off quicker than you can say Rasputin.

Biggles! says Sonia.

Sticks' head is in her hands. She doesn't know whether to laugh or cry, and comes out with a strangled sound midway between.

Too much information, are the words she says aloud to herself.

An icy crust, fit to grace Arctic realms, has accreted over proceedings, stemming the course of fluid discussion, and chilling all resident life clean to the bone. Timmy emerges from backstage and, with his trademark leap down into the stalls, breaks that ice crust.

Bless him. He has stage makeup on his face and his knees have been blackened. His costume is a parody. It is an imitation of his very first school uniform, the one he had worn when – as a terrified young pup – he had first attended primary school. Short pants were then the go. However, these *lederhosen* look-alikes are too short, failing to respect the spurts of growth a young lad experiences. The trouser legs are too tight, the crutch grips like a spanner crab, and it is basically useless anymore, hardly even for knockabout. This is painfully apparent, literally so for Timmy. Nevertheless he hurtles down the aisle towards his parents.

Mommy, he shouts. I'm in the next song. I'm in the next song.

He wriggles past Harry's knees and sinks into Sticks' lap.

I'm so pleased, Darling, says Sticks.

I'm gonna play Poppa when he was my age.

Easy peasy. He *is* your age. He suffers from arrested development.

Timmy, hands busy trying to ease the discomfort of his crutch, turns around to face Harry.

Poppa, who *is* Mulki Larka? he asks.

Harry winks at his son.

My invention, Timmy. A party pooper, I fear. Or your conscience maybe.

Turning to Sonia, he offers a placatory comment:

What do you think, Sonia? You remember Mulki Larka.

Who's he? asks Sonia.

Or she, says Harry (improbable defender of gender equality).

… and thank you, I say in all sincerity to Harry – but of course he doesn't hear – for insisting no presumptions be made about the gender of omniscient folk like us …

There was movement at the station for the word had passed around[10] … so sorry! Wrong scenario entirely. How foolish of me. None of the young colts had got away, or even wanted to. Nor was any one of them – God forbid – out of old Regret. Nevertheless,

---

10 'There was movement &etc': first line of the Australian epic poem 'The Man from Snowy River' by A B Paterson. 'Old Regret' was a brood mare.

I maintain the prevalent feeling would have been much the same: the buzz, the flurry, the itch of expectation. Why? Because the next *Stück* – and a vital one if vitality was ever to be found under the sun – is to be given over entirely to children.

They are all on stage, milling about in a state of nervous excitement. Harry and Sticks are there, like a pair of hirsute ibexes, urging the children to take up position. We know about Timmy playing his father. By similar contrivance, Timmy's cousin – Lucy – plays her own mother – Madeleine – who is Harry's younger sister. Christine, the pretty young lass playing Sonia, is the daughter of Sticks' brother who, twenty odd years ago, took Harry to court and lost. The other children, about a half dozen of them, all girls, are unrelated to the people they are playing. We can guess they are friends of friends and the like. All have had their knees blackened backstage.

Like Timmy, the girls are dressed in a mock-up of their oldest clobber. Their dresses are too short, with floral and/or check patterns washed out more keenly than a Turner seascape. Their shoes are scuffed at the toes. Their cardigans are ragged and short of buttons.

We have Matt (backstage) to thank for the makeup and costuming. Pademelons, I feel satisfied with whatever small influence I may inadvertently have had on the dear boy. There's very little he can't do when only he sets his mind to do it.

Behind the wannabe performers is a backlit screen on which is depicted the glass panels of a greenhouse containing mainly tropical plants and succulents. We are on the outside looking in. All the dubious multicoloured bling, lined up like toy soldiers in front of it, detail of which appears in close-up on the two large CCTV screens at top left and right – yes! – that could only be Main Street.

Sticks strikes a blow for stage illusion. The critical demarcation between real life and stage life must, at all costs, be razor sharp. On her say-so, the curtains are drawn and house lights are switched off. Eventually the curtains will get opened again – nothing is surer – and, when it happens, Timmy, Chrissie, Lucy, &etc. will have been transformed into youthful versions of Harry, Sonia, Madeleine, &etc. Meanwhile, pademelons, you must sit expectantly in the dark, in what could be described as theatrical limbo, neither earthly life nor theatrical paradise.

Abracadabra. Curtains open, stage lights come on, action begins.

>

Singspielstück #3: Mulki Larka

A doleful Harry is standing off to the right while the girls sit or squat around Main Street, totally absorbed in play. The flora of the tropics and of the desert watches over them from behind greenhouse glass. Looming above the rest of Mr Sheridan's extensive collection is his pride and joy, the huge *Dracaena draco*, or dragon's blood plant, which is destined – as improbable as this might sound – to assume a certain amatory significance later in Harry's young life.

CCTV captures Sonia picking up and holding between thumb and forefinger the red-painted gumnut, known by all as Red Bum. With squeaky voice, she speaks through him/her like a ventriloquist through her doll.

Chop Suey, you've been living alone for fifteen years. You need a wife.

CCTV captures Madeleine, holding and ventriloquizing Chop Suey in the same way. Chop Suey is a large blue taw.

I'm quite happy in my little house all by myself.

Why don't you marry Holey Cow?

I don't even know her.

Get in my nice new car. Me and Vic'll drive you round there.

Harry joins the circle, extracts Biggles from his pocket, bends down, and defiantly plonks him in the middle of Main Street. Sonia's hand moves deftly toward the yellow bus parked in the council depot. Soon the bus is careering down Main Street to the accompaniment of appropriate ventriloquial noises. Biggles is directly in its path. Ouch. The yellow bus is on top of Biggles.

Oh, says Red Bum, didn't you see the big yellow bus, Biggles.

Is he dead? asks Chop Suey.

I'm afraid so.

Anyone do CPR?

He doesn't need CPR. He needs a funeral.

Harry, suitably chastised, retrieves the moribund Biggles from Main Street, puts him back in his pocket and retreats to his position on the right. Don't be deceived. Harry may be smarting, but he is not defeated.

The lights dim on Main Street from where – nevertheless – a steady buzz of ventriloquism is heard as the girls continue with play. The focus shifts to Harry, on whom a spot of light falls. Simultaneously, on the left, Izzie's ghostly form is seen as his music light comes on.

While Izzie contends with the introductory bars, leading ultimately to a melody with a major key signature, an underlying rhythm of 6/8, and an irrepressibly cheerful lilt, Harry has something to say directly to you. Yes pademelons, to *you*, and to anybody else who happens to be in the audience with you. Please forgive his clumsy theatricality.

I won't give up, says Harry. I definitely won't give up. I'm going to tell a lie. It's a skill my mother taught me, and I intend to put it to good use. Watch me.

The spot on Harry goes off and full lights come up again on Main Street. The game is the focus once more. Harry struts boldly over to this game and declaims:

Have you heard the latest pop song?

Sonia, eager to get on with the game, is snappy.

What pop song? she asks.

Mulki Larka.

There's no such song.

Yes there is.

No there's not.

Yes there is, and it goes like this.

Harry begins the first verse, accompanied with bounce and vigour by Izzie on the synthesizer. Noticeably, Harry – while singing – makes frequent theatrical glances skywards, up into the flies of the stage, as if to telegraph his apprehension of some threat from that general direction.

Harry:

When there's only you and me
and you're thinking none can see, remember
Mulki Larka's lurkin' on a twig up in a tree.
So then …

Sonia interrupts him and Izzie before they can proceed any further.

That's ridiculous, she says. I told you there *is* no such song.

And I told you there is, says Harry. The Dung Beetles did it.

I don't believe you, says Sonia.

He might be right, says one of the other girls. Only I don't think it was the Dung Beetles. I think it was the Wet Nurses.

No, no, says another of the girls. It was the Arc Welders. I've got their latest album at home.

Then come on, says Harry. We'll show 'em all how it's *really* sung.

Harry flashes a glance at Izzie, and says, Play it again Sam.

Izzie raises a quick finger in acknowledgement, and reverts enthusiastically to the start of the song.

… there is a name for this time-honoured ruse, is there not, pademelons? It's called 'divide and conquer' …

Harry:

When there's only you and me
and you're thinking none can see, remember
Mulki Larka's lurkin' on a twig up in a tree.
So then when you're feeling free
and you want to make whoopee, remember
Mulki Larka's lurkin' in the tree.

The girls scramble to their feet. They have forgotten Main Street. With the exception of Sonia and apparently oblivious to the intrinsic inanity of the whole exercise, they dance. They skip in uninhibited fashion round their miniature make-believe community, raised knees impelling short skirts to flair out and up. The requirements of stage business dictate that they – like Harry – constantly flash glances and point fingers upwards towards the flies, drawing each other's attention to whatever demon is supposedly up there. Accordingly, to the utmost degree and at every opportunity, they act out the words of the song in line with whatever choreography has been deemed necessary by the adult Sonia.

The youthful Sonia stands, hands on hips, and glares. Sitting in the stalls, the adult Sonia may very well be channelling this attitude, but we cannot know for sure because her face and body are in darkness.

Harry:

On a Monday,
Boston bun day,
guess who's on your case if you're a bit inclined to stray,
or on Tuesday,
win or lose day.
Mulki Larka never ever …

One of the girls – the one who had previously spruiked the Wet Nurses – interrupts.

It should be 'breaking news day', she says.
No, says Harry. It's 'win or lose day'.
Well, says the girl, the Wet Nurses say 'breaking news day'.
Win or lose!
Breaking news!
OK, OK, says Harry. We'll do it the Wet Nurses' way. And to
Izzie he says, Play it again Sam. The song resumes at 'Monday'.
The girls resume their dance.

Harry:

On a Monday,
Boston bun day,
guess who's on your case if you're a bit inclined to stray,

Sonia, furious, tries to trip one of the girls as she passes. Glares
are exchanged. The dance continues.

Harry:

or on Tuesday,
breaking news day.

The Girls (sans Sonia):

Mulki Larka never ever takes a decent holiday.

Harry:

When the fun and games unroll
in your comfy hidey hole, remember
Mulki Larka's lurkin' up a telegraphic pole,
and if with some cherished soul
you would take a lovers' stroll, remember
Mulki Larka's lurkin' up the pole.

On a We'n'sday,
odds and ends day,
August, February, June, September, April, May,
or on Thursday,

his and hers day,

The Girls (sans Sonia):

never in a year of months will Mulki Larka stay away.

Sonia's fury has turned to desperation. Her attempts to disrupt the dancers are becoming increasingly physical, but futile nonetheless.

Harry:

When you go to talk the talk
or you're set to walk the walk, remember
Mulki Larka's lurkin' with the eagle and the hawk.
If you snitch a side of pork
or the silver carving fork, remember
Mulki Larka's lurkin' with the hawk.

On a Friday,
pigeon pie day,
sharp of eye and …

There is another interruption, from the girl who had previously spruiked the Arc Welders.
It should be 'slap your thigh day', she says.
No, says Harry. It's 'pigeon pie day'.
Well, says the girl, the Arc Welders say 'slap your thigh'.
Pigeon pie!
Slap your thigh!
OK, OK, says Harry. We'll do it the Arc Welders' way. And to Izzie he says, Play it again Sam. The song resumes at 'Friday'.

Harry:

On a Friday,
slap your thigh day,
sharp of eye and peeled of ear is Mulki Larka's way,

or on Sat'day,
tit for tat day,

The Girls (sans Sonia):

Mulki Larka's in the mood to throw you into disarray.

Harry:

When you think you have the right
to go out and pick a fight, remember
Mulki Larka's lurkin' in the nearest satellite.
When you're stealin' through the night
with intent to bash or blight, remember

(From the edges of space comes a greeting on Twitter.

Sonia pushes rudely in front of Harry to upstage him.

Sonia:

It's a hoax, mark my word, from a ground-dwelling critter.

Harry, the critter, jostles Sonia aside to reclaim his right to an upstage delivery.

Harry:

It says, I'm for real and I've never been fitter.

The Girls (sans Sonia):

Yea!)
Mulki Larka's in the satellite.

Izzie winds up the song with a couple of crisp chords. In like fashion, with foot slaps, the girls wind up their dance routine.

Harry, advancing on Main Street, whips Biggles out of his pocket, plonks him down again in the middle of Main Street, turns to Sonia and the girls, and declaims:

My name is Biggles. I have been elected mayor of Main Street. From now on everybody does exactly what I say.

Savouring the moment, he pauses for effect.

If I say 'Jump!' what do *you* say?

Stage lights go off and the curtains close.

A footnote for you pademelons: the aviator on the lapel badge was neither Rasputin nor Biggles. I have subjected the matter to close scrutiny and am sure it was Sir Charles Kingsford-Smith, a.k.a. Smithy. There is no mistaking the handsome grinning chauvinist visage behind the goggles. It is unfortunate, don't you agree, the custodians of our brand new century, despite having grown to adulthood in our last, should have so little memory of or regard for the history of our self-proclaimed lucky country?

>

The review panel (as in effect it has become) has re-convened around their card table on the right hand wing of the stage, while Izzie, his methodical fingers stumbling over what is presumably the next song, remains on the left hand wing behind his synthesizer.

Sticks – livid with rage – is standing, shouting:

Sexual politics at its most blatant! And out of the mouths of babes!

The other four are sitting, sipping their drinks in silence. Nobody dares cross swords with Sticks when she is so eager to take off a head.

The silence lasts too long and is in itself provocative. Cleverly, Elena steps in to change the subject.

She asks, Is there such person as Mulki Larka?

Only in my imagination, says Harry. Mulki Larka is fiction.

Sticks storms off in fury, up-ending her deck chair and toppling several Coke bottles on the table. A glass falls, spilling its contents, and shattering on the boards.

Another footnote for you pademelons: fiction can sometimes

be more potent than truth, especially when it has a mind to morph into truth.

<< 1ˢᵗ Unit

'Music is in the air – you simply take as much of it as you want,' Sir Edward Elgar (or one of his esteemed fraternity) is reputed to have said. *That*, pademelons, is exactly what Harry had done.

Faced, through the medium of his aeronautical avatar with the immediacy of his exile from the affairs of juvenile Bee Street, Harry had put his mind into adrenalin-fuelled overdrive. Results had arrived quickly. Out of the air so to speak, and at the tender age of nine years, he had come up with a song – music, lyrics, the lot – composing it in real time, and passing it off successfully as one of the latest pops. Should that surprise you, pademelons? Mozart composed a whole *opera* at age twelve.

Harry was never to forget this experience. Ever since that salutary moment, he was inclined to believe he could, at the drop of a hat, come up with original doggerel set to a passable tune. So, pademelons, it came to pass more than thirty years later, that Harry became obsessed with the certainty he could present his life and many deaths in strophic form. In *Singspiel*. Under a proscenium arch. As if on TV. With the help of friends, both with and without benefits.

If Harry's musical education had been extracted from a medium as thin and benign as air, then – contrariwise – his more general education – at least in his formative years – must surely have been extracted from a mire of intractable quicksand. In these early years at the local state school, he was bullied by pupils and teachers alike. A number of the pupils were children of the regulars at Delaney's pub. Even some of the teachers were regulars. Harry was persecuted for timidity, clumsiness, left-handedness, stuttering, big ears, bad breath, flatulence, no ability to do anything with a ball, even less ability to do something with a bat, not being one of the boys, not being one of the girls. This went on for three hellish years.

When he was aged eight, and up to (or should one say 'down to'?) his veritable chin in quicksand, his mother hauled him out and started him on a home schooling program. For the next three years, that is until he began his secondary education at Bunyan College, he thrived on this approach. Brenda proved able to present the curriculum to him with an intelligence and a flair way beyond what was required of her by the distance education bureaucrats. She found this activity combined well with her home duties and with the casual bookkeeping work she brought in as a means of supplementing the more-or-less regular stipend Mick (bless him) sent her from any and every corner of the country. Furthermore, the social aspects of the exercise helped her to master those soul-destroying feelings of loneliness still dogging her days.

The best moments both for Harry and for Brenda were those following the completion of the day's formal curricular requirements. Then Brenda would switch to storytelling mode. Sometimes the stories would come directly from her own head, and at other times they would come from the pages of a book she held in front of her.

>

A decade or more later, when Harry found himself with enough free time to indulge in a bit of discretionary reading, he found with amazement – when he started turning pages – he knew a lot of the 'stories' already. The old miser who lost all his hoarded gold but found instead a golden-haired girl. The lighter, laden with silver ingots, colliding in mist-shrouded seas with the hostile steamship. Penelope, who had promised her avaricious suitors to marry when she had completed her weaving, stitching by day and unstitching by night. Nasrudin Hoja, sitting astride his donkey, dispersing his wit and wisdom ('heads I win, tails you lose') like seed for crops. Where, Harry asked himself, had all these amazing stories come from? He was sure he couldn't have been *born* with them in his head.

Slowly Harry remembered. But, he asked himself, if his mother had told him these stories when he was eight years old, from where had *she* got them? In a moment of blinding insight, at odds with his native mix of narcissism and naivety, it dawned on him his mother had *not* sprung fully-formed into existence in order to become his mother. She had had a *prior* life.

He tried for a moment or two to piece this life together. There were few clues to help him, from things to which on occasion his mother had alluded adventitiously. She was an only child. Her mother and father had been schoolteachers. Her father had died young. Her mother had remarried, and had left Australia with her new husband to live in Greece. He – Harry – had, with mild interest, noticed their framed photographs at the Bee Street house, but had never met or known any of them. Also there had been books – venerable books including classics, he seemed to recollect – in the Bee Street house. Every Christmas, including the one just past, a postcard had arrived bearing foreign stamps. From Samos, Greece, he seemed to recollect.

Was *this*, Harry asked himself, the basis for something approaching a grand oral tradition? Her educated parents telling stories to her, and she in turn telling stories to her son/daughter? For him to tell to *his* son/daughter? Wonderful uplifting stories. Stories lifted from the classic literature.

If so, Harry reasoned, then perhaps there was something of great and enduring nobility about the best bits of Western civilization. Emphasis, here, on 'the best bits', thought Harry, correcting himself abruptly. Given what was happening in Iraq and Kuwait at the present moment, it was difficult to be all-embracing about such a favourable judgment. He imagined his former friend, Izzie – right there, *exactly* there, as we home here played out comfortable lives – returning fire across scorching sand dunes, breathing in the stench of dry dust, wet diesel, hot ammunition, and cold corpses. At the behest of Stormin' Norman. Where are the uplifting stories about this?

Pademelons, we are off message. My fault entirely. I should be dealing with the little tyke's early education, but instead I find myself spouting forth about the geo-politics of the early 90s. I can't imagine how I *got* there. I'll give myself a short sharp slap on the wrist and we'll get back on track immediately.

Nevertheless, you *will* get to hear some more about the redoubtable Izzie shortly. *Very* shortly.

<

At age eleven, Harry began his secondary education at John Bunyan College in a more salubrious suburb further round the bay. His mother had found she was able to afford to send him to a private school – albeit one with paltry status – and had convinced herself a move of this kind would be good for her son. She felt gratified to see Harry walking down Bee Street, doubtless in full view of the neighbours, in *that* uniform. There *was* the snob in her.

There was the snob *outside of her* too. When it became generally known in College circles that Harry was the only tradesman's child in his class, Harry was subjected to frequent and tangible reminders of those bad old days in primary school. Chanelling Dante in his infernal travels, he found himself drawn to conclude hell could come in a variety of shapes and forms. The little vulgarians making this new stage of his life difficult were the sons and daughters of the proprietors of franchise launderettes and the like. Their fathers wouldn't be seen dead at Delaney's. That made no difference to the taste in Harry's mouth of the shit sandwiches their progeny forced down his throat. Shit tends to have the same flavour no matter from which side of the tracks it comes.

After a year or so of this new hell and with – seemingly – no end in sight, Harry's life was finally made modestly bearable by a couple of friends come to him out of left field. They were – and of necessity would have *had* to be – outsiders themselves. Harry had no idea what drew them to him, but felt he was in no position to ask.

Isadore Fauntleroy Gillespie came to Harry's attention first. Indubitably, Izzie's issues with the 'yodellers' – which is what Izzie himself had dubbed those little upstarts with the temerity to presume to set the tone of the campus – had something to do with his multiply unfortunate name, but this was far from being the whole story. Izzie was an original: bold, outrageous, imaginative, enigmatic, unpredictable, and manic. Especially manic. The yodellers couldn't get a handle on him at all. He loved to spring surprises on them, because this is what he figured the yodellers hated more than anything else. Surprises.

… as for the reason Izzie had chosen to call them 'yodellers', this – in keeping with his persona generally – was difficult to fathom. In all likelihood, those who had the dubious fortune to be labelled thus were no more actual yodellers than you are actual pademelons. One might be tempted to hazard the obvious guess that Izzie's choice of epithet had something to do with his musical predisposition. But, as in all things pertaining to Izzie, the obvious guess is – more often than not – light years wide of the mark …

Getting back to it then, i.e. to 'surprises'.

Take, for example, the day Izzie announced he intended to demonstrate some 'secret boy's business'. Hordes of yodellers of both sexes descended on the stand at the back of the school oval, adjacent to the public golf course. Underneath the tiered bench seats of the sports stand, was a secluded cranny wherein much of the school's clandestine activity happened. The girls were sent packing unceremoniously, the grounds for this being it was none of their business. This is secret boy's business, they were reminded.

A phalanx of (mostly) pre-pubescent yodellers of the male gender gathered round Izzie who was ensconced in the extremity of the cranny. Through the slats behind him, the green of the oval was visible. This was the oval where, through the medium of vainglorious sporting and athletic events, the valour of the College was perennially on display and its prestige perpetually on the line. Rah, rah, rah. But nobody was here to watch sport now. Not that kind of sport, anyway.

Harry, recipient of the business end of many cruel elbows in the face and knees to the groin, retreated to the rear of the milling crowd, but still managed to get an adequate view of proceedings between bobbing heads. This was the first time he had set eyes on Izzie. His hair was jet black, boiling over with curls. His mischievous eyes darted constantly, as if looking to break free of hooked nose and thick fleshy lips. All these features were set in a cherubic face as round as the moon. He was of average height only for his age, perhaps even less, but he was stocky, and his hands and feet were huge.

When everyone was settled, and an expectant silence hung like fleecy cumuli, Izzie – without a word – pulled down his trousers, seated himself with knees spread, closed his eyes, and set Mrs Palmer and her five daughters to work. The look on his face was one of combined bliss and concentration. It wasn't long before the white creamy stuff erupted in several vigorous spurts.

The incredulous yodellers fell about. The vowel-laden responses from them were invariably accompanied by steep downwards inflexions expressive of hypocritical disgust. Those individual comments – those intelligible – were along the lines of:

Holy shit!

He's gay.

He's diseased.

Filthy bugger.

Unclean! Unclean!

Two seniors walking by, clothed in prefect's blazers and in the aloof attitude befitting their exalted station, were overheard in conversation:

That's all that was on offer? said one.

On the strength of it, said the other.

Then the little fucker sold us short, said the first.

What more could you expect from a merchant banker? replied the other.

Pademelons, it should come as no surprise to you that – from this moment on – Izzie became known among the yodellers as the 'wanking yank'. The latter portion of this colourful appellation reflected an accident of birth requiring further explanation and, if you bear with me, I shall duly supply you with such.

<

To do justice to the task, beloved pademelons, I intend to provide you with an encapsulated account of the heritage vouchsafed to Izzie via those dual conduits of nature and nurture which have affected us all. This account shall be in condensed form because – as I strive constantly to make clear – the essence of my brief is to demystify the life and many deaths of Harry McMinn, and not the exhibitionist escapades of Isadore Gillespie. In consequence, I do not feel obliged at this or at any other juncture to excurse back beyond more than one generation of Gillespies.

Who *were* the parents of this wayward child, bane of all yodellers, and exponent of secret boy's business? These are parents to whom you might – in consideration of the most recent revelations I have made to you in the course of my presentation – feel inclined to convey your deepest sympathies.

Their names were Daryl and Daphne Gillespie. For better or for worse, their marital relationship followed in the wake of a business relationship. Or was it the other way round? In any case, Daryl and Daphne were – from the outset of said conjoint relationships – the sole directors of a company registered in Oz under the cryptic name, Contrarian Promotions.

What was the business of this company?

It was to promote – often to people in realms far removed from Oz – to world-weary people who in many cases had seen it all – the varieties of entertainment to which the hoi polloi of Oz had taken – in the proving grounds of the hallowing years – with some degree of enthusiasm. In some cases, to the point of obsession.

In accordance with accepted practice among the promotions cognoscente, the principals of Contrarian Promotions would, in the normal course of events, expect to receive the lion's share of any proceeds from their ventures, but were inclined to back away from any anticipated losses quicker than a Quaker would from a general mobilization.

From the standpoint of the elitist mindset, the Gillespies were dabblers in low culture. They did races: of horses, camels, pigeons, fleas, cane-toads, bandicoots, budgerigars, crocodiles ... of anything in fact propelling itself by means of two legs, four legs, wings, wheels, flippers, paddles, inboard motors, outboard motors, and/or suitable combination thereof. They did team sports: with any kind of balls, pucks, bats, clubs, cues, fists, chains, cuffs, whips, and/or suitable combination thereof. They did gambling on any of the above or, failing that, on two coins tossed into the air.

To the credit of this worthy duo, once they had laid down (what they regarded as) a firm fiscal foundation for themselves based on the low hanging fruit alluded to above, Daryl and Daphne actively sought out (what they regarded as) the prime cut of culture: concerts, gigs, cabaret, festivals, musicals, dance, the stage ... all summed up in the single prestigious phrase, 'the performance arts'. They coveted, and set about espousing, the image of Contrarian Promotions as Patron of the Arts. On their long haul to distant shores – travelling cattle class – the Gillespies were inclined to think of themselves as dual spearheads of a noble and ambassadorial mission.

On their outward journey, they would (typically) be clutching the contract pro-formas and portfolios of a motley group of hopeful Oz-based 'event-executants' eager to exude their local colour on the international stage. On their return journey, they would hope to bring back to Oz something of the flavour of the wider world. But even a casual observer could not have failed to notice a certain imbalance between their outbound and inbound endeavours. I cite one example: they left Oz with the prospectus of a pop group known (by a handful of enthusiastic family members) as the Dubbo Doobies, and tried to return with the New York Rockettes.

They may not have persuaded the Rockettes but they *did* manage to bring *something* by way of trophy back to Oz: the new-born pink-skinned Isadore Fauntleroy Gillespie, as he was eventually (and eccentrically) to be named. I should tell you the first of Izzie's physical features to *actually* grace the wide world when the pubic curtains parted, was *not* his pink skin at all, but his tumbling jet-black and fully-formed locks of hair.

The precise geographic location of his US birthplace – not the sort of information his parents were in any great hurry to put about – was some tawdry suburb of Newark, NJ. As luck would have it, the less-than-appealing odour of his native sod had no adverse consequence for Izzie: it sufficed to qualify him for dual Oz/US citizenship, as surely as if it had been the sod of Beverley Hills or of Long Island.

On their return to Oz, Daryl and Daphne glimpsed a once-in-a-lifetime opportunity, viz. to develop baby Isadore's assumed natural talents to the point where they could be sold to an eager international audience. By Contrarian Promotions. Seated one day at her baby grand – a white Yamaha inlaid with mother-of-pearl – enjoying the sensation of Izzie gorging greedily on her milk-laden breasts, and simultaneously making a heroic effort (and with no small degree of success) to thrash Mozart's sonata *für Anfänger* to within an inch of its life, Daphne was to remark to her husband with an accompanying pianistic flourish:

Behold young Wolfgang!

I thought we named him Isadore, said Daryl.

And so we did.

So what gives with Wolfgang?

Wolfgang Amadeus Mozart.

Your point being … ?

Wake up, Australia. *He's* the prodigy and *you* get to play Leopold.

Gives *you* a chance there for a spot of bigamy. With healthy prospects for a turn at incest further down the track.

Rat!

Somehow she found a free hand. The free hand in turn found the metronome, which she hurled at Daryl's head. The metronome shaved Daryl's left ear, and fell to earth with a thwang, liberating sundry flywheels, springs, cogs, and other metallic paraphernalia from their hitherto tortured existence in the service of Time, that most pitiless of taskmasters.

I digress.

At age three, Izzie embarked on a musical education. He responded well to this, the *initial* phase of the overall process envisaged by his parents, but – to his parents' mortification – steadfastly resisted the *subsequent* phases, which involved his person being actively promoted and marketed. From the earliest days, he seemed in some canny way to sense he was being used. It became evident to blind Freddie that Izzie did not warm to the idea of being treated like some trumped-up circus animal. To cap all this off, his teen years came along and – with them – the inclination to youthful rebellion.

The upshot of it all was, aged just shy of his twenties and with said rebellion in full throat, Izzie decamped to the land/home of the free/brave, and there proceeded to join the marines. His dual citizenship proved invaluable for this purpose. Soon after making this dubious move, he was rewarded with a tour of duty in the Middle East, and was privileged to see five days of action in what became known as Operation Desert Storm.

Apropos of his experiences in this arena, there were consequences for him compelling both our discretion and our pity.

Suffice it to say at this juncture – the conclusion of this mother of all wars – Izzie managed to acquire for himself an honourable discharge from the Services, so he could return to Oz suitably buggered and bewildered.

And bald.

<

It is timely to turn our attention to the aftermath and consequences of Izzie's earlier escapade beneath the sports stand at Bunyan College, the – shall we say? – climax of which was his successful demonstration of secret boy's business to the yodellers.

As the crowd dispersed in the chaotic wake of this event, laughter – forced, macho, nervous, hyped-up – could be heard radiating out from its epicentre and eventually penetrating every corner of the campus. Harry, well able to read the signs, and aware he could so easily become a convenient outlet for pack aggression, kept out of sight as he took the long way around the oval and back to the classroom precinct. He – for his part – was mystified and more than a little uncomfortable about the black magic he had witnessed. Who was this strange Izzie person? And whence his bag of tricks? Including the white stuff.

Harry came into possession of a tiny part of the answer (together with many more questions) next morning when, at College assembly, he realized for the first time who the person was that regularly accompanied – on the school organ – the hymns they were all obliged to sing. It was the selfsame Izzie.

The manic Izzie, the compulsively exhibitionist Izzie. A picture of cool serenity as he played the instrumental line of 'Oh Love, Thou Wilt Not Let Me Go.' How very apposite! The cherubic face, its look of other-worldly absorption, the subsumption of ego into the ephemeral realms of music. Bound by love, yes, and never were shackles so willingly endured.

It was predictable the yodellers – given the dubious code of ethics to which their respective backgrounds inclined them – would include in their ranks a sprinkling of zealous laggers[11]. So – no surprise to anybody – the College administration quickly got wind of Izzie's virtuoso performance, a performance – need I remind you? – not on the school organ but on his very own.

What followed was an outpouring of verbal vomit from this administration, as it pursued the familiar ritual of dressing down and hushing up. Izzie was called in and bawled out. His parents – protesting they were snowed under – were 'invited' over, taken aside, and asked to participate in an exchange of all sorts of dodgy assurances. At the finish, it was unanimously agreed – as was inevitable from the start – that nothing more would transpire in thought, word, or deed. The matter was closed but the door was always open. And nobody knew anymore whether they were Arthur or Martha.

One day, soon after this instance of corporate inanity had run its hysterical course, Harry and Izzie made first contact. Izzie approached Harry and asked in conspiratorial voice with sardonic edge:

How can I get some uranium, professor?

… Harry, an established science nerd by now, was used to this form of address …

What they put in bombs? asked Harry.

That's the stuff.

What do you want it for?

---

11 lagger: Australian slang, derogatory, meaning 'informant'.

I'm gonna blow up this College, and I wanna make sure I do a proper job of it.

I think they make it out of lead and helium.

Helium? Like in balloons?

The same.

Can you get me some lead?

Harry – flattered to be asked – said, I'll try.

That night, back at Bee Street, Harry found some lead flashing in Mick's moribund workshop, cut a portion of it up into small pieces with tin snips, and wrapped these pieces up in an oily chamois. Next day – glancing round furtively as he did so – he extracted the chamois and its telltale contents from his port and presented the heavy bundle to Izzie.

You won't tell anyone I gave you this? asked Harry.

If that's the way you want it, fine by me.

I wouldn't want to be charged as an accessory.

Izzie laughed.

Man, this is a suicide mission. You'll be a *dead* accessory.

So, pademelons, began a beautiful friendship.

Who was the *other* friend helping to make Harry's life bearable? I'll hand over to my second unit for details of *that* one.

2nd **Unit** >>

It is Harry, Sticks, and Matt, over coffee and cakes at *La Spag*. Sticks has her laptop. The *latte* crowd is buzzing. The coffee machine is hissing. Bruno, at the desk, is content with his thoughts, which go along the lines of, ka-chink, ka-chink.

Bunion College, says Matt. Or better: Bunion Porridge. Spelt B-U-N-I-O-N. Porridge is Cockney slang for the slammer.

Sticks laughs.

I went to St Margaret's, she says. We called it St Maggot's. Then later to St Gertrude's. St Grub's.

Our head honcho at Porridge, said Harry, insisted we young ingrates would one day be singing the praises of our old school. I swear the choir never got to find the number of the page *he* was on.

How did you two get to know each other? asks Sticks.

Matt looks bemused.

Ask me how the Pope got to be a Catholic, he says.

Well, *I* remember, says Harry.

Sticks and Matt respond simultaneously.

How the Pope became a Catholic? asks Sticks. Bully for you, boyo, says Matt.

Twiggy's class, says Harry. Twiggy had us all choose a project. I chose the moons of Jupiter. Twiggy liked my choice.

Brown nose, says Matt.

Then, says Harry, it came Matt's time to choose. Remember what you chose?

No idea, says Matt.

Women's clothing, says Harry.

Matt is scornful.

Pull the other one, he says.

It's true. When Twiggy asked him why, he said, 'I like the idea of dressing women.' Remember what transpired then?

No idea, says Matt.

Not much you can remember, is there?

Get on with it, turkey.

You winked at me and said, 'I like *un*dressing them even better.' That was our first contact. That wink.

I'll rue the day, says Matt.

Harry turns to Sticks.

I was gobsmacked, he says. We were only thirteen, but Matt always seemed much older. We were sure he understated his age.

Matt is scornful.

So I could hang around playing with my own turds like you little nippers, he says.

Brass tacks time, says Sticks. Let's get down to 'em. You remember how it came about Matt taught you the facts of life?

No problem there, says Matt. This is Mr Memory himself.

Winkipops[12], says Harry.

There is silence.

Winkipops, says Harry again.

The blank look on the faces of both listeners remains unaltered. Nevertheless Sticks is writing the word on her laptop.

Harry addresses himself rhetorically to Matt.

You mean, Harry says, I'm *now* going to have to tell *you* what a winkipop is.

Matt and Sticks respond simultaneously.

A nod's as good as a wink to a blind man, says Matt. I think we can guess, says Sticks.

I'll inform you anyway, says Harry. It was in Macca's class. Macca taught us clay modelling. Remember Macca?

Macintosh?

Yes.

Vaguely, says Matt.

Me too, says Harry. I can't actually get a mental picture of him any more. Nice guy, though.

Sticks writes the name on her laptop.

Macca *tried* to teach me to make things out of clay, says Harry, but you've either got it or you don't. I didn't. But Matt was good. He was the best.

I'm short of recruits, says Sticks. I may have to dig deep to get someone to play Macca.

They are aware Bruno, who has been making courtesy calls on each table in turn, is looming over them. With his customary smile, as broad as the Mediterranean, he addresses them all simultaneously.

How is everything? he asks.

Molto bello, maestro, says Matt. *Molto bello.*

---

12 cf. Winkipop Beach, the Surf Coast, Victoria, Australia.

The coffee is good?
Molto delizioso. Molto stupendo. Molto magnifico.
Grazie mille, signore, says Bruno with a deferential bow.
Prego, mio molto buono amico, says Matt.
Bruno, in a gesture of mock impatience, puts hands on hips.
Matthew, says Bruno. You cannot take the Mickey out of me, because my name is not Mickey. It is Bruno.
Sticks, determined to put an end to this silliness, points to Roberto, behind the *espresso* machine.
Your son should be complimented, she says.
Matt interrupts.
Perchance your son the lawyer? Your son the doctor? asks Matt.
Doctor no, says Bruno. Lawyer …
Bruno's right hand, palm down, executes a side-to-side flutter.
… maybe. Roberto, he studies law.
Of course, says Matt. I foresee a future for your son as a *barista*. I foresee a future for you, Matthew, in footwear.
Bruno cups his hand over his mouth and talks, as if in an aside, to Sticks, but with the full intention all three of them should hear.
Concrete boots, he says.
Bruno leaves complimentary dinner mints on the table for all.

>

Izzie, bent over his keyboard, is engrossed in the music for the next song, a cheeky little number with a comic stride, in major key and 4/4 time.
Ranged in rough form round the stage area are a number of unusual props: slim desks with sloping benches just below shoulder height. These are clay-modelling desks. Students are expected to stand behind them kneading masterpieces.
It is rehearsal time in Sleek Street.
At centre stage, the adult Harry and Matt are goofing around

in short pants, shirt, and school necktie, angling for a reaction from Sonia and Elena in the front stalls. These two women appear a shade tipsy, which may or may not be the case, but it would certainly account for why they are disposed to be even mildly charitable towards the two unfunny clowns. Harry and Matt have no trouble getting a response of sorts, if sniggers and snide comments could be considered an adequate reward for effort.

Sticks approaches from backstage with an unfamiliar man in tow. He is about Harry's age, well groomed in an off-the-rack style, and slightly balding behind an outrageous comb-over. He is afflicted with timid blinking eyes. They light up attentively as he takes in the indications of theatrical business surrounding him. He is delighted with and amused at the bare-kneed folk.

Meet Godfrey, says Sticks. He's going to play Macca.

Harry and Matt approach. They introduce themselves.

Harry McMinn, says Harry.

He offers Godfrey his hand. They shake.

Matthew Bolton, says Matt. Call me Matt.

He offers Godfrey his hand. They shake.

Godfrey Goldsworthy, says Godfrey. Call me God.

I begin to suspect there may be more to Godfrey than meets the eye. Behind that nervous visage is a sparkle suggestive of a compulsive jokester bursting for an opportunity to unleash his clownish ego. Do you also have this sense, pademelons? Do you think he is the sort of person able to stay on message in support of Harry's grand plan? A team player, so to speak?

Godfrey is from Sandalwood Singers, says Sticks. A *local* group. They sing madrigals and the like. I'm hoping we can tap into this pool of talent whenever we need recruits.

Sticks leads Godfrey to Izzie. Izzie responds sourly when introduced. For reasons best known to himself, he has not taken kindly to Godfrey. Nevertheless, Sticks manages the situation. Soon the three of them are gathered round the synthesizer, their attention focused on the music for the next *Stück*.

Harry and Matt resume their schoolboy repartee, playing – as before – to their small audience in the stalls, bouncing remarks in quick succession off each other, and punctuating their verbal cut and thrust with wildly camped-up gesturing. We are left wondering perhaps who the real jokesters are.

Sandalwood, says Matt.

Sweet smelling wood, says Harry.

Matt tests the air with his nose.

So I have heard, boyo, he says. From where do you suppose she sniffed out these sweet smelling minstrels?

I wasn't aware myself, says Harry, madrigals had such a congenial fragrance.

Speaking more broadly, I must confess the standard repertoire for the didgeridoo has a propensity to hum. Would you agree?

I draw the line at the stench of bagpipery.

Matt screws up his nose.

Yukko! I feel the irresistible urge to apply some Chanel No. 5 in F sharp minor.

In mime, Matt squirts himself with perfume.

Have you perchance, asks Harry, experienced the odour of eucalyptus rendered with tender loving care in copperplate Braille?

Have you of recent, asks Matt, come across a person who would truly qualify as candy for the eye?

We have always, I suppose, a golden handshake to look forward to.

Or recourse to a technicolour yawn.

You, too, can enjoy a gay lifestyle with Photoshop enhancement.

Inexplicably to some perhaps, this last thrust from Harry throws Matt off his stride. He pauses. His jaw drops. He shifts his attention abruptly from the audience to Harry, and proceeds to scrutinize his side-kick's face intently. Harry, aware he is under scrutiny, does not allow himself to react. He gestures with his hand, but this is merely to remind Matt his primary duty is to his audience.

It only takes a second or two before Matt dissembles, turns back to face the audience, and delivers his riposte:

I'd rather try a bowl of crunchy quavers for brekky.

Matt bows, in order to force an end to the routine. Harry is obliged to follow suit. To outward appearances, the pair have managed to derive a deal of personal pleasure from their droll exchange, and at the least there is the pretence of amusement from Sonia and Elena in the stalls, who clap wildly.

But as the two men go their separate ways back across the stage, a sense all is not in order invades the space between them. Their developing mutual tension manages to assume an almost physical presence. Look at the body language, pademelons. Matt's pursed lips look ready to spit the mother of all dummies. Harry's gait is soldier stiff, and the furrows on his brow are so deep his eyebrows look likely to be swallowed up in them. He has the look of a person seriously worried he might have accidentally crossed a line into territory somehow off limits.

At one point in his traverse of the stage, Harry flings out his hands, palms up, in a spontaneous – and possibly involuntary – gesture of frustration, every bit as impotent as it is silent.

Can you imagine what the thought might be that, as Harry crosses the stage, is – with equal deliberation – crossing Harry's mind?

A shrewd guess might be: *So this is the pretty pass to which more than a quarter century of close friendship has led us?*

>

The hiatus does not last. A few more days of rehearsal under the gentle guidance of the genial Godfrey, has the effronted pair getting into stride again, ready to put their best into their respective contributions to the impending *Stück*. The show must go on.

Despite my initial reservations about Godfrey, he turns out to be of excellent value. Sticks has taken him on as de facto assistant. He spruiks the view – supported by evidence he claims – that, because the physical act of singing exercises the lungs and heart, it increases longevity. Can you relate to that, pademelons?

I withdraw the question, and apologize for such errant flippancy. It needs no telling our fraternity inhabit a realm appropriately described as 'timeless'. Or shall we strive for something still more appropriate and call it 'outside of time'? What use can such as we have for arcane notions such as that of longevity?

Over the next few rehearsals, the amiable Godfrey succeeds in introducing them all – including even Izzie – to a rigorous training regime designed to loosen up the vocal chords and other bodily apparatus involved in the act of singing. He has the whole team gathered round the synthesizer taking long deep breaths, rolling their shoulders, wiggling their tongues inside their mouths, do-reh-mi-so-farring, holding notes indefinitely, ascending and descending the chromatic scale, &etc, … virtually everything except swinging from the rafters.

On the eve of the performance, the members of this theatrical team are in the highest of spirits. Such an elevation of the communal soul can only bode well, not just for the imminent performance but also for the morale of my second unit in the long term. I can't help but observe that it contrasts favourably with events surrounding the previous *Stück*, in the torrid aftermath of which – as you will recall – there was a regrettable outbreak of bad feeling.

Keep your little furry digits crossed, pademelons.

>

Singspielstück #4: Winkipops

As the stage lights go up, we see at stage left, and raked at an angle of about 45° to the front of stage, a couple of rows of clay-modelling desks. This skewed view is an old cinematographer's trick, calculated to give an illusion of depth to the scene.

Behind these desks are adults dressed up as students, some male and some female, and all anonymous except for the two at the front, viz. Harry and Matt. The others, we must presume, are Sandalwood recruits. Through the magic of his backstage skills, Matt has succeeded in conferring on all of these adult performers – including himself – the extrinsics of awkward adolescence.

Stage right includes a blackboard with an electric kiln on its left and a bin for clay on its right. Macca – played by Godfrey – is sketching with chalk on blackboard an illustration of the task he has in mind for the class. He wears a plain grey apron, similar to that sometimes found on butchers and the like, fitting neatly over workday shirt and slacks.

The right hand wing is lit. Standing there, ready to translate the *Singspiel* into sign language, is a neatly-suited man, a lower ranking public servant perhaps. It appears Harry and his team are striking a blow for equal opportunity here, though I regret to say wheelchair access to this theatre can be a problem.

The left hand wing is Izzie's domain.

The two uppermost CCTV screens reveal the broader scene.

The main façade of the school appears on the upper left hand screen. Evident here is an abortive attempt to train ivy up a modern solid-brick wall. High on the wall, in silvered wrought iron, the name of the school is spelt out: **JOHN BUNYAN COLLEGE**. Beneath this is the school crest.

The upper right screen shows this school crest in magnification. Beneath the pretentious heraldic regalia is the school motto: *Nil Satis Nisi Optimum.*

The CCTV screens at bottom left and bottom right focus respectively on Harry's and Matt's work benches from above. We see shapeless lumps of clay, ready to be moulded by hand in the early stages of the task, and some simple instruments – scalpels and the like – to be used for the finishing stages.

Simple successive chords – an octave apart – comprise the musical introduction. As the song begins, two other phenomena – each in the nature of a sideshow – compete for our attention.

As if possessed by a rather unpleasant tic, the signer on the right hand wing sets his fingers and hands twitching in a furious little dance, for the benefit of those among you, pademelons, who are hearing-impaired.

Whetting our curiosity, subtitles begin to flash, white on the black excised strip over the lip of the stage.

The subtitles are at first in French but, perversely, do not stay French. In the course of the song, they move in rotation through a Babel of languages: German, Russian, Spanish, Polish, Mandarin, Korean,… Clearly this is Sticks' idea, but for whomever's benefit it is intended, the devil only knows. Unless – so we might speculate – its purpose is to provide a vehicle wherein the ostentatious display of Sticks' linguistic virtuosity might be conveyed to the unwitting.

Ultimately, as is its wont, the primary action devolving beneath the proscenium demands our attention. Macca, the floor is yours.

Macca:

The modelling of clay is now your task.
A rider on a horse is what I ask,
a-galloping along like William Tell.
The pair of them must fit together very well.

Matt:

Is it to be a woman or a man?

Macca:

Your choice. Whichever one you think you can.

Matt:

Her Ladyship Godiva's whom I'll make.
Please, Sir, to set your oven for the final bake.

Matt goes to work, and his skill – as seen on CCTV – is apparent. Separate horse and woman emerge quickly from the amorphous clay with well formed anatomical detail. The woman – naked – is in riding position, presumably in readiness to be seated, with thighs able to straddle the horse when and as required. No demure side-saddle for this Lady!

Macca, wandering round the class, pauses behind Harry, who is trying to connect several shapeless pillows of clay: one large plump pillow for the horse's body, one small plump pillow for the head, four long thin pillows for the legs, and one long thin pillow for the tail. CCTV gives us a view of this. Macca is less than impressed, but tries not to let it show too obviously on his face.

Harry:

I'm never very certain I can cope.
With clay I really feel I'm quite a dope.
Ten thumbs will never ever do the job.
The end result will be a blob.

Macca:

Well, do your level best and we shall see.
You're in the very cream of company.

Macca pauses behind Matt. His face takes on a look of delight at first, which quickly morphs into a look of mild disapproval.

My God, a masterpiece has here accrued,
but did she really need to be so nude?

Macca moves on to look at the handiwork of other students. The lyrics of the song pass to Matt and Harry. Matt's busy hands are still working. Effortlessly, he models a naked man – with full anatomical detail – from the clay.

Matt:

Girls and boys are all coming out and playing.
I'll be glad to show them how the deed is done.

Matt manipulates his models to show *Harry* how the deed is done.

A winkipop for he. A winkipop for she.
These winkipops are everybody's fun.

... the magic word 'winkipop' is not readily translatable into any of the foreign languages in circulation, so remains as 'winkipop' in the subtitles, lurking there incongruently amidst the cyphers, like a maggot turning up in a colander of green peas. We need say little about the translation into sign language. People are out there walking the streets with no more imagination than the aforesaid maggot, who would have little difficulty interpreting *these* gestures ...

Harry:

I don't understand
what a winkipop's in aid of.

Matt:

I can tell you for a fact
they're not a thing to be afraid of.
These winkies bring the stuff together
that a baby's made of.

Harry:

I don't believe that's ...

Matt:

... that a baby's made of.

Harry:

I don't believe that's …

Matt:

… that a baby's made of.

Harry:

I don't believe that's true.

Macca:

Matthew Bolton,
you get off your roller coaster!
I am mindful you are nothing but
a shabby little boaster.
It's high time for you to get back to the
matters you are s'posed ta.

Matt:

Sir, don't get in a …

Macca:

… matters you are s'posed ta.

Matt:

Sir, don't get in a …

Macca:

… matters you are s'posed ta.

Matt:

Sir, don't get in a stew.

Harry:

If that is what the game is all about
then tell me how the kiddiewink gets out.

Matt:

For months the little beastie swims around
then takes a tumble to much firmer ground.

Harry:

I don't believe a single thing you say.
I don't believe a baby comes that way.
I don't believe a winkipop can do
the mischief you presume, thank you!

Matt:

It isn't my intention just to skite.
The evidence is there though doubt you might.
Sir, Mr Macintosh, what do you say?

Macca:

I've had enough of you guys …
(Quit the ballyhoo guys.
Time to say adieu guys.
Get back to the zoo guys.)
… had enough of you guys for today.

Music stops. Stage lights go out. Curtains close.

>

Harry, Sticks, and Elena lounge on the aisle steps near one of the doors leading to front-of-house. The stage is spread out before them.

Brenda told you nothing? asks Sticks.

Brenda? asks Harry.

About winkipops.

No.

Nothing at all?

Nothing to any purpose.

I find that hard to believe.

At this moment, Izzie – at his synthesizer on the left wing of the stage – engages the keyboard with sudden vigour, belting out what we presume to be the melody for the next *Stück*. He has conjured up such a combination of instruments as will contribute the flavour of trad jazz to his rendition. Sticks' attention is diverted. She shouts to Izzie.

Sounds like The Saints are on the march, is what she shouts.

Izzie stops abruptly, becomes aware of the little group in conference on the steps, and shouts back. Not to Sticks but to Harry. His message is a bombshell, a serious threat to Harry's worldview.

By the by, Harry my best pal, is what he shouts, how many syllables are there in a haiku?

A what? shouts Harry.

Haiku.

How should I know?

Guess.

Harry can guess. He is thrown into introspective turmoil by Izzie's bald revelation. He had previously been gazing idly at Elena's shapely legs, one crossed provocatively over the other, and which – as his not-so-idle mind had ascertained – are within easy reach of fingers with a will to explore. Now, however, his gaze drifts away into some private space of his own at the other end of the universe.

Sticks is unhappy with this. She is intent on promoting discourse, not introspection. She waves a hand in front of his blank gaze.

Anyone home? she asks.

Uhh, says Harry.

I find it hard to believe Brenda didn't tell you anything.

About haikus?

About winkipops.

It takes a while, but the penny *does* drop for Harry.

That's *your* problem, he says.

You honestly didn't believe Matt when he tried to set you straight?

No.

No you did or no you didn't?

No I didn't.

Sad.

Different these days.

How so?

These days I'm a sucker, he says. I'm ready to believe any fool story.

Sticks reacts to Harry's attempt at drollery, by tilting her head as if taking aim, and shooting him a questionable look. Nevertheless, she is glad she has been able to entice him back into the real world from which he had drifted following Izzie's ill-timed remark.

When I thought about it, says Harry, it seemed as if he might be right after all.

Matt? asks Sticks.

Yes.

Hallelujah.

It was as if I'd found a missing piece of jigsaw puzzle.

Useful if you're planning to be a parent.

Useful if you're *not*.

She shoots him another withering look. Between her teeth, she says, Yes.

There is a pause.

What do you suppose is behind it all anyway? asks Harry.

Behind what?

Sex. What else might we be talking about?

Nothing behind it at all. What you see is what you get.

That's not the way I read things.

How *do* you read things?

I smell a conspiracy. Biological imperative posing as animal indulgence.

Who's the conspirator?

There is silence. When Sticks moves to break it, there is a change in her tone. She has decided to attack on another flank with the hope of taking firmer control of the agenda. This is what Sticks, the tactician, likes to do.

I'd like to put a question in all seriousness, says Sticks. To both of you.

I'll play your game, says Harry.

Elena, too, murmurs approval.

What do you suppose, asks Sticks, makes people who are more-or-less well adjusted in other respects, go to pieces when it comes to considerations of a sexual nature?

You're talking about me? asks Harry.

If the cap fits.

On the big head or the little head?

Sticks' eyes narrow. Could they, thinks Harry, be slits in the turret of a medieval fortress from which a bevy of crossbow darts are about to streak to their target?

Answer the question, Sticks says.

Obvious isn't it?

State the obvious.

Embarrassment, shame, fear, guilt. If that's not enough, there's social pressure, STDs, unwanted pregnancies, …

Elena decides to put an oar in.

Do you have hard knock school in *Avstrália*? she asks.

Harry and Sticks ask the same question simultaneously.

What do you mean? they ask.

In Russia, one learns this in hard knock school. One learns very quickly.

For a moment, Sticks and Harry are left gaping.

Sticks is the first to respond. A grand display of emotion accompanies her response. It is not at all certain how much of this emotion is genuine and how much is simulated, but it is this particular tenor of emotion Sticks always relishes the opportunity to display. She rises, steps across Harry, embraces Elena effusively, landing many wet kisses on her cheeks, even some tears, and says with quivering voice:

You're so right, darling. I *do* understand.

She turns to Harry. She has curtailed her emotion, put it back in its budgie cage ready for the moment when the next opportunity might present itself allowing it freedom of flight. Her voice takes on a resolute and much firmer tone. She says:

She's right on the money. We're totally up ourselves.

How come? asks Harry.

It's a bourgeois luxury to agonize about sexuality.

Harry is left marvelling at the magnificence of this woman who, through force of happy circumstance, has become his wife in effect and the biological mother of his child in reality. Perhaps his only regret, in respect of her, is the compulsion she apparently feels to tackle so seriously – and with such formidable intent – all the random flotsam finding its way to the surface in the pitiless wash-up of terrestrial life.

<< 1ˢᵗ Unit

Pademelons, an urge has come over me – the devil only knows why – to surprise you with a formal lecture. It is an urge I suspect I shall find impossible to contain and, consequently, any pleas from you along the lines of, What have we done to deserve this?, shall prove futile.

Equally futile from you would be a challenge to my credentials to assume such a role. My credentials are that I *have* no credentials. I have no letters after my name. I am not one of those phidiots sprouting up these days all over the shop like mother-of-millions[13]. Ask yourself, Is stale pedagoguery what you want, or would you rather have recourse to sparkling entertainment and epiphanous revelation?

I rest my case.

So, without further ado:

Economics 101. Case Study: The Micro-Economy of the Student Community on the Campus of John Bunyan College at the Height of the Antipodean Cherry Season.

Let's start with facts, of the cold and hard variety. At the beginning of the cherry season in the year under consideration (sometime in the mid to late 80s, I understand) the price of cherries was about $5 per kilo. This was exorbitant according to the dollar value of the day. For the purposes of comparison, apples, oranges, and bananas were fetching on average only about 50 cents per kilo on the retail market.

Pademelons. I hear you ask, What's the price of cherries got to do with anything?

Give me half a chance to explain.

As you will appreciate, not many people were buying cherries. The average household budget would not stretch that far. For those who *did* buy them, there were advantages. Two spring to mind:

Cherries are lolly gobble bliss bombs[14], and don't they look it! Most would agree a fat ripe sweet cherry, soft and juicy, round

---

13 mother-of-millions: an ornamental plant introduced into Australia from Madagascar and now a noxious weed in much of the country.

14 The descriptor 'lolly gobble bliss bombs' has an Australian provenance. It was/is a proprietory term used since the 1970s, not in relation to cherries, but to caramelized popcorn.

as an eyeball, and glistening with that characteristic deep purple colour, is pleasing to the palate and to the eye.

At the end of a feast of cherries, there are stones (a.k.a. pips, a.k.a. bobs) left behind. If one sucks the remnants of the flesh from these stones, then puts them out to dry, one is left with a smooth, distinctive, and not-altogether-unattractive beige-coloured object, about the size of a ... well, of a cherry bob. I put it to you several dozens of these small woody whorls, ostentatiously shown around (at the start of the cherry season) to one's friends, enemies, fellow-travellers, groupies, hangers-on, resident spongers, partners-in-crime, and other sundry associates, would serve as proof to them of the economic status of the household within whose cosseting confines one was unconditionally cherished. Excuse the pun.

Don't underestimate the power of this latter consideration. One-upmanship can be a potent economic driver. Likewise, one-upwomanship. Putting the current discussion into context, pademelons, this is where the initial appeal lay for the grubby little upstarts, a.k.a. yodellers, whose cherry-buying parents packed them off to Bunion Porridge each day.

All age cohorts were caught up in this obsession. They would arrive at Porridge in the morning, the boys with their pockets bulging, the girls with an extra bulge in their bosom. The source of the bulge would inevitably be a cloth bag with draw-strings, seemingly lifted straight out of the middle ages. Think Robin Hood and the Sheriff of Nottingham. This cloth bag, in turn, was stuffed with cherry bobs. *They*, owners of these squirreled treasures, would proudly show their fellow parvenus what fiscal powerhouses their families were. Megabobs transmuting into megawatts. A lesson in raw socio-economics.

That was, as I said pademelons, where the *initial* appeal lay. But, very quickly, unintended consequences came crowding in, throwing the scene into confusion, and marking the beginning of an economic revolution on the Porridge campus. The innocuous and supposedly inanimate little Bobbies and Pippies developed a life and a value very much of their own. They succeeded in establishing themselves – as if by their own volition – as the currency of choice among the student body. Gold and silver coins and the multi-coloured folding stuff had become *passé*, and were traded in for these drab little gems at every opportunity.

Drab little gems? Some of the more enterprising of the Porridge inmates soon hit upon the idea of baptising their Bobbies in coloured dye or ink. They theorized, I guess, the new colour made them more valuable by dint of their relative rarity. Harry and Matt found themselves pondering this question over lunch one gloriously sunny day, as they lay facing each other – heads propped on green-stained elbows – on a clover field near the wire mesh fence separating the school from the golf course. They were inspecting the contents of their cloth bags, counting their newly minted currency like a pair of old misers.

How much do you think a blue one would fetch? asked Harry.

That's for the market to say, said Matt.

The market.

Matt nodded.

Where is this market? asked Harry

Nowhere. Everywhere.

That's crazy.

But true.

Who owns it?

You. Me. Everybody. We *all* own it.

So the added value derived from colour would be determined at market time, i.e. at the time the deal was made, when some ad hoc agreement as to the degree of rarity of a blue (or red or green) cherry bob would be reached. Does anybody doubt the power of the invisible hand of a free market like this one to drive a burgeoning economy?

What deals were made? Pademelons, you name it. Anything that could be *would be* traded for cherry bobs. Food, clothing, sports gear, pornography, knickknacks from home, … Yodellers were reputed to have traded away their families' precious heirlooms, secreted from under their parents' noses. Completed homework was in great demand, and was traded wholesale. Weedy-looking plant detritus wrapped in toilet paper was traded, lit up, and consumed voraciously under the sports stand. Prescription pills and illegal substances were traded, the scope here for deceptive practises being considerable. The drug trade was up and running as never before.

Female yodellers traded favours, delivery of which would be concluded under the sports stand or in the rough of the neighbouring golf course, the latter being more private. Only a handful of girls – in defiance of everything their long-suffering mothers had been telling them since Cocky was an egg – traded the full winkipop, but those so doing would emerge triumphant, red-cheeked, and bright-eyed, their brassieres sagging under the weight of a small fortune in pithy pods. You must concede, pademelons, no flourishing economy would be complete unless the world's oldest profession got a look-in.

Usury was a going concern. One could borrow ten cherry bobs at the beginning of the day as long as one returned eleven at the end of the day. Ten percent per day was the accepted rate, and if one defaulted one was beaten up and one's stash stolen. The usurers were always tough guys as well as good accountants. Either that or the accountants hired the tough guys, at the price of a cherry bob retainer and/or a cherry bob commission. These hired guns prospered mightily.

Gambling, however, was the main game. It was the pillar of the Porridge economy during these heady times. On what did these pimply yodellers gamble? In true Oz tradition, on anything one cares to name.

Pademelons, I have arrived at a pivotal point in my lecture. It will behove you to give me your fullest attention.

There was one particular gaming operation, the *principal* one, the one *really* capturing the imagination of the Porridge community, the main game of the main game so to speak, that I intend without further delay to analyse in detail. Make no mistake, this one was a crackerjack, a doozy, a *tour de force*. At the risk of inadvertently railroading the entire discussion into a veritable maelstrom of semantic confusion, I would suggest it was a game-changer.

I should add that for all the above reasons, and for the purpose of advancing the story of the life and many deaths of Harry McMinn, my second unit shall, in their very next *Singspielstück*, apply their proven and multifarious theatrical talents to the depiction of the crucial contribution made by Harry to this ground-breaking earth-shaking market-leading game.

First, let me enlighten you by laying bare the mechanics of this deceptively simple yet stupendous little economic driver.

The game, as if needing to establish its dinkum credentials, was played down at the level of mother earth herself. What better advertisement could there be for the wholesome disposition of this enterprise, than that it was so firmly seated on its fundament?

Its principals fell into one or other of two classes, known as 'punters' and 'bookies'. According to a well-established law of nature, there were more of the former than of the latter.

The mechanics of the game … ?

While standing on a line drawn in the aforesaid soft and obliging earth, whose placement was the prerogative of the bookie, the punter would attempt to lob a bob into a hole the bookie had scooped out in this selfsame earth with his or her bare hands. If successful in his or her endeavour, the punter would receive back his bob plus some multiple, paid out fully and without question, in bobs, which multiple would have been agreed upon in advance between punter and bookie. If unsuccessful, the punter would forfeit his bob and – at his or her discretion – try again.

In this prince of games, I need hardly tell you the position of the line was crucial to the survival of the bookie. If he or she were to place it too *close* to the hole, there would be too many payouts, and bankruptcy would quickly loom. However, if he or she were to place it too *far* from the hole, all business would go to his or her competitors – of which there could be expected to be any number of eager applicants in any thriving market economy – and bankruptcy would be equally certain. There is a fine line to be drawn here, pademelons. Would you believe me if I tell you no pun is intended?

The game I have described above so managed to dominate the Porridge community some of the more reflective of the yodellers were heard to advance the view the one and only reason cherrybobs were collected and coveted in the first place was for the express purpose of playing this game. I have my doubts.

Nobody – I allow – would dispute the fact that 'the game' was the dominant paradigm in this alternative economy, but to deny the part played by all other forms of economic activity would, I feel, be a bridge too far. It would be roughly equivalent to asserting, apropos of the *mainstream* economy, that one and two dollar coins were only minted in the first place for the exclusive purpose of being shoved down the voracious slots of poker machines.

This matter is open to debate, pademelons, a debate in which I challenge you to immerse yourselves. I would just like to venture one word of caution. Before voicing an opinion, please – I urge you – give both sides of the argument your most serious consideration. The argument may well be academic but in academia the knives can be sharp.

>

That's about the strength of it really, except – to be fair – I should tell you how it all came to an end, as all good things must. What killed it – I'm sure you can guess – was the price of cherries slumping to $2 per kilo. So every Tom, Dick, and Harry could eat cherries, passing on the bobs to somebody doing time at Porridge. Sudden glut precipitated sudden panic. The currency was devalued again and again against all the indices but to no avail. First there was hyperinflation, and then the crash. Distraught yodellers, who had lost everything, hurled their heavily-laden string-drawn cloth bags into the local creek. After that, if anybody so much as mentioned cherry bobs, they got hurled into the creek also.

To think only a week previous, some of the movers and shakers at Porridge had been talking about rolling the whole operation out into the national – perhaps even the international – arena. Sadly, this was not to be.

Most of the girls went back to skipping rope and softball, and most of the boys to touch footy and British bulldog. The more savvy of both sexes indulged their preference for the newly arrived phenomenon known as Pac-Man.

Some would say sanity had been restored. But at what price?

According to one school of thought, the Porridge inmates had been given a rare opportunity to build a frontier economy from the ground up and then to set it working in their favour. The driving forces behind this economic renaissance had been the venting of pubescent imaginings, the outpouring expression of youthful individuality, and an excess of cherry-ripe happenstance. Thus was the Wild West revisited, Utopia realized. Thus was born a vibrant society, not imposed from outside to profit outside concerns, but designed from within to succour needs arising from within. Is it insanity to want this, and to feel regret when it passes, as it seems all things must?

Another school of thought maintained there had been nothing of nobility, singularity, merit, or romance about what was – when said and done – simply an ill-conceived social experiment. It was nothing more than the wider world in microcosm, mimicking all aspects of the latter's ugliness without any of its beauty, all the while pretending to be something new and wonderful. It was *déjà vu* all over again. The Wild West? That was a *wicked* place, in a *wicked time.* Utopia? More like *dys*-topia. In the final analysis, it was a house of cards deserving to come crashing down.

What's your opinion?

While you are considering which side of the fence to munch grass on, pademelons, I shall conclude the lecture and pass the baton to my second unit, who shall give us – as I promised – a theatrical depiction of the principal gaming phenomenon gripping the student body at Porridge in those halcyon days. And of the pivotal role the adolescent greenhorn Harry came to play in its unfolding.

2ⁿᵈ Unit >>

Singspielstück #5: … an' Yer Ol' Man Back

We are barely able to take our seats before the curtains part. Backstage, extending from centre to right extremity, and skewed at a 45° angle – that old cinematographer's trick again! – are the weathered chipboard panels supposedly sealing off the back of the College sports stand. In reality, there is a gap on the extreme left of the panelling – located at the centre of backstage – allowing entry to students intent on indulging their more furtive preoccupations. We are familiar with some of these.

Taking up most of the space upstage of the panels is a thick layer of artificial turf, specially brought in for the purposes of this *Stück*.

As in the previous *Stück*, the two uppermost CCTV screens reveal to us the broader scene. The main façade of the school appears again on the upper left hand screen, from which it may correctly be infered this venerable edifice has not changed since those memorable moments when – through the apposite medium of clay modelling – the world was introduced to winkipops.

On the upper right hand screen, the school oval and the front of the sports stand are seen. Students – or more correctly, adult actors *playing* students – are streaming across the oval towards the back of the sports stand. Citations are needed. Sticks, with the cooperation of the Sandalwood Singers, has done a superb job of recruiting the large cast required for what is to be a most spectacular *Stück*. And Matt – in his backstage role – has excelled in the job of stripping a decade or two (variously) from the apparent ages of these performers.

The bottom left CCTV screen shows a row of six holes the size of half oranges gouged out of the artificial turf. The function of these holes is no mystery to us. What *might* confound us is the small plot of artificial turf *sans* hole, shown on the bottom right screen. It is the place where – famously as it turns out – another hole is destined to appear in the course of this *Stück*.

Back to the stage: this is lunch break for the students of Bunyan, but there are more important things for them to do than to eat Vegemite sandwiches. Frenetic activity is taking place on the patch of stage turf. Adrenalin – God knows what else – gushes through veins. Uniformed students of both sexes surge purposefully, both singly and in groups.

The focus of attention is the line of three boy and three girl students who – backs to the panelling – are each overseeing one of the aforementioned holes in the turf at their feet, a hole each has diligently scooped out, ostensibly with bare hands. All six have bulging cloth bags slung around their necks. We can guess what their contents are.

The select six, whom we shall call 'bookmakers', are no less frenetic than the *hoi polloi*, whom we shall call 'punters'. They – the wannabe bookmakers – are shouting like hysterical and/ or drunken auctioneers. Could they be yodelling, mayhap? In any case, they are in desperate competition with each other for business, with the result each bookie's garbled repetitive chant is all but drowned out by the cacophony of his or her competitors. The chants, barely intelligible to us – uninitiated as we are –

are nevertheless very well understood by the Bunyan fraternity and sorority. Their well-attuned ears would doubtless pick up something like:

... two an' yer ol' man back, two an' yer ol' man back, two an' yer ol' man back, ...

etc, etc., competing, perhaps, with:

... four an' yer ol' man back, four an' yer ol' man back, four ...

etc, etc., competing, perhaps, with:

... seven an' yer ol' man back, seven ...

and so on. You get the picture, pademelons?

Now engage your senses, concentrate your attention, and perhaps you'll come to understand better the fatal attraction of this game.

Just as each bookie has his/her own hole in the ground, so each has his/her own line – shall we call it a 'line in the sand'? – that each has gouged in the turf with his/her heel, at something like two to three metres from his/her hole. Standing on these lines, the punters toss cherrybobs from their stash in the general direction of the scooped-out holes, with the aim of lobbing them into these holes. When they succeed, they give a whoop of delight, and are rewarded with the number of cherrybobs the bookie's odds – shouted peremptorily to the world – have promised.

Usually the bookie will place these bobs in the hole in advance of each toss, as an inducement. Typically the bobs in the hole will include a few coloured ones mixed in with the *au naturel*. As the theory goes, this draws punters of the fairer sex, in much the same way as the dowdy and supposedly colour-deprived female bowerbird is – according to the evidence – enticed into the nest of the male.

Pademelons, what wonders the world holds for those who seek them out. Verily, your seeking is rewarded, in real time, in fine detail, and in glorious colour, if only you will look at the lower left

CCTV screen. The action here is lively. Bobs – in all colours of the rainbow – are constantly being added to and removed from the holes, according to the rules of the game and the legitimate outcomes of the gaming action proceeding under our astounded eyes.

Adolescent Harry – played by the adult Harry – enters the melee from stage left. As he cuts through the throng of punters lined up waiting to toss their cherrybobs, somebody sticks their foot out, and Harry bites the turf. This gives rise to communal jeering and other crude expressions of jocularity. Students of this age, especially *en bloc*, are easily amused, and if it can be at somebody else's expense so much the better.

Humiliated, Harry gets to his feet. He is the type of person who feels these things most keenly, which is why he is so often and so obviously a target. Nobody would try this on Matt, for example, and it is Matt now – the student Matt played by the adult Matt – who appears on the scene. He saunters calmly up to the distressed Harry, and has words in his ear.

You can't beat 'em, says Matt. Your only option is to join 'em.

How? asks Harry.

Follow me, says Matt.

He leads Harry to the gap on the left extremity of the chipboard panelling.

Dig a hole, boyo, says Matt.

Wha ... , says Harry.

Matt points to the artificial turf at his feet.

Dig a hole, says Matt.

Harry obeys. With his fingernails, he scoops out a hole of the regulation size, tossing small divots to one side and the other. This hole appears in the CCTV screen at bottom right.

Matt gouges a line a couple of metres away with the heel of his shoe.

Start calling, says Matt.

How many? asks Harry.

You decide, says Matt.

One an' yer ol' man back, one an' ... , chants Harry without verve.

More, says Matt.

Two an' yer ol' man back, two an' ..., chants Harry with tentative verve.

More, says Matt.

As seen in the CCTV screen at bottom right, Harry feeds the hole with three bobs. He decides 'to hell with it', and gets into the spirit of things.

Three an' yer ol' man back, three an yer ol' man back, (&etc), chants Harry with maximum verve.

He has customers! The punters have a choice of *seven* bookies, and many are choosing *him*.

Introductory music begins, in major key and lively 4/4 time, courtesy of Izzie on the left hand wing. The trad jazz flavour is there, tribute to synthesized sounds of trumpet, trombone, and saxophone, and to Izzie's consummate skill. As the music gets underway, the black strip below the lip of the stage becomes a ticker tape, with the stock-market report crawling across it from right to left in white letters. The All Ords[15] is up already today by half a percent, and the close of trading is more than three hours away. Let the good times roll.

In this optimistic vein, the song begins. As the chorus of indigenous doggerel is taken up vigorously by all voices, the speed and fury of the on-stage action remains undiminished. The composition, naturally, is by the adult Harry.

All:

One an' yer ol' man back.
One an' yer ol' man back again. Yea,
one an' yer ol' man back.

---

15 All Ords, contraction of 'All Ordinaries', one of the principal economic indices used by the Australian Stock Exchange.

All y' think a doin' is a bobbin' an' a lobbin'
yer cherry pippin smack into the willy willy whack,
and then get
one
[*a pause of five beats*]
an' yer ol' man back.

Two an' yer ol' man back.
Two an' yer ol' man back again. Yea,
two an' yer ol' man back.
All y' think a doin' is a bobbin' an' a lobbin'
yer cherry pippin smack into the willy willy whack,
and then get
one an' two
[*a pause of five beats*]
an' yer ol' man back.

Three … &etc, …
… &etc, &etc, …
one an' two an' three
[*a pause of five beats*]
an' yer ol' man back.

The music morphs effortlessly into 'When the Saints Go Marching In'. To set the ball rolling, Harry takes up the well-known words solo. But there are significant changes to the *Urtext*.

Driven by Izzie's exuberant musicianship, the stage action changes. The muso – barely able to keep trousers on seat – charges the air with synthetic trumpet, trombone, and the like, his round bald pink head bobbing like a party balloon at the mercy of a riot of toddlers.

The bookies – Harry 'in that number' after a cherry season of desperate and intense loneliness – vacate their posts and swagger back and forth in front of their adoring crowd of punters, who clap and cheer wildly. The adulation is palpable. Harry is ecstatic. Or, perhaps the state in which he finds himself is off the scale of ecstatic, heading recklessly in the direction of sublime. In this delirious state, he finds his senses barely able to provide for him a reliable guide to reality.

Harry:

Oh when the Books go marching in,

All:

oh when the Books go marching in,

Harry:

Lord, it's so cool to be in that number,

All:

when the Books go marching in.

The frenzy of the crowd persists. A repeat of the refrain becomes obligatory:

Harry:

Oh when the Books ...& etc

The Books retreat to their holes again. The punters are unable to contain their greed. The bobs are in the air looking for a happy landing. The 'ol' man back' song resumes several verses down the track from where it left off:

All:

Eleven ... &etc, ...
... &etc, &etc, ...
one an' two an' three ... &etc ... an' ten an' eleven
[*five beats*]
an' yer ol' man back.

Twelve ... &etc, ...
... &etc, &etc, ...

one an' two an' three … &etc … an' eleven an' twelve
[*five beats*]
an' yer ol' man back.

The school siren sounds. All action is frozen in tableau. Izzie's music stops in mid-bar. The ticker-tape ceases to deliver the stock-market report, or anything else for that matter. Trading is suspended. Lunch break is over.

It takes a mere second for the tableau to degenerate into a furious scramble for the cherrybobs sitting unclaimed in the seven holes. The issue of ownership of these residual treasures is perceived by all to inhabit a legal limbo, and the previously strict demarcation between bookie and punter falls in a heap. Scuffles, even fights, break out and – desperate to keep out of it – Harry flattens his back against the chipboard panelling. But his body is blocking *the* gap, that gap so essential for the successful discharge of clandestine activity in the Porridge social scheme-of-things.

Two sheepish heads appear – of boy and then of girl – from this gap.

Can we please get out? says the boy.

Harry, taken by surprise, steps aside clumsily, and falls on his face. The guilty pair emerges, adjusting clothing. There is an outbreak of ironic cheering, catcalling, and wolf-whistling from all and sundry.

Stage lights go off, and the curtain closes.

<< 1ˢᵗ Unit

Fortescue Crescent was not far removed geographically from Bee Street, but was light-years away on any contemporary measure of relative social standing. Both were 'bayside', but Bee was 'common bayside' whereas Fortescue was of the silver-service variety. Fifteen-year-old Harry found it easy to make the journey by bus, with just a short walk at each end. His mother had insisted he be clothed in his best casual clobber for this excursion. Brenda's choice for him had been brown suede shoes, grey shorts, and short-sleeved open-necked gleaming-white shirt.

The trees in the Crescent, and those peeping over the tops of the tall stucco-rendered stone fences, were all deciduous, and hence capable – owing to some botanical equivalent of hard-wired neurones – of identifying and responding to the season. The season was summer, so leaves were in vogue. When Harry, squinting against the uncompromising sunlight, managed a glimpse through the bars of one or other of the over-arching tempered-metal gates dutifully enclosing, asserting, and guarding both privilege and territory, he could see all gardens inside were in the English style, as received – and then wholeheartedly embraced – in this salubrious suburb, in this Oz-nurtured city, in that corner of the turning globe so very remote from what, in some circles, was still being referred to as the mother country.

He stopped in front of one such gate, double, secure, in heavy ornamental wrought iron supported by solid pillars of rendered stone. He checked the number above the letter slot, and determined this must be what he was looking for, i.e. the residence of Earnest Halliwell Bolton, Esq, OA[16].

He felt small, out of place, unwanted, and wrongfully intimidated. Many years later, in his thirties, by this stage having become tolerably well read, he recalled this moment, and compared it in his mind with the moment through which Jude Fawley, by repute his brother in obscurity, must have lived when he first confronted Christminster.

He pushed the buzzer on the intercom. After all, he *was* expected. A mature male voice – too scratchy to be Matt's – answered curtly:

Close the gate behind you.

There was an electronic click, and one of the huge gates sprung

---

16 OA: Order of Australia.

open. He passed through, and didn't dare *not* to close the gate behind him.

A crescent of crunchy gravel, wide enough to take a brace of Bentleys, lead him through a grove of poplars, low hedges, and beds of annuals – their colour washed out by the flux of an unrelenting sun – till a view of the house surprised him at last. This was the house where E H Bolton, a.k.a. E H, captain of industry, lived with his younger son, Matthew.

It was a mansion according to the accepted meaning of the word circa the early 20th century, which required as a minimum that the grounds surrounding it be measurable in significant numbers of acres. The façade was in tastefully rendered stone, with elegant bay windows on the lower level of the north-facing front, an aspect deemed appropriate for the advent of a lifetime or more of inclement winters. Two levels of sash windows in hardwood frames, their panes glinting like cats' eyes, followed the rectangular profile of the house around, and told those on the outside of two more-than-ample stories inside. Hard sandstone steps, curving round a portico, funnelled visitors towards a front door fashioned from a heavy slab of oak-like material, possibly California redwood. A period semicircular fanlight graced this massive door.

The reaction all this invoked in Harry was equivocal. By dint of its height, its grandeur, and the space of its surrounds, it was intimidating. Yet the gentle pastel colours of the gravel driveway, the sandstone steps, and the rendering of the façade, conspired to lend this formidable residence a cheerful, casual, almost sporty look. Certainly to those blessed with the imprint of privilege, to whom moreover the nod had been given, it said clearly, Come right in, eschew all formality. To all others, however, it said with equal clarity, Enter at your own peril. As for 'sporty', that was well and good as long as all those who aspired to enter were invested with a proper appreciation of what the 'right' sport *was*, as accepted in privileged circles.

With trepidation, Harry pulled the bell knob at the front door, and heard a mechanical jangling from inside. Time *itself* was terrorized, and had decided the safest option was to stand still. When the door finally opened, it was – to Harry's relief – Matt who was there to welcome him across the threshold. He also was wearing shorts (in navy) and open-necked shirt (in pale blue). The shirt had several buttons undone below the neck. Shorts and shirt – by common consent it appeared – was the mode of dress best befitting the day's weather.

A hallway faced him, looming the best part of six metres vertically. A single chandelier sprouted there from the far-flung ceiling like a gigantic bleached cabbage. Its pallid facets gleamed with daylight captured and then redirected. So great was its size it was in no way belittled by the space it was intended to illuminate. A carpeted and balustraded stairway of regal breadth bisected this hallway and then executed a sweeping curve to a mezzanine balcony on the left.

Matt, presumably under instruction, led Harry down the hallway beneath the prodigious chandelier, then to the right of the staircase, then all the way down to the kitchen at the extreme rear of the house.

Noticing the look of awe on Harry's face, Matt felt obliged to say, It's only a humble abode, but we like to call it home.

He carried a wry smile on his face as they entered the kitchen.

<

I would like to call a pause while I engage in a snippet of fantasy the essence of which places you (pademelons) and me *in situ*, the site in contention being the Bolton family residence. I would appreciate it if you would indulge me in this inconsequential jot of asininity. Or, as some might be inclined to call it, marsupiality.

Let me explain. I would like to pretend – in the interests of adding colour to my presentation – we had managed to sneak unnoticed through the wrought-iron gate before Harry had closed it behind him, and then had infiltrated the house through the front door before Matt in turn had closed *it*. Incongruous though it may seem for a mob of small furry marsupials to go hip-hopping across a lustrous Persian carpet of ultra-fine weave in an Edwardian entrance hall, beneath a chandelier as large as the big red kangaroo from the Dreaming, perhaps leaving a trail of scats behind them, I would nevertheless like to have it this way. Not the least because the anticipation of such a mob bounding with exuberance through this outrageous hallway evokes in my mind a picture of irresistible bathos joining hands with irrepressible vertigo.

Yes, yes, I am aware, pademelons, it is not necessary for omniscients like us to be *actually present* at a scene in order to apprehend the detail of what is there to be observed. We have the power to sequester such things in full at whatever remove the imagination can conceive. But, grant me, doesn't it make a better story if I can say we were there? *Right there?*

Yes, yes, I am also aware you are not *actual* pademelons. The p word is nothing more than my means of expressing the tenor of the timeless affection I feel for you. But, I ask you, what is there left for the likes of us – in *our* incongruent situation – but to dream?

So, while Matt and Harry are heading right *en route* to the kitchen, we shall take the left fork and arrive at what has – variously in its history – been called the library, the smoking room, and/or the billiards room. I've been here before and – believe me – I know my way around. And, apropos of my earlier comments re sport, let me add billiards would be an example of the 'right' sport, but pool would definitely *not* be.

We negotiate the billiard table in the middle of the polished parquetry floor and make our way towards the glassed-in bookcases on the far side of the room. Can I ask one of you to pull aside those heavy satin window drapes – dyed in tones of deep magenta ever so soothing to the sun-glazed eye – so we can have some light shed on whatever volume(s) might take our fancy? Thank you. It is as I suspected: the bookcases are locked.

The bookcases, fashioned in the early 20th C out of walnut, have seldom been opened in recent times. So I am having a deal of trouble turning the key in the lock. Like an arthritic knee joint, this lock is stiff with age and lack of use. Wait, I hear you say, We don't *have* a key. How can I be turning a non-existent key?

I should not have to remind you this is *my* fantasy and, in any fantasy of *mine*, the rules are up to *me*. So what *I* say to you now is of the essence: We don't even *need* a key.

The lock yields. Glass doors swing open. We have access.

Some of you – vertically challenged creatures that you are – find yourself eyeballing the lower shelves. This is where the late Mrs Bolton kept her books. They are mainly novels – by Dickens, Hardy, Eliot, Austen, and Poe – almost certainly untouched since her death. She had taste, poor woman, and a fat lot of good it did her.

The sad truth is E H Bolton, Esq. was never interested in imaginative fiction. His books are on the *upper* shelves, and the one-and-only work of prose fiction I can see there, is *Pilgrim's Progress*. I am not about to engage in polemics at this juncture, and intend to ignore any suggestions the *Holy Bible* should be regarded as a work of fiction.

Next to *Pilgrim's Progress*, wedged between it and said Bible, is a Wesleyan hymnal. Nearby are two volumes of *The Complete Works of William Shakespeare*, looking as if they had never been opened, and perhaps only there at all because they were too tall to fit in the lower shelves. There is Gibbon, Churchill, Toynbee. There are biographies of Cecil Rhodes, Lord Kitchener, and Sir Robert Gordon Menzies. We thumb through the pages, looking for marginalia. There *are* some. We assume they can be attributed to Mr Bolton. They are written – in the residual brown of what was once blue ink – with a nibbed pen. Perchance, a Montblanc. We find a swathe of books by long-forgotten authors, each of which probably managed only one special-interest print run. One such is entitled *Do You Really Have to* **KILL** *the Child?*, with photo of bottled foetus on dust jacket and the K word emphasized in clunky black letters. Another, with a montage of Hindu, Buddhist, Islamic, and Judaic insignia on its stiff paper front, is entitled *Paganism: A Christian Perspective*. Here is *Evidence for the Ark*, flaunting on *its* jacket pairs of contented animals strutting the quarterdeck and staring from the portholes of an idealized version of Noah's seagoing sanctuary.

There is … my God! What have we here?

A monograph entitled, *The Protocols of the Learned Elders of Zion*. Leaning bold-as-brass – as if in mockery – against *The Scourge of the Swastika* by Lord Russell of Liverpool. The latter complete with those in-your-face photographs, in black-and-white, of piles of emaciated corpses, from a deranged Europe in another space and another time. We can be grateful for the conspicuous lack of colour here.

From hereon, a clearer picture begins to emerge of our Order of Oz medal-holder. We uncover Robert Conquest's, *The Great Terror*, and another monograph, with no author identified, entitled *The Case Against Evolution*. When we encounter Sir Oswald Moseley's *My Life*, we are staring at the whites of the eyes of the beast.

It comes as no surprise to us when what we are half expecting – and dreading – turns up. Here is the first unexpurgated English language edition of *Mein Kampf*, New York (1939). We thumb through its pages. Yes! There are marginalia. In the same browning ink as once poured blue off the same nibbed pen. Look. There's an example in front of our goggling eyes, adjacent to one of Adolf's many vitriolic harangues against international Jewry. It says (simply), *Too true!*

We can be certain the sentiments felt by Lord Russell, when he rushed his book off to the publishers, would have been different from the sentiments felt by the venerable E H when he rushed out to buy it.

Our attention gravitates to the *Holy Bible, Authorized King James Version*. Given what we have endured, we feel considerable relief at the prospect. What harm can come from the Good Book?

It is an oversized issue of the Bible, of the type used, one might imagine, by a preacher on his/her lectern. It is bound in creamy leather, with a cross entangled in a crown of thorns embossed on the front and spine. For ease of access, we heave this unwieldy volume over to the billiard table, where we set it down. Here we explore its bronze-edged pages.

The large print inside is in a pleasant serif font whereby the strokes are of graduated width as in good copperplate handwriting. Its appearance invites one to read it, promising numinous rewards.

We flip and flick through the shiny musty oxygen-deprived pages, from Genesis through the genealogy and the genocide, through the psalms, proverbs, and prophets, until we reach the New Testament where a shock awaits us. The text of all the direct quotes attributable to Jesus Christ – in the Gospels and beyond – is in *red type*. Red beatitudes. Red parables. The ruddy Lord's Prayer.

Does this not raise a serious question: what in God's name *did* the publisher have in mind? Is the red type there for emphasis, or does it signify blood? The words of Our Lord – every last one of them – written in blood:

Except ye eat the flesh of the Son of man, and drink his blood, ye have no life in you. Whoso eateth my flesh, and drinketh my blood, hath eternal life …

We snap the Bible shut. We are not sure we want to go there. Don't we have eternal life already, pademelons? Or what passes for such in the understanding of mortal persons (and of mortal pademelons), charged with envy, and with ignorance of and indifference to the plight of we supernal folk?

Collaterally, we experience a sense of relief at not being required to emulate the practices of vampire bats. We leave the Bible sitting on the billiard table, for the bemusement (perhaps) of the next visitor(s) to the room. Perhaps, in its myriad pages, he/she/they may chance upon chapter and verse instructive to aficionados of the billiard cue.

We turn the key in the lock, in the reverse direction. We are sealing the tomb, afraid of what further horrors we might otherwise uncover. There are limits, we feel, to what should be laid bare as the unintended consequence of our gratuitous exercise of omniscient and imaginative powers. We resolve to confine ourselves henceforth to things relating directly to our brief, i.e. the life and many deaths of Harry McMinn.

We retreat, tails between legs, although how you pademelons manage such a feat with those muscular macropod tails is beyond me. We negotiate the entrance hall, the front door, the long gravel driveway. The heavy front gates are locked.

What do we do? you ask.

Oh ye of little faith, I say. This is *fantasy* we are experiencing. *My* fantasy. Surely then you don't doubt my ability to deal with the likes of locks and keys, and their futile materiality.

Instantly we are out of the premises and out of the equation. My indulgence has ended ignominiously for all concerned. Pademelons, I offer my apology.

It is over to Harry and Matt in the kitchen.

>

... the pointy end of conservative politics, Matt was saying. That's where he and his slick-suited buddies park their feeble brains.

His business associates? asked Harry.

He has no executive function these days. Sits on the boards of a number of prominent blue-chip companies. Old boys' club. Connections. That's all he's got left.

He's done some good things in his time, hasn't he?

Some might say.

Do you?

Doing good by his country was the best move the old man ever made, because he did right well for himself as a consequence. Look around you.

Matt's eyes swivel round the room.

They were sitting at a massive wooden vintage table once used in all likelihood for food preparation. It was surfaced in unfinished planks, glued under tension by artisans of another era, the sort of job drawing comment along the lines, You don't see workmanship like *that* anymore. Rudimentary and utilitarian in comparison with the flamboyance of the rest of the house, the kitchen nevertheless boasted the full range of modern appliances bearing the best brand names, blending seamlessly with the translucent bench tops – in Italian marble – around its periphery. The table, and the voluminous pantry, were the only features of the original kitchen remaining.

What about your mother? asked Harry.

Dead. Died young. Breast cancer.

I'm sorry …

Twenty years younger than the old man, said Matt. I hardly knew her. A trophy bride, by all accounts. Meant to be win-win, but turned out lose-lose.

They must have had *some* good years together. And three children.

But only one pregnancy.

How come?

My brother and sister are twins …

Cool.

… and I'm adopted.

I didn't know that.

Dumb comment, boyo. How *could* you know?

Harry flushed. This was a conversation stopper. Matt resumed after the pause.

My mother's idea, I'm told. The old man never came to terms with it.

But he's stuck with it.

Doesn't mean he has to like it. He sent my brother and sister to the best schools. You know. Those flash sheltered workshops claiming to produce the future leaders of Oz.

Do you mean … ?

But he sent me to Porridge. That's what he considered *I* was worth.

You resent that?

Perhaps. Perhaps not.

Their attention was drawn to the kitchen door, which was opening slowly inwards, towards them. It stopped when it was sufficiently ajar to allow a head, shoulder, and arm to intrude.

It was the head of a man in his mid-sixties, with unnaturally jet-black hair, strongly suggestive of one of a number of commercial products sold in bottles to the vain. This same vanity presumably accounted for the attempts its owner had made to slick the hair back and part it unmercifully down the middle, attempts subverted to an extent by the prominent cowlick and the dark tufts curling round the ears.

The man had a thin face, jowly throat, pursed lips on a long thin line-of-mouth turned down at each end, a straight nose, and intense eyes, the latter cold and blue-grey. He was tall, judging by the height – measured along the door jamb – at which his head appeared. Despite the humid weather, he was wearing a pale blue lounge suit with vest and silk necktie.

He spoke.

Matthew. Why don't you offer your little friend a lemonade?

The head, shoulder, and arm retracted. The door closed. Matt looked at Harry, shrugged, and raised his palms skywards. The wry smile, as if always waiting in metaphoric wings, returned to his face.

Father, he said.

Father? echoed Harry's thoughts …

… thoughts stymied by a strident discord. *That* word, and Matt's unremittingly formal usage of it, was like a cacophonic assembly of off-pitch tuning forks sending their beats throbbing through the pliant jelly inside his head. Hadn't Matt – earlier on – referred to his father as 'the old man'? Why the change? Why had it now become 'Father'?

Earlier, when he had negotiated that forbidding front gate, Harry had realized he was charting unfamiliar waters, not amenable to being fathomed. It was proving to be a valid realization. The waters were becoming less and less fathomable, minute by recondite minute.

The last thing he expected was for the door to re-open, but it did, and to much the same extent. The head, shoulder, and arm intruded once again. Harry wondered if there was a body attached. A perverse idea gripped him. What he was seeing was a target presenting itself for practice.

'Father' spoke again:

Matthew, you haven't forgotten Simon and Martha are coming at the week-end. The tennis court needs rolling. Your responsibility.

The disembodied features retracted. The door closed.

Shall we roll? asked Matt.

>

On the tennis court behind the house, Harry found himself and Matt, yoked together in effect, behind the tubular metal handle of the roller, sometimes pushing and sometimes pulling, and for the most part co-operatively. The surface on which they worked was of fine gravel, becoming more and more compacted as the roller did its intended job. Glancing at the top row of windows in shade at the back of the house, Harry imagined he saw a vague shadow in one of them, the shadow perhaps of a person with sharp blue-grey eyes looking down at them.

He's up there? he asked Matt.

Probably.

Who are Simon and Martha?

My brother and sister.

Do you get on with them?

We're cool.

They swivelled the handle of the roller over the top of the heavy concrete cylinder and then heaved off in the reverse direction.

You can thank them for the sex lesson, said Matt.

Who?

Simon and Martha.

Sex lesson?

Think clay modelling. Think Macca's class.

What's your brother and sister got to do with that?

I got the info from them and, out of the goodness of my heart, passed it on to you.

Many thanks.

You didn't imagine it came from the old man did you?

In an uncharacteristic fit of anger, Matt flung the metal handle skywards causing it to flip over and rebound noisily from the gravel surface on the other side of the roller.

To hell with the old fucker, he said. Let's have that lemonade.

Harry waited while Matt retrieved a couple of bottles of 7Up from the kitchen. They climbed into the umpire's box, sat down together, and sipped from the necks of their bottles, bare thighs – raw and sweaty – wedged together in their cramped perch.

As far as his fickle memory could divine, the sensation Harry felt, when his flesh came into contact with flesh other than his own, was a new one for him. There was the taut and inviolable feeling of an extramural skin, mixed – it seemed to him incongruously – with a gentle yielding of whatever it was biology had seen fit to plant beneath that skin. There was a soporific warming effect, like a congenial emotional state, and not at all attributable to the usual suspects of heat and temperature. There was a primeval nudge, gentle but insistent, echoing back through bounteous time to an era massively pre-dating human experience, when some precocious and interloping life-force in its incipiency was determined to impress itself upon an unpromising soup of inanimate clay.

Harry wondered if Matt was having similar sensations. Then he wondered if those steely eyes were on them from above. In the grip of an uneasy guilt, he tried to shift position but, in the confines of their perch, flesh-to-flesh contact was not easy to avoid. There seemed nothing for it but to resign himself to the situation, and to the equivocal emotions it aroused in him.

What will you do when you leave Porridge? he asked.

Go into business, said Matt.

What sort of business?

Don't know. The old man promises to put up venture capital once I decide.

Useful.

Can't complain.

There it was again. The wry smile on Matt's face, as if he were laughing inwardly at himself. There was reassurance in his smile sufficient to dispatch the guilt – his recent and momentary burden – to some inaccessible cranny of his moral consciousness. As he tilted his bottle, Harry felt relaxed for the first time that day.

Years later, barely in his twenties, he would recall this moment with fondness while seated – relaxed then as now – with Matt, in the plush office he (Matt) had been destined to occupy to great purpose, the pair of them tippling shots of choice cognac from brandy balloons.

>

Harry encountered Earnest Halliwell Bolton, Esq, once more that afternoon.

It was the end of what was for Harry a memorable visit, albeit for a mixed bag of reasons. Harry and Matt were in the hallway, with the incredible chandelier behind. Powered up now, it was producing myriads of incandescent auras, haloes, and imprints on the optic nerve visible even behind closed lids. The fanlight above the front door, revealed day fading into summer twilight. Matt was showing Harry out this front door when the great man materialized as if from nowhere. The silk slippers on his feet might have explained the stealth of his approach. His obsequious manner was less explicable however, particularly in one accustomed by repute to exercising firm – even ruthless – authority over his minions.

He extended his right arm towards Harry, coughed discreetly, and said:

Young man, I believe there is a branch of the Lantern Bearers in your school, and you could do worse than to make yourself known to them.

He was not offering his right hand by way of greeting, as per the normal expectation. His right hand contained a pamphlet, and it was the *pamphlet* he was offering, not the hand.

Matt's look was dark and irritable. He made haste to usher Harry out the door. Not, however, with sufficient haste ...

... because Harry took the pamphlet. A look of exasperation enveloped Matt's face as he said to Harry, See you Monday.

>

'For the commandment is a lamp; and the law is light.' Thus spoke Solomon, singer of songs, wisest of the wise.

Matt was wrong. His father had not relinquished *all* his executive functions. He had retained *one*, though on a voluntary basis. He was CEO of an organization called Lantern Bearers Inc., whose mission it was – aside from hands-on proselytizing by any means and at every opportunity – to bring fundamentalist Christianity to the students of all privately-run schools in Oz. This excluded Catholic schools, Islamic schools, Jewish schools, and certain other fuzzy categories of school, none of whose administrations would let him or his organization get a foot in the door. Some people would say they were displaying commendable perspicacity.

As for state-run schools, E H was happy to leave responsibility for the souls of less fortunate students to somebody else. After all, he reasoned, there are limits to what one man can do. It is a wise man who knows and respects these limits.

The day had been momentous for Harry, nor was it over yet. He had climbed the mountain, seen the vision splendid, then come down safely on the other side. He was aware he had experienced things not normally vouchsafed to those of his station in society.

On the bus-ride back to the vicinity of Bee Street, rocking and bouncing gently in his seat, Harry found himself succumbing to the mesmeric qualities of the everyday suburban street scenes as they flashed past him in twilit montage. He was confident in the illusion that the toughened window glass could provide him the necessary quarantine from events outside and from any possible affront to him they might entail. People were hurrying to get bread, milk, and a cosy chat from the corner shop before it closed. Others clutched bottles of wine, clinking with promise in paper bags, as they converged on their favourite local restaurant. Lanky youths in ragged jeans displayed skills and exuded menace on skateboards. A succession of power poles, closely encountered, delivered a thump-thump-thump to his eyeballs as they whoosh-whoosh-whooshed past. Motor cars ducked and weaved as their raging drivers strived at any cost to gain that extra second or two of precious time. All these things were so ordinary, and yet each was in its small way germane to its purpose.

As if made to measure, they were germane to *his* purpose too, viz. getting the momentous events of his day into some sort of manageable perspective. Were not these ordinary goings-on outside the window glass a convenient *mise en scene* for the perceived high drama of his own life?

The bus stopped sharply at a set of traffic lights, and this precipitated his self-coddled mind into a self-referential reality check. He suddenly became aware of the flagrant self-indulgence of his train of thought. Self, self, self. Why should it always be self? Why should not the events of *his* life be part of the *mise en scene* for *somebody else's* drama? Where, after all, *was* the centre of the universe to be found?

As the bus took off again, it occurred to Harry to glance down at the pamphlet on his lap. Perhaps the answers might be found there. Improbable perhaps, certainly peripheral to the main chance, but by no means totally out of the question, and he had nothing better to do right now but to follow up this obscure possibility.

The pamphlet was folded so as to form two pages. It was glossy like a birthday card, but lacked stiffness.

On the front, as if rendered in charcoal, was a mishmash of representations in shades of grey, representations designed to be dark, depressing, and fear-inducing: of storm clouds, dark satanic mills, lightless forests of trees with stranglers' hands on the ends of their branches, and leering pock-marked creatures with obvious ill intent on tour from a mythic underworld. Across it all, in a font – stark, unadorned, and bold-black – allowing no distraction from message, were the words, **For the Wages of Sin is Death ...** The only item on the page offering any relief from overwhelming bleakness was a small monochrome logo at top right of a lighted coach lantern held aloft by a benevolent hand.

Harry turned the page. Predictably. the scene inside was different. It was all light, angels, prophets, apostles, and saints, leading down to the more common and garden keepers of the faith, and leading up through fleecy clouds and yet more angels to God in three persons, the entire holy kit and caboodle a veritable vision of Isaiah. Written across it in a cheery feather-light font of simulated freehand was the punch-line, … *but the free gift of God is eternal life through Jesus Christ our Lord.*

Signing off, at bottom right in small print, were the words, Lantern Bearers, Inc, followed by, Authorized by Earnest H Bolton, Esq, OA.

2ⁿᵈ Unit >>

Self, self, self. Unapologetic narcissistic self. Harry, nerd exemplified, trudges along the footpath of deprived and characterless Sleek Street towards the venue he has chosen to host the theatrical realization of his self-worship. He huddles to protect himself against the bitter wind this brisk Sunday afternoon in late autumn has sprung on the unwitting. Ordinarily laden with traffic fit – and perhaps bound – for hell, Sleek Street is relatively quiet right now, as if shamed into honouring God's day.

Harry's plan is to arrive hours before anybody else is due, in order to commune with himself alone in the silent darkness. He hopes thereby to conjure up aspects of his younger persona, in the interests of dramatizing the life and many deaths of Harry McMinn.

He reaches the frowzy facade of the theatre, dominated by the tall scraggly melaleuca whose bark – pale grey and peeling – hangs like dirty icicles. Paint – of the nondescript colour found in no can but which is the product of unremitting age – is peeling from fraying weatherboards. He feels the scrutiny of the pair of Janus masks decorating this facade. He has never been able to reconcile himself to their blind stare. They are masks of such stripe as –

according to some ancient and unfathomable tradition – is a mandatory adornment for premises such as these. They have been cut out as a single piece – doubtless on a band saw by some home handyman fired up with enthusiasm for amateur theatrics – from a sheet of 5-ply – then coated by the same handyman with primer, undercoat, and final finish in eggshell white and bolted just above head height to the weatherboards.

The masks inform one this unassuming venue is where theatrical dreams may be realized.

He passes through the creaking front door, closes it behind him, and switches on the lights in front-of-house. On entering the main auditorium, he leaves the doors to the stalls as he finds them, ajar.

The auditorium is quiet. Usually the doors at the back of stalls are kept closed to minimize noise from outside. But on this particular day at this particular time, even with those doors ajar, the theatre is so profoundly hushed Harry believes he can hear the cockies – on, around, and under the stage – gearing up in anticipation of nocturnal shenanigans in raunchy roach-land.

Aware these days of the properties of the Japanese poetic form known as haiku, he avoids all seats numbered seventeen. Because this number has turned out not to be so lonely after all, Harry feels betrayed, though he's not sure by whom. He is hoping to find a number truly bereft of companionship so he can take up its cause.

As was his intention, he finds himself surrounded by semi-darkness. But what an interesting semi-darkness it is. Oxygen for his imagination.

Light is cascading down the aisles from front-of-house, bringing the pebbly blood-sodden rivers to life, though we are left wondering if 'life' is the most apposite word. These are tributaries of an African river, perhaps the Limpopo or the Congo, and massive carnage is doubtless occurring somewhere upstream. The machetes are out. Their gleam is indicative of sharpness, the sharpness indicative of intent, and the intent indicative of the darkness of the human heart. Lopped-off arms, legs, heads are falling. Aortas and femoral arteries are emptying their contents into the headwaters. The bloated corpses will soon come floating by. The horror, the horror.

Within this framework, reflections beset Harry.

There are reflections of a *cognitive* nature. In Harry's mind, they take the form of toxic fantasies. He recalls his infantile fears of dominoes, yellow peril, and the like, seeing them as intrusions on comfortable life, *his* comfortable life, his comfortable life with horror waiting, horror hidden somewhere out of sight, upstream in this case, waiting for the opportune moment to ride the cascades down, to emerge from the froth and bubble, to present its ghastly face and deal its decisive blow.

There are reflections, too, of an *optical* nature. Light returns to him from the trim of the TV screens, those on and those around the proscenium, those genuine and those *faux*. Seven shiny silver borders surrround seven rectangular jet-black interiors. Seven is the number of our earlier count but, considered holistically, may there not now be *one only*, that one being a faceted alien insect eye of monstrous size? This is gestalt. This is a shape-shift worthy of Kafka. So when viewers look at TV screens, including especially *these* TV screens, maybe the screens – combined in grotesque insect-eye form – are looking straight back at the viewers.

But are they looking straight back? Can one be certain in which direction a faceted insect eye is looking? Isn't it looking in every direction at once, capturing the light from all corners and crannies of the three dimensional world mortals inhabit? Here is an observer who doesn't appear to be looking directly at anything in particular, but who – in reality – is apprehending everything at once. A frightening, alien, omniscient observer.

Apprehending? For what conceivable reason? For what spine-chilling purpose?

I've said it before, pademelons, and I'll say it again. Fiction can sometimes be more potent than truth, especially when it has a mind to morph into truth.

Harry jumps in his seat as a door behind him creaks open, then slams shut. This is the main door to the theatre, connecting the street to front-of-house. Somebody else – not merely the wind – has arrived. His fantasies evaporate. Perhaps it is as well the relief valve holding back the venomous thoughts crowding his impressionable mind has been touched off in this fortuitous manner. He turns in his seat.

He hears light footfalls, as from female shoes. Sonia – in blue jeans and matching windcheater – enters through one of the doors from front-of-house. Reality has impinged, forcing illusion to beat its retreat.

You're very early, says Harry.

I'm doing work on Matt's costumes, says Sonia.

Harry swings his body to face front again. Sonia makes her deliberate way down the centre aisle, the erstwhile and supposed Limpopo tributary.

Anyway, says Sonia, you are too.

What?

Very early.

Sonia climbs the steps at the edge of the stage area, crosses the stage, and is about to disappear backstage when she has second thoughts. Her deliberation has stalled. Turning on one hand, she vaults nimbly down from the stage, and heads back down the aisle towards Harry. She stops a couple of metres from where Harry is seated, her hands provocatively on her hips.

I'd like to have a word with you, she says.

And so you are.

You have every right to make a public spectacle of your private life if that's the way you like to get your jollies. I acknowledge that. But you don't have the same right to expose *my* private life to public gaze. I'd like you to show some respect for my privacy.

How do you propose I keep the two separate?

Two what?

My life and yours.

It's not rocket science. Do *your* life story. Leave me out of it.

Can't be done.

I don't accept that.

With pursed lips, Harry raises his hands, palms upward.

I accept your non-acceptance, he says.

What the fuck does that mean?

That we must beg to differ.

You're a dirty swine ...

Harry's response is slow and deliberate, each syllable enunciated, each separately expirated, each challenging the air. Simultaneously and perfunctorily, he slaps his wrist.

I am a dir-ty dir-ty swine.

Yes, and you know it.

How come *you* know what I know when *I* don't even know what I know?

Can we stop being a clever dick and return to the issue, which so happens to be my besieged privacy?

OK, says Harry. That's what you want, I'll spell it out.

Do so.

The reality is your life and mine have had substantial and intimate points of contact over the years, especially ...

Sonia responds with belligerent laughter, but more screech than laugh, and more spite than screech. Her words collide with those of Harry.

Intimate points of contact. That's ...

... especially in our early years, and ...

... rich. That's really fucking rich.

... consequently it will be impossible for me to do justice to my personal story without bringing in elements of *your* personal story.

Elements?

Yes, elements. On a needs basis.

Your need.

Yes.

Your need, and I can go fuck myself.

Your words, not mine.

Then what *are* your words?

You want my words? You have two options as I see it. One. You can take yourself off the team, resign from the project ...

Oh, you'd like that, wouldn't you? It'd suit you better than Fletcher Jones[17]. You and your smart set have only ever *tolerated* me, nothing more. Poor little Catholic girl, ...

Do you want to hear me out?

... toe the line, seen and not heard, taken for granted, always come running, here Sonia puss puss puss ...

Do you want to hear me out?

Sonia is silent, shoulders hunched forward.

Two, says Harry. You can stay, and we can consult, the pair of us, on all *Stücke* you are involved in. I guarantee I will give consideration to any of *your* proposals, and you can have right of reply to any of *mine*. What could be more fair?

Mister Fair and Square.

Belligerence has gone out of Sonia's voice. There is only resignation, tinged with irony. She turns to head backstage again.

Sonia, says Harry.

She stops.

We have a history, says Harry. I like to think it's a history of fondness and love. I don't want to see us falling out over this business. Or any other business for that matter.

Right you are.

... the irony once again ...

One more thing, Sonia, says Harry, I'd rather not have the sob story of how much you are despised and rejected. It's wearing very thin. Back twenty years, or whenever it was we were an item, you gave *me* the flick, not the reverse. *You* rejected *me*.

---

17 Fletcher Jones: in its heyday, an iconic Australian men's wear store.

Sonia does not reply. She is well on her way down the aisle and about to clamber back on to the stage.

Silence is in session again, joining its natural companion, the semi-darkness. Harry's wild fantasies may have fled, but realities have not, and – when slathered with the emotions to which they are prone – they can be as toxic as fantasies.

>

Harry, sitting alone, is experiencing a cocktail of such emotions related to the time when his relationship with Sonia began so promisingly, careered along so erratically, and ended so catastrophically. Both he and Sonia were in their late teens at the time. The relationship lasted some months. In some ways, it mirrored the earlier doomed tryst they had embarked upon at the more tender age of six, which had ended badly when they had simultaneously became aware of the dark forces rampaging within their respective psyches. Both events, Harry reflects, were indicative of the sorry history seeming to stalk him and Sonia through the years, determined to thwart at every turn any attempts they might make at connubiality or even at mere congeniality. He believes some relationships are like that, cursed under the stars by a malevolent black spot.

The emotions he is feeling consist of anxiety, sorrow, regret, nostalgia. Sometimes remorse, sometimes pity. Arching over them all is a sense of immense and irrecoverable loss. There have been nights, even recently, when he has dreamt he is in bed with Sonia. They are both naked, and sleeping back to back. And head to toe.

He would like a cup of coffee, but knows the only urn is backstage, where Sonia is. He makes no move from his seat. He forgoes the coffee.

He is unsure how long he has been sitting under this emotional cloudbank before he – once again – hears the front door creak then slam shut. The rest of the team are arriving is his first thought. He is grateful for the distraction. However, the footfalls are of one person only, female. He turns to see Elena enter the stalls. She wears her usual short skirt and light white blouse with colourful hand-sewn Slavic motifs. Ukrainian perhaps, he thinks.

She hip-sways down the aisle, then crab-walks along his row of seats towards him, backside towards the stage as is the polite Slavic way. Their greetings to each other are perfunctory. After that, things move more quickly.

You're early, says Harry.

You are also, says Elena.

You must be cold in that gear, says Harry.

Then you must warm me, says Elena.

Elena sits astride Harry, one creamy thigh on each side of him. Her body presses against his. Yes, she is cold, but there is warm gentle lust in her eyes. Sufficient unto the day. Harry's arms are around her. This amazes him. He can't remember putting them there. It is as if some invisible external agency had been responsible. This is the way most of his life has happened, he reflects.

Through his palms, he feels the delicate quiver of her buttocks.

Moy prikrássniy lyubímyetz, she says.

She kisses him gently, with the brush of ever-so-slightly parted lips. Harry had, on previous occasions, noticed a tendency of hers to revert to her first language when emotions of one sort or another took hold. Sweet nothings said in a foreign lingo. There is no doubting what sort of emotion is taking hold of her at this particular moment.

Sonia's out the back, he says.

Nichevó[18], she says.

The others may come at any moment, he says.

Nichevó, she says.

---

18 *nichevó*: it doesn't matter.

She undoes two, then three, then four of her blouse buttons. Buttons undone all the way down to her navel. The Slavic motifs peel back to reveal a brace of amazing fruit, one of which he cups in his hand, a hand travelling north – mysteriously and of its own volition – to make itself available for this purpose. O, amazing brace. A perfect fit in his palm, he reflects.

His gaze takes in the curves of thigh and breast, curves having every appearance – on the surface – of belonging to a continuum of those curves found commonly in habitable space, but which – *beneath* the surface – must of necessity be on the cusp of a massive discontinuity in some unseen dimension, a dimension of human susceptibility. There can, otherwise, be no way of accounting for the capacity of such curves to stun mind, will, and body into such perfect submission. This is one of Harry's more esoteric reflections at this pivotal moment.

Simultaneously he is having reflections of a more down-to-earth nature. *Nichevó* notwithstanding, he reflects ruefully, it is going to be devilishly difficult for either one of them – wedged together as they are in this unaccommodating theatre seat – to remove items of clothing as and when required. This is, one would agree, a matter of practical importance and, while he is pondering it, as doubtless she is also, he hears knocking at the front door. Not the usual creak and slam, but knocking. They both freeze and wait. There it is again, the knocking. It happens a third time. They hope after three knocks those wishing to enter will – in accordance with convention – go away and come back later or, better still, not come back at all.

This is not to be. There is the familiar creak and slam, followed by the tentative click and slap of female heels, and more than one pair at that. Has the world has been taken over by women? thinks Harry. Then into the stalls come two women known neither to Harry nor to Elena, one of them middle-aged, the other young, mother and daughter perhaps. The older woman has the look of one who has seen it all before, but the younger woman is wide-eyed.

Everything about these women is tidy, sanitized, immaculate. They are clothed identically in floral dresses to the ankles and soft fluffy cardigans to a discreet V of the neck. They wear hats – ornate with floral and faunal motifs – enclosing not just head but most of brow and ears as well. These headdresses could have passed for bonnets except for the lack of chinstraps. The observation that these woman are from another era would be too obvious. There is more to it than that. There is an outlandish element to their dress, beyond the bounds of what one would dismiss perfunctorily as old-fashioned. Judging by their get-out, Harry is thinking, these women are exercising a degree of chutzpah, tinged with gentle madness.

Elena has done up some of her blouse buttons, and has slipped discreetly into the adjacent seat. Both of them are torso-twisted so they can face the newcomers, who have proceeded down the aisle to a strategic position beside their row of seats. Harry, trying to think of something appropriate to say, ends up saying something perfectly ridiculous.

The box office is not open yet, he says.

We're not here for that, says the older woman.

Oh.

We've come about your immortal soul.

… the penny drops. Jehovah's bloody Witnesses! …

My immortal soul is *my* business, says Harry.

It most certainly is *not*.

Then we must beg to differ.

… not the first time this afternoon, Harry reflects, he has made this injunction. Can the world bear so much beggary? Or so much difference? …

The middle-aged woman responds with an emphatic 'Hmmph'. The young woman slaps a copy of the Watchtower on the seat adjacent to Elena, but not before casting a sly look in her direction.

Chalking up another rejection, the couple retreat down the aisle, and out the double doors into front-of-house. Harry and Elena twist torsos to the front again. They wait for the creak and slam from behind, and for the silence they expect will then ensue. Neither is sure any more exactly what use they might want to make of this silence, if indeed there is any judicious use to which it may be put.

There *is* no silence. After the creak and slam, there is a medley of shuffling footwear, muffled verbal exchanges, and strains of *funiculi funicula* on an unlikely accordion. Other parties have arrived and have perhaps crossed paths with the Witnesses. Then one voice, recognizably Sticks', rises above the hubhub:

Oh dear, we're all Satanists here, I'm afraid.

Gávno![19] comes the (indecorous) exclamation from Elena.

Another creak and slam from behind, and Elena retreats stage-wards – the only viable escape route – her nimble fingers working on the remaining blouse buttons as she scurries. She just makes it backstage before ...

... Sticks, Matt, Izzie, Brenda, Timmy, and Godfrey burst in. The multi-talented Godfrey is the one tickling the accordion. The gang are all here in spades. One of them flicks the theatre lights on full. Harry is momentarily blinded.

You're early.

So are you.

>

House and stage lights are on. Sticks strides the stage, in seven league boots, blocking her tackle, in preparation for the next ...

Hold it there. I apologize for my dyslexic moment. What I should have said is 'tackling her block' or something in that verbal ballpark.

---

19 *Gávno!*: Shit!

There is precious little to block. Only three people: Harry, Izzie, and Godfrey, all of whom will occupy an unchanging stage footprint throughout the *Stück*. Only three props: an accordion, a music stand, and a used king-size bed-sheet. The latter – frayed round the edges, discoloured, blotchy – is hanging high backstage. Sticks, fussing, reaches up with houseproud hands and smooths it down.

As our eyes drift further upwards, we notice another prop, a large one we had overlooked at first. It embraces the entire stage area. It comprises four interconnected surfaces, commandeering three sides and the space above in the flies. It is the colour of canvas. It is non-rigid, looking as if it might ripple at the whim of the lightest breeze.

Could it be we are inside a tent? Could this be a circus? Can we expect, at any moment, to be entertained by clowns – in multi-coloured pyjamas and fuzzy wigs – sporting humongous white-painted lips and eyes – standing on the backs of prancing piebald ponies?

Harry and Izzie are at centre stage. Izzie is not happy. He had earlier tried to argue – had pleaded – had threatened to withdraw his services – against being shanghaied into an acting role. He had been overruled. By Ms Hitler, the inconsiderate stage manager, no less. As a consequence, we see both Izzie and Harry posing as young teenage versions of themselves, neatly dressed in their Porridge uniforms, Harry lean and angular, Izzie dumpy and moon-faced.

Matt, backstage, deserves congratulations on the skilful manner in which, using his customary magic, he has transformed two grown men in their early forties into two awkward pimply adolescents.

Izzie is not a happy vegemite[20]. He contemplates his synthesizer, forlorn and abandoned, albeit still in place on the left

20 vegemite: colloquial Australian, meaning 'person in contention', perhaps one who might be inclined to eat Vegemite.

wing. Sitting on its piano seat is smug Godfrey, with music stand and accordion. Izzie would like to raise the rafters with shouts of, 'Strike-breaker!', 'Scab!' Sadly there are no rafters to be found. Remember? We concluded this was a tent.

His Scabbiness – Godfrey – is coaxing a tune out of the squeezebox, a particular tune, lively and melodious in major key and 4/4 time, sounding like a revival hymn. Which it is. Or as close to such as Harry's compositional competencies are able to deliver.

Izzie's hubris compels him to reflect *he* is the man for the job. On this score there is no question in his discomposed mind. Smarmy opportunist, Godfrey Goldsworthy, is not a contender. Or should not be, in a world able to see reason.

Fait accompli prevails over hubris. With extreme reluctance, at tortoise speed, and in opposition to instincts as insistent as those of fight and flight, Izzie is drawn closer and closer to a reality as bitter as hemlock. What he is coming to terms with is stark. Please indulge my urge to describe his angst in poetry laced with pun:

> Izzie not the only instrumentalist
> on whom calls may be made?
> Izzie's synthesizer not the only instrument
> on which tunes may be played?

Izzie has always preferred to keep reality at a distance, and his habitual position behind the synthesizer has proved ideal for this purpose. There he can – at whim and will – surround himself with a protective and pleasuring dome of pulsating and harmonious sound. So, standing on centre stage, baring his metaphoric nakedness, he is out of his comfort zone.

There are other legitimate reasons why Izzie might – in his present unwelcome situation – feel himself like a dog without its dinner. He has had to forego his amber cravat, his lemon-green jacket, and even his shaved head, which is covered by that most abominable of abominations: the regulation school cap. Only his serious lack of sideburns – incipient ones for a teenage lad, but nonetheless expected to be found peeping below the brim of the cap – hints at more extensive baldness beneath. Even with cap on, he could be mistaken for an oncology patient.

Those of the crew with no duties elsewhere are seated in the stalls. Brenda, in the front row, is trying to keep her restless grandson still. Matt and Sonia are conferring in seats further back. Elena is in the lighting box, unseen. Sticks? She is doing her best to placate Izzie.

Why should I put up with this crap? asks Izzie.

… fixing his gaze on anything but Sticks, flinging his cap on the floor, picking it up, twirling it in his hands, and then flinging it on the floor again …

We've been through that, says Sticks. It's a formative stage of Harry's life.

What about *my* life?

It's a formative stage of your life too.

It's not anything I'm fucking proud of.

Izzie, I expect …

Muted comments – perhaps not sufficiently mute – from the front row of the stalls distract Sticks.

When do I get to throw the stuff? asks Timmy.

Brenda's index finger rises to her lips.

Shhh, she says. Our little secret.

But Izzie's ears are sharp, and he doesn't like what he hears, not one little bit. Sticks flashes a disapproving look in the direction of her son. Timmy lowers his eyes.

Sticks resumes her pep talk to hangdog Izzie.

I expect, she says to Izzie, you will put aside your misgivings and rise to the occasion on the night.

Which night? asks Izzie.

This night, says Sticks. Tonight. Right now.

>

Singspielstück #6: Blood of Jesus

As house lights are dimmed, Sticks, Matt, and Sonia move discreetly to the front row of stalls, joining Timmy and Brenda. Pademelons, I don't know about you, but I have a bad feeling about this group in the front row. I suggest we keep our distance.

We choose seats as close to the back as possible.

The curtains part. Stage lights come up, illuminating the setting uniformly. We hear faint piped music, suggestive of festivities at a distant fairground.

Harry and Izzie occupy centre stage, each facing square on to the audience, each separated from the other by about a metre. Godfrey, with accordion, commands the left wing. The right wing, unoccupied, is in darkness.

Apparently information in some shape or form shall be – later on – projected onto the bed-sheet. As yet its soiled whiteness is bereft of anything intelligible.

The four CCTV screens are showing the external precinct with graduated amounts of zoom.

Top-left shows the green lawn of a municipal park adjacent to a white sandy beach on a sun-drenched summer day. There is entertainment in the park: a Ferris wheel, a carousel, a miniature train, etc. There is a large cuboid canvas tent off to one side of this entertainment.

Top-right shows the front of this tent in more detail, together with its most immediate precinct. Guy ropes are attached to pegs embedded in the lawn. The entrance to the tent is at centre front. The flaps at this entrance have been tied back to let in breeze. And punters.

Bottom left shows the entrance in more detail. At head height, attached to the tent near the left-hand flap, is a crude sign in black crayon reading 'ALL WELCOME, NO CHARGE'. Hanging above the flaps is a framed, laminated, and colourized emblem. Impish children pass by, ice creams in hands, hands feeding mouths. As their faces momentarily fill the screen, they make rude gestures at the camera, as children are wont to do.

Bottom right shows the emblem in more detail. It consists of a hand and wrist, pink and hairless, holding forth a coach lantern, painted leaf-green. The egg-yolk colour of the panes of lantern glass is meant to suggest the lantern is lit. Two intertwined characters – letters L and B – in an attractive blood-red serif font partly overwrite the lower right portion of the emblematic image. One would guess these characters in tandem stand for the words 'Lantern Bearers', indicative of the organization of the same name.

The interior of the tent? That is what the main stage depicts. Harry and Izzie are about to launch their *Singspiel*.

On the surface, this *Singspiel* appears no more than an exchange between the two of them, for internal consumption only, so to speak. The body language of the duo tells a different story. Their gesticulating hands and swaggering bodies are those of passionate evangelists. Every word spoken or sung, every gesture flung out, pierces incisively the flimsy space between them and the putative audience in the tent. The message is intended for the unwitting ears corralled under canvas.

Are you ready, asks Harry, to take the Lord Jesus Christ as your saviour?

Are you ready, asks Izzie, to confess your sins before the Lamb of God?

Are you ready, asks Harry, to join the Heaven-bound ranks of the born again?

Godfrey sounds three introductory chords on his accordion, drowning out the distant suggestion of fairground music. Then, as words are sung, they appear in projection on the bed-sheet, complete with bouncing ball.

The happy clappers are in session:

Harry:

Blood of Jesus, the elixir of salvation.

Take the cup, consume the blood, and wash your sins away.

Izzie:

The train reserved for born-agains is stopping every station.
If you believe please jump aboard. The Lord will pay.

Unison:

(all together now)
Blood of Jesus! Blood of Jesus!
Holy hallelujah! It's the only thing that frees us.
(yes sir)
All you scurvy sinners please get down upon your kneeses.
All glory be to God on high, so let us pray.

At Sticks' behest, the gang of five gathered in the front row are clapping, singing along, and swaying synchronously from side to side. Do you get the feeling, pademelons, the activity in the front row is as much a part of the performance as the activity beneath the proscenium arch? Isn't it true any good revival meeting needs both proselytizers and proselytizees?

Izzie:

Blood of Jesus, from the fountain of Jehovah,
full of mansions where He'll gladly wash your stinky feet.

Harry

If you ignore the invite then it's over Ruddy Rover.
It's down the escalator to the brimstone suite.

Unison:

(all together now)
Blood of Jesus! Blood of Jesus!
Holy hallelujah! It's the only thing that frees us.
(yes sir).
All you scurvy sinners please get down upon your kneeses.

All glory be to God on high, His will complete.

Harry:

Blood of Jesus, flowing freely for the fallen.
The Lamb of God is sacrificed atoning for our sin.

Izzie:

The welcome news is out there so forget your caterwaulin'.
Just chuck the Devil's doings in the wheelie bin.

Unison:

(all together now)
Blood of Jesus! Blood of Jesus!
Holy hallelujah! It's the only thing that frees us.
(yes sir)
All you scurvy sinners please get down upon your kneeses.
All glory be to God on high, so count me in.

Even as the last words are being sung, the tarts are flying. Arcs of flavour and colour sweep across the gap between stalls and stage: strawberry, blueberry, cherry, chocolate, and – beloved of all slapsticks – slimy yellow custard. Leaving the hands of the likes of Timmy, Sonia, Matt, Sticks, even Brenda, they end up on all presenting surfaces of Harry and Izzie. School caps go flying. Uniforms are desecrated. The bed-sheet drips ooze. Harry and Izzie stand there, wiping polychrome dribble from their chins, pictures of impotence and ignominy.

Godfrey, with accordion, makes a strategic exit left, pre-empting any inclination they might have to start in on him.

Wait on, pademelons. Do you feel in your bones something doesn't scan? Let us not be taken in by appearances. Let us peep beneath the facade erected, presumably, for our benefit. Let us exercise our special powers of omniscient perception.

Look at Harry. Ignore the tart detritus covering him from head to toe. Do you think his indisposition might be a tad contrived?

Does he not look like somebody who has been expecting these very shenanigans? More than that, has he been complicit in their management? Could it be he orchestrated the whole shebang?

This *is* Harry's very own show, is it not? Given this circumstance, the slimy overcoat he now wears should be a minor inconvenience.

Then pity the hapless Izzie – who didn't get to orchestrate anything. His howls shake the structural members of earth and sky, shatter wineglasses, curdle milk, raise dust dormant for half a century, and send cockroaches seeking out safer ground. His words, angry and embedded in the howls, are:

Shoot the fucking messenger, why don't you?

>

One way the condition of the main stage could be described is: tarted up. Mercifully, the left hand wing – including synthesizer and rightful occupant (Izzie) – appears to be a tart free zone, a small island overlooking a sea of slop.

Yes. Izzie has resumed his rightful residence behind his beloved synthesizer. Exultant, and clean of all technicolour bake, he is flaunting his lemon-green jacket and amber cravat. His bare skull is a moon of unabashed brightness shining forth from a clear night sky, a moon triumphant at last over the recent cumulo-nimbus of sorry circumstance, a formation banished now to the furthest horizon. He is teasing the secrets out of the next song – 4/4, *andante*, lyrical, and in major key – whose broad and shamelessly sentimental melodic line, is given over to synthesized saxophone. The snippets reaching our ears are tinged with romance, pride, bravado, suppressed sadness, lost love, all of these sprinkled liberally with emotional saccharine.

And the rest of the crew?

Sticks and Timmy sit on director's chairs at the card table set up on the right hand wing, also free of tart. They ignore the frightful condition of the main stage. Given the insousiance of the young, such acquiescence might be expected of Timmy, but I surprised at Sticks.

Timmy is fixated on the device in front of him, an i-this or an i-that or some such dooverlackie. He is absorbed by whatever variant of the virtual world is doing its seductive dance across the ghostly screen, that magic portal bridging the gap between cyberspace and mind, where the inordinately vibrant colours speak to the initiated of a habitat more desirable than that of our physical planet. His eyes are glued. Not so his fingers, working frenetically as they massage the on-screen apps, icons, and menus.

Sticks leans across and glances casually at the screen. She is surprised by what she sees.

Roulette? she asks.

Mm, says Timmy.

His absorption is impenetrable. Sticks reads his mood and realizes further attempts at communication with him – via any real-world interface – are likely to be unwelcome. She heaves a sigh and looks around for somewhere else to park her gaze.

Harry, carrying drinks on a tray, enters from backstage and heads towards them. He wears a full length flannelette dressing gown, and has a towel flapping loosely around his ruddy and almost luminous neck. He has only just scrubbed himself clean of all tart detritus. It shows.

As he puts the drinks down, Harry glances at Timmy's screen.

Roulette? he asks.

Mm, says Timmy.

Playing for money?

Got none!

Timmy's voice conveys youthful scorn, along with a singular determination to discourage further attempts to engage him in conversation. Harry hazards a shrug to Sticks via an upward sweep of the palms and a grimace to the face. He sits. Sticks turns to him.

Ideas for the next *Stück*? she asks him.

None filling me with any enthusiasm.

Come on. How did your life play out after you got religion?

Ugh. That didn't last. Not for me. Not for Izzie.

Answer the question.

What *was* the question?

How did fate treat you after your close encounter with God?

Good question.

He pauses for a moment, then words spurt out.

It was a bad time for me, he says. 'Fate' is the right word because *I* wasn't in control. Maybe I never have been. Chance has had more say in my past life than I care to mention. Apparently, it has much the same say in my present, which doesn't give me any great confidence in the future.

He pauses again, eyes cast down. Sticks waits.

I'm *not* the captain of my soul, nor am I the master of my fate.

She waits again.

Disempowerment. What it does is fuck the self esteem.

Yours? asks Sticks.

Anybody's, I imagine. Most certainly mine.

Sticks nods in the direction of Timmy, busy casting fake bets into cyberspace.

Some of us, she says, seem happy to put their trust in chance.

Holy shit, says Harry. Tell me this is a phase he's going through.

Sticks smiles, mildly amused, and to some extent gratified, by the display of impassioned concern Harry is showing for his son.

Give me some examples, she says, of your alleged lack of control.

O.K., says Harry. First, the Lantern Bearers arrive, take over my life, and tell me all my triumphs as I considered them to be – every single thing I'd been doing, saying, and thinking until then – have served no purpose except to guarantee me a special place in hell. So much for my self esteem. Then I flunk university. Ditto. Then the great love of my life, as I thought at the time, tells me …

Sonia?

… tells me what happened was only …

Harry pauses. He looks sideways at Timmy.

Only … ? asks Sticks.

Only, says Harry.

He looks at Timmy again, then – rolling his eyeballs – at Sticks.

I see, she says. 'Only'. I'm touched.

What's he hiding from me, Mommy? asks Timmy.

… don't you love that, pademelons? The little poseur has been listening all along …

Sticks smiles at her son. She leaves it to her embarrassed partner to field the spiky question. Harry pauses, then changes the subject. Leaning forward, he places one hand on each of Timmy's shoulders and holds his gaze, which Timmy promptly lowers.

Harry speaks with passion mingled with resolve. Or as close as Harry could ever come to resolve.

Timmy, he says. Listen to me.

Timmy is unable to do otherwise.

Take control of your fate. Have a clear idea of what you want in life, and go for it with all your might.

I know what I want, says Timmy.

You know?

Yes.

What?

I want to own a casino.

What?!

I want to own a casino.

Harry's resolve – such as it is – crumples. He lowers his head to the table, bangs it a few times, then – elbows digging in – cups the back of his head in his palms. His voice is muffled when he eventually speaks.

A casino, Harry says. The boy wants an effing casino.

God, Tim! Why? asks Sticks.

There's big money in casinos. I want to make big money.

There are better ways.

Poppa had *his* casino.

How in creation, says Harry, do you figure *that*?

Casinos have chips, don't they? asks Timmy.

So?

What are cherry bobs? Chips. That's what they are.

Harry raises his head. He presents pleading eyes to Sticks, but finds no joy there. Sticks is barely able to control her impulse to laugh aloud.

I don't believe I'm hearing this, says Harry.

Admit it, says Sticks. The logic is inescapable.

Sticks is left – as she so often is – to tame the awkward moment. To toss it on the mat, hold it with a half Nelson, and render it impotent, if not stone cold dead.

Timmy? she says.

Yes?

Sure there's big money in casinos. There are big criminals in casinos too. Who will kill to get their hands on that money. Sometimes casino operators don't get to live very long.

You know this? asks Timmy.

We do.

You know about casinos?

We know about *criminals*.

Harry backs Sticks up.

They're not nice people, Timmy, he says.

Timmy is impressed.

You've met criminals? he asks.

Sticks backs Harry up.

We've met criminals, she says. The worst sort.

Cool.

We've met them. Seen the whites of their eyes.

The front door creaks then slams shut. We hear commotion from front-of-house. Excited voices chatter. Metal clatters on metal.

A half-dozen or so Sandalwood people, including Godfrey,

come through the doors leading from front-of-house to stalls. Brenda, looking sheepish, is with them. They brandish mops, buckets, and the like. Their raucous voices overwhelm any vestige of tranquillity. On a mission, they make their exuberant way up the centre aisle towards the stage. Not before time, pademelons, we have somebody prepared to deal with that infamous colour spread like vomit across the stage.

Nearing this stage, they burst into vociferous *a cappella*, lead by Godfrey:

> Toreador,
> please don't spit on the floor.
> Use the cuspidor.
> That's what it's for.

The commotion flushes Matt, Sonia, and Elena out from backstage. Watching with amusement, they gather on stage at right front.

The bucketeers clamber noisily onto centre stage, continuing with song as they advance:

> Expectorate,
> but please adhere to proper form
> that says you
> hit the pot with your phlegm.
> Ahem!
> So
> whenever salivation comes to mind don't be a boor.
> Look for that cuspidor.

… though rendered ably by Godfrey and his bucketeers, this song, pademelons, is *not* their work. Such a conceit is attributable to one Ronnie Dash whom I referred to at the outset of my presentation. I promise to introduce you to him at an appropriate point later in my presentation …

The commotion stops Izzie. The soulful melody he had been coaxing from his synthesizer no longer hangs in the air to sooth those savage breasts in need of it. Rising from his piano seat he faces the bucketeers as they mop up the mess. Perhaps it is the look of fierce intensity on his face, or perhaps his aggressive body language – torso thrust forward, hands on hips – but, whatever it is, the bucketeers stop dead in their tracks.

Izzie addresses these bucketeers at centre stage, the happy family round the table on the right hand wing, and the spectators at stage-front, transferring his gaze back and forth from one group to the other. What he says is received breathlessly by all.

Izzie says:

Listen up, yodellers. My day will come. Its timing will be mine, not yours. I won't give you a date, but I tell you it will come when you least expect it. It will come at you out of the blue, like your dirty doings did for me. It will be swift and brutal, and for me it will be sweet. When it's over, when I've laid the beast to rest, that will be the moment when we're even.

He resumes his seat. Courtesy of his ten busy fingers, the saxophonic chords bearing the melody – chords more resolute now – hover in the chastened air. Sticks speaks for the ears of Harry and Timmy alone but – given the acuity of Izzie's auditory processes – she cannot be certain *he* does not hear also.

Thank you, Izzie, she says, for being an exemplary team player.

<< 1ˢᵗ Unit

There were two coincident universities Harry attended. One was shadow, the other corporal. One was phantom, the other actual. One was prestigious, the other nothing to write home about. One was 19ᵗʰ C sandstone, the other was 20ᵗʰ C concrete, aluminium, and glass. One had the smell of the sands of time and of the dust of ages, the other of disinfectant, window cleaner, filter coffee, and conditioned air. One spoke of matters of timeless and universal import, the other of matters immediate and local, pragmatic and vocational. One was where the oratorical spectres of famed halls and rooms could be resurrected if memory and imagination were brought to bear, the other where real contemporary lectures and tutorials – although available if required via the application of haranguing tongue to outraged ear – were likely in practice to be accessed in sterile and voiceless photostatic form.

Harry, enrolled in the first year of an electrical engineering course, was to tough it out to the end of second year. He didn't choose this course so much as drift in its general direction, whereupon it was as if a trapdoor had opened, through which he – startled – fell and watched it close above him. Consequent on this misadventure, he found himself in a dungeon, a most unlikely one, of scrubbed synthetic sound-proofed surfaces, oppressively low ceilings with fluorescent flicker to faze the eye, lacklustre lecturers pushing whiteboards on wheels, potted plants soaking up sun and liquid fertilizer in interior niches, deadlocks on all doors, and the boast of a gym, spa, sauna, and Olympic-size swimming pool somewhere out yonder, accessible to all able to flash plastic ID. All this was part of the corporal university not the shadow, the actual not the phantom.

Harry sat regularly and dutifully in small crowded lecture theatres of clinical genre, venues devoid of natural reverberance, residual organic odour, and semblance of aesthetic appeal. They paid lip surface to the model of a classical amphitheatre, but then proceeded to box up the sweeping and graceful curves of such in a low-set vision-tunnelling cuboid. They came equipped with a wall-mounted battery of touch screens and flashing LEDs, enabling those entrusted with access to a departmental codeword to operate the latest in audio-visual aids and/or climate control.

The lecturer's voice could be guaranteed to bang on soporifically for something approaching fifty minutes, during which time Harry found himself – curiously – possessed of an urge to liberate a fart.

If the delivery of the lecture was painful, the subject matter was salt to the wound. Students were taught how to pick a number for one of the myriad dimensionless ratios dreamed up by Reynolds, Mach, Rockwell, Foppl & von Karman, and others of their arcane fraternity. This was the black magic of the technocratic age. Should the *right* number be chosen – Harry was lead to believe – the engineering structure would be as sound as a bell, and would survive to face proudly the archaeologists of the far-flung future. Conversely, should the *wrong* number be chosen, the engineering structure would – instantly and inevitably – fall over, break apart, implode, explode, melt down, vaporize, descend into chaos, assume the shape of a pear, drop into a black hole, or otherwise self-destruct.

Pademelons, there was *one* memorable lecture nudging Harry's feelings – for a brief period – towards the prospect of a brighter world, a world at odds with the insistent upsurge of misgivings he usually endured. I mention this solitary instance at the risk of putting an unnecessary and undeserved gloss on the bigger picture, a picture Harry found deeply dispiriting.

The instance (and lecture) to which I refer happened in one of the species of lecture theatre of such oppressively synthetic ambience as fits my earlier description. The lecture was part of a course on electrodynamics. The subject was the differential equations of Clerk Maxwell. Unexpectedly, Harry found himself deeply moved by the breathtaking beauty of these equations.

For him no symphony, no portrait or landscape from the realm of visual art, no first hand contact with earthbound visual beauty either of natural setting or of human form, could compete, either for elegance or for grandeur, with these profound symbolic utterances when properly conceived by the human mind. The crux of them as revealed to Harry was: should all the divs, curls, and the like Maxwell had bottled up together be massaged ever so slightly, a burst of electric and magnetic energy would spout forth, djinn like, and embark on its wavy way, taking the high road to Mars and Jupiter at a speed of exactly one light-year per year, before anybody realized the universe as we know it had been shaken down for ever and a day. Oh, great God Maxwell! You foreshadowed so much, even Einstein.

But one epiphany does not a semester make, and Harry, disenchanted with the Department of Electrical Engineering, found himself searching for greener pastures. One such precinct, within which he conducted his search, was the shadow university, of earlier mention.

Here he walked through and among the pale sandstone of cloisters, ambulatories, courtyards, pointed arches, and vaulted ceilings, finding for himself what medieval humankind had known instinctively over the aeons of their prevalence: these structures were capable of imbuing their tenants with a sense of their significance in the world, with a feeling they were part of some predestined and meaningful scheme of things. Beneath the canopy of vault and arch, Harry felt a giant among men, felt himself capable of soaring through extensile space. He liked the feeling, and he liked the soaring.

There were no gowned or tweed-jacketed academics in these parts, not as one might expect, but only the bloodless ghosts of such. Living people – the men emasculated the women de-feminized – people of another ilk – people in aggressive power suits – shiny people – had assumed territorial rights here, invariably darting, plotting, gesticulating, barking at each other, threatening the air with spiral binders, busting their collective gut to fulfil their petty pecuniary missions. This was no longer a teaching precinct. This was where administration hung out, and the architectural grandeur seemed lost on them, and them on it.

Rounding the corner from a spacious quadrangle, Harry came across a pair of solid swinging doors, embedded in a sandstone wall infested with mould for want of a decent sand-blast. Words from a previous era were frosted onto the glass panel of the right-hand door: **DEPARTMENT OF NATURAL PHILOSOPHY**. This is where natural philosophers are found, he thought, whatever such strange cattle might be. He went inside.

He soared down a dimmed corridor so long it seemed eaten up in its own perspective, craning his neck in a vain attempt to discern detail in a ceiling high and dark enough to be capable of keeping its historic secrets to itself. Doors on the left and right opened onto cavernous spaces where dinosaurs – had the fact of their extinction been excised from prehistory – might once have been corralled. In one such space was an amphitheatre of staggering size. It had obviously been left unused for a considerable period, but its proud sweeping curves had been in no way thwarted as in the manner foisted on its sad contemporary cousins. Harry imagined a paper plane, launched from the galleried heights, hovering for breathless seconds, then stalling, then finally plunging floor-wards in a death dive of a dozen or so fatal fathoms.

Further down the corridor, on the right, was a small office, appearing to have been hewn out of nothing more than the oversupply of available space, as an igloo is hewn out of blocks of a superfluity of ice. Artificial light showing through opaque window glass indicated the office might be occupied. Harry knocked on the door – labelled **Overseas Students' Support Services** – then went inside.

A middle-aged Asian woman, slim, with artificially reddened hair and teeth like a piano keyboard, was seated behind a desk. She looked up, startled.

Excuse me, said Harry. I'm looking for the Natural Philosophy Department.

Not here, said the woman.

Her face was expressionless. Her abrupt tone conveyed an air of finality. Harry blushed, and retreated. He did not soar back along the corridor. There was no wind left in his sails for such a caper. Slinking was the best he could manage, and this he did all the way out into the quadrangle.

The next stop on Harry's quest for greener pastures was – shame on him, pademelons! – a lunchtime meeting of the Student Christian Movement. The Lantern Bearers had referred Harry to these people some time ago, but his interest in religion had waned considerably since those clap-happy times, and it was only his nagging loneliness driving him to this meeting. He regretted it immediately.

Minutes were read, and there was a call for office bearers, at which time Harry was savvy enough to keep his head down. After all present were exhorted by the chair to keep the faith, there was a spirited discussion about a possible return visit to Oz by the Rev. Billy Graham. Revivalist ditties were sung to a bit of vintage happy clapping, and the meeting was closed.

During the meeting, Harry's eyes had drifted in the direction of the half dozen or so coquettish young female undergrads, looking and speaking like the class of person who might have been Lantern Bearers in their respective schools. Regretfully, he concluded, there was little prospect, until they got rings on their fingers, of any one of them agreeing to come across. He smiled, a sad internal smile, from himself to himself. His lustful thoughts at this moment told of a fully-fledged Lothario rattling round inside of him who bore no relation to the greenhorn he knew was his usual persona, as presented to and seen commonly by the world. For the life of him, he couldn't think of a way to induce these two personas to swap places.

A snippet of useful information *did* come his way from one of the nymphettes. She thought the natural philosophers might be found in the Club Bar of the All Nations Hotel every Thursday evening.

The day *was* Thursday. Throwing caution to the wind and thrilled by his imagined daring, Harry rang his mother to tell her he would be home late and not to wait up for him. Brenda, unconcerned, told him it was OK and she would leave his dinner in the microwave. We all would have appreciated mothers like that, wouldn't we pademelons?

The All Nations was in the wide world outside the campus, but within easy walking distance of it. The small Club Bar, a student haunt, was tucked in behind the main bar, the latter being where all the supposed riff-raff – those who had never had the means and/or the inclination to attend university – disported themselves. Once Harry had sorted out these important matters of form and station, and had put the main bar out of sight and mind, he found himself standing with the obligatory glass of amber fluid in his hand, looking round at the various student cliques assembled in the cosy confines of this bar of young pretenders, and wondering which group were the natural philosophers.

The natural philosophers here? he asked the barman.

The barman flicked his head in the direction of a raucous all-male group gathered in a corner. Their age range suggested they might be a mix of grads and undergrads.

Dunno, said the barman. There's some pretty *un*-natural philosophers having a bash over yonder.

Harry sidled over to the periphery of this group, placing his glass on – and leaning an elbow against – a ledge about a metre away from them, hoping to be able to observe but not *be* observed. He found they were less inclined to talk about Kant, Hegel, and Wittgenstein than they were about Cleese, Gilliam, and Palin. They had appropriated one of the Pythonesque sketches for their own immediate purpose, which was to launch willy-nilly into an impromptu gig, letting the beer do the talking.

Bruce, I have a question to ask of you, said one.

I'm all ears, Bruce, said another.

What's your opinion of the proposition put by Bruce? said Bruce the first.

Got no opinion, Bruce, said Bruce the second. Better ask Bruce.

Well, what's your opinion, Bruce?

I'm not *au fait* with the proposition, Bruce, said a Bruce the third. Better ask Bruce.

Well shit, what's your opinion then, Bruce?

I don't discuss my opinions *pro bono*, Bruce, said a Bruce the fourth. Better ask Bruce.

Well, Bruce, do you think any of the other Bruces hereabouts might (a) be familiar with this proposition of Bruce's, and (b) have an opinion about said proposition, and (c) be willing to discuss said opinion? Bruce?

Bruce, I honestly couldn't say, said Bruce the second. Better ask Bruce.

Then, Bruce, what say we ask Bruce over there?

Assuming the first Bruce was looking at and pointing to someone to his rear, Harry turned his head. There was no likely person to his rear, but he *did* catch the barman's wink. When he returned his gaze to the front, he realized to his horror it was he, Harry McMinn, and nobody else, to whom the insistent Bruce the first was pointing.

Yes, you, Bruce! said Bruce the first.

He suppressed an urge to say, My name's Harry, thereby averting a social disaster of a magnitude high on the Richter scale. What he ended up saying, was far worse.

I'm an engineer, said Harry.

He flushed bright red. Sensing blood, the group homed in on their hapless prey. Bruce the first turned exultantly to Bruce the second.

Bruce, did you hear that? said Bruce the first. Bruce is an *engineer*.

We don't come across many of your stripe around here, Bruce, said Bruce the second.

Bruce, I wonder, said Bruce the first, what position an engineer like Bruce might take on issues of moment, like for example, the God debate.

He turned to Harry.

Tell me Bruce. Are you a monotheist, a polytheist, a henotheist, a pantheist? Or no sort of theist at all?

A deist, perhaps, said Bruce the second.

Or an atheist, said Bruce the third.

I hasten to warn you, Bruce, said Bruce the second, it's absolutely not kosher to be devoid of position. The concept of 'no position' is an oxymoron.

A logical vacuum, said Bruce the third by way of patronizing clarification.

I picture Bruce as an apatheist, said Bruce the fourth.

Bruce, are you serious? said Bruce the third. Do we have a lotus eater in our midst?

Permit me, Bruce, said Bruce the second, to think outside the square for the moment. Our newest Bruce could be a closet thespian.

You mean … ? said Bruce the first.

… he needs Natalie! said Bruce the second.

Let me arrange an introduction, said Bruce the first.

Harry was whisked away by Bruce the first to a different group – generally younger and of mixed gender – asserting territorial rights over a different corner of the bar. Along the way, Harry managed to pick up a fresh glass of beer and another sly wink from the barman.

At the centre of this group was a young woman called – as promised – Natalie, to whom he was introduced by Bruce the first. It turned out the group was trying to organize a student review to celebrate the approaching equinox or some such event characterized principally by its serious lack of relevance. Harry let himself be recruited, especially since it meant he could swap the company of those tiresome Bruces for the allure of Natalie, who definitely had something of the seductress about her and did not look like the sort who hankered unnecessarily after rings.

Natalie had eyes brown and mesmeric, hair black and made for stroking, limbs lean, creamy, and suggestive of acquiescence. She wore a light, loose fitting dress to just below the knees, accentuating the profile beneath to startling effect without actually exposing it. She had a disarming habit of tilting her head sideways and narrowing her eyes in deference to the person who was speaking to her. Harry was taken by her. She had no trouble persuading him to turn up for the first rehearsal next Tuesday evening.

So, pademelons, Harry's quest to locate the natural philosophers was supplanted by a quest for something far closer to the elemental than the esoteric. In his moments of fondest fantasy, a mere five barriers – and trivial barriers they were! – stood between him and the success of his newfound quest. These barriers were the days of the week taking up their residence, according to the common calendar, between Thursday and the following Tuesday.

The days passed slowly for him. Hardly less slowly did the pageant of hours, minutes, and seconds comprising them. These selfsame seconds, in fact, seemed to tick away at the frequency of a ponderous cathedral bell. Nobody should ask, pademelons, for whom *this* bell tolled.

Tuesday evening arrived.

The venue Harry hoped would bear witness to his anticipated amatory success was a drab meeting hall, with a small proscenium stage, in the Student Union building. About ten or twelve punters arrived for rehearsals, young men and young women in an acceptable gender balance. Harry's eyes found Natalie, presenting more or less as he had anticipated in his five nights of fervid dreams under tousled blankets. Discreetly, he ticked off the choicest details in his head: eyes, hair, limbs, tilting head, loose fitting dress. Perhaps not discreetly enough as it turned out because, appearing to catch him at it, she flashed a confidential smile in his exclusive direction.

A young wannabe film-maker, Michel, was in charge of proceedings. He spoke to the group with marked condescension for about ten minutes. They would start, he told them, with the introductory number, an unstructured dance. Choreography, presently not required, was to be added later. For preliminaries, dancers should go with the flow, absorbed osmotically by the music. Let structure emerge spontaneously in the absence of imposed boundaries.

Harry looked around. Natalie was gone.

Piped music started up: *O Fortuna* from *Carmina Burana*.

The opening section, with its loud sallies of percussion, inspired some moments of wild revel from the dozen or so participants. Then the music mutated to the stuff of quiet incipient devilry, less of the wild revel, but extremely potent nonetheless. Those who previously had leapt now lurched from one threatening pose to another. Or else they lay in wait, muscles taut, ready to launch ambush. As the music progressed towards orgasm, the dancers had no trouble picking up the cue. The sexual element in their movements became clear, as did the intent of their threats and ambushes. The covert assumed the form of the overt. All in psychotic strobe light as delivered from on high, from somewhere behind and above the stalls.

What was Harry's reaction to this – his inaugural – encounter with the pointy end of live theatre? In a word: terrified. Terrified by the emerging subtext of the event, by the ominous subliminals behind the action. He went through the motions hoping the relentless strobing would disguise his ineptitude, the iterative shafts of darkness somehow hiding him. But he felt his anxiety growing to catastrophic levels, and knew things were going to end badly.

Climax and consummation arrived, heralded by a massive eruption of cymbalic and timpanic violence. At this moment of musical rampage, Natalie appeared naked and full-frontal from behind a backstage scrim. She moved rapidly to centre stage, striking a pose amidst the throng of circling dancers. A sharp spot set her apart from all peripheral action and from the strobe lighting, throwing her furry triangle into graphic relief against her creamy flesh. Harry felt an instant marasmus invade his body. Where was his Lothario now?

He had never before been so close at hand to anything so beautiful or desirable, but the other side of the coin was the concurrent and certain threat he perceived. He wanted to cut and run – as he had done years earlier in that blind alley – but found he couldn't. All he could do was freeze stupidly, like a big red kangaroo in the sights of a grazier's shotgun. Vermin. That's precisely what he felt like.

As music and dance of such vitality must end, so the white-hot intensity of one's moments of thrall must give way to hues more typical of one's pale world. The vividness of dreams must give way to humdrum wakefulness. The preternatural must give way to the natural. So, when the curtains closed on this thespian romp, the sweaty stagers faced a reluctant return to their day jobs.

But first: a small task.

All participants joined Michel in the stalls to help script other items for the revue. Natalie was dressed now, but Harry couldn't bring himself to look at her, except with the eye of his tortured mind. This eye saw, in her face, compassion one moment, contempt the next. And at times something far worse. Gross indifference.

As regards script development, suggestions were advanced and duly accepted, most of them excruciatingly vapid and unfunny.

To prove this rule by way of outrageous exception, there *was* a person present who turned out to be more than adequate to the task. This person was Ronald Dash, whom I have mentioned a couple of times already. Ronnie was a perennial student who never enrolled for courses or paid fees, preferring the irregular – and more affordable – approach of dropping in at whim on the available broad church of lectures and tutorials the campus had on offer. He had a special talent for devising lyrics to recognizable tunes, lyrics with the capacity – especially off campus – to cause outrage. For example:

Who flipped the frangers[21] into Mrs Murphy's chowder?
Not the sort of stupid prank to make a mother prouder.
I've two bones to pick with you:
they're so difficult to chew,
and the inner tube has issues with the outer.

---

21 franger: Australian slang, meaning 'condom'.

Michel, aware such a lyricist – though not necessarily family friendly – might be an asset to the revue, made overtures, but found Ronnie a difficult steer to keep in the paddock. Ronnie liked hanging around on the fringes of things, keeping a low profile, and shying away from unnecessary commitment. Pushy people like Michel got up his nostrils.

On this particular Tuesday evening, Michel wielded the long lasso, but true to form Ronnie slipped the noose. He was not to be corralled. Michel cut his losses.

So, he said, next week, same time, same place? The group disbanded, many of them heading to the All Nations for an ale or two before closing time. Harry headed home to his microwave dinner.

Harry didn't attend next week's rehearsal. He didn't attend *any more* rehearsals. He had decided the revue wasn't for him.

He stayed on at university for almost another year, before deciding it wasn't for him either.

2nd Unit >>

Sticks has discovered another reason why she likes *La Spag*. Somehow, she muses silently, the acoustics have turned out right. The background buzz of combined conversation from all other tables in the premises intrudes minimally onto hers, with the fortunate result she and her tablemates have no difficulty hearing their own conversation. In fact, this background buzz has useful attributes. This is buzz with a positive purpose. It provides the cover necessary to ensure any fragment of conversation escaping from her table does not penetrate to other tables. And vice versa. It is as if – while things are buzzing – each table at *La Spag* is enclosed in a confidential cone of silence. How does Bruno – not known to be an acoustic engineer – achieve this sublime balance? The man is a homespun genius.

Sharing the table with her is Harry, who is pontificating.

... organized religion might have some use as a monument to our collective dysfunction, or perhaps as a negative role model, letting us know what *not* to do, like abusing choirboys, indulging latent chauvinism, holding ceremonies simulating the eating of flesh and blood, and so on *ad infinitum.*

Quite a mouthful, feller, says Sticks. If I were you, I'd say less and eat more.

They are eating *zuppe inglese*, a house specialty. They each wolf down another spoonful, licking their lips afterwards. Sticks changes the subject.

Remember, she says, when we sat down with Timmy after the last performance. There was something you were unable to say in front of him.

There was?

Something Sonia told you in your uni days.

Sonia didn't go to university.

Did I say she did?

Following a pause, Sticks breaks the silence.

It involved the word 'only', she says.

Harry puts down his eating utensils abruptly. His speech is distant.

Only, he says.

Sticks waits, convinced Harry is ready to spill the beans. When, after some moments, he *does* break the silence, there is a look on his face, suggestive of a plan to undertake the cerebral equivalent of a high dive into the deep end.

When she broke off our ailing relationship, he says, she used the word 'only'.

Go on.

She told me what happened was *only* a fuck.

This requires some digestion by the mind. Perversely they each take a spoonful for the stomach. Sticks speaks.

So. *That's* the story.

Sticks breaks the inevitable pause.

I might have guessed.

But you didn't.

Didn't I?

Another pause insinuates itself. Perhaps the whole occasion is best regarded as one long pause interrupted by sporadic verbal snippets.

It stuck with me, says Harry. That word 'only'.

Why?

It devalues the fuck. Would you say '*Only* a nine on the Richter scale'? '*Only* a small supernova'? '*Only* a historical glitch known as World War Three'?

... pademelons! Permit me a digression. I, too, can play this game: '*Only* the pile-driver of heavy irony powering home the point of a needle'...

Do I detect the romantic in you? asks Sticks.

Are you devaluing it also?

Not at all. I don't devalue such things. But I would prefer to call it lovemaking.

Why?

Let's say personal eccentricity.

She finds his hand across the table. They enjoy a few moments of non-verbal communication. Then Harry speaks.

Perhaps, says Harry, this will be the subject of the next *Stück*.

What will you call it?

'Only'.

Of course.

Bruno's daughter, Giulietta, is hovering, with a mind to gather plates. Sticks, noticing this, stacks them for her. Giulietta thanks her, and departs with the stack.

Pademelons, I see a question poised on your marsupial lips. We know Bruno has plans for his sons. Roberto will be a lawyer. Rinaldo will be a doctor. What will Giulietta be?

I shall tell you.

We deal here, paddies, with the Mediterranean diaspora. 'Mediterranea' is a country with long-standing traditions ensuring no *signorina* need trouble herself with doubts about her place. Apropos of a plan for Giulietta, I ruefully predict:

> *For* her, no plan is needed,
> and, *to* her, none is ceded.

<< 1st Unit

'The way it's always done' had been the credo of the female line of Sonia's family down the generations.

Every Christmas, in the Bee Street household, Mrs Sheridan cooked a ham for the family, to supplement the obligatory roast turkey, ignoring – as citizens of Oz are prone to do – the forty degree heat blanketing festive suburbia. And every Christmas, Mrs Sheridan would cut the ends off the ham and bin them, before the ham went into the oven.

When Sonia – an only child – was ten years old, she started to help her mother in the kitchen. Come Christmas then, and seeing her mother cut the ends off the ham as usual, she asked, Why do you cut the ends off the ham? Her mother replied, That's the way it's always done. When pressed, she modified her response to, That's the way *my* mother taught *me*.

When Sonia next saw her grandmother she asked, Why do you cut the ends off the ham? Grandmother responded, That's the way it's always done. Later modified to, That's the way *my* mother taught *me*.

Sonia's great-grandmother was still alive back then. The old dear had clear memories of two world wars and of the depression in between, but only fuzzy memories of the events tweaking the fabric of history from the trials at Nuremberg and Maralinga[22] up until those importunate trials playing havoc in this day and age. Not even the events of family history were exempt from this fuzziness. So, by prior arrangement all parties agreed it would be kosher for this venerable ancestor to address Sonia and all other small children around the traps – family members or not – by that fragment of generic gibberish rendered more-or-less as 'Diddums'.

It transpired when Sonia next saw her great-grandmother and asked her, Why do you cut the ends off the ham?, great-grammy's response – delivered by quivering vocal chords, cleared for passage by bare and bleeding gums, and mouthed to the world by lips pallid and purplish – was, I only had one pan, Diddums, and it was too small, so what would you do? I cut the ends off the ham to make it fit.

>

Sonia – in her mid teens – knew 'the drill'. Otherwise known as 'the way it's always done'. She signalled Travis with her eyes, lids lowered but eyeballs dead level. Travis knew what the signal meant. He *also* knew the drill.

Travis was one of Sonia's three male cousins, sons of one or other of her father's brothers, and each a few years older than she was. All her cousins knew the drill. Opportunists they assuredly were, and they kept each other in the loop via the established and active grapevine of colluding cousinhood.

So Travis turned to Sonia's father and said, How's the dragon's blood plant, Uncle Steve?

Mr Sheridan – embraced by the folds of his comfortable armchair, sucking like a baby at a can of beer, subsumed by the

---

22 Maralinga: a location in the Australian desert, site of British nuclear test-ing in the 1950s and 1960s.

football replay on TV – muttered in reluctant reply, You mean *Dracaena draco?*

Yes, said Travis.

Going ahead in leaps and bounds.

I'd really like to see it.

It was Saturday afternoon. Travis and Mr Sheridan had returned from the live match between the Cats and the Dogs, with mandatory team scarves dangling at their heels. Mr Sheridan was a Dogs supporter, and all three cousins were Cats supporters. The cousins took turns to accompany Mr Sheridan to Saturday football matches, and to watch the replay and post mortem afterwards in the Sheridans' living room. One of the cousins would usually turn up again the next day after mass, when there would be roast dinner followed by still more football analysis by the pundits on TV. Football – of the variety played with a laced-up spheroidal ball – was a big deal in the Sheridan household, at any rate in the one-third of the household comprising Mr Sheridan.

When Travis asked his Uncle Steve after the welfare of the dragon's blood plant, he knew exactly what he was doing. He was wedging the older man between his two over-riding interests: football and horticulture.

… Mr Sheridan did regular paid work, but only to keep the wolf from the door. Beyond the pay packet it held little interest for him. Whenever asked, he would describe himself as an engineer. Within a broad ambit, he *was* an engineer, if such ambit were stretched to include the supervision of road gangs for the local shire …

Getting back to the wedge. The wedge was a strategy used and understood by Travis, Sonia, and the other two cousins. The wedge was part of the drill, the way it's always done. Courtesy of the wedge, Travis and Sonia now elicited the response they were seeking from her father.

Honeybunch, said Mr Sheridan. You know where the key is. Show the boy.

Mrs Sheridan was slicing onions in the kitchen. Through the door to the living room, she could see and hear everything. There was a look of disquiet on her face. She wasn't sure whether or not the developments she observed were the way it's always done. She certainly had a strong sense of the historical imperative because her Catholic faith informed it, and was in turn informed *by* it. But she too was wedged by circumstances. To contradict one's husband is assuredly *not* the way it's always done.

So, without saying boo, she watched Sonia retrieve the key to the greenhouse. She kept watching as Sonia – with an unmistakeable look of anticipation – smoothed down the front of her skirt with the palms of both hands from the top of her thighs to the knees. This was the very skirt she – Mrs Sheridan – had pressed only last night! She kept watching as Sonia and Travis went out the back door, and would have continued watching out the kitchen window as they wended their way to the greenhouse if only the view out that wretched window had *included* the wretched greenhouse and the wretched path leading to it.

If she *had* been able to watch, she would have seen the eager pair walking side by side toward the greenhouse, Sonia with an arm draped around Travis' shoulders, and Travis with a hand placed confidently on Sonia's right buttock.

>

I have an inclination, pademelons, to use lecture mode to proceed further with my presentation. You will recall I have used this mode before and – dare I suggest? – have pulled it off with aplomb. Accordingly, I invite you to take your places in the amphitheatre while I take the lectern. You never can know. What you may learn from this lecture could be of value to you in a bizarre set of circumstances as yet unforseen by you, your omniscience notwithstanding.

Psychology 101, Module 32b: Human Sexuality, as Informed by 'The Method', and as Elucidated by a Case Study of the Coming of Age of an Inexperienced Young Person of the Male Gender upon Entering into Commerce with a More Experienced Young Person of the Female Gender.

Has it crossed your mind the young man under consideration here might be Harry McMinn, nerd, and the young woman his sexually awakened neighbour, Sonia Sheridan? Congratulations on your prescience.

Before proceeding with the case study, it is fitting I provide you with a summary of the elements of what is being referred to in the literature as 'The Method'. I have spelt out these elements in advance for you on the whiteboard. Please excuse my scrawl ...

... uuuhhh. Uuuhhh. This blessed board refuses to budge. Bear with me while I set myself up to give it an almighty heave. UUUHHH – ahhhh. Success. Here are the goods ...

The Method:
§ proximity § contiguity § social kissing § sexual kissing
§ genital play § petting to climax § copulation.

I can't pretend I am happy with that unfortunate title, even though it is pre-eminent in the peer-review literature. In my opinion, such a lacklustre choice of title could only have come about through regrettable default to a serious lack of imagination. 'The Method'? Really! Give me a break.

Consider it in isolation: to what might this so-called 'Method' refer? A system of that obsolete art once known in the world of commerce as stenographic shorthand? Or a procedure for preparing a Cape Barren goose for the pleasure of a celebratory moment round the dinner table? Perhaps it is a scheme for clipping one's toenails with both hands tied behind one's back. As it stands, this title gives no clue as to what in the devil's name the stuff following it is all about. Not one iota of a clue. It is a pair of conjoined weasel words, in deliberate pursuit of vagueness.

I have come up with my preferred title, which I suggest is more reflective of the subject matter, and certainly more redolent of colour, than something as amorphous as 'The Method'. I would like to share it with you. My alternative title is: 'The Stations of the Crotch'. What do you think? Indelicate, I agree, if not downright crude. Explicit, I agree, if not downright anatomical. Irreligious, I agree, if not downright profane. But you must allow the metaphor it employs is apt. It packs a punch. Below the belt, one might say. Have not pundits down the ages – poets, pedagogues, philosophers, philanderers – described coitus as *le petite mort?* By way of qualification here, it is doubtful if death by crucifixion is what any of the good folk who coined this phrase had in mind.

Let us take a good long look at the 'Stations', as I have chosen to call them. At the risk of seeming unnecessarily clinical, I put two questions to you: (a) are they *necessary?* (b) are they *sufficient?*

Necessary for what? Sufficient for what? Successful coition, of course. That's what the exercise is all about. There's nothing to be gained by being precious about these matters.

Would any of you like to argue the Stations as listed here, shall not – when applied *in toto* and in the order stated – deliver the desired effect, i.e. prove *sufficient?* I thought not. Such a sequence of events – self evidently – must lead at the very least to satisfactory sexual congress and, with a modicum of luck and will, to congress rather more than satisfactory.

Are all the Stations as listed absolutely *necessary?* And, by way of corollary, is the order in which they are stated necessary? In the parallel case of the *biblical* Stations, from which – by analogy and with trepidation – I derive *my* Stations, there is *doctrinal* necessity. But I doubt, in any instance of sexual adventurism taken through to completion, doctrine is a consideration. What is called for here

– I maintain – is a degree of flexibility, along lines I list for you here …

… uuuhhh. This board again. Uuuhhh. May the curse of the galloping goitre be upon those responsible, as it is upon my gormless granny. Won't said powers permit me to take a trick for once? UUUHHH – ahhh. The beast moves …

§ Stations may be omitted if such is desired.

§ Stations may be visited in a different order if such is desired.

§ Stations may be re-visited if such is desired.

§ New Stations may even be added willy nilly, according to the celebrated powers of human invention.

One is lead to conclude there is little of necessity about the nature, number, and order of these Stations. When the coital curtain finally descends, the important thing is the amatory purposes of any ardent pilgrim should have been met, and met well. In consequence, this joyous pilgrimage shall find itself in need of repetition …

… again, and again, and again, and once again …

… oops! Agggggghhhhhh! …

… sorry, paddies. My notes appear to have taken wing. Be so good as to help me gather up these loose pages.

I can't believe I did that. I know some of my mannerisms have of recent been verging on the extravagant. But to engage physically with the lectern, do an imitation of a whirling dervish, and end up spreadeagled on the floor in front of you, pushes the bounds of extravagance.

Perhaps the titillatory nature of the subject matter has stirred up old fires in my supernal loins. You are sceptical? I understand your doubts. I, too, would have imagined those ancient flames had long ago gone to ashes and, in such friable form, been dispersed to all points by the eddies of time. But I suspect reminiscences of old – even for the likes of us – still contain unquenched sparks.

Which may no longer find much by way of combustible burden to ignite, but can nevertheless deliver a red-hot sting.

Thank you very much for your forbearance. Thank you. Give me a moment to catch my breath and gather my wits.

>

Let us resume. Where was I?

Oh, yes. Pilgrimage.

How may we assume Henry Athol McMinn disported himself on his first pilgrimage of the nature I discuss?

Harry had known Sonia since early childhood. But there would have come a point in his life – out of a clear blue sky I imagine – when he began to see Sonia in a different light. The old Sonia – of the blind alley, of Main Street, of Mulki Larka – was a relic expunged from his consciousness. A new Sonia had come forward via some strange magic working its way outwards from the curve, bulk, and bounce of upright breasts and from the flexing expanse of lap, groin, and thigh. How did Harry McMinn react to this new Sonia presenting itself?

To put himself in the way of this magic, Harry began to pay calls on the Sheridan residence, which – as you are aware – was only a few doors from his own in Bee Street. Here, cups of Twinings tea were pressed on him, as he found himself swept up in games of four-handed canasta. The Sheridans no longer held his family's shady past against him. His status as an (apparently) industrious student at university, with (presumably) a rosy future ahead of him, redeemed him in their eyes, or so appearances suggested.

The games of canasta were problematic. Inevitably, there would be a curt exchange or two – between Mr and Mrs – of the type:

You can't make a meld out of threes, mother, Mr Sheridan would say.

Oh, Mrs Sheridan would reply, why not, dear?

It's the rules of canasta, mother.

Is that really in the rules, dear?

Always has been.

Sometimes, Uncle Steve – as Mr Sheridan was known to young visitors whether family or not – invited Harry to the greenhouse to inspect the *Dracaena draco*, whose progress this proud parent had monitored assiduously over a period of twenty years or so. It was a flourishing specimen, grown almost to the height of a person, and shaped like a gigantic flat-topped mushroom. Its silvery trunk rose straight, before branching into a labyrinth of twisted trunk-lets, which collectively bore a thick canopy of long grey-green leaves contriving to be both fleshy and pointy at the same time. Mr Sheridan insisted – but declined to demonstrate – the sap of this tree was blood-red in colour. Hence, he explained, the reason for the common name: dragon's blood plant.

This was the plant from nowhere. To any person with a psyche habituated to the usual range of botanical specimens found in Oz, whether native or introduced, this plant was bound to seem foreign, even sinister. Harry, who fell into this category, was glad when Mr Sheridan ushered him out and locked the greenhouse door behind him.

As for Uncle Steve's other great passion – his beloved football-playing Dogs – Harry did not share it. Sport had never been his bag, not even as spectator. We may speculate this deficiency in his makeup derived from his lack of a male role model in his formative years.

At about this time, Harry became the proud owner of a pre-loved six-cylinder two-tone Torana, in jaunty red and white. Looking at the vehicle on his first day of ownership, Harry felt a thrill invade his body, not the least because he expected this was a rite-of-passage moment for him, especially as regards Sonia.

At last, he and Sonia could escape from the bottomless cups of tea, from the tedious games of canasta, from Uncle Steve and his subservient spouse, to find adventures of their own in the wider world, preferably right across the other side of town. Most importantly, he knew the chance he would get to tick boxes against some of the Stations was significantly enhanced. Everybody knew what one could get up to in a car.

Pademelons, as we proceed with this case study, I trust you *too* will be poised with your pencils to tick boxes.

Harry started by dropping Sonia off and picking her up from ballet class. Sonia had persevered with these lessons ever since she was six years old. Her teacher, Mrs Grigorova, who claimed to be a veteran of *Ballet Russes*, taught an amalgam of classical and modern dance. Sometimes Harry sat in on the lesson. Afterwards, they would drive somewhere for cappuccinos. Harry loved the freedom his Torana afforded him.

… to Mrs Grigorova's disappointment, Sonia – her star pupil – was to persevere for only one more year. Coincidentally, this was about how long Harry was to persist with his university studies. They were both persuaded by life's various and insistent pressures to abandon what had become increasingly irrelevant to them …

Harry was gratified to find coffee houses were a hit with Sonia. Settled in such congenial surroundings with whatever brew was her choice, a loose-tongued Sonia would abandon herself to self-absorbed chatter. Harry found all he had to do was sit back, pretend to listen, and hold her hand across the table.

Harry floated on air. The sequence of dreary and repetitive events making up the bulk of everyday life for most people became infused – for him – with a mellow yet unaccountable charm. Mundane things around him became objects of great beauty. Even the drizzly skies typical of this location on the globe at this time of year radiated warmth and light as he walked oblivious beneath them. Sonia was in his thoughts and that was sufficient unto the day with – moreover – bright prospects for tomorrow.

Harry decided to show Sonia what life was like in the student precinct near his university. Accordingly, they descended one evening on a well known student haunt, ostensibly to sample cappuccino and cake. The trappings of the place were – befitting the clientele – cheap, funky, and tawdry, but the coffee was excellent.

Sonia was excited by the new world she saw: bright young things dashing around, talking with animation – but no understanding – on arcane subjects, pouring over old-growth forests of lecture notes, surreptitiously sharing joints in hidden corners, attempting desperately to school themselves in upmarket accents, and engaging in all the other subterfuges part and parcel of being a hopelessly insecure student. She held hands with Harry across the table of scuffed plastic laminate, her eyes sparkling while they soaked up the sight of a milieu she never knew existed. Torrents of conversation poured out of her, with only an occasional interjection by Harry required to keep the flow going.

Then her eyes dulled. She let go of his hand.

What's the matter? he asked.

They're all wearing black, she replied.

Harry looked around him. She was right. It was like a uniform. Trouser or skirt: it was black. Blouse, jumper, or jacket: it was black. Footware, headware: it was black. Some wore dark glasses, with frames and lenses the colour of crannies in a termite mound on a moonless midnight.

What of it? he asked.

A pall had descended. Black.

We're not, she replied.

She was right again. He wore blue jeans. She wore a suede skirt in olive green. Both of them had white shirts showing beneath windcheaters in pastel shades. They were not wearing 'the uniform'. They were obvious ring-ins, tourists, voyeurs.

Let's get out, she said.

They left. The wind had gone from Harry's metaphoric sails. To him, it was immaterial whether they were wearing bitumen black or the full shrieking spectrum. To him, it was immaterial whether they were seen as gauche tourists or as cool insiders. Hadn't they paid for their coffee?

Back at Bee Street, on the dark front porch of the Sheridan house, Harry moved to kiss Sonia on the lips, but she turned her head sideways, and he ended up planting a chaste kiss on her cheek instead.

One of his next excursions with Sonia was to an art cinema close to the university and patronized – for the most part – by young people of the echelon they had encountered in that coffee house those nights back. This time our couple – the subject of my brief – were clothed in empathetic black. No surprise there, pademelons. Sonia seemed comfortable, and her tendency to animation was beginning to bubble to the surface.

Seated near the front of the cinema, Harry swivelled his trunk to get a view of those behind him. He swept his eyes in swift arcs back and forth across the audience, fearful lest he should find Natalie, Michel, or others of his former thespian associates in attendance. He located nobody of concern.

Looking for somebody? asked Sonia.

Nobody, he replied.

Somebody fart?

Not really.

Is there a bull loose in the paddock?

He felt sheepish. Why should he fret about people who would certainly not waste time fretting about him? He was in the company of the beautiful clever young woman of his choice, so what need had he for the ghosts of his past? He took Sonia's hand in his, and kept holding it for the duration of the film.

Afterwards, they went for coffee, this time to a more upmarket venue. Here, over steaming mugs of a milky-brown decoction laced with Irish whiskey they discussed the film they had seen.

Which one was Peter Sellers? Sonia asked.

He played three roles, Harry replied.

Three?

That's right.

Good God.

Could you pick them?

I'm not sure.

Guess.

Well … Doctor Strangeglove … but after that I'm not sure.

OK. There's Mandrake, the dapper English guy with the moustache.

Him? I never would have guessed.

And the President of the United States. That makes three.

I guess so.

By the way, it's Doctor Strange*love*, not Doctor Strange*glove*.

But he certainly had a strange *glove*.

That wasn't a glove. That was a prosthesis.

Sonia looked blank.

An artificial arm, said Harry.

Oh.

An embarrassing pause followed. Sonia broke the ice.

I think I liked him better in Pink Panther, she said.

Back at Bee Street, on that dark porch again, he managed at last to kiss Sonia on full and willing lips. She tilted her head, opened her mouth ever so slightly, used a tiny bit of tongue, and generally contrived to prolong and intensify the kiss. Afterwards, there was consensus it bore repeating, and they did so. Again and again.

For Harry, these kisses reverberated through his body with electric urgency, delivering to him an intense pleasure mixed with a profound sense of his own worth. He had the delicious feeling the engines of control and responsibility – normally spinning monotonously and at his behest – were now being impelled by some universal and benign animalism, both inside and outside of him. It was a new deal for him and he felt excited by it.

That night, in his lone bed, a twang like the mellowest musings of classical guitar soothed his body. Sleep, deep and delicious, quickly overtook him. He woke to a tomorrow foreshadowing limitless prospects. For Harry McMinn, the life and times were very very good.

From this point on, the evening outings enjoyed by this increasingly amorous couple ended in the back seat of the Torana, parked – for what minimal seclusion it might offer – beneath one of the legendary oleanders of Bee Street. In the interests of their privacy, pademelons, I urge you to bring your imaginings to bear when deciding which Stations need ticking off. I suggest to you the number of them might be counted in a prolific plural.

I shall give a brief account of another of their outings because it was a *coup* of sorts for Harry. David Bowie was doing a one-off gig in town, and Harry – aware this event would appeal to Sonia though perhaps not so much to him – had scored tickets. Seventeen was an auspicious number for Harry and – *voila* – on the night before Sonia's seventeenth birthday, they took their seats near the back of the crowded venue. Here they waited expectantly for the appearance on stage of the revered celebrity and for the moment when walls, floor, and ceiling would disgorge over-amplified sound, in wilful disregard for the integrity of thousands of young ear canals.

The Man dutifully appeared but, from where Harry and Sonia were seated, it would have been difficult without the assistance of the Hubble telescope to ascertain who it *was* on stage. So this Bowie of Lilliputian proportions pranced around on a shoebox stage, his voice delivered by disproportionate electronic means, while Sonia (and thousands of others of like mind) exercised their lungs with abandon. Harry watched the antics with bemusement.

But if Bowie himself hadn't actually prophesied by song, then Harry's head, heart, skin, breath, and eyes should have told: the prospects for this enamoured pair would most likely include a miracle goodnight.[23]

Past the witching hour in the back of the Torana, Harry

---

23 cf. Bowie's song 'Miracle Goodnight'.

turned to Sonia and said, Happy birthday. Sonia – through lips disengaged momentarily from the prerogative of passion – replied, I might have to start taking my little wishful-thinking pill.

The following evening they celebrated Sonia's birthday with her parents. The cake was cut, toasts were proposed. Then Mr Sheridan suggested a game of canasta. The cards were in his hands when Sonia rose abruptly to her feet and said, May I show Harry the dragon's blood plant?

You know where the key is, honeybunch, said Mr Sheridan.

They did the walk, Sonia leading. She fumbled with the key, but eventually got the door of the greenhouse open. Propitious moonlight penetrated the framed glass panels, illuminating the tangled boughs of the *Dracaena draco* and row-upon-row of smaller plants. Harry tried to embrace Sonia, but she repulsed him.

Wait, she said.

Harry picked up the faint tremor in her voice.

Sonia collected a couple of blankets stashed on a shelf, for the purposes – as required – of protecting the more delicate plants from excessive heat or cold. She laid these at the foot of the dragon's blood plant, and proceeded to take off her clothes. When completely naked, she laid herself down on the blankets, and looked up at Harry with eyes behind which lust stalked the territory. These eyes conveyed her feelings on immediate matters more succinctly than spoken words could have.

She spoke anyway. Hazard a guess, pademelons, at the degree of astonishment Harry felt even *before* she opened her mouth. Then consider: to this base was added acute surprise at the tone of her voice. Harry had never before heard this tone from her. In its uncharacteristically husky timbre, he detected riot and rampage out-running control.

Get yours off, she said.

Henceforth, it was as if all mundane fragments of experience – such as *his* turn to shed clothes and *their* subsequent sleights of body – were relegated to autonomous realms outside of Harry's consciousness, and other fragments more germane to the moment contrived to fill the space they left behind in his sensible universe. What might it have been that was germane to his moment? Sublimity, I suggest to you. Sublimity of a degree and kind impervious to guesswork and incapable of reconstruction through human verbalization. As I have already intimated, pademelons, our immortal and omniscient status shall be of little use to us in this context. The best we can do is bring to bear our imaginings and ancient recollections in a futile attempt to re-create something of the flavour of this earthbound aspect of perfection.

We have left all this behind, pademelons, and it is not given to us to know it again. This is our sorry lot.

Afterwards, enjoying the abandonment of his senses to languid tides washing dreamy post-coital shores, Harry wondered: where to now? where else is there to go? is this literally *le petite mort*? Then, contemplating the real live world, and especially that wonder of all wonders, her sated body – benign, beguiling, bewildering – by his side beneath those twisted conduits of dragon's blood, he realized all dread, guilt, and fear had forever been expunged from his putative Garden-of-Eden. There was nothing of the blind alley or of Natalie anywhere to be found in such precincts.

Looking up, he was aware even *Dracaena draco* had lost its sinister aspect.

>

Scudding along unobserved in the wake of our young turtledoves, pademelons, we have arrived at the last of the Stations. It follows we have arrived at the end of our case study. Nonetheless, you might be interested in the aftermath, i.e. at what lay *beyond* the ultimate Station. At the supra-ultimate, so to speak.

Time presses, as the wall-clock insists. In the meagre minutes remaining, I shall cobble together an epilogue for you. You must be content with this for today and – one never knows, does one? – tomorrow may bring another lecture.

It was Harry himself who asked the question, where to now? Perhaps you are inclined to ask the same question, and to hope for an answer.

The answer, in a word, is: nowhere.

Sonia did not share Harry's ecstatic feelings about the carnal event to which they had given themselves over. Whereas Harry found himself soaring free of earthbound concerns, Sonia had no trouble keeping her feet grounded. Business as usual was her credo. She found Harry needlessly obsessed with the whole affair and his obsession tedious. It struck her dalliance with one or other of her randy cousins was much less bother than dalliance with a love-stricken Harry.

If, as some would contend, sexuality is all in the mind, then arguably there was a serious mismatch of minds here.

It took only a week for Sonia's exasperation with the resolute nerd in Harry to reach the unendurable stage. The moment had come, she felt, to cut herself loose from him. Then, from the recesses of her psyche, doubt arose: a rogue thought, taking the form of a pressing question. What, she asked herself, if the exalted realms in which Harry revelled were not accessible to her? What if a quirk of fate, or perhaps the vicissitudes of nature and nurture, had contrived to place the wonders in which Harry was so obviously immersed beyond her reach? Or, to couch her query in popular parlance, what if she were temperamentally incapable of falling in love?

By inclination, Sonia was not given to introspection. She gave such short shrift to this rogue thought one might have expected it would quit its cosy nesting place in her unwilling head for ever and anon. Mostly it did. However, Sonia could not entirely avoid the *remnants* of this thought: tinges of envy, bitterness, and self-doubt, especially at moments when her guard was down. As she would find throughout her subsequent life, always in the most toxic of contexts, these remnants would erupt through a fissure of vulnerability in her mind to demand her reluctant attention.

But here and now, the whole rotten deal devolving upon Sonia – first the necessity of giving Harry the flick and then the inconvenient rogue thought – irritated the b'Jesus out of her. Its culmination was her brutal remark set to resonate with Harry down the years: 'Mate, it was only a fuck.'

Only.

What was Harry's take on the matter? Fortune took a mere week to cast him down without ceremony from delirious heights to a world spelling out comprehensive rout and ruin for him. He had lost the main game. The frightful pain he experienced was as sharp as acid in the face, and as persistent as the cycle of dismal day followed by fretful night. Consider those endless nights. The attacks of anguish didn't go to sleep, and nor did he. As his mother had learnt years ago when *she* was beset with adverse circumstances, so *he* was to learn the technique of crying into his pillow to prevent anyone from hearing him.

… Brenda knew what was up, but refrained from action other than sympathetic and silent communion via eye contact and body language. She would go so far as to put a comforting arm around him, but she knew better than to pry …

Compulsive analysis, foisted on Harry by some malevolent goblin inside his head, was superseded by another and yet another round of compulsive analysis, the insane repetition sandpaper to his synapses. The same question – 'What went wrong?' – in myriad guises, burst forth *from* himself *to* himself, *from* himself *to* himself. Then came the myriad answers *to* himself *from* himself, *to* himself *from* himself, a devil's dance done in merciless disregard for his fevered brain.

One of the putative answers bedevilling Harry during this cruel time for him deserves special mention, because – paradoxically – it mirrored Sonia's rogue thought. Unbeknown to both parties, the same thought in essence was washing up on the fringes of both his and her consciousness at more-or-less the same moment. The answer to which I refer informed Harry of the possibility Sonia might suffer from a pathological inability to seize the moment whenever feelings of wonder about the gamut of human experience were up for grabs. Sonia's version of this train of thought was an irritation to her. Harry's parallel version provided a miniscule consolation to him.

Maybe the break-up wasn't his fault, he thought. Maybe the problem lay outside his jurisdiction. Maybe all along there was nothing he could have done about it. But how could a universe of miniscule consolations tip the scales when stacked up against the enormity of the single wretched event foisted upon him?

What were the repercussions outside the immediate ambit of the unhappy pair? These were few. When Mr and Mrs Sheridan were discussing the break-up of the relationship one evening over tea and canasta, the conversation went like this:

Admit it, mother, said Mr Sheridan. The boy *was* a bit of a wuss.

This provoked Mrs Sheridan to a rare moment of defiance.

Nonsense, dear, she said. He was a *nice* boy. Not at all like those rough nephews of yours.

That's the strength of it, pademelons. We have – you will agree – shared an instructive journey in the company of Harry and Sonia, the principals of this case study. Our journey has been along a much-travelled route visiting the Stations it has been my pleasure to demystify for your benefit. We have even travelled a tad beyond the last of these Stations, into regions warranting further exploration at a date to be determined. But all the best journeys must come to an end. So too has this one.

Here endeth the lesson. Last to leave turns out the lights.

… I must let maintenance know about this troublesome whiteboard. It needs to be re-hung …

‖

Hung. Past tense of the verb 'to hang'.

One can hang a whiteboard. Or one can hang a person. Oneself if one has a mind to. There's a proper way to do each of these.

The late Albert Pierpoint, Esq, professional hangman from a previous era, in that sovereign state some people like to call the mother country, knew the way one should hang people. He had studied the matter closely, as befits a professional of his calibre. He took all variables into account: strength of rope, thickness of rope, type of knot, position of knot, weight of client, height of client, &etc. Thus he was able to calculate the drop required in order to facilitate – in the very best interests of the client – an instantaneous broken neck. Death was as quick as the click of a finger. Or should I say the snap of a spine.

Pierpoint's studies were apposite. If one failed to get the drop right, the spine wouldn't snap, and the client would dangle helplessly while strangling painfully at the end of the rope, perhaps over a period of several excruciating minutes. It would have been a dreadful way to go. No way to turn the clock back. No way to turn it forward. A mockery of life, and an affront to death. Swing, twitch, and endure agony mixed with indignity, until the end arrived at its pleasure, delivering belated mercy.

Oh, my poor darling! My poor, poor darling! Whatever made you think you could try *this* at home?

If only …

2ⁿᵈ Unit >>

Singspielstück #7: Only

Harry:

Only a rainbow against a storm-stricken sky,
with birdsong air-shattering in the dawning.
Only the smell of rain and earth conjoining.
Only feel the touch of velvet breezes passing by.

Such is Harry's heavy-handed take on irony.

For reasons we can't fathom, the stage setting is sparse and dark. Harry is illuminated but nothing else on the main stage is. Scrubs up well, some might have said of him. Indeed, he *does* seem to have taken a tad more trouble than usual with his dress. He wears pale grey slacks, white shirt open at the neck, and a closely woven V-neck jumper in charcoal.

We are barely conscious of Izzie's music light, off to the left of the main stage. It is like the faint iridescent emanation given out by certain fungi on a dark night. Likewise, the blank CCTV screens and the white strip below the lip of the stage are barely distinguishable in the pervasive darkness.

Harry occupies a customized spot on stage left. Elena has composed it out of warm yellow tones with fuzzy edges, presumably in keeping with the mood of the song we are hearing. Its words, the baritone voice conveying them, and the broad melodic line supporting them, are soporific and congenial. The key of the melodic line is an affable major and its tone is that of synthetic saxophone.

All else is stark and pitiless.

Why so stark? Sticks had asked during rehearsals.

Bear with me, Harry had answered. I have my reasons.

We deduce this episode of amateur stagecraft of which we are the audience, is one of these rehearsals. Why, otherwise, would Harry be singing from those sheaves of paper he holds in front of his nose?

Seated in the stalls a few rows from the front, we see something else.

The backs of the heads of four people in the front row are

silhouetted against the spot Elena has thrown. One of them is small. Timmy, we might guess. On each side of him sits a woman, betrayed as such by her *coiffure*. Timmy's mother and grandmother, we might guess, with Sticks the one who sits so erect. Seated next to this conjectural Sticks, at the left extremity of the group, is a tall man, whom we might speculate is Matt.

Their silhouettes are not stationary. Heads, shoulders, and sometimes arms pitch, thrust, bob, and roll about as their owners whisper to each other with a mixture of enthusiasm and concern. The gentle rhythmic movements of their upper bodies choreograph their unheard conversation. What we see here is a shadow play in competition with the main stage-centric production.

Nor does Harry stand still. While massaging the song with his baritone voice, he brings to bear the whole gamut of theatrical posturing. Where the object of his eulogy is some identifiable feature or other – take the rainbow as a case in point – Harry turns his body with emphasis towards the imaginary location of that feature. He follows up with an extravagant gaze and/or gesture in that direction, and may even take a step or two towards it, the spot tracking him at all times. All his movements, particularly his gestures, are smooth, sweeping, and declamatory.

Some of his gazes and gestures are directed to the heavens, others to some limited patch of earth near his feet.

Harry:

Only the dew-dappled cobwebs, spirals of sunlit tears,
such spidery lacework populating pliant spaces.
Staggers of butterflies claim air's embraces.
Bees provide such company as only favours ears.

… what do you suppose, pademelons, is the provenance of Harry's sudden passion for irony? I have a theory. Irony is close kin to misstatement, misstatement is cousin to lying, and lying is a talent Harry learnt at his mother's breast. However this theory floats, Harry's ironic take on affairs fails to convince me. Its tone seems forced and stubbornly self-serving ...

Elena has the next call.

Extinguishing the spot on stage left, she simultaneously throws a spot on stage right. This spot has a much different character. Warm tones are replaced by the chill blue of the Dog Star on a moonless winter night. Edges are as sharp as a blade.

Harry's business is over for now. He stands unobtrusive in the darkness colonizing stage left. Sonia, inhabiting the newly-thrown spot, takes over. Like Harry, she has script in hand. Her gear is an uncompromising black. Blouse, short skirt, fish-net stockings, and knee-high boots match the sable of her hair. We speculate she has been lurking there at stage right all along, invisible for practical purposes until now.

The visual austerity of stage right has its echo in Izzie's music. While retaining the same meter and cadence as before, it has been recast in dismal minor key, with soulful oboe replacing soporific saxophone.

Though Sonia sings with delicacy in soprano voice her mood, as seen in face and body language, is dark, as befits her bleak oratorio. Irony is absent. The singer's movements are forced, awkward, and minimal, bearing resemblance to those of a puppet on strings.

Sonia:

Only the mediocre prosper underneath these skies.
Mundane are humanity's workings since creation.
Only those bereft of innovative station
rise up to the challenge of the *petit bourgeois* prize.

... galloping goitre of my gormless granny! These, pademelons, are not the words of the Sonia *we* know. They are lamentations of the likes of Jeremiah ...

Only the creak of the treadmill trod by humankind,
a thousand moons the desultory toll ...

Sonia stops singing. Her hands fall to her sides. She turns her body towards Harry in the darkness at stage left. The expression on her face is sardonic and quizzical. Izzie, sensing a problem, stops playing.

I need direction from the Director, says Sonia.

Your problem? asks Harry, his disembodied voice vented by darkness.

Are you moonstruck?

What are you driving at?

One thousand moons. That's a shitload of moons. The sky must be ablaze.

Sonia, you've got it wrong. It's not …

Harry emerges from the gloom at stage left. He approaches Sonia with light tread and a dead weight of condescension.

… a thousand different moons in the sky all at once. Its the same old moon seen a thousand different times.

I don't get …

Harry, having joined Sonia in her spot, elaborates.

A thousand sightings of the moon. At intervals of a month. A *lunar* month. What does that give you?

A hairy chest?

Forescore years. The human lifespan. Do your maths.

Sonia looks bemused.

Back to the start of the verse, says Harry. Give her the cue, Izzie.

Izzie strikes a couple of chords. Harry retreats to his shroud of darkness at stage left.

Sonia:

Only the creak of the treadmill trod by humankind,
a thousand moons the desultory toll exacted.
Brutish routine is mindlessly enacted.
Only withered souls prevail where governance is blind.

Elena and Izzie ring the changes. Sharp cold spot on the right morphs to fuzzy warm spot on the left. Harry is in focus and

Sonia is in darkness. Minor key morphs to major key. Oboe morphs to saxophone. Irony resumes.

Harry:

Only the universe revealed in star-speckled night,
bold moonlets of Jupiter twisting, turning.
Only trace the arch of constellations burning.
Swiftly streaks a shooting star in transitory flight.

Again Elena and Izzie work together to snatch Harry from us on the left and return Sonia to us on the right. There are 'only' two sides to a coin, and what we are about to see is the other side.

But in what devilish currency are we trading here?

Sonia looks distinctly uneasy. As she sings her way bravely through the misanthropic line and verse inconsiderately thrust into her hand, her unease intensifies, coming to resemble something like distress. This has not escaped the attention of the folk in the front row of stalls, judging by the shadowy head-bobs and stifled mutter going on forward of us.

Sonia:

Only rank brutality can be found in nature's orb.
The cannibal throat its very own kind engorges.
Fear finesses fair, and forward boldly forges.
Only so much venom can humanity absorb.

Wielding their relentless sound and light show, Elena and Izzie whisk Sonia with her unlovely message away. Harry with his bonhomie is ushered in.

But perhaps not swiftly enough. Before Sonia is plunged into darkness, we see her sink on to her haunches. Just for the briefest of moments we catch a glimpse of her, an abject and diminished figure, consisting of head buried in hands atop a pair of black boots. We observe considerable agitation in the ranks of the shadow players, and we hope it shall be followed up by a suitable and sympathetic response.

Is it time yet to shout, Fire?

We are gratified to see the person we suppose to be Sticks rise abruptly to her feet. We recognize her upright gait and the swish of her long skirt as she moves swiftly off towards the left aisle, and thence up steps towards backstage.

Meanwhile Harry, deftly oblivious, stands ready to resume his eulogy, determined to guide our eye with his theatrical gestures and our ear with his hyperbolic phrases. We, the increasingly anxious audience, are to be invited yet again to applaud his tedious ironies and warm to his soporific homilies, accompanied by saxophonic tones and major key.

We hear Sticks' emphatic whisper, from behind the drawn curtains on stage left: 'Cut! Now!' We see Harry hesitate, indicating he has heard her. He decides to continue nonetheless. Izzie's music comes in on cue.

Harry:

Only the querulous loins of ...

Sticks backs away from the stage curtain to her front stall seat. Her movement is choreographed fury. Resuming her seat, she leans in conversation toward the silhouette we suppose to be Matt's. Then, turning in her seat, cell phone at her ear, she raises a hand. This gesture to the lighting box is urgent, angry, and emphatic.

> ... adamant desire,
> challenging the necessity to maintain breathing.
> Only the brew of thought ...

Sticks gets an ambiguous response from Elena. A warm fuzzy spot comes up on Sonia, still squatting on her haunches at stage right. Harry remains illuminated as before. The quality of spot previously enjoyed exclusively by Harry is now shed on both performers.

It is doubtful at this late stage if the new lighting regime works to Sonia's advantage. The damage has been done. It is equally doubtful it is part of Harry's grand plan. Nevertheless, his singing doesn't miss a beat, and nor does Izzie's music. Sticks, silhouetted, still has the cell phone pressed to her ear.

We are left wondering, pademelons, could this be a mutiny of sorts?

... set simmering and seething.
Only senses alchemized, traduced by carnal fire.

Izzie's music changes to oboe and minor key, the cue for Sonia to take over from Harry. Shaken and cowed, her hands unsteady, the stricken woman rises to her feet.

Sonia:

Only the ...

House lights come up. Izzie stops playing. Sonia stops singing. Harry, bewildered, looks first at Sonia, then at Izzie. The identities of the shadow players are revealed, and we get full marks for our inspired guesswork.

The garb worn by Harry and Sonia, is slave to monochrome: from virginal white through shades of grey to blackest jet. Nor does the austere stage on which the pair strut add colour to the monochrome base. But now, in the house lighting, we see Sticks in rainbow hues, Matt in coordinated shades of blue, and Izzie favouring orange and lime green.

Colour, previously in abeyance, is now king.

Sticks is on her feet. We could not have anticipated the fearsome stamp of aggression of her hands-on-hips stance, not even when we knew all the time something of the sort was on the cards. Because her back is to us, we cannot see the look she must be flashing in Harry's direction, but we sense its frightful power as it threatens the fabric of the space between them.

Sonia reacts. Her script becomes airborne, sheaves fluttering to all points of the compass, from which diverse locations they begin their slow waft to the floor like feathers that have lost their bird. Out of control, lungs bellowing, limbs flailing, torso heaving, the mind in seizure but the mouth spitting out phrases of abuse, Sonia directs her tirade across stage from right to left, towards a hapless and disoriented Harry.

Pathetic little fucker, she shouts.

Then again:

Pathetic little fucker. You want to do the story of your life? I'll tell you what the story of your fucking life is. Couldn't get your willy up a windsock. That's the story of your life.

All residents of the precinct – human, marsupial, and cockroach – freeze in grotesque tableau, while the passing seconds throb like a communal heartbeat.

Sonia gathers up handfuls of the sheaves as they land. Like a child enjoying a party game, she flings them into the air again. There is, however, none of the gleeful child in the venom she spits out.

Who the fuck owns these? she shouts.

She waits for an answer. None is forthcoming. She continues.

They're *your* words, not mine, and so *you* should own them, you cowardly shitbag, not me. Did you hear me, shitbag? *Own* your fucking words, for Christ's sake. Don't fucking foist them on me, you steaming dump of dromedary dung.

With apparent purpose, Matt rises to his feet, but his purpose promptly evaporates. He does nothing except stand still, uncertain, infected by the generic state of dread. Timmy and Brenda sit things out in the front row of stalls, stunned into immobility and silenced by circumstances. It remains to Sticks to make some form of conciliatory move towards Sonia. She advances a step or two but, before she is able to mount the stage, Sonia's tongue is up and running again with its lunatic rant.

I'm out of here, Sonia shouts. Dead. D-E-A-D. Understand that, McMinimum, you freak? Your project is dead in the fucking water, and I won't be part of it. Not for a minute longer. Not ever again. Not in this incarnation. Not in any.

She hurls herself off the edge of the stage and into the pebbly river, which she then takes upstream, her pace a blistering, albeit undisciplined, freestyle. She hurtles through the door opening onto front-of-house. We hear the creak and clunk of the entrance door. Sonia, we may safely assume, is no longer in the building.

Izzie begins to play 'Chopsticks' on his synthesizer, choosing clunky xylophonic tones. Mounting the stage, Sticks rounds on him.

Cut the crap, you misanthropic gnome, she says.

The gnome desists.

Seconds of fevered silence pass before Sticks turns her attention back to Harry. She speaks brusquely, but with a cool equanimity – or is it resignation? – whose restraint surprises everyone.

Well, she says, it remains for us to give it a decent burial.

Bury what? asks Harry.

Your whole self-serving project, turkey.

You can't do that.

Harry, a child deprived not only of bat and ball but also of people with whom to field a team, is unable to engage as the principal in the beloved game he has always imagined was his to play by natural accession. Gone is the private pleasure he was able to enjoy *vis-a-vis* his play, too tricky by half, on the word 'only'. He stands at the edge of an abyss, staring into the void, stricken with terminal vertigo.

Matt, who has been nursing fierce anger, leaps up onto the stage. Taking Harry by the shoulders, he speaks to him with undisguised severity.

You poor sad sicko, Matt says. What has four decades on this earth taught you? S-F-A! How could you *think* of treating a fellow human being this way? Jesus, boyo. I'm not talking here about a*ny* human being. I'm talking about one you've supposedly *loved* at some stage in your dysfunctional existence.

I'm sorry, says Harry.

You think 'sorry' will do the trick?

What *more* can I do?

This catastrophe calls for consideration *before* not sorrow *after*.
Then let's give it another shot.
Give what a shot?
Get her back.
I'm not sure I catch your drift.
Get Sonia back.

Zounds, pademelons. We hear the faint ring tone of a cell phone from somewhere behind us. Bye Bye Miss American Pie. We reflect on the bad form of the presumed member of the audience who has failed to turn off his/her device.

Matt turns away from Harry and – arms outstretched, palms upright, gaze flitting from one person to the next – appeals to the others. *Sans* Izzie, who is sitting behind him at his synthesizer, silently nursing his humiliation. Mad laughter wracks Matt's voice, the laughter of disbelief. Disbelief at the implausible plea Harry has just made.

Get her back? Matt asks of everyone. You know him as well as I. Is this guy living in the real world?

As if this is not enough drama, the stage erupts in psychedelic colour. Spots in a variety of bold bright hues blind our eyes from backstage while, on stage, crew and players encounter a similar visual onslaught from myriad sources: flies, footlights, right, left. Dust in the air scatters the beams. Those from overhead resemble sprays of iridescent water from diabolic shower roses. This colourful show does not stand still. Spots and beams rotate, pulse, duck, weave, dance, cavort. The stage is an out-of-control discotheque.

… here, pademelons, is what irony *really* looks like. Harry's efforts to convey bleakest austerity onstage have been rewarded by this outrageous light show …

Harry ignores the rogue display of colour. He is determined to make his point. Angst crazing his features, face neck and arms bathed in kryptonitic green, he approaches Matt, grasps him by the shoulder, and heaves his body around roughly until the pair of them are face to face again.

Use your influence with her, says Harry.

Matt shakes off the green devil.

Mad bastard, he says.

Please get her back.

Matt, in exasperation, raises his arms and eyes skywards in another flamboyant gesture and is caught full in the face by a beam of hellish vermillion.

Halifax, he says. What does Elena think she's playing at?

Meanwhile Timmy has been waiting for the right moment to put a nagging question to his grandmother.

Did Poppa do something wrong, Grammy? he asks.

Nothing, darling, Brenda replies. Been a bit thoughtless, that's all.

>

We deserve to take a turn in the great outdoors, do we not pademelons?

We have had as much as we can take of the Beast. The Beast to which I here refer is the one whose wrath runs rampant inside the premises overseen by the two-faced Janus. We suspect the jurisdiction of this Beast does not extend beyond the entrance door through which Sonia recently made her retreat. We follow her example.

Once we are outside, the assault on our optic processes, consequence of that Bacchanalian riot of colour at large inside, is no more. In its place are muted tones, various shades of grey, so very gentle to the eye, typical of a day in decline. Calling the shots here is the balm of cool fresh air, restorative dusk, and the other forces nature has in store. We are thankful to all of them. All too keenly, we have suffered frazzle from the *human* component of the mortal world. Now we seek solace at the discretion of the mother of *all* mortal life.

The gentle 'woo' of a tawny frogmouth, call to action for the benefit of a mate close by, tickles the air. This bird could, ungraciously perhaps, be mistaken for a deformed owl. Mimicking the architecture of the peeling strips of white bark – strips part and parcel of the ungainly overhang of the melaleuca – the overhang within whose foliage birds of all varieties choose to nest – this frogmouth is instantly at one with its surroundings. Its camouflage serves to confound the gaze of all inclined to harass or merely show benign curiosity.

The frogmouth pair are making ready to gorge silently on insects. These insects are full of dart and dash, their temperament skittish. Skittish to the extent of putting their puny lives in danger. Danger only too happy to oblige.

Another critter, blue tongued and scaly seen in the full light of day, has already had its fill of insects. Bloated and lethargic, it waits not for a reptilian Godot but for the regenerative radiance of the morning sun. The wait will be long. Blood cooling rapidly, muscles flirting with seizure, and biosystems threatening shutdown, the lizard shuffles around feebly in the mulch beneath the melaleuca, where it hopes it may chance upon the entrance to its warm burrow, hibernacle for the night.

Whatever scratchy decibels the lizard's claws lend to the topsoil, is enough to incline a timid resident of the loam's uppermost layer to a temporary curfew. This small creature, all saw-tooth appendages and silky-soft feelers, will wait for the lizard to settle before resuming its piccolo call for a mate. It is not in a hurry. It will bide its time. The night will be long. Sufficient unto it.

Meanwhile that frightful Beast, avatar of human angst and uproar, continues to run amok behind those doors.

<

Our invisible presences reluctantly back inside, we recall the question Matt had asked earlier, along the lines of, What *has* Elena been playing at in her lighting box?

My second unit's best guesses, and our own omniscient sorcery, are able to ascertain in essence what it was she had been up to. Turn the clocks back a few minutes. We find Elena, confident purveyor of light, on top of her game. On top until unforeseen events bring her down.

>

Elena signs off on the call Sticks had made to her re the infamous double act involving Harry and Sonia. On Sticks' instruction then, she turns the house lights on full. Stowing her cell phone down the front of her Slavic blouse, she waits for further orders from the stage manager.

The lighting box, barely fit for purpose, is typical of similar facilities found elsewhere in theatrical venues harking from the period. The space it encapsulates, and 'capsule' you will grant is the right notion here, is barely enough for a smallish person to move around in, especially after a complement has been set aside for technical components deemed to be essential.

Her window to the stage is about the size found in a typical tank of the type frequenting battlefields. Such comparison suggest drivers of such clunky war machines, in common with lighting technicians in theatres, are not in any great necessity of seeing what is going on in front of them. Nevertheless, we observe through Elena's inadequate window the cast and crew down below moving about in an agitated state.

Elena's equipment is what one could expect in a lighting box of this vintage. Wedged onto a narrow shelf beneath the window, and close at hand, are panels for switching, mixing, dimming, and the like. Swept into an out-of-the-way corner is a tangle of relics from a forgotten time: sundry unwanted fuses, circuit breakers, walkie-talkies, headphones, and other electronic paraphernalia, mostly of unknown purpose and doubtful working order.

Of all the equipment on hand, only one item is state-of-the-art, standing out from its ancient fellows like a digital snap might from a collection of fading nitrate negatives. It is a bank of switches used for throwing spots, incorporated into and controlled by icons on a touch screen. Elena finds it a joy to use. It is what she had been using just now to execute the various, and sometimes contradictory, directives of Harry and Sticks.

Elena's cell phone rings again. Her right hand dives down the front of her blouse before she realizes that it is her *personal* phone ringing, *not* the one she uses to communicate with the stage manager. Shit, says Elena. Somewhere, God knows where, the errant phone plays its preset rendition of Bye Bye Miss American Pie. Insistently.

Lighting duties on hold for the moment Elena, exasperated, flaps around trying to remember where she put the wretched device only minutes ago, and hoping she will find it in time to take the call. She feels an irrational compulsion to locate it post-haste, despite her nagging fear of who the caller might be. Such is the slavery of her generation to the seductive pull of technology.

With peremptory abandon, she upends her handbag, emptying its contents onto the touch screen. She fails completely to notice the chaotic and colourful effect this has on the theatre lights down below. She rummages through these contents. The phone is not there. Unceremoniously, she upends the adjacent dimmer board.

Hallelujah. There it is. It had slipped out of sight under the dimmer board in the tricky way to which small things are inclined. She reaches for it, stabs a button, and puts the recalcitrant device to her ear. Trepidaciously. The call is not from downstairs. She concludes it is unlikely to be a benign call.

Allô, she says.

We cannot hear the reply, but can deduce from the increase in the rigidity of her frame her worst fears have been realized. She slides into her swivel chair to take things sitting down.

What we hear is a succession of verbal snippets by Elena, punctuated by pauses, some long, some short. We do not hear her caller's responses. I regret I am unable to communicate with Elena asking her to switch on her speakerphone. Or, as things stand, for any purpose.

Verbal snippets it is then, exclusively from Elena's mouth. Snippets which, rendered chronologically, resemble a disjointed monologue, lacking in continuity perhaps, but making up for this by the urgency of its existential appeal:

> I'm in lighting box. ... I'm ripping up. ... *Konyéshna*[24]. I am wrapping up. I apologize my English is so poor. ... Sal, I'm sorry. I don't want to do no more work for you. ... Michelangelo? ... Sal, I didn't come to *Avstrália* to work in Michelangelo way. ... You threaten me. ... You tell me I don't have no choice. ... What right have you to tell me I never have no choice? ... Sal, I want my freedom.

The pause now is much longer. We infer Sal – could it be *the* Sal, the hefty one, who so ruthlessly sidelined Mick McMinn almost four decades ago? – is reading the riot act to the unfortunate Elena.

Elena supports her beaten brow with the hand not holding the cell phone, a brow lustrous with perspiration. She resumes speaking in a voice seething with frustration, tinged nevertheless with resignation.

> You haven't given me no choice. So one more job only ... Sal, please may I finish? ... One more job. This I will do. But then my freedom. ... A guarantee of freedom for good ... Sal, do you give me guarantee? ... Tell me who I must do dirty on. ... Do you mean ... ? ... But he is famous man. ...

---

24 *konyéshna*: of course.

Elena, distraught, slams the phone face down on the bench. Her face follows, nestling in her folded arms. She waits some seconds until able to dissemble, then sits up, and returns the phone to her ear.

> I'm here. I haven't gone nowhere. If I will go, you only would hunt me down. ... I am very unhappy but you twist my arm. It must be my last job. *Óchin poslyédnyaya*[25]. ... No! ... Sal, I cannot. ... Please, Sal, why must you never not have no pity? ... *Nikogdá!* Not Michelangelo!

Elena, in a frenzy, howls and smashes the cell phone against the wall, driven by distress exceeding all reasonable allowances. Then, head in hands, she expresses her feelings *soto vocce*. Her muffled whimper resembles the plea of a terminally injured animal.

She doesn't maintain this huddle for long. She dissembles again. Calmly, on automatic pilot, she rises from her chair, turns off the stage lights including the unintentional colour extravaganza, and prepares to join her colleagues downstairs, to participate in *their* fun-and-games. She is back in control again. She has presence of mind. She is lucid. So outward appearances suggest.

But her fixed visage, forged from the grimmest meld of circumstances, is dominated by unblinking eyes able to settle on nothing.

What might she be thinking? A suggestion for you, pademelons: she thinks no situation could be worse than the personal bind in which she now finds herself. Certainly not the pathetic skirmish happening below, into the midst of which she descends.

>

The moon is up.

Insects, and those hunting them, are out and about, striving

---

25 *óchin poslyédnyaya*: the very last; *nikogdá!*: never!

to be unobtrusive. Critters living below ground, having retired, are unobtrusive *sans* the striving, deeming their lairs impregnable. Some ground huggers are abroad and not concerned one way or the other. This includes people and some noisy dogs from the apartments. And some invisible pademelons.

Matt stands alone beneath the melaleuca. His fellow thespians have dispersed.

Behind him, the moonlight shows a tendency to congeal. A waxy formless wraith appears, moving towards him. At closer quarters, it assumes the form of a man: slim, young, of medium height, his hair a halo of muted gold. Matt seems to be expecting him. Eyeball meets eyeball. The slim man speaks.

How's tricks?

Don't ask, says Matt.

Hands meet hands. Lips meet lips.

Problems? asks the slim man.

Frigging meltdown.

Want to tell me?

Where to start? Harry with his ego trip …

The usual suspect.

… got right up Sonia's nostrils. Remember Sonia?

Come on.

Well she spat the dummy and did a runner.

You're joking.

That's not all. Elena, in the lighting box, was visited by demons. She totally freaked out.

Russian demons?

Presumably. Then Sticks stuck it up Izzie. Called him a misanthropic gnome. He's sulking big time.

Was that fair comment?

Matt, exasperated, lowers himself to a sitting position at the base of the melaleuca. Leaning back on its trunk, one arm a cushion for his head, he crosses his legs. Averse to terrestrial disturbances, the underground piper ceases its piccolo song abruptly.

Matt casts an upward glance at the slim man.

Look. How to put it? he says. You weren't there, boyo. It was like everybody had caught Harry's disease. Nobody showed any empathy. Nobody was reading anyone else's mood. Me included, I guess. Everybody seemed determined to wear their sense of personal affront like a badge of honour, regardless of the plight of their fellows.

The slim man lowers himself, squatting side-on to Matt, his haunches supporting his frame. He plants a sympathetic hand on Matt's shoulder, and holds it there.

Poor darling, he says. What did you do?

What you would expect. I laid into Harry. So did Sticks. We all tried to settle Elena. As for Izzie, he needs to get over it.

Is this the end of the line?

For what?

Harry's show.

We were on the verge, I tell you. But Sticks put in a plea for Harry. Brenda supported her.

Family solidarity?

Not darling Timothy, I'll have you know. Little tosser had the right idea. Eyes glued the whole time to his i-device, swapping earthly shemozzle for a skerrick or two of virtual peace.

Bully for him.

Tell you something about Brenda. She says very little, but when she *does* speak, it makes an impact. Everybody stops to listen.

So who won the war of words?

Sticks wants me to get Sonia back.

You're not for real.

Better believe it. She figures I'm the only one still in Sonia's good books.

How does she get that?

I employed her for the best part of two years. My personal fucking secretary. Remember? She left when you came on the scene.

So *I'm* the villain.

Not you. The green-eyed monster.

Sonia? Planning to move in on you?

You be the judge.

Far out.

Leaning across, he kisses Matt firmly on the lips.

So you agreed to bring the lamb back into the fold?

No way. I agreed to *consider* it. Reluctantly. Sticks can be very persuasive. Likes to have things her own way.

Don't we all.

The *quid pro quo* was Harry must agree to a brand new directorial style. Much less of the self-absorption. Fairer to all stakeholders. Opportunities for all of us to make an input.

Pigs might take wing.

We agreed on a break. Meet again at *La Spag* in three weeks. Then see how the land lies.

Could I be a fly on the wall?

Matt springs to his feet, dusts himself down, fumbles in his pocket, finds his cell phone.

Let's get that taxi, says Matt.

The slim man rises slowly. Matt spends time attacking the keyboard before returning the phone to his pocket.

By the way, he says. A point of curiousity. Just when they were about to go their separate ways for three weeks, Elena pipes up. Quite chirpy. Perhaps her demons took a break too. Guess what she says.

You tell me.

She says, 'What's going to happen to Izzie?'

What was her point?

Milk of human kindness, boyo. Poor guy's treated like a doormat. Then gets put in his place by Sticks. Wouldn't you think he deserved a taste?

Taste of what?

Milk. Of human kindness.

The slim man says nothing, so Matt continues.

He's an abject soul, he says. Harry's project is his life. What is *he* to do for three weeks? Where is *he* to go?

A taxi, moon-blessed spectre, glides to the curb in Sleek Street. Your place or mine? asks the slim man.

<< 1ˢᵗ Unit

Brenda McMinn, in her early forties, was eating a ham and salad roll in a small park on the fringes of a light-industrial estate of such vintage as flaunts its benignly moribund character. Weather permitting, she often parked her car here on the way back from midweek shopping, and ate lunch in the sunshine at one of several small wooden picnic tables. She, lonely soul, enjoyed the anonymous company she found here. Invariably, she managed to strike up a conversation with somebody or other. Usually, the somebody-or-other worked nearby.

Many of the streets criss-crossing the estate were named, perhaps by some founding father with ornithological predilections, after varieties of bird. Brenda's attention drifted absently in the direction of the corner of Cockatoo and Ibis Streets, not because this corner was of any special interest, but because it happened to be in her line of sight, across the street (Cockatoo) from where she sat.

On this corner, front entrance abutting Cockatoo and a powder blue Holden Commodore parked outside, were the unprepossessing premises of Unthank Engineering.

Built a considerable time ago out of cement-rendered brick, capped by a corrugated fibreglass roof, and opening onto the world through windows by Stegbar, it was certainly no architectural masterpiece. Two out-of-plumb supports fashioned from vintage four-by-four struggled to keep the sagging shop awning from collapsing onto the footpath. A weathered sign, out of peeling

Dulux Hi-Gloss paint coaxed reluctantly onto warped tinplate, was propped up precariously on the roof by gangly struts of angle-iron.

The sign enabled the public at large to identify the premises, for whatever obscure reason they might have, with confidence. Given the listless stretch of Ibis Street to their left and the desolate expanse of vacant land to their right, the premises exemplified the proverbial shag on rock. Perhaps one should say the *effigy* of a shag because, to all appearances, it had been standing there forever and was not about to fly away anytime soon.

Most sunny lunchtimes, a man in his late fifties but looking much older, would lock up shop, and shuffle from these premises across Cockatoo Street to the park. His lunch was a clumsy affair consisting of stale bread slices slapped hastily around a thick slab of pressed meat, the whole sorry issue hauled by him out of a greasy paper bag. On this particular day Brenda, with intent, moved closer to him and asked him if he came here often.

Oh, yes, he said.

Then silence.

Brenda McMinn, said Brenda.

She offered her hand.

Nigel Unthank, said the man.

He didn't take her hand, nor did he offer his.

Brenda wasn't fazed. She had a knack for dragging recalcitrant curmudgeons into polite conversation, to the point where the intimate details of their lives began to spill out like vomit. So it was with Nigel. Soon he was saying:

… not a well man. On my third triple by-pass. Only thing can save me is a transplant. I'm on the list.

Are you married? asked Brenda.

Michelle passed away two months back.

I'm truly sorry.

Asthma attack.

After a discreet pause, Brenda pointed across the street.

Your business? she asked.

It's been my life. I'd like to retire but my shit-useless kids don't give a toss. And the only hired help I can get are prone to getting fingers caught in the till.

Tell me about your children.

What would you like to know?

How many?

Three.

What sort?

Two boys and a girl.

Lovely.

She paused, taking a deep breath before resuming.

I've got a son, she said. Looking for a job.

Silence. Bird noises only. Nigel was wary, but couldn't endure Brenda's insistent gaze. He made a play for the initiative.

My sons run their own business these days, said Nigel. Useless pair of buggers. Wouldn't recognize their arseholes if they were advertised on Channel Seven. You think they could give a shit about their old man? Who the hell's he? Only the dickhead who set 'em up.

And the girl?

The girl?

The girl.

She's just started uni.

You must be proud.

Tell you a secret. She's a king-sized pain in the butt.

Brenda lowered her eyes and let another strategic pause take effect. She was rewarded.

What did you say your son's name was? Nigel asked.

Harry.

Is he honest?

As the day.

Poor sucker.

II

In The Round

... Sal steps forward. He interposes his substantial body between Elena – on her knees – and the two Russian men.

Leave her, says Sal. She stays.

The boss will not like this, says R.

Say again, pal? says Sal.

The boss will not like this, says G.

Snow, oesophagus *in extremis* but mind sharp, slaps his brow with his palm, in mockery of the two Russians. Addressing them, he speaks, with downward inflexion on his key word.

Oh, you mean the *boss*, says Snow.

The *boss*, say R and G in unison.

Snow, turning to Sal, continues to mock the Russians.

Mr R and Mr G are concerned about what the *boss* might think, says Snow.

Get a good squiz[26] of my fucking face, you Bolshie bludgers, says Sal. *There's* your boss.

II

For the sake of granny's galloping goitre, cut.

... I can't believe this is happening ...

Should I play nursemaid to idiots? Correction. Make that idiot, *singular*.

Who? You! Scotty!

... in charge of continuity, but couldn't put his left foot in front of his right if his piss-poor excuse for a life depended on it ...

Of *course* I know you're not alive, you dipstick. I speak metaphorically.

Let's not have this conversation. It is beyond dispute, true to form, you've ejaculated prematurely.

---

26 squiz: Australian slang, meaning 'eyeful'; bludger: Australian slang, derogatory, meaning 'idler, sponger'.

Yes, Scotty. You're sharp today. That *is* in fact another metaphor. For which we can all be thankful.

Now put me back in control.

When? Like now, turkey. I want you to put *me* on that freaking podium. *Me*. Not that other pack of degenerates.

Yes. If it suits me, I *shall* refer to my second unit as degenerates.

Are you ready?

Sure of it?

Do *I* count down or do *you*?

Why the eff should I trust *you* to do a better job?

... oops! ...

<< 1ˢᵗ

On Harry's first day of work, Nigel Unthank said to him:

I'm buggered if I can squeeze a cent of profit, lawful or otherwise, out of this venture, so consider yourself and these poxy premises on a six-month trial. If there's no prospect of a profit after that, I'm selling up. Oh ... and keep your fingers out of the till.

Harry's physical appearance at this phase of his life was stark, reflecting his recent disappointments. His build was unnaturally slender, making him look taller than he was. He had parted his mouse-brown hair on the left, ruthlessly and with stiletto sharpness. The expression on his face was intense, solemn, and forbidding. It seemed to be fixed permanently in this guise. Should he look one full in the face, one might get the impression his eyes had got stuck there somehow (in mute appeal?) and he was fighting to un-glue them. His dress was conventional to the point of parody, as if his penultimate fear was to experiment with his wardrobe and his ultimate fear a failed experiment. These days, he clung slavishly to home-knitted cardigans (Brenda's handiwork, of course), neckties with a subdued stripe, neatly-pressed brown slacks, suede shoes of the Hush Puppy brand, and dark socks one of which was usually inside out.

If regression is the refuge of the uncertain, the evidence was plain for all eyes to see. Harry had joined the ranks of those who are not sure any more if eggs are eggs.

Harry quickly realized nothing resembling engineering went on at Unthank Engineering, nor had it for some time. Little of *anything* went on there anymore. The ostensible reason for the existence of the Unthank enterprise was the repair and reconditioning of intractable TV sets and other like items. Those of its meagre customer base who still remained loyal would drop off their defunct TVs or whatever at the front desk and come back some days? weeks? later to collect their – should one say? – funct ones.

Although he kept a low profile himself, Harry got to overhear many snippets of interest from the more communicative of his occasional customers. For example, he learnt 'old no-thanks and his no-account sons' were making a tidy profit from an offshoot of the old firm going under the preposterous name of Positronic Solutions. 'PS Inc.' had sprouted recently on the other more salubrious side of town. It had succeeded in extracting loose shekels from the pockets of its cashed-up customers via the effortless strategy of importing and selling prestige electronic goods. Neither Unthank nor his sons were interested in repairing TV sets anymore. That was far too difficult. That was a mug's game. Harry, the mug, was on his own. The Cockatoo Street premises were his exclusive domain.

Nevertheless, and certainly at the old man's insistence, Harry *did* receive visits from the male members of the Unthank family. These visits occurred roughly once per month and (mercifully) were of short duration. Typically, it would be a tripartite delegation, consisting of Nigel in his worn suit – denizen of many days as the shiny patches proved – and his two sons, Jared and Jerome, in their slick new suits intended to reflect their status as sales representatives with exclusive up-market products to spruik. Nigel would deliver a few homilies to the effect dedication would prove to be its own reward, invariably rounding this off with a few words of encouragement ('keep up the good work, son'). Meanwhile, the younger Unthanks would hang back with distaste, resentful at being forced to associate with this nerdish representative of an unacceptable social order.

The younger sister didn't put in an appearance on these occasions, nor was there the slightest reason why she should do so. But Harry found his excessively garrulous customers, from whom he could be certain to glean a great deal of gossip about the Unthank family (and about much else besides), had something of interest to say about her. For the record, she was not the cat's mother. Her name – cropping up frequently in the gossip – was Annalise.

I reckon that outburst of hers, said one loose-lipped biddy to another, helped send poor Michelle to an early grave.

The girl *did* have a tendency to voice her opinion where it was never going to be appreciated, said the other biddy. But the young always expect to be heard.

One a them uni freaks now, I hear?

Yes. A good brain, I understand. And a photographic memory. I expect she'll go places when she learns to control her tongue.

Oh, and what do you think of that poor Mrs Wintergreen?

Wasn't it a shame!

At this stage, Harry handed an invoice to the first biddy and carried her ailing TV set through the concertina partition behind him and into the workshop.

What were the 'poxy premises' of which Harry now found himself master?

There was a neat-and-tidy front counter, opening on to Cockatoo Street, with a cash register, a clunky computer, a black Bakelite rotary-dial phone, and a machine for registering the imprint – in paper triplicate – of a credit card. This was where people dropped stuff off and picked it up again. But the front office – the public face of Unthank Engineering – was not the problem. Not by a long shot. The problem lay behind the concertina partition – always kept closed – separating the front counter from the workshop where technical support 'talked' to the recalcitrant items. Harry was that technical support. The gizmo whisperer.

Let's cross the Rubicon and get to the problematic workshop.

Dust was king in this realm. Two dusty workbenches ran its entire length with dusty aisles vaguely separating one from the other. Stacks of dusty open shelves colonized the space beneath the dusty benches. Dust-laden overhead fans scraped and groaned overhead. Dust-sprinkled cobwebs were to be found wherever there was faint chance of a living for a spider. Occupying the shelves and appropriating their fair share of dust, black boxes of all varieties – amplifiers, tape recorders, turntables, photocopiers, teleprinters, even one seismograph, but mainly TV sets – were crammed like oysters in a bottle, with no respect for what was up, down, or sideways.

Despite their impressive diversity, these black boxes *did* have one thing in common: each had a 'lifeline', its power cord, which sadly did not deliver life anymore, but which instead dangled pathetically into the aisle inviting technical support to trip over it. If technical support's face *did* happen – as a consequence – to hit the deck, it would in all likelihood find itself intimately engaged with a stale rodent-nibbled piece of pizza crust still in its Pizza Hut cardboard and keeping company perhaps with a few blackened banana skins. His face would have to bear the ignominy and the bruises.

Covering the tops of the workbenches, and spilling over their edges, was a fearsome tangle of black boxes, gizzards exposed, in many cases waiting their turn for last rites to be administered. Also on these benches were the inevitable tools of trade of technical support: soldering irons, pliers, power boards, multimeters, transformers, wire strippers, oscilloscopes, odd fragments of circuitry, &etc, but never forgetting the plastic-laminated cardboard drink holders with half-consumed Coke-to-go inside with layers of penicillin mould floating on their menisci. Everywhere one looked, TV sets would be competing for one's attention with their version of the selfsame mid-day movie, with added snow perhaps, or rollover, or vertical compression, or massive zigzag distortion. In every case the sound, however, would be impossible to fault, and going at a deafening blast.

Old Unthank had made a canny choice in hiring Harry. Harry had little claim to a personal life anymore, so he took to this job of technical support with relish. It *became* his life. And, although – at this stage of his social development – he found big-picture issues (no pun intended) threatening, especially those involving contact with real people, he proved to be a whiz at repairing intractable TV sets. Within weeks, a modest cash flow began to salve the parched and cracked riverbed of the Unthank Engineering watercourse. Unthank himself was impressed, and showed it in a grumpy sort of way. His sons remained openly contemptuous.

One day, the powder blue Commodore pulled up outside the premises. Nigel Unthank had come to seek Harry out, and he had come alone.

I've had a request from my golf club, Unthank said, for an extra large TV display in the dining room, about the height of a man if that's possible. I'm not sure if it can be done.

Harry didn't take the bait. Unthank continued.

If it could be done at all, it would require the use of multiple screens and split images. You've got a bit of a flair. Would you like to have a crack at it?

I'll try, said Harry.

Unthank slapped Harry on the back.

That's the style, boy, he said. I'll make sure you get the necessary raw materials from Positronics first thing tomorrow. Anything else you want, don't be afraid. You just ask.

With nothing much else in his life, Harry cleared space on one of the workbenches and began a two-month-long vigil on the premises after hours. Sometimes he even slept on site. During these lonely hours, with late night Doris Day movies on TVs all over the shop keeping the treacherous silence at bay, he managed to jig together a workable arrangement using the said multiple screens and split images. I expect these days, the same effect would be achieved with a single flat plasma screen. But who are we to belittle Harry's accomplishment as per *l'ancien régime*?

Harry's creation was duly delivered. The hardest part was getting the beast out the front door into Cockatoo Street. Though not as large as what the General Manager of the golf club had hoped for, it was enough to impress him and induce him to pay Unthank a handsome fee. Unthank came around to slap Harry on the back again, and to slap a small bonus on the table. That was that. Done and dusted. A one-off event, so Harry assumed. He went back to repairing intractable TVs.

A few days later, the six month ultimatum fell due. Unthank decided to keep Harry and the poxy premises on. Then, a few more days later, the old curmudgeon died in his bed.

His children and the wider community expressed their grief outwardly according to the conventions, but sadly when it came to genuine feelings nobody gave a rat's arse. The hard truth was Harry, who felt some residual gratitude towards the person who had given him his first paying job, missed him as much as, or perhaps more than, anyone else.

Nigel Unthank's will was read. Essentially it split the assets three ways. The sons wanted to keep Positronic Solutions – their cash cow – so grudgingly they had to buy Annalise out. But there *was* one small surprise. The business interest in Unthank Engineering – *sans* the real estate housing it – was bequeathed to Harry. Nobody objected at the time the will was read. Doubtless the sons regarded this business as a poisoned chalice. In all likelihood, the father had also regarded it as such when in his final days he had come to revise the will.

Harry, having no expectations, was not present at the reading of the will. He only learnt he was to become a small businessperson through Jared, the elder brother.

Don't expect any special privileges, said Jared. You get a lease consistent with current rental values in the district. At the end of the lease, rents get adjusted according to CPI. We expect to get our rent on time. I'll instruct our lawyers to watch that.

The bereaved sons settled back, waiting for Harry's business to crash.

>

A few days later, Harry was himself consulting lawyers. He was sitting at a small boardroom table in a modern suite on the 29th floor of one of the tallest buildings in the CBD, of the type his mother referred to as 'tents', because – by her reckoning – they were put up and pulled down as quickly as tents and as often. He was alone, waiting to sign the documents giving him proprietary rights to the Unthank Engineering business.

There was a sweeping panorama from the two adjacent windows he was facing. He stared up at dismal clouds persisting to distant horizons and down at grey mist swirling through shadowless canyons of concrete and glass. Below him, birds in flight were buffeted cruelly by winds merciless and cold. Poor creatures they were, with as much control over their trajectories as the upwelling sheets of discarded newspaper.

Harry shivered involuntarily, before remembering he, in situ, was actually feeling warm and cosy. The centralized climate control made sure of that. Safely and comfortably ensconced here with 28 floors of vertical depth below him, he tried to conjure up pictures of what his single-story home in Bee Street and his single-story workplace in Cockatoo Street might look like should they happen to find themselves transported, by the devil knows what means, to the precincts of the frigid maelstrom running amok below him.

He shuddered.

In a sudden revelation, it occurred to him he had spent all his life thus far confined essentially to a horizontal plane. Thus far, a whole dimension had been missing from his life. He allowed his eyes to track both horizontally and vertically through and around the environment enveloping him, and relished the sensation.

One day, he thought, I'm going to live in a place like this.

A woman aged about twenty-five, in black gown and white wig, burst into the room as a warm breeze might, a document folder under her arm. She smiled broadly at him as if they were familiars.

Hello Harry, she said.

Harry was confused. He was certain he had never met this woman before in his life. She placed the folder on the table in front of him.

These are the documents you need to sign, she said.

Harry was still confused. She appeared, in an engaging sort of way, to be enjoying his confusion. She held out her hand to him and he took it.

Martha Singleton, she said. Matthew Bolton's sister.

Oh yes, said Harry. He's talked about you. How is he?

Matt talks a lot about *you*, she said. I'm glad to have tracked you down. The pair of you should make contact again.

She fumbled in her handbag.

Here's his card, she said.

She handed it to him. He glanced at it. It said '**Matthew Bolton**' then, underneath his name, '*Dress Rules*', which was from all appearances a business name. Underneath this business name were contact details.

Thank you, he said. I *will* get in touch.

Her eyes softened.

Please do, she said. He needs you more than you know.

I can't imagine …

She interrupted him.

I'm a barrister, she said. The solicitor you're waiting for will be in soon. I only came in here because I happened to glance at their lists, and saw your name.

Thank you, he said. I'm pleased you did.

With a parting smile, conveying much warmth, she left him alone. Inexplicably, he felt his life was returning to him and the prospect of rejoining the fold of humankind might now be on his table, the metaphoric one. In front of him was a more substantial table, not at all metaphoric, a table of sufficient materiality to support his elbows. What was on *that* table, i.e. the folder of paperwork awaiting his signature, heralded prospects for him of an exciting new era.

2nd >>

In the early evening, three weeks to the day since the debacle that was *Singspielstück #7*, a party of eight pedestrians makes its way along the unkempt footpath running as if begrudgingly alongside Sleek Street. These folk have emerged on to this dismal thoroughfare from one of the many small lively streets collectively making up the trendy enclave within which *La Spag* occupies a strategic location. Dare I suggest they have been enjoying refreshments and conversation at the illustrious establishment of that name, run by the Gervasoni family? They plod laboriously towards the un-named amateur theatrical premises with which we (and they) are familiar.

It is cold, wet, and windy. Mercedes buses swish along the sodden street, their defective piston rings coughing foul fumes into hoarse tailpipes for onward delivery to the sweet wet air.

The wind and rain sting the faces of those who make up this

party. They use umbrellas in a futile attempt to keep themselves dry. It seems likely some of these umbrellas – were they to be exposed to the full light of day – would flaunt bright and cheerful hues, as can be the habit of umbrellas, but this is not our destiny to know. The relentless fluorescence gushing from the street lighting has put the kibosh on brightness and cheer, reducing all colours to the same shade, to the sombre hue of cold steel.

To avoid a stab in the eye by a recalcitrant prong, the members of this party string themselves out along the footpath, travelling singly or (at most) in pairs. Harry and Sticks lead the way. Brenda follows, holding Timmy's hand. Elena comes next. Izzie is behind her. Matt and Sonia bring up the rear.

Yes! Sonia! It would appear Matt has managed the necessary miracle.

Eventually and gladly, the party find some shelter beneath the tall gnarly melaleuca and beside the decaying façade boasting its Janus masks. Harry, fumbling for the key, finds it. On cue, they shake out and collapse their umbrellas, wiping their sodden footwear on the fraying doormat, before seeking dryness and warmth in the darkness behind the clunky front door. Elena feels for the switch, finds it, and brings up light on front-of-house.

For a while, nobody notices the changes. They are too busy depositing umbrellas and wet apparel behind the cloak counter. This counter stands on the right beneath the spiral staircase leading up to the lighting box. On the left is the ticket box and beside it a sales counter from which programs, ice creams, &etc may on the night be served at interval to the paying public.

Sticks speaks.

The carpet is gone, she says.

Yes, they all realize, she speaks the truth. Beneath their feet, where there was once that unlovely carpet with the river-pebble motif, there is now the feel – firm yet smooth – of polished Baltic pine, the original flooring, exposed here to good effect.

Nor is that the whole story. The walls and ceiling are painted freshly in warm pastel colours. Where previously those walls were conspicuously bare, there hang now framed prints of contemporary art, undoubtedly of local origin. Perhaps not art of great moment, art amateurish certainly, but art prone to catch the eye, stimulate the mind, and cheer the heart. Art replete with vibrant geometry and colour.

A question springs to the mind of all present: who might be the good fairy responsible for this salubrity? Then – as if ungrateful for small mercies – they flirt with an amplified version of this question: has this fairy by any chance been blessed with such excess of goodness as would incline her/him to extend these improvements beyond front-of-house and into the main body of the theatre? This irresistible prospect precipitates a general rush to the two doors accessing the performance arena.

At the back of stalls, focusing their attention on the space the proscenium arch once dominated, they all stand gobsmacked. Brenda and Sonia are moved to make extravagant vowel-laden responses. The others are awed into breathless silence.

The arch is gone. The former stage has gone. The wings are gone. The curtains are gone. The TV screens – both fake and real – have gone. The huge insect eye is no more. The man in the songkok is no more. And, at first sight, it appears Izzie's synthesizer is no more.

A large circular turntable replaces the proscenium stage. This new performance space has no curtains or screens to define its boundaries. Instead it blends almost seamlessly with the viewing area immediately external to it. The insubstantial height differential between turntable and floor – fifteen centimetres or so – accentuates the cosy intimacy of this arrangement.

As expected, and apropos of this surrounding floor, the river-pebble carpet has given way to the warmth of polished timber, a natural extension of identical appointments vouchsafed to front-of-house. This re-vamped floor leads all eyes towards a further wonder: the re-vamped stalls seats.

Without ceremony or scruple, the entire configuration of these seats has been usurped. The plush royal-green back-swivelling seats are no more. In their place are bench seats, following the curve of the turntable stage like planetary orbits, sloping steeply upwards as they go backwards like the seating in a circus tent. Each bench is colourfully cushioned in a style evoking the best traditions of Turkey or Central Asia.

The benches sweep out arcs of almost three-quarters of a full circle, the result being the nearest practicable thing to absolute theatre in the round. No upstage, no downstage, no stage left, no stage right. It is theatre with intimacy, theatre with depth, theatre expansive and expandable, theatre capable of apprehension from any allowable viewpoint. Not from one angle only. Regretably, my cinematographer's tricks are irrelevant in this environment.

As was *always* going to happen, Izzie makes a distressed appeal.

Where's my synthesizer? he asks.

Harry has found it. Arm round Izzie's shoulder, he points towards the very back of the turntable where – sure enough – situated just off the stage area proper, on its own elevated platform, is the item in contention. The muso is vastly relieved, though not entirely satisfied.

Not prominent, he says.

Sticks and Matt speak together.

Leave vanity for the actors, says Sticks.

Grow a bigger snozz, boyo, says Matt.

They have been moving slowly – as befits the awe they feel – towards the stage area, until they take the final step up onto the magic turntable. Like children at Christmas, they look up, down, and around, for what new things they might find. Except Elena. She has retraced her steps through front-of-house to her lighting box, to see what wonders lie there.

We become aware of one of these wonders when the turntable actually starts to turn. It does so with a slight jerk – giving a start to those standing on it – and then continues ponderously but purposefully. Sticks raises her cell phone to her face.

Touché, Elena, she says. Does it turn the other way?

Sure enough, the turntable slows down, stops, and starts off in the reverse direction.

Timmy impresses with a sequence of cartwheels and handstands.

>

Pademelons, let's take leave of our second unit, giving them time to become acquainted with their new toy. Our presence is not necessary while they indulge their fancy in such innocent and fetching fashion. Nor shall they come to any mischief thereby.

Moreover, I sense your growing concern about the situation and frankly I am not surprised.

I believe the substance of your concern can be boiled down to two pertinent questions. They are:

Who *is* the good fairy responsible for the largesse we have observed?

Even with the aid of such a generous member of the tiny folk, how could the necessary renovations and refurbishments have been accomplished in a mere three weeks?

Congratulations, pademelons. You have asked the right questions. Can you come up with the right answers? Please apply your marsupial minds to the problem.

Think ... think ... think.

Let those minds churn purposefully.

Think ... think ... think.

Ah ... do I detect the light-bulb moment in your eyes?

Am I to understand the penny has begun its drop?

Do I hear you say 'Yes!'?

I *am* impressed.

Correct me if I am wrong, pademelons, but I would be prepared to lay bets on the direction in which your respective trains of thought nudge you. You are inclined to think the activities of my second unit, from the outset, have *not* been taking place in dreary Sleek Street and its surrounds at all, but inside the nerdy head of Harry McMinn.

You might at a stretch be prepared to acknowledge the objective reality of *La Spag*, and even of Sleek Street itself. Even of the unfortunate façade flaunting its Janus masks, so obviously the victim of deferred maintenance.

But as regards the activity of my second unit allegedly occurring in these places, the episodes of drama both on and off stage allegedly enacted by these mummers and players, the theatre fixtures and stage props allegedly existing behind that two-faced façade, the alleged Godfrey with his loyal Sandalwood troupe, and the three-week pause allegedly agreed to by all …

… these events, artefacts, persons, and schedules are likely to have been dreams infesting Harry's fertile brain. I believe you are increasingly inclined to entertain this point of view.

No revolving stage. No proscenium arch. No synthesizer. No CCTV. No *Singspielstücke*. No review panels. No singers of madrigals. No egotistical outbursts. No debacles.

Only dreams.

Once again, pademelons, congratulations. Are you ready to take this proposition one step further?

May not this explain how Harry had managed, with apparent ease, to recruit his crew for the purpose of re-enacting his life and many deaths? Sticks. Matt. Sonia. Izzie. Elena. All busy busy people in their prime, with lives of their own to lead. Why should they waste precious time gratifying Harry's narcissistic predilections?

May not this explain, also, how Sonia was enticed so readily back into the fold? Enticed when the prospect seemed well nigh impossible?

Has your mind churn come up with these explanations?

Yes! you say.

Voila. The penny, I believe, has dropped deep into the bowels of the infernal mechanism. It is impossible to get so much as a brass farthing back from such a place.

Pademelons, let me make a suggestion. The origin of my second unit's contributions to my evolving presentation is irrelevant. It matters not a bean to me, and nor should it to you, whether the activities of Harry and his thespian team have happened in the reverberatory blaze of reality or in the lightless confines of Harry's cerebral corridors. Either way, the end product shall be satisfactory for our purposes.

Finally, let me quell any lingering doubts in your marsupial minds. If we immortals question the validity of earthly dreams, we must question also our very own existence. For is not our existence nurtured by such earthly dreams?

Heed this existential warning, pademelons. Fiction can sometimes be more potent than truth, especially when it has a mind to morph into truth.

<< 1ˢᵗ

'Give ear to the words of my mouth ...' saith the Psalmist. Such an exhortation would likely have been voiced by the General Manager of the golf club once frequented by the now late Nigel Unthank.

A week after Unthank died, Harry answered the phone at his new business premises. It was the local RSL[27] club, wondering if he could build them a public display system similar to the one he had built for the golf club.

Next day, there were two such calls. The day after that, there

---

27 RSL: the Returned and Services League, an organisation representing the interests of people who have served or who are serving currently in the armed forces of Australia.

were five. The day after that, there were nine. By Harry's reckoning, that added up to seventeen. Suddenly Harry had visions of every pub and club in town wanting a public display system. Surprise turned to worry. Worry turned to panic.

That evening found Harry pounding on double glass doors carrying the logo '*Dress Rules*' frosted on to the transparent surfaces in mock art deco style. This was Matt Bolton's fashion house. Read *women's* fashion, of course.

His business occupied the ground floor of an elegant building of vintage early 20th C on the corner of Lyceum Street and Echo Lane in a desirable suburb replete with fashionable restaurants, galleries, and the like. The plate glass façade of the premises, slotting elegantly on to the corner as if it had always been there, formed three sides of an octagonal prism. The doors on which Harry was pounding so insistently were slung in the centrepiece, i.e. the side lopping a diagonal slice and the incipient sharpness off the corner, as does a bevelled edge.

A light came on at the back of the dark interior, throwing into relief a showroom full of dressed-up mannequins. Matt emerged from the back office, at first with a mix of irritation and bewilderment on his face, which changed – at the moment of recognition – to a broad grin. His blue bow-tie, his masthead these days, and one familiar to his well-heeled customers, had been loosened and was hanging off-centre like a wilting flower as he advanced to the doors. He unlocked them, and pulled on the one free to swing.

It opened inwards. As it did so, Harry was treated to a montage of reflected light sweeping across its glassy surface at subliminal speed. The montage, composed of accidental vignettes captured from the night-lit streetscape outside, told Harry – in a moment almost over before it began – of a good life beckoning to him, a life he surely deserved, a life ever at arm's length from him, kept there cruelly and unfairly by invidious problems such as the one presently tormenting him.

These dark thoughts vanished from his mind when Matt, face-to-face with him now, embraced him.

Matt led Harry to his office, past the mobility-challenged mannequins sporting their glamorous emblems of high fashion. These mannequins were arranged in tableaux to great effect. It dawned on Harry the hand and mind fashioning these tableaux were versed by nature in prodigious design skills. The tableaux contrived – as if by strange magic – to graft on to these intrinsically static mannequins the element of rippling movement they lacked otherwise. Harry realized he had, earlier in his life, witnessed a demonstration of these same uncommon skills, but in a different context, that of a memorable clay-modelling class.

The garments adorning the mannequins bore testimony both to the target group and to the marketing ploy embraced by Matt. Celebrating art nouveaux, they were of elegant cut, with a full-length sweep, out of natural fibre, in colours as bright as nature but in no way showy. Each of them exclaimed its uniqueness. Although the moulded figures they clung to exemplified youthful pzazz, the creations themselves were intended to appeal in general to women of middle age, say in excess of thirty-five, and cashed-up. Needless to say, such a juxtaposition – in the marketplace – proved a deadly one.

With obvious and genuine pleasure, the architect of this strategy opened the door of his office to Harry, revealing to him a desk arranged the way his clientele had come to expect, with catalogues and elite fashion magazines spread about strategically, open at carefully selected pages. This was a lesson in meticulously controlled disorder, in shameless *sprezzatura*.

Matt sensed the anxiety bedevilling his visitor, not that such an observation would have required special ability. He directed Harry to the leather divan reserved for his special clients, insisting he stay calm. With Harry seated, he found brandy balloons and the good stuff to fill them, in a cabinet beneath the desk. He poured, sitting himself sideways on the front of his desk, facing Harry.

What's this? asked Harry.

Matt passed one of the balloons to Harry.

Bisquit. An engaging drop. A gift from one of my regulars.

Harry's story poured out of him like the cognac out of the neck of the bottle, in breathless fits and spasmodic starts. Matt swirled, sniffed, sipped, and savoured his *Bisquit* as he listened. He found himself veering towards incredulity, but not for the reasons Harry might have expected. When Harry was done, Matt's astonishment found voice.

Any other business got word of mouth like that, he said, they'd be cracking open the champagne and the lobsters.

Harry did not respond. The divan had qualities inviting languor, but Harry sat stiffly on its edge, regarding his cognac as if it were spiked.

Matt spent a moment deep in thought. Suddenly, he rose, went behind his desk, scooped a pad of paper and a pen from a drawer, and shepherded them across to Harry on the divan.

Write this down, Matt said.

He returned to the front of his desk, sat there, and waited for Harry to show himself ready.

One, said Matt. Clean the bloody place up. By your own account it's a brothel. I'll get some bodies and we'll help you over the weekend.

Harry sat there looking at him.

Chop chop, said Matt. Write it down!

Harry wrote.

Two, said Matt. Unthank Engineering? That's a joke. Change the name. We'll think of one. The business *is yours* now, for Christ's sake.

Harry wrote.

Three. Learn to work the phones. I'll come over tomorrow and show you how. Watch me and learn.

Harry wrote.

Four. Come to grips with business basics. Capital raising, cash flow management, and the like. I'm the guy to shine some light on that path. Been there, done that.

Harry wrote.

Four, was it? Jesus, I've lost count.

Five.

O.K. Five. Hire assistants. You'll need a few good technical folk and a secretary. I'll help you get the best.

Harry wrote.

Six. You *will* owe me for this, mate.

Harry wrote.

Don't write that down, turkey.

Harry smiled weakly. He sunk back in the divan, prepared finally to succumb to its tactile magic. He cupped his hands round his brandy balloon, sipped its contents, ready now to surrender to their soporific qualities. He reflected on events. History was repeating itself. Matt was telling him how to set up shop, just as he had done at Porridge during the cherry season. Relieved, he acknowledged he was more relaxed than he had been all day, with prospects of becoming still more so.

OK, said Matt. About that secretary. No, come to think of it, 'business manager' sounds better. I've a suggestion. More cognac?

Harry nodded. Matt poured.

Somebody who worked for me recently, said Matt. Ideal for the job.

Harry nodded perfunctorily.

Sonia's her name, said Matt. Young woman. Sonia Sheridan.

Harry stiffened. By way of total regression, he sat up, slid forward, and balanced his buttocks on the edge of the divan again. Matt was startled by his reaction.

You *know* her? he asked.

The blood drained out of Harry's face.

What's wrong? asked Matt. She's one smart cookie.

Harry hung his head.

Halifax, said Matt under his breath.

Harry hung his head lower.

Let me guess ... , said Matt.

Harry's nose nuzzled his kneecaps.

... you two were an item, and she's broken it off.

The back of Harry's head jerked. Matt took this as a nod. He rose from his desk, approached Harry, sat next to him on the divan, saved his brandy balloon from an ignominious fate, and put a gentle hand on his shoulder.

It happens, boyo, said Matt. It need not be fatal. Or even final. Especially when things are on the up and up as they are for you.

Matt, moving to his chair behind the desk, slid down in it in a futile attempt to catch Harry's downcast eye.

I've got a proposal to make, said Matt. Tell me if I'm out of order.

Harry's head jerked again.

You listening?

Another jerk.

Then look up.

Slowly and reluctantly, Harry levelled his gaze. His features were as stiff and pale as plaster. Matt moved to him, handed him back his cognac, and sat on the front of his desk again.

Let me speak to Sonia, said Matt. You need her. She needs you. Don't get me wrong. I'm talking about a business relationship here.

Harry was unable or unwilling to speak.

You can't really blame the girl. Your prospects haven't been real flash, not until now anyway. For Christ's sake, you're still living with your Mum.

Harry was still not speaking.

It calls for a degree of maturity on your part. Do you think you could manage to summon it up? The necessary maturity, I mean. Be honest with me.

Harry nod was barely perceptible. But worries began to form in his head. He took a sip of cognac.

How come you know Sonia? he asked.

I told you. She worked for me.

How long for?

A couple of years.

And then?

She moved on. People do. I didn't ask her why. Not my business.

What did you make of her?

She was good value. We got along like a house on fire.

There was silence. They were eyeball to eyeball, two pairs of hands warming two brandy balloons.

Harry struggled to corral the thoughts slewing around in his head, confronting thoughts, suspicious thoughts, jealous thoughts, thoughts wrapped in the heady swirl of cognac vapour. Could it be ... ? Are you ... ? Is she ... ? Do you and Sonia ... ? were some of their fragments, none managing to form into a precise question, and certainly none yet ready to make the gigantic leap from synaptic chatter to vibrations in the air.

Matt's wry smile was a giveaway. He had a fair idea of the full form of these questions. Pademelons, I know the sly devil well. He was enjoying the sense of power consequential on his guesswork, even though he realized Harry might soon want answers.

But the cognac was coursing in Harry's veins, lapping against the levy banks of his headspace, and finally sweeping away the last skerrick of disturbed thought, like flotsam on a flood tide. The only thing left in the backwash was an overwhelming sense of wellbeing. Was he not in the presence of someone who knew the ways of the world much better than he did? Was this someone not an old school friend, and a successful one at that? Was not this person, for reasons best known to said person, favourably inclined towards him? Literally smiling on him? So did this not bode well for a fortunate future?

He eased his body into the folds of the divan.

He felt sufficiently relaxed now to examine his surroundings in detail. What he saw reinforced his warm and fuzzy feelings, unaccountable feelings of having 'come home', of having arrived at a place he was certain he should always have been.

His eyes could not avoid the large commercial print, framed in black for emphasis, and dominating the wall space behind Matt's desk. Its style was art nouveaux, its prominent caption *Belle Femme Français*. Its subject was a woman in profile, elegant of dress and of natural attributes, from wasp waist to outlandish headdress out of peacock feathers. Her downcast eye followed the line of her long Grecian nose to a string of fine beads she held between fingers as slender as spider legs. Her outfit of severest black, of matchless cut, and of dateless fashion exposed creamy curves of cleavage and of arm from wrist to biceps. Here was evidence of yet another judgment call Matt had made regarding the tastes of his well-fixed clients.

Elsewhere, the walls of the office were adorned with sketches, in frames as unobtrusive as the air one breathes. They were Matt's sketches of his creations, hanging off the protuberances of idealized loose-limbed pouting sylphs.

He regarded the furnishings with approval: desk, chairs, divan, sideboard, and some minor decorative items. Out of matching New Guinea rosewood, they were custom built in a style screaming 'contemporary' and 'designer', but which nevertheless managed to retain some semblance of the solidly traditional. Again, this was an obvious strategy aimed squarely at Matt's clientele. Two decades or so later, the inimitable Sticks would find herself campaigning vigorously, on ecological grounds, against the harvesting of rain forest timber of this kind.

Before long, he found himself in conversation with Matt about their common acquaintances, starting with family. Matt's father, it transpired, was trying to drum up financial support for the Lantern Bearers by spruiking its virtues to his former business colleagues, and to anybody else he thought might have the spare shekels. No surprises here.

Then it was old school friends and associates. Conversation went along the lines of, What happened to … ? followed by, I believe he went into … There were constant refillings of his brandy balloon, sometimes by himself. There was a discussion of Izzie, in which consensus was reached he had joined the US marines and had finished a tour of duty in the Persian Gulf. For Harry, the curious thing about these conversations was he didn't seem to be part of them. He was as if outside of himself, an observer, watching the movement of his own lips and the language of his own body.

Through the shutters on the window to his left – also of New Guinea hardwood – trickled a gentle evening breeze, bearing olfactory tidings of light rain, and playing briefly with the brown satin drapes before wafting into the room to appease the senses of its human occupants. The breeze also carried with it urban traffic sounds, distant but reassuring. At regular intervals Harry would hear the unapologetic clatter of a tram and would absently wonder if it had square wheels.

He began a relaxed descent into languorous depths full of idle imaginings. The room became cave-like, akin to something out of Plato, on whose authority it is to be understood all impressions are mere shadows on the wall, misleading as to the reality they blithely mimic.

The gentle patter on the window panes behind the shutters was not raindrops but condoms. The Pope – having had a change of heart – was broadcasting the ravioli-like packages from his bullet-proof dirigible high up in the troposphere.

The evening breeze was – in reality – the combined wake of flocks of distressed birds fleeing the city in blind panic. They had heard the entire Australasian Chapter of the One-Armed Dove Shooters was in town and couldn't tell a dove from a dodo.

What might have passed for tram noises was a convoy of coal-skips, their wheels arrant hexagons thumping and lurching on hardened-steel hypotenuses. They carried not coal but cognac, crates and crates of it, bottles smashing open under the impact of the bone-shattering ride. The gutters were running with *Bisquit*

...

... a voice, distant and reverberative, from deep in the cave, penetrated the addled wetware inside his head, bringing back to him memories of the soothing sound-play of adult voices – of Mick and Brenda? – filtering through childhood drowsiness. Again he experienced the delicious sensation of having come home. Only after some time did he realize it was Matt's voice he was hearing.

Crash here if you like, said the voice. There's a sofa-bed in the annexe at the back of the showroom.

Cool.

Slowly, he raised his legless body from the divan.

Just don't interfere with the mannequins, said Matt. I get jealous.

>

Harry woke, on what he might have acknowledged to be the next morning, had he been capable of giving a damn. His eyelids felt leaden and his brain felt as nimble as an engine running on tar. His entire body ached.

He did manage to get his left eye open. The hands on the traveller's clock at his head were blurry, but the time was immaterial to him anyway, so he was happy to let the issue ride. He was aware also he was in a strange bed, but even that was something whose possible implications he was happy to ignore.

He thought he saw a framed photograph beside the clock. Through his reluctant left eye it was blurry, but even so he could tell it was a head-shot of a man. For a moment – miraculously – it came into focus, and he saw the man was youngish, neat, tidy, fresh-faced, fair-headed. A real cleanskin. Then it went out of focus again.

Something – the devil knows what – made him lean his aching body on one elbow, reach out for the frame and draw it close to his face. There was a handwritten inscription at the bottom of the photo. He opened both eyes and made a valiant effort to focus. It read 'With you always. Snapper.'

He replaced the frame on the bedside table and slumped back in a stupor. The sun was high before he woke again. Matt had materialized beside him offering coffee. As he raised himself on one elbow to take the coffee, he noticed the clock was there on the bedside table as before, but the framed photo was not.

Thanks, he said.

Matt left him alone.

Over his coffee, he thought about the missing photo He was puzzled by its absence, even a shade disturbed. Eventually he convinced himself it had never existed, a cognac-fuelled illusion perhaps. He gave it no further thought, finished drinking the coffee, and made the first tentative effort to rise. Dizziness and nausea made this adventure problematic, and he concluded it would be prudent to fall back on the bed and try again later.

But hold your horses, pademelons. At this point, let's leave the unfortunate Harry to his own devices. I have a different row to hoe.

I'm not prepared to dismiss the issue of the missing photograph with the same alacrity as did Harry. I can tell you the photo *did* exist. I know because I happen to be the talent whose effort conjured it into existence. In my days as a mortal being, I was the photographer.

And, as photographer, I happen to be in a position to know who the guy in the photograph is.

C'est moi. It is me. Snapper. A self-portrait in cellulose acetate.

>

Over the next fortnight, Harry went along with everything on Matt's list, bar the name change which needed more time. Assisted by Matt and – on occasion – a complement of able bodies shanghaied by Matt, he found his evenings and weekends very much taken up. The 'brothel' was swept clean, and he learnt to 'work the phones', acquire start-up funds, and manage the flow of orders. A trio of 'techies' presented for work, this number increasing steadily as weeks passed. The techies donned grey coats, rolled sleeves up, and began to churn out customized public display systems at a rate almost matching that of the burgeoning demand.

And he hired Sonia as business manager.

For a while, Harry didn't know where to put her. His first thoughts were *he* should have a desk at reception, near the revamped front counter, while *she* should be relegated to the workshop with the techies. With such a configuration in place, he reasoned, potential friction between the pair of them and the distress this would entail, possibly for both parties, would be minimized. But more level heads persuaded him such an arrangement was unworkable.

Matt and Sonia joined forces to insist on the obvious, i.e. he (Harry) and his business manager would need at all times to work closely together. So, recalling Matt's earlier injunction to him about summoning up the necessary degree of maturity, he decided to bite the bullet and install Sonia at a desk beside his own at reception. He was determined to show his mettle, to resign himself to the one-thousand cuts and – when things got beyond what he could endure – to take a turn in the workshop.

If there *were* one-thousand cuts abroad waiting to lacerate him in his weak moments, he was too busy by day either to notice the cuts or to have the weak moments. Part of the reason for this was Sonia really *did* know her job. Early in the piece, she put in place an effective outreach strategy, so demand for public display systems increased at a gallop. Across the length and breadth of the city, awareness of and desire for public display systems were spreading like those other scourges of the times: HIV, and the fear of such.

So Harry and his team (with a single exception, about whom we shall hear more shortly), were kept on the hop by production schedules. More and more techies needed hiring, overtime established itself as the norm, and – on a note less sweet – it became increasingly obvious to all stakeholders that the workshop – revamped though it might be – was inadequate to handle the throughput.

All clutter had been cleared including the content of the dusty shelves. All non-performing electronic paraphernalia had been dumped without mercy. The overhead fans had been replaced with air-con. The floors and bench tops had been resurfaced. But the aisles were too narrow to be negotiated by trolleys or fork-lifts, which meant the product required manipulation by three or four strong human bodies. Entrances and exits were barely adequate to take anything except light-weight hand-held equipment. Only at a pinch could the finished product be cajoled out the front door. People kept getting in each other's way, limbs tangling with limbs, bodies falling over each other. Nevertheless, through the determination of Harry and Ramon, the semblance of a production line was established and maintained.

Who was Ramon?

Ramon Contreras had become Harry's most trusted techie. He was a man Harry's age and height, but solidly built, swarthy, with balding pate encroaching on the receding remnants of deepest black hair. A pair of large hazel eyes, each as glossy as a glazed almond, was sandwiched between his prominent brow and the ridge formed when one high cheekbone saluted the other across the bridge of his nose. His speech betrayed his English language (especially of the Oz variety) as a work in progress but, by way of compensation, it had the melody and cadence of a middle-class European accent.

His origin was Argentina, not Europe. His father was an *estanciero* in the province of Buenos Aires. His mother was an academic in the city itself. Ramon had moved to Oz to escape the economic chaos in his home country, hoping to find better prospects in this neck of the woods.

None of Harry's team had a problem with Ramon's background. Quite the contrary. As a consequence of his naturally gracious manner, and his firm but fair way of interacting with his fellow workers, he engendered respect in one and all. The men liked him, and the women were charmed by him.

Ramon proved time and again he could think beyond the square. Using his native ingenuity, he devised a technique for moving finished product from one end of the workshop to the other and finally out the front door and into transport. Ramon dubbed this technique the 'Cockatoo Roll'. Maybe, when he coined the phrase, he had in mind the way the rowdy sulphur-crested marauders frequenting these parts disported themselves after feasting on fermented fruit. Or maybe not. He might simply have been thinking of the street address of his workplace.

Whatever the case, the Cockatoo Roll, as designed by Ramon and then acted out in the workshop, became an established routine. I shall leave a detailed account of its *modus operandi*, and of the enthusiasm with which the workforce received it, to my second unit. I am informed they propose to make such things the basis of their next *Stück*. It is not my intention to steal their thunder, but suffice it to say when a Roll was in progress, the techies pitched themselves into the event – some would say 'game' – with a deal of animalistic huff and grunt. Wild applause, and other more physical expressions of delight, from participants and spectators alike, marked the game's completion.

As you will have gathered, pademelons, morale was high in the camp, despite the physical limitations of the working environment.

Harry, Ramon, and all the other techies (with one exception whom I have already flagged) got a buzz out of working on production. Everybody felt they were treated fairly and respectfully, free from the gratuitous game-playing bedevilling many workplaces. Moreover, they felt pride tempered by awe from the realization they were producing a unique item much coveted by the world outside.

This was not a production line churning out a standard everyday one-size-fits-all widget. Indeed no. This was a production line flaunting its output of *the* Public Display System, a system routinely tailored to exacting customer requirements, and thought not to be happening anywhere else in the known universe.

So what I have presented here for your benefit, pademelons, is an encapsulation of the triumphs and tribulations transpiring on each day at the coalface of the enterprise of which Harry McMinn had – to an extent – become the accidental proprietor.

But the nights – not the days – were the biggest problem for Harry. That's when the demons of old returned to torment him. That's when his grief glowed white hot inside his belly. That's when sleep was replaced by relentless repetitive analysis. That's when nostalgic images appeared uninvited beneath the lids of his somnambulant eyes, eyes kept busy stalking the best and the worst of his amatory and post-amatory memories. Exhausted when morning light finally and mercifully intruded on his bed of agony, he never failed to thank providence over his Weeties he was about to reconnect with his day job.

2nd >>

Singspielstück #8: The Cockatoo Rollers

We take up positions front-on to the turntable stage, choosing bench seats towards the back, elevated above stage level, affording us a panoramic view. But not so far back we cannot realize a degree of proximity to and intimacy with the performers. We judge the seating appointments – the plump cushions inscribed with motifs in middle-eastern style – cater most adequately to creature comfort and gratify our tastes.

What we anticipate, with exhilaration we can barely contain, is a display of virtuosity by Harry and his theatrical team, the likes of which neither we nor they would have formerly dared to hope for even in the delirious depths of dream. It is to be inspired, of course, by the new performance space of which they are now custodians. With such cutting edge accoutrements at their disposal, and the potential for technical versatility promised by such wonders as these, we can expect a performance of such lucidity as shall cut to the rampaging chase, of such intensity as would sear a cryogenic heart, of such presence as would breathe life into the bygone dead. Oh, for the sake of my poor old granny – the gormless one – with whose plight you must all be familiar – let stage business roll! Let it roll! Let it roll! LET IT R-R-R-R-R-R-R-R-R-ROLL!

Yes, yes, pademelons. I hear you. What you say is undeniable. I *am* allowing myself to be carried away by my own disproportionate enthusiasm. I *do* run the risk, thereby, of making a spectacle of myself. But, rest assured, I shall – in robust fashion – take the necessary self-disciplinary measures to bring myself into line. I shall rein in my worst excesses of enthusiasm. I shall disport myself with dignity. And we shall – in accordance with your advice – born of wisdom more in keeping with owls than with pademelons – but very much appreciated nonetheless – wait and see.

So shall we, with due composure, turn our attention to the turntable stage, unobscured by curtain, and unsullied at present by human presence?

Represented on this stage, and crammed into the smallest practicable segment at its front, are the barest bones of an office. Sticks, the stage manager, has opted for minimal furnishings, presumably in order to maintain an open stage, and to ensure the audience shall not be distracted by irrelevancies. These furnishings consist of two small desks and a partition. Yet to be occupied, the desks are on our left, facing off to our right, one in front of the other. The partition, behind the desks, is of concertina design and presently closed off. It divides the stage from left to right, comprehensively blocking our view, despite our favourable elevation, of everything lurking behind it.

Everything, that is, except Izzie and his synthesizer. We see him behind the turntable stage, on his discrete platform, also elevated, sitting still but alert behind his console, his articulate hands by his sides. In readiness.

Lighting, on house, on stage, and on Izzie's platform, is uniform but subdued, suggesting time is in abeyance pending the start of stage action.

We do not have long to wait for action. Elena turns house lighting off and stage lighting up a notch or two. Harry and Sonia enter from our left, to take up positions at their desks. Harry takes the desk closer to the partition, and Sonia the desk closer to us. They are dressed casually, groomed nevertheless to be presentable to the anonymous but pernickety public with whom they would like to do business.

Both adopt poses of studied silence, of deep immersion in paperwork. At this moment, courtesy of Elena's skills, afternoon sunlight the shape of window panes appears, falling across the desks from a source apparently located upwards and offstage front. For a few seconds, the only sound we hear is the rustle of paper from the desk jockeys, but moments later we become aware of heavy footfall behind the partition, bearing down with determination on the office.

On its right extremity, curling fingers drag the partition open, but only far enough for a balding head to poke through. Neck and head swivel in the direction of Harry and Sonia. Energetic hazel eyes flash. We recognize this person. It is Ramon Contreras, about to play himself. Here is yet another recruit to Harry's dreamt theatrics.

Buenas tardes, says Ramon.

Good afternoon to you, Ramon, says Harry.

Good afternoon, Sonia, says Ramon.

Hi, big boy, says Sonia.

I'm sorry to disturb you, says Ramon, but we are ready for a Roll.

A Cockatoo Roll? asks Harry.

A Cockatoo Roll.

Transport has been arranged?

Yes.

Then don't let us stop you.

Ramon gives a 'thumbs up'. Squeezing through the partition, he enters the office. We see him head-to-toe now, clothed in a light-weight knee-length pale-grey coat buttoning down the front. With vigour, he pushes the folds of the partition aside from right to left, giving us our first view of everything and everybody on stage behind it. We see ...

... two long benches running parallel to each other, all the way from the partition to the back of stage. Narrow aisles give access to both sides of these benches.

The front end of the left-hand bench abuts Harry's desk. Clutter is scattered willy nilly along the surface of this bench. This clutter is work in progress, consisting of partially completed public display systems and associated paraphernalia. Some of the systems have their multiple screens facing us, others have their chunky backs turned to us, and for others again the edge-on aspect commands our view revealing to us the black trim holding their screens in place. The majority are two-by-two systems consisting of four conjoined screens, but one – going by sheer size – looks destined to evolve into a fully-fledged three-by-three model. On completion, all of nine screens will make up its monstrous insect eye.

In the aisles hugging the sides of this bench, upwards of a dozen actors – we assume recruits from Sandalwood – mill around, playing the part of technical personnel, a.k.a. techies. They are going full bore at the guts of the display systems with screwdrivers, soldering irons, and welding equipment. Genders are mixed, though leaning numerically towards male. We identify them as bona fide techies by the grey coats – similar to Ramon's – they wear over their clothing of choice, their glad rags.

In contrast, the right-hand bench is uncluttered. No display systems, complete or otherwise, nor items of ancillary equipment, occupy the bench-top. No techies attend it. There is clear passage along its length, and along the aisles, for any traffic with a mind to traverse them.

Appearances suggest this situation is about to change. Backstage, four techies are in the process of transferring a two-by-two display system from left-hand bench to right-hand bench. We get the impression the object they move is heavy, and they have – at some stage, in another context – officiated as pall-bearers. Grounds for both impressions are dubious.

Given its bright shiny finish, the object these four techies are about to deposit on the right-hand bench is in a state of completion. Ready for delivery to an eager customer with full blessings and the security of a three-year warranty.

Let us return our attention to Ramon. It is clear he shall be the centre of action for the duration of this *Stück*.

Having opened the partition, Ramon strides purposefully forward past the two desks and their occupants. He stops at the very edge of stage, where he flings open a make-believe door. Here we are beholden to Elena again. Sunlight taking the shape of an open doorway falls onto the stage to the right of the two desks, grazing the front end of the right-hand bench-top. The impression we get is of an open front door to which the right-hand bench leads. Since there is no such door onstage, we are obliged to imagine it.

Ramon turns, and propels himself down the aisle to the place where the ersatz pall-bearers are about to place their load, i.e. at the backstage end of the right-hand bench. With an athletic bound, he mounts this bench to help his fellow techies manoeuvre the unwieldy object with care into position on the bench. The multiple screens end up facing off to the right, so that we – sadly – have to make do with a less engaging edge-on view.

Three other techies join Ramon atop the bench. Four more techies hang out in the aisles to help support the device and lay down thick mats on the bench in front of it. These are mats of the type gymnasts use to practice the art of dropping and rolling. And it is rolling I believe we are about to witness, but not the roll of a gymnast. Pademelons, we are about to see the roll of the device occupying the far end of the right-hand bench. The one resembling an oversize four-faceted insect eye.

What might the implications be – from the standpoint of occupational health and safety – of the procedure about to unfold before us? It is best not to think about such matters.

When Izzie begins his musical introduction – which he does with fanfare and flourish – it is evident everything is poised for a Cockatoo Roll to proceed.

We hear from him an impetuous melody in 6/8 time. Its pace signals to us the vigour of stage business we are about to see. Among the many moods the melody evokes, we discern a gypsy flavour, distinctly edgy, particularly at those moments when the key has a mind to change from major to minor. Our impression is said 'mind' has not decided which of these two modes shall prevail. Perhaps equivocation and uncertainty are part of the intended musical mix.

To enhance the gypsy feel of the music, Izzie coaxes a sound like that of an accordion from his synthesizer, augmented by thwacks of high-pitched percussion. Tambourines and castanets mayhap.

At this much anticipated moment, when we are about to be entertained by *Sing* – joined perchance by *Tanz* – my eyes, pademelons, are drawn to a curiosity backstage, off to the left of the left-hand bench.

The curiosity in question attracts my attention because it jars with the overall scene of resolute activity. It sits – languid, benign, unobtrusive – amidst all the hubhub, trying to pretend it has every right to be there. Its superfluity, and not less its incongruity, demands explanation.

You see it too, do you not? Look closely. A small table poised on the edge of stage. Right at the back. A table. See it?

Resting on the table is something resembling a malformed pyramid, with the semblance of a square base tapering to an imprecise point on top. It is a metre high, give or take a tad. It is enclosed in a black cloth the size of a sheet. Did I say 'sheet'? More like a shroud! Do you see it, pademelons? OK. Now keep your eyes on it. Do you see it move?

Yes. I said 'move'.

I know the object in question is some distance away. I know it is tucked away into a badly lit cranny. But at certain moments it seems to me this black thingummy has a mind to shift and heave. As if something or other is bobbing around beneath that putative shroud. Something alive.

Yes. I said 'alive'.

What monstrous mistake of nature could this be? A golem? A hobyah? A yeti?

Oops. This is wild paranoiac speculation. Mainstream action on stage is about to take a decisive turn. This action demands our attention now. We hope for an opportunity, at some spare moment in the future course of events, enabling us to delve further into the mystery of the creature clothed in black.

Right now … it's show time.

Ramon, his back to us as he controls the leading edge of the display system, heaves with all the might he can muster. One techie on each side, and one on the trailing edge, help him with a similar contribution by way of heave, might, and muster. A couple of techies stationed in the aisles help to keep the whole unwieldy issue on an even keel, moving alongside it in the process. Another couple are engaged in moving the mats as required from the back to the front in the direction of travel.

The object yields. Balancing on its trim, it moves like a square wheel, lurching from one straight section of this trim to the next, with much gentle skill required from the drivers of this strange conveyance in order to bring each quarter-turn to completion without inflicting impact damage on the precious device. Soft landings are *de rigueur* in the practice of the Cockatoo Roll.

Sonia's choreography is evident here. The object being rolled is – if I may be forgiven for exploding stage illusion – made of polystyrene and papier-mache. The movements of those who manipulate it, however, suggest it has the weight of an anvil. Such movements do not come naturally. They must be learnt, and Sonia – at rehearsal time – was the teacher.

The turntable rotates, ponderously and clockwise. Its motion is a circle, that miraculous line *sans* beginning or end, that perfect parable on eternal return, about which we – pademelons – know a thing or two. This is our first demonstration of the theatrical possibilities of stage rotation. We shall be exposed to an ever-changing view of the activity in Harry's workshop, until we have seen the action from every angle possible within horizontal constraints. No aspect of the action shall escape our scrutiny.

Just as the rotation of the workshop celebrates the 'tune' *Elena* has called, so song – delivered by lusty human voice – honours the tune *Izzie* has called. Initially the voices are those of Ramon and his chorus of rollers:

Ramon:

Roll.
It's a cockatoo roll.
There's nothing so likely to excite as,
or able to set the shop alight as,

Rollers:

the cockatoo roll.

Ramon:

Our goal
is to get the stuff out
of the spit of the spout
with a holy moly
rock and roly.

Rollers:

Holy moly
rock and roly.

The slow rotation of the stage brings the front of the insect eye to our view. We are chuffed by this. Those of you with an eye for technical flair will not fail to pick up on a vital feature of the assembly process of these gizmos: the criss-cross trim separating the individual TV screens has been kept cleverly to a minimum, to enable the composite image to be viewed by the eventual client without unsightly black bars obtruding to any significant degree.

Rollers:

Roll.

Ramon:

It's a cockatoo roll.

Rollers:

Don't matter a holler where the crew's from,
Ramon's the man they'll take their cues from.
Let it all roll.

Ramon:

The soul
of this show on the road
is a dirty great load.
So go easy peasy,
bend the kneesy.

Rollers:

Easy peasy,
bend the kneesy.

Danger looms down the track.

This improbable train has gathered momentum. Those techies loitering in the aisles are at risk of being trampled underfoot or otherwise subjected to significant personal inconvenience. This train stops for nobody. Ramon and his crew take responsibility through the medium of song, to warn the unwary of this hazard.

Simultaneously and dramatically, the music resolves its former ambiguity decisively, coming down in favour of a frenetic minor key. The pads of Izzie's fingers rain massive hammer-blows on the defenceless keyboard, while his entire frame shudders, appearing at times to rebound from his piano seat. If his vigour is anything to go by, then one could imagine Izzie as pacesetter for all the peril of the on-stage action.

Ramon:

Avast!

Rollers:

Disencumber the decks so we can pass.

Ramon:

We're not in a humour to take any prisoners.
Get out of our way if you value your arse.

Rollers:

We're not in a humour to take any prisoners.
Get out of our way if you value your arse.

Despite warnings, bodies tangle with bodies and limbs with limbs. Those techies with tardy reflexes topple to the floor, to get a taste of the dust there, and to feel delicate parts of their bodies yielding to the boots of their fellow techies. We are grateful to Sonia's choreography for our chance to experience such vicarious excitement.

The mood changes.

Danger has passed. Setting their ignominy and bruises aside, those techies who were floored pick themselves up and dust themselves down.

Through Elena's contrivance, the turntable has travelled through a quarter revolution. Here, it pauses. Ramon and the rollers, as if needing a break, pause also. Sweating and panting, they turn to face us squarely. Then a surprise. Harry and Sonia, as if caught up in an act of spontaneous enthusiasm, scramble onto their desktops, stand upright on them, and face us also.

So this is the tableau we view ...

What was formerly the right-hand bench now occupies stage front. Ramon, the rollers, and the insect eye occupy a position midway along its top. The four facets of the eye stare up at us blankly. The rectangular shaft of golden light indicating the open front door illuminates the left extremity of the bench.

Harry and Sonia, standing on their desks, are at back left.

As regards that unidentified interloper, he/she/it is ensconced pharaoh-like in his/her/its dark pyramid, still very much a presence in need of an explanation. He/she/it occupies a position at back right, having got there by rotation from his/her/its previous position at back left.

... and this is the music we hear ...

At Izzie's behest, the song undergoes a mutation. Minor key morphs to to unabashed major key. In place of the folksy sound of accordion &etc., we hear a synthesized brass band. The declamatory mood of a triumphal hymn emerges from what lingers in our minds of the former gypsy strains.

Everybody on stage lends impassioned voice to this hymn: Harry, Sonia, Ramon, the rollers, and the sundry techies not involved in the roll. This is a moment of celebration. Ramon, hero of the moment, is worshipped accordingly.

Harry:

To get from A to B,

Ramon:

finished product as company,

Sonia:

the quickest way must be

All:

via cockatoo roll.

Harry:

To go from whoa

Ramon:

with a difficult load in tow

Sonia:

then the row to hoe

All:

is the cockatoo roll.

Harry:

He whose hand is steadiest,

Ramon:

the willingest man and the readiest,

Sonia:

whose *je ne sais quoi* is the headiest,

All:

shall manage the cockatoo roll.

All eyes and a frenzy of hand gestures are directed to Ramon, who accepts the accolades with modesty and discreet bows to every point of the compass. One feels he is across the etiquette appropriate to occasions like this, a tribute perhaps to his previous (Argentinean) incarnation. Generously, he extends a hand to his fellow rollers on the bench top, indicating they should take their share of the accolades.

Harry & Sonia:

Ramon!

All (*sans* Ramon):

The Don!

Harry & Sonia:

Ramon!

All (*sans* Ramon):

The Don!

Harry & Sonia:

Ramon!

All (*sans* Ramon):

The Don!

Uproar erupts: of applause, foot stomping, whistles, bravos, and catcalls. Pademelons, do you not feel compelled to join in?

Ramon, too modest to accept easily the role of celebrity so freely offered to him, is overwhelmed. It is a bridge too far for him, and his confusion shows. His hands fall limply to his sides, indicative of his silent plea for this unnecessary carnival to desist.

When it eventually does, Ramon – his demeanour channelling his relief – springs to work again. The job is only half done. The display system is not yet out the door. Celebrations are premature. The roll must resume. The cockatoo roll.

Climbing sheepishly down from their desktops, Harry and Sonia resume their seats and their sedentary mien. Ramon resumes his position forward of the insect eye. Taking their cue from Ramon, the other rollers position themselves.

The turntable resumes its clockwise rotation. The melodic line of the song reverts to the earlier ambiguous moment, when it was unable to make up its mind which modality it should pursue. Edginess has the drop on triumphalism. Gypsy strains elbow out the brass band.

Ramon:

Heave
or get up and leave.
Work to be done, so put your skates on.
What do you think our client waits on?

Rollers:

The cockatoo roll!

Ramon:

Behold
the sassy panache
of our marathon bash,
with its hoppo bumpo,

move the lumpo.

Rollers:

Hoppo bumpo,
move the lumpo.

Ramon:

Shove.

Rollers:

A labour of love.

Ramon:

We've got a top product to deliver.
They're the receiver. We're the giver,

Rollers:

by cockatoo roll.

Ramon:

The bole
of this task, you'll discern
is a twist and a turn, a
hurdy gurdy.
Hold her sturdy.

Rollers:

hurdy gurdy.
Hold her sturdy.

Again, musical ambiguity is resolved in favour of furious amok and changes to a vehement minor key. Repeating his earlier performance, Izzie vents spleen on an unwitting keyboard, a sure sign things on-stage are about to get dangerous again. Any techie careless enough to loiter in the aisle is fair game.

Ramon:

Fore!

Rollers:

Out of the way or cop some more!

Ramon:

Flapping your arms is a fool of a trick.
Surfing the air? No! You'll surface the floor.

Rollers:

Flapping your arms is a fool of a trick.
Surfing the air? No! You'll surface the floor.

The momentum of the rollers is unstoppable. Tardy techies get bowled over and find their faces attending to the tongue and groove of the stage decking.

Danger passes.

Having turned through another quarter revolution, the stage pauses once more. Having ceased their activity, Ramon, the rollers, and all other techies turn to face us. So do Harry and Sonia, who have clambered onto their desktops again.

As everybody prepares to engage in vocal tribute to the cockatoo roll and to Ramon, the arrangement of the tableau stands as follows ...

The bench used for rolling is at left. Ramon, the rollers and the insect eye occupy the top of this bench near its back left extremity. Beyond them is the rectangular shaft of golden light indicating the open front door.

Harry, Sonia, and the desks on which they stand are at back right.

The den of black cloth, within whose confines that ominous

inhabitant with a propensity to lurch has found shelter, is at front right, in proximity to us. We are thrilled to be at such close range. Apparently we deal here not so much with a pyramid as with a small tepee, held aloft in makeshift fashion on its tabletop, with a couple of broomsticks or the like doubling as tent-poles.

Forget pyramid. Forget tepee. Compare it to a cocoon, then live in hope/fear the chrysalis shall emerge.

Harry:

To maintain supply

Ramon:

we're very much on the fly,

Sonia:

as we hurtle by

All:

on a cockatoo roll.

Harry:

Getting underway

Ramon:

with this swine of a game to play

Sonia:

shall be a.o.k.

All:

with a cockatoo roll.

Harry:

He who's gentle to a fault

Ramon:

but could tame a thoroughbred yearling colt

Sonia:

or bring a stampede to a screaming halt

All:

shall manage the cockatoo roll.

Wild acclamation demands a repeat display of embarrassment and etiquette by Ramon.

Harry & Sonia:

Ramon!

All (*sans* Ramon):

The Don!

Harry & Sonia:

Ramon!

All (*sans* Ramon):

The Don!

Harry & Sonia:

Ramon!

All (*sans* Ramon):

The Don!

The music stops abruptly. Everybody on stage freezes. This suspended moment lasts for some seconds, before the final eruption of action and music, involving all performers *sans* Ramon. The conclusion of this cathartic moment has the cast flinging their arms skywards, to the accompaniment of a glissando of percussive sounds delivered with relish by Izzie.

All (*sans* Ramon):

Ramo-o-o-o-o-o-o-on!
The ineffable Don!

While the bulk of the cast remain frozen with hands in air, the appointed group of four techies take on pall-bearing roles again. In silence, and bathed in the rectangle of golden afternoon light, they wangle the insect eye from the end of the bench out through what we have presumed is the front door, ready for transportation to an eager customer.

Actors disperse. Stage lights go off, except for a spot on the contentious pyramid/tepee/cocoon, whose enshrouded occupant is lurching and heaving with undiminished enthusiasm. The spot rests on this dark enigma for a few provocative seconds.

Then this light goes out too. We are left in darkness to ponder in vexation a phenomenon still to be explained.

<< 1st

On only the second night in his new living quarters, Harry received his first guest, who was unexpected, unannounced, and (initially) unrecognized.

New living quarters? With mixed feelings, Brenda had reconciled herself to the reality of Harry, *her* Harry, leaving Bee Street. She was glad he had made a success of his new career, one she had been instrumental in setting up for him. She was glad he was able, as a result, to make his own way in the world, including as regards domestic arrangements. But she was only too aware loneliness more severe than ever before awaited her. Mick had gone, then Madeleine had gone, and now Harry was going …

Not to worry, Mum, Harry had said. I'll see you once a week. More often if I can manage.

Come for dinner then, had been Brenda's reply.

... an irresistible inducement to Harry, as Brenda knew it would be ...

It was Brenda, of course, who had redirected Harry's first visitor. When Harry opened his door, this visitor, a stocky man of about his own age, stood there sporting a shaved head in lieu of hair. Somehow, he had slipped through the ground floor security system.

The yodellers not giving you any stick, bro? asked the visitor.

After the penny had dropped for Harry, they found themselves needful of a few beers. Harry poured, then seated himself, but Izzie – restless – paced the floor. The 17th floor.

Harry had realized his ambition to add the vertical dimension to his life's manifest. If the lights of the CBD – winking at him as he sat in his living area – were indicative, then 'vertical' was the only game going. He derived comfort (and sometimes awe) from knowing the lucent rectangle, cast by his very own window out into the darkening sky, was one of many similar rectangles of light, collectively tracing out a line from ground level halfway to heaven and, in the process, defining one edge of a canyon on whose edge he now lived in a state of delicious dubiety.

If he moved so close to his window the tip of his nose smeared the glass, he could look to the bottom of this canyon to see, in aerial perspective and two dimensions, city life asserting itself. To his delight, everything was miniaturized and thereby demystified from up here. Toy cars chased toy headlight beams benignly through the mish-mash of criss-crossing toy roads. The compressed scale of the action, he felt, was as it should be.

The aboriginal paintings – with names like 'My Country' or 'My Mother's Country' – gracing the walls of his apartment were aerial perspectives also. Perspectives of expanses of parched desert. Desert intersected by sinuous dried-up creek beds. Done in dots.

Miniaturized and demystified. Perhaps the perspective he found himself sharing vicariously with these indigenous artists had drawn him to buy the paintings in the first place. He imagined himself, at his window, transformed into some latter-day archaeologist with X-ray vision, whose precocious power of sight was able to penetrate the patina of technological modernity, to find ancient layers beneath, layers replete with waterholes, middens, campfires, sacred sites, …

Cool set-up you've got here, said Izzie. This was as close an approach to acclamation as Izzie, the iconoclast, ever ventured.

Izzie had recently returned from the Persian Gulf. It was inevitable the conversation would turn to his exploits in the First Gulf War.

What was the war like? asked Harry.

Izzie sat down. This was his serious moment, the moment he had been waiting for, his moment of high theatre, the moment when he would be called upon to spill his gut, the moment when he would be only too glad to do so.

A gas, said Izzie. Won't hear any complaints from me. Top notch outfit. Firefights before brekky. Reconnaissance all arvo[28]. Stealth raids before lights out. Friendly fire at any time of day or night.

Was it dangerous?

Of course it was bloody dangerous. There were psychotics out there wielding assault weapons. And sane guys determined to kill me with them. I preferred the sane guys, to be honest, even though – rumour had it – they were the enemy.

Were you afraid?

Of course I wasn't afraid. Marines aren't allowed to be afraid. You'll likely get put on a charge just for *looking* afraid. But inside my head, white flags were flapping like fucking flamingos. 24/7. And inside my bowels shit was doing a merry dance trying to find a quick exit. 24/7.

---

28 arvo: Australian shorthand, meaning 'afternoon'.

I heard it was very short.

Less than a week of ground combat. That's all it took to shake down Saddam. But there's the preparatory phase before and the debriefing after. Fucking intense shit, both of those, I tell you.

Did you get injured?

Depends on what passes for injury.

Izzie paused. Slowly and deliberately, he drew a battered photograph from his wallet. He passed it across the glass coffee table to Harry.

This is me, said Izzie, just before I joined the US marines.

Harry looked at the photo. It showed, in portrait, a younger fresh-faced Izzie, with black curls boiling over onto his wide brow. This was Izzie as Harry remembered him from Porridge.

See any difference? asked Izzie.

You had hair then.

I'd have hair *now* if I let it grow. Just I'm no longer enthusiastic about its colour.

Izzie took the photo back from Harry and returned it to his wallet.

What I am about to say, said Izzie, is confidential.

Harry nodded assent.

One morning – good morning Kuwait! – I woke up, looked in the mirror, and it was white. The colour of milk squeezed from an Arab brood mare. The colour of a sheikh's glad rags.

Your hair?

No, dumb-arse. It was my bloody prick.

Izzie rose to his feet, beer in hand, and began to pace again. Arriving at the window, he turned his back on Harry, and looked down into the canyon, to the streetscape seventeen floors below.

Who's the joker[29], he asked, drives a brand-new white Ferrari round here?

---

29 joker: Australian slang, meaning 'person in contention'.

>

Hefty was no longer Mr Big of the bayside. Those days had been a fabulous apprenticeship for him. But recently he – grand wizard of his trade – had relocated his command centre to the big end of town, from whence it could nourish tentacles servicing every cranny of the inner city while reaching to the remotest outliers of suburbia. Delaney's was small bickies compared with his new empire. Nowadays it was just a historical patch of turf, ceded to a lesser operative over which Sal – as was his way – exercised invisible control.

The ambit of his influence, the strength of his ambition, and the style of his management changed in tandem with this territorial expansion. These days, his approach had more of the 'white collar' about it. Money laundering, all types of fraud, and the grooming of corruptible figures of officialdom/establishment were his forte. And, although his direct involvement in the tactics of such things as warehouse heists and illegal drug distribution was minimal and diminishing by the day, strategic control, albeit remote, over these bread-and-butter activities was still important in his priorities.

He persisted in keeping Snow by his side, despite the latter's pronounced – and often vocal – nostalgia for the old days.

His taste in white Ferraris had not changed.

>

We have identified the owner of the white Ferrari. A no brainer really. For creatures of your mental acuity, pademelons, blindingly obvious.

But unaided, it may not be so easy for you to identify that person to whom I have alluded on occasion, such allusion being to the one-and-only person unwilling/unable to be swept up in the intoxicating busyness of daily activity at (soon to be renamed) Unthank Engineering. Let me spell things out.

He was a most singular techie by the name of Ronald Dash. Having encountered him *en passant* in his university days, Harry had – subsequently and on a whim – hired him.

In the arena of Unthank Engineering, if not of life in general, Ronnie was a loner and a techno-nerd, driven by a preference for doing his own thing. The production line was not to his liking. If scheduled onto it, by Harry and/or Ramon, Ronnie would proceed to desert it discreetly when an opportune moment presented itself, retiring unobtrusively to a small table in a secluded corner of the workshop, hidden from view by a strategically placed black tarpaulin.

What *was* Ronnie's 'own thing'? Well, as a matter of fact, quite a variety of 'things' were to surface over time. The particular 'own thing' intriguing Harry first up was a technical challenge of his own conception. He was determined to develop a transparent interface whose viewing direction could be changed with the flick of a switch.

Ronnie had been pressed from many quarters to elaborate on his project. He was always evasive and, if leaned upon to the point where evasion was no longer a comfortable option for him, he would give an explanation designed to confuse. Nevertheless, over time, those sufficiently curious began to perceive a pattern in his litany of obfuscations and, if you will excuse my anhydrous description, the story they pieced together went thus:

Assume a glass panel, not necessarily given over to transparency. Assume A and B are on opposite sides of this panel. Four possible viewing scenarios are possible. They are (1) A can see B but not vice versa, and (2) B can see A but not vice versa, and (3) both A and B can see each other (as through normal window glass), and (4) neither A nor B can see the other (as through a brick wall).

Ronnie's aim was to enable the selection of any one of these four possibilities using a remote four-way control, and to have the selection realized as close to instantly as practicable.

Why did this project grab Ronnie? You may have to ask him.

The other techies said Ronnie was 'Aspergers'. It is true Ronnie uttered hardly a word to anybody all day. But some aspects of his behaviour did not conform to the usual clinical description of a person with this alleged condition.

For example, seated at his secluded bench, engrossed in his esoteric project, Ronnie might remain silent for the best part of a day before, without apparent reason, emerging from behind his tarpaulin to burst into song. Not *any* song, understand, but some dubious and derivative piece of doggerel with sufficient corruption of its lyrics as to indicate the machinations of a rogue imagination.

Earlier in my presentation, you will remember, I entertained you with some choice examples. Now it is my pleasure to amuse you with a further example, one Ronnie used to assail the ears of the unwitting techies at Unthank Engineering ...

> She'll preside in sexy corsets when she strums.
> She'll preside in sexy corsets when she strums.
> For a bed and a square meal daily
> she'll keep flogging that ukulele.
> She'll preside in those sexy corsets when she strums.

... after the delivery of which, and oblivious to the bemusement he had provoked among his fellow workers, Ronnie would retreat behind his tarpaulin and resume his silence.

That Sonia had Ronnie in the gun will not surprise you. Her advice to Harry was to 'let him go'. She had grounds. It was not good business practice to develop a product before establishing a market for it. She continued to pressure Harry along these lines. Finally, Harry felt he had no option but to confront Ronnie.

Ronnie was in his den. The black tarpaulin shielding from view his person, his table, and his equipment, was rigged up more like a simple curtain than like the tepee my second unit – presumably for theatrical effect – would have. The shape of a head bobbing against the curtain was noticeable on occasion, suggestive of the antics of a photographer from Edwardian times.

Ronnie, said Harry.

The head, sporting a mop of dishevelled fair hair and a small well-trimmed honey-coloured goatee beard, peeped from behind the curtain. It spoke in exasperated reply to Harry.

Uhhh? it said.

Can we speak?

Ronnie flung the curtain aside with vexation. He glared at Harry, his blue eyes bright with anger. His equipment, revealed, consisted of a motley assembly of mirrors, lasers, sheets of glass, lenses, prisms, clamps, hinges, collimators, &etc. A miniature laboratory, no less.

How did you come by your equipment? asked Harry.

Scrounged it.

He lowered his eyebrows, contorted his freckled face, bared his teeth, thrust his chin forward and stroked his beard, as if to say, Want to make an issue of it?!

What's the market for this contraption? asked Harry.

Contraption! Mate, it's an anisotropane. And you're a frigging turkey!

… Harry, nonplussed, experienced a flashback to his childhood days when Izzie had drawn him into plans to make a nuclear device …

Ronnie waved an index finger in Harry's face like a weapon.

The day will come, and you'd better believe it, said Ronnie, when you'll be fucking glad to have this contraption …

(At this point, he withdrew the index finger, so he could work a pair of fingers on each hand to simulate quotation marks.)

… at your disposal.

Two barely compatible feelings afflicted Harry. One was a feeling of frustration arising from thwarted purpose. The other was an incipient feeling he and Ronnie might actually be kindred souls, belonging perhaps to some unsung fellowship of nerds.

Consequently, Harry stood open-mouthed for a few seconds trying to conjure up a response. Only one suggested itself and he was unsure it was appropriate to the circumstances. He went with it anyway.

OK, said Harry. We'll make it official. I'll find you some funding.

Ronnie's eyes, narrowing significantly, expressed disbelief.

Funding? he asked.

Fiscal stimulus, said Harry. The wherewithal.

Where might *you* find that?

An ironic smile spread across Harry's lean face, tempering his naturally solemn countenance with momentary warmth.

I'll scrounge it, he said.

Pademelons. As things panned out, Ronnie's prophecy re the vindication of his 'anisotropane' would be realized within the lifetime of all the principals in my presentation. All the principals, that is to say, bar one.

The anisotropane would have its day.

<

' ... but every bird that cuts the airy way is an immense world of delight ...' saith a poet of some distinction. So thought the city fathers, I presume, when they named those dreary streets whose cross-hatch defines the light industrial zone in which Nigel Unthank set up shop and sold his services to the willing. Cockatoo, Currawong, and Curlew running north-south. Ibis, Emu, and Egret running east-west.

Which leads me, pademelons, to make a proposal you are bound to consider preposterous. You shall earn my eternal gratitude should you accede to my proposal. In any event, you have no choice. This is *my* presentation, and we shall proceed in the way I propose. Get used to it.

Do you see the thick wooden poles on the edge of Cockatoo Street opposite the Unthank premises? You've got it. The power poles.

I propose we ascend these poles and roost there in an orderly row on the wires, in imitation of our feathered friends. Then, after we have come to terms with our vertigo, we can get right down (up?) to the business at hand, watching with the eyes of eagles the day-to-day comings and goings to and from the premises below. The Unthank premises.

What is the thinking behind my proposal? I shall tell you. It is to add a fresh perspective to my presentation, a perspective enabling us all to view events with the advantage of a bird's eye. Harry's flirtation with the vertical serves to vindicate my position.

Yes, yes. I know, I know. What I propose violates your natural instincts such as befit a ground-hugging animal of the specie – in accord with another of my fancies – till now proxy for you. Yes, and I do know what equipment I might have organized for you had I meant you to fly.

As consolation for you, I believe I am capable of anticipating the tone and tenor of your objections. They would be many, varied, strident, pitiful, plaintive, and (frankly) perfectly reasonable, going along the lines of:

What place is a high wire surging with amps for a mob of macropods like us – heavy-boned and unfeathered – to perch upon? What should we do for food given our staple, viz. grass, is unlikely to grow up there? What should we do to quench our thirst given there is no natural watershed up there? What would be the consequences if one of us should sneeze, lose grip, and end up either plummeting earthwards or straddling a lethal voltage?

It is dangerous. It is bad for health. It is humiliating. It is embarrassing. It is frightening. It is something for which we are inadequately equipped. Etcetera.

Put aside your qualms. Join me. It will hardly diminish us should we take on a tad of altitude, and by such means get to comprehend the fearsome voids populating the very air we breathe, voids seeking to swallow us on every ambient quarter. I shall be alongside you at all moments. Then, when we have installed ourselves with confidence on this high wire, we shall have the duty and the pleasure of maintaining a vigil for the best part of a decade. Do you imagine an extended tour of duty such as this will be a problem for supernal folk like us who are not fazed by the passage of time?

I offer my apologies but I do not resile. End of story.

∧

Up. Up.

Hold tight. Don't look down. *Don't*, I implore you.

>

We are in position. Installed at an altitude beneath which the awesome depths – when plumbed by our fevered minds – could induce us to forget to breathe. The hostile ambience is enough to congeal the marrow of the backbones we were not sure anymore we had. We should ignore the adverse gusts buffeting us from the south-west. We should ignore our jelly legs. We should take in the view. Look at it! Be impressed! Around us, the gleaming metal roofs of the industrial estate, scattered like a confusion of children's toys. Beyond, a bewildering excrescence of identical red-tiled roofs stretching to the stripe of turquoise bay in one direction and to the smudge of purple mountain in the other.

What can we learn from this privileged vantage point, traditionally enjoyed only by those capable of propelling themselves with the aid of feathered limbs?

Regretfully, our capacity to interpret what is unfolding below us is limited in ways we might not have anticipated. It is a massive blind spot for us. We see many of these red-tiled roofs, but cannot discern what goes on beneath the structural planches of even *one* of them. We see the tops of the heads of many people moving about the streets but – without access to the secrets inside those skulls – can only guess at what motives might propel the owners of them. We enjoy panorama without narrative. Effect without cause. Surface without substance.

No matter. We must make do with what we have, not what we might hope for. A bird in the hand, as they say.

Pademelons, I know we could employ our omniscient powers to penetrate these mysteries. So, yet again, I remind you who it is rolls the dice here, and who decides the rules of the game. And *I* decree we shall observe, for the duration of the spectacle we shall enjoy from on high, *only* what is capable of observation through the eyes of these terrors of the troposphere, these shoguns of the skies, replete with the limitations – sharp though their beady eyes may be – such a view entails.

>

In the beginning there was Unthank Engineering.

Every weekday morning, no matter what the elements flung in their face, a man and woman in their fifties drove up at precisely 8:30 a.m. in a powder blue Commodore to occupy the premises – identifiable as Unthank Engineering – below and opposite us. They stayed there until precisely 5:30 p.m. This couple, unremarkable in all respects bar one, was Nigel Unthank and his dutiful wife, Michelle. The one respect worthy of remark was her jungle of bottle-fed russet-red hair.

Each fine day, and only on fine days, at precisely 12:30 p.m., they locked up shop and crossed Cockatoo Street passing directly beneath our quivering frames and loosening bowels to a picnic table in the small park. Here they ate an artistically packed lunch from a Tupperware container, plucking at it with stainless-steel forks, and washing it down with a hot beverage – presumably tea – poured by Michelle from a Thermos flask into plastic floral teacups. Then, at precisely 1:15 p.m., they packed up and returned to shop.

Evidently, the shop's business was related to the arrival of all-and-sundry from near-and-far bearing electronic paraphernalia, which they lugged in through the Cockatoo Street entrance and, after some days (or in difficult cases never), lugged out again.

Saturdays were different. They arrived – at opening time – with their lean-faced son, Jared, in tow. Jared wore his school uniform and a scowl. They shut up shop for the day at 12:30 p.m.

On Sunday, God bless them, they rested.

This routine evolved over the years. Jared was replaced in time by a younger model, Jerome, likewise in school uniform with the same scowl on *his* lean face. Then after a couple more years, Jerome was replaced by his younger sister, Annalise, an irrepressible eruption of primal vigour, haughty demeanour, and determined rebellion. All three children were reluctant conscripts to the Saturday morning routine. But, whereas both Jared and Jerome had borne the burden of the tedious ritual with mindless stoicism (and the scowl), Annalise was prepared (literally on some occasions) to be dragged kicking and screaming.

The school uniform – deemed mandatory by her parents on these occasions – in particular irked her, but on this point her father wouldn't budge. The uniform itself seemed inoffensive enough. It consisted of a tartan skirt in rust tones, a plain white blouse with necktie to echo the skirt, a matching broad-brimmed crinoline hat, and thick stockings in a pink tone to round off the whole kit. But we, forming a judgment from on high, were inclined to believe the uniform *per se* was not the problem, but rather what it represented. To Mr Unthank, it shouted to the world, I can afford private school education for my children. To Annalise, it shouted to the world, I am not my own person.

From our height, with the wind stinging our cheeks and the wire biting into our soft paws, we watched the young girl's chronic and sullen protest each Saturday morning and the frequent impassioned outbursts punctuating these protests. On the occasion of one such outburst, a fragment of her angry tirade drifted in our direction, viz. upwards, to shock our vigilant ears: 'It's all one fucking humungous gi-normous suck-hole!' From this choice morsel of artless verbosity we gathered she was given by nature to humungous hyperbole.

We observed her progression from junior student to senior student and her simultaneous blossoming from girlhood to womanhood. As she did so, we saw her pert young body filling out the detested uniform in fine fashion.

Over the years, we counted three periods, each lasting a month or two, during which Mr Unthank failed to put in his regular appearance. During these periods, it was *Mrs* Unthank – Michelle of the red hair – who drove up in the Commodore to open shop. At mid-day, she ate a lonely lunch at the picnic table, courtesy of Tupperware, Thermos, and the whim of the weather. For reasons not immediately apparent to us, these were dark days for the Unthank dynasty in general and for Mr Unthank in particular, but the good wife was valiant. She held the fort.

When Mr Unthank presented again after each of his absences, he looked drawn and sallow, depending for his mobility on a walking stick and Mrs Unthank's obliging shoulder. It was around two months before he could dispense with this assistance and drive the Commodore again.

One Saturday morning, we noticed a seemingly insignificant matter we felt intuitively had implications broader than appearances suggested. Hopeful of relief from the monotony of our vigil, we gave it our fullest attention.

The matter was this. Annalise arrived as usual with her parents and her snarling reluctance, but the school uniform she was wearing had changed. It was now a full-length pleated tunic in deep green, drawn at the waist with a cloth belt. With necktie and boater to match. Even the stockings had changed colour: from pink to beige.

What do you make of it, pademelons? I asked at the time. And, peering down with trepidation through the frightful chasm between wires, we speculated these modifications to her apparel meant young Annalise had changed school. This shrewd guess was supported by a snippet of conversation we overheard from Mr Unthank in the street as he took time out to chide his daughter: ' ... at this rate there won't be a respectable school left in the country prepared to take you.'

We noticed about this time a succession of people we couldn't identify arriving at Unthank Engineering, sometimes in lieu of the Unthanks themselves, apparently to take charge of day-to-day dealings. Our best guess was they were hired help. Often they fronted up well after 8:30, and locked up shop well shy of 5:30. We sometimes saw Mr Unthank in the street below us expressing his displeasure with one or other of them to his/her face. Aphorisms like 'You couldn't lie straight in bed,' assailed our ears as we struggled to remain erect on the high wire.

Then Mrs Unthank stopped coming altogether and, shortly after this, so did Annalise. For the days following Mrs Unthank's no-show, Mr wore a black armband, so we were able to infer the sad demise of the family matriarch. On the other hand, Annalise's failure to show was *not* occasion for an armband, which was as well. We had grown fond of the fiery little devil in skirts.

Following the decease of his wife, Mr Unthank assumed the full burden of duty. He drove up alone in his Commodore. His lunches were no longer an art form, and no longer in Tupperware. No Thermos flask either. Nor stainless-steel fork. Nor floral teacup. The feminine touch had gone to the dogs. Lunch was flung together willy nilly, perhaps like the breakfast of the very same dogs, and stuffed any old how, *sans* utensils, into a grotty paper bag.

This, of course, was how Brenda McMinn caught him one sunny lunchtime on the day life changed for her son Harry. We were up there, furry ears flapping, hanging on every word as we were onto our precarious roost, witness to the shining moment.

Harry was hired.

We know already Harry was to turn out a different kettle of fish from the previous hired assistants. We were nevertheless gratified to have our birds' eyes confirm this. The boy was punctual to a fault. Diligent too. He put in the full complement of expected hours, then more besides.

Huddled together on our wire in an attempt to mitigate the chill of the night air, we often saw Harry's Torana parked outside the premises at midnight and beyond. Sometimes it remained there round the clock. It was not unknown, when grey dawn pushed back the black vault of the night sky, for us to find the Torana standing there immobile, like a faithful hound, to greet the new day. Both we and the Torana shared the same sprinkling of frost.

Occasionally these days, Jared and Jerome appeared, always together, and always with father. We had trouble at first recognizing them out of school uniform. As young men about town now, they flaunted the power of their presence by dint of the swish suits they wore and the sporty cars they drove. Their efforts in this regard were undermined by their increasingly lean faces which made them look like famished ferrets. Clearly the beauty in the family had passed to Annalise.

We were there to see the first product of Harry's technical ingenuity emerge into Cockatoo street. Harry and old Unthank watched while workers bundled it into a Hertz van. From the top it looked like a small rhinoceros (*sans* the horn), but side on more like a large insect eye.

Then Unthank died. We knew a death had taken place as we

had those months earlier when time ran out for *Mrs* Unthank. Not that we saw or heard anything specific up here on the wire. We didn't need to. The pall of death is a tangible and obdurate presence able to make itself felt through channels independent of the normal senses. One can always know when death is at large even though the means by which it makes itself apparent remain mysterious. Death shall not be denied its audience or its moment on centre stage.

Nevertheless, life goes on.

As the working days followed relentlessly on each other's heels, more and more replicas of Harry's creation – each of them paying homage to the multi-faceted eye of an inordinately large insect – emerged from what had by this time become *Harry's* business premises, to be loaded into Hertz vans for delivery to grateful clients.

The average throughput of ten insect eyes per week was do-able because the numbers in the workforce had increased from one (Harry) to something like twelve paid personnel. We watched with interest as they arrived for work each day. Most of them were techies in grey coats, predominantly but not exclusively male. We recognized Ronnie Dash and Ramon Contreras in their number. So I guess it was around this time the Cockatoo Roll was devised, and subsequently embraced with relish as standard operating procedure.

There was *one* female who was not a techie and not in a grey coat. We knew her. Sonia Sheridan.

We were surprised to see how pally Harry and Sonia had become. We had expected the bad blood of earlier days to re-emerge. We had expected to see Harry cowering before those one thousand cuts. It was not to be. Lunch at the picnic tables appeared always to be a pleasant social occasion, in which Harry, Sonia, and the techies shared what seemed mostly to be shop talk.

Sometimes Matt appeared. It could be at any time of day. He arrived by taxi, because he didn't drive. He was always made welcome. However, I have it on the best of authority – from the man himself – he was never on the payroll.

The monotonous predictability of these productive times was interrupted, one memorable day, by an unexpected development. We watched spellbound from our vantage point, as the large vacant lot on the right hand side of the premises sprouted a high security fence – with locked gate – around its extensive perimeter.

With miraculous speed, the space inside the fence was concreted over. From footings set in this concrete a cuboid structure in sheet steel arose, enclosing at least ten times the plan area of Harry's little shop and at least twice the height.

The shorter sides, abutting Cockatoo and Currawong, had large opposing automated doors resembling – when fully open – the mouths of gigantic ventriloquist's dolls. These doors could usher in loaded shipping containers, and usher out the empties. Before long, this manoeuvre was happening several times a day.

The longer sides, one of which abutted Harry's premises, had small opposing doors catering for traffic dependent on legs.

The shag on the rock had company.

Pademelons, this analogy needs updating. The two premises in juxtaposition were better compared to a big fish and a little fish. Had I been the little fish in that situation, I'd have felt nervous.

Equipment – shelving, forklifts, overhead rail with cranes – arrived. So did men in loud business suits, driving Audis. They supervised. Then came the stock. That yawning mouth, constantly open to Cockatoo Street, gorged itself on container loads of all varieties of kitchen and laundry appliances at all hours of day and night. Our 24/7 vigilance attested to this. Even after sunset, we could – courtesy of our insentient companions, the mercury vapour streetlights – peep in through that mouth to see busy men in blue overalls unloading washing machines, fridges, &etc.

We, seasoned observers of externals, assumed this massive structure was an active clearinghouse for white goods. It was big.

It was modern. It was dynamic. It had everything Harry's modest operation lacked, and more besides. Except for one thing.

Except a name. The operation remained steadfastly anonymous.

One day, perhaps a month after deliveries of white goods had begun, a white Ferrari pulled up outside the security fence. If we had taken the trouble to look at the numberplate we might have known exactly what to expect. Sal Heffernan, a.k.a. Hefty, emerged from the driver's side and his subordinate, Snow, from the passenger's side. If their general notoriety had not made them instantly recognizable, our personal experience of them – way back at the time they made Mick McMinn's life a misery – would have sufficed.

Almost two decades had passed since then, so we saw them now in life's prime and on good living's bed of nails. Hefty's hairline was receding and he had developed a (hefty?) paunch. Snow, stooping and more wizened than ever, was – if the grimace on his face and his constant popping of pills were indications – nursing a hiatus hernia or worse. Neither man had lost the inclination (nor the means) for dressing in ways that shouted wealth and power without crossing the line into overt crassness. The habit would have been second nature to Hefty, but Snow would – one might guess – have been inducted into it.

Hefty, with Snow in tow, walked in through the front gate and through the mouth of the huge automated door (at present engorging a trailer-load of containers) with an air of composure that would have done the owners of the place proud. About five minutes elapsed, no more. Then Hefty emerged – Snow in tow again – sporting the same air of composure. The pair was soon back in the Ferrari and driving away.

Everything, apparently, reverted to normal. One might have been left wondering what it was all about. Was it imagination? Had Hefty paid a visit at all? Or had he paid a visit but to no effect? We know better, don't we pademelons? Such wonderings are vapid, naïve, and wishful. And redolent of steaming bullshit. No visit of Hefty is *ever* 'to no effect'.

The effect came later that week, the hour early, our cheeks still retaining hints of the sting of a frigid dawn. We had a ringside seat so to speak, except we were not sitting. Pademelons, I shall have no trouble convincing you what we saw down there made all the endless years of languishing up here in this rarefied and inhospitable precinct, with all its chill, privation, vertigo, danger, ennui, and worse ... it made all those endless years upon endless years totally worthwhile. Almost worth repeating.

Fleets of white Ford Falcons sped recklessly round corners from all points, homing in on the Cockatoo Street clearinghouse, tyres squealing and sirens hammering eardrums. As the plain clothes brigade, in medium grey suits and trilby hats, emerged with intent from the Falcons, the loud-suited folk piled, panic stricken, into their Audis. These automotive icons of Teutonic diligence sped off, only to screech to a halt in front of phalanxes of stationary white Falcons blocking exit in all adjoining streets.

... by this time, Harry, Sonia, and the techies – even Ronnie Dash – were crowding the entrance to Harry's shop, watching the spectacle unfold before their wide eyes ...

One of the fleeing Audis, faced with one of the extemporized roadblocks, managed to skirt it by mounting the footpath, taking out a red pillar box in the process. Some distance beyond the roadblock, the Audi was abandoned by its occupants, who then dispersed like leaves – or, more appositely, like Her Majesty's Mail – before the autumn breeze.

They were the exceptions. Most of the loud-suits were plucked from their Audis and escorted in no dainty fashion, handcuffed and disconsolate, to the white Falcons, where – one by one – their heads were shoved down unceremoniously as they were invited to take a seat. In an act of special generosity, their seat belts were done up for them.

Two of the plain-clothes officers put heavy-duty padlocks on all four entrances to the clearinghouse and wrapped its entire perimeter in crime scene tape. Operation 'Busted Arse', over in less than one frenetic hour, was hailed as a textbook exercise in law enforcement, executed with a professionalism destined to be rewarded with multiple citations.

Lunchtime at the picnic tables was a buzz the likes of which had not been heard before in the industrial estate. Part of the buzz our eager overhead ears picked up was:

Flawed business model, said an anonymous picnicker.

How do you make that out? asked Harry.

Turkeys got their definition of white goods wrong, said the picnicker.

How? asked Harry.

They presumed it covered the white powder inside the panelling.

For the rest of the day and through the following night, two plain-clothes men sat in a white Falcon guarding the premises. We could see cigarette smoke and steam from hot drinks spiralling chaotically from a front window of the vehicle. We could hear low muttering voices and snores. We presided over the changing of the guard at about 2 a.m.

As the new day advanced, we were faced with a problem of our own up here on the wire. One of you pademelons – I shall not mention names – was feeling indisposed. It was all the rest of us could do to prevent this distressed member of our mob from plummeting headlong into Cockatoo Street, falling off the twig so to speak. Consequently we were unable to give our fullest attention to the action below, which – in essence – involved two uniformed police unlocking the padlock on the huge front door, and retrieving from the scene plastic bag after plastic bag full of a powdery-white stuff we presumed to be the intended spoils of crime. They seemed oblivious to the drama being played out over their heads.

The next day, our compatriot had recovered to the extent he/

she was capable of maintaining his/her balance unaided. We were relieved. Now we were treated to another sight.

A fresh contingent of suited men arrived, escorted by a fresh pair of uniformed police. The suits of these new arrivals boasted a smarter cut and weave than those of the plain-clothes folk two days earlier. Furthermore, the outfits on show came in a variety of colours and textures, and trilbies were not part of the deal. The public face of those so adorned was certainly warmer and more user-friendly than that of the plain-clothes men.

Straining our ears, we picked up words of warning Matt gave to Harry as the pair of them stood rubbernecking in front of Harry's shop.

Don't be taken in, he said. These are vultures.

The 'vultures' carried clipboards, calculators, and ballpoint pens. Were they some sort of bean counter? is what we up in the Gods speculated.

Receivers, said Matt from down below.

In the weeks following, all stock in the clearinghouse – the merchandise intended as decoy – was flogged off at fire-sale prices. We saw fridges and washing machines exit the doors by the truckload. And word got about, even to those of us on high, that the clearinghouse itself, together with all internal accoutrements, and with a couple of small delivery vans thrown in, was to be sold off as a job lot to the highest bidder.

Very soon after the stock had all gone off to new owners, we were witness to the extension of the high security fence. Its perimeter now came to embrace not only the premises of the former purveyors of white goods but those of Harry's shop as well. Though we were not ourselves privy to it, our intuition told us some very smart footwork had been done by someone in Harry's camp. Not one of us imagined for a moment this person might have been Harry.

Soon after this, we saw the old shop get a thorough makeover. We presumed the idea was to imbue its decrepit features with a quaint and trendy ambience, so it could pose as a transplanted country-town shopfront, of a fashionable vintage, opening on to a state-of-the-art light manufacturing facility.

With the new identity should, of course, go a new name. So the final observation I shall require you to make from these accursed wires is the new sign atop the renovated iron roof of the old shop. Look across, pademelons. Not down. Yes, there. It says: 'Integrated Electronic Imagery'.

Nature is turned on its head. You, dear pademelons, get to mimic birds. And the little fish gets to eat the big fish.

But isn't it time for us to come down from our ignominious perch? The storyline from this point is best taken up by my second unit, ensconced as they are in *their* new premises.

2nd >>

Singspielstück #9: Courtroom Shenanigans

We – creatures of habit – take up seating positions identical to those we occupied during the last *Stück*, and find ourselves rewarded with an excellent compromise between close presence to the actors and panoramic view of the action.

Stage and house lights are up. Illumination, the colour of sunlight, washes evenly over the turntable stage, as if from skylights set in the roof. This is a staging trick. There are no actual skylights. The simulated sunlight is very much under Elena's control as she sits up there in her space-age facility.

We contemplate the stage setting and, after conjecture, decide it is a courtroom in representation. The impression it conveys is of a clean-cut and airy venue in a pleasant contemporary style. All appointments are in pale hardwood, mountain ash perhaps.

The back half of the turntable is separated from the front half by a barrier resembling an up-market post-and-rail fence with matching gate. The public gallery, consisting of gently raked seating, occupies this back half. The areas where court business happens occupy the front half. Facing us, just forward of the putative fence, are desks and chairs intended for prosecution and defence. Prosecution is to our left and defence to our right.

Closest to us, at the very front of the turntable, and in rear view, are the judge's bench (centre), the witness stand (to the right of it), and the small desk of the stenotypist (to the left of it). Looking at the rear of such furniture is about as rewarding as licking the label on a bottle of whiskey, but I happen to know, pademelons, that those responsible for blocking the stage have a purpose in mind to justify this arrangement. Trust me.

Focus on the extreme rear of the turntable. There, in central position, behind the public gallery, and supported at a height of about three metres by an almost invisible framework attached to and arising from the stage, is a large clock dial with prominent numbers in Roman style. We see this timepiece in full frontal view. It is 'pretending' to be attached to a non-existent back wall, the aforementioned framework being an artifice necessary to achieve such an illusion.

At present, no direct lighting falls on the clock, so we struggle to make out what time it tells.

Pademelons, a trade secret. Whenever the stage presents itself to us in this manner tacitly denying us a view of the faces of judge, witness, and stenotypist, we are being encouraged to focus on this clock. Given its dominant position, we can scarcely ignore it. We may infer that the chronology of the action to be represented on stage will help us interpret such action.

Behind this clock, clear of the turntable, at a slight elevation, and on its own purpose-built platform, is the synthesizer, with Izzie seated at the ready.

Since I am privy to the machinations of my second unit, I can tell you more trade secrets, this time about the intentions behind the regime of stage movement about to unfold. Intentions arguably conceived by a mind nerdish, obsessive, controlling, and anal.

At times, the stage shall rotate anticlockwise through a quarter turn. This is the signal we are about to be entertained by a fragment of *Sing*, as opposed to *Spiel*. At other times, there shall be a quarter turn clockwise. We can then expect a fragment of *Spiel* as opposed to *Sing*. Should the stage revert to its starting position, viz. what you are seeing right now, we are being persuaded gently to note the time.

Zounds, pademelons. We are adults. Are we to be treated like stupid young joeys fresh from the pouch?

House lights go off and stage lights are dimmed. We see the stage furniture only in silhouette. Action is to begin.

A spot appears on the clock face. The time is 9:30. We assume this is the start time of the current court session. A.m not p.m. Justice keeps bankers' hours.

Izzie begins a chirpy melodic introduction in major key, in 4/4 time, and with a rhythm as relentless as that of – wouldn't you know it? – a ticking timepiece. This melody is a musical 'holding pattern', its purpose being to buy enough time to allow the performers to enter.

But, before any such thespian invasion can proceed, the stage rotates anticlockwise with speed through a quarter turn, then stops abruptly. The spot on the clock disappears. Stage lighting is raised. We see the stage setting in a new perspective. The judge's bench, the witness stand, and the stenotypist's desk are on our right, in profile. Of these three, the desk of the stenotypist is closest to us. The public gallery and (behind it) the clock are on our left.

We can anticipate *Sing* not *Spiel*. Them's the rules.

The stenotypist's desk supports a bulky and ancient stenotype machine, whose function is the manual recording of transcripts. This dooverlackie from a bygone age leads me to reflect on the troglodyte mentality of the legal fraternity. Why are they, technologically speaking, dragging their feet to this extent?

Let's forego futile speculation. The performers are entering the stage from left and right to take up positions. Let's see them seated.

From the left:

Matt and Sonia come in chatting. They sit in the front row of the public gallery.

Behind them comes a contingent of Sandalwood Singers, who take up seats dispersed throughout the gallery. We assume they represent the disinterested public with a sprinkling of those who anticipate being called as witnesses.

Behind them comes Sticks, who steals in as if not wanting to be noticed. Sitting towards the back, she extracts pen and notebook from her handbag.

… yes! It is Sticks! She is to make her inaugural appearance in the unfolding chronology of Harry's life and many deaths. Pademelons, what do you suppose is her relationship to the business of this courtroom? And to the principals, as yet to emerge, who are about to slug it out in this courtroom contretemps? She surely could not be a casual visitor …

From the right:

Godfrey – playing the judge! – comes in wearing wig, gown, and an uncustomary air of solemnity. He goes to his bench and fiddles with his gavel.

Behind him comes one of his Sandalwood colleagues – playing the stenotypist – a small, wiry, middle-aged man in a business suit of conservative cut. Heavy spectacles, with frames out of faux amber and with lenses as thick as bottle-bottoms, balance on his nose. He sits behind the stenotype machine at his small desk, and practices looking invisible.

Behind him, comes Martha Singleton, Matt's barrister sister, playing herself. Her client accompanies her. Harry McMinn. She leads him to their allotted place. As learned counsel for the defence, Martha is wearing wig and gown. She lays out sheaves of paper from her briefcase in front of her. Harry fidgets.

Last in line is another Sandalwood Singer, in wig and gown, to play counsel for the prosecution, whose name we understand is Justin. Trailing him are his clients, Jared and Jerome Unthank, playing themselves. He leads this pair to *their* allotted place, and takes papers out of *his* briefcase. The demeanour of his clients is confident and jaunty. Their faces are ferrety.

Justin and Martha salute each other with smiles across the gap separating their desks, thereby demonstrating the triumph of collegiate solidarity over adversarial expectations.

For the seconds it takes the performers to enter, Izzie maintains the holding pattern. When all actors are settled in position, the stage lights are dimmed. The actors, in silhouette now, freeze in tableau.

This frozen moment holds for a few seconds. Then the lights are raised, which is the cue for action to resume, for the tableau to un-freeze, and for song to evolve from out of the monotonous tick-tock of the holding pattern. Stage action consists of much strutting and gesturing, as is appropriate to the words of the song, but arguably less appropriate to the etiquette expected in an *actual* courtroom. Of the actors, only the stenotypist doesn't join in.

Justin:

In the case of Unthank brothers as the plaintiffs

Martha:

up against defendant, Harry A McMinn,

Judge:

intellectual property's in question, and
who takes grip
of ownership.

Jared and Jerome:

In the case of Unthank brothers as the plaintiffs

Harry:

up against defendant, Harry A McMinn,

Matt and Sonia:

intellectual property's in question.

Sticks:

Let the trial begin.

Judge:

Justice merely seen to be isn't justice done,
and isn't the way for a court of the law to be run.

Justin:

In the case of Unthank brothers as the plaintiffs,

Martha:

ring the bell and let the trial begin.

All (except stenotypist):

Ears lent,
listening to the patter of the argument
bouncing off the furniture and firmament.

Matt and Sonia:

Waffle, tommyrot, and mumbo

Sticks:

share the air with brother jumbo.

All (except stenotypist):

Eyes front,
not to miss the drama of the legal stunt,
nor the money-grubbery of the treasure hunt,

Sticks:

a nod to *numero uno*!

Izzie's fingers re-activate the holding pattern, Elena's fingers dim the stage lights, and the frozen tableau of actors is re-visited. The stage rotates clockwise through a quarter turn, bringing it back to the starting position. The clock face is in full frontal view.

A spot lights this clock face. The hands make a rapid clockwise sweep of the dial, simulating time-lapse photography, to bring up a time of 2:30. Afternoon. We are at the mercy of my second unit, pademelons, who have decided we shall jump forward in time.

The stage rotates again: another quarter turn clockwise. The spot disappears from the clock face. Elena brings stage lights up. Izzie lifts his fingers from the keyboard. There is silence. We see the stage setting from yet another angle. The public gallery is on our right, the judge's bench &etc is on our left, with the witness stand in closest proximity to us. It is a mirror image of the perspective we saw earlier when we were entertained by *Sing*.

But it is *Spiel* we can expect now, not *Sing*.

The tableau unfreezes. Actors resume their designated places. Their demeanour during this episode of *Spiel* conforms more closely to the dignity and bearing expected in a courtroom. But rest assured: theatricality has not been abandoned entirely.

Harry takes the witness stand. The stenotypist, hunched, prepares for action. The judge proceeds to question Harry.

I understand, says the judge, your full name is Henry Athol McMinn, the name under which you took the oath.

Yes, Your Honour, says Harry.

Your learned counsel, says the judge, has briefed the court on the activities of what was formerly known as Unthank Engineering and latterly as Integrated Electronic Imagery. I would like to hear some of this from your own mouth, Mr McMinn. Could you start by telling me about the time when you began to do something of a more innovative nature than the simple repair of television sets?

The first thing was the public display system based on ...

Whose idea was that, Mr McMinn?

Mr Unthank's, Your Honour.

Would that be Mr *Jared* Unthank?

No. It was ...

Mr *Jerome* Unthank, perhaps?

No. It was ...

Neither of the plaintiffs?

It was *old* Mr Unthank, Your Honour.

Mr *Nigel* Unthank, now deceased?

Yes, Your Honour.

The judge pauses to write something down. The ferret faces of the Unthank brothers twitch.

Mr McMinn, are you aware, says the judge, the plaintiffs have testified under oath *they* put the idea into your head?

Yes, Your Honour.

You maintain they were lying?

I ... suppose I might be forced to ...

Come, Mr McMinn. The issue is contempt of court. This is not the time or the place for supposition on your part, or coercion on mine. Give the court a simple 'Yes' or 'No'.

Yes, Your Honour.

So is it 'Yes' or is it 'No', Mr McMinn?

'Yes', Your Honour.

The judge pauses to write something down.

I wonder, says the judge, if you would mind giving the court a run-down of *all* the developments of an innovative nature transpiring under the auspices of Unthank Engineering or possibly of Integrated Electronic Imagery since the moment of your first association with those institutions.

Innovations?

Innovations.

Yes, Your Honour.

Harry pauses for thought.

Well ... after the public display systems, says Harry, we had a go at electronic text strips and bulletin boards ...

Text strips?

Yes. Otherwise known as crawls.

Crawls?

You sometimes see them running ... or crawling, I guess ... from right to left along the bottom of a TV screen during scheduled programming. And in all sorts of other places. News summaries in text form. Or the weather, or sports results, ...

Or the stock market?

Yes, Your Honour. Anything that can be told in text form and updated in real time. Bulletin boards are similar, except they scroll up and down. You see them at airports. Arrivals and departures. And train stations. In sports stadiums too. Cinemas, TABs, supermarkets. All over the place. There's no limit to the potential applications.

Do go on.

We're developing a sur-text system for opera.

Really? Opera?

We've run up against a problem there. We don't have any language experts on our technical team. We'll have to look at ...

How many on your team, Mr McMinn?

Seventeen, Your Honour. Including myself.

The judge pauses to jot something down.

Proceed with the innovations, says the judge. If you please.

I was about to say, says Harry, we're going to have to address the issue of languages, because of the overwhelming interest in electronic bulletin boards coming out of ...

The judge looks down his nose, and chuckles discreetly.

Overwhelming?   Being carried away by your own hype, perhaps?

No, Your Honour. The interest is from all over Asia. They want bi- and multi- lingual systems for their airports and the like.

The judge nods, but says nothing. His enthusiasm getting the better of him, Harry takes this as an invitation to continue.

We hope to get into high definition holographic systems, one hundred percent digital of course, to facilitate remote conferencing, or perhaps even virtual reality where participants get to interact via proxies in all three dimensions ...

That will suffice for now, Mr McMinn. It gives us an overview. We wouldn't want you to reveal any trade secrets.

No, Your Honour.

You put me in awe. I dread the day when courtrooms the length and breadth of our wide brown land are replaced by conference facilities in virtual reality, within which context judges, juries, and counsel are nevertheless required in all seriousness to perform their prescribed duties.

Both learned counsels titter politely at what they assume has been a feeble attempt by His Honour to crack a joke. The judge pretends not to notice their obsequious confusion. He pauses strategically before continuing to address Harry.

One more thing if I may. Were these recent innovations your own ideas? The crawls ... the bulletin boards ... the sur-text ... et alia?

Yes, Your Honour.

No input from anybody else?

No, Your Honour.

Lights are dimmed, actors freeze, and the holding pattern resumes. The stage rotates anticlockwise, this time through a half turn.

Then lights are raised. The actors un-freeze. The orientation of the stage signals we are to be entertained by another fragment of exuberant *Sing*. If that were not enough, Izzie's accompaniment provides the cue for full-blooded song to begin again, embellished by extravagant gestures and struts from the singers.

Justin and Martha:

When the learned counsels spruik unlikely stories

Judge:

then the learned judge must rein the ponies in,

Matt:

lest the consequence of due process be

Sticks:

far-fetched tale
gets to prevail.

Jared & Jerome:

When the learned counsels spruik unlikely stories

Harry:

then the learned judge must rein the ponies in,

Sonia:

lest the consequence of due process be

Sticks:

truth outfoxed by spin.

Justin:

Keen interrogation's certain to flush things out,

Martha:

some with an odour inclined to get right up the snout.

Judge:

When the learned counsels spruik unlikely stories

Sticks:

truth will need a hand to outdo spin.

Lights are dimmed, actors freeze, holding pattern resumes. The stage rotates clockwise through a quarter turn. We see the clock in full frontal view, with a spot illuminating its face. Its hands sweep rapidly clockwise, the hour hand traversing a full revolution and more before stopping at 10:30. We are informed the best part of a day has passed, and it is morning of the next day.

The stage rotates a further quarter turn clockwise. The spot disappears from the clock face. The holding pattern gives way to silence. Stage lights are raised. The stage is ready for another fragment of *Spiel*.

The frozen tableau thaws. Actors resume their appointed places.

The ferrets, nervous, crowd round Justin, perhaps under the illusion their counsel can provide them with a much needed morale boost. Justin, anxious to avoid the dumb appeal in his clients' eyes, pretends to be busy shuffling papers.

Harry listens while Martha, *his* counsel, gives advice in a low voice with confidential tone. Since her desk is adjacent to us now, we are able to hear her.

Play it cool, she says. He will be a desperate man by now. That makes him dangerous. Expect mud to be slung. Don't let him lead you. Give short simple answers to his questions. Don't gild the lily.

Harry nods agreement. He walks with trepidation to the witness stand. Justin comes forward to cross-examine.

Mr McMinn, says Justin, I remind you of the innovatory developments you allege to have devised single-handedly under the auspices of Unthank Engineering and latterly of Integrated Electronic Imagery. According to a statement you made to this court, you received no input from any other person. Do you confirm you made such a statement?

Yes, says Harry.

Is it true?

Yes.

Mr McMinn, do you know a Mr Matthew Bolton?

Yes.

Harry is startled. He glances at Matt in the public gallery. Matt's face is impassive, as if Justin were talking about somebody else. But his body has stiffened.

What do you understand is his occupation?

He runs a business called Dress Rules.

And what kind of business might that be?

Women's fashion.

There is veiled insinuation in Justin's tone as he replies:

Oh, indeed.

If I may interrupt my learned colleague, says the judge, I would like to get the spelling of that name.

Bolton. B-O-L-T-O-N, your honour.

The judge writes this down.

You may proceed, says the judge.

Thank you, Your Honour, says Justin.

Justin turns again to Harry.

Mr McMinn, isn't it true Mr Matthew Bolton has made an input to your business?

Harry is lost for words.

You must answer the question, Mr McMinn, says the judge.

Yes ...

Harry stumbles. Sweat breaks out on his brow.

... yes, but not a technical one.

An *input*, nevertheless.

Justin pauses strategically.

What kind of input might that *be*?

Moral support. Mainly.

Mainly? What was the rest?

Again, Harry is lost for words.

You must answer the question, Mr McMinn, says the judge.

Harry finds voice. His face registers surprise, as if he is not sure exactly *whose* voice he has found, but has decided *any* voice will do.

Some logical ... I mean logistical support, says the voice. Nothing technical.

Moral *and* logistical support, says Justin. What would be his motive in giving moral and logistical support?

Objection, says Martha. Witness is being asked to read minds.

Upheld, says the judge.

At this moment Sonia, with an ambiguous gesture to Matt, excuses herself, then discreetly exits the public gallery.

I'll rephrase the question, says Justin. What do you *presume* was the motive driving Mr Bolton to give you his moral and logistic support?

I presume because he's an old school friend, says Harry.

Again, veiled insinuation colours Justin's tone, especially noticeable in the downward inflexion of his voice:

Old ... school ... friend.

Justin forces another strategic pause. Through his nervous and sweat-stung eyes, Harry flashes glances, first at Matt (sitting impassively), and then at the judge. The latter has gone on full alert. A look of unease, or possibly distaste, transforms his bewigged face.

Was Mr Bolton a director of your Company? asks Justin.

No.

Was he on the payroll?

No.

He received no material advantage whatsoever?

No.

Then it would come down to the – ahem – relationship between old school friends ...

Harry's face expresses his bewilderment. A toxic silence

invades the courtroom, reinforced by the lack of movement even of the minutest muscle of the most restless person in the room, presumably Harry. We do not hear the usual light shuffle of leather soles on the floor. We imagine we hear the breath of the fly alighting on Jared's anxious brow.

… with benefits mayhap?

Jared's slap as he moves the fly on has the impact of a thunderclap.

Martha, irate and in breach of her own edict re playing it cool, springs to her feet, shouting:

Objection. Irrelevant and offensive innuendo.

Sustained, says the judge. Does the plaintiffs' counsel intend the purpose of his line of questioning shall become apparent this side of doomsday?

Justin sputters.

Your Honour, he says, I intend to maintain Messrs McMinn and Bolton conspired conjointly, for the purposes of personal profit, to apply undue pressure on the now deceased Mr Nigel Unthank, in order to induce him to alter his will in their favour.

My most learned colleague, says the judge, you are indeed at liberty to *maintain*, but there is no evidence currently before the court to *support* what you maintain.

He turns to Harry.

Is there any truth in what the plaintiffs' counsel has asserted?

No, says Harry.

The judge turns back to Justin.

I suggest to my esteemed colleague his current line of questioning has the potential to be profitable neither to himself nor to the court.

I have no further questions, Your Honour.

Justin, shattered, returns to his desk. There he and his two clients give a convincing impression of straw men who have lost their stuffing to a pack of wild dogs. Whereas Harry and Martha at their desk are like cats doing their best to dispose of an excess of cream.

Lights are dimmed. Izzie's nimble fingers coax the holding pattern from the keyboard. Actors freeze. The stage rotates anticlockwise through a half turn. When the lights are raised, the stage is ready for an episode of *Sing*.

Izzie's music morphs into the cue for song. The actors un-freeze and, with notable exceptions, launch into vocals accompanied by enthusiastic gesturing and strutting. Exceptions? you ask. Yes, pademelons, I reply. Let's take each of them in turn:

The stenotypist, who knows his place, maintains a professional distance.

The prosecuting team have collapsed in a heap.

Matt is, to all appearances, rooted to his seat.

Sonia is no longer present.

Martha:

In the case of Harry as the sole defendant

Harry:

up against the brothers Jared and Jerome,

Judge:

he who cooked up the pudding in the first place

Sticks:

should hold sway
and win the day.

Judge:

In the case of Harry as the sole defendant

Martha:

up against the brothers Jared and Jerome,

Harry:

he who cooked up the pudding in the first place

Sticks:

should be hosed and home.

Martha:

The law's truly asinine if the law can find
merit in prejudice, slander, and slur of this kind.

Judge:

In the case of Harry as the sole defendant

Sticks:

it's a moral[30] Harry's hosed and home.

All (except stenotypist):

Ears lent,
listening to the patter of the argument
bouncing off the furniture and firmament.

Martha:

Waffle, tommyrot, and mumbo

Sticks:

share the air with brother jumbo.

All (except stenotypist):

Eyes front,
not to miss the drama of the legal stunt,
nor the money-grubbery of the treasure hunt,

---

30 'moral': colloquial Australian, meaning (in this context) 'certainty'.

Sticks:

a nod to *numero uno*!

Lights are dimmed. Actors freeze. Izzie sounds the final chords. And – whether by design or accident, the devil only knows – a spot comes up on the stenotypist, hunched over his archaic contraption. The lenses of his spectacles catch the bright light of the spot and reflect it back in part to various corners and crannies of the theatre. The spot lingers on him for a few seconds – perhaps a shade longer than it should have had the lingering been purely accidental – and then it too goes off.

House lights come up. The actors un-freeze and leave the stage.

II

O, steadfast stenotypist. O, zealous warrior. Spurning fame and fortune, indifferent to the accolades of sycophants and to the machinations of the legal fraternity, but concerned merely to hurl yourself into the fray of perpetual battle, despite odds stacked so heavily against you by Those who exercise power over the verities of the time-spun universe! We honour you with this tribute.

Your quest? To capture, and preserve for posterity, those will-o-the-wisp moments of present time so managing to elude, and thereby to vex, each one of us, when we once trod the turf and found ourselves slaves to the perilous portent of mortal life.

As these discrete moments break off successively like fractious icebergs from that mythic glacial mass known as the future, determined to hold their brief sway over both you and the entire world you inhabit, you see your task as being to take these icy invaders hostage one by one, and to encapsulate their essence in your transcript. But they have different plans. They have a mind, once they have enjoyed their moment in the sun, to dissolve into that great salt ocean of prior moments known as the past, from whence never to return.

So, like the Don of legend, slashing with his sword at windmills, you flail at fragments of time with whatever flimsy weapons you can bring to bear: your clunky keyboard, and the cogs and gears grinding away at your behest inside that ancient and infernal machinery of yours. You do not pause to contemplate the futility of your task, not to acknowledge applause, not to gather up bouquets, not to receive medals, not even to partake of bodily refreshment for the purposes of your invigoration for onslaughts still to come.

No, noble being. To you, the battle, together with the cause for which this battle must be fought, is the totality of everything of importance. We stand in awe. And we salute you.

But, of course, our plaudits do not reach you. You are unaware, even of our existence.

<< 1ˢᵗ

Harry won the case. The Unthank brothers seethed inwardly, but paid the costs *in toto*, as required by court order. They were so cash strapped as a result of their comprehensive drubbing, Harry – evidently in the thrall of an 'old school friend' – felt free to put a daring offer to them, viz. an offer for the outright purchase of the archetypal Cockatoo Street premises. They accepted this offer with neither argument nor good grace. Afterwards they – so it was heard said – were 'fucking glad to be out of it.'

Pademelons, you cannot doubt a win for Harry was always destined to be the outcome. Nobody needs to peruse a full transcript of the court proceedings in order to be persuaded of the inevitability of such a result beyond reasonable doubt. The juicy snippets my second unit have presented to you, though in themselves far from a complete record, shall be more than adequate to persuade you. Armed with these snippets and nothing more, you may deduce with impunity that, from the start, a fast-gathering wind – or more aptly, a gale – was holding hard in a direction less than favourable to Jared and Jerome. It duly blew them away.

Nevertheless one other event, not covered by the theatrics of my second unit, but of sufficient significance to make it worth reporting, *did* occur at the time of the court proceedings, though not actually *in* the courtroom as such.

The occasion of it was a lunch recess called by the judge. This recess came immediately after Martha had made things extremely uncomfortable for the hapless Unthank brothers in the process of her cross-examination of them, a cross-examination not actually taken up – for whatever reasons they might have had – by my second unit as part of their re-enactment. It came immediately before the prosecuting counsel's ill-conceived cross-examination of Harry, re-enacted in full – as you have witnessed – with such theatrical panache by Harry and his fellow actors.

The venue was the precinct immediately outside the courtroom, a modern anteroom masquerading as a cloister, looking out through a pretentious array of colonnades on to a quadrangle open to the sky and planted with bonsai.

I draw your attention to a quirk of human nature, pademelons, of which you may or may not be aware. Whenever people gather in such a public forum for whatever purpose, they tend to coalesce in groups *around the columns*, rather than populate the wide-open spaces *between them*. Is it a territorial thing, I wonder? Along the lines of: '*This* is our column, and *that* is yours.' Or maybe it can be attributed to incipient agoraphobia. Or are they perhaps expecting an earthquake? Speculation could become rife on this point if we were to make no attempt to rein it in.

In any event, the McMinn camp – consisting of Harry, Matt, and Sonia – gathered themselves around one column, and the Unthank camp around another. The two opposing counsels – Martha, and Justin – had found themselves a third column. An animated group of people from the public gallery – a group of students I believe – had commandeered a fourth column. All groups were taken up with chatting, eating sandwiches, and washing down the edibles with spoon coffee in polystyrene cups.

Pretence was rife in this venue. The columns in the faux cloister were plain tapered cylinders of rendered concrete pretending to be marble. The floor was baked clay pretending to be granite. As for the deftly manicured bonsai, one could not doubt they represented a significant departure from the real botanical McCoy.

But there was nothing fake about the acoustic qualities of the cloister. These were very real, startlingly effective, and presumably an unintended consequence devolving willy-nilly from an ill-considered construction process. I mention this fact – seeming on the surface to be neither here nor there – because I'm not sure too many of the determined word-spinners gathered in the cloister during this recess had bothered to take sufficient account of this technicality. They might have been alarmed had they known how readily their supposed private conversations were inclined to waft on the receptive air, even over a distance.

We found ourselves hanging out – invisible, as it is our fate to be – with Harry's group while we made our discreet observations. What we were privileged to see and hear from this vantage point might be summarized as follows.

Looking from Harry's group towards the counsels, we saw the bewigged pair – having temporarily abandoned their antagonist roles – talking amiably to each other in low tones. We heard the buzz of their conversation but not the precise words. We presumed they were comparing notes about the generalities of shop.

Looking from Harry's group towards the Unthanks, we saw the two brothers looking distinctly uneasy as they leaned against the column in profile view. A third person was with them, her back turned to us, and we presumed this to be the sister, Annalise. Our inadequate glimpse of her was sufficient for us to ascertain she was quite the young woman now, *sans* school uniform to cramp her style.

Conversation in the McMinn camp was proceeding along lines we expected.

… shoved it right up the noses of those pretentious little turds, said Matt. Siss knows her job, and does it with style.

You won't find me complaining, said Harry.

I *am* glad, boyo. It's so refreshing to find a customer happy with the services rendered.

How could I not be?

Let's see if you can find the prosecution as much to your liking.

Aye, said Sonia. There's the rub.

Matt pointed towards the Unthank camp.

Who's the *Fraulein*? he asked.

The sister, replied Harry. I believe her name's Annalise.

Sonia shifted nervously.

What sort of name is that? she asked.

Ever met her? asked Matt.

Harry and Sonia responded simultaneously.

Never, said Harry.

Never! said Sonia.

… but the disproportionate emphasis in Sonia's denial could lead one to speculate on the veracity of this lady's protestation …

Striking … said Matt.

At this point Sonia interrupted him with alarm.

She's coming this way, she said.

She was. When she turned to face our direction, we had her in full-frontal view. To say we were surprised would undervalue the acuity of the shock delivered to us in that moment. Pademelons, were we not tossed, tumbled, rattled, and rearranged by events to the extent we were inclined to question even the special nature of what might loosely be termed our existence? At first gasp we had difficulty believing what we saw but – by way of turning difficulty on its head – it transpired we were *not* mistaken, were we?

The young woman walking towards us had every appearance of being a younger version of Sticks. The same Sticks with whom we had developed such familiarity, as invisible observers of Harry's *Singspielstücke* on the occasions we made excursions into the next millennium. The Sticks who, with command of authority, had blocked the stage. The Sticks who had engendered fear in the hearts of grown adults, even of such as Matt and Izzie. Sticks, the mother. Sticks, the saviour of the world. Sticks, volatile, explosive, gratuitously emotional. Our very own Sticks, no less.

She approached Harry's group with a posture so upright not a single drop of liquid – not water, not whiskey, not nitroglycerine – would have spilt from a hypothetical glass poised on the crown of her head. Her dress – angora cardigan in aquamarine, floral skirt in muted colours to below her knees, and flat heels – could be described politely as 'outside of fashion'. But – here again is an object lesson for Matt – she did not need to assert her dominance via the style of her clothes. The presence she exuded did the job.

Where did she learn to walk like that? asked Matt.

'She' was with them now, and answered the question herself.

St Maggot's had me balance books on my skull, she said. Guess I'd have a head start selling encyclopaedias.

You here to suss out the enemy? asked Matt.

Perhaps.

Matt stuck out his hand. She took it.

I'm Matt. This is Harry. This is Sonia.

I know. I've done my homework.

You are Annalise?

Calls me Sticks.

Sticks? asked Harry

Let's say I played hockey at school.

This comment warranted a pause in conversation. Harry forced its resumption.

What do *you* think about the way things are going? he asked.

Fine for you guys, she said. My brothers were fools to take you on.

From the moment Sticks arrived, Sonia had seemed unnerved,

pallid in the face, and unsteady on the feet. Now she ventured a timorous question.

Aren't you here to support them? she asked.

Sticks laughed.

You'd have me support fools?

Then why *are* you here? asked Harry.

Fixing Harry with her eyes, she replied.

To ask you for a job.

This was a conversation stopper. Suddenly, Sonia – afflicted with buckling legs – needed the column for support. And, from a neighbouring column, where the temperature of the conversation between opposing counsels had – over the last few seconds – increased several notches, Martha's shrill voice carried on the treacherous acoustics:

... advice to you, Justin, is don't go there. Bad career move.

Bells rang. Around the cloister, half-eaten sandwiches were gulped, coffee slurped.

Let's make tracks, said Matt.

... as for what happened next, my second unit has already shown you, through the revelatory lens of live theatrical performance, how the plan of the prosecuting counsel came to grief in the courtroom ...

>

'I wouldn't want to be Prime Minister of a country that didn't *make* things,' said an aspirant for this high office in Oz early in the 21st C.

Harry McMinn, who was a split generation younger than this man, made things. He started making things with his bare hands in the early 90s when barely out of his teens, with old Nigel Unthank his mentor. By the time the above-mentioned aspiring person got to fulfil his aspiration, Harry had had an assembly line going for over a decade for the purpose of making things. His assembly line was in Cockatoo Street, in the former clearinghouse for white goods he, with a little help from a friend, had picked up for a song.

Regrettably, making things ceased to be cool some months after this amiable pretender became Prime Minister. Egged on by certain other of their political masters, by figureheads of the mining fraternity such as E H Bolton, OA, and by sundry scurrilous fliers-by-night, the good folk of Oz – cargo cultists in the main – decided their salvation lay more in flogging off stuff extracted from the wide brown land than it did in making things. Flying in the face of the cargo cult, Harry's enterprise, by way of exception, managed an unlikely success. As for the aspirant for high office, he got his wish. He ceased to be Prime Minister.

May the galloping goitre of my gormless granny be roundly cursed! Before this particular axe fell (and on more heads than one, I might say), Harry suffered his many deaths, and I suffered my one and only. Yet again, I catch myself wandering off message, neglecting my brief. For this I apologize.

To get this presentation back on track, pademelons, we should shift our omniscient gaze to an unseasonably sunny afternoon a few days after Harry won his court case. We shall find Harry and Sticks approaching the threshold of the former clearinghouse, i.e. the mouth of the ventriloquist's doll.

Harry was about to show Sticks how Integrated Electronic Imagery made things. The searing sun hung behind them in a cloudless sky at a position signifying 4 p.m. or thereabouts. What they were about to see, Harry had seen many times. For Sticks it would be a revelation.

Astonishing changes had been made since the days when it had been a clearinghouse for a variety of categories, some dubious, of white goods.

The sheet steel of the four interior walls and ceiling were unrelieved except for two large doors at front and back, two small doors at the sides, and a couple of insignificant high-set windows. Had these metal surfaces been transmuted into canvas, one might have felt tempted to compare these premises to a circus pavilion, such was the expansiveness of the space enclosed and the hullabaloo filling it. Harry, so tempted, had dubbed it the 'Big Top'.

Two heavy-duty overhead rail lines, from each of which a bevy of cranes hung, ran lengthwise from one huge mouth to the other. Workstations, peopled by grey-coated techies in hard hats, were positioned strategically beneath these rails. Dangling from the cranes, like carcasses in a slaughterhouse, were public display systems, at various stages of completion, the left-hand rail line being devoted exclusively to multi-screen systems, and the right-hand line to electronic bulletin boards. The assembly lines so formed progressed slowly and steadily from the front of the premises to the back, at which point the finished product underwent quality control before being swept up by a fork-lift and loaded for delivery.

The days of the Cockatoo Roll were nothing more than a memory, albeit one with the indelible imprint of nostalgia.

As each 'carcass' moved into position adjacent to a workstation, the responsible techie would anchor the swaying frame to the workbench and, having thus secured it safely, would begin work on it with whatever implement(s) the occasion demanded: multimeter, soldering iron, welding tools, and/or screwdriver. Or – in reserve for abortive cases – multi-grips, jemmy, and/or wrecking bar.

Workbenches not part of the assembly lines ran the interior perimeter of the premises. Techies with more advanced skills were busy here. From these benches, 'crawls', sur-text for opera, and other niche items would emerge.

Whirligigs embedded in the ceiling, overhead fans, and fluorescent lighting were necessary evils, especially so because of the lack of windows.

Another evil – apparently necessary – was the insidious accumulation of incidental detritus in the form of wooden pallets and crates, packaging out of cardboard and Styrofoam, drums/bottles of fuel/solvent in various stages of depletion, overflowing dumpsters, &etc, of which it was fair to say its removal from the premises never seemed to keep pace with its arrival. Such items are exemplars of the anarchic tyranny of the shop floor.

Pademelons, having detailed the paraphernalia of the workplace and the mechanics of its operation, I follow up now with mention of the human component. Harry did not neglect to exchange shy cordial greetings with each of the techies as he and Sticks passed easily among them. One employee, Ramon, in bright yellow overalls, whom these days Harry referred to as his Operations Manager, mingled with the other techies, checking progress, issuing instructions, and proffering advice with the gentle courtesy second nature to him.

Harry introduced Sticks to him and afterwards remarked the obvious to her: Ramon was 'worth his weight in gold.'

For a few moments – destined to be treasured by him – Harry forgot he was entertaining a visitor, so carried away was he with the sight before his eyes. It was, of course, much the same sight confronting him every day of the week, but on this occasion it was as if he were seeing it for the first time, through Sticks' eyes perhaps. It was, despite its propensity for repetition, a miraculous sight, replete with liberating space, invigorating noise, breathless action, purposeful design, ruthless efficiency, safe working conditions, and harmonious workplace relations.

It was a far cry from the days of the Cockatoo Roll when the production line, if one could call it such, was housed in more claustrophobic premises. Premises, should one delve into ancient history, established proudly in some forgotten era by a then youthful Nigel Unthank and his compliant wife Michelle.

How had it come about? Harry asked himself. He knew the answer. It was luck, unimaginable luck, luck he had no right to expect, luck at every turn, luck falling into place as he rounded each corner, luck blessing him for no reason. It *had* to be luck, because he knew it was not within his capacity to set up an operation such as this off his own bat. True to form – he was his mother's son after all – he had been happy for illusion to stand uncorrected.

Finding names to which this luck might be apportioned, he came up with such as 'Matt', 'Ramon' and now (potentially) 'Sticks'. Not to forget doting Brenda and crusty old Unthank himself.

As if channelling his thoughts, Sticks – appropriately overcome – said, My father would have loved to see this.

To which, pademelons, I follow up with the question (which she cannot hear): What makes you suppose he isn't?

<

I hear you ask, Are we to understand Sticks is part of this operation? The short answer is, Yes. For the longer answer, we must turn the clock back forty minutes or so, to when Sticks – seated in Harry's office – tried to explain to Harry the particular and prodigious talents she could bring to bear on the everyday operations of Integrated Electronic Imagery.

If *I* tried to explain the nature of these talents to you, pademelons, I would fail for want of an inkling. Likewise Harry, I suspect. So the only recourse I have is to go back to their source, viz. Sticks, and have her speak for herself, assuming – of course – *she* understands.

Here are the words of explanation she uttered to Harry. Her pitch. Verbatim. Make of it what you can.

It's not a photographic process at all, Sticks said. *Look, this is difficult to describe, but if you imagine a narrative of some sort, to which the information in need of memorizing can be related in some codified manner, all you have to remember is the narrative. Not the information. When you want to get the information back, you re-tell the narrative. Record then replay. Code then decode. That's the gist of how it works to the best of my knowledge. I'm afraid this is the best explanation I can give.*

This conversation happened in a space formerly the front counter of Unthank Engineering, but which since those early days had been thoroughly made over into an office. In the process, no overtures, not in deed, word, or thought – not so much as a sly wink in her direction – had been made to the goddess of style. Functionality, cheap and nerdish, was king here. Functionality fit to sap and shrivel delicate souls.

The small desk across which Sticks spoke to Harry was one of two placed side-by-side in the office. Both were shoddy steel-framed affairs with plastic laminate surfaces behind which were cheap swivel chairs. Apple Macs and telephones doubling as DIY switchboards sat on both. Bookshelves out of unpainted chipboard, crammed to overflowing with technical manuals and the like, spilt their unruly contents without ceremony on to the desktops they adjoined. An air conditioner whirred.

The paintwork on walls and ceiling was uniform, and of the blandest beige. Hanging on the walls were certificates in plain frames out of cheap moulding, informing all who could be bothered to look that this small business had been the recipient of industry awards. An 'antique' clock – a flagrant fake running on batteries – hung amongst them, ticking purely for effect. Behind Harry was a whiteboard flaunting diagrams of electronic circuitry and related jottings. A heading, scrawled at the top, read 'THE NERD CENTRE'.

Are you aware of this process while it is happening? asked Harry.

... after Sticks had made her pitch ...

Not consciously, said Sticks.

It decides to happen of its own volition?

Look, I find it hard to believe anything out of the ordinary is happening. I'd hazard a guess it's been happening to me right from the moment I first drew breath. For some time I assumed it happened like this for everybody.

I wish.

Ramon burst in through the front door, brandishing a sheaf of papers. When he realized he had intruded upon a private interview, he showed his embarrassment.

I am sorry, he said. Excuse me please.

He started to back out.

What's brewing, Ramon? asked Harry.

Ramon approached again and handed Harry the papers.

Today's dispatches, he said. Do you have the work schedule for tomorrow?

Harry indicated the vacant desk.

On Sonia's desk, he said.

Sonia is not in today? asked Ramon.

There was a look of mild vexation on Harry's face.

So it has transpired, he said.

Ramon rummaged through the papers on Sonia's desk until he found what he was looking for.

Ramon, said Harry.

Yes.

Thank you for taking the helm while I was in court. Much appreciated.

Not even worth mentioning, chief, said Ramon.

Ramon went out the way he had come.

Harry recollected his thoughts, then addressed Sticks again.

Like a tour of the premises? he asked. We can talk as we walk.

They went out the front door as Ramon had just done. Out there, blinded temporarily by merciless sunlight, they took refuge in the partial shade afforded by the shop awning. Here they stood for a while and continued their conversation.

Sticks told Harry her first school – St Maggot's – had pointed her in the direction of language studies when they became aware of her prodigious if not freakish memory skills. Her second school – St Grub's – saw no reason to press for a change of direction. She did not explain to Harry why she had changed schools.

At university, she had studied linguistics with enthusiasm, simultaneously becoming fluent in several Asian and European languages. However, she was having second thoughts about taking on a Master's degree.

Why's that? asked Harry.

It's not the real world in that rarefied precinct, she said. It's so incestuous. A sheltered workshop, and not even able to function properly in *that* modest capacity, but pretending nevertheless to be a repository of everything worth knowing. It's populated in the main by male academic sleazebags who've never known the outside of an educational institution and can't control their big dicks. If you're a woman, they want to get into your pants. If you're pretty, and a man, half the time too. To be honest, I've had it up to *here*.

She indicated 'up to where' with her hand.

These are gutsy accusations …

Fully justified, I assure you.

… and they sound like gross generalisations.

There's nothing so gross or so general as those sleazebags.

You don't feel you're overstating the case?

Have you ever been there?

Yes.

Sticks, never one to admit defeat in an argument, changed the subject.

Is Matt gay? she asked.

How should I know? said Harry.

Give me a break, she said. How could you *not* know? You've been friends for yonks.

He's very secretive.

And you're not very perceptive.

He's never made a pass at *me*.

Means nothing. Gays learn to pick their targets very carefully.
It's all about survival.

I'm not a promising target?

You think you are?

Harry let the ambiguity ride. *He* changed the subject.

When do you need to make up your mind? he asked.

About what?

Your Master's degree.

In about three months.

Well, said Harry, that's not a problem. We can put you on a
three-month trial. God knows, we need your talents.

Deciding it was time to run the sun's gauntlet, they headed off
in the direction of the former clearinghouse …

… which, in their company, we visited earlier, pademelons. We
need not go there again.

>

They were back in the Nerd Centre, suitably exhilarated by the
stunning performance they had seen under the Big Top, a.k.a. the
production facility of Integrated Electronic Imagery.

Harry drew the Holland blind on the west facing window
because the awning outside gave no protection to the office and
its occupants when the sun's rays were on such a slant. Though
lower in the sky, the sun had lost none of its ferocity.

We'll put you out the back with Ronnie, said Harry (pointing),
where you'll get plenty …

Who's Ronnie? asked Sticks.

… of peace and quiet. Ronnie Dash.

Who's Ronnie Dash?

Oh, he's harmless. It's changed a lot back there since you last
saw it. These days you could say it's given over to R & D, provided
you stretched the definition a bit.

What are my duties?

Please. Let's not use that word.

What word should I use?

Harry, assuming the question was rhetorical, chose not to answer it.

We need bulletin boards in a variety of foreign languages, he said. Do you know Malay?

I can learn.

OK. When you've got the basis of a Malay bulletin board, you can supervise its assembly in the Big Top. But I wouldn't want to rush you. Take it one small step at a time.

You'll be available?

What for?

Consultation.

24/7. My time is yours.

He paused, weighing his next words.

Starting tonight, he said. I'd like to take you out to dinner if you're free. Celebrate this moment.

Sticks' stratagem, typically, was to ignore the invitation.

You're aware you have an enemy in your camp? she asked.

What do you mean? asked Harry.

A spy. Somebody who's spilling the beans.

What gave you *that* idea?

Well, how do you imagine the prosecuting counsel got to know the minute details of your operations? Including Matt's involvement. Including Matt's supposed sexual orientation.

I don't know. You tell me.

Think.

I've honestly got no idea.

It should be obvious.

Not to me.

Sticks, relishing the control she had over the drift of the conversation, paused, tilted her head to the left, and shot him a quizzical glance.

For a while there, she said, I lived in an annex at the back of my brothers' business premises.

Positronic Solutions?

My brothers liked the idea because of the extra security a live-in person provided. So I often happened to be there when this little spy came creeping by. To tell *your* secrets to *my* brothers. Mostly after hours.

Who?

Well, who's not here today? Who's too afraid to front?

Sticks paused again, head tilted, looking at him intently, waiting until she was certain the penny had dropped.

Sonia, said Harry.

Sticks nodded, once, twice, three times. Harry felt the sudden freeze of his thought processes, their lurch into panic mode, and finally their scramble for cover. For a skerrick of time the insane idea occurred to him Stick's head might continue nodding until it fell off.

Why ... would she do such a thing? asked Harry.

That's a question *you're* better equipped to answer. I'm merely presenting you with the bald facts.

A long pause followed. The pain and bewilderment Harry felt showed themselves to the immediate world through the medium of his long angular face. Its muscles contracted, drawing the flesh back, emphasizing the stark frame supporting it. Unable to hold hard in this position for any length of time, they convulsed. Salvos of small tics erupted across his mouth and lower jaw.

He spoke with quivering lips.

I guess ... I'll need to fire her.

Won't be necessary, said Sticks. My guess is you've seen the last of her. She didn't come down in the last shower. She knows she's been sprung.

Harry folded his arms on his desk, and buried his head in the pillow they presented. Sticks waited with uncharacteristic patience. In the silence, the ticking of the wall clock sounded – to both of them – like some mutated variety of water torture that had learnt to do without the water. Boom, boom, boom, until …

… Matt burst in with a bottle of *Bisquit*. Sticks rose to her feet and, to Matt's confusion, ushered him out again. The day was almost spent. The sun – fierce alchemist – was transmuting the earth's horizon into liquid gold. Sticks leaned against the half closed door and whispered:

Can this matter wait?

Sonia? asked Matt.

You know?

Of course.

How?

Sticks! Think! The trial?

Sticks nodded almost imperceptibly.

She's one mixed up little vegemite, she said.

It was a bad call on my part, said Matt.

What do you mean?

I recommended Sonia to him.

Sticks touched Matt gently on the shoulder.

Never mind, she said. It backfired on her. Ask yourself: if it *hadn't* happened, would Harry now be in such a favourable position?

She paused, tilted her head, and watched Matt ponder this question.

>

The sun had done its dash for the day, conceding the field to an emergent moon bleeding into low cloud. As if such a change of the celestial guard had been the cue for them, Harry and Sticks appeared outside the Dress Rules showroom. Matt, expecting them, unlocked the heavy glass doors, greeted them with enthusiasm, and led them through. The mannequins were clad in raunchier garb than when Harry had made his first frantic visit to Matt at that other, more desperate time. Raunchy garb, yes, and impertinent manner. Harry imagined they were whispering snidely to each other, perhaps about Sticks' putative need for a comprehensive wardrobe makeover.

Harry hung back morosely. He was still smarting from the revelations Sticks had forced on him apropos of Sonia of the cloak and dagger.

Sticks, by contrast, ran the gauntlet of haughty mannequins with panache, the jut of her chin high. She wore an outfit covering her body from conservative neckline to calf-hugging hemline. Impressed by Matt's creations, and willing to concede their originality, she concluded nevertheless with due respect they were not for her. Matt sensed she was, on this point as on others, not one to be contradicted lightly.

Matt led his guests to his office, where changes were in progress. *Belle Femme Française*, apparently out of favour, had come down, and lay forlornly on its side, wallowing in the ignominy of dereliction, waiting for its trip to some dusty backroom repository for discarded props. A film poster – from '*Prêt-a-Porter*' – hung there in its stead, claiming pride of place behind Matt's desk. This new poster had leggy models revealing a greater expanse of bare skin than of fabric. The prostrate *Femme* with the peacock headdress and stiletto fingers would never have approved.

This substitution drew comment from Harry, despite his inclination to taciturnity.

Why the change? he asked.

… pointing to the 'before' and 'after' posters …

To stay on top of the game, boyo, said Matt. To stay on top of the game. So I won't end up out on the street with my begging bowl.

Harry looked unconvinced. Matt – a raw nerve tweaked – forgot to invite his guests to sit. His harangue was heated:

This is the *fashion* industry. It's not like the electronic widgetry you lot are playing with. This trade doesn't obey the laws of physics. Fickle? You've no idea, boyo. It's as fickle as all get-out. My clients these days demand a touch of the risqué when they strut their stuff in the glare of their fucked-up social milieu. Believe me, a more unforgiving milieu you'd crawl to Bourke and back on broken glass to find. I fancied I saw the latest trend coming months ago before even the clients had an inkling, and I was right. That's the sort of foresight I need to have if I want to stick around in this game long enough to draw my next breath.

What's the next trend going to be? asked Sticks.

Ask the oracle, said Matt. I have no idea as of now. But, make no mistake, I *will* be around to claim first option when the goddess of fashion decides to make her play. Then you watch me shift my arse.

>

Later that evening, it was candlelight and *Bisquit* for three in a smart restaurant off Echo Lane near Matt's showroom. Harry brightened up after an interval, especially as this interval included good food, a few cognacs thrown back, and the embrace of an ameliorative ambience. *Off* the agenda for everybody were Sonia and her antics, and *on* it were a clutch of bright plans. After Harry and Sticks had laid theirs on the table, it turned out Matt had some too. Upon finishing their *crème brûlée*, and as they relaxed into their third or fourth cognac, Matt opened up.

I'm off to Russia in a couple of months, he said. When the apparatchiks pull the finger out and organize a frigging visa for me.

He was going north, to the little known city of Petrozavodsk. At present, here in the southern half of the globe, it was early summer. Add two months and early spring could be expected to greet him there, bringing with it serious cold, including unthawed ice in the sub-Arctic rivers and lakes. To keep his ears warm, he would find it necessary, in accordance with the perennial joke, to 'wear the fox hat'.

... you *do* know the joke, of course, pademelons. Everybody does. 'Petrozavodsk? Wear the fox hat?' ...

His mission was to bring back live models which, for that neck of the woods, is apt to conjure up expectations of golden-haired Nordic princesses with thighs reaching all the way to heaven. Harry, of course, put in a request for one.

Matt, in inimitable fashion, seemed to have it organized. He claimed to have contacts in Petrozavodsk (the supply side) and here in Oz (the demand side). The Oz 'contacts' proved to be one contact only, but potentially a very useful one: a colleague by the name of Penelope Galatano, who had recently launched a fashion display house, including catwalk, in the refurbished Wintergarden building round the corner in Lyceum Street. Matt could envisage having his creations draped to great effect around real live female bodies imbued with erotic grace and charged with voluptuous motion.

Who will look after your business while you're gone? asked Sticks.

He explained the responsibility for this would devolve to Penny and Mark, then went on to explain Mark was his occasional fashion photographer, a Taswegian[31] who had arrived on mainland shores a couple of years back fresh from a course in cinematography. Jobs in film and television were thin on the ground, so he had had to settle for any crumbs he could find. Matt was convinced Mark had a flair for composition of still subjects like dressed-up mannequins, a flair he expected would transfer well to Dress Rules' new regime involving live models.

Matt was having trouble with his sibilants by now, so his next statement was a challenge.

---

31 Taswegian: colloquialism, meaning 'citizen of Tasmania'.

No worries, he said. I'm leaving my business in the very best of hands.

So, as the alcohol-fuelled evening drew to an incoherent close, these eager exponents of the entrepreneurial ethic (of whom it might loosely be said one was born to it, one had strived to achieve it, and one had had it thrust upon him) considered they had anticipated all problems conceivably arising in a well augured future.

Had they not laid their plans out for all eyes as if literally on the starched and food-stained tablecloth lying crumpled before them? Had even one plan – when put to the test – been found wanting, in any respect? What else needed doing by this starry-eyed trio except ride their snow-white steeds with confidence into a dawn full of promise in order to corral those elusive but biddable rewards theirs by right?

Pademelons, it was never going to work out like that, not for any one of these hopeful yet naive souls. But perhaps it is too early yet to weep for them.

And Matt's photographer? Mark, alias Snapper, was – need I mention – me, your narrator, condemned in this dismal role to fumble about in a timeless realm unseen and unseeable by the inhabitants of the mortal and time-spun world.

<

I cannot begin to impress on you, pademelons, the extent of my adverse feelings when Matt first told me he was going to Russia to bring back live models. Frankly, I was horrified, and I see the same horror spreading across *your* usually genial marsupial features. Russia: a place where government-sanctioned corruption is part and parcel of the standard operating procedure for transacting any business deal. Russia: a place where bureaucratic heavy-handedness pummels the b'Jesus out of the legitimate hopes and expectations of foreign operatives. Russia: a place where what one is buying into is never what one *thinks* one is buying into.

Oh, Matt, was my passionate cry, think again for the sake of my gormless granny. Can't you make do with live models of the *local* variety, of which there is an abundance?

Matt didn't listen. He was thralled by the artist's vision of his creations wrapped around the vivified flesh of imagined Russian beauties, and he would not settle for less than this perceived ideal.

2nd >>

It is turbulent times on the turntable stage. Sticks is to make her directorial debut. Harry – predictably – is not ready to surrender power quietly. It is war. Interrogation is his weapon of choice.

Are you prepared, he asks, to let us in on your grubby little secrets?

No more than *you* were, she says, when they were *your* grubby little secrets.

Why be so difficult?

Call it revenge.

How can I stage manage this *Stück* when I don't know what it's about?

You'll find out on a 'need to know' basis.

On that basis, what will you deign to tell me right now?

What I've already told you.

Which is?

Sticks' hands-on-hips stance is aggressive.

This *Stück* is about how I came by my nickname, she says.

Sticks?

Sticks.

How *did* you come by it?

You don't need to know that yet.

Harry's exasperation has reached a tipping point. So he topples a lectern, one of the stage props intended for the next *Stück*.

Fuck you! he shouts. Take control out of my hands when this is supposed to be about *my* life. Incite my crew to mutiny. Tell me nothing worth knowing. Flip the storyline backwards in time the best part of a decade, muck up the whole frigging chronology I've been at pains …

Sticks can match his histrionics. She removes the crinoline hat from her head, and slams it down hard on his. The point of his scalp splits the crown of the hat, and its brim is left sitting forlornly on the bridge of his nose, a significant impediment to his vision.

You into chronology? asks Sticks.

Yes, says Harry. Chronology. No apologies. Chronology with a capital C.

Well I know a place with a capital A where you can shove it.

Harry plucks the wreckage of the hat from his face, flings it to the floor, stamps about like a madman, and looks around for another stage prop to topple. There are none.

Fuck you! he shouts again.

If you intend, says Sticks, to precipitate a walkout by the crew, you're going about it the right way.

Matt, Sonia, and Elena – also on stage – look on with varying degrees of bewilderment and disappointment at this display from their fractious principals. Izzie looks similarly bemused from the vantage point of his synthesizer behind the turntable. He is hammering out a cheeky march tune, destined we presume for use in the next *Stück*, assuming such is going to happen.

I should explain why Sticks was wearing a crinoline hat. Wearing it – that is to say – before she chose to use it to add some vigour to the point she was making. This hat was part of the St Margaret's uniform, as prescribed by the venerable school board two decades ago or thereabouts. Sticks, who will have an important on-stage role in this next *Stück*, has been decked out like the St Maggot's schoolgirl she was at that time, then in her mid teens, a time when the only name she answered to was Annalise.

Pademelons. Hark back to those exciting times when we observed the fabric of the world from on high. Perched on electric wires. Pretending to be birds.

Recall the uniform worn reluctantly by Annalise, young rebel that she was. It consisted of tartan skirt in rust tones, plain white blouse, broad-brimmed crinoline hat, and thick stockings in a pink tone. That is how Sticks is dressed now. *Sans* the hat, lying torn and crumpled at her feet.

This is not the whole story of Sticks' get-out. There is more. She has been given a radical 'Sleek Street makeover'. Decades have been stripped from her appearance, courtesy of Matt and his skills in the art that conceals art.

A dozen or so female actors emerge from the backstage dressing rooms. They huddle together on the turntable to await orders. They wear the same uniform as Sticks, and have had the same makeover. They are Sandalwood people, and Sticks intends they will represent on stage the more mature students of the St Maggot's sorority, the repository of much of the school's prestige.

One of them is *not* dressed as a schoolgirl, and Matt has not bothered to tamper with her age. She is an elderly woman intended to represent an elderly woman. Dowdy and dumpy, with arthritic joints, with unflattering folds around her neck and chin, and with strict notions in her head re the husbandry of minors, she is done out in a conservative manner such as might get the nod of approval from the administration of a school like St Margaret's with lofty pretensions to uphold.

For example, she has drab skirts down to her ankles, clunky patent leather shoes, fading hair bleached to a sickly honeycomb colour, and a bosom-full of frilly lace. This person shall, at Sticks' behest, depict the redoubtable, the one-and-only 'Mrs Wintergreen', of whom we shall find out more anon.

Sticks has not finished battle with her recalcitrant stage

manager. She continues to harangue him forcefully. The huddled women, including the woman playing Agnes Wintergreen, find themselves caught in the crossfire. What have we blundered into? they must be thinking. Bewildered, they look for direction from the rest of the crew. They do not find it.

You should not need reminding, pal, so goes Sticks' harangue, that after a recent bunfight posing as one of your *Stücke*, you were forced, kicking and screaming, to allow we should *all* be given the chance to present events in *our* lives, including events in our formative years, even if that means upsetting your precious chronology.

She pauses for breath.

That means me ... , she says,

(thumping her chest)

... or Matt ...

(stabbing the air)

... or Sonia ...

(stabbing the air)

... or Elena ...

(stabbing the air)

... or ...

No! says Elena.

Her protestation is loud, assertive, and unexpected. It startles everybody. She repeats it.

No!

All game plans are off. All space, tenanted or capable of being tenanted, has been taken hostage. Pairs of eyes *en masse* focus on Elena. Even Izzie's. He has stopped playing mid-bar.

Pozháluista. Éta nye hochú[32], says Elena. I don't never want to.

Time, breathless, holds itself in abeyance.

Elena's shoulders slump. Her knees bend. Tears well up behind rampant lids. Through the flood of moisture, swimming eyes plead for mercy.

---

32 *Pozháluista. Éta nye hochú.*: Please. I don't want this.

Sticks, shocked by the turn of events, races to her side.

Darling, she says, I never meant it was compulsory. It's your choice, and your choice alone, whether …

Elena repels Sticks' advances. She dashes offstage, heading towards the doors to front-of-house, beyond which she evidently hopes for sanctuary in her lighting box. Nobody follows her. Nobody has been expecting this. All people onstage freeze in a state of bewilderment. In response to the drama foisted on them with the shock and finality of a train wreck, the crew look from one to the other, wondering whether they should be flashing accusatory glances or fending them off.

Matt steps forward.

Let's call it a day, he says.

>

Elena – traumatized by demons inside her head – lurches into the lighting box, slams the door behind her, rams the latch shut, slumps heavily into her swivel chair, sweeps equipment aside willy-nilly, makes a pillow out of her arms, and buries her head in its soft folds.

The state-of-the-art lighting box to which she has fled resembles the cockpit of a Boeing, given its broad 'windscreen' opening on to a pilot's eye view of the wide curve of the world. Or, in this instance, the light technician's view of the turntable stage. Through it, the Sandalwood people are seen to have retreated to the dressing rooms. The crew are sitting – disconsolate and silent – on the edge of the turntable, hands supporting chins.

Pademelons. We have looked down before from the inside of a lighting box onto my demoralized and dejected second unit, flaunting their mental strife on stage. Looked down, while we kept company with this same Elena, beset (then as now) with an excess of unresolved emotion. Is this *déjà vu*, or is this *déjà vu*?

Inside *this* lighting box, a broad flat bench follows the curve of the 'windscreen'. Upon this bench Elena's bedevilled head – cushioned in the fold of her arms – rests amidst a dazzling array of state-of-the-art equipment, none of it (ironically) in any way sensitive to her current plight.

There are mixer panels, dimmer panels, control panels, banks of fuses, banks of switches, banks of dial knobs, and even some small CCTV screens. Much of it is back-lit, so as to minimally disturb those on stage spinning dreams and those in the audience wearing them. To the left of this equipment is a jumble of scripts, manuals, and spare parts. To the right, in spiral binding, is a single script, the one in current use we presume, open at page one, annotated appropriately, and illuminated by the impersonal blue of an LED lamp. Recessed into the ceiling, is a more diffuse light: soft, warm, friendly, discreet, and kind to the optic nerve.

To Elena, even this light scalds. She shields her moist eyes from it, seeing only darkness. In such darkness she hopes for safety. But the eye of the *mind* is apt to see more than bland darkness, because it shepherds all ambient thought processes in the direction of ... memories? ... visions? ... dreams? ... nightmares? ... imaginings? ... and then projects such horrors ruthlessly onto the darkness – the darkness Elena believed was safe – as if onto some everyday servile screen.

She trawls her mind for a word. A particular word, an ugly foreign word Sticks has taught her recently ... ? ... ?

Stücke!

That's the word.

Stücke!

It is *Stücke* Elena sees flitting uninvited across her mantle of darkness. These are home-grown *Stücke*, playing themselves back to her in the idiom of her native language and culture. Each *Stück* has montage as sharp as a paper cut, colour as bold as a monkey's bum, sound as strident as a gazillion simultaneous cicadas, and three robust dimensions with the collective impregnability of a vault. To Elena's way of thinking, inflamed though her synapses are at this moment, these are djinn that should *never* have been let out of the bottle. And *never never* should they be played out on Harry's stage.

But, zounds, they *shall* play out on *our* supernal stage. Here is their gist:

Stück the First: – hybrid family – gross dysfunction – systematic abuse – violent alcoholic orgies – curse of having been born female – curse of having been born at all – thrust out into numbing cold – twenty below zero – scavenging for food – fighting others for limited shelter – clothing in tatters – footwear *sans* soles – bronchitis – pleurisy – chilblains – frostbite – icicles dangling from eaves – blood-spotted phlegm – red blotches in snow – longing for death –

Stück the Second: – this all-too-friendly stranger – treachery of his friendship – inducted into wrong crowd – ship on frozen lake – Jolly Roger aloft – survival through slavery – rough trade – many more strangers – in bed with them – in bed with strangers sleaze and degradation – boredom of perpetual personal violation – *moy khozyáin*[33] giving orders – evil so banal – longing for death –

Stück the Third: – relocation to strange country – Oz by name – fear of unknown – never trust no-one – keep low profile – spies for Immigration Police are abroad – play dumb – plead inability to understand language – '*ya nye panimáyu po-anglíski*' – but *podozhdítye!* – need for rethink – realization of certain fate of witless beauty – possibility of Michelangelo all over again – hovering arm of sexual slavery – double take – about face – **WRONG WAY GO BACK!** –

Stück the Fourth: – learn English – learn it fast – hope it's not too late – be smart not dumb – dumb is not never smart – know thine enemy – Sal is his name – learn his criminal trade – I am pupil – he is mentor – practice his trade – practice makes perfect –

---

33 *moy khozyáin*: my master; *ya nye panimáyu po-anglíski*: I don't under-stand English; *podozhdítye!*: wait!

become better at his trade than he is – take control of his squalid game – be power behind throne – tell Michelangelo to go bite his bum – walk tightrope – walk it lightly – don't never look down – *Bórzhe moy!* – not never –

Elena, instantly alert, sits upright. For a moment, she has the impression she is in endless free fall.

Then she realizes her uninvited reverie, despite the tenacity of its hold on her, has been penetrated irrevocably and without warning. Penetrated by a deafening crash from downstairs, from front-of-house.

The taste of bitter almond – hemlock of loathsome reminiscence – has fled from Elena's palate. The flavour of the real and present – as coarse as camel's shit – has taken its place, without compunction or gentility of manner. And who among us, pademelons, would predict her circumstances will have shown improvement thereby?

Prediction? Let us have done with prediction. It is a fool's game. Let us follow her downstairs and like her come face to face with certainty.

>

Harry and his crew, licking their wounds on the edge of the turntable, hear the crash also. It being the species of crash that may only be ignored at peril, they leap as one to their feet, as if a puppet-master has jerked their strings. Sticks is first out the door to front-of-house. She is amazed by what she sees.

The front door, snapped clean off its hinges, lies flat on the Baltic pine floor. Two uniformed male police-persons – one lanky, one burly – have stepped over it. The burly one nurses a painful shoulder.

Law enforcement is caught off guard by the sight of Sticks dressed as a schoolgirl. But the Keystone duo quickly put appearances back in their place, retreating to the safety of their regular and rehearsed routine. They are ready as always to play it by the book.

Where is she? asks the lanky cop.

Who? asks Sticks.

The lanky cop consults a notebook.

Élena, he says. (He mispronounces, in accordance with common practice, putting stress on the first syllable.)

Sticks steals a swift glance upwards and catches the eye of Elena, cowering at the top of the spiral staircase leading to the lighting box. Just as swiftly, Sticks lowers her gaze, hoping the law enforcers will not have noticed the furtive swoop of her eyeballs.

There's nobody by that name here, she says. Please come through and talk to my colleagues.

As she leads them through to the performance arena, she catches a glimpse – out of the corner of her eye – of Elena making her escape through the gaping hole where the front door had been.

There was no need to break down the door, says Sticks. It was open.

We go by the manual, says the burly cop. Appendix Four. The paragraph on gaining entry to premises.

Sticks and the two cops halt at the back of stalls. The rest of the crew, incredulous, gather round.

Do we know anybody here by the name of Eleanor? asks Sticks.

We hear a chorus of 'No' from the crew, accompanied by head shaking. The lanky cop consults his notebook again.

Her full name, says the lanky cop, is Él ... en ... ah. Pét ...

The burly cop is speaking with satisfaction over a walkie-talkie retrieved from his belt.

... gained entry to the premises, says the burly cop, but are still to make ourselves known to the person of interest.

... ro ... vich. Rus ... al ... kóvah[34].

Do you think they mean Eléna? asks Sticks of the crew.

---

34 The stem of the family name, Rusalkóva, is *rusálka* which, in Russian, means 'mermaid'.

Where would she be? asks the burly cop.

Last time I saw her, says Sticks, she was in the lighting box.

Where's that?

Sticks points back they way they had come.

Out there, to the left and up the stairs.

As of one mind, the two cops race back through the door to front-of-house. The crew stand aghast, not able to believe Sticks has betrayed Elena. She reassures them.

She's well away, says Sticks.

Will she be back? asks Harry.

Not any time soon, if she's got the sense God gave a goat.

<< 1st

Sticks stood behind the desk, formerly Sonia's, covering the telephone mouthpiece with her hand. The expression on her face was a mix of incredulity and amusement.

You'd never guess who this is, she said.

Who? asked Harry.

Malaysia calling.

Who in Malaysia?

The Sultan of Kick My Arse Around.

Who?

Some long word starting with K I didn't catch.

A Sultan?

The Sultan of K.

What does he want?

Speak to him.

Sticks held the handpiece at arm's length. Harry came from behind his desk to take it.

Harry McMinn speaking, he said.

For the next five minutes or so, all Sticks could hear was the occasional 'Mmm' from Harry punctuating long and steady silences. Then, to Sticks' annoyance, the phone on Harry's desk rang. While Sticks was busy tending to this call, she lost track of the conversation between Harry and the Sultan. She *did* manage at one stage to hear Harry utter the words 'technical expert' but didn't catch the context.

By the time Sticks had concluded her call, Harry was in the process of winding up his.

Can I get back to you ... Excellency?

There was a short silence.

Yes, Your Excellency. End of week at the latest.

Harry, muttering numbers under his breath, scribbled something down on a slip of paper, before reading the whole thing back to the Sultan. There was another brief pause, after which:

Thank you, Your Excellency. *Selemat tinggal.*

... indicating, pademelons, that Harry – to his credit – had been consulting his phrasebook ...

Harry passed the handpiece back to Sticks who returned it to its cradle.

Is 'Excellency' the correct form of address for a Sultan? asked Harry.

I'm sure it will do, said Sticks. What did he want?

You'll never guess.

>

This is what Harry told Sticks the Sultan of K had said he wanted.

The Sultan wanted Harry to make a virtual reality system for the amusement of his nephew and heir apparent. He had seen the bulletin boards Integrated Electronic Imagery had installed, in airports and the like all around Malaysia and was royally impressed.

Harry had, of course, broached the subject of a virtual reality system before: in the public domain and on more than one occasion. Remember, pademelons, when he aired the concept in the district courtroom, making an impression on the learned judge in the process. 'I have a dream,' is what he might have said in such moments. They were rosy moments so redolent of promise, but *sans* the disquieting prospect of firm demands on him.

Now, when pressed by this Sultan to deliver on the *substance* of his dream, he felt a chill in his feet and a weakness in his knees. For a congenitally tentative person like Harry, the suggestion he should take a virtual reality system all the way through to the done-and-dusted stage was a tad outside his comfort zone. Better off left as a dream, he thought.

So, bringing delaying tactics to bear, he had told His Excellency over the phone he needed to consult with technical experts before making a decision.

When Sticks finally coaxed the truth out of Harry, she was ropable.

You bloody fool! she said. With this sort of thing, you say 'Yes' first, and call in technical experts afterwards. Get back on the phone this instant and say loud and clear to His Excellency ... listen to me and don't dare get it wrong ... 'I - can - do.'

Harry hesitated. Hesitation was a mistake. Sticks thumped the desk so hard the objects on it bounced. She bellowed.

Like me to spell it?!

Harry made the call. Then and there. The upshot was, after the expected ritual of petty to-ing and fro-ing, he entered into a verbal contract to make a virtual reality system for the Sultan's nephew. A contract into which he felt he had been stampeded. A contract on which, left to his own devices, he was not likely to have signed off. A contract whose path from dream to fulfilment he found difficult to envisage.

Why, he mused at the time, should reality be allowed to spoil a perfectly good fantasy?

>

Pademelons. I am about to indulge one of *my* fabulous fantasies. It places you all in the cabin of a Boeing, accompanying Harry and Sticks on one of the many flights they made around this time from their home country to the Federation of Malaysia.

I hold a wonderful picture of you in my imaginings, pademelons. I see you taking up all available cattle-class seats in the aircraft, except for those occupied by our two human passengers. I see bobbing macropod heads shedding fine fur on customized antimacassars in row upon row of identical seats; alert macropod bodies belted up and ready for the adventure of this high altitude hoppity skip; muscular macropod tails folded neatly beneath macropod haunches or dangling carelessly into aisles bristling with the bluster of the flight crew; furry macropod paws clutching at complimentary vodkas or stabbing the button for refills; pricked macropod ears listening to the safety drill or to the captain's cheery messages or maybe just to the mournful whine of the jet stream; glazed macropod eyes vaguely following the formulaic plot of the in-flight movie and occasionally getting waylaid by the waggling behinds of pretty Asian hostesses heaving trolleys laden with candied nuts and the like ...

I see you at your destination, scurrying after Harry and Sticks as they negotiate the formalities of customs and immigration; straining your marsupial necks to see to the top of the gigantic photographic image of an unctuous and corrupt Prime Minister welcoming to his country all-comers prepared to toe his autocratic line; emptying out the contents of your congenitally front-slung pouches for the benefit of surly officialdom; struggling at passport desks way too high for the vertically-challenged and certainly so for pademelons; facing off – eye to beady eye – with sniffer dogs who are itching for a game with such sport as you; surfing the wobbly suitcases on the carousel on the pretext of pursuing your checked bags before they fall into the hands of thieves, gypsies, drug-mules, or whatever; wincing at the sharp pain of a tail snarled in the wheels of a wayward baggage trolley; trying pathetically to hail a taxi with a paw-in-mouth whistle not coming naturally to members of your breed ...

(I warm to this game, pademelons. I am inclined to continue with it for a tad longer. Accordingly, I beg your indulgence. I shall have you, at your pleasure, tagging along behind Harry and Sticks as they enter the precincts of the royal palace of the Sultan of K.)

I see each of you playing the role and striking the pose of uninvited guest of His Excellency the Sultan of K, whose full title consists not of a single letter K but of ten to twelve consecutive and difficult-to-pronounce names variously of Malay and Arabic origin. I see you slinking surreptitiously behind Harry and Sticks, marvelling at the grandeur of the palace. I see the awe in your rust-red eyes as you take in the sight of the expensive gifts lavished upon the Sultanate by wealthy sycophants – each gift received with gratitude from whatever tin-pot potentate happened to be appropriating for venal purposes whatever festering corner of the globe he inhabited – each gift duly acknowledged and then labelled according to the protocols of the office of the Sultanate – each gift groaning under the weight of lashings of gold and jewels – each gift meticulously stored away in its individual security-alarmed glass case. I see you coming to grips with the Islamic austerity of the majority of the rooms, eschewing any form of adornment involving images of humans or of animals (including pademelons), such strategy being seen by adherents of the Prophet as a disincentive to the temptations of idolatry. I see you trying to reconcile this systemic austerity with the excessive prodigality of the high-tech 'entertainment centre', the domain of choice of the Sultan's nephew, who is Baharudin by name, spoilt by nature, Oxbridge by education, and amiable by predilection. I see you socializing with this heir apparent, and on occasion with the Sultan himself, over a glass of iced lime-juice and a game of checkers, a game at which pademelons (though it may surprise many) can always be expected to excel ...

>

These are my father's plantations, said Baharudin. His comment went unremarked, but not unnoticed.

From horizon to horizon, Harry and Sticks saw nothing but a monotony of lush greenery covering an ocean of gentle hills and valleys. It was the greenery of plantation, not of rainforest. The latter, in all its natural glory, had long gone. Replacing it, after aeons of its predominance in the natural scheme of things, was row upon row of equi-spaced palms compliant with human intentions of mixed merit at best. The trunks of these palms – dead straight and bearded with epiphytes – had the scaly texture and the organic colour of crocodile skin. The droopy fronds atop each trunk adhered determinedly to an impressive symmetry, insofar as (collectively) their tips traced out an envelope the shape of a near-perfect sphere. These fronds were dense enough to hide beneath their collective skirt any manner of evil.

Evil? Hold that word. Taken – as is my intention here – in its idiomatic context, the word is not to be feared. But strip away the idiom, leaving the word naked and exposed, and that same word carries with it a powerful condemnation. In the minds of those not inclined to flexibility or compromise on matters relating to the protection of the natural environment, the fruit of this tree was indeed the embodiment of evil.

Evil or no, everything about the plantations seemed designed to pander to the aesthetics of people who liked things to be neat and tidy. Accountants, one might imagine. Certainly this was a cash crop to invigorate an accountant's soul. The product was palm oil.

They could see plantations out the side windows, and (turning their heads) out the back window, and (looking over the head and shoulders of the chrome lady on the verge of taking flight) out the front window. Palm oil plants were everywhere the eye could impel its gaze.

Embraced by flounces of leather, and waves of conditioned air, Harry and Sticks rode in the back seat of a Rolls Royce. Baharudin, in the front passenger seat, had swivelled his body so he could face his foreign guests. Presenting themselves to Harry and Sticks from between the two front head-rests were dancing brown eyes, perfect white teeth, and a well-trimmed goatee beard. These amiable features complemented a face wearing a practiced smile, a face both youthful and handsome, a face resident beneath the golden tones of a royal songkok.

This was the context in which Baharudin, golden boy, made his unremarked, but not unnoticed comment: 'These are my father's plantations.'

A chauffeur was driving, the back of his head visible to the back-seat passengers. He wore a more plebeian songkok, in black.

The Rolls purred sedately along a two-lane sealed road with minimal traffic. Occasionally it would pass a beat-up open-tray truck chugging along geriatrically in the opposite direction. Invariably the piston rings of this vehicle were in serious need of attention. It was loaded to the gunnels with tonnes of a bizarre botanical excrescence, each in size like a soccer ball but in appearance like a compote of blood-shot eyeballs.

Palm oil fruit, said Baharudin. Ready for crushing.

Who is your father? asked Sticks.

Baharudin winked.

The man who laid down with my mother, he said.

I mean, how does he fit into the scheme of things?

He doesn't. He is not approved of. He is a black sheep.

If it's not a personal question, asked Harry, how come you're the heir given you're not in the Sultan's direct line?

Of course it is a personal question, but not one I am afraid to answer. It is simple. My uncle has six wives. But no sons. Not even daughters.

He gave a wry smile.

My uncle fires blanks, he said.

A village appeared on the horizon in front of them, looming larger and larger, until it became apparent the road they were on would pass through its centre. Baharudin and the driver exchanged a few words in Malay. Then Baharudin turned his attention once more to the back-seat passengers.

We shall pause here, said Bahurudin. Hussein must pray.

Turning a corner, they were suddenly exposed to that sensual ambush characterizing and comprising a South East Asian village. Goats, chickens, bare-bottomed urchins, laden two-stroke bicycles and tricars, men in traditional dress, women in burquas, dust, flies, fumes: all of this scattered before them as if caught up in a willy willy[35]. The unmistakable stench of durian assaulted nasal membranes with a ripe feculency. Loudspeakers from on high carried the imam's acoustically distorted message, the ubiquitous call to prayer. Fingernails across fly-wire would have been more soothing to the ear.

Hussein parked the Rolls in the main street, outside the local mosque. As was customary, its minarets housed the scratchy loudspeakers. The chaotic produce-market opposite was the undoubted source of the durians. Curious locals gaped as Hussein emerged from the driver's seat and made for the mosque. If to them the vehicle was incongruous, then Hussein – in everyday samping and songkok – blended in perfectly.

With Hussein swallowed up by the mosque, and his three passengers insulated from the sounds, smells, and dust of the village (but not from the gawks of the villagers), Sticks felt free to ask her next question.

You don't feel the need to pray? she asked.

No, said Baharudin.

Aware Sticks expected more from him than a blunt monosyllable, he continued expansively.

I'm content for the moment to lead the life of Riley, he said, and this much my uncle tolerates. Even encourages, I believe.

---

35 willy willy: colloquial Australian, meaning small whirlwind.

But we are both aware the time is fast approaching when I shall be required, God willing, to show more circumspection in my behaviour. A time for setting an example to my subjects. That will be my moment for prayer.

Baharudin gave a sharp nod, and another wry smile. Then, feeling perhaps he might have spilled a tad too many beans, he turned to face the front windscreen, contemplating in silence the Spirit of Ecstasy as she prepared to launch herself from the bonnet. Perhaps he was wondering what, according to protocol, he might and might not say to these *balanda*.

Hussein back behind the wheel, they left the turmoil of the village in their wake. The landscape, till now dominated by the plantations, increasingly tolerated an admixture of something a little more wild, the vestiges of original rainforest. Baharudin's purpose – to show his visitors something of the natural beauty of the untrammelled Malay countryside – was about to be realized.

In mid afternoon, the Rolls pulled up at what – decades later – would come to assume the euphemistic sobriquet of 'eco-resort'. It nestled on the edge of the rainforest beside a swiftly flowing brown river. Darters and hornbills spread their wings high in the resident ironwood trees and strangler vines. Sharing this habitat, silver-tailed monkeys bided their time, waiting for unguarded human leavings below. The shrill cries of gibbons could be heard slicing the still air from the depths of distant jungle.

Flunkies, in exaggerated – and mostly fake – traditional costume, appeared from everywhere, eager to bow and scrape before the young heir to the Sultanate and his guests. While Hussein fished around in the boot, Baharudin, Harry, and Sticks were lead to a private *al fresco* table some distance from where the paying guests, mostly well-heeled Westerners, were enjoying drinks. For the first time that day, Baharudin's visitors were treated to a full view of his frame from royal head to royal toe as he strutted his regalia unselfconsciously. He wore light shirt, loose leggings, samping, and songkok, all in different shades of gold. With leather shoes, black and hand-crafted.

Harry and Sticks were struck by Baharudin's composure as, with no evident hassle but with lashings of nonchalance, he accepted the services of the flunkies as if they were as much a part of his entitlement as the contingency of birds, monkeys, and the muddy wash of the river itself.

When all were seated, the multi-skilled Hussein appeared, flanked by yet more flunkies bearing the makings of a picnic: several giant Thermoses from China, a couple of stainless-steel Eskies from Oz, and a wicker basket rattling with utensils. The utensils turned out to be genuine Delft crockery, fine Riedel glassware, and solid silver cutlery of a traditional pattern harking from the early part of the 20th century.

Hussein served up cucumber sandwiches out of white bread cut into small triangles, delicate English cakes barely larger than bite-size, Jacob's biscuits direct from Fortnum and Mason, figs from Jordan, pomegranates from Uzbekistan, juice from local limes, and individual pots of Twinning's tea. When he had finished serving, Hussein retreated discreetly to a suitable distance where, squatting with his back to a dipterocarp tree, he proceeded to consume a bowl of spicy noodles using plastic chopsticks.

At table, Baharudin – munching enthusiastically on a cucumber sandwich – was first to find voice.

I should like to visit you in Australia, he said.

A moment of uncertainty followed.

I am in earnest, said Baharudin. I have discussed the matter with my uncle.

Harry, in confusion as to how the heir to a Sultanate might be billeted, responded tentatively.

You would be most welcome, he said.

Baharudin smiled, having guessed the reason for Harry's embarrassment.

He is of the opinion, said Baharudin, I should be present to commission the virtual reality system. He believes I, as future Sultan, God willing, should embrace every opportunity to position myself in the international arena.

Your uncle is a wise man, said Sticks. We will be honoured to have you.

Baharudin nodded deferentially in her direction.

It shall be *my* pleasure, he said.

Some moments of casual conversation, ranging over a number of inconsequential subjects, followed as they investigated the sweet treats in front of them. Sticks waited for the opportune moment to venture another searching question. She found it.

Do you still see your father? she asked

Of course I do, replied Baharudin. He is part of me. One cannot deny one's blood. To put him out of my life would be an unnatural act on my part.

A matter of filial loyalty, said Sticks.

My father is a trader, said Baharudin, without regard for ethics or legality. He survives because he is a ruthless man and can always pull rank. Nevertheless he is my father.

The shriek of an invisible gibbon pierced the air and the conversation. Baharudin stood up.

We should try to see rainforest while there is light, he said. We shall need a water taxi to cross the river.

Hussein understood. He was already heading off to organize one.

Tinkle and clatter dared to compete with the jungle noises. Subjected to processing by the human brain, these foreign sounds confessed to their domestic associations. It was Sticks gathering up the used dishes. Baharudin extended his hand by way of gentle admonition.

Please, he said. There is no need. Hussein will deal with this matter.

2nd >>

Time courses in the lives of my second unit via the channels in place for those governed by the rules of earth-bound ephemerality. But, on this occasion, time does bring a significant mercy for my co-presenters. The bumptious play-it-by-the-book police do not return. Not after one hour. Not after one day. Not after one week. Would it be too much to assume, pademelons, they will never be seen again?

Instead, it is Elena who stages a return. Five days is all it takes. On the evening appointed by whatever Fates decide such matters, she pokes her head cautiously around the door to the performance arena, gives the assembled crew a wave and a cheery little 'Hi', and proceeds to mingle with them as if nothing had happened. As if the trauma of the circumstances under which she chose to depart had been consumed by its own virulence. To Harry and the crew, she seems none the worse for wear. Careful not to ask her too many questions, they take pains to make her welcome.

Her reappearance leaves the crew with a problem. To allow Elena back in the lighting box as things stand could invite a catastrophic ambush should the premises be raided by police again, given the number of escape routes for her would be limited to one narrow spiral staircase. Elena, as much as anybody, is swayed by the potency of this consideration. So general consent has it Matt should assume responsibility for lighting until there is no earthly possibility of the lighting box coming under siege.

Matt proves himself no slouch in this new role. Nor is Elena a spare part in the safe haven backstage where she now hangs out. She throws herself enthusiastically into her new duties, principally in costuming (as Matt's proxy), but to some extent also (as Sonia's assistant) in choreography.

<< 1st

One day, back in Oz now, Sticks burst through the doors of what was formerly the workshop of what was formerly Unthank Engineering, and stood with hands on hips in the middle of the Nerd Centre looking ready to bite off heads. She proceeded to bark at rather than speak to Harry, the hapless one, trapped behind his desk phone.

Where did you say you unearthed that living national treasure? she asked.

Harry quickly cupped his hand over the mouthpiece, and looked at her with irritation. Seeing she was not about to go away, he decided to wind up his conversation.

Can I get back to you? he said into the mouthpiece. Ronnie, I'm presuming, was what he then said to Sticks as he hung up.

Do you know what that turkey spends his money on? said Sticks.

I'm his employer, not his keeper.

On escort services. Every last cent.

His choice, said Harry.

That's not the whole story, said Sticks. You know what his other hobby is?

You tell me.

Tennis.

Sounds healthy.

Don't you believe it. He frequents a prestigious church tennis club, because that's where he figures he's most likely to find himself a suitable wife. Who, according to his chauvinist demands, must be a virgin.

Harry shrugged.

Don't get it, do you? said Sticks. He fucks prostitutes on a regular basis, but when he deigns to get married, he goes and insists on a virgin bride.

This is not such an unusual story, I believe, said Harry.

It reeks to high heaven. Of hypocrisy.

Harry shrugged.

Wait, said Sticks. There's more. When I asked him if he'd give up prostitutes once he got married, know what his answer was?

No idea.

'Don't see any harm mixing a dash of off-the-shelf in with the home-grown.'

Traces of mild amusement appeared around the corners of Harry's mouth, but the issue was not something Sticks was prepared to find funny.

Oh, I see, she said. Happy to go along with this sort of caper, are we?

Sticks, said Harry, do you think it's possible he might be having a lend of you[36]?

Sticks gaped.

And in any event succeeding, said Harry.

Sticks' hands were, until this moment, anchored firmly, one on each of side of her pelvis. In a flash, they – palms upwards, fingers tensed, in dramatic gesticulation – terrorized the air in front of her.

Well screw you, squire, she said. Excuse me while I go and find some place with a bit of integrity where I can park my butt.

She stormed through the front door, slamming it with a crash as resounding as her physical strength could muster.

2ⁿᵈ >>

Singspielstück #10: The Rebadging of Annalise Unthank

As stage lights wash over the performance space, the person playing Agnes Wintergreen commands the centre of the turntable.

---

36 'having a lend of you': Australian slang, meaning 'having you on', 'taking the piss'.

Her dress and makeover are as described earlier. She stands behind a lectern from which hangs a velvet drape in a tangerine tone designed to blend amiably with the St Margaret's colours as exemplified by the school uniform. The drape bears two logos: the school crest (suitably emblematic), and the identifier of the Lantern Bearers. The latter consists (as we know already) of a hand holding aloft a coach lantern adorned with the intertwined letters **L** and **B**.

Mrs Wintergreen projects her voice, which spurts from her compressed lips as a deep-throated vibrato:

Young women, she says. There are many millstones along the road of life over which it will be your misfortune to trip. I want to talk to you frankly about one of these today. It is self-abuse, otherwise known as masturbation.

The people representing her audience, as it would have been in the early 90s, occupy the two front rows of stalls. They are grown women, actors, representing young women in their late teens, the senior sorority of St Margaret's, dressed in full school uniform as would befit an important extracurricular occasion. One of them – centrally placed – is Sticks, representing Annalise, which is the name by which we are (at present) obliged to call her, it being the only name to which she knew back then – her salad days in retrospect – how to answer.

... the *other* audience hugging the back of the auditorium are those of us, pademelons, who represent nobody, but are merely unseen blow-ins from the timeless spaceless zone we have the misfortune to inhabit, come here for the purpose – gratuitous though it may be – of acquainting ourselves further with the life and many deaths of Harry McMinn, as interpreted – with mixed enthusiasm at present – by my second unit ...

The schoolgirls titter in response to the linguistic barbarism and salacious potential of Mrs Wintergreen's introductory remarks, but the good lady quells such sport to effect with the aid of quivering chins and a fearsome scowl. Thereby she engineers a pause, which gives her time to extract, from the bulging black-leather handbag balancing on the lectern beside her, a pair of spectacles, thick-framed and embellished with floral motifs. She wipes their lenses, then balances them on the bridge of her flabellate nose. She consults her notes, also on the lectern. This done to her satisfaction, she feels able to continue:

Once considered a taboo subject, Mrs W says, we live these days in enlightened times where many such mute points get regularly chewed over. Let me tell you some good news, girls. In one foul swoop, we can put to bed all those old chestnuts doing the proverbial traps in certain circles. I refer to those old chestnuts about masturbation being bad for your health.

Allow me, she says, to put your young minds to rest. Masturbation *does not* leave you infertile. You *will*, one fine day, go forth and multiply in combobulation with an upright husband. Masturbation *does not* send you blind. You will still be able to observe with your very own eyes the full splendour of God's estate as you make your way along its well-honed byways. Masturbation *does not* lower your IQ. If you put in the midnight oil and burn up the hard yards, there will be acolytes in flying colours for all of you. You have my word for that, and I speak from 20/20 hindsight.

Mrs Wintergreen pauses, licks a finger, lowers her eyes, flips through her notes, raises her eyes, and conjures up a menacing look.

However ... , she says.

She pauses with intent to overawe.

However ... , she repeats, ... although a young woman may suffer no *physical* harm when she chooses to abuse herself, there are still some issues – issues of spirit – issues of character – lurking like Joe Blakes among the apples. They can't wait to sink their fangs into the heart of the will and the spirit – those priceless gifts from God – as she, the unwary young woman – ahem – lies pleasuring herself. Don't doubt me girls, masturbation can poison the spirit, the character, and the high esteem in which you hold yourself and in which others hold *you*.

Let me give you an example, Mrs W says.

We, she says, all love our sporting heroes, don't we girls? Heroes *and* heroines. Our admiration for them knows no leaps and bounds. We hold them in the highest possible esteem. Praise be to the Lord, this is how it was meant to be. As we lift up our eyes with reverence to those harrowed halls of sporting fame, I *know* it would be the members of our much acclaimed women's hockey teams causing us – from north to south, from east to west, from sweeping plains to ragged mountains, from pillow to post – to swell up with fulsome pride like – ahem – toads.

What, she asks, do the scriptures tell us about this?

… Mrs Wintergreen clearly revels in the power an inquisitor can derive from the process of breathing life into a rhetorical question …

Well girls, she says, from the gospel according to St Matthew we learn these heroines are pearls of great price He, the good Lord Himself, has seen fit to cast before us. And this venereal Saint also teaches us that reckless bushels – in the habit I fear of throwing their weight around – should not extinguish the lights of these young players.

We love, she says, to watch the loathsome arms of these brave girls as they sweep the field with their sticks. We love to watch their plucky bodies, hungry for victory, as they surge towards the net. We love to watch as the pick gets flucked – I mean the flick gets pucked – I mean the puck gets flicked – from one loyal team member to the next. We feel the team spirit, like eagles, soaring to wuthering heights.

They are role models for us all, she says. Ask yourself girls. Is this the type of young woman we would want ourselves to be if we had our druthers?

Mrs Wintergreen pauses, checks her notes. A look of satisfaction, like that of an avenging angel, spreads over her jowly features as she contemplates the salutary effect the next stage of her argument will have on her young charges.

But girls, she asks, how would you feel about these women if they emerged to the wild cheers of an adoring crowd, like they were ready and eager to play the sort of game for which they are justly renounced, and then, instead of taking up their team positions, they all lay flat out on the field and started masturbating?

Would you, she asks, hold them in high esteem now? Would you ... ?

Until this moment, Mrs Wintergreen had successfully gauged the measure of her young charges and, through the use of her formidable glare, had quelled any tendency to titter. But the dam has burst. Uproarious laughter spreads, her fierce scowl unable to contain it. She is at a loss to know what has gone wrong and what to do about it. This outbreak of ribaldry threatens to destroy the integrity of proceedings as certainly as would an insurgent flood.

On the cliff-edge of panic, her desperate eyes scan her young audience from left to right then from right to left. She sees an arm shoot up, stabbing the air repeatedly and vigorously. Desperate for a diversion, she indicates with hand and eye that the girl to whom this arm belongs has permission to ask her putative question.

The girl is Annalise ...

Yes, young lady, says Mrs Wintergreen.

... and the question Annalise poses is:

With or without hockey sticks, Mrs W?

It is not titter anymore. It is not laughter any more. It is aural mayhem. The shock wave of instant uproar strikes like a grenade burst. Shards of auditory shrapnel shred the air. Fledgling vocal cords launch crossfire that has every angle covered. Savage decibels stalk the halls of learning.

'Sticks' is born. 'Annalise' is consigned to history.

As regards the unfortunate Mrs Wintergreen in the brief seconds of cognition remaining to her in this earthly life, it is impossible for her to comprehend that her moment has been stolen from her grasp with such breathtaking effrontery. Her jaw drops as far as her multiple chins will allow. Her formidable glare morphs to a vacant stare. She staggers forward and slumps against the lectern, which becomes the sole means of support for her stricken frame, a frame become totally rigid, repository from head to toe of full-on catalepsy.

... I shall give you the medical lowdown, pademelons, based on intelligence I glean from impeccable sources. For Mrs Wintergreen, the issue is more than comprehensive rout by a vicious cabal of pubescent schoolgirls. It is total personal demolition, the aftermath for her being a mind whose whereabouts nobody can pinpoint anymore, and a body destined for an intensive-care bed at the mercy of life-support systems ...

But by what law should her young charges give a toss for *her* plight? This is very much *their* moment, a moment of empowerment, a moment of riot, a moment to rejoice, a rare moment, a moment these gals do not intend to squander. And that squirreled moment, in brazen re-enactment, is on display here and now in suburban Sleek Street, set to bright music on a rotatable stage together with the chill unconcern and brute cruelty of raw youth, *en masse* and free of rein.

Izzie pumps out the introductory bars of his music, *tempo di marcia*, though sounding more festive than martial. *Spiel* surrenders to *Sing*, in this moment of dubious celebration.

Music is the cue for Sticks to lead a surge of schoolgirls – those making up the two front rows of the audience – onto stage front, each wielding a hockey stick. The spot, previously illuminating the solo Mrs Wintergreen, expands to take in Sticks and her throng of ardent admirers, her disciples. Gathering these disciples round her, Sticks opens the song, brandishing her hockey stick with youthful vigour:

Sticks:

Hundreds of ways a sister can
abuse a hockey stick,

put in a hat and shaken up
and then you take your pick, e.g.

The thread of song devolves to one of her disciples, interpreting the imagined conversion of Sticks' hockey stick into a fishing rod. The other disciples crowd round watching with interest. Behind them poor Agnes W hugs the lectern, partially enfolded in the drape bearing the school crest and the logo of the Lantern Bearers. This tableau resembles a piece of tortured statuary tangled around its plinth. Agnes W, its subject, appears (illusorily) to direct her lifeless stare to the same purpose as the disciples.

Disciple 1:

attach a hook and line and sinker.
Certainly that'll suffice for a trick, and then

Sticks mimes casting her 'line' and hauling in a fish, which miraculously appears at the end of the line as a holographic image. Its colours arise like a cold flame from deep within, glimmering diffusely like sun striking through raindrops. This technical triumph, originating in the flies, is doubtless under control from the lighting box, a collaborative effort – with inputs one presumes – from Matt, Harry, and Elena.

Sticks:

catch some trevallies to fill up the bellies
of Thomas and Harry and Dick.

Another of the disciples examines the catch closely. She says, That's no trevally, sister. That's a mullet.

Yet another disciple examines the catch and says, She's right on, sister. That fish *is* a mullet.

Sticks turns to Izzie and says, Play it again, Sam.

The music and the song resume at 'catch'.

Disciple 2:

catch some fat mullets to gladden the gullets

of Thomas and Harry and Dick.

The music marks time for a few bars. Sticks launches into another verse:

Sticks:

What can a sister do with a

Disciple 1:

hockey stick around the home?

A huge holographic spider appears, dangling on its silken thread.

Disciple 2:

Squash the creepy crawlies.

Disciple 2 demolishes the spider with her hockey stick. A hologram of a grotesque garden gnome, sporting a salacious leer, appears.

Sticks:

Pulverize the garden gnome.

Sticks wields her hockey stick. The garden gnome vanishes in a puff of plaster of Paris. For a split second, its leer lingers like the grin of the Cheshire cat. In place of the gnome, a television set appears. Federal Parliament is in session for Question Time. Proceedings are going out live for the benefit of viewers with a penchant for masochism and/or a fetish for un-funny clowns.

Disciple 1:

Assume attack position, when

Disciple 2:

flat out on your belly, you're watching the telly.

Sticks and the two disciples lie prone facing the TV set.

Sticks:

All is inanity, threatening sanity.

Disciple 1:

Sister, just drive the stick home.

Sticks drives the stick home. The TV set disintegrates in a flash of electric blue.

The stage begins a slow clockwise rotation. The music switches from tonic to dominant.

Lead by Sticks, the girls march in formation, thrusting their hockey sticks vigorously and vertically. Their direction is anticlockwise. Relative to their audience, viz. us, the phalanx they form merely marks time. Only the frozen tableau, consisting of lectern and Mrs Wintergreen, moves relative to us, like the spindle of a carousel, sometimes with front to us, sometimes with back to us, itself always spinning while – in turn – its macabre tale is being spun.

As they march, the girls sing a refrain and act it out with vigour to choreography by Sonia:

All Girls:

Girls and hockey sticks forever,
bonding mere time shall never sever.
When we get the wink,
we scarcely stop to think.
Libidinous scurry, all sticks in a flurry.
We relish the action, just never you worry.
(Go!)

Girls and hockey sticks forever,
the combination doubly clever.
When the two convene
they make a mean machine.
A bit of a jiggle, an innocent giggle,

and life's OK.

The stage stops rotating. The girls stop marching. The music reverts to the tonic.

A holographic kite appears above the girls' heads. Disciple 1 gathers its string. The other girls crowd round her. Though totally out of the equation, Mrs Wintergreen appears to be subjecting the matter to – one might say – religious scrutiny.

Sticks opens a new verse:

Sticks:

Picture Benjy Franklin with
his kite up in the air.

Disciple 2:

His wife, she loved her hockey,
was a fan *extraordinaire*,

Several holographic hockey sticks appear, adorning the length of the kite's string.

Sticks:

so naturally it was never a key
attracted the lightning, and give him a fright'ning.

Thunder crashes. Lightning flashes. Charged with electricity, the kite, string, and hockey sticks exude a vivid incandescence. Disciple 1 staggers.

Disciple 2:

The hockey sticks frizzled and Benjamin grizzled,

The holographic representations of pieces of frizzled hockey stick fall from kite string to stage.

Sticks:

Dear God, you dumb dude, play it fair.

The stage resumes its rotation. The music chooses the dominant. The girls march in formation as before. As they do so, they sing the refrain with alternative words:

All Girls:

Hockey sticks and girls united,
sisters around the world delighted.
When the prigs descend,
to bring our game to end,
we'll give 'em a poke in the vitreous humor
to show 'em the stick is one hell of a rumour.
(Go!)

Hockey sticks and girls united,
universal honour plighted.
We shall get right down
with neither pout nor frown.
A touch of the crook is a trick for the book
to start our day.

The stage stops rotating. The girls stop marching. The music chooses the tonic. Sticks opens a new verse:

Sticks:

Stratford-born Anne Hathaway
played hockey all her days.
She kept a boyfriend Willie
who was keen on writing plays ...

Disciple 1 interjects. Hold on, she says. Hockey wasn't even invented back then.

I do believe you're right, says Sticks. She turns to Izzie and says, Play it again, Sam.

The verse begins again:

Sticks:

Florence Nightingale indulged

in hockey as a whim,
then crafted splints from hockey kit,
two sticks for every limb ...

Blackout!

>

Candlelight at the card table. Crowded round this table are more chairs than will fit comfortably. Few are occupied. Only Sticks and Sonia are making use of them. Oh ... and Izzie. His synthesizer doesn't work without power, so he has joined them at the card table. This option, for him, is second-best.

Sticks, uncharacteristically, is in pensive mood.

What I did to Mrs Wintergreen, she says, is something I'm not proud of.

She deserved it, I'd say, says Sonia.

None of us is blameless, says Sticks. Silly old biddy she may have been, but she didn't deserve what I dished out.

The flicker of candlelight plays on Sticks' lowered lids.

It was youthful arrogance, she says, and I'm deeply ashamed of it.

Harry and Elena, entering from front of house, find their way down the aisle by the light of the torch Elena holds. Harry shouts to the group at the table.

All Sleek Street is out, is his news.

Well that lets you off the hook, says Sticks.

What do you mean?

Suspicion of sabotage?

Give me a break!

Throwing fantastic shadows in front of them, Harry and Elena mount the stage and find seats for themselves. Elena switches off her torch. Then Matt emerges from backstage, torch in hand, and conjoint at the feet with a gigantic black effigy of himself.

Matt squeezes into a seat and switches off his torch. Sticks resumes her introspective musings.

Anyway, she says, I paid for my sins. With a nickname for life.

And you got expelled, says Harry.

The private school system doesn't expel students. They merely exchange prisoners. 'You give me your bad girls, and I'll give you mine.'

So you moved from St Maggot's to St Grub's? asks Matt.

Sticks responds with the barest of nods. Then deciding reminiscence and introspection have limited shelf life, she changes the subject, addressing the whole team.

I've squared things with Elena, says Sticks. She's ready to tread the boards, so long as there's no mention of her former life in Russia.

I can relate to that, says Matt.

True, isn't it? asks Sticks of Elena.

It is true, says Elena.

So, says Sticks, we'll be seeing a lot of Elena from here on. She'll be prominent in the next two *Stücke*.

The rest of the crew offer Elena their congratulations, except for Harry who looks glum. With her eyes, then with her voice, Sticks invites comment.

Want to know about them? she asks.

About what? asks Harry.

The *Stücke*.

Harry responds with a fascist salute, and a click of the heels. *Jawohl!* he says.

Sticks gives him a look suggesting she will hold the hounds of her ire in abeyance, until the moment arrives when she can safely let them loose without risk of collateral damage.

The first one, she says, deals with the jiggery-pokery surrounding the strange disappearance of Matt's models.

Except one, says Elena.

Sticks, with a warm smile, nods.

Bar one, she says. The second is about the commissioning of the virtual reality system for the Sultan's nephew, says Sticks.

Who plays the nephew? asks Matt.

The man himself. He's on the plane from K L as we speak.

Elena's eyes light up.

Barry? she asks.

Sticks nods.

Baharudin, she says.

Shit, says Izzie. A real live Sultan. His right royal person slumming it with yodellers down under.

He ain't no Sultan yet, says Sticks.

<< 1st

The icy covering of Lake Onega was cracking under clear blue skies.

Matt had observed this same ice – or at any rate its anonymous precursors – as floes in the Neva River, when he was in St Petersburg some days earlier, in transit to the Karelian capital. These floes had found their way downstream through a series of interconnected rivers and lakes bringing a belated resurgence of winter chill to the ghost-ridden city of Dostoevsky, of Repin, of Mariinsky.

But Matt had since taken the train northeast, and was now here in Petrozavodsk. Wrapped up tightly in multiple layers, with furry gloves to keep frostbite from his fingers, and with the flaps of his *ushánka* folded down to protect his neck and ears from twenty or more degrees below zero, he walked along a paved pedestrian embankment, the lake on his left and the city streets some way off on his right. Walls of fresh snow, pushed up earlier on each side of the embankment by some benevolent machinery, guided him to his intended destination.

The time was midday, but the sun was showing a distinct

preference for the southerly aspect of the sky. Its rays, at such low incidence they seemed to be having difficulty making landfall, set off the soft pastel colours of the neoclassical public buildings so that, from a distance, they resembled iced confections.

Slender archipelagos, almost flush with the ice, and thick with snow-mantled *taigá*, marked the far reaches of the lake, except where distance or glacial mists consumed them.

Matt's walk – as his youth decreed – was jaunty. His breaths, expelled with energy, lived briefly as a succession of small white clouds, each contriving to be icy and steamy at the same time, each part of his presence like a ghostly shadow waxing then waning. Bent on an unexplained vengeance, the folds of his heavy tweed overcoat thwacked the frigid air. Impotent against the sting his exposed features felt, the weak sun on his face nevertheless buoyed his spirits.

Pedestrian traffic along the embankment was limited to the occasional derelict soul passing by in silence, with torso in comprehensive retreat beneath thick folds of drapery. Indicative of years of wear and extremes of weather, this drapery was invariably torn, faded, and shapeless. Its saving graces were its familiarity and a sweat-stained fleeciness.

Traffic on the lake itself was nonexistent. Had any intrepid skater been inclined on impulse to attempt an icy frolic, he/she would have been brought undone by the frozen wind-driven wavelets, spoiling the slick surface. And, months earlier, all vessels had been repatriated to dry dock to await the spring thaw ...

... except for one, stuck fast at the bank, about two hundred metres in front of Matt. This was where Matt was headed. Inside this vessel, he would have the rare pleasure of doing business in the international arena. Or, more specifically, this dear brave friend of mine was about to cross swords with the oligarchy from which this country – to the chagrin of many – derives notoriety.

At this point, pademelons, let us take a break from our narrative journey. I put a proposal to you for your consideration.

As part of the process for coming to terms with the premises Matt was making for, let us give ourselves over to illusion for a moment, as we have done many times before, and as befits our sojourn in this problematic land. After all, the sobering realities of this country are palatable to sensibilities like ours only if we retain the option of a retreat into the soft bordellos of art and illusion.

Here is the illusion I propose.

At first glance, it is not a ship we see at the embankment. It is a scarab beetle. A beetle oversized, overturned, and over-endowed with colour, marooned on a frosty and frictionless mirror, also oversized. This entomological disaster is compounded by the hapless insect's diffuse – and thereby fantastical – reflection in the irresolute mirror.

Let us hold fast to this mirage for as long as circumstances allow. The reality it masks is unlikely to be pretty.

Nyet. Our first glance has no shelf life. Our resolve is thwarted.

A couple of sceptical blinks of the eye is all it takes for reality to assert itself. In the scheme of things reality must ultimately explode illusion. So much for soft bordellos.

There *is* no upturned beetle. All along, it was a converted freighter from the early Soviet era, moored in the lake, and held fast against the embankment by an unrelenting collar of ice. For carapace read hull. For legs read masts.

As if transplanted from a family-friendly fun-fare, she was a kaleidoscope of shameless colour. Her entire hull was striped in the Russian tricolour. Flags of all allegiances, including a prominent Jolly Roger, decorated her masts and rigging. They didn't flap. Unfurled, but immobile, they were held in place as if in readiness for a moon landing. Immobility, in fact, was written all over this nautical parody. This ship would never again brave the northern seas, her gangplank would never be raised, and her present moorings were doomed to be her final resting place. Her mission was to adorn the Petrozavodsk embankment, servicing the needs of inveterate landlubbers.

What, precisely, was the nature of the business Matt was determined to transact within these mock-maritime premises, heated throughout – as he would soon find – to convivially tropical temperatures? Well, to put it in O's brutal terms, Matt was about to buy six gorgeous young Russian women. Buy? Matt would have preferred to describe the impending transaction in a manner less suggestive of the recycled version of an ancient and disreputable trade. He would have liked the world to know his plan was to buy the right to offer these women gainful employment back in Oz.

But the S word and what it stood for had a propensity to echo through time, making it (viz. time) infamous thereby. So, even before he had left Oz enroute to the Republic of Karelia – territory assuredly outside the comfort zone of most punters – Matt had found himself on the defensive, seeking to justify his prospective venture to his colleagues and, in particular, to a suspicious and much-concerned Penny.

What's your game, Matthew? she had asked.

You must know it's not my intent to enslave any of these women, Matt had replied.

You must know intent like yours famously paves the road to hell.

But, without intent, none of us would bother dragging their arse along any road *at all*.

Better pick the right one then, my dear.

Matt thought he had. His road would lead him to the realization of a professional dream, and O was the guide he had chosen here in Petrozavodsk to help him with this realization.

... exactly who *was* this O? ...

O was the proprieter of these premises with colourful externals and lapsed seafaring credentials. By dint of assiduous duplication, he had established many similar premises throughout the length and breadth of the motherland, from Archangelsk to Astrakhan, and from Vyborg to Vladivostok. In addition to his business operations, O could claim ownership of:

a family name, Ogorodnikov[37], with at last count five syllables, and hence 'O' for the sake of tractability,

a stump in lieu of a right hand,

the ability to roll his own Sobranie look-alikes despite his shortage of the necessary tactile equipment, and

a mix of insouciance with menace befitting a fellow of the Russian godfatherhood.

Matt found O on board this Good Ship Lollipop with difficulty. As soon as he crossed her gangplank, close to where her name in inscrutable Cyrillic was painted in vivid colours on her prow, he began to swelter under waves of artificial heat. He stuffed his gloves and *ushánka* into the pocket of his coat, but the problem was where to put the coat. Although it was clear to him he was privy to a commercial operation here, dedicated to the provision of services to paying customers, he could find no obvious place, such as a cloakroom, in which clients could hand over coats to an obliging person.

Putrid as a navvy, he traversed the boat from fore to aft and from port to starboard. Making enquiries was problematic. There was much verbal stumbling and many fitful pauses, involving his retreat again and again to the sanctuary of his phrasebook. When Matt finally located his quarry, O's command of English turned out to be excellent, albeit accented.

Your trip was interesting? asked O.

Most, said Matt.

You have a hotel?

The Metropol.

O, expecting him, took immediate charge. Using his left hand to unbutton the jacket of his dark suit and adjust the dark glasses on his face – square, staunchly Slavic, and granite-hard – he ushered Matt to a room cobbled together by boxing in space on the forward deck. The door was locked. Fumbling for the key

---

37 This name has a provenance. *Ogoródnik* means 'vegetable grower' or 'market gardener'.

in the left-hand pocket of his jacket, then finding it, O unlocked the door. He turned to Matt and, indicating unselfconsciously with his stump, said, *Pryámo*. Taking this as an invitation to enter, Matt did so, while O returned the key to his pocket and followed.

Inside, Matt was faced with an austere stateroom, painted steel-blue, and with minimal furnishings. Smack dab in the centre was a teak table of contemporary vintage – square with a side of about two metres – on which eight matching chairs danced attendance. It was bare except for a dial-phone in black Bakelite and a cast-iron devil's head ashtray. The latter was an exercise in vulgarity having – one could imagine – seen use by many old salts.

Directly in front of him, mounted at eye level on the wall, was an antique aneroid barometer, its glass marooned in an annulus of clunky brass. Undoubtedly, it was a relic from the bridge and from the glory days when the ship's business was the dominion of the open waters.

To his right was a large retrofitted window, the room's feature, half again as broad as the table, with dazzling views over the lake.

To his left, again mounted at eye level, was a framed life-size headshot in black and white of a middle-aged couple with an icon of the Eastern Church looming importantly to their rear. They were clothed in the style of the Soviet era, he with a cloth cap arranged with studied symmetry on his head, and she with a scarf draped fastidiously around hers. Matt imagined keen intelligence lived behind these two pairs of steady eyes, just as the ingrained grime of the *kolkhóz* lived beneath their twenty collective fingernails. Facing the lake view as it did, this photograph occupied pride of place, chosen – it would appear – out of deep respect for its subjects.

Behind him was the door through which he had come and, to its right, a carved oak wardrobe of early 20th century vintage, probably pre-revolutionary.

Matt had seen enough of the ship to conclude this room was like no other on board. Not one skerrick of garish colour resided here to lay siege to his optics. Beneath his feet, he felt the solidity of the crafted decking, exposed and polished. The generous space around him evoked a comfortable sense of uncluttered airiness, not to be expected in a vessel originally intended for the high seas.

In here, there are no bugs, said O.

Matt's heavy clothing was soon hanging in the wardrobe beside O's winter jacket. He felt more at ease in shirtsleeves. A thought, shod in hob-nails, galumphed across his mind. When O talked about bugs, he did not mean mosquitoes.

<

If the stateroom was a standout, what *were* the other rooms on the ship like? Let us retrace the steps Matt had taken some thirty minutes earlier when he had combed the vessel from stem to stern in search of O, thereby encountering by accident much of her interior.

So, let the minute hand of some cosmic timepiece, presumed to be out there and counting down the machinations of the known universe, describe the arc of a semicircle in an anticlockwise direction.

>

Matt's overwhelming impression in his wanderings was that all the ship's original purpose had been comprehensively subverted. The same perverse intelligence gone into remodelling the ship's exterior had been given similar license when applied to its interior. For example, the deck area throughout the vessel, including the bridge and quarterdeck, had been transformed into a multiplex of rooms exhibiting a variety of shapes, sizes, and colours, according to the intended purpose of each. To complete the travesty, even the former cargo hold had fallen foul of this relentless process of subdivision.

Matt searched the lower deck first because, from these nether regions, the signs of activity first grabbed his attention. Brute colour, and other varieties of visual insalubrity, were everywhere to be found down there. Disco lights ushered in and then celebrated the advent of sensory disorientation. A claustrophobic labyrinth of internal gangways, ladders, and tiny airless cabins, was slathered with carpet, plush cheap and gaudy. Here flourished the habitat of innumerable pretty young women flitting around in brief negligees, their eyes downcast, avoiding his at all costs. Could these be the Nordic princesses he had come here to buy?

What might have been mistaken for the noise of ship's engines turned out to be the purr of diesel generators pushing out electrical power in prodigal abundance for heating and for whatever nefarious activities might decide to take root amidships. This purr was masked by piped music, pervasive, intended to numb the mind and inflame the passions, a medley of the very worst Russian pop songs. Everywhere there was the combined stench of stale vodka and inferior tobacco.

Since O was not to be found down here in the depths, Matt returned to the main deck. Here there were larger rooms, though none so large as the stateroom. They housed gaming activities. In some, pokies flaunted their inane sound and light show, in others, blackjack its green and sleazy tables. Small bars were in all. Sadness and misfortune hung everywhere like sides of beef.

The clients were dumpy and middle-aged: the men in shoddy suits and the women in much-faded off-the-shelf floral fabrics. Each of them seemed unaware of the existence of their fellows, comfortable in the skin of the lone wolf or she-wolf. Easy money was all they had eyes for, the thrill of its acquisition their drug of choice.

Shall we let these miserable punters be? They are a worldwide phenomenon and much to be pitied.

Matt might have been thinking along similar lines. He was about to proceed to the upper deck, where he thought the high rollers might be, when he came across O. Or was it O came across him? Whichever it was, we may return with impunity to the stateroom, to take things up where we left things off. We have satisfied our curiosity re the interior layout of the vessel and Matt's first bewildering steps on board.

>

The moving and shaking in the stateroom was playing out.

... dealing with Immigration in my country? we found Matt asking.

When O spoke interrogatively in reply, derision was detectable in his voice as was a rhetorical tone in his question.

Akh, he said. Petty bureaucracy?

Matt, prudent, remained silent.

You need not concern yourself, said O, with the trifling details of our procedures for the distribution of our merchandise. Please rest your mind. There are many back doors, I assure you, and our procedures are well tested.

O and Matt were seated at the square table. O had the window behind and Matt opposite him. This, we may presume, was also a well tested procedure. O could see Matt clearly, and also the framed photograph of the peasant couple on the wall directly behind Matt. But Matt – through blinking eyes – could see little more than a silhouette of O against the glare of the lake's icy surface.

Master of his domain, O proceeded to inform Matt with perverse pleasure that his firm's representatives, the multisyllabic R and G, were already installed in Oz ready to 'expedite delivery'. There was more. O had organised the services of a local identity, born and bred in Oz, to help R and G with their task. He flicked a card across the table to Matt, suggesting he, on his return to Oz, might like to make himself known to this person. Matt put the card in his shirtfront pocket.

A knock came at the door. *Voidítye!* O shouted.

One of the pretty young women with downcast eyes entered, a flimsy housecoat slung discreetly over her negligee. She appeared about seventeen years of age, perhaps less. Her hair was of the sober hue gold might take on were it to be relieved of its vulgar excess of gloss. Her frame was so evidently fragile her mere presence was a cry for protection. Her immature breasts looked as if they could at any moment take fright and scamper away to skulk in some secure corner as timid animals might. The curves of her exquisite figure seemed ready to be subsumed by the salience of the space they dared to dissect.

She carried a silver tray on which was a photograph album, a document folder, two pens whose prestige was announced by a distinctive Russian rebus, two *stakána* of tea in pewter holders, and serving plates out of fine China (and in duplicate) bearing crackers, black caviar, and jam. She divvied these items out to the men, the album and documents going to O's left hand.

Spasíbo, Eléna, said O. While she was serving, he addressed her in Russian, of which Matt was able to understand nothing save for two words standing out like beacons in the sea of verbiage: *Avstrália* and (cryptically) Michelangelo. An occasional nod was her only response to what O was saying. Her downcast eyes and expressionless features were steadfast.

O turned to Matt.

This is Elena, he said. Of course, you cannot assume this is her real name. Perhaps you would like to buy her.

Although this was precisely what he had come to this neck of the woods to do, Matt was appalled by the effrontery of the suggestion. Elena did not raise her eyes.

If you will buy her, said O, naturally you may name her anything you please.

Could it be, pademelons, O was a man of such attenuated conscience he could relish so consummately the absolute control over Elena he was exerting? Matt and Elena were silent on this score, so O continued to speak in lieu of their silence. Indicating Elena with his stump, he said to Matt:

This one is smart. Not just a pretty face.

He turned to Elena and, one raised eyebrow visible above the rim of his dark glasses, said with condescension, *Iskusnáya rabóta, da?*[38]

Elena gave a weak smile but kept her eyes lowered. She had finished serving, and was hanging around awkwardly, waiting to be dismissed. O, enjoying her embarrassment, kept her in limbo for a few seconds more. A look of self-satisfaction spreading across his stony face, he tapped the document folder, and turned to Matt.

These, he said, are the documents.

Matt's features remained staunchly blank.

Documents, said O, signed off by your lawyer.

My lawyer ... , said Matt.

O turned back to Elena.

Poká, he said.

Elena gave a curtsey, and a '*Poká*' barely perceptible to the ear. She left with relief, carrying the empty tray out the door with her. When the door closed behind her, O allowed a tantalizing silence to prevail, broken only by the crunch of his straight white teeth coming down on a cracker loaded with caviar.

My lawyer ... , said Matt.

This is *ikrá*, said O. From the Caspian Sea. Try some.

My lawyer, said Matt, advised me to have nothing to do with this deal.

Akh, of course he did, said O. But he has prepared the papers nonetheless. And you are here.

Once again, O let silence preside, during which Matt treated

---

38 *Iskusnáya rabóta, da?*: You're a clever piece of work, aren't you?

himself tentatively to some caviar. O chose the moment to launch into polemics.

In my experience, said O, our legal colleagues are inclined to meddle in business affairs when what is required of them is they confine themselves strictly to the *legal* aspects of those business affairs. We have here a violation of the separation of powers, I maintain. Would you agree?

A loose interpretation, said Matt.

I am in favour of loose interpretations, said O. Speaking of which, it is modelling you are planning for these girls. Is not so?

Yes.

Fashion modelling?

Yes.

My girls will suit your purpose. They are most versatile.

O engineered yet another silence. Matt, who had reached the conclusion these silences were traps laid for the unwary, declined this time to take the bait. O indicated the photo album.

So, asked O, how shall we go about things?

Matt wasn't falling for it.

I suggest, said O, you look through this catalogue and make your six choices. I understand it is six?

Yes.

You may have more if you wish. There are plenty here.

Six will do nicely.

O.K. We settle on six. When you have made your selections, I shall call in the girls, and you can see for yourself they are as beautiful in their skin as they look in the pictures.

O slid the album across the table. Extracting a tobacco pouch from his trouser pocket, he proceeded to roll a cigarette with five fingers and a stump, a trick for which he was renowned in the circles of his dubious brotherhood and beyond. With this distraction close at hand, Matt was unable to give his undivided attention to the task at hand, not even when it involved the allure of these photographic representations of physical perfection.

The rolling process was neither quick nor pretty. Shreds of tobacco leaf took flight willy nilly, becoming dispersed – like the debris from a miniature volcano – over a space about the size and shape of a ship's helm. Matt fought back an urge to offer help. When the operation was complete, and O was able with satisfaction to raise finished product to eager lips, it turned out – contrary to Matt's expectations – to be a near perfect job.

Matt speculated. Was O's missing forearm the result of an industrial accident? Or was it some unspeakable legacy of the torrid times O had lived through? Perhaps a badge of honour he had acquired in the process of rising to his present position in whatever nefarious hierarchy?

Fanciful? Not if there was any truth in stories he'd been told in recent days.

While O leaned back in his chair, staring as if unconcerned at the ceiling, and giving himself over to tobacco-induced euphoria, Matt – playing God – proceeded to choose his six princesses. Elena was in the catalogue, and she was one of his choices. Selection completed, it remained for O to get on the blower, and arrange for the chosen six to come forth from the bowels of the ship to parade before their new owner.

They came, Elena among them. The other five were close physical replicas of Elena, custodians of the same brand of fragile beauty, and of the same flimsy housecoats thrown over their negligees.

Their eyes were downcast.

So were Matt's. Mortified and embarrassed, he found himself suddenly and unexpectedly overwhelmed by the evident helplessness of the young women, obviously cowed and uncertain of what sort of debut they were making. Inwardly, he questioned the equivocal nature of his own role in this barbaric ritual. He suppressed with difficulty the tremor taking hold of him.

For O, who had seen it all before, it was business as usual.

A spiralling wisp of smoke rose between the men. It came

from the gaping mouth of that monstrous effigy of a satiated Satan, an artefact Matt found confrontational. Because this cast-iron excrescence resided in the centre of the table, it was hard for him to ignore.

He traced the source of the smoke back, within its yawning mouth, to O's cigarette, now crushed there. Once a potent firestick, it was now burnt out, its back broken. It occurred to Matt this imagery held some intransigent symbolism whose meaning – if and when deciphered – he doubted he would find welcome.

O looked in Matt's direction for a response. Despite his emergent misgivings, Matt summoned one up. With diminished enthusiasm, and trying not to appear hesitant, he delivered the clumsy line he thought O expected from him.

These women, he said, are as beautiful in the flesh as they appear in their photographs.

I am pleased you think so, said O. Often it is said we in Russia have more beautiful women than it is possible to put to good use.

Inferring Matt had given him the nod, O sent the princesses on their way back to the nautical depths from which they had briefly surfaced. In a moment of fancy, Matt thought they might be mermaids. Scrutinizing each face closely as they passed in single file out the door, he could not detect a skerrick of excitement or joy residing on any one of them.

Their features were inclined neither to receive nor transmit information with any alacrity. Yet Matt imagined he could see *something* of significance written on them. Yes. Something was discernible. Uncertainty? Fear? Yearning? Secret knowledge to which he was not privy? All of the above?

Their downcast bearing was as if bolted on. The depth of their resignation could not be plumbed. With an air of ineluctability chilling Matt to the core, they had turned their faces decisively to the metaphoric wall.

He felt guilty. He felt dirty. He felt sick. He felt this entire venture had been a disaster of such magnitude it lacked any capacity for exaggeration.

>

The light from the window in front of Matt diminished suddenly in intensity. Over the shoulders of O's profile, he saw murky grey clouds, hinting of snow, taming the sun and effacing the defenceless sky. It occurred to Matt he might have to find the way back to his hotel in the mother of all blizzards.

His potpourri of adverse thoughts found a way to his stomach. The whole room seemed in the thrall of a gut-wrenching pitch and roll. For an insane moment, the thought crossed his mind anchor had been weighed and they were headed for the open seas. Fighting his nausea, Matt stumbled through the remaining formalities. He signed the forms. He paid his roubles. He rose, his full frame teetering on groggy feet. He shook O's hand, his left one, his only one. Near the door, he let O help him on with his coat.

Then, as if a voice spoke within him other than his own, he surprised himself by asking O a question.

Does this ship have a name? Matt asked.

All ships must have a name, said O. So must this one.

What is its name?

Her name. Ships must be referred to in the feminine.

Oh, yes. *Her* name.

Her name is Anna Akhmatova.

Is she a real person?

One of the great Russian poets. My parents knew her, or so I have been led to believe.

At this moment, Matt imagined he detected – despite the dark glasses – a quick back-and-forth movement of O's eyeballs in the direction of the wall-hung photograph, and of the amiable couple who were its subjects.

She was some time ago claimed by God, said O, but her immortal spirit still stalks the holy turf of *Rus*.

O contrived a pause to which Matt did not respond.

She brings tears, said O, to the eyes of all who lay claim to a Russian soul.

This time around the pause was not contrived. It struck Matt O was no longer playing his regular game. A noticeable, perhaps profound, change had come over him.

This case hardened man, who – believably – sank his teeth into heavy gauge nails every morning for breakfast, had relinquished control, even of the presentation of his own body. His guard had come crashing down around his now vulnerable person. His posture, formerly resolute, had taken on all the slackness of the wisp of smoke still hanging in the expectant air. His lips could not control an involuntary quiver. He had whipped the dark glasses from off the bridge of his nose, and they were dangling loose in the fingers of his left hand.

As a consequence, O's pallid blue eyes were exposed to Matt's view for the first time. Their gaze – lachrymal, distant, unfocused – simultaneously unnerved and intrigued him. As one could expect, there was authority in that gaze, but, for the first and only time in his brief engagement with O, Matt's sentiment informed him of an inner composure driving that authority, the composure of resignation.

O's lips moved. Barely discernible sounds emerged, sounds he whispered softly to himself, sounds composed of those earthy vowels and swishing sibilants Matt, despite his ignorance of the language, was certain were of Russian provenance.

O's whispering held several slow seconds siege until …

… his lips stopped moving. He transferred his gaze to Matt. It was as if he were seeing Matt for the first time.

Of course, said O, you will want this in *your* language. So I must translate.

In a hesitant declamatory style, the style a person might use when translating on the run, O spoke directly to Matt in English, his left hand supplying emphasis:

> My life … resembles a river
> whose course has been changed by the … severity of the age.
> For me, one life has been … substituted for another.
> The river now flows in a different … bed
> and I no longer recognize its banks.

Over O's shoulder, Matt glimpsed the wall-mounted barometer. Everyday utilitarian object though it was, its clear glass had acquired a dazzling amber halo, whose source of lustre was the reflection – directly into his eyes – of the waning sunshine, the sun's last gasp perhaps. For an instant, his mind's eye saw this venerable instrument mounted in prominent position on the bridge, as the ship and its then captain together braved the swell of the rogue sea. He found himself wondering cryptically along such lines as: Does this ship, moored permanently as it is by the edge of Lake Onega, … does this ship recognize its banks?

From this point on, question burst upon question in his restless head. Was it conceivable, he asked himself, that O and the ship, Anna and the river … and why not all four? … have had their courses changed by the severity of the age holding sway over them? Nobody could doubt the inclemency of the times that had afflicted Russia over the past century. If it could be true for Anna that she found herself no longer able to recognize her banks, could this not also be true for O?

O must have been thinking along congruent lines, because he spoke, with irony tingeing his voice, and a smile ghosting his lips:

If she will be alive today, he said, she would compare her life to my ship instead of to a river. *Bórzhe moy*, it bears her name.

In a flash, Matt conceived a bold scenario to explain the changes in O's behaviour, a scenario not merely plausible, not merely compelling, but inescapable. The gist of it was that O had been beset, here and in his presence, by the re-emergence of a stifled innocence, sense of wonder, common culture, and benign humanity, all of this imbibed in infancy along with mother's milk. O's entire childhood milieu had resurfaced, taking him in its thrall, and reminding him he was one of a breed of men expected to stand tall in the exemplary trappings of honourable behaviour.

Look at the man now, and then at the man who might have been. Which man would recognize his banks?

Matt suddenly felt embarrassed to be present. He was not certain he had the right to be hanging around in this man's stateroom, uninvited witness to his struggle with devils. It's not as if one has no devils of one's own, he reasoned. He fancied he was seeing – spying on, no less – an aspect of O's most intimate nature seldom prey to observation. He was seeing clear through to a private sanctum within the embattlements of this pitiless man's innermost self.

As this frozen moment thawed, and as Matt turned sheepishly to go, O stopped him in his tracks with his outstretched hand. The hand implored, as did O's words thundering their finality in Matt's brain.

Akh, said O, the tears Anna brings to my eyes! But when it is the turn of Fyodor Andreevitch to be counted, all eyes shall be dry. Dry eyes, every one of them. Their narrowness shrieking judgment upon me. No, not even …

Here Matt was sure he heard a stifled sob.

… my divine Creator in His infinite grace would condescend for an instant to shed tears on my account.

Matt left.

>

Harry and Sticks were an item. Perhaps the romance of the recent trip to Malaysia, together with the taste of luxury consequential upon the Sultan's hospitality, had hastened their union.

One humid Friday afternoon in early autumn, this pair of de facto connubials left their workplace – Integrated Electronic Imagery – bound for Harry's 'vertical' living quarters. Harry was ferrying Sticks, his cherished cargo, in a brand new Alpha Romeo. He had come a long way since the days when he made do with a humble Torana, and an unbecoming vanity compelled him to show he had done so.

His vanity however took a back seat – pardon the semantic confusion – when confronted with the repetitive stop/start of gridlocked traffic. Sleek Street, a stretch of arterial road well known by commuters for all the wrong reasons, had found a new victim. The Alpha was hostage. Neither Harry nor Sticks were enjoying the experience, especially since their air conditioner had decided just now to pack it in. Air-con was not a standard fixture on Toranas and, Harry reflected ruefully, it might as well not have been on Alphas.

Looking for a speedier passage, he turned off Sleek Street. They found themselves negotiating unfamiliar streets, lined with tawdry apartment blocks, tenanted by people not spoilt for choice of accommodation. The humid air, laden with moisture, bore deprivation as well, poison to the sensibilities of those exposed to it, not least the hapless tenants. Harry and Sticks, blow-ins, sought escape.

Beyond a couple of strategically placed speed bumps the ambience changed dramatically. From out of the sea of disadvantage, an island of gentility beckoned this pair of privileged commuters. Within this enclave, the air was free of poison. A bland colony of upmarket shops forged a square around a manicured patch of parkland. Sculptured streets gave access to stylishly renovated town houses and boutique restaurants. Gentrification flourished. Here was panacea to the bourgeois mindset.

Harry and Sticks could not resist a small trattoria, *La Spag*. It conjured thoughts of cool conditioned air, a refreshing glass or two of *vino bianco*, green salads, and light meals in the Mediterranean style. They stopped, relaxed, indulged, imbibed.

Sitting opposite Harry, over her meal of stuffed calamari, under a poster of the Venice Carnival, Sticks ventured a remark and her hand across the table.

Luck pursues you, she said.

Meaning? asked Harry.

Just that. You're the luckiest person I know. You do nothing. You wait. And luck comes to your door.

You think so?

If you run from it, which you have been known to do, luck comes right on after you at a gallop. Where Harry McMinn is concerned, luck will not be brushed off.

I don't see myself as any luckier than the next person.

Oh, but you are.

You're being fanciful.

Those people down the road. On the way here. In the run-down apartments. Tell me. When was the last time luck crossed their paths?

Harry let this comment ride, preferring to address his spaghetti vongole. Sticks smiled. Equilibrium restored, they drove home in light traffic.

Thanks to my second unit, pademelons, you are already acquainted with the establishment known as *La Spag*, managed by the genial Bruno Gervasoni and his family. From the moment Harry and Sticks discovered it – by luck, one might say – they became habitués. Moreover, they persuaded people like Matt, Ramon, and some of the other techies, of its special delights. Many a time, on a week night after work, and always to Bruno's delight, a contingent from Integrated Electronic Imagery arrived to check out the ambience and cuisine.

Matt was a noteworthy devotee. Following his return from Russia, he would often arrive by taxi from Lyceum Street, sporting a bottle of *Bisquit*, intent on meeting up with Harry, Sticks, and company. Once ensconced, and with a few drinks under his belt, he would engage in one of his favourite pastimes: taking the piss out of the good-natured Bruno.

His favourite ploy was speaking Strine[39] to Bruno whenever he appeared at their table and then sitting back to watch the reaction. To questions such as 'Have you the wherewithal to satisfy our ebb tides?' or 'Would you mind turning down the egg nishning?' Bruno would flash a broad smile to mask his total bemusement. He fielded Matt's cheap shots with grace. They were paying customers after all.

These were moments redolent of entitlement. The luckless poor were at a convenient remove. They were stacked away neatly in their incommodious apartments back down the road.

<

Pademelons, I am ahead of myself. Matt has yet to return from Russia. We have left him in a hostile environment, with his story not yet concluded. I assume responsibility for this shemozzle. We have no business swanning it in Oz while he languishes in limbo. We must rattle our dags[40] and get back there. No ifs or buts. It is our signal duty to rejoin him …

>

… the *Anna Akhmatova* was behind Matt. He trudged listlessly,

---

39 'Strine': an adjectival noun coined in the 60s by journalist Alistair Morrison, and syncope of 'Australian' (i.e. the supposed Australian language). In Strine speak, 'ebb tide' translates as 'appetite', and 'egg nishning' as 'air conditioning'.

40 'rattle the dags': Australian slang meaning 'hurry up'.

retracing steps taken earlier in the day. The snow walls, frozen solid, snaked before him, guiding him. The sun, weaker, and in danger of being snuffed out, fell on his back. From the weave of this rear aspect of his tweed coat, the shallow rays picked up flecks of colour, suggestive of scintillations. A fertile imagination might conclude these scintillations were a colony of tiny phosphorescent creatures resident among the fibres.

It was colder. Smears of cloud like curdled grease – precursors of snow – proceeded to blot out the sky and pressure such sun as dared to persist into inglorious demise. The wind, from the north off the icy lake, flung itself without mercy in Matt's face. He had tucked a handkerchief inside his *ushánka* in a vain attempt to protect his exposed features from a chill bent on freezing all life resident in his body.

Seen in back view, Matt was uncharacteristically tentative in both posture and motion. Gone was the youthful pzazz evident earlier that day. His carriage was hesitant, his gait awkward. He had withdrawn his head into the hunch of his shoulders, a demeanour apt to be conspicuous in a tall man. An observer some distance off might have mistaken him for a brown bear, driven from the depths of the *taigá* by pangs of hunger to scavenge in this urban excrescence.

Excrescence? Indeed. Excrescence after the inimitable Russian style. Those neo-classical buildings, resplendent in their pastel tones at an earlier and more hopeful hour, now looked shabby if not sordid in the struggling light.

As he turned off the embankment towards this city centre – precinct of innumerable provincial tyrannies – the signs of excrescence became more profound. Peeling lead-based paint held together diseased masonry, whose rusty reinforcing rods protruded like complex bone fractures. Intractable potholes, full of toxic oil-stained thaw, blighted all thoroughfares, aggravating motorized traffic, pedestrians, and the not infrequent rodent. Abandoned machinery, stripped of its copper wiring in the dead of night by hungry vagabonds, succumbed to ruin on every vacant lot. The need for a modicum of upkeep and public order was evidently beyond the capabilities of whatever hapless civic authority was able to eke out an existence in parallel with the reality of the insistent grab of the oligarchs.

Matt was beset not only with the bitter conditions, and with his disagreeable impressions of the environs, but also with disturbing thoughts stemming from his business transactions aboard the *Anna Ahkmatova*. These thoughts drained his morale. They threatened the autonomous mechanisms designed to preserve his mortal existence. His feet were as heavy as the bloodless chunks of crumbling concrete surrounding him. His head was as light as the air taking orders from the billowing gale. His body ached although (or perhaps because) his cryogenically challenged mind had left it. His soul, whose existence depended at the best of times on dubious theological considerations, was not about to declare itself at the worst of times. Hypothermia hovered, with death close by in its wintry vortex.

He was spared disaster. In timely fashion, and without the ghost of an imprint on his brain to remind him how such a miracle had occurred, Matt found himself leaning over a steaming bowl at a table in a small *restorán* only doors from his hotel. What kindly Slav, he speculated, had rescued him?

The bowl contained chunks of chewy reindeer meat, swimming in brown broth, with portions of cabbage and potato for company. He washed this restorative dish down with mouthfuls of Baltika No. 4, a fine ale, straight from the bottle. Snow, unsurprisingly, fell outside. The *restorán*, heated by communal hot water, invited him to enjoy its cosiness. His heavy coat was behind him, draped over the back of his chair. His *ushánka* was stuffed into a coat pocket. Once again, he was in shirtsleeves. This was survival, Karelian style.

A postcard, tatty leftover from some past summer tourist season, lay beside his bowl. He wiped its surface clean of food spatter with the edge of the gingham tablecloth, flipped it, read what he had just now written on its back, sighed, and placed it on top of a stack of several postcards he intended to send. The picture on the postcard showed the lake and the embankment, but not the marooned freighter. Instead there was a sleek hydrofoil, doubtless brimming with sightseers, slicing its way through ice-free waters, bound for fabulous Kizhi Island. He had bought these postcards yesterday from a *magazín* across from his hotel.

Pademelons, that top postcard was a love letter written to *me*!

>

Though subject to the vagaries of the Russian postal service, the postcard *did* reach me. Penny and I were holding the fort for Matt half way round the world. Pademelons, when it arrived I was chuffed.

Is there nothing, I asked, my man *can't* do?

It appears, said Penny, he has bearded the Russian bear.

The card told of the weather. It told of the triumphs of Matt's dealings in Petrozavodsk. It told of the impending dispatch of a half dozen young female models to Oz. It told of his loneliness, not failing in this context to mention he was pining for me. It told of his feelings for me, in terms likely to cause him embarrassment when he came later to reflect on its libidinous phraseology. It was signed off, *Yours longingly, Matt, who will love you to the death.*

How very prescient.

A confidence, pademelons. For the brief time remaining to me on as opposed to under terra firma, I kept that postcard close by. I treasured it. I drooled over it daily. I feasted my eyes on it. I smelt it. I kissed it. It was a fragment of special joy for me come all the way from my dearest, albeit not my nearest, a godforsaken corner of the globe having swallowed him up for the foreseeable.

I no longer have this treasured article with me. My grip on it was loosened by circumstances and it drifted far from me. It is no longer within my orbit, whose spaceless ellipse – I had dared to hope – would entrap an item so deficient in compass or substantiality. What price hope?

How did this loss come to pass, an event the mention of which rends my heart to a degree and in a manner only capable of appreciation by supernal folk such as we? I shall tell you:

> One's bound to find, within one's breast,
> those fateful words so often said
> and, once occasioned, mostly fed
> (I'm loath to say) with ribald jest:
> 'One cannot take it with one, man.'
> They scorch one's soul, the words ablaze,
> or morph to mordant paraphrase:
> 'What life entreasures, death shall ban.'

Pademelons, I hate that!

<

The other postcards in the stack?

As you know, pademelons, there are things I could never know while I was mortal, which my omniscient powers can now penetrate. In my superlunary incarnation, I can know all things knowable, including things my curiosity and jealous predisposition *incline* me to know.

Zounds. By the goitre that gallops, change that word to '*compel*'!

What *are* these things I am compelled to know? Let me enlighten you. They are the intended destinations of these postcards. And more besides.

So let us sneak a guilty glance at the accommodating pile of greetings, that rectangular stack of good cheer, hovering beside

Matt's bowl, in the cosy *restorán* in central Petrozavodsk, late in the snow-bedevilled afternoon in question. Matt need have no inkling he is being spied upon, nor by whom.

Some of what our prying eyes find is to be expected. There are postcards from Matt to his father and siblings. There are postcards from Matt to colleagues like Penny and me. But that's not all. Oh, no.

In the stack, is a postcard to someone familiar to all of us, but whom my mortal self has yet to meet. I refer to Harry A McMinn, Esq.

I need not reveal the content of this postcard chapter and verse. But I shall say this. Between the lines a jealous mind could readily construe a degree of gratuitous – and, I would hope, unrequited – sentiment. Matt, love of my life, you are a duplicitous dog.

Pademelons, I put this question to you. Is it my fate to be haunted by retrospective jealousy for the best part of my tenure in this eternal realm? (My meagre grasp of mathematical theory informs me the best part of eternity is *itself* eternity.)

Be more precise, you say. What exactly am I afraid shall haunt me? I shall tell you. Thoughts, replete with vivid mental pictures, shall haunt me. Of Matt and Harry playing the roles of old school friends. Of Matt and Harry yoked together to roll a tennis court. Of Matt and Harry squeezed together, thigh against thigh, in the umpires' box. Of Matt teaching Harry the ins and outs of cherrybobs and winkipops. Of Harry and Matt probing the meaning of life over a *Bisquit* or three. Of Matt rescuing Harry from a moribund future with Unthank Engineering. Of Matt steering Harry towards the bright prosperous new reality of Integrated Electronic Imagery.

Oh, pademelons, pademelons. A can of worms, a can of worms. This is the how and why of the undoing of my earthly sojourn. My susceptibilities – as do yours – defy computation. The soundings of mortals cannot fathom them. How shall I bear the unbearable?

>

Snow carpetted the main street of downtown Petrozavodsk and took a stranglehold on the afternoon. Premature darkness shrouded the streetscape. Evening had muscled out afternoon in a fashion typical of this time of year and extremity of latitude.

This was *not* Nevsky Prospect. The brightest light in the street, barely enough to read one's watch by, came from the *restorán* almost at the junction of said street with a stagnant lane. I say 'almost' because, wedged into the masonry between the *restorán* and the lane, was a decrepit ATM. Its console – in better days a harbinger of ready cash – was littered with broken bottles, its slot jammed with foreign objects ranging from the impish to the downright dangerous. Needless to say, it would have been the height of personal fiscal irresponsibility to even *think* of inserting a card into this slot.

Had this street been a desert, the *restorán* would have been its oasis. Its wan light, spilling onto its bleak environs, was a drawcard. In spite of (or perhaps because of) the condensation obscuring it, the plate-glass facade told of warmth, conviviality, and freely-flowing vodka inside. Never was a welcome call from inside in so much contrast with the conditions prevailing outside.

Once inside, the heart's cockles (whatever they may be) were reassured, and made deliciously warm besides. At tables, absorbed groups, mostly men, were at play. The more inebriated groups played some Slavic variant of euchre noisily. The more sober played chess silently. A pleasant buzz of those uniquely Russian vowel sounds provided a soothing background upon which the occasional jagged-edged consonant might sometimes intrude.

Matt, with his postcards, sat alone at the small table where earlier he had enjoyed reindeer goulash. He was not, however, *left* alone. That was not the Russian way. He was a curiosity and, as such, needed to be plied with cheap vodka and riotous song. Especially vodka. He counted his drinks warily. Through comparable experience in Oz, he figured if he downed more than five or six shot-glasses-full of the rough and ready stuff on offer, he would spend the night under the table, resurfacing mid-morning with a throbbing head and an emerging apprehension his tweed overcoat was gone and his pockets picked. And an inkling somebody – Gogol? – had forewarned him.

His thoughts turned to the *Anna Akhmatova* flying her colours on the embankment. She surely carried the brightest lights in town. He wondered how festivities below deck were progressing. He feared for the pretty young princesses, and began to feel his mission was justified after all because he was rescuing a handful of them. He hastened to explain to himself the moral ground he occupied would suit the likes of Mother Teresa. His earlier qualms were a joke.

Suddenly he remembered the card O had given him, purporting to provide details of an Australian contact willing to work alongside the anonymous R and G, to 'expedite delivery' of the 'merchandise'. He thrust his hand into his shirt pocket. It came out with the item in contention.

He examined the card. Its contents rang a tiny bell in the reverberant recesses of his memory. It said: **Sal Heffernan, Esq, International Operative**, and gave contact details.

2nd >>

Singspielstück #11: Catwalkery

We sit just to the right of centre in the front row. House lights go down, and stage lights come up. Mostly uniform illumination exposes to us an enigmatic setting. Of course, enigma being our natural condition, we take it in our stride.

Imagine a diameter on the turntable stage extending from 8 o'clock near the front to 2 o'clock near the back. A red carpet runs its ten metres of length. About a metre wide, this select walkway is a step higher than its surrounds. Rows of individual seats, two on each side, face it.

The seats eschew sleaze resolutely. They are elegantly designed, high backed, and devoid of cheap synthetics. Oaken structural members support soft felt cushions. Shifts as soft as muslin and as light as gossamer enclose the chair legs as a sarong might enclose human legs. God forbid the legs of either should offend decency.

Actors playing well-heeled mostly female spectators pack the seats. At first glance, we find no familiar faces. We conclude this is the usual rent-a-crowd from Sandalwood.

At the decree of a Sleek Street guru by now familiar to us, each woman is conspicuous by the outlandish high fashion fitting her out. We intuit the guru's rationale. He seeks to underscore the current of malevolent competition swirling among and between these ladies. Self-styled sophisticates, ladies putatively of high calibre, they are determined at any cost to out-gun their rivals in the fashion stakes.

We wonder what might come hurtling down the red track. A mechanical lure pursued by a pack of salivating greyhounds?

We identify – on second glance – some familiar faces. Eyeballing us at 8 o'clock, and sitting next to each other at the near end of the walkway on its left, are Matt and Penny. That's Penny Galatano, of course, whom we first encountered in *Stück* #2. Penny Galatano, who you may remember played a young Brenda McMinn. Penny Galatano, Matt's colleague in the rag trade, who runs a house of *haute couture* down the road from Dress Rules. Penny Galatano who, together with yours truly, looked after Matt's interests while he was gallivanting around Russia.

So the penny – pun unintended – drops. The stage setting we see represents a catwalk in Penny's establishment, the recently renovated Wintergarden building in Lyceum Street. In depiction, the catwalk is foreshortened, as stage size dictates. At her premises, we are likely to encounter Matt's newly acquired models from Russia. We look forward to the prospect.

We may have cleared up *one* enigma, but plenty more await us, one of them composed of flesh and blood.

A case in point, pademelons, apropos of enigmas. The seating area to the right of the far end of the catwalk is in partial shadow. We suspect this is a deliberate ploy by Sticks, the director. We suspect she is setting us up for a surprise to be sprung at a later moment. Try as we might, we cannot make out the occupants of this shadow. But we *are* distracted at times by stabs of laser-sharp light of a warmish hue, as if from small lustrous objects, reflected from this quarter.

A fresh-faced young man, who would – take my word – be considered extremely cute in certain circles, leaps onto the stage from the left, digital SLR camera in hand. We have met him before. He is the slim golden-haired youth inclined to liaise with Matt outside these Sleek Street premises post *Singspielstücke*.

Matt and Penny, nearby, acknowledge his entrance with exaggerated gestures of approbation, including extravagant hugs. He crouches in front of them, and begins setting up shots down the catwalk.

This is Mark. Mark, a.k.a. Snapper, fashion photographer from the Apple Isle[41]. Mark, recently discovered by Matt. Mark, object of Matt's affections. Mark, reciprocator of such affections.

Here we are faced not so much with an enigma as with a paradox. Mark, apparently, is in two places at once. Mark, the mortal, is on stage. Mark, the supernal, none other than me, is in the theatre audience, chuffed to see his alter ego strut the stage. That my second unit has recruited Mark to play himself only reinforces the paradox. We have a deceased person onstage.

Pademelons. Listen to the clapping and enthusiastic vowel sounds from those who play the onstage spectators. Models,

---

41 Tasmania.

I believe, are about to make their entrance. Please resolve the erstwhile paradox as best you may.

They come. Just Elena at first, from backstage onto the far end of the catwalk, savouring spots of light placed for her benefit. She is playing herself as she would have graced the world some ten or twelve years earlier. The *actor*, Elena, aged about thirty years is playing the *character*, Elena, aged in her late teens.

... of course, the same may be said of the other principals in Sticks' troupe. They too have had makeovers reducing their apparent age by an similar amount ...

More models of Nordic appearance follow in Elena's footsteps, six of them all up, their svelte young frames spaced two metres apart along the catwalk. They have learnt their new trade well. Flaunting their fair complexion, their practiced pout, and their mincing gait – each of them affecting superior knowledge as regards all things fashionable – these Karelian princesses lope long-leggedly down the catwalk towards Matt and Penny. Each contender is clad in one of the fabulous creations *de rigueur* in the house of Dress Rules.

One of the hacks writing for that glossy mag known as '*Catwalkery*' might have chosen words like these to describe Matt's creations:

... when offset to stupendous effect by the ambience of lighting and venue, they exude subtlety of colour, integrity of weave, fluidity of line, and singularity of cut, effectively invoking mother nature herself, with all her terrifying beauty, coupled with her unique ability to meld the simple and the complex into a gestalt both magnificent and coherent. Hanging loose in appearance while in reality remaining taut to the nth degree, these quintessential garments invest the chaste yet nubile bodies of these fairest-of-fair Eves with the redolence of taste, salubrity, flamboyance, and eco-friendliness ...

Irrespective of what flapdoodle these imitable scribblers write, the aim of the exercise is, of course, economic. It is to groom the minds of cashed-up clients in their late thirties and upwards –

doctors' wives as Matt calls them – for blithe transference of what they see on the catwalk to their own less likely bodies, thereby inducing them to open their purses wide.

Mark ducks and weaves with vigour, his camera throwing forth spitballs of light in rapid fire. Izzie, from behind the turntable, makes magic in the shape of introductory bars in 3/4 time and major key. The turntable lurches into slow clockwise rotation.

Elena, in sweetly accented soprano, and on cue, projects song as she struts:

Elena:

Our heels are hurling,
our pert lips curling,
our hemlines swirling,
our midriffs whirling,
our skirts unfurling.
We're walking on plank, bearing insolent swank, making scowl.

Reaching the other end of the catwalk, adjacent to Matt and Penny, Elena swivels on high heels with balletic grace, setting course in the reverse direction. The other five models, taking their lead from Elena, do the same, one by one and in their turn.

Fake faces frigid,
arms straight and rigid,
no moment to fidget,
no twitching of digit,
blink must be so midget.
We venture on mats like some malnourished cats having prowl.

Meanwhile, the stage has turned through a half circle, bringing the mysterious parties, previously obscured by inadequate lighting, closer to us. When rotation brings them to a position adjacent to us, in the same relation to us as were Matt and Penny at the start of the session, i.e. almost full in our faces, we are able to identify them.

There are four of them, men, hiding behind dark glasses.

One, seated, is portly and balding, his image redeemed to an extent by his immaculate dress after the Italian style. His aura of prosperity dazzles, as do the emanations from the topaz and ruby rings on the fourth and fifth fingers of his right hand, rings hurling their glints with abandon round the precincts.

Sal Heffernan! Otherwise known as Hefty! Who else?

Two dour men, palpably of foreign origin, stand to Sal's right in ill-fitting suits lending them the appearance of on-course bookmakers *sans* bags. They are virtually indistinguishable one from the other. Tweedledum and Tweedledee? No. My guess is they are letter R and letter G, recent arrivals from Russia. To borrow Sal's phraseology: '... useless commie stooges I keep finding under my fucking feet.'

A small man, frail and emaciated, sits alert and mournful on Sal's left. Turned side-on he would be invisible. This is Snow, afflicted these days with oesophageal cancer. For him the prognosis is bleak. Today is one of his rare good days. It would be a cruel joke to wish him well, but we can perhaps feel comfortable extending our sympathies.

Are these four people playing themselves? you ask. How could this be? I reply. Harry has never met any of them in his life. If he cannot construct a stage presence for them from the cache in his head known as memory, then he must resort to the alternative cache known as imagination, read 'Sandalwood'. Look closely. Sal is played by that most versatile of imagined actors, Godfrey Goldsworthy, erstwhile singer of madrigals.

The enigma now facing us is: what brings this criminal coterie to this unlikely venue? We dread to think.

Elena, adjacent to the men, flashes them an equivocal look, reflective of both scorn and fear. She effects another elegant

U-turn, challenging the five protégés following on her heels to do as well or better when their turn comes.

In response, there is widespread applause from the spectators, including from the four men with an undeclared interest in proceedings. Continuing her song, Elena stays on message for the benefit of those punters who have no need to declare their interest. Clearly, these moneyed folk are happy to immerse themselves in creative couture with a soupçon of backbiting stirred in to add colour and flavour.

Elena:

Youth and fashion are here on display for you.
Fashion you pay for though youth mightn't stay for you.
Nevertheless it's such wonderful day for you.
Open your cashbook and jump into fray.

Four of the five models who follow Elena strut past the four men, affecting nonchalance, doing their stuff. But, as the fifth approaches, R and G step forward as one and beckon her with curling forefingers. Her face registers alarm. As she is about to bolt, the wannabe twins snatch her from the catwalk. They manoeuvre the struggling princess off the edge of the turntable and away to someplace backstage, presaging for her a future we can only guess at while fearing the worst.

At the other end of the catwalk, Elena swivels on her heels again, in time to witness the ambush. In disbelief, she covers her mouth momentarily with her hand, then quickly dissembles. She continues her strut gamely towards this putative press gang, the other four models trailing – not so gamely – behind.

After a few seconds, R and G return *sans* the abducted model or any show of concern. Situation normal. Mission accomplished. They take up their places again beside Sal and Snow.

The stage stops rotating. Matt and Penny, having travelled full circle, are adjacent to us again. To say they look bemused by the recent turn of events, i.e. by the brazen snatch and grab of one of their models from under their noses, would be a bald understatement.

Mark also shows concern. But, like a professional – for which cachet I am happy to vouch – he continues to take photographs. On his knees at the near end of the catwalk, he contorts his body, striving to achieve shots of the (now only five) models, lead by Elena, as they exit the catwalk at the far end before heading backstage. He does not fail, while at it, to get shots of the abductors.

While the last model exits, this quartet of miscreant intent, well illuminated now and standing to face us, celebrate their triumph with song, the metre of which is now 4/4 time:

Quartet:

Six lean models go mincing down the mall.
Six lean models go mincing down the mall,
and if one lean model should chance to get the call,

... R and G step forward and beckon with curling forefingers
...

then there'll be
five lean models go mincing down the mall.

Sal and Snow resume their seats. R and G resume their standing position to the right of Sal. Lights on the four men go down, leaving them in shadow again. The stage now looks the same as it did when the session started.

Adjacent to their nemeses, and with wary eyes on them, the five remaining models re-emerge from backstage with fresh outfits to flaunt, Elena leading the way. The audience sounds its approval with applause and vowel-laden vocals. The stage resumes its clockwise rotation, the music reverts to 3/4 time, the models resume their strut, and Elena resumes her song.

Elena:

Mark our devotion
to zealous promotion

of youth's magic potion
through elegant motion.
We've traversed whole ocean
to promenade here so as better to peddle our wares.

... she turns neatly on her heels and heads back the way she came ...

Models are walking,
and not never baulking.
So vendors are stalking,
and clients are gawking,
and chequebooks are talking.
We're better off running with bulls than go sulking with bears.

... she swivels and changes direction again ...

Live in your dream world. These outfits are made for it.
Why hesitate when sly bitches have bayed for it?
Your treasure for taking as soon as you've paid for it.
Show your credentials. Don't never delay.

Swivelling and changing direction again, Elena is horrified to see R and G snatch another model from the end of the line and drag her offstage.

Stage rotation stops. The four remaining models exit backstage from the far end of the catwalk. Having disposed of their latest abductee, R and G return to take their positions in the notorious quartet. Well illuminated, and standing once more to face the theatre audience, the four men sing in 4/4 time:

Quartet:

Five lean models go mincing down the mall.
Five lean models go mincing down the mall,
and if one lean model should chance to get the call,

... R and G again with curling forefingers ...

then there'll be
four lean models go mincing down the mall.

The music stops. Stage lights go down. The turntable stage is inky dark. What gives? you ask. I am unable to enlighten you.

Two spots are thrown, to positions on the immediate left and right of the stage platform. Visible now but dimly lit, the catwalk milieu is a frozen tableau.

Harry appears in the left spot and Sticks in the right. Their clobber, by contrast with that of the frozen people, is everyday. Both have hands on hips in assertive postures, as if neither one is willing to brook argument from the other.

Their discourse is theatrical. They speak sharp words to each other, but the language of eye and body is directed to the theatre audience, which happens to be us.

Like my directorial style? asks Sticks.

What's to like? asks Harry.

Why do I bother? Might as well get back to the action.

No need.

Why 'no need'?

Everybody knows how things go from here.

How?

It's a countdown.

O.K., wise-guy. Tell me how the countdown goes.

Like all countdowns go.

Tell me.

Four models … three models … two models … one …

Stop right there!

At 'one'?

At 'one'!

Not 'zero'?

At 'one'!

That's where the action resumes?

You've got it, pal.

The spots on Harry and Sticks go off. The warring pair have

de-materialized. Stage lights come up on the catwalk and on the well-heeled spectators, no longer frozen. Their placements are as they were when the session began.

Elena enters the catwalk, adjacent to the sinister foursome. Yet another outfit from Dress Rules is draped around her, to the delight of the clients, who respond with the usual applause and vocals.

Izzie plays it again in 3/4 time, the stage rotates clockwise, and Elena lopes down the catwalk towards Matt and Penny. But, pademelons, a shock is in store for us. We wait for an indeterminate number of other models to emerge and follow in Elena's footsteps. None do!

Elena, last model standing, shall brave the catwalk alone.

Her demeanor tells us she is aware of this. Her façade of nonchalance has evaporated. Taking its place is anxiety, barely disguised. She is clothed not only in creations of *haute couture*, but also in her own fragility.

Elena:

Total confusion
and grim disillusion
from growing profusion
of wicked collusion
whose only conclusion
will shackle me, body and soul, and with throw-away key.

... she turns on her heels and heads back towards the gang of four ...

Determination
to honour my station,
oppose relocation,
avoid sequestration,
embrace liberation,
for living in world where my will and my fancy are free.

We, immediately adjacent, see it all. R and G step forward to beckon Elena. She falters, her legs crumbling beneath her like a deer that has taken a shot to the heart.

The stage stops rotating. Izzie stops playing. Stage lights go down and a broad spot is thrown on the crucial events unfolding before our eyes. Unexpectedly, Sal steps forward. He interposes his substantial body between Elena – on her knees – and the two Russian men.

Leave her, says Sal. She stays.

The boss will not like this, says R.

Say again, pal? says Sal.

The boss will not like this, says G.

Snow, oesophagus *in extremis* but mind sharp, slaps his brow with his palm, in mockery of the two Russians. Addressing them, he speaks, with downward inflexion on his key word.

Oh, you mean the *boss*, says Snow.

The *boss*, say R and G in unison.

Snow, turning to Sal, continues to mock the Russians.

Mr R and Mr G are concerned about what the *boss* might think, says Snow.

Get a good squiz of my fucking face, you Bolshie bludgers, says Sal. *There's* your boss.

Stage action is frozen as the spot goes off and theatre lights come up. We stifle an urge to clap.

>

Pop.

It's champagne time.

House lights and stage lights provide illumination for all who may need it.

Izzie, behind stage at his synthesizer, works on a variety of pieces set to romance our auditory processes at some time down the track.

Clockwise from right, going round the card table at stage front, are: Harry, Sticks, Matt, Mark, Elena, and Godfrey. It is a cosy fit. They, all six, still wear their costumes and grease paint from the *Stück* just finished. Godfrey's dark glasses sit low on the bridge of his nose. Peering over the top of them, he is pleased to make eye contact with all and sundry.

We conclude these ardent thespians are reluctant to part with the voluptuous theatrical moment.

Penny, also in costume, hovers behind their backs, serving the bubbly. Godfrey twists in his seat to speak to her.

Is it her directorial debut? he asks.

No, says Penny. You missed that one. But she's overdue for plaudits.

Crossing the stage, she mounts Izzie's platform to offer him a glass. He tosses it back in one with his right hand, while his left continues to riffle the keyboard. She returns, and manages somehow to squeeze between Matt and Mark at the table. Harry decides to muddy the waters.

We all know, he says, that's not the way things happened.

Say again, says Sticks.

The abductions didn't happen right off the catwalk.

How *did* they happen perchance?

A friendly call at 3 a.m. is my guess.

Well I'll be hung, drawn, and quartered, ...

She follows up her feigned surprise with unfeigned anger.

... when I'm ready to engage with naturalism, I'll send you, registered post, a hefty dose of reality in the form of a gift wrapped steaming turd.

Penny raises her glass.

To Sticks, she says. Always ready to turn a phrase. And to ...

There are echos all around the table of 'To Sticks'.

... Elena. Not only the actor of a model but also the model of an actor.

All, Harry grudgingly, raise their glasses and mumble indecipherable toasts.

Mark is reviewing the shots he has taken. Sticks questions him.

Did you get good ones of the crims? she asks.

Mark passes the camera to her.

It wasn't easy, he says. They're somewhat camera averse.

The dark glasses?

And they like to lurk in shadows.

Hang on, Mark. These are *good*.

Wanting to see for themselves, everybody (except Izzie) gathers behind Sticks. Appreciative vowel sounds and hisses of aspirated breath fill the air. Harry points.

That one ... , says Harry.

Hefty, says Matt.

I thought it was Godfrey, says Harry.

Over the top of his glasses, Godfrey glares at Harry.

Some of us here, he says, see value in stage illusion.

The badly dressed pair? asks Penny.

Russians, says Elena.

The little guy? asks Sticks.

Got to be Snow, says Penny.

He looks sick.

Cancer, says Matt. He died. Hung on for quite a few years. Tough little bugger.

Mark, says Sticks, you have talent. These are wonderful photos. They deserve international acclaim. They should travel.

They have, says Matt. They caused a stir in Russia. They won *prizes* in Petrozavodsk.

In Malaysia also, I hear, says Penny.

Barry tells me, says Elena, his father makes life-size posters from them. Useful for target practice.

<< 1st

At the buzz of the intercom, they – not expecting company that evening – quizzed each other with their eyeballs.

Who? asked Sticks.

She was pregnant, into the second trimester. She insisted, and a reluctant Harry conceded, his city apartment, fit for purpose till now, would no longer be adequate when there were three of them. It was fine for one, passable for two, but for three … ? Especially when the third person would likely be a mischievous little tyke, preferring to wreak his/her havoc in the down, dirty, and open spaces of suburban terra firma.

Harry knew he would miss this pad. Resignation remained his only option. When he needed a reminder, he told himself, of what life in the vertical had been like, his aboriginal paintings would provide it.

Hello, said Harry into the intercom.

The voice on the other end was female, tinged with anxiety, with hesitancy, and with a foreign accent neither Harry nor Sticks recognized.

You are Harry McMinn? the voice asked.

Yes.

Menyá zovút … Izvinítye![42] I am so sorry. My name is Elena Rusalkova. May I come in to talk with you?

Yes … ah … who sent you?

The voice contained sobs.

Nobody never sent me. I seek asylum.

Placing his hand over the intercom, Harry – bewildered – turned to Sticks.

She says she seeks asylum, he said.

I heard, turkey, said Sticks. Invite her up.

Harry spoke into the intercom.

Come up, he said.

---

42 *Menyá zovút … Izvinítye!*: My name is … Excuse me!

Harry pressed the button to open the downstairs security door. He and Sticks exchanged more quizzical looks. Seconds later came the timid knock at the door.

Come in, said Harry and Sticks simultaneously.

For the first time, they cast eyes on Elena, a person who was to turn their lives upside down. Winter was barely over, but she was dressed only in a flimsy shift with light sandals, apparently her sole possessions. Her knees were blue. She shivered involuntarily.

They ushered her to a lounge seat next to the fan heater, and fixed her a hot toddy. Wrapping her frozen hands round the mug, Elena told them how Matt, in cahoots with someone called Sal Heffernan, together with a slew of Russian criminals from Petrozavodsk, had duped her and her fellow models, selling them into prostitution.

>

It was, said Matt, as if they were snatched off the catwalk under my very own eyes.

The glimpse those eyes caught in the mirror across from where their owner sat revealed all. He was under siege, a person of interest, a prime suspect, the accused, the co-perpetrator. It was there in the anxious lines, the tense mouth, the wide pupils. He felt surprised yet thankful there was no trace of sweat on his brow. But that haunted? hunted? look said better than words, 'Guilty, Your Honour.'

He had not brought his customary bottle of *Bisquit*. The occasion was serious, and demanded sobriety.

So where were you, sport, when these helpless girls needed you? asked Sticks.

By prior arrangement, Sticks was taking the role of inquisitor, sparing Harry the odium of putting the boot into his 'old school friend'. Harry's role was to lend silent support. Good cop, bad cop. Matt felt the pressure.

Shit, this has been a disaster, he said.

Of your making, said Sticks.

You've got me wrong.

Give us your version.

Matt sighed.

My idea, he said, was they would work as models. That was plan A. I *had* no plan B. But *somebody* did. Because five of them disappeared into thin air. All except Elena.

...whom you claim is *lying* to us about your criminal intent? asked Sticks.

Do you believe I'd be involved in stuff like that? asked Matt.

Sticks softened her stance.

I don't know, Matt. I don't know any longer, she said.

She sighed. Not Newton, not Einstein would have been able to compute the gravity of the silence ensuing.

Sticks broke it.

Feeling maligned? she asked.

A tad.

I'm only trying to get to the bottom of this ugly mess.

I know that.

Matt palmed his heavy eyes. He paraphrased Sticks' earlier question, following up with an inconclusive answer.

Is Elena lying? Maybe she is. Or ...

Why might she lie?

... perhaps she misunderstands my role.

Why might she lie?

Look, I hesitate to disabuse you, but has it occurred to you she may not be the innocent she makes herself out to be?

Be my guest. Disabuse me.

Let me ask *you* a question. Are you and Harry thinking of billeting her?

Maybe.

A word of advice. Don't let her anywhere near your business records.

Would you like to explain yourself?

Glad to. On the morning of the day Elena knocked on your door, I caught her out in a devious scheme she and that rogue Heffernan dreamt up between them.

Sticks and Harry reacted simultaneously.

This Sal guy? Harry asked. The hefty one? Sticks asked.

The same, said Matt.

Enlighten us, said Harry.

O.K., said Matt. Get this. She used my records to steal the identities of a number of my well-heeled clients. Then she made property investments in their names, using their loan accounts to take out mortgages. Sal paid off the mortgages, Elena sold the properties, and – bingo – his money is clean.

She did *that*?! was Sticks' response.

Many many times, said Matt.

She wouldn't be up to it, said Harry.

I found it hard to believe myself. But the facts have a persuasive voice. Come to my office. See those facts for yourself and let the same voice persuade *you*.

The interrogation had reached an impasse mere spoken word can find no way around. Silence held until it became sufficient of an embarrassment. Then Matt resumed.

Nor can I be certain, said Matt, Sal wasn't channelling other criminal operations through my premises. Not just money laundering.

Wait, said Harry. There's more.

If my suspicions are correct, said Matt.

Involving Elena? asked Sticks.

I'm pretty damn sure Elena has been using my office as a way station for offloading smack and methamphetamines to the local dealers.

Sheba! said Sticks. The little floosie has been in the country less than a year.

She'll be running it soon enough, said Matt.

Apparently.

Rising from her chair, Sticks paced the room. Suddenly she swung around to face Matt.

No bulldust? she asked.

None, said Matt.

She turned to the window, her palms supporting her lower back, her profile in silhouette. She looked bigger in the belly than her four months would have it. Outside, the setting sun lit up the window panes of the neighbouring buildings. A cityscape of towering infernos.

She turned again to face Matt.

We owe you an apology, she said.

Forget it, said Matt.

No, no, said Harry. Accept our apology for Christ's sake. We had no right to question your integrity as we did.

In your place, said Matt, I'd have done the same.

A celebratory round or two of *Bisquit* could have filled the silent moment marking the immense relief Matt was feeling. Tragically, there was none to be had.

Let me ask you one more question, said Sticks. Who is Michelangelo?

I'll play your game, said Matt. Could it be Mr Buonarotti, renaissance painter and sculptor?

Why should a dead painter be a threat to Elena?

She finds him a threat?

The word is poison to her.

A wry smile appeared on Matt's lips.

I have a theory, he said.

Share it?

Her minders back in Russia made their girls work like Michelangelo.

In who's universe?

How do you think he painted the Sistine Chapel?

... the penny took its time to drop ...

Sticks gasped and raised a hand to her mouth. Harry spoke.

Very little wriggle room for the man with the paintbrush, he said.

Even less for our Karelian gal, said Sticks.

Nothing for her but to reach for the hand of God, said Matt.

>

Had one been watching late in the afternoon on a particular mild spring day, one might have seen Elena, draped in a grey techie's coat, emerge from the huge mouth metaphorizing the front entrance to the Big Top, and set off with an armload of crushed cardboard towards a dumpster in front of the premises.

As she reached the dumpster, a taxi pulled up. Matt emerged, *Bisquit* in hand.

Hello, said Matt.

Hello, said Elena.

... but her regard was for the pebbles on the ground, her pose reminiscent of her days aboard the *Anna Akhmatova*, a pose reflecting an entrenched attitude of fear, resignation, and silent resentment, a pose familiar to Matt ...

Depositing her load in the dumpster, she scurried back inside the Big Top. Matt headed to the old shopfront, the former premises of Unthank Engineering, to seek out Harry and Sticks.

Soon after Matt entered the front door, Sticks – big in the belly and on a mission – erupted from it. She headed for, then broached, the front entrance of the Big Top. Seconds later, she re-emerged, Elena trailing reluctantly behind her. In tortured formation, the two women made for the old shopfront, and entered.

>

In the Nerd Centre, it was Harry, Matt, Sticks, and Elena. Harry sat behind his desk, regarding the unopened bottle of *Bisquit* Matt had placed before him. Elena sat beside Sticks' desk, scrutinizing the scratches on its laminate surface. Sticks stood defiantly over Elena. Matt, also on his feet, his discomfort showing, kept his distance from everybody.

Sticks opened the conversation, directing her comment and her determined gaze to Elena. Acid was in her words, acid such as might be flung with intent to injure, by a party with an aversion to being played for a fool.

Mr Bolton, she said, is *not* in collusion with Mr Heffernan, not for any purpose under the sun. Mr Bolton has never met the gentleman. None of us have had the pleasure except you. I accept Mr Bolton has colluded with your criminal associates in Russia, but only to recruit models for his fashion house. That is why he brought you here. Not for any other purpose. Do you read me?

Elena's eyes avoided those of Sticks. She continued to regard the surface of the desk in front of her, as if its texture contained some hidden meaning.

Go easy on her, said Harry.

Sticks was not ready for 'easy'. She continued to put the boot into Elena.

Mr Bolton, she said, owes you no apology. On the other hand, there are many apologies you owe Mr Bolton. For example, …

Halifax, said Matt. Call me Matt.

… *you* have colluded with the odious Mr Heffernan to use Mr Bolton's premises and his business records unlawfully. To abuse them for illegal purposes. Is this not true?

Silence held sway. Sticks repeated her question at higher volume.

Is this not true?!

Without looking up, Elena gave a barely perceptible nod. Matt spoke.

We need to cut this process short, he said. I'm across Elena's problem because I've seen her *in situ*. In Petrozavodsk. It's not a good place. I understand why she did what she did. I'm sure we'd all do something similar in her circumstances, if we didn't slit our throats first. For my part I'm happy to put it behind me. My affairs are easily repaired.

Moving towards Elena, he addressed her.

Can we bury the hatchet?

Elena looked up. Her face reflected the confusion in her mind. Matt rephrased his question.

Can we be friends?

Elena scanned the entire company, then returned her gaze to Matt. She gave another barely perceptible nod.

Matt shot a significant glance in Stick's direction, catching her eye.

All is settled, he said.

Everyone took the silence to signify unanimous agreement. Then Harry posed a question to Elena.

What made you seek refuge in our digs? he asked.

Digs? asked Elena.

Our apartment.

Elena became more forthcoming, possibly because she saw Harry's inquiry as a malice-free question to which the answer should have been self-evident.

I knew you were nice man because I saw you at Matt's shop one night. You were talking jokes and drinking this cognac …

She indicated the *Bisquit*.

… together.

I didn't see you, said Harry.

I hid myself. But I learnt your name. Harry McMinn.

How did you find out where I lived? asked Harry.

Sheba, said Sticks, you can be such a turkey. How do you think the girl knew?

Matt had opened the *Bisquit*, found tumblers, wiped their insides clean with a tissue, and poured drinks for four. As he passed Harry his glass, he enlightened him.

My records, boyo, he said.

>

' ... so work the honey-bees, creatures that by a rule in nature teach the act of order to a peopled kingdom.' One could imagine these fine words resonating down the ages to anticipate the punctilious activity within Harry's Big Top on a typical working day at the sparrow fart of the 21ˢᵗ century.

This peopled kingdom resembled a house of all nations. As electronic bulletin boards lurched along their designated assembly line, each in turn confessed its national allegiance. East and southeast Asian pictograms gleamed white hot on the torsos of these metallic beasts. This electronic lexigraphy was the product of Sticks' prodigious linguistic ability, the engine of which was the freakish way she was able by birthright to exercise to advantage the arcane mechanism of her memory. Sticks' skills had opened doors to lucrative international trade. Her contribution to Integrated Electronic Imagery was the stuff of legend.

Getting back to insects. If bees are symbolic of order, then butterflies, specifically the flap of their wings, are the reputed harbingers of chaos. Which brings me, pademelons, to the particular day when not one but *three* occurrences of lepidopteral flappery occurred within moments of each other beneath the roof of the Big Top. They feathered the air in such quick succession they might have been participants in some inscrutable act of collusion.

Real live butterflies? If these three occurrences could not

be traced back to the wings of *actual* butterflies, then they were assuredly ascribable to their metaphoric cousins.

Let us deal with them one by one. The first occurrence was the burst of inane music from Ramon's cell phone, the one he used for work purposes. The tune was the William Tell Overture, a musical cliché in its own right, and – in ringtone form – doubly so. Ramon, clipboard in hand, was monitoring the assembly lines when the phone affronted his ear, with an insistence inclined to impel its owner to find the bloody thing and crush it with a well-directed heel.

The phone was a clunky first-generation job, the size and shape of a shrivelled house brick, but nevertheless the technological wonder of the brand new millennium. Ramon normally had it stuffed into the back pocket of his yellow overalls but, on this occasion, when he fumbled for it, nothing was there. He suspected the call was a directive of some importance from the Nerd Centre across the way. Since he figured the phone's alert came from somewhere within arm's length, he swivelled his head and body energetically in all directions in the hope of pinpointing the recalcitrant device in timely fashion.

Voila! He located it. The phone had insinuated itself onto the opposite edge of the assembly line against which he stood, the one relentlessly churning out multi-screen systems. As he leaned awkwardly to retrieve it, his heavy boot made contact with something soft and furry beneath the workbench: the inevitable factory cat.

A mature female, she belonged to the select breed known in veterinarian circles as 'Common House Cat'. Until a few days ago she had survived *sans* a name, which oversight had caused her no grief. Nevertheless, by way of unsolicited redress, recent days had gifted her a moniker of considerable chic, though not one to which she was inclined to answer. She became known as Koshechka[43].

---

43 This name has a provenance. *Koshéchka* is an affectionate diminutive of *kóshka* which, in Russian, means 'cat'.

Now came the second instance of flappery. Despite her advancing years, Koshechka was capable of lively moments, especially when finding herself on the receiving end of an unceremonious boot. Screeching rupture to all eardrums, with claws extended for mayhem, and like the scalded cat of legend, she hurled herself onto the other assembly line, the one churning out bulletin boards.

Ramon, phone in hand, reacted by falling backwards heavily onto his bum. Ouch! But with good grace, and making a virtue of necessity, he remained seated, nursing bruises while he fielded the call. Meanwhile Koshechka looked set to be crushed under the looming weight of an incipient bulletin board dangling from the overhead crane.

Rescue was imminent. A grey-coated techie – a new chum – leapt into action, snatching the cat clear with moments to spare. Showing foresight, another techie hit the red emergency button. Both assembly lines ground to an ignominious halt, carcasses left swinging in the air like synchronous pendulums.

The third instance of flappery? Sonia Sheridan, carrying a cardboard carton, entered through the front vehicular door, testament to ventriloquism. Looking around to get her bearings, she headed towards Ramon, sitting with knees apart on the shop floor, phone pressed to ear.

Yes, said Ramon into the phone. She's here now.

The techie, patron saint apparent of small cats, who had effected the rescue, headed with the struggling moggy tucked under her arm towards the front (north-west) corner of the Big Top. A portion of this corner adjacent to the vehicular entrance, had been partitioned off in makeshift fashion with bamboo screens bound together with basket weave. As she approached this small shanty – tent within a tent? – she removed her hard hat, revealing tresses of fair hair tied up into a bun. And her identity.

Elena.

Her temporary living quarters were in this corner, behind the screens. The quarters were basic, immaculate, and obsessively neat. There was a low set bunk bed with a milk crate for a bedside table, a set of open shelves containing sundry utensils and personal effects, a collapsible table and chair, a mini-fridge, and a camp stove with gas bottle. A bowl and a dirt tray, with newspaper spread beneath them, met the modest needs of a small feline. An untidy jumble of books, audiotapes, tools, and other sundries, somebody else's evidently, had been swept without ceremony into a corner.

Elena entered. She put her hard hat on the table, then released her grip on Koshechka who took the opportunity to break for freedom. She had scarcely enough time to pour milk from the fridge into the cat's bowl, when she was startled by Sonia coming in behind her, with her cardboard carton and her proprietorial manner.

Hello, said Sonia. I'm Sonia.

My name is Elena, said Elena.

Sonia indicated the jumble in the corner.

I'm here to collect my belongings, she said. I used to work here. Please.

Stepping over the feeding cat, Sonia set about sorting through this confusion of items, every now and again transferring one to her cardboard carton. There was silence for a time. Then Sonia spoke.

You live here? she asked.

Since one week.

You are Russian?

You can tell?

I had a Russian ballet teacher.

She blew the dust off a videotape, packed it in her box, then looked up at Elena, scrutinizing her face pointedly.

These days there are plenty of Russians around the traps, said Sonia. I keep falling over them. Especially near where I work. In Lyceum Street.

Where is Lyceum Street? asked Elena.

... a card she played with insouciance as if Lyceum Street had not been her old stomping ground ...

The fashion district, said Sonia. South of the CBD.

I haven't never been there.

Her denial did not convince Sonia, on whose face the look of satisfaction was evidence what she had come for was not all she would be taking away.

Their *tête-a-tête* was interrupted by the voice of benign authority – Ramon's – powerful enough to penetrate the furthest reaches of the factory floor. He was calling the peopled kingdom of the Big Top to order.

Boys and girls, said Ramon. Party's over. The day's target must be met.

Elena grabbed her hard hat from the table.

Excuse me, she said. I must go.

2nd >>

Singspielstück #12: Be Beside the Seaside

We take our usual position in the stalls, eager for action to begin. As the theatre lights go down, stage lights flood the turntable uniformly.

The stage is carpeted in yellow, suggestive perhaps of beach sand. Reinforcing this suggestion are some of the paraphernalia of the seaside: beach umbrellas, banana lounges, colourful balls, and the like, strewn randomly around the periphery of the stage.

An anomalous black edifice, the size and shape of a small room, occupies centre stage. Essentially opaque, it is nonetheless composed of a glass-like material. It has four walls but no obvious door. For the want at present of any more suitable descriptor, I shall refer to it as the 'enclosure'.

What – one might ask – does it enclose? More-or-less opaque

it may be, but there *is* – if one looks closely – the suggestion of some shadowy creature – perhaps human – moving around inside.

Elena enters from left and mounts the turntable. The manner of her dress is familiar to us: short skirt and Slavic top in bright colours. Seemingly oblivious to the presence of the enclosure, she strolls across front of stage, absorbed in the small device in shocking pink she holds in her hand, something the size and shape of a cell phone. She stops to the right of centre front. The device has her undivided attention.

I alert you, pademelons, to an item of intelligence vouchsafed me by my second unit, an item of curiosity value only, but one which I shall share with you for what it is worth. The *Stück* we are about to see is unusual – though not unique – insofar as its four actors – Elena among them – shall play themselves. Play themselves, I hasten to inform you, as the wide world would have seen them some ten or so years prior to the date of the performance.

The second of these actors/characters, Ronnie Dash, drifts onto stage from the right. His appearance and manner – broad shorts, dishevelled fair hair, and nonchalance – apes the mien of a leisured surfer. Elena, sensing his approach, edges away nervously, not altogether glad to see him.

He speaks.

I've been sent, says Ronnie, to help you with the control you're wrestling with there but, between you and me, I'd rather a spot of the old SP bookie. Feel inclined?

The phraseology may confuse Elena, but she fathoms his intentions.

Ronnie, she says, I'm seeing Barry. You know that.

Barry? The future Sultan?

Yes.

Fancy yourself as a future Sultana?

You're being silly.

The favourite wife perhaps?

A hefty thump from inside the enclosure startles them.

Holy suffering of Christ, says Ronnie. Is the dude in there?
I think.

Ronnie covers his mouth with his hand, pretending shock.
However, it is in the nature of Ronnie and his ilk that a close
encounter with alien abduction would not unnerve them.

Look, says Ronnie. I want out of here. Let's cut it short.

Sidling up to Elena, he points to the buttons on the device she
clutches.

Four buttons, four functions, says Ronnie. One, two, three,
four. Choose the function you want, and press the button.

Elena looks dubious.

Try, says Ronnie.

Elena points her device at the enclosure, stabs a button, and
Voila! No longer is the enclosure black and opaque.

Colour gushes from its interior, washing over stage and
audience. Baharudin is inside. In wet suit, flippers, and scuba gear,
with virtual reality goggles in lieu of mask, he hangs, supported
by slings around shoulders and hips, like a submarine version of
Mary Poppins. A holographic diorama of a tropical reef surrounds
him. This diorama – with coral, clown fish, blue sea, and bubbles
in attendance – is suffused with that eerie kaleidoscopic glimmer
bringing to mind such unfortunate misalliances as Obi-Wan
Kenobi.

Ronnie skedaddles.

What gives here, pademelons? As will transpire, the enclosure is
a demonstration model of the virtual reality system commissioned
by the Sultan of K for the use of his nephew, brought to technical
fruition by Integrated Electronic Imagery, and depicted here in
Sleek Street with some degree of theatrical licence. Moreover,
the interface between the virtual world inhabited by Baharudin,
and the non-virtual world we all inhabit or have inhabited,
is nothing less than Ronnie Dash's long-awaited and much-
vaunted anisotropane. That we find ourselves overwhelmed by

technological miracles is a feature of the age we deal with. Get used to it, guys!

Baharudin is rapturous over his faux environment. Elena gives him a gentle wave. But, seemingly immersed in his own world, he fails to return the wave. She ups the ante. Her waving becomes progressively more-and-more furious and frantic. It is to no avail. He seems unable to observe her or, what in her mind would doubtless be far worse, unwilling to acknowledge her.

The splash of holographic colour is the cue for the stage to begin a slow clockwise turn, enabling us – the audience – to view the aquatic conurbation from all four sides, and forcing Elena to walk slowly anticlockwise to stay put. It is the cue, also, for Izzie's music to start. In bold major key and 4/4 time, it has a declamatory – almost operatic – flavour. Simulated percussion suggests the crash of surf. The tubas and trombones Izzie lets loose lurk like whales trawling fathomless depths.

Suspended in space, Baharudin bides his time until the musical introduction gives him his cue, at which time he breaks into ecstatic song, surprising us with his mellow and tutored tenor:

Baharudin:

Ocean wallow of tropic kind
serves to mollify my restive mind.
Blithe minnows skelter through the coral ways,
like roguish thoughts that cross and commandeer my pensive gaze.

Inside the enclosure, faux fish slither gracefully in their coral playground. Outside the enclosure, Elena resorts to handstands and other gymnastic devices to attract Baharudin's attention. But only the fish get from him the response she desires so frantically.

Fallow waters in pristine tones
soothe the marrow gel of jaded bones.
Svelte floral look-alikes beguile the eye.
The radiant totality shall shame the far-flung sky.

Frustrated, Elena points the control and stabs a button. The effect is immediate. Baharudin sees and acknowledges her. Delighted, he waves. Massively delighted, she waves back. A flurry of hand waving follows as he continues his song:

> Sea as blue as a trove of jewels
> spawns such multi-coloured fish in schools,
> rude reef's insurgency, a worthy sphere
> for rays and sharks successfully inciting mortal fear.

As sharks and rays swarm, Elena covers mouth with hand, mimicking fright. Baharudin hastens to reassure her with a confident pair of thumbs in the air.

> Colour, psychedelic revelry,
> such is oceanic devilry.
> Graffiti, dastardy of Davy Jones,
> is painted by the swirling seagrass strands in nature's tones.

While Elena and Baharudin throw kisses to each other across that magic interface between real and virtual worlds, Izzie – in his world – engineers a change from tonic to dominant, and from declamatory 4/4 time to a more prosaic 3/4 time. Baharudin continues to carry the lyrics, his message received with elation by Elena:

Baharudin:

> Mystery, the spur of my passion,
> presents as this indigent girl,
> maid without fetish for fashion,
> the grit apprehending the pearl.

... to which Elena, chuffed, replies in kind ...

Elena:

> Star-crossed, at sixes and sevens,
> I thrall to this credulous man.
> Childlike, he prays to God's heavens.
> Uncertain, he searches for plan.

... which message, with some trepedation, is more-or-less gratifying to Baharudin.

Elena points the control and stabs another button. To her feigned horror, the holographic display disappears from view. No longer is the stage washed by the brilliant but fugitive colour of the virtual world. Only the enclosure, flaunting its opacity, is visible. But if the shadowy movement from within is an indication Baharudin has not left the building.

His shadowy movement ... *and* his singing! At Izzie's wont, the music has reverted to tonic and to full-blooded 4/4 time. Baharudin, or perhaps one could say his shadow, takes up the lyrics:

Baharudin:

Mangrove mazes hanging pendulous,
grey green gardens waxing tendrilous,
sea shells fantastical, their ossuary
a final place for salt soaked squatters and attendant scree.

Distressed, Elena thumps the walls of the enclosure with fists, and kicks it with high heels.

Catch a glimpse of gentle dugong cows,
blissful in the grassy beds they browse.

Realizing the futility of her blows, Elena points and stabs once more. Baharudin reappears in full visual splendour amid a herd of dugongs the size of torpedos. But it is clear he is unable to see her. Elena points and stabs yet again.

For barramundi in this sanctuary
always to eat but not be eaten is their tendency.

Exit dugongs. Enter barramundi the size of baseball bats. Significantly, the human couple are able to resume their mutual communication across the interface between their two worlds. They bounce delight off each other, indulging in an ostentatious display of hand waving and kiss throwing ...

… and of singing to each other. The music switches once more to the dominant key and 3/4 time …

Baharudin:

Shared stuff is better than solo.
Mutual pleasure's divine.
I'm the example to follow.
Come in please. The water is fine.

Elena:

Sand in my crotch is big burden.
Brine in my hair isn't grand.
So, if you will please keep your shirt on
I'll join you for drinks on dry land.

The music stops. The virtual reality machine shuts down. Hussein, in his usual Malaysian gear, hurries from left, carrying a colourful beach towel He is almost brought to ground by a wayward beach ball.

Baharudin opens a disguised door in the enclosure and steps out, shedding all but his wet suit as he does so. He is, of course, bone dry. Nevertheless Hussein wraps the towel around his master and pats him down. Baharudin then takes the towel from Hussein and 'dries' his exposed skin: head, neck, hands, and feet.

Elena approaches and embraces him. The couple walk off together, arms round each other, wet suit mixing it with Slavic blouse. Hussein tags along behind.

Stage lights go off.

<< 1st

At this point in my presentation, pademelons, I propose we sharpen up those special powers, with which we are blessed, for the purposes of penetrating the heads of several of our protagonists in this tale and, so to speak, spy on their private reflections. What better way could there be to find out precisely where they are at in life's journey, faced with what is – as events shall make clear – a crucial juncture for them? If you will permit me a grandiose metaphor, these private reflections are the bonsai of the persona, pruned into grotesque shape by the secateurs of rabid introspection.

So ...

... in the execution of our scheme, we find one of the heads – guess whose? – full of bourgeois claptrap of the type:

... the bland hand dealt to me face down a relationship creeping up on me Sticks her name where I ask is the sign why no angelic choir instead a deal full of sixes and sevens no big deal at all creeping up by degrees no moment of glory the earth not shaken down no indication this woman is the one will I go to the grave never in receipt of a sign story of my sorry life no picture cards no aces but creeping up I am at pains to tell by stealth not at all like the way it played out that time once before love of Jesus the first time me a virgin is that perhaps why her name Sonia that was a wallop and a half won't you give me a sign Mulki the larker apropos of the one they call Sticks give me a sign any sign ...

What have we here aside from my name rendered in vain? Confusion. Like several voices in the head all talking at once. Like the 'stream of consciousness' fad all the rage among scribblers in the first half of the 20th century, its success mixed at best. Regardless, we shall press on. For I ask you, pademelons, apropos of what we have uncovered here: is not this the real thing, raw and unexpurgated? Is not this exactly the way private reflections shall present?

In whose head might we have been messing around? No prizes for this one, pademelons. We have just tapped the shambolic wetware resident in the headspace of Harry A McMinn.

Are you enjoying this game? O.K. Let's move on to the next head:

... parallel universes boyo one pure one perverse name of the father

must keep separate never the twain the old man insisting and father knows best and knows he knows best but bulldust he knows fuck all so twin universes Halifax isn't two enough face off across the divide this chasm of sexual preference father get fucked likewise Porridge these dual worlds I insist have no right no inclination to stay separate hear that father if the one I'm in dared speak its name it might declare itself homogeneous Mark there in spades fathers not admitted for me overlap of universes a consummation devoutly old school friend stuck fast in the other one a back door to be wished yes father stick that *up your mean little quoit* ...

Getting the idea? O.K. Try another:

... asphyxiation of the soul is virtual reality with a royal touch Oz my bolt hole never in a fit was it King's College no plighting of my troth to Classics nor to a Malayan throne delaying such plight an issue needing address in which respect my friends in low places in two words Big Top acknowledge me I them they wanting me waiting for me and never doubting I shall return oxygen there in the offing for the last gasp of my inner man Harry Sticks Elena et al all golden hearts but on the Peninsula only the pretence of a golden throne the throne a pretender for *a pretender how may I contrive to get out of this my commitment since birth wait I must and shall for a sign imprinted with Heaven's name God willing* ...

In the interests of gender equality:

... what sort of prize booby have I become a Babel fish a baby machine a freak a geek worse still I fear I have become a prude yes prude who would believe not always as you see me now once upon a time in a maggoty place faraway I was a blasphemous firebrand my name Annalise ask Agnes Wintergreen if you can ever find the woman at home not to complain no point denying Harry Matt and the rest treat me well but where were they when my mojo went missing and whence for me now sans mojo me practitioner of many tongues always more of such metaphor out of control simmer on the back burner waiting to be devoured by malnourished nerds but who can't for dear life find

her own *true lingo only option left seems to be mute appeal to a vision-impaired providence ...*

Oh my! So many ardent souls seeking signs!

There is another head we might investigate – female? – but this one is difficult to get into. Determined to keep its horrors to itself, it resists intrusion, as folk in recent times on opposite sides of the globe have determined. You should not find it impossible, pademelons, to guess the owner of this head.

There is yet another female head into which we might not *want* to get. Inside is a Sodom likely to daunt even the supernal crew it is our fate to be.

>

It's happened, said Elena, since that woman came. I didn't never trust her.

Sonia? asked Sticks.

... looking massively pregnant, Sticks was effectually desk-bound ...

Elena nodded. The door to the back room opened slightly, and Ronnie's head appeared in the gap, his inquiring eyes taking in all particulars of the confab proceeding in the Nerd Centre. Sticks instantly went on her guard, but Ronnie's attention was directed to Elena.

I'm with you there, sunshine, he said. I didn't never trust her neither.

You talking about the strange black car parked outside? Harry asked of Elena.

It is Chaika, said Elena.

Chaika?

Russian car. Very posh.

The door to the back room was fully open now, Ronnie framed by the jamb.

VIPs? he asked.

Doubtful, said Harry. Two spooks in dark glasses. They just sit there. They don't get out. They just sit there.

Russian spooks, said Elena.

Sticks' eyes swept all present.

How do we intend to get these goons off our case? she asked.

You know something else about that Sonia chick? said Ronnie. She's a legend. Does a neat job installing condoms using lips and teeth, nothing more. A final flick of the tongue and Bob's your uncle. Ready for action.

Harry looked like somebody having difficulty keeping down his breakfast. Sticks, exasperation on show, reset her voice to a higher volume and a sterner tone.

Ronnie, she said, we are trying to be serious here.

Harry turned to Ronnie.

How, asked Harry, might *you* have come by that sort of information?

Word of mouth, said Ronnie.

Temper in tatters, Sticks stabbed the air with a forefinger directed squarely at the space between Ronnie's eyes. Her voice as she shouted went right off the decibel scale.

Out!!! she said.

Ronnie proceeded to come in.

Not until you've heard my roundelay, he said.

Ronnie, don't dare …

As Sticks – awkward in her pregnancy but battle ready – rose from her desk, Ronnie strode across the office, positioning himself next to a steel filing cabinet. With deliberation, he placed his left hand on top of the cabinet. He used his right hand to smooth his hair, before redirecting it to the small of his back. Then, upon tilting his nose and chin upwards, his pose was complete. The attitude he struck conveyed an air of affected solemnity. He might have been standing beside an upright piano in a cosy Victorian drawing room, about to deliver a recitation to a select soirée.

Instead he delivered a song in melodious tenor voice:

I dreamt I'd developed twin marzipan balls,
and a phallus of praline besides.
So all who'd give head to me savoured withal
the sweetness of such a ride.
They'd flock from the east,
they'd blow in from the west,
for the sugar fest I'd provide.
(Sweet – Je – sus!)
From the full gamut my dreams could deploy,
there wasn't a frown on
a face going down on
my saccharine tackle
– a face going down on
my saccharine tackle –
my joy.

Ronnie concluded with a curtsy and a flourish of his right hand as if doffing a cap to an enthusiastic audience. Sticks picked up a stapler and flung it at his head. He ducked reflexively. The stapler hit the wall, releasing a spray of shrapnel.

Ronnie, unfazed, feigned offence.

If *that's* the way you feel, he said, I'll withhold the pearls of wisdom I *had* intended to share with you.

What freaking pearls of wisdom? asked Sticks.

Well, since you insist. Why shouldn't the Sultan condescend to take this piece of Russian fluff off our hands? He has a suite in the city centre large enough to be visible from space. He's a living breathing ticket to the life to which she's itching to become accustomed. I'm sure there'd be no hanky panky involved.

Ronnie winked at Elena.

None whatsoever, he said.

>

The powder-blue Bentley was being tailed by the black car identified by Elena as a Chaika. The boulevard they travelled along was illuminated extravagantly so headlights were unnecessary for safety. Nonetheless, headlight beams still served to announce presence. Those of the Chaika did this in spades, especially to the driver of the Bentley.

Hussein was this driver. Given his traditional Malay costume, one could imagine him wrestling with impossible gridlock in downtown Kuala Lumpur. Here tonight, in urban Oz, he enjoyed free flowing traffic.

By contrast, Baharudin – one of his back-seat passengers – had assumed the guise of playboy. Perhaps it was no guise, but a clue to his true identity.

His dress was evidence he had adapted well to his new environment. He had discovered superfine merino wool, which is what his pale grey slacks and matching jacket were made of. As a sop to his origins, he had supplemented this top-of-the-range western garb with his perennial gold songkok and shoes custom-crafted by royal decree in his home province.

The other back-seat passenger was Elena. Baharudin had cosied up to her, whispering suave nothings in her pink ear.

For the first time in her life, Elena was indulging a 'fetish for fashion'. She had concluded the loud two-piece clobber with Slavic blouse – her preference until now – was not appropriate for a date with a Sultan-to-be. In its place, she wore a one-piece outfit in demure apricot, such as would have passed muster even in Matt's discerning eyes. However, she had not gone so far along the path of 'demure' as to disguise her natural attributes of thigh and cleavage. The garment in question sported a hemline well north of her knees and boasted a generous declivity south of her chin. And the allure of her cow eyes was undiminished.

Hussein pointed to the rear-vision mirror. Baharudin nodded.

He said something to Hussein in Malay and, turning to Elena, said, Hold on.

Instantly, the vehicle executed a left turn of breathtaking acuity, veering onto a lesser road without reduction in speed nor trace of tyre squeal. It followed up with an equally sharp right into a one-way street – presenting, as things turned out, in the wrong direction – and almost immediately with a sharp left into a dark, narrow, and blind alley.

Bringing the vehicle to a halt, Hussein switched off the lights. The motion of his arm – downwards, limp-wristed, and emphatic – indicated they should all lay low.

They ducked. Seconds later, they saw the Chaika drift slowly past the entrance to the alley, almost silently it seemed, cruising the one-way street in the legal direction. Heads down, they waited. The Chaika did not return. Hussein raised his head. The others followed suit.

We cannot continue to do this, said Baharudin. It will only work the first time.

>

The following evening, the Bentley was tailed again. This time, responding to instructions from Baharudin, Hussein pulled off the boulevard at the Tomb of the Unknown Soldier.

This much-venerated monument, a tableau in verdigris-encrusted bronze astride a plinth of speckled granite, was situated in an oasis of well-established greenery, accompanied by an Eternal Flame. The tableau comprised a tripod of .303-calibre rifles with attached bayonets spearing the granite turf. Around this show of antiquated weaponry, spirals of faux barbed wire coiled. Poised on the conjoined butts, a digger's[44] slouch hat hung jauntily. Leaning against them, a Somme-weary digger found welcome support.

A moat hugged the perimeter of the monument. An amphitheatre of granite steps faced the moat.

This will do nicely, said Baharudin.

Elena thought she detected in his tone a resolve of which she had not before been aware. It worried her.

For what purpose? she asked.

He made no reply. She seated herself beside him on the lowest of the granite steps, facing the monument obliquely. Light, from a gibbous moon and from the Eternal Flame, illuminated one side of their respective faces, leaving the other in darkness, in mimicry of the moon itself perhaps. Hussein, tagging along behind, brought with him Baharudin's briefcase, crafted from premium crocodile skin, darkly stained. Placing this briefcase on the step beside his master, Hussein stood discreetly to one side as if on guard. Doubtless he was.

They waited for the Russian contingent to arrive.

The Chaika pulled up behind the Bentley. R and G emerged in their ill-fitting dark suits. Dry leaves rustled beneath feet as they walked towards their quarry. When they were close enough, there were rough acknowledgements all round via nods of the head. Not a word was spoken.

The stars of the southern sky, framed by the branches of majestic elms, bore witness to the pervasive silence and to events as they unfolded.

Baharudin motioned to the Russians, inviting them to sit. Perhaps slave to some sort of protocol, they chose to squat on their haunches facing him and Elena. Over their hunched shoulders, the tired digger directed sunken eye sockets towards nothing in particular, the moon perhaps. The Russians remained silent, waiting for Baharudin to play his cards.

---

44 digger: Australian slang, meaning an Australian soldier harking from the other ranks.

Baharudin broke the silence.

I am of the opinion, he said, there is possibility for compromise here.

He opened his briefcase and, to the accompaniment of gasps from both R and G, withdrew from it a Magnum 44. It gleamed – grotesque – bellicose – in the flickering light from the Eternal Flame. He set the weapon down with a loud clunk – metallic – deliberate – on the hard granite between Elena and himself, letting the muzzle point idly in the direction of the Russian duo.

Elena, dissembling well, showed neither surprise nor concern, but the standard emoticons for such would surely have been a fair representation of her inner state. One can imagine, at that moment, she was revisiting the assessment she had made of her eminently eligible and extravagantly courteous escort.

How … how you got *that* into country? asked R.

Same way you got yours in, I would think, said Baharudin.

The silence – broken by Baharudin after breathless seconds – was more fearsome than any sound would have been.

On the table with them! said Baharudin.

Chto … ? said G.

Gentlemen, said Baharudin, I insist!

Slowly, reluctantly, R and G produced their secreted handpieces from beneath the jackets of their suits, pieces smaller in calibre than the Magnum but lethal nonetheless. They placed them down on the granite slab between their feet.

O.K., said Baharudin. Here's the deal. I get Elena. You get a *hundred* Elenas. Read this.

Baharudin rummaged in his briefcase. R and G looked wary. Presumably they were wondering what rabbit would emerge from the hat this time.

The rabbit was a sheet of white A4 paper. Baharudin waved it in the air with a flourish before handing it to R. The Russian duo moved to the Eternal Flame to read it. They strained to do so in the poor light, the anxiety on their faces evident in the flicker of the sacred flame. R put on a pair of spectacles from the Soviet era.

Looks like contract, said R.

It is a draft, said Baharudin. The real one is with my father in Malaysia. It shall be necessary for you to travel there to complete the deal. Of course your business class fares shall be paid.

R and G exchanged glances redolent with doubt.

What is the problem? asked Baharudin.

We must consult our boss, said G.

Do so. The deal is an excellent one, for you and for him. I have no doubt he will give his consent.

At the base of the monument, a dark shadow stirred, a shadow none of them had noticed until now. Was the Unknown Soldier making a ghostly return to life? Was Don Giovanni's stone nemesis abroad? Reaching for their handguns, R and G sprang to their feet.

A derelict man wrapped in a threadbare blanket had been sleeping rough. Rubbing his eyes, he rose slowly to his feet. Suddenly, he was on full alert, staring down the barrels of the artillery wielded by the Russians. In a fitful heartbeat, his body had gone from slack to bone rigid. He cowered against the cool granite of the monument's plinth.

Fellers, fellers, he said, give a poor old bugger a break, for the love of Christ.

What did you hear? asked R.

Wha ... ?

What did you see? asked G.

I ... nothing, squire, I swear. Didn't hear nothing. Didn't see nothing. *Now* look what you tossers have done. Gone and made me piss myself.

Baharudin came forward, *sans* Magnum. Hussein and Elena watched intently as he did so. Hussein was ready to spring into action should the necessity arise. Elena was equally ready to show a clean pair of heels.

Taking charge of the situation, Baharudin addressed the derelict man.

In the morning, he said, when you wake, all these things that have happened, and to which you have been witness, will seem like a bad dream. Nothing more. Is that not true?

Yes ... yes, sir. Right on. That's how it'll be. A bad dream.

Baharudin fumbled for his wallet in the pocket of his slacks. From it, he extracted a fifty dollar bill. A smile, signalling the dawn of irony, crossed his lips as he pressed the note into the quaking hand of this man whom terror had induced to deny reality.

You may find it difficult in your dream to account for *this*, he said.

On this point, the bronze digger, looking on in silence, seemed to agree.

>

The email R and G received from O in due course went:

Továrishchi R i G:

... but, pademelons, we must forgo *Rúskiy yazík*[45]. This, my presentation, must be delivered for the most part in the language whose stamp of approval has been affixed by generations of inbred British monarchs, so ...

Comrades R and G:

You have failed to snare our mermaid. This is most unsatisfactory. Redouble your efforts. I demand the child be in your custody next time we communicate. Much is at stake here, not least for you.

A warning. Fail me now and you will never again play happy families or smell the sod of Mother Russia. I can and will make sure of that. If you will let me down again, your

---

45 *Rúskiy yazík*: the Russian language.

best prospect is eking out your days in *zhárkiy Sibír*[46]. Your worst? I leave that to your imagination.

Your proposal interests me. I have contacted the gentleman in Malaysia to whom you have been referred, and have also made independent background checks. The prognosis is good. The man appears to have credentials. I am inclined to believe he is legitimate. Nonetheless we must exercise extreme caution. I shall continue to keep him under close scrutiny.

I authorize you to travel to Malaysia to close the deal. Go with my blessing. And take all necessary care.

Be aware of your station. Remember the reins are in my hands. Experienced hands. Yours, frankly, lack the necessary finesse. For your own health, never presume you can cut me out of any deal you make.

Observe all necessary protocols when communicating with me by email. Use only the secure server. Do not use any medium such as telephone whose integrity may be subject to compromise.

I raise a glass to my lips and toast your success. But don't imagine I have forgotten your other assignment. I will have my mermaid.

Fyodor Andreevich Ogorodnikov.

>

Sticks was absent from her desk in the Nerd Centre. Her time had arrived. She was an unwitting participant in the grand plan sustaining the survival on earth of the flawed species to which we all belong or have belonged. She had given birth.

---

46 *zhárkiy Sibír*: the hot Siberia, a.k.a. Australia. The phrase was coined (reputedly) by the poet Yevgeny Yevtushenko, himself Siberian by birth, around the time of his visits to Australia in the 1960s and 1970s.

Harry, holding the fort, was at his desk. Elena, sitting opposite him, was dressed in the chic apricot outfit she reserved these days for Baharudin. Whom she was expecting.

Pademelons, your indulgence. By any standard of physical beauty, Elena embodied such a quality to a prodigious degree.

Unsurprisingly, Harry was in the thrall of involuntary sexual arousal. Peripherally, he felt guilty about the distraction she posed for him, especially since Sticks would be at this moment recuperating in a maternity ward, in custody of a child half of whose genes were his. He felt keenly the injustice of the biological imperative putting him in the way of an irrepressible distraction at a time like this. At the same time he felt keenly the distraction itself.

Dominating the visual banality of the room, and occupying a more-or-less central position in it, were two brand new Samsonite suitcases in brilliant magenta and aquamarine respectively, looking like a pair of oversized party balloons *sans* helium. Harry indicated them.

Hefty have anything to do with these? he asked.

Sal? said Elena.

Who else?

He bought them.

I thought we'd agreed, said Harry, you'd have nothing to do with Sal once you came here to the Big Top.

I did not never intend this, Harry. Russians tracked me down here, and Sal tracked Russians. They led him to me.

Harry was bemused. How could he argue with the owner of this creamy planch of exposed flesh? Or of the cow eyes, luminous with promise both inescapable and indeterminate?

When he looked into those eyes, Harry felt his entire body galvanize autonomously, clearing the coast for precipitate action. With difficulty, he would avert his eyes, corral the unruly urges, and dissemble. Then he would tempt fate by looking once again into those dangerous eyes. And the whole wretched cycle would begin again.

How is Sticks? asked Elena.

She is fine. You heard we have a boy?

Does he have name yet?

We're thinking Timothy.

That is nice name.

A pause. The spoken word – not so the unspoken – had stalled. Harry restarted it.

Tell me again, he said. What do the Russian stooges plan to do in Malaysia?

Meet with Barry's father, who is big-time criminal in that country.

What does he do?

Many things. Not pretty things. Like selling young women for prostitution.

Women like you.

Yes.

You're helping them do this job. Bring unfortunate women here to Australia to work as sex slaves.

This is their plan.

Your plan also.

No, Harry. Is *not* my plan.

Explain why not.

The Russians won't never meet Barry's father. They won't never get past airport.

Why won't they?

Elena rose. Harry watched, intoxicated, as she steered her body – confusion for the male mind if there ever was such – across the room to the suitcases. She placed one hand on each. They were a pianist's hands, the fingers long yet dainty. They caressed the suitcases fondly, as if trying to coax an etude from them. Harry was overtaken by an absurd jealousy. What right had these suitcases to treatment denied him?

Sal has hidden one hundred grams of methamphetamine in each of these, Elena said.

Harry's jaw dropped to the floorboards.

Sal has ... what?

We will not never see those Russians again.

Jesus Christ!

For several seconds, only the tick of the wall clock was heard. When this became unbearable, Harry drowned it with speech.

How much meths can you take into Malaysia without risking the death penalty? he asked.

Barry tells me it is fifty grams.

Elena, you can't do this to them. This is murder.

And what would they do to *me* if they will stay here?

Once more, the only sound heard was the tick of the timepiece, counting down the realizations as they sunk in.

Will you perhaps miss them? asked Elena.

No.

Perhaps I also shall not.

Harry looked at the suitcases and shuddered. To him their lustrous colours resembled those of poisonous berries of the type lurking lethally in untrammelled Oz bushland, their lustre advertising their toxicity. Snacks to be avoided under pain of death by all wary birds and beasts who call such habitat home.

2nd >>

While we sit in the amphitheatre, waiting for the thespians to launch their next *Stück*, I have a couple of footnotes for your consideration.

The first footnote concerns directorial control which – as you are aware – had – over the course of the last few *Stücke* – been assumed peremptorily by Sticks. It is about to revert back to Harry which, you may imagine, brings joy to his heart. As my presentation hurtles towards its penultimate phase – beyond which lies only the end game – necessarily involving Harry's many deaths – it is appropriate that Harry assume control of my second unit.

The second footnote relates to the identities of the two men hitherto known to us as R and G and presumably, as the chronology advances, not never to be known neither to us nor to the mortal world again. I shall share with you my theory regarding their identities. I put it to you their real names are Rosencrantz and Guildenstern, despite the absence of any Slavic resonance therein.

Fiction can sometimes be more potent than truth, especially when it has a mind to morph into truth.

>

Singspielstück #13: Love and the Awry Senses

House lights go down. We are restless for action but as yet the stage is unoccupied.

A spot comes up at stage front, illuminating a fragment of ill-defined circular track. The track, half a metre wide and dimly lit, sweeps a clear space around the perimeter of the turntable. Harry strolls in from left and occupies the spot.

He is dressed sloppily, as he might be in the security of his own home, which – in theatrical representation – is where he happens to be. Some specifics of his dress are: a worn T-shirt tucked loosely into tattered jeans, an uncool fisher's hat in faded cotton, sandals slapping the floor, and socks round his ankles.

Behind Harry, occupying the circular space the track encloses, and at present in semi-darkness, is a stage set whose roofless construction suggests an open-plan house. The rooms – four of them divided from each other by radial partitions – take the shape, in plan view, of trapeziums, fitting together like blunt wedges round the full arc of the stage. They communicate with each other via imaginary doors understood to exist in the surrounding track, and large open hatches – windows *sans* glass – contained in the partitions. Each hatch, wider than it is high, exemplifies 'landscape' aspect.

Each room abuts a small space straddling the geometric centre of stage, and whose plan view approximates a square. What this space represents is not immediately clear. I shall refer to it as a 'study'. Its interface to each of the trapezoidal rooms is a partition with a slight convexity. These four partitions define the extent of the study. They *also* contain open hatches, but the aspect of *these* hatches is 'portrait'.

The only piece of furniture in this study – in line-of-sight through each of its four hatches – is a wooden chair, stiff and straight-backed. A shadowy figure sits there in the gloom.

Aboriginal dot paintings adorn the two radial partitions of the particular trapezoidal room Harry occupies. Within this room he paces back and forth, the spot following him. He seems in a trance, talking to himself, directing his voice not to anyone on stage or in the audience, but to the unconcerned air surrounding him.

What he says is of a transcendental nature, the product of an altered state of mind. I shall give no oxygen to speculation this altered state has been pharmacologically induced.

His words are:

Ever get this feeling, he asks, I sometimes get? The feeling there are dead people out there watching everything you do? Late relatives. Late friends. Late in the sense of dead. Watching. Listening. Hanging on your every thought, word, and deed. Omniscient.

... startled, we nonetheless resist the temptation to do a bunk. To slink soundlessly, tails between legs, out of the theatre. Helplessly, we wait, expecting any moment to be sprung ...

A female voice, dreamy and distracted, replies to Harry from the study. We recognize the voice. It is Sticks'. Apparently, *she* is the shadowy figure seated inside. But, pademelons, this is a most uncharacteristic Sticks, whose repertoire in my experience doesn't include 'dreamy' or 'distracted'.

Can't say I do, she says.

Harry continues to pace and harangue the air.

Ever have the sense, he asks, all things are dissociated? Effect disowns cause? Thoughts are out and about with no mind to contain them? Colours have an urge to desert their rainbow? Birdsong won't adhere to the bird? When the cat quits the scene, it leaves its grin behind?

... that's quite a relief to us, pademelons, although a tad schizoid on Harry's part. We breathe freely again. No need to skedaddle yet ...

Can't say I have, says Sticks.

... dreamily ... distractedly ...

Ever possessed by this hunch, asks Harry, the senses are out of kilter? Sounds have vibrant colour? The touch of a hand resounds like a big brass gong? Words leave a taste behind as they fly off the tongue? Thoughts exude an odour as if seeping into the sinuses? Numbers buzz like bees as their swarm overwhelms the brain?

... is Harry the full quid? we find ourselves wondering ...

Can't say I am, says Sticks.

... distractedly ... dreamily ...

A spot comes up on the interior of the study and, in particular, on the shadowy figure occupying it. We have visual confirmation now. The figure is indeed Sticks. We see her, in profile, facing left, seated on the chair, clad in a brief satin negligee, with child at breast, her right one, the one furthest from us. The hatch connecting the study with the room Harry paces frames this adult/infant pair artistically, as if designed to do so. This is mother and child, emulating the eternal archetypes in their sublime moment of bonding.

The light reflected from Sticks to us, is soft, warm, diffuse, and ethereally radiant, effects achieved – we presume by Elena who is back in the lighting box these days – through the clever use of light filtered by scrims. Moreover, framed as she is in dimensions akin to those of the magic ratio, Sticks resembles a Madonna with child as might have been painted by Raphael or Da Vinci. As she feeds her child – proxy for the newborn Timmy – her gaze turns inward and her downturned face reflects a most striking serenity. This is an aspect of Sticks we have not seen before. Neither, we suspect, has Harry.

Harry stops in his tracks, rooted to the spot, moved to rapture by the tableau Sticks and child present.

Sticks, for her part, gives no indication she notices Harry.

Izzie's fingers massage the keyboard gently. Harry, voice melding seamlessly with synthesized music, relates the salient moment in song. The music is in 4/4 time and major key, without trace of staccato, each note lovingly but briefly sustained. The vocal line is little more than a succession of slow quavers. With rhythm almost totally absent, harmonized melody alone remains to capture the ambience of the tableau to which both we and Harry are unobserved witnesses:

Harry:

Beauty, in its secularity,
from all numinosity set free,
sans religious trappings and the rest,
lauds the sweet brave earth that's first and best.

The stage rotates slowly clockwise. Harry, still singing, walks anticlockwise, so as to stay in front of us. In relativistic terms, one might say he is strolling slowly round the house, taking us – his rapt audience – in tow, from one trapezoidal room to the next, exposing himself and ourselves to constantly shifting views of the tableau of Sticks, child, and chair. Perhaps this tableau by virtue of its now overt solidity bears a closer similarity to a sculpture by Michelangelo or Rodin than it does to a flat representation on canvas by the likes of Raphael or Da Vinci.

When rude senses thrall my feelings,
there's confusion in their dealings.
Mix and match, their piquant feature,
turns the mind of me, poor creature.
What's to see I'm prone to hear,
and what's to hear afflicts my eye.
I taste what I should touch, I fear,
and smell all beauty I come by.

We – and Harry – have Sticks in back view.

If such heady apparition
swerves my senses from their mission,
what remains is flawed sensation
subject to interpretation.
Nose shall sniff out aural vibes.
The twisted tongue's in vision's maw.
Deft fingers stroke what taste describes,
and I am left to swallow awe.

To this moment, both the stage and Harry have rotated 180^0 in opposition to each other. Now their rotations pause.

We see Sticks, framed by a hatch, in reverse profile, i.e. facing right. Her exposed breast is the one closest to us. The curve of the child's cheek, chin, and neck is congruent with the curve of this exposed breast. The tandem of Izzie's melodic line and Harry's lyrics celebrates the rapturous synaesthetic episode to which Harry is hostage.

Beauty seen's a fragrance for the eye.
Beauty heard's a flame across the sky.
Beauty's feel is music welling high.
So you send my senses all awry.

At the word 'you', Harry gestures emphatically with his arm and upturned palm towards Sticks who remains blithely ignorant of his presence.

The opposed rotations of Harry and stage resume.

Harry's song changes its 'shape', each stanza defined by a longer succession of quavers, picked over by Izzie's practiced hands then entrusted to the pliant air:

> May my rainbows ricochet from perspicacious touch.
> Peddle me the perfumes I can see or hear as such.
> Feast with me on spectral food from red to violet.
> Sing me scents in dulcet tones so I shall not forget.

We – and Harry – have Sticks in front view.

> Paint for me a velvet symphony or saraband.
> Spoil me with sweetness I can hear with sleight of hand.
> Feed me reek of roses as it thunders through the air.
> Massage me with gentleness and culinary stare.

To this moment, Harry and the stage have each turned 360^0. Things are back to where they started. The aboriginal dot paintings on the partitions are back. Behind Harry, we see Sticks – framed in the hatch – in the same left-facing profile she had owned at the outset.

Rotations stop. Harry's song reverts to shorter phrasing. We are not sure to whom he pleads:

> Pity me the plight in which I'm found,
> everything upturned and mixed around.
> Won't you extricate me from this spell
> to a sober life in which to dwell?

Izzie's fingers float from the keyboard. The sated child drops off the breast. Sticks fastens the top buttons of her negligee.

Elena wields her magic. The light on Sticks and the child changes from ethereal to everyday, from diffuse to distinct. The sublime moment has passed.

Sticks rises from the chair. She burps the child with gentle pats to his back. She cradles him with one arm while pushing the partition in front of her with the other. It swings open, as a door might. From the study, she moves to Harry in the room he occupies, sharing with him his spot of light.

I think I can oblige, feller, she says.

How? Harry asks.

If you'll condescend to come down off your metaphysical perch for a moment, you might like to change your son's nappy.

She hands the child across to Harry, who resembles the stunned mullet of lore.

<< 1st

'If you'll condescend to come down off your metaphysical perch for a moment, you might like to change your son's nappy.'

Sticks spoke these words as she passed from the 'study' where she had been feeding Timothy to the room where Harry had been pleading. Here she thrust the baby into Harry's arms, a ploy taking Harry – and perhaps Timmy also – by no small skerrick of surprise.

We know all this, pademelons, thanks to the *Stück* we have just seen, a *Stück* apparently set in the new family home of Harry, Sticks, and Timmy. As you would have guessed, the rooms in stage representation were stylized. Real rooms in real houses do *not* look like that. My second unit – nothing if not inventive – had resorted to theatrical license and, for that, apology from them is unwarranted.

What did the 'real' rooms look like? I shall tell you.

Consider the study from which Sticks had emerged with Timmy cradled in her arm. It was not the small room, entrapped and airless, depicted in the *Stück*, but a room of generous size. A feature window drew attention to an outdoors overwhelmed with greenery. Some of this *out*doors – in particular, a massive blue gum whose territory this had been for yonks – had been invited *in*, via a floor-to-ceiling enclave set into the feature window.

Then consider the room where Harry had aired exotic thoughts. Conforming to the whim of the architect commissioned by Harry and Sticks, this room was indeed trapezoidal in shape, with ceilings to match set on a rakish slant. Here flourished a colony of accursed Dutch angles, if you will excuse my recourse to the jargon of the cinematographer.

… why on earth had Harry and Sticks consented to go along with such pretentious architectural foibles? …

Contrary to what one might inadvertently have inferred from the *Stück*, the room contained furnishings. Still redolent of the newness of the showroom, they shrieked their character: swank and contemporary, big ticket and brand flaunting.

They included:

A leather lounge suite – low-set, chunky, modular – bleached to the blandest of eggshell white. A coffee table – austere to the point of invisibility – out of moulded glass. Standard lamps sprouting like chrome-plated strangler-vines from a floor of jungle-nourished hardwood. A phalanx of black boxes – sleek and knobless clones – comprising a home theatre system.

For Harry, sadly, and perhaps for Sticks also, these were the trappings of an apparent regression to an upmarket version of the likes of Bee Street. It was as if taste were talking to them, but they – not listening – went with the crowd instead. The rich crowd.

By way of minor concession to said taste, Harry's aboriginal paintings were there, transplanted from his former abode, and dominating the walls of this present-day one. Events may have compelled his return to a flat earth existence, but his artworks stood tribute to the vertical life he had once embraced.

So – to remind you, pademelons – it was in this precinct Sticks had spoken – in the very same breath – of nappies and metaphysics.

Perhaps Sticks regretted the brusque tone and brute phrasing of her suggestion to Harry, because now she softened her verbal stance. Placing a gentle hand on his shoulder and turning her body in towards his, she added some words of placatory intent and effect.

You've said some weird and wonderful things just now, pal, she said, but I gather the gist of them is I float your boat.

You do, said Harry. That is exactly the gist.

His free arm, the one not cradling the baby, ventured to the small of her waist. She responded by pulling yet closer to him, subjecting the baby to a gentle familial pressure. As close to each other as nostrils to the scent of hair, as lips to the flutter of lashes, one face raised, the other lowered, they spoke to each other with visual cues in place of words, touch in place of sound. In ratification, perhaps, of Harry's thesis re the awry senses.

Sticks reached for a control on the wall, to manage the simulated daylight washing over them from above. In mimicry of small critters retreating to their burrows, points of illumination dimmed all over the slant of the trapezoidal ceiling. A gentler light now blunted the angles of the room, caressed its enamoured occupants, softened the air between them, and lubricated the channels of their discourse.

There's no woman I can think of, said Sticks, who, on hearing the words you have gifted me, would not find herself testing the limits of her restraint.

She grazed his lips with hers. Harry regarded the bundle nestled peacefully in the crook of his arm. His impression was of a miraculous cynosure in miniature of an adult human person, a cynosure inclined to shit at inconvenient moments.

Screwing up his nose, he slid himself gently from Sticks' orbit.

I've a job to do, he said. First.

II

Shall we, pademelons, withdraw discreetly from the premises, respecting the privacy of these turtle-doves and leaving them to their vices/devices? We shall have the opportunity, as we do so, of observing the environs of their dovecote, of surveying the neighbourhood.

>

Outside, a gibbous moon in pewter tones invaded the daylight sky. Everywhere beneath, flashy architect-designed mansions, demanding membership of the modernist oeuvre, shouted sweet success and willing money.

Facades consisting of sweeping curves of marbled concrete embraced cliff faces of plate glass. Enclaves open to the sky welcomed pre-existing trees into the bosom of the home. Triple and quadruple garages housed prestige cars, which vehicles – by dint of brand – were big cats and the like. Modish outdoor furniture infested rooftop recreation areas, inviting one to take in the view while clutching a stem of chardonnay. Hostile Dutch angles were ubiquitous.

In this fine new suburb were found people who had 'arrived'. How long they might stay was conjectural, as would be the circumstances of their departure.

>

The trap was not sprung. The bait was not taken. R and G, clutching their colourful suitcases, waltzed through Kuala Lumpur airport without a hitch, as if their status were privileged. The best laid plans of the conspirators (Baharudin?, Elena?, Hefty?) had apparently come to nought.

Was there, perhaps, a counter-conspiracy in play to account for such an unexpected setback in plans? Had Customs been paid off? Had the sniffer dogs been nobbled?

If so, who was the counter-conspirator? And how had he/ she gotten wind of the devilish plan conceived in faraway Oz? I guess, pademelons, if one were sufficiently curious on this point, one might ask who stood to benefit most by countermanding the progenitory conspiracy. Ogorodnikov? Baharudin? Baharudin's father? The Sultan of K? One of the Sultan's wives? Murphy?

In any case, R and G, free as breezes, checked in soon after at the lavish accommodation, overseen by clunky twin towers, reserved for them by Baharudin's father. The man himself, whose direct line tenanted nothing less than a future Sultan, arrived later that evening. Flesh was pressed. Fruitful discussions were enjoined. Contracts were signed. Vodka was consumed.

Sal's and Elena's names and details were tabled and – via such resource sharing – an understanding was reached by both parties as to the preferred way of touching base in Oz. Re connections with the Russian motherland, both parties agreed to notify O – through appropriately secure channels – informing him of the favourable outcome of their discourse.

R and G spent the next few days at leisure, exploring the precincts, stocking up on souvenirs, seeking the services of female escorts, but mostly drinking vodka in the bars set aside for infidels. Then, when time was up, they headed, with their psychedelic suitcases, to the airport for the return flight to Oz.

But, pademelons, what doesn't assail one on the way north may do so on the way south. Customs were on their game when R and G fronted up for the second time, and so were the cute little canines. Neither the Slavic pair, nor – post firing squad – their bleached bones, made landfall either in Oz or their cherished motherland.

>

Sticks took ill. It happened when she and Harry were out

socializing with Ramon and his Argentinean friends. Brenda was babysitting young Timmy, the arrangement being Sticks would be back in time for his regular grapple with the breast.

Over the course of the evening, Sticks became progressively more irritable for no apparent reason. When her face began to register signs of significant pain, Harry realized he had no option but to get her home.

At home, her condition deteriorated. She had lost all interest in her surroundings, as if about to lapse into coma. Harry, frantic, called the doctor. Brenda arrived also, very anxious, and with baby.

The doctor listened to Sticks' heart, took her blood pressure, shone a light into each eye in turn. Then he turned to Harry.

I suspect meningitis, he said. May I use your phone?

Harry, listening to the doctor's words over the phone, heard disturbing phrases such as 'priority case', 'mobile IC unit', 'infectious diseases ward'. Yet he felt calm. Matters, though serious, were beyond his control. He felt unusually alert and, at the same time, detached from events, as if in the thrall of one of his altered states of mind.

The baby? he asked.

He goes with her, said the doctor. He needs to be checked out too. And you should watch *yourself* for symptoms.

For the next few days, Harry – in the grip of an identity crisis colonized by Arthur and Martha – spent most of his time by Sticks' hospital bed. Fretful days stretched into weeks, during which he was gratified to see her respond gradually to treatment, some of which, e.g. lumbar puncture, did not bear contemplation. Towards the end of her hospitalization, she seemed fully alert, reading avidly from the detective fiction he brought her from the local library.

After about three weeks, she and Timmy were discharged. Timmy, having suffered no symptoms, was fine, but she was extremely fragile. For a further three weeks, she was confined to bed, deeply disappointed by the adverse impact events had had on her breast-feeding program. Harry spent a lot of time heating formula milk and changing nappies.

When Sticks finally rose, and attempted short walks, she could struggle no further than spitting distance from her front gate, before seeking Harry's shoulder to guide her to bed. Several gruesome months were to pass – during which time she resorted to a wheelchair for mobility – before she achieved an adequate degree of physical independence. Everybody then agreed it was a great relief to have her back *intacta*, and said so.

So: had she lost nothing more than a few months from her life, and a few kilograms from her frame? Was this the end of it? No siree. One day – in which context she had ironically forgotten – a realization dawned informing her the freakish memory skills she thought she owned were no more. The meningitis had scuttled them as it had her breast-feeding ambitions.

As regards her exercise of memory, she was now just an ordinary person with a plebeian range of abilities. A cerebral shape-shift had occurred – from *Wunderkind* to *Durchschnittsmensch* as she might herself have said – with which she had no option but to come to terms. This development laid siege to her thought processes. Idle musings got short shrift.

In her mind, she enacted a catechistic dialogue with herself:

How, she asked, shall I conduct myself as an ordinary person with the power of memory of an ordinary person?

Like the vast majority of people in the world are obliged to do on every single day of their ordinary lives, she answered.

But ordinary people have their past life as a precedent to guide them. Where is *my* precedent?

Perhaps you have none.

What sort of answer is that?

An answer in accordance with the evidence.

Then shall I be thrown to the wolves?

If the wolves will have you.

2nd >>

My second unit has assembled in force: Matt, Sonia, Elena, Izzie, Brenda, Penny, Ronnie, … and Baharudin. Yes, Baharudin is back in town, assuming he ever left.

They are goofing around in front-of-house, amidst the pleasant but un-noteworthy works of art adorning the walls. House lights are up, and the doors to the performance arena are open. The turntable stage, proxy for theatre-in-the-round in all its glory, is visible beyond, inviting all with a mind to tread the boards and strut their stuff to get amongst it.

Izzie is entertaining the assembly with a vocalise on the Harry Lime theme, executed with a sheet of paper folded loosely over the teeth of a comb. They wait for Harry (McMinn not Lime) to arrive with information they will need to know about the next *Stück*.

When Harry *does* arrive he looks a tad unstrung. He barrels through the front door, with Timmy, hooked up via 'ears' to an iPod, trailing him. Harry, hands on hips, lobs his verbal bombshell into the exhuberant throng.

Sticks has meningitis, he says.

Action winds down. Nobody knows what to say, or what to do with their arms, legs, hands, feet. Harry repeats his statement.

Sticks has meningitis, he says.

The concern shown is genuine and across the board.

Doesn't sound real flash, says Matt.

Where is she? asks Brenda.

Hospital obviously, says Sonia.

In Infectious Diseases, says Harry.

She is O.K.? asks Elena.

Recovering, says Harry. It's expected to be slow.

Everybody is still and silent, at a loss for words, their sails *sans* wind.

May we visit? asks Baharudin.

Not a problem, says Harry. Any time.

How will the show go on without her? asks Sonia.

Harry shakes his head. He raises his arms, palms upwards. As he speaks, his face is a grimace, palliated by bemusement.

We'll have to suspend operations, he says. Disband.

How long for? asks Izzie.

No telling, says Harry. Weeks, perhaps months, they say, before she's on her feet. I'm open to suggestions.

Shall we take a break? asks Matt. Regroup in three weeks time. Review the situation at that time. Like we did once before.

We have a plan here, says Harry. Is it acceptable?

Murmurs, incoherent, are abroad.

Can we agree then? asks Matt.

The murmurs coalesce into a single word, oft repeated: 'Agreed'.

Pademelons, something doesn't scan. If Sticks had contracted meningitis around the outset of the millennium at a time Timmy was a mere babe in arms, can she then go on to contract it a *second* time, ten years later, with Timmy a web-savvy pre-teen nurturing a predilection for casinos? Is this not a medical impossibility, like having mumps or measles twice in a lifetime?

The far greater likelihood – I suggest – is my second unit's director has his wires crossed. Harry, stickler for chronology, is nevertheless having trouble with the order of events, with continuity. Perhaps this is a consequence of the emotional impact the (single) occasion of Sticks' illness had on him all those years prior.

We must forgive him this aberration, go along with his unlikely fiction, and resign ourselves to my second unit being out of action for some time.

III

Studio

Matt emerges at front right, his smart clothes dishevelled, his cravat askew. His left arm is bloodied and held to his chest by a hastily improvized sling. His movements are tentative. His legs are wobbly. He is distraught.

He walks, as if in a pharmacologically induced stupor, towards Mark's body. When he gets there, he kneels. His face and Mark's draw level with each other, his living eyes engaging with Mark's dead eyes.

Why this? he asks.

Nobody, certainly not Mark, answers. Matt repeats his question.

Why this, boyo? he asks.

The moment is assuredly grotesque, but one small detail, a detail screaming out for mention, seems especially so. Matt's face is the right way up whereas Mark's hangs upside down.

Is this, then, the way they must greet each other for their most final of farewells? Such a perverse juxtaposition, decreed as it is by geometry, is by any measure a wicked travesty.

||

Cut.

I regret to inform you, Scotty, you prize wingnut, you sad disgrace to our exalted realm of everywhere and everywhen, you have gone and stuffed up once more.

Yes. Stuffed up. Stuffed up big time.

Can you please put *me* on the podium?

You want the freaking thing spelt out? Me, M-E, on the podium, P-O-D-I ...

(Oops!)

<<

Open grave. Bitter weather. Casket about to be lowered. Priest and mourners in attendance. We are familiar with this scenario, pademelons, if not from recollections of some of the less auspicious moments of our personal life, then certainly from the clichéd depictions of such moments in any number of B-grade films we have seen.

Snow was dead.

> There once was a bloke,
> and he answered to Snow.
> He lived then he died.
> That's as much as we know.

The mourners, few in number, and – judging by appearances – all intimates, were suitably solemn. But one some of you would least expect was distraught. Beside himself. Inconsolable. Weeping tears into the grave to mingle, at a future moment, with the clods of clay destined to be shovelled there. These were the tears not of a habitual mourner, but of a soul in extremity. This was distress such as precluded effective awareness of the presence of any other person at the ceremony.

Hefty.

True to form, his was a presence to be reckoned with, duly amplified by the rings on his right hand. It was these rings he removed now and let fall – tears of topaz and ruby to supplement those of brine – on to the oaken casket. Once the damp earth was filled in over them, it would be game over for these plucky gems. No more would they favour this tropospheric life with their glint and sparkle.

The presiding priest, in long black habit, approached Sal to put a comforting arm round his shoulders, shoulders bent, shoulders stiff with grief. But Sal swept the clerical arm aside, with what seemed to the others huddled around the grave like an uncalled-for degree of brusqueness.

Attend to your job, Father, said Sal, and let me be.

Balancing on the lip of the grave, Sal extracted from a deep pocket in his oilskin overcoat a globe of solid glass – a paperweight perhaps? or a crystal ball? – of a size fitting comfortably in the palm of his hand. He let it fall onto the casket, which it did with an affirmative clunk. The oak, courtesy of its natural elasticity, was able to cushion its impact and prevent its shatter. Sal watched as it rolled into the crevice between earth and casket hugging the long edge of the casket nearest to him. Then he turned decisively away from the grave – and from Snow – forever, his stony face etched with indelible sadness, his ashen pallor unremitting.

But why should a man such as Sal ('Hefty') Heffernan – whose life might be compared – in both temper and resilience – to a blade of hardened black steel – why should a man of such stripe – display emotion – emotion not at all in character – upon the death – fully expected in any case – of a mere minion such as Snow? Pademelons, recourse to an historical exhumation will be necessary to uncover the answer. We must get down on our hands and knees, and scrabble around in the deep scree of the past, a past adept at burying – if you will forgive my choice of metaphor – so many of these riddles …

II

… the fifties, Scotty. The 1950s. The potent post-war era of which some who recall it are stricken with nostalgia, whereas others have few regrets at its passing. Can we presume on your capabilities, limited though they have proven to be on many a crucial occasion, to set me down fairly and squarely in those obdurate fifties?

Attaboy, Scotty!

??

Not far enough, Scotty, not far enough …

??

I tell you, Scotty, not frigging far enough. Jesus mate,

get your shit together. You're short by a country mile. Get it right for fuck's sake. Get it right for the sake of what little remains of your good standing. Get it right for the sake of my old granny's galloping ...
(Oops!)

<

On the day the unfortunate incident was laid bare, the irrepressible sun was busy sketching out the lines of the rural landscape, as only an Australian sun in collusion with an Australian landscape can do. Sketching out lines, yes, and then filling in colours. Colours selected from a palette of stupendous vibrancy. Colours formed as ingots might, from molten sunshine flowing and then congealing. Colours pure, bold, devoid of haze, and undiluted with atmospheric detritus, captured from the emanations of our daystar at their moment of incidence, and then reflected in tones and hues unlikely to be found elsewhere in this universe.

Ah, this is Oz. Let us savour its essence. Imbibe its unique yet ordinary charm.

The orphanage where (allegedly) the crime had occurred was run by the Christian Brothers at a location remote from major cities or towns. A number of reports were filed by law enforcement called from the nearest of these towns, and they all brought down the same verdict.

Suicide.

At cock crow, a young novice, Brother Bill, had been found hanging by the cord of his cassock from a water pipe skirting the ceiling of a communal shower block in the orphanage.

Some of his fellow Brothers had private doubts about the conclusion reached by the law, on the grounds no member of their Order would have chosen to depart this world in a manner deemed by the ultimate Authority to be sinful, and which manner (moreover) precluded any prospect of absolution. But private doubts were kept private, in accordance with the rule that what happens in the orphanage stays in the orphanage.

||

Pademelons. The truth of such monasterial mysteries as this resides not with the police and not with the Brothers. If it resides anywhere, it must reside with those omniscients in whose select company you and I belong. Therefore, in the interests of accurate disclosure, let each of us bring his/her power to bear.

<

Some hours earlier, well before any birdcall had penetrated the land of nod, and most certainly at such time as all orphan boys would or should have been asleep in their dorm beds, Brother Bill – in what was to be his last act of service to the Lord – was doing his regular rounds. In his long black cassock, he seemed – and doubtless was content to seem – an inseparable part of the darkness. His movements were smooth and silent, so much so one might have imagined he was propelled by a set of small well-oiled wheels, tucked discreetly under the hem of his habit.

All appeared to be in shipshape and Bristol fashion. To some, it might have come across as odd that a few of the poor lads slept with their heads tucked determinedly under their pillows. Perhaps only the initiated would have found this an ominous sign.

Brother Bill paused for a moment beside one particular bunk in the long line of bunks. He nudged the boy therein, who stirred slightly. Might it be said, reluctantly? Brother Bill, with a shhh on his lips, pulled the boy firmly to his feet, and steered him in the direction of the shower block. The boy, looking vulnerable in his baggy striped pyjamas, shuffled along compliantly, his face expressionless, and his eyes glued to the floor. He was thirteen years old, but big and strong for his age. On the grounds of these attributes, his fellow orphans had gifted him a nickname.

Hefty.

As they entered the shower block, Brother Bill switched on the lights and closed the door quietly behind them. Then it was game on. The Brother undid the cord of his cassock. The cassock hung open. It was apparent this brotherly noviciate was propelled less by a set of wheels than by an overweening lust, whose physical evidence was on display and ready for immediate action.

The boy sprang to action first. For him, the stakes were high. Half measures would not cut the mustard. He decked the randy Brother with a backhand delivery of his forearm and elbow. Then he sat astride the fraternal chest and wrapped the cord of the cassock tightly around the fraternal neck: once, twice, three times. This was not a moment to be taking prisoners. He gathered in the slack of the cord, allowing no possibility for the passage of air down the monkish throat. The cord was soon as taut as a hawser round a capstan. The Brother jerked, bucked, groaned, croaked, and became blue in the face. Then he went quiet.

Well, thought the boy, this time I've killed someone. It ain't no big deal. This is another of them Charlies was pushing his luck too far.

Drained both physically and emotionally, he allowed his head to sink limply onto Brother Bill's breast, an inert breast from which there was no longer any trace of a heartbeat, and much less of an amorous inclination. He lay in this position for some inchoate seconds, before realizing with a start this was not the moment to be resting. He knew what must be done next, and he knew it must be done in timely fashion. Before he was discovered.

Scanning his environs quickly, he saw a heavy-duty water pipe passing high and long through the body of the shower block. He jumped to his feet. After several vain attempts, he managed to flip the free end of the cord over an angle joint in the pipe. Then, hauling with full might and muscle, he managed to lift the Brother to his knees but – try as he would – no further. Exhausted and demoralized, he tied off the cord on a shower tap. A cold tap. There *were* no hot taps in the orphans' blocks.

Suddenly, his worst fears were realized. He was sprung. The door to the shower block creaked open, and a small boy, in what were obviously regulation pyjamas, headed somnambulistically towards the toilet block yonder, in response to the call of the great god, Bladder. He (the small boy) seemed not to notice the singular tussle occupying the attention of the larger boy. To wit, a tussle with a freshly strangled Man of God, still warm, and hanging heavy on the end of his own cassock cord.

I need your help, said Hefty.

The small boy saw. Did he understand? Did he sympathize? Maybe, but he had more immediate concerns.

I need your help, said Hefty.

I need to pee, said the small boy.

Get back here quickly, said Hefty. And bring a chair.

A chair?

The small boy was hopping from one foot to the other.

A chair, dumb-arse.

Where do I find a chair?

Plan to play the fool all your life? asked Hefty.

The small boy ran off. Imagine, pademelons, the anxiety Hefty must have felt at that moment. Would the small boy come back at all? And if he did, would he come with chair, or with a platoon of randy black-habited Brothers?

When the small boy returned (with chair!), he found Hefty squatting with head in hands, apparently unable to comprehend the presenting scene, a scene illuminated by cold fluorescence, a scene not altogether family friendly, a scene largely of his own making.

Here's the chair, said the small boy.

Hefty looked up, saw, and found new strength. Aided by the small boy, he set about the task of raising Brother Bill to such a height as would make it appear he had hung himself. The incentive was huge as were the surges of adrenalin they both felt in their veins. The small boy proved – unexpectedly perhaps – to be of good value. Eventually, the two boys in tandem managed to hoist Brother Bill up until his feet dangled free of the floor. *Sans* its cord, the dead Brother's cassock hung loose and open, giving rise to a display – impotent, derelict, yet strangely compelling to the eye – of his genitals.

Well, bugger me dead, said the small boy, if these holy men ain't got knackers and a prick like any regular geezer.

Mate, said Hefty, you ought to get down on your knees and give thanks to the friggin' tooth fairy you ain't found *that* out before today.

Hefty toppled the chair, completing the intended fabrication. Then, possessed of a new-found clear-headedness, he proceeded to set a plan in place.

Listen to me, titch, he said. We ain't welcome around here no more. Let's make like greased lightning. To our bunks. Gather our rags. To the kitchen. Gather some grub. Then to the hills. Mind, not a squeak out of you, or we're toast.

Things went more smoothly than they dared hope. Outside in their ragged orphan's clothes, they tossed their swags over the high wall. Hefty virtually threw the little guy over before scrambling over himself. Bruised, scratched, and limping, they hauled themselves several kilometres on foot through scrub before reaching a railway siding.

A soft and mellow dawn smiled on them as they watched the engineer of an interstate goods train dismount to change the points. In a flash, and unseen, they were snug and secure inside a covered bogie. The prospect of a journey of hundreds perhaps thousands of kilometres did not daunt them. It thrilled them.

Back at the orphanage there was the expected hue and cry.

Brother Bill was mourned, and the two boys missed, but – for reasons difficult to fathom – no causal connection was made between these two significant and contemporaneous events. With regard to Brother Bill's demise, perhaps the interested parties were inclined towards an explanation making minimum waves. In any event, a few days later, when the situation had stabilized, the law having concluded what it perceived to be its job, the fraternity of orphan boys (*sans* two) felt free to own – albeit each privately – relief in the knowledge Brother Bill had gone, struck down – it would appear – by his own guilty conscience.

Their relief was short lived.

Old Brother Brian, renowned for his lecherous ways, was first in the queue of applicants for young Brother Bill's workload with its attendant benefits. This should have come as no surprise to anybody with a feeling for historical accretion. Tradition, laid down slowly over two millennia – laid down as sedimentary rock would be – had not failed to allocate a perverse ecclesiastical variation on *droit du seigneur* to institutions like this orphanage. Said variation was an established article such as no man could presume to put asunder.

Let us return to our two young fly-by-nighters.

Enduring the monotonous da-da-de-dum, da-da-de-dum of the train rattling over its tracks, relishing the rattling in fact as a harbinger of their freedom, the boys spent many pleasant days and nights eating, sleeping, massaging sore muscles, dreaming, planning, talking, cementing their relationship. This latter activity, to wit cementing, devolved mainly on the small boy, Hefty's manner, by nature and for most of the time, being gruff and uncommunicative.

Let us catch them in one iconic moment.

What you got in your pocket? asked Hefty.

… he was referring to a bulge beneath the small boy's clothing, in more-or-less the territory where privates might ordinarily have staked their anatomical claim …

The small boy dived into his pocket and produced a clear-glass paperweight. Embedded in the glass – like an insect trapped in amber – was the likeness of a small, rustic, and ever-so-quaint European village. Dominating the village was a parish church sporting its mandatory spire atop an ancient stone tower.

Where'd you get it? asked Hefty.

None of your business, said the small boy.

Just curious.

Always had it. Look.

The small boy up-ended the paperweight, then righted it again. Silvery flakes – glistening – fell in and all around the village, mirroring the delight spreading across the boy's face, the glass globe his portal to a fabled world.

Snow, said the small boy.

Give it here, said Hefty.

Hefty up-ended the paperweight, then righted it again. The silvery flakes dutifully repeated their performance.

Snow, said Hefty.

He handed the treasure back to the small boy, who was chuffed at having been able to engage his taciturn companion so completely and in such effortless manner.

Snow, said the small boy.

Hefty's response had a sardonic edge.

O.K., Snow, he said. How d'you think we're goin' to support ourselves when we make it to wherever we're heading?

We'll manage fine, said Snow.

Snow's opinion was put to the test. A halt followed by prolonged silence signalled the train was going no further. The two country-bred lads, with grass seeds in their hair to prove it, emerged to find themselves in the big smoke. The big *unfamiliar* smoke.

A decade or more of bitter experience with the Brotherhood had led them to presume the institutions, of which the wider world was comprised, were not likely to be a source of joy to them. In the single example they knew, they had only ever seen depravity, treachery, and exploitation. Nevertheless, prepared to allow better angels might prevail, they elected to endure a trial stint as builder's labourers on a construction site. It was a bad move. Before first smoko[47], they felt the full measure of self-interested backhanded bastardry, channelled their way by management, unions, maverick committees, fractious work teams, and the like.

Who do these jokers think they are? was Hefty's response. So they walked off the job, appropriating for themselves, on their way out, whatever tools and equipment they could lay their hands on. That might have included one decent vehicle apiece, had they been a shade less circumspect, and/or had they been able to master the institutional mechanism of licenses, registration plates, engine numbers, and the like.

One need not doubt they began without delay to research this mechanism.

For those with the appropriate résumé, a life of crime has a mind to beckon. Or – perhaps more appositely – the life beckoning matched the definition of crime in the manner of thinking of the graft-ridden establishment against which these two likely lads found themselves pitted.

Dog eat dog world it surely was. Hefty and Snow were hot on the olfactory trails left by said dogs, trails leading them in time to the burial place of the choicest bones.

II

Scotty. Beam me up and out pronto. I've had a gutful

---

47 smoko: colloquial Australian, meaning 'scheduled teabreak in the work-place'.

of the fifties. Beam me to a time when I can ply my trade without recourse to the vomitorium.

??

Not far enough, Scotty. This is *not* where I need to be. Try the 21st century. Twenty one. Can you count beyond ten? Oh, and out of mild curiosity, where did you souvenir that watch?

Brother Bill?

You mean you whipped it off of a freaking corpse, you dead beat?

What use would a timepiece be to you and your motley crowd, even presuming any of you knew how to tell the time?

Between friends, I'd very much like to know how you managed to secrete an article like that from out of the sublunary world. Share your dirty little secret, comrade. Come clean.

Come clean, you wacko.

(Oops!)

>

After the funeral, Hefty needed a right-hand-man. Snow, irreplaceable, nevertheless had to be replaced. Death has paradoxic consequences. This is one of them.

Snow's replacement was a person who in no way resembled Snow. Hefty's annointed was known in criminal circles as The Poet. This was a 'Poet' who didn't write and seldom spoke. This 'Poet' was a man of action. His action was his poetry, his poetry his action.

The recruit's action was *sans* ruth, i.e. he liked to act ruthlessly. With international interests threatening his territory these days,

Hefty figured a ruthless sidekick could be a useful adjunct to the firm.

Hefty always liked to shy away from hands-on stuff, except – one might argue – when it came to Christian Brothers. Action at a distance was Hefty's preferred style. By way of contrast, the sidekick preferred action up close and personal.

This recruit was a devotee of ruthless hands-on action.

Hail The Poet.

>

The poster behind Matt's desk – his mission statement in pictorial form – had changed again. Where previously *Prêt-a-Porter* had hung (and before that *Belle Femme Français*), the space was now filled by an enlarged photographic representation of a wiry young dark-haired woman, in frame from the waist up. Her torso was naked except for a raspberry coloured revolutionary's beret on her head, a silver-hued amulet round her neck, a bandolier over each shoulder, and a look on her face saying, Don't mess with me. The bandoliers bristled with what seemed, at first sight, to be live ammunition.

Matt, his back to this young warrior, sat behind his desk. Harry, facing towards both her and Matt, sat in front, engulfed in the folds of the leather divan. In accordance with a well-established routine, a routine verging on the religious, each of the men was sipping from a brandy balloon.

Is Sticks out of danger? asked Matt.

Completely, said Harry.

When will she be up and about?

Comes home day after tomorrow. She'll need rehab.

The baby. Timothy, is it?

Harry nodded.

Fit and well, he said. Never in any trouble.

A pause in conversation lent itself, for both of these happy imbibers, to a rediscovery of the aroma and flavour of the *Bisquit*. Then Harry pointed to the framed photograph behind Matt.

Why the change? asked Harry. This was not the first time he had had cause to ask this question.

One must leave oneself open to fresh developments.

What development might we be talking about here?

Know who that gal is?

No idea.

Matt gave Harry a smug look, as might someone in possession of privileged information. Of intelligence calculated to arouse gratuitous interest.

Che Guevara's grand-daughter, he said. Her name is Lydia.

You're having me on.

Look her up yourself on Google.

What have guns and bullets got to do with the rag trade?

Mate, the fashion industry is not just about fancy bits of fabric, elegantly spliced together. It's a state of mind.

A most warlike state of mind, to all appearances.

You may be surprised to know what goes on in the heads of bored doctor's wives. The romantic allure of revolution. The need to escape from the mind-numbing banality of the status quo. The craving for a new and exciting world order.

Post nine-eleven?

You bet your sweet Nellie.

What makes you so sure?

Because, driven as always by my own pecuniary interests, I happen to be monitoring the situation very very closely ...

Matt stabbed the air with an emphatic upright forefinger.

... unlike you, boyo.

Meaning?

Get up off your backside, why don't you, and take a long close-up look at yonder shiksa.

Matt jabbed his thumb emphatically over his shoulder towards the object of reference, the portrait of Lydia. Harry, obedient soul, rose and walked over to it. Lydia seemed to look back at him with fierce disdain.

After a moment or two of scrutiny, Harry reacted with incredulity.

They're not bullets at all, he said. It's just they're meant to *look like* bullets.

And what, perchance, are they actually?

They're fucking carrots.

… which on examination, pademelons, was true. The slender orange phallo-analogues filling Lydia's bandoliers were not rounds of ammunition, but rabbit fodder. If one were to look closely, one could even see tiny green stalks peeping out …

Right you are, said Matt. So what message is this young revolutionary selling?

Lydia?

Lydia.

Uh … meat is murder?

More than that, turkey. The complete new age deal. The primacy of nature. Gaia. Deep green. Mother earth. Make love not war. Self realization. Meditation. Toot if you're a vegan. The whole kit and caboodle.

Clever.

Not just clever. Brilliant.

I concede. Brilliant.

And just the ticket for those doctor's wives.

Harry returned to the divan. Carried away by the audacious *trompe l'oeil* perpetrated by the rogue image, an image continuing to hold him in hypnotic capture from over Matt's shoulder, he paused to take in a deep breath and to gather his thoughts.

So you think this is the new direction for the fashion industry? he asked.

I'm staking my livelihood on it, said Matt.

For the first time that evening, Harry noticed the glossy

magazines spread across Matt's desk in deliberate disorder, many of them managing to fall open at strategic pages. The titles he could read were **New Age Storefront, Kinesiology and Fashion**, and **The Astral Aardvark**. He speculated these rags would be replete with articles both pretentious and alternative – but nonetheless purporting to be evidence-based – articles fit for the eyes of the wives of medical practitioners – practitioners wedded not only to them (viz. the wives) but also to a solid scientific culture.

You know who introduced me to Lydia? asked Matt.

Mark, I would guess, said Harry.

Clever boy. Here's your reward.

Matt rose, walked over to Harry on the divan, and poured him another *Bisquit*. Then he poured himself one, but did not return to the seat behind his desk. Instead, brandy balloon in hand, he walked over to the rosewood shutters. Standing in front of them, and turning to face Harry, he spoke with great deliberation.

Mark is my lover, he said.

Jesus, tell me something I *don't* know.

I'll make a point of introducing you to him one of these days.

Looking forward to it ...

Harry delivered his corollary:

... and it's not before time, either.

Matt turned his back on Harry. He opened the rosewood shutters, surveyed the streetscape outside, the hesitant traffic, the bourgeoning nightlife, anything at this juncture not involving eye contact with Harry.

You must forgive me, said Matt. I've felt so acutely awkward about the matter.

About Mark?

Yes.

Why?

Lots of reasons.

Matt paused strategically.

False hope, ...

He paused again.

... a sense of betrayal.

Betrayal? Who's betrayed who? asked Harry.

Who's betrayed whom!

O.K. Whom.

Harry was alert. He sensed an uncharacteristic fragility in his companion. Matt appeared to be in the process of overcoming a reticence. Reticence due to be replaced – in painful stages, in forced gradations – by the overwhelming need to spit things out.

I've betrayed *you*, said Matt.

You'll need to explain that one, mate.

Matt walked – swirling his brandy balloon as he did so – until he faced Lydia's portrait. Harry's eyes were boring holes into the back of his head.

I guess, said Matt, it's always been my hope ... you might one day become ... available.

Harry was not expecting a revelation of precisely this complexion.

Me?

Your name's Harry McMinn?

You're not being serious.

I'm afraid I am.

Harry sat stiffly upright, gripping the edge of the couch with both hands.

Jesus, I'm ... flabbergasted. All these years?

Each and every one of them.

Porridge, your father's place, *my* business, *your* business ... ?

All of that.

You must have known nothing was ever going to come of it?

Of course I did. My resignation has been steadfast. But resignation ...

Why don't you shake ...

... doesn't quench hope.

... the monkey off your back? You've got Mark, for Christ's sake.

You've got Sticks too, but I've seen the way you look at Elena.

Well, for me, neither possibility has any traction.

Not ... ?

Not me with Elena. Not me with you.

The silence ensuing was inevitable and toxic. Harry broke it with words hardly less toxic.

Matt, he said, I'm so sorry.

Forget I mentioned it.

Matt. I truly mean it.

Matt turned suddenly to face Harry. The smile on his face was thin and tortured, the travesty of a smile. Although they were looking directly at each other, neither man was able to say anything capable of safe passage through the air. No word *could* be spoken.

But the corrosive silence needed to be neutralized somehow, *any*how, perhaps by the distraction of benevolent extraneity, and suddenly Harry thought he had a way of conjuring this up. He rose, fumbling in the pocket of the lightweight suede jacket he was wearing.

I've had a letter from Izzie, he said.

Matt seemed, for a moment, not to understand. Perhaps he was not yet able to wrench himself free of the trauma riding the wake of their recent discourse.

Izzie, said Harry. Remember him from Porridge?

Of course I do.

Harry was pleased Matt had taken the bait.

How is he? Matt asked.

Harry thrust the letter – a single crumpled sheet – under Matt's nose. Matt took the letter, unfolded it, and read:

>

Harry my friend:

Greetings bro. I write from this hole which is some sort of privately run funny farm. No fucking technology here, so it's HB pencil on blue-lined paper going out snail mail from me to yours truly. Apologies.

The joint's called Passant House, but I call it Pissant House, and that's when I'm in a _good_ mood. Actually I'm being a tad harsh. It's O.K. here except the food is crap and it's full of mad people. There is a dude down the corridor who draws cows all day. Draws a cow, flushes it down the toot, and draws another cow. Never says a word, just keeps drawing cows. All fucking day, draws cows. No bull.

Here's how I got here. It pains me to tell. I trashed my parents' digs, and also roughed up the old stagers a treat in the process. The law duly puts in an appearance, pepper sprays me, throws me in the drunk tank, though no alcohol is involved, not a drop I swear.

Next day, yodellers in white coats appear, women among them with serious death stares. Scary stuff. I cannot help but reflect with sadness on the fact it was my very own flesh and blood sprung this surprise party on me. So here I am putting up a tad of resistance, as you naturally would, giving them some stick too, no more than they richly deserved, and here's where the tossers up and straight jacket me, and give me a swift jab in the hindquarters with an unsolicited hypo, what you might call a parting shot.

Wans't no fun, that jab. No way was it about to shake up the street trade, I can tell you. Nothing at all like the scratch-my-back on offer in Basra base camp. Great shit, that. The crap them yodellers jabbed me with was an anti-psychotic or somesuch, so the maddies tell me. Anyways, next thing I know's my mind's in serious meltdown. Bro, I tell you, my head felt like it was full to the tip of my hairless pate with congealed camel drool, no bulldust.

Anyway upshot is, after living through the mother of all bad trips, me and my arse wake up in what the locals are delighted to inform me is sunny downtown Pissant.

The shrinks say what I've got is PTSD, but personally I think it's _them_ are pissed. When I figure out some way of checking myself out of this lunie bin, I might drop by and sink a beer or two with someone halfway sane. Until then, hold the thought.

Izzie.

>

Matt handed the letter back to Harry.

Halifax, he said, we've got to get the poor bugger out of that shithole.

> >

As an exercise in alienation, the residential precinct bordering Sleek Street has little serious competition. Here, decaying cement-clad town houses, possible precursors of modern-day McMansions, rise up through four stories, affirming the worst of the 1920s. They are shoddy emulations of an art deco model that had been worthless in the first place.

Abutting each other with barely room between them for a person to move without turning sideways, they speak in this millennium of hotchpotched families living on top of each other, drunkenness hand in glove with domestic violence, social insalubrity hidden behind scraggles of prickly border hedge, clunky utility meters with chisel-sharp corners perched dangerously on side walls at head height, security alarms set to trip at the footfall of a cockroach, and (out back and out of sight) grease-engorged gully traps surrounded by seas of sprouting concrete.

Sleek Street itself, a cruel slash bisecting this apology for a residential quarter, allows the injury and insult of torrential traffic to flood its faltering heart. It is an artery *sans* bypasses, through which intransigent local authorities have funnelled – without regard for amenity – all motorized movement to, from, and between two encroaching and recently gentrified neighbourhoods.

As a consequence, the ears of residents are assaulted, day and night, by the shriek and shudder of air brakes, the peremptory wail of emergency sirens, and the horn honk of road ragers. The recurrent instances of gridlock are an offense to human dignity. Exhaust vapours launch pathogenic assaults on any presenting brain or lung tissue.

Mercifully in some respects, developers have recently focused their avaricious eyes on this hapless neighbourhood. Through their importunity, the entire quarter is likely – at a time only the future can know – to be demolished and replaced by up-market air-conditioned double-glazed condominiums flanking a multi-lane freeway.

My second unit, returning after a break of three weeks, and strung out along the footpath of blithe unconcern, is not inclined to dawdle. They have no desire to partake of the barbarous mid afternoon ambience. The sanctuary toward which they make tracks, is the weatherworn theatrical premises, announced by Janus masks and overhung by an ancient melaleuca, a venue destined – by some perverse accident – to flaunt its derelict existence between two of the very saddest of the town houses.

Here my second unit plan to ensconce themselves behind heavy doors, in which refuge they shall entertain hopes. Hopes of *relief from* the hell of urban estrangement. Hopes of *solace in* esoteric theatrical pursuits.

II

Which brings me to speculate idly about the cognitive processes of the embattled residents of these Sleek Street precincts. I am especially interested in the way they grapple with the mysteries of past, present, and future time as they spin their lives of futility and dark desperation. Mysteries you and I, pademelons, are famously at a loss to comprehend.

Let us liken their 'now' to a single teardrop in a sequence of teardrops. Given the sheer desolation of their everyday experience, can there realistically be any disagreement between the 'now' of their present moment as it traces its salty trail down the curve of an indifferent cheek, the many previous 'nows' that have splashed at their uncaring toes before becoming one with the stagnant pool of their squandered past, and the many pending 'nows' due to well up and cloud their dispassionate eyes as befits the watersheds of their irredeemable future?

I think not, pademelons.

What this means, then, is past, present, and future are as one to these poor souls. For them, there is no fretting for the past, because the present recreates it. There is no speculating about the future, because the present foretells it. Time is homogeneous for them, its tripartite divisions indistinguishable one from the other. All time is one, and one time is all. This is *their* problem. It is also *ours.* The downtrodden everymen and everywomen of Sleek Street are trapped in the *everywhen*, as are we, pademelons.

Who owns the vale of tears? They do. And we do.

>

Harry, pushing a wheelchair containing Sticks and a suitable proxy for her infant Timothy, leads the entourage. It appears the director of my second unit has managed to sort out that little problem of continuity.

Following him in order are: Brenda, Sonia, Izzie, Elena, Godfrey, Matt, and Mark.

Mark? you ask.

Yes, I mean Mark. No big deal. Mark, you will recall, has strutted the stage once before. In an early *Stück* depicting a contentious catwalk.

It is Mark, the living breathing version, plucked from out of Harry McMinn's memory bank. Faced with the crying need for a suitable literary convention, I shall refer to him in the third person. I do *not* mean here the insubstantial shade – the insinuative presence of the long deceased Mark – frequently found hanging out in the company of pademelons – who happens to be none other than yours truly. I shall continue to refer to this Mark in the *first* person.

At the front door of the theatre, Brenda takes the baby from Sticks. Bubs registers his protest loudly. Harry assists Sticks from her wheelchair and walks her up the two front steps obtruding so inconveniently. Inside front-of-house, with the house lights switched on, Sticks is able to re-unite with her wheelchair and baby. As we have had occasion to remark at an earlier juncture, the venue is no friend to disability.

Front-of-house is unchanged. The spiral staircase, the ticket box, and the naive artworks extend greetings, as before, like old acquaintances. But go any deeper into the precincts – for example, into the performance space – and a different story unfolds. As Harry throws open the doors to this space, the resumptive party stands bewildered, stunned for a moment into silence and immobility. Fast-moving fairies, it appears, have been at work once again.

Gone are the gracious curves, of a stripe such as theatre-in-the-round is bound by its nature to provide in abundance. They have been replaced by the shock of a matrix unapologetically rectangular. And unapologetically functional. What confronts my second unit – and confronts us also, pademelons, as we hang about close by but unseen – is a fully equipped TV production studio, on which little expense has been spared, but lacking at present the personnel who might run it or the sets with which they might work.

Brackets of powerful stand-alone light sources sprout atop their metallic stalks, tracing out the perimeter of this dormant studio, as it waits to be powered up. Auxiliary lighting – each unit of which zealous grips must have spent hours bolting securely into place on a steel frame – lurks in the flies overhead. Other natural denizens found in this new theatrical space are the strategically placed cameras and sausage microphones, awaiting activation by their absentee technicians.

The active area of the studio is flexible in size, to allow the staging of a goodly range of production scenarios, from intimate moments dependent on close shots, to dynamic situations requiring more space and wider angles.

Positioned centrally in the active space, is a rectangular dais, raised about twelve centimetres. It is a dedicated performance precinct designed to ensure acting talent strutting on it shall stand tall against the lenses of the cameras lurking outside it.

Neither we nor my incredulous second unit can overlook the seating arrangements intended for a studio audience should such be called for. Currently empty, this accommodation consists of dual rectangular banks arranged in gently raked tiers, one such bank angled to the left and the other to the right of the active space. Each bank consists of identical plastic bucket-seats in an unappealing olive green, ostensibly shaped to receive human backsides. Plush carpeting in bland beige has colonized the space under, around, and between each seat.

The bucket-seats are frequently referred to in the trade as 'one-hour seats', on the grounds anybody who has the misfortune to occupy them for longer will, most likely, come away with acute numbness of their posterior region.

Production studios must always have a control room. There is no prize, pademelons, for guessing where such a room might be located. It *has* to be in the former lighting box. Though unable to confirm this with our own eyes, we guess the paraphernalia of this revamped lighting box, along with Elena's role in respect of it, is bound to have undergone considerable revision.

We find ourselves regretting we shall never again see the turntable stage. During the era of its ascendency, we were privileged to experience – and this in a vicarious sense only, such being the limited lot of an audience – some truly memorable moments of high theatre, the like of which it is doubtful we shall experience again except in our fond memories.

For the participants themselves, i.e. for the members of my second unit, the experience would have been another thing, an enhanced experience indeed. In those halcyon days, the likes of Harry, Sticks, Elena, &etc. would – we may imagine – have received a sense of personal vindication, accompanied by insights of a profound and revelatory nature into aspects of their innermost lives. Or, at any rate, of those *alleged* lives that were played out in the wilds of Harry's imagination.

We regret also the passing of the resplendent seating furniture, finished in designs borrowed from Asia and Byzantium. Now such frivolity is redundant. Let's face facts. The performance arena in its present incarnation is to be viewed not so much by a live audience as by passive couch dwellers in the thrall of a remote and impersonal screen. A screen, one might imagine, scorning the presumed privacy of the living room and of its resident potatoes. A screen Harry, in a moment of raw imagination laced with paranoia, once regarded as a single facet of a ginormous insect eye, an insidious conflation surveilling whole unthinking neighbourhoods.

After a long hard look at the new theatrical space, the alleged Sticks turns in her wheelchair to face the alleged Harry.

Herr Direktor, she asks, how do you propose we deal with *this* situation?

It's a challenge, I concede, but we'll rise to the occasion, says Harry. For example, we already have a fledgling DOP waiting in the wings.

DOP? asks Sonia.

Matt indicates Mark by placing a hand on his shoulder.

Director of Photography, he says.

Mark reddens.

<<

Australian History 101, (xxi) Immigration circa The White Australia Policy, (g) The £75 Pom: Case Study of Mr & Mrs L and Son.

'Who sees his true-love in her naked bed/ Teaching the sheets a whiter hue than white,/ But when his glutton eye so full hath fed,/ His other agents aim at like delight?'

So asketh the Bard. Well might those who can lay claim to the appropriate gender, orientation, and inclination answer, Amen!

Pademelons. This racy poetic fragment is no unnecessary digression on my part. I intend to use it as kick-off in the game plan of my lecture. If one seeks 'a whiter hue than white', there's nobody more likely than a home-grown pom to pass the Persil test. Such was the credo adopted by the Immigration gurus who prevailed in Oz during much of the last century.

The Australian public at this time, aided and abetted by their policymakers, were seduced by the above credo. Skin of a 'proper' colour, and preferably the Anglo-Celtic provenance to go with it, was of great importance to the majority of these worthy citizens, and was certainly something they expected of their immigrants.

Accordingly, the Oz public was prepared – at public expense – to subsidize the travel of 'the right type of pom' from his/her home country to theirs, for the purposes of permanent residency in the lucky country, the land of oranges and sunshine. Whence arose the concept of the '£10 pom', a tenner being the price initially asked of the prospective adult immigrant for a journey half way round the world by ocean liner.

Enter Mr and Mrs L and son, the subjects of my case study. They were poms of the right type, living in the mother country, who decided (with the exception of the young lad, who by virtue of his tender age, was privileged to have all decisions made *for* him) to migrate to an obliging Oz in the mid to late 70s.

To the chagrin of the adult couple, the Oz government upped the asking price from £10 to £75 only one week before Mr and Mrs L lodged their application. They grudgingly bit the bullet, making a virtue out of necessity by putting it about – in the circles of the wantonly gullible – that they – the L family no less – must *sine qua non* be 7.5 times more worthy than your everyday family of ten-pound poms.

Let it be shouted to the heavens – because, given the skerrick of a chance, *they* would have raised their voices to such purpose – that both Mr and Mrs had passed through one of the most prestigious universities in the land. I shall refrain from specifying exactly *which* university, for fear of igniting acrimonious debate. In the technical sense, the couple were alumni of this university, their passage through these venerable precincts having been accomplished astride bicycles. On any working day over the past fifteen years, those up and about might have observed them flitting across the academic landscape like friendly pedal pushing ghosts. During this period, he had been deputy curator in the archives of the Museum of the Department of Natural History, and she had been a clerical assistant in these same archives.

His job had been to tend to the preservation of the biological specimens housed therein and, in particular, of specimens from the collection of Alfred Russel Wallace, co-proponent along with Charles Darwin of the theory of evolution through natural selection. The Department was fortunate enough to be custodian of a substantial fragment of the Wallace collection.

Her job had been to catalogue these same specimens.

These were not mean tasks. Wallace's specimens, crumbling under dusty glass, were vulnerable. And the annotations were written in copperplate so small as to be impossible to read except with a powerful magnifying glass, which made one wonder how Wallace had written them in the first place.

Things were not to last for the L family.

Given their predilection for indiscriminate downsizing, new brooms in university administration are the scourge of academia and its sundry hangers-on. Driven by an overweening obsession for a balance sheet blacker than a baboon's snout, such new brooms are prone to overlook the strategic importance of such a prestigious collection as that of Wallace. So, in the early 70s, Mr and Mrs L found themselves no longer needful of regular cycling commutes to and from the university, not for any reason, and certainly not for remunerative purposes.

With their young male first-born to feed and clothe, they quickly saw value in the investment of a mere £10 per adult person for the purposes of transportation to a new life in a new world reportedly full of promise. They were horrified when the required amount of the investment increased overnight by that aforementioned factor, but could not but agree the value for them still remained.

On board the boat – Italian – they overcame their initial aversion to the 'dago' crew, and settled in to enjoy the food and service. Mr L discovered if he raised his finger in the air and shouted, Boy!, he would be promptly delivered of a pint of Worthington's (accompanied by a Pimms No. 1 Cup for *madame*) by a 'boy' with balding pate, greying moustache, yellowing teeth, and stooping frame. Though their name was L, they were leading the life of Riley.

Mr L thought this floating life was all 'jolly good fun'. First, the captain's cocktail party, with endless pints of free Worthington's. Deck quoits when unaccountably one felt the need for physical activity. Shore leave, first at Cairo and then at Colombo, both a universe away from South Anglia. The crossing of the line, at which ceremony King Neptune – looking suspiciously like the Italian captain – surfaced with his three-pronged fork to check the credentials of all new arrivals to the southern half of the globe.

Then – oh yes – next stop Australia fair.

Mr and Mrs L found the hot dry weather on the west coast did not suit them. Nor did the derisory response they received pursuant on a finger in the air and the shout of 'Boy!' So they chose to remain on the boat. They found the east coast suited them no better, but here they were required to disembark. The boat was about to return to the motherland with a cargo of young Oz backpackers and the like who, in their quest for The Great Adventure, had squirreled away hundreds of dollars apiece. The disillusioned Ls might have been tempted to go back with these young colonials but for the financial disincentive.

Searching for cooler weather, they went south, found Tasmania, cut their losses, and settled. Admin jobs in a local brewery were up for grabs. They grabbed. Their workplace was not the famed university of their former life any more than the beer they helped produce was Worthington's. A slow and painful adjustment process ensued.

We shall leave the parents to wallow in their disgruntled and advancing dotage.

The young lad – their son – also had adjustments to make. There were the recalcitrant parents he sought to shake off. And there was the street culture to which he sought to adapt.

The locals found his patois problematic. His preference for 'shall' and its derivatives, his predisposition to use 'one' as a pronoun, and his other grammatical quirks, bothered the local Taswegians, who found such modes of expression foreign or worse elitist. Over time, they realized he was not trying to put on dog, and dismissed him as an oddity, a self-styled grammar tragic.

Some other matters were to surface, including his sexual preferences. These they would find more difficult to dismiss.

As for primary and secondary school, much of his effort was taken up avoiding bullies. His long legs and nimble feet helped him avoid a comprehensive thumping and the bullies the occasion of sin. When puberty arrived, in the absence of fanfare as it mostly does, he was mortified to discover he had a preference for boys rather than girls, an inclination he suspected certain of his male cohorts shared to a degree, in a transitionary sense at least. Of course, none of the latter was eager to admit to such an 'unnatural' leaning.

Mark – that was his name – found the inclination persisted despite the passage of months and years. Finally he realized there was nothing of a transitionary nature about *his* inclinations. He cherished his sexual feelings, but squaring up to their nature was painful. The uncomfortable fact of his sexuality was apparently something he would be stuck with for life.

… this was a turn-up for the books, on which those White Australia supremos surely had not reckoned …

After completing a creditable year 11, Mark enrolled in 'Snapper School', an establishment having no association – unless adventitious – with actual fish. The school in question was the Institute of Still Photography and Cinematography. The Tasmanian Chapter thereof.

ISPAC was a happy choice for Mark, his parents' disapproval notwithstanding. In the wider world, he was the target of bigotry on account of his unconventional sexual leanings, which the bigots seemed to have an uncanny knack of sussing out. Yet, within the Institute, he rarely found himself bedevilled by such prejudice.

Unapologetic gay blade he may have been, but a culture of benign tolerance had somehow arisen and then flourished at Snapper School. He found he was able to swim there in a current of his own choosing with snapper of similar stripe. Life was good.

One of the mandatory performance objectives at Snapper School, was the production of a cinematographic project on a subject of the student's choosing. When it came to making *his* choice, Mark was at a loss. His supervisor came to the rescue with the idea Mark should produce a documentary on The White Australia Policy. What could be more appropriate, said the supervisor, in the case of somebody who had come to Oz under the auspices of said Policy? Mark was happy to run with this suggestion.

He began. While constructing a storyboard, Mark rediscovered a talent he had consistently undervalued in the past. He could draw. He was adept at the pictorial representation of people, places, and events. What was a struggle for many other students came effortlessly to him. He reflected that if his preferred career in cinematography did not work out for one reason or another, he could always try his hand as a cartoonist or book illustrator.

Pre-production over, Mark began to trawl the streets in the vicinity of Snapper School wielding a hand-held camera. A fellow of the student body (and of his bed), whom he had persuaded to hold a microphone, accompanied him. On interviewing people at random re The White Australia Policy, he encountered – time and again – a response along the lines of, What the fuck sort a question's that meant to be mate?, which response at the very least gave Mark the opportunity to demonstrate to his supervisor his skills in the interpolation of bleeps into the sound track rushes.

He consulted the abundant archival footage, including that epigrammatical gem, attributed to The Hon. A A Caldwell, Minister for Immigration in the 1940s, an avowed supporter of the White Australia Policy: 'Two Wongs don't make a white.'[48] It may come as a surprise to some of you to learn the two Wongs were real people. Assiduously, Mark tracked them down and researched their background. The choice quotation from the Hon. A A re these redoubtable Wongs, and the harrowing experiences of the Wongs themselves, were to become the centrepieces of his completed documentary.

He received a High Distinction for his project.

For Mark, a significant unintended consequence was to flow from his cinematographic triumph. Formerly staunchly apolitical, Mark became radicalized. Generalizing with reckless abandon, he began to see the White Australia Policy in the broader context of rampant colonialism. It needs be said, whenever presenting as a political animal, he did not bother to budge from his armchair. He was no bare-knuckled agent for the cause.

The plight of full-blood Tasmanian aborigines as a specimen of applied colonialism would have been the closest to home for him. Then he uncovered other instances – some current, some historical – some local, some remote – instances whose chords – sometimes plaintive, sometimes strident – resonated with an identifiable harmonic relation to the Tasmanian exemplar. There was Sinn Fein, the struggle for Tibetan independence, the Viet Cong, Castroite Cuba, West Irian, Fretilin, the Chechen insurgency, &etc. Each of these diverse crusades came at him complete with its quota of freedom fighters of whatever political flavour, for whatever zealous cause, in whatever corner of the seething globe.

He found himself regretting Australia's allegiance to the British crown, as reflected in the constitution, the national anthem, and

---

48 The Hon. Caldwell had always asserted his statement – judged to be in-
    flammatory down the ensuing decades – had been wilfully and consistently
    quoted out of context, in that 'white' should have been read as 'White', this
    being in reference to his fellow parliamentarian on the opposition benches,
    the Hon. T W White. Official transcripts support this assertion. Never-
    theless, neither his (Caldwell's) insistence, nor the transcripts to prove it,
    resulted in his becoming disengaged from his petard.

the Oz flag. He was sobered to realize all of his latter-day views on such matters were in opposition to those of his £75 pom parents.

... and, though it would seem to fall outside the ambit of colonialism, being more in the nature of hostile action *sans frontières*, the scourge of gay oppression was an enemy against which he was more than willing to register his protest, from his armchair of course ...

Stop right there!

Pademelons, let's put aside any further pretence. Nobody is fooled. This lecture of mine is an outrageous charade, an impropriety to which I plead guilty.

Mark L is, of course, me. Me, your unhappy narrator, in an earlier and mortal incarnation, his death poised ready at a moment's notice to facilitate the necessary transformation. The transformation from him to me, from third person to first, from life's eager participant to life's reluctant narrator. Forever fated to narrate life at a significant remove from it.

As for the White Australia Policy, let us leave it to historians better equipped for the task, and for relegation to the shameful backwaters of their discipline.

I quit the lectern.

>

Early evening inside the Big Top. The soft patter of warm light rain on a Colorbond roof.

The techies whose habit it was to occupy the venue during normal working hours would have found it eerily quiet in its dim after-hours guise, lacking as it did the daily hustle and hullaballoo. This contrast in ambience was creepy. Dimly lit metallo-electronic carcasses, their inards incomplete, hung with not even a breeze to swing in, from overhead rails on which nothing rolled. The putative carcasses were wrapped in plastic jackets, as if they had been put to bed for the night. They had no option but to await the Operations Manager – Ramon Contreras – scheduled to put in an appearance at seven on the dot the following morning at which time they and the whole cadaverous concern would be re-activated.

… Operations Manager? Of what, pray? An abattoir for androids? A slaughterhouse for cyborgs? We, of course, are in a position to know better …

The carcasses threw menacing shadows in the meagre fluorescence filtering down from security lights in the ceiling. Supplementary lights at floor level, as if emulating votive candles, made paltry attempts to dispel gloom. These ground-dwelling pinpoints of apologetic illumination, almost lost in the immensity of the precincts, came from two bamboo shanties, one in the front northwest corner, the other in the back southeast corner of the Big Top.

This was the moment of repose for the dynamic enterprise known as Integrated Electronic Imagery. In such abeyance, IEI had the capacity to startle. Then again, it also had the capacity to startle when, in broad daylight, it operated at full throttle.

The sound of a zither – determinedly *noir* – came from the shanty in the southeast corner. The Harry Lime theme. But, if one lent one's ear to closer scrutiny, it was not the exact sound of a zither. It was a counterfeit sound. The twangy musical line came with a subtle distortion of the zither's signature quality, a distortion clipping the sharp edges of its notes and homogenizing its crisp resonances.

This was a rendering in a style on the point of heading off down the revisionist road towards that tacky cul-de-sac known as Muzak. But, regardless of this rogue retreat from authenticity, one might easily have imagined Orson Welles, flitting between carcasses, as might a fugitive from justice, under cover of the prevailing semi-darkness.

From outside, came the scratch of a key turning in a lock,

followed by a louder grating noise. The large vehicular door, the one at front of shop, was rolling up. The 'zither' music ceased abruptly.

Shock to the coddled mechanism of our marsupial eyes, the main lights snapped full on. The full glare revealed the source of intrusion. Visitors, sporting umbrellas, were making their entrance through the wide-open front door. They were: Harry (pushing wheelchair), Sticks (sitting in wheelchair), Brenda (tagging along behind), and Timmy (babe in Brenda's arms). Simultaneously, Izzie emerged from the shanty at the back, source until recently of the Harry Lime music, and Elena emerged from the shanty at the front. A determined cat seeking food – known by those in the loop as Koshechka – was twisting and twirling at Elena's ankles, as if making every attempt to trip her up and lay her out flat as a corpse.

The full lights served also to dispel our illusions apropos of sinister slaughterhouses and the like. This was an engineering production line – sleek and bloodless – of vintage late 20th/early 21st century.

We became aware changes had been made to the precincts, changes not evident in the dim light, but obvious when exposed to the riot of relentless kilowatts. *Two* changes, one apparently of a transitory nature, the other with a more permanent feel to it:

Balloons, and festoons of paper streamers, in rainbow colours, had been strung from and between whatever protuberances could be found on high. A couple of dozens bottles of champagne, their pear-shaped profiles promises of palative pleasure, were laid out like a single rank of soldiers on one of the dormant assembly lines. China plates, loaded with a variety of gourmet finger food, adorned a stack of wooden pallets. The goodies on each plate were covered with a crocheted doily, the handiwork, one might guess, of Brenda. A celebration of sorts seemed imminent.

The long sides of the Big Top had been retrofitted with enormous windows, four in all, taking up most of the available wall space. This was the only substantial modification the frame of the building had seen since Harry had assumed ownership almost a decade ago. Personnel ensconced in the premises during the day could now expect to enjoy a constant and reassuring view of the outside world as it progressed through its cycle of quotidian activity. Regrettably, about all that was visible at present of the outside world through these windows were a few desolate street lamps, these lamps struggling blobs of diffuse light shimmering through the steadfast drizzle.

The five people – early arrivals for the festivities – coalesced beneath the festoons as if compelled by gravity. They stood silently in their huddle, intimidated perhaps by the immense space and the unorthodox time. Brenda, while jiggling/juggling baby, offered a plate around to the others. Sticks broke the silence, addressing Izzie and Elena from her wheelchair.

Well boys and girls, she asked, how do you rate the Cockatoo Street refuge for the abjectly orphaned and the seriously down at heel?

Khorosho[49], said Elena. We now have music.

There's a better class of yodeller here than at Pissant House, said Izzie.

But this was no time for such pleasantries. More guests were arriving through the front door.

Penny, on her own, came in first, her accoutrements colour-coordinated down/up? to the umbrella she was collapsing. As expected, everything about her was elegant and fashionable. She would never be seen out and about in anything other than the finest and latest.

… pademelons, do you wonder about Penny? Penny Galatano: well scrubbed, personable, empathetic, witty? But very much a private person. Why does she always arrive alone on social occasions? Could there be some deep dark tragic secret in her

---

49 *Khorosho*: It's good.

past? It is beyond *my* brief to delve into this intriguing mystery, pademelons, but one of you might feel inclined to follow it up ...

Scanning the company, Penny greeted everybody with a collective wave. Then she saw Izzie standing alone and apart. In a manner typical of her, she made a beeline for him. She considered misfortune, and the lost souls inhabiting such territory, to be her special responsibility.

She spoke to Izzie in a manner cultivated over the years, a manner designed to ensure the subject of her attentions felt he/she was a special person.

Word has it, she said, you are hunkered down here with a brand new nickelodeon.

Don't know that particular animal, said Izzie.

Penny repeated herself, with emphasis on each syllable.

A nick-el-od-e-on.

You mean a polyphonic multi-modal electro-acoustic synthesizer?

Penny clapping hand over mouth, winked at him.

Oh, she said, how unspeakably gauche of me.

Behind Penny, dealing with superfluous umbrellas, Matt's siblings – Simon and Martha – entered. Simon was dressed as would an academic, in tweed jacket with leather elbows. Martha, familiar with the corridors of the corporate world, wore a conservative skirt and jacket. For what seemed to her like forever, she was enduring the tribulations of a messy divorce, and was glad tonight to have her twin brother as an escort.

They exchanged greetings and then mingled with those already present.

Having done her duty by Izzie, Penny sought out Sticks. Communication demanded she kneel beside the wheelchair. After voicing her commiserations (re Sticks' illness) and congratulations (re Sticks' newborn), she broached – in a confidential tone – the issue bugging her.

Izzie saw action in the Iraq War, I understand, she said.

A few years back now, said Sticks.

He O.K.?

Sticks shrugged.

There's a look in his eye, said Penny. Intent at times. Distant at others.

He's always like that.

Soldiers sometimes bring war back with them, said Penny, and try to re-enact their former battles in Civvy Street. It happens. You're not worried having him here as a tenant?

Sticks laughed dismissively.

I don't think he's a problem, she said.

Others were arriving. Baharudin came in first, with Hussein at his heels. Hussein, as usual in traditional Malaysian garb, shook the excess water from the umbrella he was holding over his master's head and folded it.

Ramon, travelling solo, entered a matter of seconds behind them. Yes, pademelons, you were not mistaken. That *was* Señor Contreras who entered the premises, disproving our earlier presumption he might not make his appearance until seven next morning. Shedding his raincoat, then folding it over his arm, he hurried to draw level with Baharudin. So Ramon and the Sultan-to-be proceeded together to join the assembled throng, looking for all the world like competitors in some unsung sartorial stakes.

Hussein, ever conscious of protocol, positioned himself at the 'correct' distance from the throng, facing them with feet apart and hands clasped behind his back.

Gravity was still a force to be reckoned with. Baharudin, gravitating to Elena, grasped her right hand, raised it to his lips with an extravagant flourish, and kissed it. Nothing as singular as this gesture had ever been seen before around *these* traps. Elena was chuffed.

Ramon, gravitating to Harry, engaged him and was engaged *by* him in shop talk and sundry frivolities.

In her ongoing conversation with Sticks, Penny switched the subject of her polite concern to Sticks herself.

Everything on the up and up with you? she asked.

Most certainly, said Sticks.

I hear you have lost your superhuman skills since the illness.

My memory skills?

How do you feel about that?

It's been a challenge. But, of late, I've begun to see it as an opportunity.

How so?

Ever since I first became aware of my freakish talents, I've felt trapped by them. Now I'm free. The meningitis has actually liberated me.

Penny looked at Sticks as at one who had lost her mind, but she managed nevertheless to dissemble.

How wonderful, she said.

Sticks was not fooled.

It must be difficult, she said, for somebody else to see it from my point of view. Let me try to explain.

She gathered her thoughts.

Right from the outset, everybody assumed there was only one future for me. A future in linguistics and its applications. Providence via my DNA had given me a rare gift. How can you deny a gift of that nature? Like it or not, I was obliged to accept it as my destiny.

She looked up at Penny with clear eyes.

But the Lord giveth and the Lord taketh away.

Are you religious?

Sticks laughed.

Let's say my options are now wide open.

Glancing sideways at Harry, she lowered her voice to a whisper.

I'm not obliged to work for Harry any more.

You will, of course.

Not necessarily.

Where *would* you work?

I'm thinking seriously of taking on a cause.

What sort of cause?

The environment. More specifically, the threat to Malaysian rainforest. I've mentioned it to Baharudin.

What does he think?

He thinks it's dangerous.

You'd do it *in situ*? In Malaysia?

Where else?

There are plenty of worthy causes to be found in *this* country.

Penny. The Malaysian rainforest is the cause I know and care about.

Again Sticks paused to collect her thoughts.

Palm oil is the big threat. If the rainforest disappears, so does the habitat of thousands upon thousands of species of fauna. You've heard about the orang-utans?

Of course.

It's not *only* orang-utans. It's the whole gamut. It's critters as small as fireflies. As large as elephants.

What about Timmy?

I'm not planning to leave *tomorrow*.

She slapped the side of the wheelchair.

Maybe in two years, said Sticks. Brenda would look after Timmy. And Harry would do his bit.

What does *he* think?

Not keen. But he's reconciled.

Sticks responded to the dubious look on Penny's face.

Look, she said. Harry is a great person to work with. I've got no complaints on that score. But, post meningitis, I must think of myself. And this is the right course for me to take.

Why?

It's my vision. My passion.

Penny's riposte was stinging.

Matt's line precisely, she said.

Uh ... ?

When he took himself off to Russia.

There were more arrivals. Amidst a flurry of activity, noise, and loud conversation – some of it in accented Spanish – Ramon's expat Argentinean friends entered. They were eight in number: four men, accompanied by women whose status – wives? girl friends? – was ambiguous. All were well groomed, of Latin appearance, and ready for a good time. They had brought their own six-packs of beer and pre-mixed beverages, which they wasted no time putting to the taste test.

They gravitated to where Ramon, Harry, and Sticks were in session. Here they showed a deal of polite concern over Sticks' condition.

Brenda, who had settled baby into bassinette and stowed the bassinette in a quiet corner, continued to press food on all takers. She insisted the champagne must wait until the guests of honour arrived. Elena took the opportunity to relieve her of a choice piece of smoked salmon on a cracker, then let the salmon slide surreptitiously to the floor at her feet, where Koshechka disposed of it greedily.

... and, because Brenda deigned to speak of the devil, the devil (in duplicate) found it necessary to arrive. Through the front door came Matt and Mark, dealing with sodden umbrellas. Both were dressed to the standard one might expect of representatives of a fashion house. They were a stylish duo – Matt the dark twin and Mark the fair – with matching bow ties in blue, a colour suiting both complexions.

Matt had brought his bottle of *Bisquit*, an indication he had perhaps anticipated meeting up tonight with no more than three select people, say Harry, Sticks, and Sticks' newborn. All four adults would then enjoy an intimate evening in which Mark would make his social debut within the confines of a small and manageable circle. With impunity, and no intimation of threat.

That was not to be.

Instead, an oversized throng confronted them with a barrage of lusty greetings. The eager punters had been awaiting this moment. Harry let a whopping 'Bravo!' escape his lungs. Ramon let loose a piercing wolf whistle. Others stamped feet. And, seemingly from nowhere, paper streamers in rainbow colours sliced the air, coiling themselves around the embarrassed couple.

Matt and Mark looked as if they might be of a mind to do a runner.

The champagne corks started popping as the new arrivals began their faltering approach to the throng. They had conceded their only option at this late stage was to face the music. The frothy stuff filled plastic cups to the brim, which were passed around until everyone could claim to have received at least one. Of course, Brenda made sure Hussein got orange juice and Timmy his formula.

Everybody now saw a clear path to a good booze-up, and was inclined to tread this path with enthusiasm. Apropos of paths, the buzz of animated conversation soared up the steep boulevard of sound best named 'Crescendo'. Only Matt and Mark remained subdued. They each engaged in sly touches of the other's hand when they imagined they were not being observed. Perhaps those sly touches carried messages of support for each other in a situation they were finding to be fraught with possibilities for humiliation.

Harry – who else should we blame for the plastic cups? – decided the moment had arrived to quell the rising tide of sound. He tapped the handle of a serendipitous screwdriver against the side of a champagne bottle until the noise of conversation had dropped back to a level he felt might enable him to get his words heard. Then he assaulted all ears with what had the hallmarks of a rehearsed spiel.

I believe Mark, the long-awaited one, is with us tonight, he said. We have all heard about Mark, but few of us have met him. Matt, will you be so good as to introduce this mythic person, until now kept under more wraps than Tutankhamen?

Matt, clearly embarrassed and with rising irritation, indicated the hapless Mark with a deferential wave of an upturned hand.

Pademelons. I have it on authority – of the type being the prerogative of a rank insider – that Mark was mortified by all this flapdoodle. His most fervent desire was to melt into the air, to fall into a non-existent crack in the floor, to gain entree to some parallel universe, to become totally invisible. One or all of the above. And Matt, paragon of empathy, knew without doubt exactly how Mark felt at this moment.

Loud interpositions of 'Right on, Mark' and/or 'Attaboy, Mark' and/or 'Bully for you, Mark' billowed to the conversational surface. Crescendo reasserted itself. Harry tapped the champagne bottle again.

Mark comes from Tasmania, said Harry. It's fitting we toast him with Tassie's finest vintage. A *cuvée* ...

(pronouncing it with an -ee- sound)

... from Clover Hill, the drop served up to Frederik and Mary, Prince and Princess elect of Denmark, beloved of all paparazzi, on the occasion of their wedding.

I'll bet *they* didn't get to drink it out of plastic cups, said Penny.

Let us toast the happy couple, said Harry.

He raised his cup.

Which happy couple might that be? asked Penny.

Matt and Mark, said Harry.

All around, cups were raised and there were echoes of 'Matt and Mark'.

Nobody noticed Izzie slip away from the throng. The moment everybody realized Izzie had vanished, was the same moment the sounds of synthesized saxophone filled the premises with an instrumental version of a vintage song once popular and recently blessed with a revival. The lyrics, though not making actual vibrations in the air, managed to insinuate themselves into many heads:

... that's why, darling, it's incredible

that someone so unforgettable
thinks that I am unforgettable too ...

Matt looked homicidal. Mark looked bewildered.

Matt's words forced their way out from between clenched teeth.

There are those among us, said Matt, who would have hoped for some delicacy in relation to this matter.

The words fell on deaf ears. Perhaps in the light of day when heads recharged with the hair of the dog were less fuzzy, regrets would surface.

Sticks turned in her wheelchair, beckoning Harry. Harry obliged by bending his knees to bring his ear down to the level of her tongue. Into this ear, she delivered her admonitory words.

Should you want my honest opinion, sport, she said, this event could have been conducted with a tad more circumspection.

>

Apropos of circumspection, Ronnie Dash put in a late appearance to festivities. The formalities were all but over when he did so, which was possibly his precise intention.

With him was a young woman of indisputable allure, in loose blouse and short diaphanous skirt. She was endowed with natural physical attributes guaranteed to incite envy in every woman, and lust in every man. Nonetheless, her make-up and coiffure were of such discreet and tasteful mien as would placate her very own mother. Those already gathered speculated: was she the virgin from the parish tennis club or the paid escort?

The floor was littered with champagne corks, twisted rainbows of paper streamer, food scraps, and burst balloons. Negotiating their way through this charnel, and fending off a number of near legless people, the late arriving pair managed to get their eager hands around plastic cups of royal wedding bubbly.

The throng, each person presenting in turn, was feting Mark, who had unwittingly stolen the show. There was no escape for him. After all, with the exception of Matt, Penny, and Elena, nobody had met him before. Nevertheless, to the last man/woman they *had* all heard about him. Everybody was friendly if a tad tipsy, and Mark – putting aside earlier trepidations – was beginning to enjoy his moment of fame.

Izzie had rejoined the company, the possibilities of his 'unforgettable' rendition exhausted.

Sticks indicated to Matt she would like a word in private with him, so he took charge of her wheelchair. He steered her away from the throng to a bench on the north side of the Big Top, a bench where, in daylight hours, items such as sur-text for opera, items of low demand but high prestige, would be assembled. He sat himself down behind the bench, facing her across it.

She opened the conversation.

I'm sorry, she said, if you feel you have been treated with disrespect.

Don't concern yourself unduly, Matt said. My behaviour may have been a little too precious. It's all good now. Look at him. A pig in mud.

He waved his hand towards Mark.

I'm pleased to have met him, she said.

I'm sure it's mutual.

You love him?

Of course.

Outside, through one of the large windows, the rain was easing. The dark outline of the former premises of Unthank Engineering, wherein was housed the Nerd Centre, was beginning to become visible over Matt's right shoulder.

There was a pause before Sticks broached the subject that was the purpose of her setting up this *tête-a-tête*.

You, she said, have been very good to Izzie …

The least we could do.

… and credit is due to you in spades.

Not only to me, I'll have you know.

Harry also?

Harry is the one providing the shelter.

And, between the pair of you, you've bought him a synthesizer.

Well, apropos of that …

You trying to deny it?

… there's potential for some lucrative spin-off to justify the purchase.

Oh?

We're not the philanthropists we might seem.

Matt, I know the story.

You … ?

Harry told me.

The sound of Ronnie's voice suddenly assailed them, it having somehow managed to pierce the shroud of conversation woven by that fabulous word-factory yonder, whose auspices they had quit. Arm around the shoulders of his female companion, Ronnie was in the process of introducing himself to Mark.

Guessing you must be Mark, he said. Hi.

Hi, said Mark.

The name's Ronnie.

Pleased to meet you, Ronnie. You work here also?

Ronnie, nodding extravagantly, indicated one of the large windows.

That's one of my creations, he said.

The window?

It's an anisotropane.

An an- an- …

Anisotropane. Give you a demo if you like.

Right now?

Good a time as any.

Ronnie suddenly realized he hadn't introduced his companion.

Oh, and this is Desiree, he said.

Glad to meet you, Desiree, said Mark.

Glad to meet *you*, Mark, said Desiree.

… Desiree!? Pademelons, is this the sort of name to which one might expect an ingénue of the tennis courts would answer? …

The conversation between this threesome was subsumed into the general alcohol fuelled buzz. Matt and Sticks, having lost its verbal thread, felt able to resume their own.

You said Harry told you the story, said Matt. About the synthesizer.

He did, said Sticks.

What *exactly* did he tell you?

He told me Izzie can now provide musical entertainment for the techies while they work.

Is that all?

He told me Izzie might be leaned upon to provide lunchtime recitals for the techies.

Is that all?

Sticks, to press home her main point, raised her eyes so they engaged with his.

And he told me, she said, the manufacture of synthesizers tailored to specific needs, might be the makings of a good plan B in the event the market for multi-screen systems collapses.

I like his idea.

A wry smile sculpted Sticks' lips.

Funny that. I *knew* you would, she said.

Matt, uncomfortable with Sticks' sarcasm and where it might be heading, tried to deflect her assault.

Why should the market collapse? he asked.

Quit the charade. We both *know* this conversation.

No. Tell me. Why should it collapse?

Sticks took a deep breath. She re-established the challenging eye contact with Matt.

Harry talked about the probability, she said, of competition from cheap single-screen plasma TVs of unlimited size, imported from Asia.

Full marks to him.

Indeed? For passing on *your* thoughts?

Mine?

Yours.

Great minds think alike.

Don't bullshit me, Matt. It's a good strategic plan. Could be a brilliant one. But *Harry* didn't dream it up. Harry is no strategic thinker. By his own admission, he's a techno nerd.

And a bloody good one.

But the *ideas*, Matt. The *ideas*. My father gave Harry the idea for a multi-screen system, and Harry went with it. Then *you* gave him every idea since then. Electronic bulletin boards, crawls, surtext, virtual reality, ...

She gestured with her arms, palms upward.

... all *your* ideas, Matt. Every last one of them.

Not virtual reality. That was the Sultan's idea.

But not Harry's. That's my point.

But he *makes* the stuff, Sticks. He *makes* it all happen.

Matt. You protest too much.

Silence held until the moment when silence itself became intolerable.

Why do you *do* it? asked Sticks. You're not on the payroll.

Matt, both elbows on the bench, dropped his brow onto his upright palms to hide his face from Sticks' insistent view. He could not bear the thought of Sticks being privy to his nervous eyes and tense lips.

What's the special relationship between you and Harry? asked Sticks.

Matt did not stir.

Spit it out! said Sticks.

Matt did not stir.

My brothers' lawyer was right on the money, said Sticks.

>>

Singspielstück #14: Izzie Trigger Happy?

We, invisible to mortal life, comprise the entire studio audience. We look across at the active space of the studio, a space flooded with light from above. A generous expanse. Actors shall find room to swing cats when and if necessary. Within it, the crew are gearing up for the next *Stück*. We recognize many of them: the Sandalwood push, familiar to us from previous *Stücke*.

Cameras, supported on pedestals, cover the space from three sides, their operators lounging beside them, with studied nonchalance, and an uncanny resemblance to suburban council workers leaning on their shovels. The fourth side, void of cameras, contains a constructed backdrop, proxy for a large pane of clear glass framed by sheet steel. This backdrop represents the wall of a particular light industrial enterprise with which we should be familiar.

Through the putative pane of glass, we see an illuminated streetlight. We are meant to believe it is evening in the imaginary world of this *Stück*.

Clustered round a camera on our left are Harry (trying to appear in charge of proceedings), Mark (my mortal self in the role of DOP), and a male camera operator whom we identify as that self-proclaimed deity, Godfrey Goldsworthy. All three wear the casual clothes and communications headgear a studio crew might be expected to wear.

The active space boasts a minimal set. A narrow shelf shaves the back right corner on a shallow diagonal. Poised above this shelf, and hanging from the flies, are a couple of metal housings crammed with electronic spaghetti. A stack of wooden pallets claims the mid-distance on the right. Littering the floor, shelf, and pallets are the remnants of a celebration: empty bottles, plastic cups, paper streamers, uneaten food, etc. We conclude this set represents an excision from the interior of the Big Top, in the dying stages of that memorable party held in honour of Mark's coming out.

We are surprised to find Izzie's synthesizer occupying the back left of the performance space. What the devil is it doing there?

Harry turns to the left and speaks softly – into the mike forming part of his headgear – to somebody unseen by us, presumably off set.

Send in the talent, he says.

The 'talent' enters from the left. It comprises quite a bunch: Matt, Martha, Simon, Penny, Ramon, Baharudin, Ronnie, Sonia, Brenda, and toddler Timmy, supplemented by a contingent of the Sandalwood folk. Oh, and Izzie. He proceeds directly to his synthesizer where, seating himself, he arranges his sheet music.

… but why *toddler* Timmy? Shouldn't he be a babe-in-arms? Nor are we aware Sonia was invited to this shindig. We are confused but – we suspect – not nearly as confused as Harry …

Sticks, *sans* wheelchair, follows them on. In her role as floor manager, she also wears headgear. She busies herself with the placement of talent, directing them to positions scattered more or less evenly round the performance space. In the process, she is cognisant of likely social groupings: for example, Timmy with Brenda.

This done to her satisfaction, she heads with intent toward Harry lurking near the camera on the left. We gather she has something of importance to say to him. Getting his attention, she beckons with a flick of her head. Then she changes direction, heading towards the studio audience, i.e. us. She drops her headgear as she moves, leaving it to dangle loosely around her neck. Apparently, the words she wants with Harry are intended to be private.

Harry follows her and, taking the hint, drops his headgear also. Seating themselves within our earshot, they speak to each other in lowered voices. But, zounds, they have invisible eavesdroppers.

I smell a rat, says Sticks.

I'll call pest control, says Harry.

Spare me the wisecracks, she says. You're keeping something up your sleeve and I'm not happy about it.

What might I be hiding?

Something you and Izzie have concocted together.

I can't imagine what it could be.

Sticks is irate. Words, dollops of lava, erupt from her lips.

Don't piss on me and call it rain. *You*, whose capacity to engineer your own version of the truth is legendary? *You* can't imagine? Odds on your rogue imagination is planning as we speak to trump reality yet again. Like it did back at the time of your big debacle.

Debacle?

Debacle.

When was that?

When you dumped on Sonia.

When did I dump on Sonia?

Don't play dumb-arse.

When?

When we did the *Stück* you called 'Only'.

Harry is displeased at being reminded of the occasion on which his theatrical troupe, to the last soul, had seriously contemplated jumping ship.

That's history, he says. A little mistake of mine you had no business bringing up.

Spare me your *big* mistakes.

They hear Mark's raised voice from across the floor.

Do you think our esteemed executive, he says, might deign to apply themselves to the production at hand?

Sticks purses her lips and shakes her head. But Mark's plea has the desired effect. Adjusting their headgear, Sticks and Harry make their way back to where Mark and Godfrey wait impatiently. As if suddenly aware they are on a tight schedule, they do not dawdle. Action starts the very moment they are back in position.

Camera One, says Mark. At your leisure, zoom to keyboard. Then roll.

A production assistant with clapperboard approaches. Godfrey raises a finger in the air. Harry gives the thumbs up. The clapperboard 'claps'.

Take One of the *Stück* begins.

Izzie coaxes three chords from the keyboard, the opening bars of Rachmaninov's prelude in C sharp minor. Strangely, he neglects to imbue them with any of the drama they deserve. Having executed them in lacklustre fashion, his drooping fingers dangle over the keyboard like switches of a weeping willow over a languid watercourse. It is uncharacteristic of Izzie to be so reticent.

He rises half-heartedly to his feet.

Cut, says Harry.

Things grind to an ignominious halt. So much for Take One. Sticks and Harry vent their spleen on Izzie.

Sheba, says Sticks, what's eating you? Put some life into it, man.

You are *Il Maestro*, says Harry. Play the part. Your hands, mate, your hands.

Izzie, not happy, sits. The clapper signals the start of Take Two. The three dramatic chords are to get a replay.

This time around, Izzie camps things up with flamboyant hand gestures, fingers poised high in the air between each successive assault on the keyboard. When *Il Maestro* has hammered the last chord home, and while the sustain mechanism of his synthesizer is in the process of working its magic, his pianist's hands float high, and stay there, as if under the control of a puppet master who has taken up residence in the flies.

He rises abruptly to his feet, and flashes a glare in the direction of Sticks and Harry, a glare that asks with disdain, Satisfied now, yodellers?

Harry gives Izzie thumbs up. Sticks, puzzled, shakes her head, unable to figure out what is bugging Izzie. Pademelons, we also sense a problem, don't we, but can't quite put a finger/paw on it.

Harry and Sticks shed their headgear and stride nimbly into the performance space to join the festivities. They are actors now, not crew.

… but if they are actors where is Sticks' wheelchair? And as for Mark, guest of honour for these festivities as we understand, why doesn't he join them? We suspect Harry, in charge of continuity, has once again stuffed up and in spades …

Camera Two, says Mark. Set up wide shot on entire space. Then roll.

The clapper again. Take Three begins.

All actors *ad lib* conversation with accompanying hand gestures. We pick up no actual words because what they say coalesces into an incoherent background buzz. Brenda and Timmy move about among the throng as they party, offering drinks and finger food.

Pre-recorded music, staged by Izzie at some ealier time, begins. Rudely contemptuous of the Rachmaninov, it consists of a melodic line – in 4/4 and major key – of such childlike simplicity it could double as the Mickey Mouse song.

Izzie opens his piano seat and extracts an AK47. We stifle a tendency to gasp. Gripping the trigger guard with one hand, he heaves the weapon vigorously in the air above his head: once, twice, three times. He holds it up there for a moment, before lowering the butt to his shoulder. He is ready for action.

Harry turns towards the studio audience (invisible us) and lip-syncs along with the pre-recorded lyrics:

Harry:

Izzie fully armed against a sea of troubled vibe?
Contumely is hard to take as is the constant jibe.
Bold as brass and twice as ugly, Izzie with that gun
brings to mind a paranoiac out to have some fun.

Izzie lets off a few rounds into the air over the actors' heads, then – in lip-sync – takes up the refrain:

Izzie:

Finger wakes the trigger,
preface to explosive vigour,
pounding jackets,
sounding clackets,
letting bullets burn.

Harry:

His Kalashnikov is apt to prompt some grave concerns.
Repercussions will be felt when sanity returns.

Pademelons, perhaps this explains Izzie's earlier reticence. What soul with any vestige of sensitivity *wouldn't* be reluctant to brandish a fully armed AK47 for the purposes of hijacking a celebratory gathering? But zounds. Whatever Izzie's feelings might have been at the outset, he seems now to be getting right with it. There is no longer a smidgeon of reticence in his demeanour.

The music changes key from tonic to dominant. Between each phrase of the lyrics, Izzie lets off a burst of gunfire … at head and chest height.

Lethal bursts.

Mayhem follows. Bodies begin to fall, twitching weirdly at first, then lying still in contorted shapes, as bodies might, and certainly in accordance with theatrical traditions. The horrified survivors try to help the fallen but, on realizing their own peril, flee for cover instead. But where is cover to be found?

Mere words are not fit for purpose, pademelons. One cannot use words to depict adequately the existential grip on the mind this moment brings to bear as it squeezes the substance out of all empathetic tendency, heroic zeal, and resolute action. Somebody persuaded of the efficacy of verbalise might incline towards palilalia, repeating words over and over, in the vain hope their effect might as a consequence be magnified. The horror, the horror, the horror, and so on. But no. The mustard is not cut. The auditory hieroglyphs of spoken language must fail before the outrage that resists any telling.

Izzie:

Life.
What endless strife.
Not worth the candle you're so hopeful sheds some light upon it.

The crack of gunfire. The ping of ricochet. Screams. The thud of falling bodies. Izzie's mad laughter.

Peace.
A glad release.
The gun delivers it more surely than your sweetest sonnet.

More gunfire. Screams. More falling bodies. Women and children are not immune.

Brenda falls across Timmy to protect him. Izzie takes her out with a single shot, rolls her aside with the toe of his boot, then takes Timmy out with a single shot. The muso-turned-assassin is ecstatic.

Death.
A dearth of breath.
So with such panacea and weaponry I will pursue you.

Of the 'talent', only Sticks, Harry, (and Izzie) still stand. Sticks, barely able to comprehend, looks crazed, her face a mirror held to the horror of the scene unfolding before her. Harry's face is a portrait of induced catalepsy, of one unable or unwilling to absorb the enormity of events.

Soul,
it's blatant fiction on the whole,

and I'm the guy who's gonna prove it to you.

Izzie, exultant, takes out Sticks with a head shot. Weapon raised high, he struts his triumph.

The musical line, carrier of the pre-recorded lyrics, passes from dominant back to tonic, and from Izzie back to Harry, who has (inexplicably) turned dispassionate commentator. As is an actor's prerogative, he embraces understatement and eschews naturalism. Standing at the front of the performance space, he delivers his message (in lip-sync) to us, the audience.

Harry:

Izzie pleased to spill the blood of all his faithful friends,
seemingly to gratify his own ignoble ends?
Should you really feel the need to know what drives his spree,
take these fateful letters down, that's P T S and D.

Izzie sprays the air over his head with a burst of rapid fire, then takes over the lyrics again from Harry.

Izzie:

Finger wakes the trigger,
preface to explosive vigour,
pounding jackets,
sounding clackets,
letting bullets spray.

Harry:

His Kalashnikov is bound to cause some deep dismay.
Repercussions will be felt forever and a day.

Izzie, felling Harry with a shot to the back, is now the sole actor left standing. The twisted bodies of all the others litter the performance space.

Pademelons, this is a slaughter of Homeric scale. We find ourselves bereft of appropriate response other than to pay homage to the fallen. Let them be named then and, as this solemn roll-call proceeds, let us join paws and bow our marsupial heads in remembrance.

Our eyes panning back and forth, we are mortified to find the crumpled remains of ... Matt ... Penny ... Simon ... Martha ... Ramon ... Baharudin ... Sonia ... Ronnie ... Timmy ... Brenda ... Sticks ... Harry ... and sundry Sandlewood people.

Izzie's eyes also pan as he surveys his handiwork. He is incredulous rather then penitent.

Oh, shit, he says.

He lowers his gun to his side, its business end scraping the floor. He has accomplished his dark mission. Dragging his feet, he moves slowly back to his synthesizer, flings the AK47 laconically into the still open piano seat, lets the lid fall shut, and seats himself. Almost instantly, his fingers are poised over his instrument. His *musical* instrument.

Mark, despite the apparent demise of his lover, is the model of professional detachment.

Camera One, he says. At your leisure, zoom to keyboard. Then roll.

The clapper sounds. Take Four begins.

Izzie, epitomising *sang-froid*, plays the coda of the Rachmaninov prelude. These concluding bars are quiet and subdued, *as per* the composer's intentions, and *as if* to add credence to the understatement hanging heavily in the theatrical air.

As the coda tails off, the premises plunge into total darkness. Silence prevails.

Some moments of darkness and silence pass. We hear the disinterested mutterings of Mark, DOP. From them, we gather a new Take is about to begin. A Take in wide angle.

Emerging like wraiths from the gloom, come Harry, Sticks, Matt, and Elena, seated in that clockwise order on director's chairs round a card table. Sonia, on a camp stool, is wedged onto the corner between Sticks and Matt. This wedge is symbolic, as it was at an earlier time, of her social isolation. Izzie, at back right and wedded predictably to his synthesizer, is interpreting the main body of the Rachmaninov prelude with gusto.

An exemplary G-rated scene has replaced the killing fields.

Hark back to Bunion Porridge, says Harry.

Do we have to? asks Matt.

There was a time, says Harry, when Mr Guthrie, our humanities teacher ...

Old Misery Guts, says Matt.

The same, says Harry. Anyway, said person of the crook gut decreed the class would write a story in serial form, so we could all chance our hand at devising cliffhangers and at engineering suitable recoveries from them.

Fun and games, says Sticks.

Harry and Sonia speak simultaneously.

A bad joke, says Harry.

One way of getting your jollies, says Sonia.

Izzie has reached a fortissimo passage in his recital. It is drowning out conversation. Sticks intervenes, shouting to him.

Put a cork in it, *Maestro*, she says.

Izzie stops mid-bar. He folds his arms in a display of pique. We expect him at any moment to open up the piano seat and retrieve the Kalashnikov.

As I was saying ... , Harry says.

He looks around, making sure he has regained full attention.

... the serial turned out to be a doozie while it lasted. Brimming with action. The good guys were James Bond types. The bad guys were terrorists. A background of international intrigue and risky intelligence gathering. Blokes in death defying situations. Boy's Own stuff. One of us students would write ...

Any girls get a look-in? asks Sticks.

... an episode, leave it hanging over a cliff, and pass it on to the next student. It went on like this for weeks. Misery Guts loved it.

The suspense would have been killing, says Matt.

Precisely the right word, says Harry.

A new episode every day? asks Sticks.

Harry nods.

Days we had a class, he says.

What happened when it was the turn of the master storyteller? asks Sonia.

Me? asks Harry.

Acceded to so modestly, says Sonia.

Well, says Harry, first let me tell you the deal I got. Goodies ...

Matt interjects with appropriate vocalise.

Da dum-m-m-m-m! he says, The story so far.

... and baddies aboard a luxury yacht in mid Pacific. The goodies had been entrusted with a mission of crucial importance. The prestige of the nation hung in the balance. The baddies were trying to thwart their mission.

As they would, says Sonia.

I arranged, says Harry, for the yacht to go down in a category five cyclone. The perfect storm. After a massive rescue effort involving an impromptu alliance of Pacific nations, every passenger was accounted for. But, alas, there were no survivors among them.

They all died? asks Sticks.

Drowned, says Harry.

Goodies *and* baddies? asks Sticks.

Dead goodies and baddies, says Harry.

Elena gasps and puts her hand to her mouth.

Katastróffa! she says.

Then, says Harry, I passed the baton to the next student in line. I figured I had left him with a pretty neat cliffhanger.

You killed off all the characters? asks Sticks.

Every last one.

Sheba, says Sticks. We have in our midst the epitome of a team player.

What became of national prestige? asks Matt.

Buggered, I suspect, says Sticks.

Matt turns to Harry.

Well what happened next? he asks. Don't keep me dangling.

Mate, they all died.

I mean, what happened to the storytelling, boyo?

You don't remember?

Not a clue.

You were part of the class.

Matt shrugs.

After my effort, says Harry, the story was dead in the water. In the Pacific Ocean, to be exact. Nobody could dream up a continuation. Lack of imagination, I'd call it. Misery Guts was ready to slit my throat.

I'd have held you down, says Sticks.

I'd have sharpened the razor, says Sonia.

That's the response I'd *expect* from barbarians, says Harry.

Izzie pipes in.

Yodellers, he says.

This nautical tale having been told, and all comment exhausted, a pause is called for, and duly it arrives. Sticks eventually breaks the silence.

Let's deal with present problems, she says.

Which are? asks Harry

We, here in this studio, face the same intractable dilemma as those cruise junkies. Courtesy of Izzie, *we're* all dead too.

Éta lózhno![50] *I* am not dead, says Elena. *I* was in control room.

Sticks ignores her.

So where does *our* story go from here? she asks.

A solution stares us in the face, says Harry.

Don't mock the dead, says Sticks.

I'm not. The answer's bloody obvious.

Not to me, it isn't. And I doubt I'm alone.

So. Who wants to hear it?

Listen up, folks. A voice from beyond the grave's about to tell us how we can all rise again.

---

50 *Éta lózhno!*: This is untrue!

O.K. Consider this. Is Elena alive?

Of course, says Sticks. She was in the control room. As she insists.

The perfect place to leave her, says Harry. We'll get her to play the rushes backwards.

Once more, the premises plunge into darkness and silence. After a few moments like this, we fancy we can hear Mark's barely audible mutterings disturbing the quiet.

When the lights come up again, we find the studio configured as it had been in Take Four with Izzie, at his synthesizer, just finishing the coda of the Rachmaninov prelude.

Izzie sits still, his fingers itching for some new task. Silence holds sway as our eyes scan the performance space. It is littered with bodies, familiar bodies, twisted and contorted in the grotesque manner death is wont to impose on mortal remains recently fallen. The bodies occupy the positions to which they had dropped at that earlier time. We are privy here to a recap of the moment Harry, intent on depicting his very own life, succeeded in depicting his very own death, and the concurrent deaths of many of his associates.

The camera crew are poised (unnecessarily as it happens) for the call to action. Mark, my living breathing persona, hovers near Camera One, whose operator is Godfrey. Take Four is over. At Mark's discretion, a new Take will begin.

… fear not. Things can't get any worse. To suppose otherwise would indeed challenge the imagination …

Plans have changed. The new Take does not happen. Mark, gazing up at the control room, speaks softly into his headgear.

Control, he says. At your leisure, reverse play.

By the galloping goitre of my gormless granny, we are witness it seems to the last judgment. Resurrection is *de rigueur*. Bodies spring to erect positions as if manipulated by that hypothetical puppet-master in the flies. What is more, these latter-day Lazaruses are living breathing replicas of the people they once were. Harry is

Harry again. Sticks is Sticks again. &etc. The only real problem, certainly apropos of the gravity the moment demands, is they all have a disconcerting tendency to walk backwards.

Let's take things chronologically. Izzie rises from his seat, which then opens itself. The AK47 springs into his hand and, walking backwards, he repeats his deadly mission in reverse. One by one his victims rise, always prior to Izzie pointing and firing his weapon.

While doing his own bizarre backwards dance, Harry lip-syncs along with the pre-recorded music and lyrics:

Harry:

Sometimes when the Reaper makes an unexpected play,
those cut down can come to life to fight another day.
Everything's reversible, and that includes a stiff.
Feather dusters shall be turned to roosters in a jiff.

Actors retrace their earlier steps but in reverse. That includes Izzie who, back at his synthesizer, does a backwards rendition of heaving the AK47 three times in the air, before returning the weapon to the piano seat and sitting.

Every player is back where they were at the start of the fateful Take Three. Mark, gazing up at the control room, speaks softly into his headgear.

Thank you, Control, he says. That should suffice.

Indeed it should, pademelons. We have before us a tableau of living breathing persons. Nothing less. Who would have expected it?

<<

How, pademelons, could I have anticipated the power and prehensility of those marsupial forelegs of yours, attributes apparent on the tennis courts behind the Bolton residence?

With a mix of amazement and awe, I stood watching your games proceed from love all to deuce and beyond. I cheered each time one of you – while pivoting on a spring-loaded tail – delivered – with confident though white-knuckled grip of the racquet – one of those devastating forepaw or backpaw return volleys. Your petite frames, petite but never puny, were no impediment to a tenacious display of court skills. I could not help but admire the speed of your hip-hoppity approach to ball and net, an approach never lacking poise or balance.

The onset of dusk was our enemy. Regrettably, there were no night-lights available for use after hours. Darkness forced us to retire prematurely, via the tradesman's entrance of course, to the kitchen of the Bolton household, for well-earned refreshment of the 7Up variety.

We were not alone in that kitchen. At the table, the one blessed with workmanship one never sees anymore, a Bolton family conference was in progress, conspicuous for the seriousness of its intent. There was more being discussed here than whose responsibility it was to put the cat out at night …

>

Father, said Martha, this little caper has the legs to travel up one side of the legal system and down the other.

I don't doubt it, said E H Bolton.

E H sat between Martha and Simon. Matt faced his adoptive father at a distance from the other end of the table. All three children were sipping from bottles of 7Up. Simon and Martha, in tennis gear, were both sweaty from the competitive rubber they had recently played. Matt – not a tennis player – merely the bunny who got to roll the gravel – was fresh, dry, and clean smelling in his swanky gear, which of course included a bow tie.

E H had called the meeting. He was dressed determinedly in

black pin-stripe business suit with conservative navy tie. For all the impregnable solidity of the power-dressed image he was at pains to impress on his children, anxiety wracked his person. As if under an irrational compulsion to do so, he kept sweeping back imaginary locks of dark hair from the furrows of his brow. He exuded frailty and an uncharacteristic vulnerability.

A tabloid newspaper was in front of him, open to page three. The page leader declared boldly:

MINING CHIEF LINKED TO CRIME BOSS

If I am to represent you, said Martha, you must level with me. What is the extent of your complicity?

I have none, said E H.

Are you complicit when you draw breath?

Listen to Siss, said Simon. She has your best interests at heart.

… neither Simon (marine biologist) nor Matt (fashion designer) had any other reasonable option but to defer to Martha in this situation. A lawyer was needed. She was the lawyer …

As Martha continued to interrogate, E H continued to evade. But Martha was not discouraged by his petulance. Breaking from the task at hand, she asked Simon to fetch the large leather bound Bible from the library where – you will recall pademelons – it – in dubious company – was locked away behind glass. Matt watched the stubborn set of his father's face take on the appearance of granite.

When Simon arrived back with the Good Book weighing heavily on his biceps, Martha asked him to place it on the table between her and her father.

Father, said Martha, this is what it will be like when you face the bench, except they will not be nearly so kind to you as I am being.

Martha picked up her father's hand – spotted with age – and planted it on the Bible. The embossed crown of thorns was visible between his splayed fingers. He held his hand there for a moment, then capriciously removed it. Martha was not going to stand for this. She picked up the errant hand again, put it back where it had been on the Bible, and held it firmly in place, her hand on top of his.

O.K. Father. The whole story. The truth and nothing but.

E H wept. It was like the blubber of a small child. But the ploy worked. He was ready to spill beans.

>

What were the beans? E H – on the strength of his confession before God – was indeed implicated, along with many of his establishment colleagues, and much of the executive of the Lantern Bearers. And one Sal Heffernan, Esq.

E H's 'caper', as Martha termed it, had legs fit not only for the corridors of the law, but also for those of the fourth estate. The press loved this triumvirate of big business, criminality, and religion. The only thing missing was a 'dirt angle', meaning sex, and before much time had passed some assiduous investigative reporting was able to dredge up material of *this* stripe also.

The nature of the caper?

It went thus. E H and his buddies were to be guaranteed a lucrative return on investment, the *quid pro quo* being Hefty would get to launder his illegal booty. It was a simple arrangement on the surface, but in these situations the devil always prefers to reside below the surface, i.e. where the detail is known to be. In these murky depths, things were *not* so simple.

The detail?

It consisted of the precise nature of the contractual arrangements linking consenting parties. By mutual agreement, such links – perceived by all parties to be incriminating – were to be kept from the prying eyes of auditors and the like through a scheme dubbed 'spaghetti bolognaise', i.e. the deliberate entanglement of essential links with vast numbers of misleading and irrelevant links.

Martha extracted from E H the name of the person who had masterminded this attempt at obfuscation. The person who had cooked the spaghetti.

The name was Elena Rusalkova.

Matt, said Martha, I believe you know this woman.

Matt sighed.

Yes, he replied, I'm sorry to say. I know her only too well.

I need to speak to her.

Matt pointed to the newspaper on the table.

I'll see what I can do, he said. But throw the hounds off the scent.

I'll try.

>

Perhaps she *did* try, but her cause was doomed.

It was inevitable the media would latch onto this turn of events. When they did so, they were delighted to find it involved a mystery woman, who was young, photogenic, and capable of inciting much prurient interest amongst the readers and viewers of shock-jock journalism.

The focus of the action moved rapidly and decisively away from that kitchen table on that fine but fast fading day, away from tennis, away from 7Up, away from the laying on of hands, away from E H's tearful confessions. At the whim of a frenetic camera-toting scrum/scum, interest shifted to Elena and the Big Top, then to the relentless stake-out of courtroom precincts, and ultimately to the grave.

Hefty was not called upon to answer questions. He had covered his tracks well. Always destined to take the rap, Elena was the person of interest. But she couldn't be found.

Martha, not to mention every hack reporter in town, sought her at the Big Top, but she had long since vacated *those* premises.

So it transpired Harry, Sticks, and all the other Big Top personnel were drawn into the drama.

Harry and Sticks were not pleased with this unwanted attention.

Their reaction was equivocal. They cursed Elena silently. They reflected that retaining her as an absentee tenant was akin to inviting an enemy – albeit one whose heart was not in it – to sup at their table. But they stopped short of evicting her *in absentia*. They figured even Matt was unlikely to agree to such action, though he was the one who had up to now lost the most through her treachery and bloody-minded recidivism.

They worried on Elena's behalf. Though not eager to advertise the fact, they hoped she would sooner or later put in an appearance, e.g. when the heat from all quarters no longer had fire to sustain it. Perhaps her worldly possessions, though meagre, might nonetheless draw her back. Or perhaps it was her cosy world *in toto* she would be reluctant to abandon. A world inclusive of the secure and comfortable milieu of the Big Top, including a cuddly Koshechka.

Could I see the place where she bunks down? asked Martha.

I'm not comfortable with that, said Sticks. It would infringe on her privacy.

Fair call, said Martha. But you understand I was obliged to ask you.

One of the news sources managed a scoop in the form of a purported photograph of Elena. In point of fact, it was *not* a photo of Elena at all. It was of one of the five *other* Russian nymphettes, whisked away from the catwalk, and from under Matt's nose, by the late R and G. The photo was undoubtedly one of the many publicity shots Mark, my avatar in the mortal world, had been commissioned to take at that earlier time. Doubtless it had been spirited away through an act of bald chicanery, probably from Penny's premises in the refurbished Wintergarden, site of the aforesaid catwalk.

Authenticity was never an issue for the editor of the rag

publishing the photograph. Regardless of whomever the image represented, it would sell papers.

As his day in court approached, E H found himself snubbed by his colleagues. Snubbed by those implicated *and* those not. Snubbed as a diseased person might be. Habituated as he was to bask in a degree of respect as essential as oxygen for figures of his stature in the establishment, E H was finding such ostracism hard to take. His family – viz. his children – noticed the effect on him and, to afford the man a modicum of consolation and distraction, closed ranks behind him.

In this context Matt, with trepidation, invited E H to Dress Rules. Even though the Old Man had bankrolled Matt's venture, he had never set foot in the premises until now. The mannequins, whose gauntlet he ran as he entered, disturbed him. Interpolated into the mock-up of a pastoral setting, they were dressed in long flowing diaphanous gowns, striking poses typical of a Norman Lindsay[51] sketch or the like. The themes they espoused were environmental and revolutionary, not causes E H might have been expected to embrace.

To top things off, when E H reached Matt's office, the large and mischievously deceptive photographic representation of a semi-naked Lydia, descendant of Che Guevara, confronted him. He blanched.

In the office, Matt introduced him to Penny and Mark. E H was impressed with Penny's businesslike manner. He was not so sure of Mark. On leaving, which one might imagine would have been a relief to the old fellow, he aired his doubts to Matt.

Do you know that photographer of yours is a fairy? said E H.

Do you really think so? was Matt's rejoinder, a masterful dissemblance.

I know one when I see one, boy.

E H's departure from the premises resembled that of one who,

---

51 Norman Lindsay was an Australian artist, sculptor, writer, and cartoonist in the first half of the 20th C.

in biblical times, fled Sodom, which begs the natural question, Did he look back? Had he done so, he might have seen Matt, his stance pensive, as he attempted to wrestle his demon thoughts re the fragile bigotry of his adoptive father.

This event, always in the nature of a sociological experiment, was the first and last occasion on which E H was to grace the doors of Dress Rules. Afterwards, on analysis, Matt was to make a surprising discovery about himself. Beneath his surface loathing, he harboured, and always had harboured, a strong affection for the old misanthrope.

Despite the efforts of his children, E H succumbed to a crisis. Of one part morale and one part physiology. He didn't make it to the finish of court proceedings. Days before verdicts were to be announced, he had three massive strokes in quick succession, the last of which took him out. The attendance at his funeral, orchestrated from go to woe by the Lantern Bearers, was epic. The colleagues who refused to have a bar of him in the last months of his life, turned up in droves for his death. His children were there of course, Matt in the company of Mark and Harry.

Some suspected the shady figure, shielded from view behind dark glasses and the lapels of a heavy overcoat, may have been Sal Heffernan.

>

Harry paid a visit to his doctor – a visit he assumed would be routine – to review the results of a number of tests the doctor had ordered for him. It transpired the visit was anything but routine. Harry should have expected there might be a problem, because it was the doctor himself who had requested the visit.

Some hours later, back at the Nerd Centre, he looked distracted to the extent Sticks was at first surprised and then alarmed. He flopped heavily into his swivel chair, tossed his head back, and stared at the ceiling.

What is it? asked Sticks.

Harry gave a deep drawn-out sigh.

I don't know how to say it, he said.

Try putting one word in front of the other.

He sat upright, planted his elbows on his desk and his brow in the palms of his hands. As one might expect from his posture, his voice – when he found it – sounded muffled.

You know those tests I had done last week?

On your knee?

Well, yes, initially, my knee. But then they insisted on taking more. In the end, they scanned my whole body.

Sticks was now on full alert.

The scans are not good? she asked.

You might say.

A short silence seemed warranted, so they both let it happen. Then Harry looked up. His eyes, reflecting a mix of anger and resignation, caught those of Sticks.

Jesus, he said, I'm buggered. Pathology says it's a really aggressive cancer. Stage four. Metastasized. Rampaging through my system. I might have three months if I'm lucky.

Who says?

The fucking doctor.

This is on the level?

Would I joke about it?

You'll get a second opinion, of course.

I guess.

Sticks rose from her desk, walked around to Harry, straddled him with her thighs, and cradled his head in her bosom. Her hands and lips caressed his uncharacteristically dishevelled hair. They struck this affecting pose – a sort of inverted Pieta – for the best part of a minute before Sticks broke the silence.

Now *I* don't know how to say it, she said.

Believe me, said Harry, you're saying it OK.

... such precious moments of wordless communication were to become a ritual for them over the weeks and months as the import of Harry's bleak news sunk in. The only upside they could see in the whole wretched affair was the physical solace they were able to derive from it ...

Lifting his head from Sticks' bosom, Harry engaged her visually. Each could see clear through to the agony entrapped behind the other's optics. There was no escape for this agony, only the futility of the writhing it spawned.

I've got a jar, said Harry, with ninety beans in it, and I get to pluck one bean out every day until the jar is empty. That's my lot.

Darling, it's *my* lot too, said Sticks.

Trying to pull herself together without sounding unduly cold and analytical, Sticks asked the obvious question:

Do you feel any symptoms?

Harry laughed bitterly.

I've never felt better, he said.

But, come evening in the comfort of his new home, he believed he *could* detect symptoms, vague twinges from inside the lower trunk of his body, a physiological realm he didn't fathom, and didn't care to fathom. By morning, he did not doubt the twinges, only the precise origin of them. Lungs? Liver? Kidneys? How would he know? Pains shot the rapids of his legs, following the muscles? or the blood vessels? or the nerves? How would he know?

All he knew was the pain itself. In the days following, this pain became his constant companion. The relationship between Harry and the pain was consummated within his domestic precincts. Seldom did he, or the pain to which he was wedded, leave his bed in those anxious days and even less his house. Sticks held the fort at the Nerd Centre.

When he slept – less and less often these days – he woke to pain. When he moved from his bed, the pain moved with him.

When he stopped to think, pain overwhelmed his thoughts. Pain, always around the corner, contrived to pre-emt the corner.

Sticks' attention was a comfort to him at night. And the palliative care – care authorized by a medical fraternity that had otherwise given him away – care assuming the form of a confusion of pills with disagreeable side effects – this care actually did – when one looked at the bottom line – a shade more good than harm. But as the pain increased over time, so did the degree of attention he sought from the long-suffering Sticks, and so did the concentration of the pills required for palliation.

It wasn't only the pain. It was also what Harry imagined the pain signified, viz. the invasion of his body by a malign force and his body's subsequent disintegration. He believed he could feel the disgusting riot of rogue tissue, growing like Topsy, in every vital organ of his body. He believed he could detect its stench in his nostrils, taste its putrefaction at the back of his throat.

Curled up in bed one day, nursing his pain, Harry was visited by his family. There was Brenda, of course. But she brought along some visitors Harry saw only on rare occasions: his sister Madeleine and his two nieces. Harry guessed the pair of sly-eyed young nymphettes had been strenuously cajoled into paying their respects to their ailing Uncle Harry. To them, it must have been a duty, a dismal chore.

Harry reflected ruefully. When seldom-seen family members began to make bedside visits, it was time to activate the funeral plan.

One evening Sticks, having only that hour retrieved the six-year-old Timmy from school, arrived home to find Harry sitting at the glass coffee table in the living room, eyeing off a couple of ominous looking medicine bottles. One brown and large, one green and small, they nestled in a flurry of crumpled wrapping paper and bubble wrap. Instructions in Mandarin and Chinglish were close at hand. Sticks guessed immediately what they were, and what his intentions were regarding them. She burst into a flood of tears even before she had had time to whisk Timmy away. When she returned *sans* Timmy, to sit opposite Harry at the table, her words were sobs.

Why has it come to this? she said.

It's time, he said.

Where did you get it?

The internet.

Have you thought things through?

No. I'm doing this purely on impulse.

His sarcasm was a scant source of warmth when tears needed drying. She sniffled a bit in the silence, then used a tissue to dab her face, which looked all the more fetching for letting the misery shine through. Harry spoke first.

If, he said, I really wanted to lay claim to the sixty or so days the gurus in their wisdom estimate I have left, I'm sure I could set about invoking them in my dreams.

Dreaming your life?

Seems a good alternative to living it.

Can you be sure of that?

If my dreams don't turn out better than the real thing, I've only myself to blame.

Fine for *you*. But where does that leave *me*?

He didn't answer. He assumed her question was rhetorical, indicative of angry resignation. He rose, came round the table to her, and put his arm round her shoulder. In a show of bravado, she brushed the arm aside, then indicated the two bottles on the table in front of them.

Why two? she asked.

One's an anti-emetic to help me keep the stuff down while it absobs.

Trust the ghouls to think of everything.

Nothing left to chance when you're playing for keeps.

You really sure you want to follow through?

Dead sure.

Harry was startled at the inadvertent escape from his lips of the D word. Sticks rolled her eyes. She liberated a long sigh.

Then I would like to be present.

Are *you* sure?

Somebody has to attend to … the corpse.

Be my guest. The whole frigging crew if they want. It's their choice.

They could fall foul of the law.

I'll write a note indemnifying them.

How do *you* feel about having company?

Harry reply was a shrug of the shoulders. Sticks forced a sardonic chuckle, tinged with bitterness, from her vocals.

Like in the Canadian film, she said.

The Barbarians … ?

'The Barbarian Invasions'.

Suddenly, Sticks was brave no more. It was not only tears – there were certainly enough of those – but howls, whose genesis was a place within her head, a head finding itself forced to think the unthinkable. Her words, when she eventually uttered them, came out as an anguished staccato descant to these howls.

Oh, Harry, she said, can … this … really be … happening?

Come to bed.

<

Whenever a significant event has a mind to occur, another event of similar moment will conspire to join it. This is how things panned out at this stage in the lives of Harry and Sticks.

Only the day after the couple received the grim news of Harry's medical prognosis and, as a consequence, became busy agonizing over the way they might be able or willing to deal with it, Elena put in an appearance at the Big Top to reclaim her bamboo shanty and her career as a techie. To know more about this audaciously intrusive event, the event that might fairly be accused of surfing the other's wave, we need, pademelons, to turn back the clock by about a month to the moment when Elena, as if nothing had happened, strolled nonchalantly into the Big Top premises. She was dressed in her grey coat and hard hat, as if expecting Ramon would, on the spot, reassign her a place on the Big Top production line.

When Ramon passed on the news of Elena's return, Sticks – furious – frogmarched the returning prodigal to the Nerd Centre. Harry was sitting behind his desk, literally contemplating his navel, awaiting intimations there of pain from within. Sticks sat down at her desk and indicated with a terse wave of the hand that Elena should also sit. Elena obeyed, looking sheepish.

Becoming a habit, wouldn't you say? asked Sticks.

I don't understand, said Elena.

Oh yes, you do, little minx. Along comes a crisis, invariably of your own making, and you do a runner, leaving mugs like us to pick up the pieces.

Elena chose to be silent.

The door to the back room creaked open slightly, and Ronnie's head insinuated itself into the gap. Sticks hurled such a scowl in this direction the head retreated immediately. However, the door failed to close behind the head, credible evidence that Ronnie's peeled ear was still within range.

Harry and Sticks revisited their roles of good and bad cop.

Elena, said Harry, you're smart enough to know it is not in our nature to toss you out into the street. So perhaps you could learn to trust us a little.

Sticks, ostensibly addressing Harry, even going so far as to make eye contact with him, clearly intended her next remark for Elena's ears.

I'd like to know, said Sticks, why she still does the bidding of that pathological malfeasant.

... words, chosen deliberately by Sticks, who knew they would confound a relative newcomer to the language ...

You mean Heffernan? asked Harry.

Elena's response was her downcast eyes, a favourite tactic.

You don't understand, she said. Sal is powerful man.

Are you afraid of him? asked Harry.

Yes. I am most afraid.

Why not let us help you?

Sticks fixed her gaze firmly on Elena. It might have been iron hands rather than gelatinous eyeballs assailing the younger woman. Eyeballs determined to exert their steely grip on her slouching shoulders. Eyeballs determined to shake down her slender frame.

Conditions apply, girl, said Sticks. You want our help, you don't do anything anymore without warning us the instant the idea enters your pretty head. Not anything. We intend to be the *first* to know, not the last. We intend to know *before* the event, not after it. Has that message got through your precious skull?

I ...

You have something to say?

No.

>

Elena *did* have something to say. She waited a few days until such time as she could corral Harry alone, i.e. Harry *sans* the intimidatory Sticks. The latter happened to be busy that day, consulting parties able to boast credentials re the matter of Malaysian rainforests.

Once again, the venue was the Nerd Centre. Once again, the door to the back room was ajar, suggesting the proximity of a certain avid eavesdropper.

Elena brought Baharudin with her. After a sojourn of some months in his home country, the prospective Sultan was back in Oz, disturbing news having reached his ears of Elena's fresh dalliance with criminals.

Between them, they had some disturbing news for *Harry's* ears. All three of them seated, Baharudin opened the conversation.

You are ill? he asked.

So they tell me, Harry replied.

I am sorry to hear it.

I appreciate your concern.

It is in God's hands. I shall ask Hussein to pray for you. His prayers are always answered.

A natural pause ensued. Elena allowed it a plenitude of free rein, before bringing discussion round abruptly to the point she wished to make.

Ogorodnikov knows what happened to R and G, she said. He is not happy vegemite.

Who is this Ogre person? asked Harry.

Not Ogre. He is Ogorodnikov. The man who kept me slave in Russia.

He knows the truth?

Yes.

Shit.

Harry's elbows were on his desk. His palms cradled his forehead.

How did you come by this news? he asked.

Sal told me.

So what does Ogre-man intend to do about it?

He will send more Russians. They will come looking for me.

Is that worth his while? You're small fry.

He is vengeful man.

Harry said nothing. He did not lift his head. He tried to imagine the ramifications of this news. None seemed pretty.

Is not all, said Elena. Barry has other news.

Baharudin cleared his throat.

My father, he said, succeeded in having talks with the two

Russians in Kuala Lumpur before they were detained. I have no idea how that happened. It was not part of our plan.

Harry, confounded, was trying to measure the ramifications of this second news bite against those of the first. Baharudin rose from his seat and began to pace.

I am sorry, he said. I must take responsibility for this.

Harry raised his head, making eye contact with Baharudin.

But surely no harm is done, said Harry.

My father, said Baharudin, as a consequence would like to establish a trafficking venture channelling young women from all over south-east Asia through his operational hub in K L.

Sex slaves?

Yes.

Bound for Australia, I'm supposing.

Largely.

A charming man, your father, said Harry. But I don't see how this can affect us?

My father thinks Elena can be useful to his operation.

That's ridiculous.

I've tried to tell him that.

Harry was overwhelmed with ramifications for his mind to work on. Somehow terminal cancer seemed so much easier to deal with. He heaved a deep sigh.

We thought we'd nailed this, he said, when we sent R and G off with all that methamphetamine. But, b'Jesus, has it backfired on us!

It is a Hydra, said Baharudin. We cut off its head. Ergo. It grows many new heads. We need a Heracles.

Harry and Elena, for want of a classical education, looked quizzically at Baharudin, who declined to enlighten them.

So, said Baharudin, to sum up our position, there are two criminal groups ...

Three, said Elena. Sal will send men too.

... *three* criminal groups, not likely to be well disposed towards each other, who will soon come looking for Elena. If *this* is where she lives, *this* is where they will come. So, Harry, we may *all* of us have a problem here. I am sorry.

Could *you* hide her? asked Harry.

I could try. But, if possible, I would like to avoid this. I have my reasons.

You don't want to cross swords with your father?

That's part of the story.

Well, the way I see it, things are dandy. Who'd want to be dead? Trafficking in people brought to our front door. Turf wars between mobs determined to fight them on my territory. Why don't we put out a bulletin on the World Wide Web inviting the whole international criminal community? Let's be multicultural.

I am sorry, said Elena. Is all because of me.

No point being sorry. You did the right thing by telling me. That's a good start. Now all we need is a plan. A bloody good plan.

I have a plan, said Baharudin.

Let's hear it, said Harry.

Do you happen to have a spare virtual reality system on site?

I can rustle one up.

May I take a spell in the deepest subterranean cave on the planet?

Harry thought about this. All things considered, a cave seemed the ideal solution. No people, no situations. Lightless, except for candle flicker in the whisper of an unsourced breeze. Soundless, except for the slow reverberating plunk of water dripping in some unseen cranny. Motionless, except for the unfelt swoop of continents around the earth's axis. Matterless, except for stalactites and stalagmites among which the upright human frame might become inconspicuous. Lifeless, except for myriad bent-winged bats with which one might commune peacefully. Timeless, to the extent even the threat of death might fail here to remember its mission.

Mind if I join you? he asked.

>

The day after Harry un-wrapped his consignment of poison from China, unexpected visitors turned up at his home. They arrived about mid-day, to find Harry lying sprawled on the sofa of the white lounge suite, clad in a white chenille dressing gown complete with cord, tassels, and fraying edges. In front of him, on the moulded glass coffee table, were blister packs of painkillers. The flurry of dots on an expanse of unframed canvass on the wall behind him was one of his aboriginal paintings, his ode to the vertical as he himself lay horizontal.

The visitors were Matt, Ramon, and Ronnie. They bore gifts. Harry was not aware he had a resemblance to the Christ child, and did not consider his visitors to be preternaturally wise.

He was glad to see Matt. He had not seen him since E H's funeral, and was concerned all might not be right with him. But Matt seemed fine.

He had a fleeting concern about Ramon's presence. Who, he wondered, was in charge of operations at the Big Top? Then he felt guilty at having had such an unworthy thought. Ramon would certainly have selected an adequate stand-in.

Ronnie's presence puzzled him. He had intuited Ronnie was antisocial. Or aloof. Or reclusive. He had not decided which of these descriptors best fitted the man. Or whether, a combination wouldn't suit the purpose.

Matt's gift was not the usual *Bisquit*. It was a large print, on stiff paper scrolled up and tied with a blue ribbon.

It was Ramon who brought a bottle. The label said Pisco. Ramon extolled it as the Peruvian equivalent of cognac. Harry was dubious.

Ronnie's offering was a DVD. He placed it on the table next to the Pisco. Harry glanced at the title.

'Gran Torino'? asked Harry.

Clint Eastwood, said Ronnie. It could be relevant.

Harry didn't ask why.

When Harry unrolled Matt's print, he discovered it to be a familiar item, not at all unwelcome. It was the print of Lydia, the bellicose likeness that had graced the wall behind Matt's desk, witness to Matt's confession of endearment to him.

It's yours now, said Matt.

Despised and rejected already? asked Harry.

Matt nodded.

Doctor's wives are fickle, he said. The idle shiksas have decided fashion these days must pay lip service to multiculturalism. For them, it's socially enabling. So, when they chance to say things like, 'I'm not a racist, but ... ', nobody will question their right to the moral high ground.

Pisco also is socially enabling, said Ramon. Best enjoyed neat. No ice. No water. No soda. It will cure your pain.

This was the signal to crack the bottle. Harry eased himself off the sofa to find glasses. Then the four amigos proceeded to get themselves mildly plastered. The afternoon passed quickly, pleasantly, and – as Ramon had foreseen – painlessly.

>

Early that evening, soon after Sticks came home, the pain returned to Harry in spades. As Harry had previously observed, it had a life and a mind of its own. But assuredly no soul.

Sticks had wanted to enthuse to Harry about her plans to engage in a spot of activism on behalf of the rainforests of Malaysia and its cute fauna. She was distressed to find he was in no mood for her confidences on this subject or any other. He would not even respond to her attempts at erotic consolation.

Later in the evening, Harry counted up the beans remaining in his jar, and came to the conclusion he might as well forfeit them.

>

Pademelons. Shall we partake of a little R & R? You deserve such a treat, considering the unrelenting demands my weighty presentation must be making on your powers of endurance. Don't fret. We have time to spare. An eternity, in fact.

Let us adjourn with our popcorn and choc-tops[52] to that dimly lit pleasure dome known as the cinema. You may find the plush seats with collapsible arm-rests a deal too large for your small marsupial frames, but at least there shall be space available for your retractable hind legs and curled-up tails. In any case, once the house lights are extinguished, our attention shall be captive to the purposes of whomever may be director of the imagined reality about to flood the silver screen. Which is a misnomer. The screen shows no preference for silver. It reflects all colours inhabiting the electromagnetic spectrum with equal enthusiasm.

You may have expected we would view 'The Barbarian Invasions', the film to which Sticks had alluded a few weeks earlier. Instead, we are confronted with the septuagenarian frame, tall and gaunt, of Clint Eastwood. Under his own self-assured direction, he plays a character called Walt Kowalski.

The opening credits tell us the title of the film: 'Gran Torino'. The title fails (initially) to enlighten us.

It is the first decade of the 21ˢᵗ century. White, Caucasian, and curmudgeonly, Walt lives alone in a working class neighbourhood, where lawnmowers are king, in Michigan, USA. As the story

---

52 'choc-top': an Australian sweet treat consisting of a cone of ice cream dipped in chocolate, traditionally eaten at the cinema.

begins, and to Walt's considerable chagrin, his immediate neighbours turn out to be immigrants belonging to an ethnic group known as the Hmong. But slowly, as the story unfolds, he grows to appreciate some of the virtues of these worthy tribespeople. One of these worthies – his favourite Hmong, one might say – is a teenage lad called Thao.

What Walt does *not* appreciate are the gun-toting gangland-emulating street thugs, themselves Hmong, standing over the hard-working families of their own community, armed with weapons and arrogance. He is drawn into confrontation with these thugs, managing in the process to flaunt weaponry of his own – including an ex Vietnam war M1 rifle – and his expertise in using it.

Over time, the tensions between Walt and the thuggish gang escalate to crisis proportions. This is the development phase of the film's gripping action. I sense your mounting excitement, pademelons. Your red marsupial eyes, primed to be precursors of fight or flight, are nailed to the screen. Your hind legs, ready to propel you hoppity-skip through the landscape, are balanced on the edges of your seats. Your teeth, better suited to chomping on stems of grass, are carelessly grinding popcorn.

Is that a scuffle breaking out in your ranks, pademelons, coming from the row of seats immediately behind me, and slightly to my left? I crane my neck in that direction. Two of you appear to be at sixes and sevens. Apparently an ice cream in the hand of one had engaged somehow with the nostrils of the other.

The resulting hullaballoo attracts the attention of the usher, a grown man looking faintly ridiculous in his bell-hop uniform. A pencil of light from his torch scorches the darkness, pin-pointing the source of the kerfuffle. Pademelons, I am not your keeper but, if pressed by authority, I shall explain away your behaviour as the high jinx natural to your species.

Thankfully, I need make no response. You, the perpetrators,

having been exposed to view, desist promptly, and that is where wise heads choose to leave the matter.

Our attention returns to the movie.

Walt has health problems. He is a smoker who frequently coughs up blood. Knowing he has not long to live, he devises a plan for ridding the community of the thugs once and for all.

Walt visits his tailor, his barber, and his confessor, in that order. The priest, new young and wet behind the ears, is surprised by the appearance of this crusty old heathen. Then he (Walt) confronts the thugs noisily in their residential headquarters, first making sure the neighbours, law abiding Hmong, are watching. They can be counted on to alert the police.

Now Clint Eastwood enacts the type of scene for which he is legendary. We see Walt plant a cigarette casually between his lips. Then we see him withdraw, slowly and deliberately, from an inside pocket, what the gang members believe to be a weapon.

The gang members shoot him dead in a bee-swarm of bullets. What Walt had withdrawn from his pocket was a cigarette lighter.

Arrests are made. Charges of killing an unarmed person are laid. There is no shortage of witnesses. We are led to believe the gang members will serve long custodial sentences.

What, I hear you ask, with expletive-laden bemusement unbefitting a pademelon, is the significance of the cryptic title 'Gran Torino'? Let me tell you. Gran Torino is a motor vehicle. Specifically, it is a 1972 model Ford, sporty and convertible, much cherished by Walt while he lived, and coveted since puberty by Thao. Subsequent to Walt's death, as revealed in his will, the vehicle is bequeathed to Thao who, as the film concludes, is seen driving it proudly along a lakeside boulevard.

Let me make a comment while the end credits roll, a comment in the nature of a message for Harry. Indications are he, like Walt, is planning to cash in his chips. Might it not be incumbent upon Harry to leave behind a valid will, ensuring *his* most cherished possession – say, the going concern known as Integrated Electronic

Imagery – would on his death fall into the hands of parties *he* might choose? Not fall arbitrarily into the hands of any old person, a distant relative perhaps, with the temerity to emerge in timely fashion from the woodwork, a person with whom Harry has no special relationship?

Your unhealthy obsession with the trappings of the mortal world has not escaped my attention, pademelons. So, while the matter of last testaments is at the forefront of your minds, I shall turn to the subject of the inheritance Matt received in the course of events from the estate of his deceased father, a subject I imagine has prompted a degree of unrequited curiosity within your ranks of late. I shall enlighten you.

You may be bemused by what you shall learn. Under the terms of E H's will, the lion's share of his wealth was to pass to his two biological children, Simon and Martin, with only a token consideration going to Matt. Simon and Martha were never going to have a bar of such an arrangement and, despite Matt's vigorous protestations, engineered an even three-way split after the event. Consequently, Matt became a person of considerable and independent means. Posthumously, E H was shown the finger.

All was well that ended well in the Bolton camp.

But what of Harry?

> >

Singspielstück #15: Poisonous Posturing

We are seated and, the clappers having done their job, it is time for the actors to ply their trade. All nine of them occupy the raised dais in the studio space which, in its present incarnation, represents that living room with whose unruly angles we are already familiar, the domestic domain of Harry and Sticks when entertaining. The nine actors gather in a rough circle round the glass coffee table, sitting either on the chunky white lounge suite or nearby on the floor.

The lighting is subdued.

Three of the four sides of the performance space are taken up by backdrop representing the interior walls of the living room. The fourth side is open to our view and the view of strategically placed cameras.

On one of the pretend walls is a dot painting by an indigene of Oz, one of several such paintings Harry brought with him from the days when he harboured a passion for high-rise living.

The actors, playing themselves, are Harry, Sticks, Brenda, Matt, Penny, Izzie, Ramon, Ronnie, and Baharudin. Elena, Mark, and Godfrey do not have acting roles because their services are required elsewhere. Mark (DOP) and Godfrey (camera operator) hover near the camera at front left. Elena is out of sight in the control room.

Harry, in central position on a lounge chair, surveys the suicide kit – large brown bottle, small green bottle, two glasses, carafe of water, and box of tissues – sitting squarely in front of him within easy reach on the coffee table.

If by some contrivance there could have chanced to be an extra quartet of participants, what we would see might well pass – should one draw a long bow – for a latter-day Last Supper.

Everybody is in solemn mood, silent except for the occasional discreet cough. Matt is tense, his body as rigid as a ramrod. The women look fragile. Sticks is already dabbing her eyes with a tissue.

Ronnie breaks this silence. He looks squarely at Harry as he speaks.

Your call, squire, he says.

Without hesitation, Harry unscrews the lid of the small green bottle and downs its contents straight from the bottle. Jaws drop.

Gasps are passed. Despite her own mounting anxiety, Sticks reassures the assembly.

The anti-emetic, she says.

Harry screws up his face.

Tastes foul, he says.

Pouring water from the carafe into a glass, he washes the taste down with theatrical enthusiasm. Silence resumes. It is broken after a few seconds, this time by Harry.

Now we must wait, he says.

Pre-recorded music begins, of Izzie on his synthesizer. The melody we hear is tender, a balm to bleeding hearts, with a tendency to cloy, in major key and 4/4 time, given over to simulated strings and clarinet. It is of the same genre as Abide with Me, but more elemental than religious.

After the introductory bars Harry, gesturing with upturned palm, indicates the kit on the table in front of him. Then, lip-syncing along in solo, he accompanies the melody that is to be exclusively his for the duration of the *Stück*:

Harry:

Death when I choose
is the right kind of news.

He gesticulates vigorously.

Get this show
on the road,
'cause there's no
time to lose.

The brown bottle is the focus of everybody's attention. Harry picks it up and brandishes it. It is Sticks' turn to gasp.

This is the wine
from some unlikely vine,
ending strife
that derives

from a life
in decline.

The music changes key, from tonic to dominant …

Don't weep for me now.
Please succour better paradigms,
and dwell on those remembered times
we've shared within this troposphere
devoid of favour and of fear.

… and from dominant back to tonic …

So …
I'll drink the cup

Unscrewing the cap on the bottle, Harry pours its contents, clear liquid gurgling like a newborn babe, into one of the glasses. He raises this glass.

for my sojourn is up.
Bearing pain
like a man's
a refrain
so fucked up.

Such is my lot,
this my last angry shot.
I'll endure
this foul glug

… Harry scrutinizes the glug with fondness …

to ensure
I will rot.

… tonic back to dominant …

Life's all but over.
My word, it's been a wondrous ride,
a privilege I'll not deride.

542 | Where Pademelons Play

I'll toast it with due reverence,

... Harry raises his glass ...

then take my bow and severance.

... and the final key change, from dominant back to tonic ...

So ...

Live well, or die,
it's our choice, you and I,
at the toll
of the bell,
on a shoal
quite close by.

Harry raises the glass to his lips with intent. There are gapes and gasps from all, and a pitiful moan from Sticks. The song and the pre-recorded music stop abruptly, underscoring the fatal moment, and accommodating the interjection from Ronnie.

Hold those brumbies[53] right there, says Ronnie.

Harry freezes with the glass at his lips.

You talk big about living well, says Ronnie. How about *dying* well?

Harry remains frozen, not able to credit what he is seeing and hearing.

Topping yourself's fine by me, says Ronnie. But you want to throw away the opportunity of a lifetime? Your death could be useful, man.

Harry lowers the glass to the table.

You want me to donate my fucking organs? he asks.

Ronnie's immediate response is non-verbal, achieved by throwing his hands in the air, palms upwards. After a second or two, he lets his hands and arms go limp. Then he makes his verbal point.

---

53 brumby: in Australia, a feral horse.

Be ever mindful, he says, of what Mr Make-My-Day would do. Clint Eastwood?

That's the dude.

Meanwhile, Sticks is in a state of acute distress. The moans she emits resemble those of a mortally wounded animal. Brenda and Penny are at her side, but their attempts to comfort her are fruitless. Shock has robbed her of presence of mind and awareness of surroundings.

In a sudden rush of determination, Harry raises the glass to his lips again, but hesitates at the crucial moment. He holds the glass where his eyeballs can focus on it, peruses its contents as if for the first time, becomes aware of Sticks' discomposure, then slams the glass down fiercely on the table. Some of its contents splash out onto his hand. Transparent liquid, looking as innocent as water from a babbling brook, dribbles from his shaking hand onto the transparent surface of the coffee table. The look on Harry's face, as he contemplates the elixir of death, liberated from both bottle and glass, tells the story. What Ronnie has been driving at has dawned on him in the nick of time.

Apologies, folks, says Harry.

He looks sheepish. The others, *sans* Sticks, look mildly bemused. Sticks looks incapable of holding an attitude.

The Reaper has moved on, says Harry.

To return at a later date by all reports, says Matt.

With distaste, Harry flicks his hand to dislodge the remaining drops, then wipes his fingers dry with a handful of tissues. Confusion shrouds his features. He is not at all sure how he should dispose of the soggy mess he holds, certain to be inimical to life on earth.

Sticks' moans are replaced by hysterical sobbing, of a degree not amenable to penetration by any attempt at consolation, no matter how sympathetic.

Lights go out.

>

Light glares bright on the scene post-*Singspielstück*.

Casual and relaxed, Harry, Sticks, Matt, Penny, Ronnie, Timmy, Elena, Sonia, and Mark sit amidst the studio set, as yet not dismantled. Those who played parts in the *Stück* – Harry, Sticks, Matt, Penny, and Ronnie – have shed the personas of their respective characters. For example, Sticks, the actor, is not showing any of the distress recently overwhelming Sticks, the character.

Timmy, with ears in his ears, is zoned in, switched on, as cool as.

A petition, begging signatures, circulates. Matt, pen poised ready to sign, directs a question to Sticks.

Why not *Australian* rainforests? he asks.

I'm inclined to ask the same question, says Penny. In point of fact, I *have* done so on at least one past occasion.

I take your point, says Sticks. But it's difficult for me to get my head and heart around more than one worthy cause at a time, says Sticks. Good enough?

Nobody responds. Matt signs and passes the petition to Penny. The clipboard does the rounds: from Penny to Ronnie to Timmy to Elena to Sonia and finally to Mark. As Ronnie passes to Timmy, he nudges him. Predictably, he is gambling online.

Game of chance, says Ronnie.

Uh, says Timmy.

Blackjack.

Uh.

Helps to count the cards.

Uh.

I can teach you how if you like.

Uh.

Sticks, alert to the possible threat this conversation might pose, interpolates a cautionary comment.

My son already knows how, she says. His memory skills come from his mum. Courtesy of a game of chance called heredity.

Mark interrupts this exchange, returning the petition to her. She glances at it, squints to read his signature, then turns to him.

So *that's* your last name, she says.

Always has been, says Mark.

Larker, she says.

By name and by nature, says Mark.

Harry takes charge of the interrogation.

So, says Harry, your name is Mark Larker.

I cannot lie.

It rhymes.

Pademelons. There is something more than poetic contrivance on Harry's mind. As if to check out this mind, his eyeballs roll upwards. When they roll downwards again, they fix themselves intently on Mark.

What's your middle name? asks Harry.

Mark is mildly embarrassed.

Why is it important? he asks.

Don't be shy, says Harry. Out of curiosity, what is it?

Eugene, if you must know, says Mark.

Harry's eyeballs roll upwards again, remain fixed in this elevated position for an instant, then roll down again.

So you are Mark Eugene Larker? asks Harry.

Mark is puzzled, but nods.

Mark E Larker? asks Harry.

Mark nods.

Mulk … i … lark … a, says Harry. Mulki Larka

You, pademelons, cherished creatures of my company, should not be surprised by Harry's revelation. Nevertheless, it behoves me to say what I have said many times before, and which I am always glad of the opportunity of saying again.

Fiction can sometimes be more potent than truth, especially when it has a mind to morph into truth.

<<

Harry, Sticks, and Matt sat on swivel chairs in the Nerd Centre.

Harry and Sticks sat behind their desks. Matt sat facing Harry across his desk. Over Harry's shoulders, he could see the poster, formerly his, of the vegetarian firebrand known as Lydia. It had been Blu-Tacked to the whiteboard by her new owner. The door to the back room was ajar. Behind it lurked an unseen spook.

No *Bisquit* was on offer. The occasion did not demand it. This was not a social occasion.

Some minutes earlier, Matt had felt obliged to check on Harry's state of health.

How are you feeling? he had asked.

Don't ask, Harry had replied.

Are you up to it?

I'm going to have to be.

All preliminaries having been dealt with and small talk exhausted, it was down to business. Indeed this *was* no social occasion. This was a council of war. So often her lot, Sticks opened discussion.

Our problem, said Sticks, is the virtual certainty we will have no less than *three*, I repeat *three*, criminal gangs arriving on our doorstep at some time in the not too distant future.

Nobody responds.

Like public education, says Sticks. It comes free and compulsory.

Any idea how soon? asked Matt.

No way of knowing, said Sticks.

What will they be after? asked Harry.

You mean *who* will they be after.

O.K. Who?

A particular female person who brought this trouble with her from a distant land, and whose name I need not mention.

Are they expected to arrive together? asked Matt.

The gangs?

Yes.

I certainly hope not. That's the worst case scenario. Best not contemplated.

A cough from the back room massaged the air all the way round the door jamb to the three pairs of ears in the Nerd Centre. Three pairs of eyes were drawn in the direction of the cough. Sticks' response was sharp.

Ronnie, she said, quit the charade. Get out here right away.

Ronnie, feigning sheepishness, opened the door wide, and emerged. Behind his back, as if hiding a weapon, he held a scrolled-up A3 sheet of stiff white paper. Finding a seat near the window, out of direct view of the other three, he sat, the scroll between his knees. Sticks found it necessary to swivel on her seat in order to face him. She addressed him with disdain.

O.K., rubberneck, she said, *your* take on these matters?

You won't like it.

Give it anyway.

You *really* won't like it.

Try us.

Well, said Ronnie, in contradistinction to Your Highness personally and your two airhead lackeys here, I think it could be to our advantage if the three lots of crims arrive together.

Harry and Matt swivelled on *their* chairs to face Ronnie, effectively ceding him the floor. By skilful contrivance, Ronnie had changed the geometry of the communication channels in the room so as to place himself firmly at the centre of things. Sticks, annoyed at being so blatantly sidelined in this way, scrabbled desperately to find a response capable of wresting the initiative back from him. After a pause, she settled for an attempt to kill the suggestion he had made.

An academic point, she said. It's beyond our control.

I beg to differ. It's my gut feeling you could, if you put your mind to it, get the Russian floosie to make the necessary arrangements.

Elena?

Don't know any other Russians. No floosies neither.

And suppose she came across, genius?

What? Offer me a head job?

Sticks, furious, rose to her feet.

Sheba, she said, don't you play *me* for a fool.

Ronnie muttered under his breath.

Don't need to, were his words.

Matt takes charge, attempting to defuse the explosive egos.

She means suppose Elena got all the crims here together, he said. Your idea, boyo.

I'd say if she did, we'd have a real fucking fight on our hands …

Sticks single word reply was derisive, and carried with it such a burden of downward inflexion, its vowel sound serenaded the termites in the floorboards.

No-o-o-o, she said.

… and every chance of coming out top flake in the Weeties pack by knocking all our assailants out of contention with a single blow, especially …

You've got to be …

… given we have a person here prepared to die for the cause.

Sticks, visibly shaken, almost swallowed her last word.

… joking.

She fell back in her chair. There were gasps from all in the room except Ronnie. The room was as if drained of air by the massive communal inhalation. When Sticks eventually ventured a response, she had difficulty holding both voice and accusing finger steady.

You, she said, … are talking about … the father of my child?

Sorry, ma'am. Couldn't find any other contenders.

A cocktail of emotions overcame Sticks. Exasperation, fury, and grief were all part of the mix. Tears streamed down her face as she rose, upset the chair, grabbed at a box of tissues, and fled the room. Nursing his pain, Harry rose and scurried after her.

It was a two-way flow. As people and their emotions vacated

the room, silence invaded it. Matt allowed the silence time to settle before breaking it.

Halifax, he said, that was insensitive even for you.

Apologies were not part of Ronnie's repertoire. He stared at the ceiling. Matt continued.

What in the name of fortune did you think you were going to achieve? he asked.

A round of applause wouldn't go astray, said Ronnie.

Well, said Matt, as a consequence of your gross insensitivity, you've got an audience of *one* to provide it.

Much obliged, comrade, said Ronnie.

Imperturbable, he rode his swivel chair like a scooter over to Harry's desk. With a flourish, he un-scrolled the A3 sheet under Matt's nose, anchoring its curling ends with a couple of weighty catalogues.

Behold, he said.

Side by side, shoulders bent, palms and elbows braced on the desk, the two men poured over Ronnie's exhibit. On the white expanse of paper in front of them, flaunting its rectangularity, was the draughted plan view of a building, executed skillfully and signed off with all the professional niceties. The drawing represented the Big Top. Depicted according to accepted conventions, were doors, windows, benches, the assembly lines, the two makeshift shanties, and the south external wall of the premises they presently occupied. Solid arrows swept in from both vehicular entrances, and then swirled around like smoke inside the Big Top itself, as if meant to indicate hypothetical troop movements.

Despite his misgivings, Matt was impressed with Ronnie's drawing. If this had been a war room, and the drawing had been the outline of a military strategy begging consideration, then the only thing missing were the colour-coded thumb tacks to represent deployments.

Matt came to attention and conjured up the parody of a salute.

O.K., field marshal, said Matt, you've gone to a lot of trouble here, but what frigging point are you trying to make?

>

Later in the week, Ronnie found himself invited for the first time to that palace of modernist pretention in which Harry, Sticks, and Timmy lived. Again, the occasion was not social. Should it have been, Sticks would never have countenanced his visit. Ronnie was not on her list.

This was a reconvention of the council of war. Ronnie had been co-opted onto that council.

Harry was lying on the sofa of the lounge suite, robed in chenille, and almost comatose from pain, painkillers, or both. Sticks sat on a lounge chair on Harry's left, Ronnie on the floor on his right. Matt, Elena, and Ramon completed the putative council. The six adults sat in a circle.

Then there was Timmy. Scorning all adult company, he lay full length and face down on the floor on the other side of the room, eyes stalking the action on the screen in front of him, fingers thrusting as he placed bets, phonic ears inserted into his fleshy ears.

But, pademelons, we may be certain he had half an ear, of the fleshy variety, peeled in order to keep abreast of developments in the planning of scenario occupying the adult circle. Crime, no less, was involved here. Crime fascinated Timmy. Perhaps this was a throwback to his grandfather, Mick.

Re the 'planning of scenario', the broad issues had been dealt with. Predictably, there had been hot debate. Sticks was resigned. She conceded if Harry was going to die anyway he might as well die in his chosen manner. Some detail needed fleshing out, but otherwise this was the moment to sit back and reflect with awe on the effrontery of the plan on which they had decided, and on the difficulty of its execution.

The risk is mind-blowing, said Sticks.

Whatever response we choose is risky, said Matt.

Just to breathe is risky, said Ramon.

Not to breathe is more risky, said Matt.

There was a lull in conversation while the council cogitated on the ubiquity of risk.

What is my role? asked Ramon.

To dismiss all personnel on the day, said Sticks. Including yourself, Ramon. Make yourself scarce. We need to quarantine the risk.

What about Izzie?

Get rid of him, too, if you possibly can, though I realize that's easier said than done. He can be a king-sized pain in the butt when he likes.

What is my role? asked Elena.

To set the date, said Sticks. Make sure they know. Make sure they are all resolved to come. Then clear the hell out.

But it is for *me* they will come.

Precisely.

Can you persuade Baharudin to shelter you? asked Matt.

Barry is unsuitable choice, said Elena. They would go looking for him if they will not find me. And they will find him for sure. Then *he* will be at risk.

Fair point.

She can stay in my digs, said Ronnie.

Sticks pounced.

And what might *your* game be, Charlie? she asked.

The name's Ronnie. And it's not *my* game. Yours I believe. *You're* the one wants to hide her?

Is your place secure? asked Matt.

Don't know about secure. But it's like the waiter who spits in the soup.

Uh?

Nobody knows about it.

Bear in mind, said Sticks, she *will* be there on her own.

Alone?

Yes.

Why so?

Because you'll be needed on deck, turkey.

Oh, shit yes, said Ronnie. What a bummer. For a moment, I could see myself in there with a chance.

All avenues having been exhausted, the planning process had reached nexus. Silence held court. Then, to the surprise of the meeting, Ronnie rose to his feet, sauntered across to Timmy, and squatted on his haunches in front of the young gambler. Timmy pretended not to notice him.

Don't tell me you haven't been listening in all along, you tricky little poser, said Ronnie.

Timmy made no response. Ronnie peered over his shoulder.

Trying to hypnotize the cards? asked Ronnie.

Timmy made no response. Ronnie tried another tack.

I've made up a song especially for you, said Ronnie.

Timmy didn't respond, but Sticks was alarmed.

Is this necessary? she asked.

If need was all that mattered, said Ronnie, we'd be swinging on lantana vines beneath the rhubarb trees.

Then make sure you keep it decent and age appropriate.

Ronnie's response was to launch forthwith into unaccompanied song, the lyrics intended specifically for Timmy's ears but heard by all present.

> Now you can't play all the tables so you only play the best.
> The rabble play the rest.
> You can put it to the test.
> So ring the floor staff right away.
> You'll be so pleased to hear them say,
> Just settle your hips and peddle your chips with Ron-nie.

Timmy was not inclined normally to be pleasantly surprised by initiatives coming from the generations preceding his. He was nonetheless impressed by what he had heard from Ronnie. Delight spread involuntarily across his youthful features. The accolade springing spontaneously to his lips was praise indeed, and rare coming from him.

Far out, he said.

Their right hands rising as one, the pair executed a high five.

>

Thursday next at 2 p.m. By agreement, this was to be the date and time. The venue, of course, would be the Big Top. Elena, clever girl, had negotiated separate trysts with each of the criminal gangs, in the process leaving each gang believing it was the only one coming to the party. Such was the deal she made with them.

Deal? Singular?

More correctly, three deals, albeit identical. Fateful clones.

Time to sit back and wait. Time for anxiety attacks to override the imperative to stay calm. Time for the importunity of a mental diarrhoea of second thoughts. Time for multiple pairs of feet to shuffle off to colder climes, occasioned by the looming prospect of violent confrontation.

Time also for nightmares. Harry invited them to his sick bed each night leading to that fateful Thursday. The nightmares spooked the pain he had come to regard as his bosom companion, causing it to duck for cover into the blind ditch of temporary irrelevance.

Nightmares? Plural?

More correctly, the same nightmare, over and over. Ruthless reiteration.

What was the gist of this nightmare? The plot was chilling and minimal.

A limousine, sleek and black as a hearse, would cruise smoothly and silently along Cockatoo Street, turn the corner into Ibis Street, go round the block, and re-emerge in Cockatoo Street. Its circuit round the block would replay over and over, an unwanted and terrifying repetition. Nothing contained within could be seen through its heavily tinted windows. It might have been self-driven.

The movement of this limousine defied the laws of physics. Its motion didn't slow down as it turned corners, and was so deathly silent, the faint hum of an eerie tinnitus became the de facto aural background.

This non-visual aura, was persistent, pervasive, portentous, and low pitched. It didn't come from internal combustion or any other automotive process. It was unrelenting, unhinging, and unfathomable. It had no reason to exist. Like the dream.

It all played itself out while Harry lay sweating and writhing on his bed of unremitting terror. As nightmares go, he concluded this one was at the sinister end of sinister.

Between these oppressive nights, in the daytime hours through whose fabric reality was able to peer, Harry became aware of real cars cruising Cockatoo Street. These cars were not of the usual stripe seen around the industrial estate. Nor was Harry the only person who noticed them.

There was a large black sedan, the Chaika, containing likenesses, complete with dark glasses and ill-fitting suits, of the late R and G, except there were three of them.

There was a blue Ford Fairmont, with a Malaysian flag flapping on its powderized bonnet, peopled by three men of Asian appearance, wearing black songkoks and white sampings. One might imagine they were lackeys of some tin god from across the Straits of Malacca.

Perhaps more familiar, there was a white Ferrari, with two occupants, difficult to distinguish, but the driver would surely have been Hefty, well into his 60s. We could presume the other, whose craggy face was overrun with unsightly eruptions suggestive of a close encounter with a swarm of unfriendly bees, was The Poet of some notoriety.

These vehicles would cruise by, slowing to a crawl as they came abreast of the Big Top. Sometimes the glint of binoculars, from the interior of the vehicle as it passed by, would tweak the eyeballs of bystanders.

Then on the Tuesday the Fairmont stopped, and the three Malaysian lackeys alighted. Zounds, it wasn't Thursday yet. Did they intend to jump the gun?

Harry, fighting back pain, hobbled from his desk to the window of the Nerd Centre, where he was joined promptly by Sticks. Together, they saw the Malaysians approach the yawning mouth of the vehicular entrance of the Big Top, before becoming swallowed up in its oral immensity.

A short time later, he saw them exit, return to the Fairmont, and drive off.

Several moons later, Harry revisited this moment in a suite of dreams, cousins to his earlier nightmare. In these dreams, the three Malaysians were leading animals through arable terrain by ropes tied around their necks. Strictly one animal per man, one man per animal. But what an animal! This animal belonged to some dubious hybrid species, resulting surely from a ghastly biological accident. A species construable in only one of two ways, either as untenable or as profane.

The cross of a leopard with a giraffe.

This dream metamorphosed. The new form, became a particular obsession for Harry. The Malaysians, and the strange animals they lead, were embroidered repetitiously onto the fabric of a stiff curtain whose function was to open and close as required on theatrical events performed under a proscenium arch …

<

Pademelons. Are you curious to know what business was transacted by the three Malaysian lackeys in the course of their brief sojourn beneath the steel canopy of the Big Top on that prefiguring Tuesday? I, the custodian of omniscient powers, can satisfy your curiosity.

As they entered, the visitors were confronted by assembly lines buzzing, as usual, with disinterested activity.

Changes had occurred, changes the visitors could not have been expected to notice, this being their first time in this neck of the woods. Multi-screen systems were no longer in demand and so had no further need of being produced. The era of giant insect eyes had been superseded, with brute finality, by the era of cheap imported flat screen TVs. Both assembly lines were now devoted exclusively to the manufacture of custom-built electronic bulletin boards and their near relations. Some enterprising techies were attempting to develop new prospects, music synthesizers among them, on the surrounding benches.

... the end of the era of the giant insect eye, an era spanning almost fifteen years, did not go unheralded in Harry's camp. How could such a worthy vehicle of prosperity and good fortune be allowed to go the way of all things without due ceremony? Elena, a decorative addition to the Big Top team in recent times, had been chosen by her workmates to operate the mechanism that sent a ceremonial bottle of *Biscuit* smashing itself to pieces against the very last multi-screen system to roll off the assembly line. She felt honoured to have been so chosen ...

I digress.

The trio of impatient visitors, the devil knows what surprises lurking beneath their bulging sampings, sought out the person in charge and found him in the person of Ramon. He greeted the strangers warmly, pretending ignorance of who they might be or what they might want. One of the three, acting as spokesperson, and whose name I happen to know was Abdullah, addressed Ramon in terse English, accented of course.

We are looking for Elena Rusalkova, said Abdullah.

She won't be back until Thursday, said Ramon. Would you like to leave a message?

That will not be necessary. We will come again on Thursday.

Shall I tell her who called?

That will not be necessary. She is expecting us.

Abdullah turned on his heels. The other two men did likewise. All three men left the building. As they did so, Ramon's cheery voice caught up with them.

Have a nice day, the voice said.

>

Thursday arrived. This was not a day like any other. No, *non, nein, nyet, nada.* The day was much anticipated and much dreaded. And most trepidations with regard to it were eventually to be realized.

It was noon. All morning, those unlikely cars had been cruising Cockatoo and the other streets of the immediate neighbourhood. At the moments when, as they were bound to do, these vehicles strayed across each other's path, eruptions of profanity from the occupants, to which our marsupial ears were not privy, spewed forth in at least three languages. Even *sans* words however, the poses struck by the occupants of the cars were consistent with a question on their lips such as, What the **** are *they* doing here?

Within the Big Top, a shock awaited both us and (later) possibly them. Operations within the premises were suspended for the day. The assembly lines were silent and still. Hanging lifelessly, the electronic carcasses showed no appetite even to emulate pendulums. To the senses, there was no evidence human presence had ever graced these precincts. For those with no inkling of its history, this particular nook of the hemisphere might have been mistaken for the exclusive province of phantoms.

The vehicular doors adjoining Cockatoo and Currawong were

open wide. Nobody took this as an invitation to drive through. All parties had apparently and independently agreed shenanigans would not begin until the agreed time of 2 p.m. Pending that moment, inspection was achievable at a distance, discreetly, through the mechanism of binoculars.

No other orifices in these premises, not doors, not windows, not anisotropanes, spoke to the wider world of what was within. The not-so-little house on the prairie had drawn its shutters.

Then the clock struck two.

Harry emerged from the Nerd Centre and crossed to the small door serving pedestrian traffic on the north side of the Big Top. He was dressed, uncharacteristically, in a bulging flak jacket and lightweight camouflage trousers. He opened the door, entered the Big Top, closed it behind him, and positioned himself at the geometric centre of the floor space between the two assembly lines. He stood still and waited calmly.

The three cars closed in. First, the white Ferrari drew up to the gaping jaws of the Cockatoo Street entrance. The Poet, granite faced and pock marked, emerged from the front passenger seat, and two sub-operatives from the rear seats. One of these sub-operatives, known as Mad Dog, was the designated mouthpiece of The Poet who, famously, preferred not to talk.

The Ferrari, driven by Hefty, backed out, and drove away, not to be seen again for the duration. Hefty knew his place.

Next, the powder blue vehicle, its flag advertising the national allegiance of its occupants, pulled up at the the Currawong Street entrance. Abdullah and his two offsiders alighted.

Last, the black Chaika arrived at the Cockatoo Street entrance. The replacements for the late R and G emerged. Good authority informs me they may conveniently be referred to as Sh, T, and N. They were about to mix it with The Poet and his entourage. The Russian contingent seemed a tad nervous. I am told The Poet, can have this effect on people.

The Poet and his crew were wrapped in long lightweight

overcoats in beige to calf level, the Russians in dark ill-fitting suits. For the hitherto impatient Malaysians it was white sampings. All these garments bulged ominously, as if straining to accommodate the bulk of whatever weaponry the visitors thought they might require for this adventure. We are tempted to speculate on the nature of these sinister accessories, as we might also wonder what Harry was hiding under his flak jacket.

Wordlessly, as was his wont, The Poet indicated by a hand gesture, managing to tick the boxes of both protocol and politeness, that the Russians should precede him into the Big Top. With a nod of acknowledgment from Sh, they did so, in the process casting nervous backward glances at The Poet &etc taking up the rear.

A minor miracle for you, pademelons, indicative perhaps of the supraliminal behaviour we are informed holds sway in a congregation of like minds. As if by a form of telepathy, Sh, The Poet, and Abdullah simultaneously withdrew cell phones from somewhere within the warp and weave of their clothing and began speaking on them. I swear they did it in unison. Even The Poet spoke, or so it would appear from the rare sight of his moving lips.

Were they contacting their respective HQs to report their unexpected encounter with rival parties bent on similar but competing objectives? We can only speculate.

As the Russians passed Elena's shanty on their left, with The Poet and his men pressing close on their heels, so the Malaysians passed Izzie's shanty on *their* left. With solemn deliberation the three groups drew closer to Harry and to each other.

Minor miracle followed on minor miracle, this latest one startling the b'Jesus out of the visitors. Music burst forth from speakers installed in the ceiling of the Big Top. The ears of three nations were assailed by a melodic line given over to synthesized strings only. It was pure melody, uncorrupted by words. Nevertheless, lyrics could readily be added by any mind conversant with the rich mythology of the Wild West:

Do not forsake me, oh, my darling
on this our wedding da-ay …

… so, pademelons, it would appear Ramon had not been able to persuade Izzie to stay clear of the action. But where was this loose cannon hiding himself away? And what might be his next move? …

It was not long before all interlopers in the Big Top could see the whites of the eyes of all the other interlopers. They could also see the whites of Harry's eyes, and Harry could see the whites of theirs. A mass exposition of ocular whiteness was in play.

Instead of keeping straight ahead, the Russian trio tacked hard to their right. As they did so, Sh indicated to The Poet and his crew, by means of a cautionary flick or two of a trailing hand, that they should not insist on following. The Poet complied, wordlessly of course. The Poet was not inclined by nature to be compliant, so we must assume the request suited his purpose.

Before long, everybody agreed to stop where they were. They had Harry covered on three of four sides, his only unguarded side being the one containing the door through which he had entered. The Malaysians were on his east, the Russians on his south, and Hefty's henchmen were on his west. Harry looked surprisingly calm for somebody in such an obvious life-threatening situation. By contrast, those threatening him seemed decidedly edgy. Their discomfort at the presence of rival gangs was evident, and was to become increasingly so.

The music ceased mid-bar. A threatening silence took its place which, in that cavernous enclave, settled on events like treacle.

Foreplay was over. The deed was about to be done.

Pademelons. I am overcome with dread. With possibilities so portentous, I intend to pass the baton. My second unit are more than adequately equipped to carry the story forward from this point. By contrast with them, I feel I lack the emotional resilience to portray to effect the development of events as they escalate towards their tragic *denouement*. We have feelings – do we not pademelons? – and there is a black stump[54] in my cognitive terrain, and perhaps in yours also, beyond which sensitive psyches fear to advance.

> >

Singspielstück #16: The Genesis of 'I'

We, inhabitants of the supernal, make up the bulk of the studio audience. What we see in front of us fortells the epic not the intimate. Lit from above, and pushing its boundaries to the limit, the active space has subsumed every skerrick of studio territory that can be brought into service.

We guess this space is intended to represent a substantial excision from the factory floor of the Big Top. Cameras cover it on three of four sides. The cameras in front of us, to left and to right, have been pulled back some distance, in order to facilitate as required effective wide-angle shots of the entire active space.

The fourth side – void of cameras – the intended backdrop – is an expanse of grey sheet-steel in proxy, framing a rectangular expanse of lightweight scrim. This scrim is apparently intended to simulate heavily tinted window-glass. Nothing is visible through it. Ghostly reflections of much of what is in front of it – including us, pademelons – dance on its smooth dark surface. We, the audience, are accidental intrusions upon the active space. Intrusions visible only to our eyes.

Immediately forward of the backdrop, extending from extreme left to extreme right, is an assembly line for electronic bulletin boards in representation. Hanging from the flies, several 'carcasses' sway forlornly above rigid metal shelving.

---

54 The 'black stump' is a mythical feature of the Australian landscape, be-yond which 'woop woop', (i.e. the Outback) begins, and the niceties of civilization are unlikely to be found.

From out of view on both left and right, simulated sunlight seeps in. We presume this is meant to suggest wide-open vehicular doors.

Crew stroll in from the right. First to arrive are the camera operators, moving promptly to their stations. Harry, director for now, comes next, dressed in flak jacket and camouflage trousers. His communications headgear, incongruous against such clobber, hangs loose around his neck.

Behind Harry come Sticks and Mark, dressed as crew might. Their headgear also hangs loose. All three gather round the camera at left front.

Muttered words pass between them. Then Harry, handing over his headgear to Sticks, moves to a central position in the active space. Close behind is the assembly line. Harry has, for the forthcoming action of this *Stück*, abandoned his directorial role in favour of an acting role. He is to be talent, not crew.

Sticks and Mark secure their headgear and are ready for action. They are poised to be crew, not talent.

Sticks speaks to her microphone. A number of Sandalwood recruits appear on the right, Godfrey among them. They will make up the bulk of the cast. There are nine of them, three lots of three, representing the criminal gangs. Those playing Malaysians move to Harry's left. Those playing Russians take up position behind him, all but sitting on the assembly line. Hefty's band press him on his right. Godfrey, one of the latter group, will play The Poet, judging by his makeup and demeanour.

Mere metres separate the gangs from each other and from Harry.

Credit for costuming is thanks not so much to Matt but, as with all my second unit's enterprises, to Harry's memory and/or imagination. The Malaysians are black and white in their songkoks and sampings. The Russians are wholly black in their ill-fitting suits. Those representing Hefty's interests are beige. Their sinister overcoats cover them from lapels framing their chins to pleats lapping their shins.

The voluminous costumes appear to contain more than just the bodies of their occupants.

All actors in place, the clapper sounds and pre-recorded music, rendered *in camera* at some earlier time by Izzie, begins to spin magic. In minor key, ¾ time, and the colour of a full orchestra, it is tense, vital, and impossible to ignore.

A warning, pademelons. As the drama unfolds, the crew may come to represent for us an irritating distraction. They will be busy reducing action to a sequence of close shots, two shots, long shots, and the like. At certain moments, Mark and Sticks may even demand re-takes of this action which, from our point of view, would have the capacity to disrupt continuity in a most disconcerting way. Pademelons, a studio audience must agree to bear this cross. It is our *privilege* to be here, not our *right*. With time, I trust we will learn to take these moments of unavoidable delay in their stride, and perhaps eventually to ignore their existence entirely.

A holographic apparition appears beside Harry. It is a representation of Elena. She turns slowly, giving cheeky waves, hand engaged but not eyes, in each new direction she faces. Those in the gangs – e.g. the Malaysians – who do not immediately recognize this female pseudo-presence, this luminous embodiment, are nevertheless quickly able to figure out who she is. She is their quarry, for Allah's sake.

The criminal invaders, already extremely edgy, are thrown decidedly off balance by her unheralded and insubstantial appearance. Instinctively, their hands scrabble beneath the folds of their garments in search of comfort in the form of trigger mechanisms fashioned from cold hard steel.

To superstitious minds not schooled by science, this airy sculpture, proxy for Elena, with its ghostly shimmer, its multi-coloured fringing, and its ephemerality, belongs in the family of occult phenomena inclusive of Saharan mirages, northern lights, migrainous auras, St Elmo's fire, and the Min Min light[55]. If one happens to be of this primitive turn of mind, avoidance would seem the best tactic. To confront such wraiths head on would be sure to invoke terror. But, in the scenario my second unit talent enacts here, avoidance is not an option, so terror numbs their minds. With the exception of Harry, who is cool.

A melodic cue marks the end of the introductory bars of Harry's musical creation, and the start of the creation proper. It is a feisty Überwalzer with staccato bursts, like gunshots one might say, of naked rhythm and energy. Harry adds lip-sync to the pre-recorded lyrics of which he was erstwhile author:

Harry:

Gentlemen, I presume this is what you've come to claim.

Harry gestures at the apparition.

I deal in images.

Harry gestures towards the criminal gangs.

Put me in the picture. Tell me what your game is.

Mad Dog takes a tentative step forward, indicates the hologram with trembling hand, and adds his lip-synced contribution to the lyrics:

Mad Dog:

Can we be sure you're not just another phantom like her?

It is Sh's turn. He steps forward:

Sh:

How in hell are we to know it?

---

55 Min Min light: harking from the western parts of New South Wales and Queensland, it is categorized sometimes as an Australian version of will-o-the-wisp and/or of similar aural phenomena.

It is Abdullah's turn:

Abdullah:

Simple shake of hands should show it.

He steps forward and offers his trembling hand.

Pressing flesh, the way to go. It's
the proof of the pudding. Don't forego it.

Harry shakes Abdullah's hand.

Harry:

My *bona fides* are here for all the world to see.
So it is your turn to put upon the table your credentials for me.

Sh responds to Harry's request.

Sh:

Glad to oblige since you turn a phrase so very nicely.

Sh extracts a small pistol from an inside pocket of his jacket, and displays it in the palm of his (trembling) hand.

Meet my beautiful Beretta.
You ain't likely to forget 'er.
Fits in hand of the jet setter,
and she cleaves flesh like feta, only better.

Harry:

Do you make threats, because this is what I'm apt to glean?

Sh:

Only if you put yourself between us and this girl we're sorta keen on.

Abdullah addresses himself to Harry.

Abdullah:

Bring us the lady if you'd prefer to have a future.

This incites Mad Dog to aggressive contention with Abdullah.

Mad Dog:

Go to hell, you piss-weak poser.
We're the outfit who first chose her.

Abdullah extracts a double-barrelled shotgun from the depths of his bulging samping.

Abdullah:

Take a look at my bulldozer.

Mad Dog extracts a shoulder-held missile launcher from the depths of *his* bulging overcoat.

Mad Dog:

I'll be honoured to preside at your disposure.

We are distracted for a moment from these lively theatrics, looking instead at the exchange occurring between Sticks and Mark near the camera at front left. Headgear down around their necks, they are conversing privately with each other.

Mark passes his headgear to Sticks as Harry had done earlier. Careful to stay behind the cameras, he exits to the right, in front of us. Sticks readjusts her headgear, and returns her attention to the production. She, it would appear, will take over the role of DOP.

We are left wondering why.

But wondering to no effect is unproductive. We transfer our attention back to the theatrics.

Harry, against all odds, is putting on a brave face. Understand his dilemma. Abdullah to his left menaces him with a shotgun, Mad Dog to his right trains a rocket launcher on his vitals, and Sh behind him, having put away his Beretta, has opted for firepower proportionate to what the other gangs are wielding. He has

III Studio | 567

produced a Kalashnikov – what else? – from beneath the folds of his suit.

Despite the weaponry directed prejudicially at him, Harry stays doggedly on message:

Harry:

Troops of all banners, please listen up to what I say.
I have surprises
for all and sundry sure to brighten up their stay here.

Sh:

What kind of scam do you fucking try to spring upon us?

Harry turns to face Sh.

Harry:

Just a certain little trifle.
Makes a monkey of that rifle.
It's a doozy of an eyeful.

Things happen fast from this point, events given added emphasis by a climactic lurch in the music.

Whipping off his flak jacket, Harry flings it to the floor. He now stands in navy blue singlet, camouflage trousers, and a broad khaki belt supporting the latter. Hanging from this belt on each side of its brass buckle, each of them packing menace are – can we be seeing right? – a total of a dozen or so khaki spheroids, each of a size that would fit snugly in the palm of a hand.

Grenades.

The criminal gangs fall back. Disbelief is rife. Harry turns to his left to engage the Malaysian gang.

… in what follows, each time Harry utters the word 'one', he is accompanied by the clash of synthesized percussion, dominated by cymbals …

Harry:

One is for you guys, and

Harry takes a grenade from his belt and – did he draw the pin first? – tosses it vertically, following through with a simple 'one-ball' juggle. All eyes are on this 'ball'. All lower jaws are on the floor.

Harry turns to his right to address the gang here at the pleasure of Sal Heffernan, Esq.

one is for you guys, and

Plucking a second grenade from his belt, Harry tosses it into the air. It joins its friend, making up the numbers for a 'two-ball' juggle. He swings to face the Russian gang behind him, managing meanwhile to keep the two 'balls' in the air.

one is for you guys.

Harry liberates a third grenade. It teams up with the others to complete a classic 'three-ball' juggle. Pademelons, it has emerged Harry is no mean juggler.

Quicker than the eye reads action, and with three deft flicks of the wrist, Harry concludes the juggling act by launching the grenades into steep trajectories, one directed towards each of the three criminal gangs.

Enjoy!

Pre-recorded music and lip-sync cease.

Harry falls on his haunches. Bending his head, then covering it with forearms and elbows, he adopts a foetal position. It is a futile defence, and we suspect he knows it.

Panic has a mind to enliven the action. All nine visitors drop, roll, and take whatever meagre cover they can find, some under the assembly line, some behind hanging 'carcasses', some spreadeagled on the floor. Simultaneously, and with the speed of – pardon the analogy – bullets, they produce automatic weapons and start shooting off frantic bursts. Harry crouches calmly at the epicentre of it all, waiting to collect the round bearing his name.

They seem to take an age, but the grenades eventually hit the floor. *Voila*! They are not grenades. They don't explode and they don't bounce. They splatter and form pools with the appearance of frog spawn in a lather of green slime.

Kiwi fruit.

The first to fall from a bullet is Mad Dog. A head shot, it has from indications taken him out in decisive fashion. This young puppy will show no more frisk. He lies twitching on the floor, his hair in a pool of pulsing blood. The Poet shoots a ferocious death stare in the direction of the Malaysians, from whence he figures the bullet is most likely to have come. His granite lips form the shape of a single soundless word. We have no trouble reading the word.

Motherfucker!

Standing with feet apart, knees slightly bent, unwavering, assuredly a man chiselled from stone, The Poet liberates several serious bursts of fire in the direction of the Malaysians. One of them falls, his songkok rolling loose across the floor. Abdullah dashes forward, retrieves the rocket launcher dropped by Mad Dog, raises it to his shoulder, braces himself, and squeezes one off in the direction of Hefty's crew. A swoosh and a fiery flash precede a massive explosion, off right and out of our view, presumably beyond the vehicular door, out in Cockatoo Street.

Fuck, says Sh. They took out Chaika.

Indiscriminate three-way fire breaks out, with Harry intact against all odds still crouching in the middle of it all, head bent, eyes closed, awaiting his moment of violent dispatch. The interloping gangs have forgotten all about their mission, a holographic reminder of which still graces the air with spectral shimmer, rewarding each gang in turn with a wave such as royalty might bestow on their subjects.

The gangs have turned on each other.

A door we didn't know was there opens in the sheet-steel backdrop. Daylight floods in. Matt bursts through this door, framed momentarily in a rectangular halo of light. He is dressed immaculately in white shirt, loose blue cravat, cream slacks, and brown dress shoes. Ducking under the assembly line, he dodges the warring gang members, defies the furious zing of live rounds, and swoops on Harry. Employing a rugby tackle, Matt sweeps this wannabe martyr before him. Winged at one stage, Matt staggers under the impact. But he keeps on, without care for himself, half dragging and half carrying Harry's reluctant frame beyond camera range towards us.

We can only presume this pair has escaped successfully via the door through which Harry had originally entered the premises.

The scrim representing window glass suddenly sheds its opacity. Where previously we saw on its surface only idle reflections, we can now see through it to the outside world. It is populated by police, an elite squad from the Special Forces, a Tactical Response Unit no less, fitted out from head to foot in bulging black riot gear, each member of the Unit looking as if he had stepped out from a bath of sticky black bubbles. The bristle of their weapons, exudes lethality, enough to make macropod hearts leap.

Irony is abroad, pademelons. Those who portray these Special Forces for our benefit, and adopt their fearsome guise, are thespians from the Sandalwood push, former singers of madrigals.

The Special Forces are observing with more than casual interest the events unfolding within the Big Top. Specifically, what they see is: a factory floor strewn with bodies and firearms, a handful of warriors, including The Poet, still standing, and weapons being discharged by these warriors in the direction of each other.

One particular body, illuminated by light shafting through the open door, the door through which Matt had recently burst, lies fallen on its back across the assembly line. It is the body of a man we imagine we know, but curiously *not* one of the gang members. Its legs dangle lifelessly at the back of the assembly line. Its head and arms dangle lifelessly at the front. Connecting arms with legs is a spinal cord arched seemingly to the point of fracture. Blank eyes stare upwards. If these eyes could see, the image confronting them would be of an upended studio space, with the disposition of floor and flies reversed. Those gang members not fallen in battle would be standing on their heads, those fallen adhering like geckos to a de facto ceiling.

In deference to gravity, blood trickles from the chest of this corpse, past its left ear, to the point of its chin, and onto the floor.

Only a truly dead body *looks* like a dead body. This one fits the bill.

We scan the face for clues to identity. It is Mark's face.

Yes. Mark's face. I should know. Sadly, it was once mine.

Those warriors still standing see the tactical responders. Internecine grievances are promptly forgotten. Other priorities demand their attention now. The fat lady is ready to sing. Some flee left and some right, towards the vehicular doors. There they stop in their tracks, uncertain which way to turn. We infer law enforcement, anticipating them, have reached the doors first and have the criminals surrounded.

We hear authoritarian voices off, from both left and right, demanding compliance.

Drop your weapons!

Raise your hands!

Do it now!

The Poet is the last to drop his weapon, the last to raise hands. In his brief moment of hesitation, he may have entertained a plan to fight to the death, taking as many as possible of the tactical response crew with him. Instead, not a second too soon for the integrity of his vitals, his feet nudge his grounded weapon and his raised hands glove the empty air. This word-shy poet lets a soundless riposte ripple his lips of stone.

Motherfuckers!

In the final reckoning, where does this leave Mark and me?

Watsón, il est élémentaire. Mark's misfortune is his exodus. Mine is my genesis.

Lights on both active space and audience go off. The holographic representation of Elena evaporates. We are in darkness, unable to see our hand/paw in front of our face.

But we are not yet done with this gut wrenching *Stück*. As we sit wrapped in total darkness, we hear the shuffling of crew assiduously re-arranging the set. We huddle in fear more horrors will soon confront us.

When the lights resume, the excision from the factory floor is much reduced in size. We see only the portion of the assembly line across which Mark's back is arched so cruelly, his body stiffening in the pose it had assumed following the crossfire to which he had succumbed. As the cameras take stock of this smaller precinct and its grizzly content, the intimacy of the scene startles us. An intimacy we would not have sought had it been up to us.

As the *Stück* enters its new phase, and at the discretion of whoever takes on the role of DOP, we expect to view the corpse from a variety of camera angles, including one straight into its lifeless eyes. We notice a camera mounted in the flies ready to serve this purpose.

Harry, Sticks, and a camera operator, all with headgear on, enter from front right. They proceed to the camera at front left. We guess Harry will resume the role of director. Sticks will retain the role of floor manager, to which she will add the responsibilities of DOP.

The clapper sounds. Pre-recorded music resumes: the same waltz as before but in abbreviated form and much more sombre. Sticks talks to her headgear, inviting an unseen person off on her right to enter.

Matt emerges at front right, his smart clothes dishevelled, his cravat askew. His left arm is bloodied and held to his chest by a hastily improvized sling. His movements are tentative. His legs are wobbly. He is distraught.

He walks, as if in a pharmacologically induced stupor, towards Mark's body. When he gets there, he kneels. His face and Mark's draw level with each other, his living eyes engaging with Mark's dead eyes.

Why this? he asks.

Nobody, certainly not Mark, answers. Matt repeats his question.

Why this, boyo? he asks.

The moment is assuredly grotesque, but one small detail, a detail screaming out for mention, seems especially so. Matt's face is the right way up whereas Mark's hangs upside down.

Is this, then, the way they must greet each other for their most final of farewells? Such a perverse juxtaposition, decreed as it is by geometry, is by any measure a wicked travesty.

With emotion, Matt lends lip-sync and gestures to the pre-recorded song:

Matt:

Why did I not tell you straight
I love you most dearly?
Why was I never moved to state
my feelings more clearly?

Timely words I was loath to declare
so you never got to hear them.
Duplicity and deceitful fare
was the way I rewarded the light of my life,
who stayed faithful to me in the face of oblivion.

Some would say the chance has passed,
and I'm, by half, too clever.
But I shall blurt it out at last.
It's better now than never.

Fielding a rush of tears, Matt supports the head of his deceased lover between his palms.

I love you, he says.

He plants a passionate kiss on dead lips. It is an incongruent kiss, upper lip finding lower lip, lower finding upper, warm finding cold, cold finding warm. His action – this gloss I push with a mixture of wonder and remorse – is a tribute to the irony of love whose realization peaks only after its opportunities are cut short.

Cut, says Sticks.

All lights go out.

< <

Pademelons. Not since the bare-breasted Lydia made her graphic espousal, accessible to all via the World Wide Web, had veganism enjoyed such good press. The explosive message delivered via the humble kiwi fruit was more than flesh-eating gourmands could be expected to withstand.

By the same token you would not have failed to pick up on the role played by Ronnie Dash's inimitable anisotropane. By means of this fabulous invention, those outside the Big Top, including especially the elite police quad, got to play the part of *unobserved* observers until the moment, judged by Ronnie to be appropriate, when the mere flip of a switch transformed them into *observed* observers. In this manner, the murderous deeds of the criminal gangs (those intended and those accomplished) were laid bare to the eyes of the elite police squad, and the selfsame criminal gangs were obliged to realize they were busted.

I hear you objecting: did not the script, inspired by Clint Eastwood no less, foreshadow the murder of Harry McMinn? Not a luckless stray by the name of Mark Larker?

Mark and I have, by dint of his murder, unwittingly come to form the inseparable components of a duality spanning both sub and superlunary realms. The very fact I am here with you, pademelons, attests to this duality. Accordingly, I feel authorized to speak on behalf of myself, *and also* on behalf of the deceased Mark, when I tell you *we* are touched by the concern you show *us*.

So how did the fatal switch occur? How did Mark collect the bullet destined for Harry?

This, pademelons, is how. After Matt made his impetuous dash to save Harry from impending death, an equally impetuous Mark followed close on *his* heels to save *him* from a similar fate. Kinship notwithstanding, I doubt I have the capacity to illuminate fully Mark's motives. So you must necessarily be left wondering what in Heaven's name was going on in his mind at that mad moment.

What I *can* tell you is, chance having had its decisive say, the bullet caught Mark full in the chest, fatally wounding him. Involuntary muscular spasms twirled him round in such manner as left him splayed on his back in a less than elegant pose across the assembly line. Neither Matt nor Harry knew of this collateral tragedy until Sticks informed them after the shootout.

Consequently, Matt only got to mourn the event some thirty minutes or so later, at which time he said his anguished goodbyes to Mark via that grotesquely misaligned kiss. A potent mix of guilt and grief overwhelmed Matt, so much so he felt obliged, the next day, to close the doors of Dress Rules and go to ground for a few weeks. Rumour had it he sat it out alone and inconsolable in his sister's rural hideaway.

When Matt returned from self-imposed exile, the consensus among his friends and associates decreed he was his old self again. But, pademelons, one does not, in so brief a time, disengage oneself from beasts as powerful as those with which he had been obliged to wrestle. One does not dispel grief so quickly as that. Nor guilt. I am sure the returning prodigal was, in those moments to which his friends defer, dissembling in valiant style, and with conscious deliberation. The brave face was what his friends saw. The brave face, not the inner struggles. On this, I would stake my life if I had one to stake.

Nevertheless, on occasion, flashes of deep malaise in Matt's eyes would bear witness to the true picture. Despite the limits of their perception, even his friends were privy to these inadvertent displays of inner angst.

And what was Izzie's role in the drama played out in the Big Top on that fateful day? You would certainly have sensed his unauthorized presence from the moment when the music to the ballad of High Noon resounded on around and above the factory floor, flailing all ears from the rafters as it were. Where, then, was Izzie hiding out during the furious exchange of fire? The fire following close on the heels of his premonitory intermezzo?

His story did not come to light until much later, in conversation with Sticks. All along, he had been hunkered down in his shanty, intending to observe the excitement through gaps in the bamboo weave. When stray bullets had begun to splinter the bamboo and tickle his earlobes, he had sought cover behind his synthesizer. As one would.

Yodellers, he told Sticks. Yodellers with automatic weapons and funny accents blew in. They opened hostilities, and sprayed bullets like they were scattering confetti. Before I could say 'General Schwartzkopf', it was like I was drawing fire again back in the Euphrates Valley. Blood oath, it was fierce. I thought I was a gone guy.

What did you do? asked Sticks.

Well, without my M16, what the toss *could* I do? I snuck in behind my synthesizer, and listened to it getting shot to pieces. Interesting sound that. Like a piano dropping off of a frigging cliff. But over and over. The same frigging piano.

>>

Harry, Sticks, and Matt occupy a table at *La Spag*. They are in fine fettle. Believing they have grounds for celebration, they are determined to make hay. *Bisquit* is available to invigorate the coffee. Bruno, standing nearby, has been favoured with a nip of this beverage and with access to their circle. Apropos of the beverage, he has made clear his preference for grappa.

Harry, who has the floor, is holding forth to Bruno. For all the others present, his information is not new.

... bit of a surprise, all said and done, how little damage was done. Those snoops, the homicide squad, took their own sweet time gathering evidence. Otherwise, we could have been back in production within a week. As things transpired, of course ...

Suddenly, glancing at Matt, he realizes how insensitive his words make him sound.

Sorry, best mate, he says to Matt.

It's OK, says Matt. Life goes on. For those of us lucky enough to have dodged the bullets.

Sticks, aware of the delicate poise of this moment, is eager to change the subject. Glancing nervously at Matt, she is relieved to see, if appearances count for anything, he has taken Harry's remarks with good grace.

Harry certainly dodged a few, she says. Luck embraces him like an invisible shield.

How about the big C? asks Bruno. This a bullet difficult to dodge.

Matt winks at Harry.

Bruno means the Cosa Nostra, he says.

Bruno, flexing his eyebrows into the form of a frown, regards Matt with feigned savagery.

Is a brave man, says Bruno, who talks big in the trattoria. He may end up face down in his minestrone.

Sticks, amused, nevertheless steers the conversation back onto what she has determined will be its course.

Bruno, she says, I'm sorry to disappoint you, but Harry *has* managed to dodge cancer. For which, by the way, I am extremely grateful.

This a true? asks Bruno.

Bruno looks at Harry, but it is Sticks who speaks.

The pathology lab got their samples mixed up. He had nothing wrong with him except fluid on the knee.

Matt does not resist the opportunity to stick the knife in.

Strangely, he said, the excruciating pain he was feeling 24/7 did a runner the instant he got the correct diagnosis.

Bruno is ecstatic. His arms dance.

This a wonderful, he says. I am so glad for you, Harry. This a real miracle.

Not a miracle, says Matt, for the other guy.

Which guy you mean?

The guy who believed the only thing *he* had wrong with him was fluid on the knee.

Sticks administers a gentle reprove.

'He' might have been a 'she', she says.

But, says Bruno, this not for Harry to feel bad about. Harry, he's a *good* man. He wouldn' a hurt a soul. This other man, he had the cancer all the time. Was *his* problem.

Sticks, insistent, clenches her teeth.

It might have been a woman, she says.

If a woman, is sad. But she must face her destiny.

Sticks decides the time has come to take Bruno to task.

Bruno, she says

Signora?

We think ourselves good people, don't we?

Of course we all good people.

Then shouldn't we show a little compassion for a fellow human?

Which human you mean?

The one we don't even know, who's got the big C.

Then *signora*, I ask you, why you not more *simpatico* with my good friend Harry?

What do you mean?

Bruno, glad to have found a worthy parry to Sticks' thrust, flings his hands out to the air in a gesture combining bewilderment and feigned disgust.

You leave him and go overseas to a foreign place, he says. You leave him and your beautiful son behind in this beautiful country. Then you say you love them both.

I do. The beautiful country as well.

Bruno's hands are in the air again.

So I ask why you do it, he says.

I always come back, says Sticks. Admit it.

Bruno's silent shake of the head reflects his dubiety.

Do you know my reason? asks Sticks.

Per favore?

The reason I come back.

You must tell me.

I can't resist your wife's wonderful gnocchi.

Harry, sitting across the table from Sticks, seeks and finds her hand. He catches Bruno's eye.

Bruno, he says, we *do* love each other. Sticks and I. We only realized our love late in life, but it is true love. Believe me.

Then why you let her go?

I have my life to live and she has hers. This is the only way we can both achieve our goals.

You talk to me of football?

Life goals, Bruno. Not a game of football. Like Roberto wanting to become a lawyer.

Bruno's eyes tell the story. He doesn't get it. He shakes his head again. Then, catching out of the corner of his eye a customer at a distant table demanding attention, he raises a cautionary palm to present company by way of apology, as if to say, Don't go away. He moves off, with intent, across the room.

There is a pause at Harry's table marking the end of this phase of conversation and the beginning of the next.

Shouldn't we get down to business? asks Matt.

What business? asks Harry.

Didn't we come here to discuss the next *Stück*?

Of course.

The last *Stück*, says Sticks.

The *seventeenth Stück*, says Harry.

<<

Monday morning. Overnight rain had left puddles on the ground.

The production line was working at diminished capacity. Damage to the premises was still under repair, and competition from rival enterprises in Asian countries to the north of Oz was beginning to bite. Integrated Electronic Imagery no longer enjoyed a monopoly on the manufacture of bulletin boards and the like. Although it gratified Harry et al to see the cogs and wheels turning again, it was clear to both observers and insiders management at IEI would soon be called upon to execute some fancy footwork to maintain a competitive advantage.

A month had passed since blood had been spilt in the Big Top, three weeks since Mark had been laid to rest, and two weeks since Harry had learnt the cancer he thought he owned was somebody else's. Among the techies, Harry was known as Harry the Hoax. A *number* of instances in his recent calendar might have served to earn him this appellation.

Mark's funeral, delayed by police investigations and the rituals of autopsy and coroner's report, proved suitably therapeutic for most of his friends. Matt was a notable absentee from the funeral. He declared he 'didn't do funerals'. In truth, he was not ready for public catarthis, especially one involving people like Mark's family from Tasmania, the £75 poms.

Inevitably, the gang violence of four weeks prior and its repercussions were grist to the grimy mill of the popular press. Crews camped outside both vehicular entrances for eight to ten days following the shootout. Anything that moved, even

Koshechka some swore, were coerced for an interview. Under the circumstances, it was a minor miracle those involved in the day-to-day business of Integrated Electronic Imagery kept their cool.

Elena had had the best ploy, albeit an obvious one. She told the news hounds she didn't speak the lingo. They fell about in any case in their quest for video footage of her most congenial person. Invariably, this footage made it to front and centre of the morning and/or evening news bites and talk shows.

Some astute investigative journalists suspected the existence of a link between the recent clash of the Titans under the roof of the Big Top and last year's story of E H Bolton and his criminal associates. However, nobody was able to connect enough of the dots to establish anything tangible. Reluctantly, they were obliged to let the matter ride for the present, or else resort to unscrupulous innuendo.

On this propitious Monday morning, Harry and Sticks sat at their desks in the Nerd Centre easing themselves into a return to business as usual. They assumed the bulk of the media hullabaloo was behind them. From their demeanour, suggestive of nerveless application to task, one could scarcely believe a significant seismic event, a turf war between multiple criminal gangs, had conspired recently and on these premises *in extensor*, to disrupt the well-honed standard operating procedures of the enterprise.

Harry glanced at Sticks' desktop, on which resided a document wallet out of stiff paper bearing the logo of Malaysian Airlines.

When do you leave? he asked.

The day after tomorrow, Sticks replied.

How long for *this* time?

Almost three weeks.

Harry pricked up his ears. From outside, in Cockatoo Street, came the throaty song with which a largish vehicle might hold forth were it to pull up at the vehicular entrance to the Big Top. He went to the window to investigate.

It was a bus, a fifty-seat luxury tourist job, fully air-conditioned with onboard loo one would imagine. It was disgorging leisured passengers with loud shirts, photographic equipment, and holiday ebullience. Emblazoned in blood red along the flank were the words:

CRIME SCENE TOURS

What the fuck … ? said Harry.

Sticks joined him at the window to gape.

A guide doubling as driver emerged from the bus with a handheld megaphone. He was chubby and sweaty. Dressed for effect like a ship's captain, flat braided hat perched on head and golden chevrons adorning jacket, he was not looking especially comfortable in any of his assumed roles.

Some of the passengers gathered round him to listen, but most were intent on photography. The enthusiasts in this latter category aimed their cameras and cell phones obsessively at everything in sight, some up and down the street, some at proceedings inside the Big Top, some at the charred ground where the hapless Chaika had been obliterated, some at the clear blue sky. The window of the Nerd Centre, the one framing Harry and Sticks, was a popular target. Harry, mortified, ducked out of sight. Sticks, dumfounded, stood her ground.

Ramon emerged from the Big Top to see what the fuss was about. Suddenly, the photographic brigade had a new subject: male, handsome, Latin, photogenic, and putatively criminal. They went for it. Ramon stood with dropped jaw.

The message, as formed on the lips of the faux ship's captain and duly enhanced by megaphone, was:

'Ladies and gentlemen, welcome to Integrated Electronic Imagery. Here is the cold hard reality of what you good folk have been seeing on your television screens over the last few weeks. Only a month ago, on the premises you see before you, three crime gangs, representing three international syndicates, became locked together in deadly armed combat. Multiple casualties were sustained before law enforcement was able to bring the situation under control. Citizens, I ask you, is

this type of activity set to become the norm for civic behaviour on our peaceful shores? Can we expect an exponential rise in such events is what our future will hold? Are we safe in our own houses? Does this sort of atrocity pass the pub test?

Inside the Nerd Centre, Sticks turned to Harry.

Get out there and put an end to this, she said. I don't like the tone of what I'm hearing.

She shepherded Harry toward the door and opened it. In no mood to be brooked, she shoved him out backwards. He stumbled into sunlight, protesting vehemently. The door slammed shut behind him.

Harry did an impromptu dance on the doorstep. The megaphone message ratcheted up another hysteric notch. Harry turned to face the maverick commercial operation whose pursuits intruded on his premises.

'*The Company, Integrated Electronic Imagery, has been cleared of any criminal involvement in the incident. But is there smoke without fire? If this Company is not a front for criminal activity, I ask, what could its function be? What does it make? Where is its product? Perhaps the CEO of this Company is the real Mr Big here. The real criminal supremo. The register of Proprietary Limited Companies shows the CEO to be one Harry A McMinn, who – good grief! – I do believe is approaching us as I speak …*'

Harry *was* approaching. Ramon, recovering his wits, provided verbal support.

Go for it, Boss, he said. You're Mr Big so you won't have any trouble sticking it right up 'em.

Perception is everything. Harry's approach to the crime scene tourists was not threatening. This was a man whose most serious crime to date was the occasional practical application of a lesson his mother had once taught him on her knee, i.e. how to lie. This was a man who had turned indecision into an art form to the extent chance and/or the whims of others had governed his life.

This was a man for whom the consequences of actions taken were never planned or intended.

So it was now.

The tourists, happy voyeurs to this point, stopped what they were doing and froze. They were spooked. Nemesis was approaching. All pairs of eyes turned in Harry's direction. Their body language spoke of their uncertainty: about what the outcomes might possibly be, of where they stood personally in respect of these outcomes, of what options might remain open to them and for how long.

Go on, Boss, said Ramon. Give 'em a run for their money.

'Run' it was. There was a dash for the bus. The captain, caught up in the crush at the door, lost his megaphone and his hat. Others, in their panic, dropped telephoto lenses and the like into the slush. The captain scrambled on all fours up the steps, fingers at the mercy of spiked heels. Reaching the driver's seat, he closed the bus door forthwith. This left several paying passengers outside, bruising their knuckles on the panels of the bus, in fear, one must assume, for their lives.

Harry advanced on the bus.

The starter motor whined. The engine roared into life. And promptly stalled.

Harry continued to advance.

From behind him came a sadistic cackle. Sticks had followed him out from the Nerd Centre, shouting her improvident delight to Harry and the world. Her words choked on laughter.

Enjoy it, my darling, were her strangled words. Who'd have thought? You …

She stopped in her tracks, bent over, rested her hands on her kneecaps. Oh dear, pademelons. Was it a gastric attack?

What spurted out was belly laugh, not vomit.

The engine started up again. There was a crunch of gears. Metal tore metal. Tyres squealing, clutch shuddering, the vehicle slithered sideways in the mud as it reversed with a shattering lurch, inflicting whiplash or worse on its passengers. Somehow it slalomed out of the driveway and into Cockatoo Street. The frantic passengers left behind chased the retreating bus, muddied by its spinning rear wheels.

Sticks straightened up. Glee enlivened her face. Glee reckless, wicked, vocal, and out of control.

Street cred, were the words she shouted to nobody in particular. First time in your life, Harry McMinn, you've got street cred. Never had it before, …

She hurled herself at Ramon, and took him in tow. Together, arms round each other's waist, Ramon sheepish, Sticks hysterical, they chased after Harry who, with the resolute gait of a zombie, paced it out with the bus and its occupants in his sights.

… and, Sheba, you'll never have it again. Celebrate …

The bus roared off down Cockatoo Street, leaving the smell of scorched clutch lining, a trail of ex passengers, and a determined Harry in its wake. Triumphant Sticks and bewildered Ramon released their hold on each other. Sticks flung her arms skywards and bellowed.

… your street cred. Cherish the moment.

Later that day, Harry declared this had been his finest hour.

>

A few days later, the incident still fresh in their minds, Harry and Ramon were eating lunch in the park opposite their respective domains. The fare was ham sandwiches and coffee-to-go, bought from a van doing the rounds of the industrial estate.

Brenda, having dropped Timmy off at school, was in charge at the Nerd Centre. She had taken over Sticks' office duties while the latter was off playing environmental activist in Malaysia.

They could hear the mechanical whirr of activity from the Big Top across the street, and felt vindicated by it. This was the sound of their livelihood.

You enjoyed playing Mr Big the other day, Boss? asked Ramon.

Awesome, said Harry. It's something special to feel as powerful as that.

I believe you are developing a taste for it.

Harry laughed.

Once in a lifetime will do, he said.

They spent a few quiet moments munching on their sandwiches before Harry spoke.

I'm glad we've seen the last of the criminal gangs, he said.

I wouldn't be so sure, said Ramon.

What makes you say that?

Crime's an infestation. Once it's wormed its way into the blood stream of its host, it likes to stay put. You might think you're free of crims for all time, but most likely they'll be biding their time. When the moment's right, they'll come right back again bigger and bolder than ever.

Right here?

To this table.

The same three?

The same and perhaps more.

Harry looked demoralized.

That's terrible, he says. You're saying there's no point taking any action.

Don't get me wrong, Boss. It makes good sense to give organized crime a haircut once in a while. So you can see the whites of their eyes.

Harry looked confused. Ramon felt obliged to elaborate.

In the country of my birth, it became so bad ...

Argentina?

Argentina. It became so bad the government and its instrumentalities weren't able to see straight any more. Crime had become institutionalized. *Con*stitutionalized. That's why I fled to Australia.

I know. Difficult times. I remember in the papers.

My point is, Boss, if people don't fight it, the same could happen here.

In Oz?

In Oz. Take my word.

They had food for thought now, as well as for their stomachs. They munched on their sandwiches quietly, while their minds ruminated. Ramon eventually broke the silence, changing the subject.

Speaking of infestation, when do we fumigate the joint? he asked.

It took Harry a moment before the penny dropped. Then he replied.

Saturday, he said. We seal the place up. Leave the fumes overnight to do the dirty work. Flush out the critters and their happy families. That way we have the time to make the place habitable again before the working week. What are your thoughts?

Sounds like a plan.

They spent a few quiet moments masticating. Then Harry remembered Ramon had requested this *tête-a-tête* because there was something he needed to say. Apparently, now though, when the moment was ripe, he was reticent about saying it.

Tell me, Ramon, asked Harry. What's on your mind?

I'm afraid it could be delicate.

Don't be shy. Fire away.

There was a moment of hesitation before Ramon replied.

I'm seeing Sonia. I'd like to know if it's OK with you.

Sonia Sheridan?

Yes, Boss.

Harry was not expecting this. A smile curled his lips.

I don't own her, Ramon, he said. Please feel free.

But you *were* going out with her at one time.

In a previous life. A long time ago now.

I thought you might feel upset …

It matters not a jot to me now, and even if it *did* matter I'd have no right ...

So it's alright with you, Boss?

You're a real gentleman, Ramon. My mother would call you thoughtful. But, Jesus, I wish you'd stop calling me 'Boss'.

There was another episode of quiet mastication. Harry lowered his eyes.

What you get up to with Sonia, he said, really is none of my concern. Go for it. I wish you the best.

I am most grateful to you.

Don't even mention it.

Harry looked up again.

By the way, what is she doing with herself these days?

What do you mean, Boss?

Where is she living? Where does she work?

She lives with her parents. And she works in a pathology lab.

The conversation, flowing smoothly until this point had, with these words, reached a hiatus. The ham sandwich fell out of Harry's hand into his coffee, making a splash, and fouling the picnic table. For a moment, Harry felt impelled to retrieve the sandwich. Then, leaving it to its soggy fate, he stared at the sky. When his gaze returned to the horizontal, he treated Ramon to a single drawn-out word, its vowel inflected emphatically downwards.

Ri ... i ... ight, was the word Harry said.

Boss?

Which pathology lab, Ramon?

The one in Lyceum Street. Near Mr Bolton's shop.

Shit.

Once again, the sky served as a retreat for Harry's eyeballs. Then, after a few seconds, he rose. Looking down on Ramon, he addressed him with faltering voice.

I think we'd better be getting back, he said. I'm a bit afraid my mother may not be coping.

Anything wrong, Boss?

They walked back across the street. Ramon clutched ham sandwich in one hand and coffee in the other. Harry put an arm round the shoulder of his Operations Manager and said some final words *vis-a-vis* the matter at hand:

Nothing. As for Sonia, mate, you have my blessing.

>

Early evening. After closing time. A light at the back of shop. Matt's desk.

The space behind this desk, a space Lydia of the line of Guevara had previously occupied, sported a new resident. Multicultural woman was the replacement. The framed poster boasted a female face, but whether in profile or in full-frontal view depended on whether one believed the nose or the eye. Picasso and his school, one trusts, had known what chaos they were letting loose when they foisted this fashion on the world.

The face was a pastiche of bold colours: in various shades of red, yellow, orange, brown, with a touch of ash grey. On closer inspection, shades of improbable green, blue, and purple came to light. The confusion of colours was somewhat at odds with the simple underlying message: a celebration of the multiplicity of possible, or even impossible, skin complexions.

The mannequins, forming a guard of honour for all visitors to Dress Rules, exemplified this quest for cultural and racial elan. Tableaux of these mannequins – mannequins clad in costumes whose ethnic couture complemented skin complexion – costumes Matt had designed with his innate and inimitable skill – these tableaux purported to demonstrate through astute juxtaposition the ease with which diversity could morph into unity.

Matt, in contrast to the mannequins, was slumped awkwardly at his desk. He was alone, except for a bottle of *Bisquit*. It was almost empty. What was once for Matt a social lubricant had become a private solace.

Sentiments of one sort or another, all difficult to corral, roamed the allotment of his mind. Grief only the passage of time could attenuate, was central to these sentiments. His grief was recent and therefore not attenuated.

Booze, he had found, was no substitute for the passage of time. Booze allayed the immediacy but not the immensity of the grief.

He fancied he saw Mark once again, backbone arched, arms dangling, eyes dead. This image played itself over, but never out, in his mind. He heard himself ask that futile question, the one he had asked on an earlier and more cogent occasion:

Why this?

Why this, boyo?

It occurred to him the end point of human life was nothing more than a conglomerate of accumulated episodes of grief, each of them attenuated to a degree determined by its age. It was sobering to think life, in the final analysis, was so nugatory.

Gleaming nacreous in the light filtering in from the street, the phalanx of mannequins in their tableaux stretched before him. Perusing them, he fancied he saw Penny Galatano. She threaded her way between the female effigies, effigies still and silent, effigies incapable of enjoining him in grief, effigies determined only to spruik the cause of multiculturalism.

She approached him with intent. She even waved. He reflected with satisfaction that many people – the push from Cockatoo Street, his neighbours in Lyceum Street, his regular customers – had shown concern for his welfare since his loss, but none so much as Penny. Nor had he been able to detect a hint of homophobia from any of these well-wishers. Assuredly not from Penny.

Penny had, more than anybody, jollied him through his crisis. Penny had strived to make it possible for him, though grieving inwardly, to act out the brave face in his workaday dealings with all and sundry. Penny had enabled him, despite everything, to confront the outside world with the confidence it so ruthlessly demanded of its supplicants.

Penny. Darling Penny. Lovely Penny. At times like this, he wished a tiny spark of latent heterosexuality had been able to light his tinderbox. He suspected Penny also might have wished for such a circumstance.

He suddenly felt a need to look more closely at the apparition making its way to him so eagerly. Doubts had surfaced. Surely it *was* Penny, was it not? He lifted his swimming head.

It wasn't Penny. It was Mark.

>

It had happened before. What played out was a re-run of an earlier idyllic scenario. *Sans* Harry.

Playing out were: the soon-to-be eco-resort in the Malaysian rainforest, the swift-flowing muddy river, the obsequious costumed flunkies, the well-heeled Western guests, the *al fresco* snack spread out on the table before them. Et al.

Déjà vu.

Sticks was dressed as always in defiance of fashion. Baharudin paraded his royal regalia unselfconsciously. Hussein, ever aware of his place, sat beneath a dipterocarb tree devouring noodles.

Away in the background, the sounds of monkeys, of gibbons, and of joyous nature generally, quelled any tension with a mind to develop.

… your opinion of Al Qaida? Sticks was saying.

The same opinion you have, I imagine, said Baharudin. It is not civilized. It is not Islam.

Many things are not Islam. These cucumber sandwiches, for example.

Yes, but *they* don't leave a bad taste in the mouth.

They paused, the better to savour the taste.

You know you are playing hopscotch in a minefield, said Baharudin.

Of course.

I am too, said Baharudin. Any day, I may be called upon to fulfil my destiny.

As Sultan? asked Sticks.

Baharudin nodded.

It will be a mixed blessing, he said. But it shall put me in a better position to help you with your cause, and perhaps deflect some of the danger from you.

It may put you in opposition to your own father.

It *will* put me in opposition to my father. But my father is in the wrong. May I pour you some lime juice?

Thank you.

Baharudin poured juice for both of them.

What will you do about Elena? asked Sticks.

I would always hope to see her when I come to Australia. But ...

She knows it was never to be. She is a resourceful young woman. She is a survivor. She will find her way better than any of us.

He took a long sip of his juice.

Perhaps, said Baharudin, you think I am – in the Australian vernacular – a right bastard.

A ring tone from Sticks' handbag interrupted this conversation, relieving Sticks of the duty of finding a rejoinder to Baharudin's self-deprecatory remark. She scrabbled in her handbag for the phone, found it, observed the call was from Harry, then answered.

Yes, darling? she said.

Baharudin rose, and moved off discreetly in the direction of Hussein. Sticks listened silently for a time to what Harry had to say, the expression on her face meanwhile changing from relaxed to concerned to alarmed. When she finally responded, her voice reflected this alarm in spades.

Harry, she said, you poor darling. I'm on the first flight back.

She returned the phone to her handbag, rose, and joined Baharudin at the dipterocarb tree. She looked distressed.

I'm sorry, she said to Baharudin. An emergency at home. I must get back.

<

The propellant was flammable. An essential preliminary to the use of these 'bombs' was that all pilot flames, and electrical devices capable of producing a spark, be turned off. The Company was strict about this. Accidents had happened.

The logo of the Company, cast in iceberg blue on all promotional material, was **Bombe Alaska**. BA specialized in the eradication of insect pests from light industrial facilities and the more spacious variety of commercial premises. Their modus operandi was the controlled release of powerful insecticide, the active ingredient in their bombs, into the air in lethal quantities. Hence the propellant.

Another necessary preliminary was vacation of the premises under fumigation before the bombs were primed. It was not *essence de rose* being dispensed here. The insecticide was an insidious poison to humans as well as insects. Should a living creature exposed to it have the dubious luck to survive its initial onslaught, the liver and other vital organs would likely be sites for pathological re-emergence of its poisonous effect for the remainder of the victim's miserable and attenuated lifetime.

Harry called in Bombe Alaska because the Big Top had an ongoing problem with cockroaches, wasps, ants, and other creepy crawlies. Worst of all were the red-back spiders[56], which critters seemed to relish the dry conditions around the factory floor.

So, late afternoon Saturday, Harry insisted the human lodgers

---

56 red-back spider: a common and venomous Australian spider, almost an icon, but not fun to get bitten by.

quit the premises for the weekend. For Elena this was no problem. She never seemed to have trouble finding alternative accommodation, averse though she was to alerting the prurient of the options at her disposal. Izzie was a different kettle of fish. Harry agreed he could bunk down in the Nerd Centre.

The personnel from Bombe Alaska, suited up as if to fight the black death, arrived to plant the bombs, prime them, and then seal the premises. It didn't take them long. Between their coming and going, no more than fifteen minutes elapsed.

So began the final night in the lives of the thousands of six and eight-legged residents of the Big Top. However, as things turned out, their dispatch was not achieved by the means intended.

Blasts began around midnight. They were loud, but did not disturb Izzie in the slightest. He heard them alright, but imagined they were part of his regular regime of nightmares, unwelcome legacy of his five days of active service in Iraq. He rolled over in his bed and slept on.

An explosive mixture of propellant and air had ignited. The Colorbond roof of the Big Top ruptured like a burst paper bag. Doors, windows, and anisotropanes blew out. Fire took hold inside, fuelled by bamboo shanties, piles of wooden pallets, Styrofoam packing, hard plastic trim, flammable liquids, books, paper, &etc. By the time the fire brigade arrived, the heat had become so intense cylinders of acetylene and LPG were streaking like Roman candles into the wintry night sky.

The fire fighters could do nothing but wait it out at a safe distance, hosing down the neighbouring premises, including that in which Izzie slept.

Harry arrived in the wee hours, as did stakeholders in properties situated on and around the industrial estate. Ramon arrived soon after. By this time, the red-hot structural members of the Big Top were giving way in showers of sparks. Fervid air, sucked in for the purpose, was happy to participate in the promotion of full-on firestorm.

It was Ramon who remembered Izzie might be inside the Nerd Centre. Harry watched. It was as if time, for him, had become warped by his sense of shock. He imagined he saw Ramon emerge from the Nerd centre with Izzie, and only afterwards race in to find him. One might describe it as dyslexia of the chronologic faculty. But, irrespective of whether chronology, as it played itself out in Harry's tortured mind, was right way round or arse about, the befuddled muso found himself turned out peremptorily into the flame-lit and waterlogged street, clutching a tangle of pre-worn clothes to his naked body, his bare skin subject to stings by falling embers, his mind far away, willing hostage to the murmurings of Morpheus.

Gesturing somnambulistically in the direction of the tornado of sparks and the orchestra of explosions, Izzie let his mind speak through the congealed porridge of his sleep.

Wilco out, is what his mind said out aloud. Watch me and my platoon. We'll show that tosser Saddam how this man's army fights a fucking war.

Best if you put your clothes on first, said Ramon.

The fire continued to pulse and swirl, bursting in fearsome saffron waves over its immediate quarry, and lighting up more distant environs in chaotic strobe. One moment it would entice the firefighters to move in close, the next it would send them scurrying back for their lives. Tongues of flames lashed speechlessly, and hence without warning. The infernal foe declined to play by the rules, whether of Geneva or Queensbury.

Harry's reaction to the calamitous event playing itself out in front of him ranged from initial shock, through cognitive paralysis, through bitter resignation, and finally to a peaceful Zen-like acceptance. He began with the excruciating thought of two decades of his precious endeavour going up literally in smoke. He ended by embracing the mantra 'Easy come, easy go.' At the starting barrier, he was itching to dash into the premises to put a stop to the conflagration or die trying. In the homestretch, he had settled down calmly at a table in the park and, chin cupped in hands, was content to enjoy the spectacle for what it was.

Chance, fate, destiny, he reflected, as he gave himself over to the hypnotism of the flames. Call it what you will. If you can't beat it, the only option is join it. That's the option my recalcitrant son has chosen, and from which he is determined to profit. I'll swear by the Almighty, or by the goddess of fortune should you prefer, he's on the right team. He'll do well.

The next morning, amidst the dull-red smoulder, and the faecal stench always accompanying sodden char, two male firefighters in heat resistant boots and fire retardant clothing, crunched their way through the scorched tangle of buckle and crumble. One of them ducked under a fallen steel beam, twisted back on itself by the heat. He stopped, and called to the other.

Over here, Dave, he said. I've found the arsonist.

The two firefighters contemplated what the first had found. A small blackened skeleton, swaddled in shreds of blackened hide. A grinning visage, the static grin of violent death. Teeth still engaged with the three-phase electrical cable, putative conduit of death. Deep dark pockets in the hide, pockets having once contained the sharpest of night eyes, and from where the firefighters imagined green slits glaring out at them. Four clawed appendages, stiff as dildos, telling of the involuntary throes of a final futile struggle.

Koshechka.

Beside her remains was a sludge of semi-molten metal, printed circuitry, and the suggestion of a musical keyboard. These remnants, presenting to the world in the brutish here and now, were a metaphor for the thwart of civilization. The cable, agency of Koshechka's gruesome death, had its origins here. It ran to a switch. Though heat damaged, this switch was, in the professional opinion of the firefighters, turned on at the moment feline teeth had engaged with cable.

Even my gormless granny would agree, galloping goitre

notwithstanding, a case of sorts was proven here beyond reasonable doubt.

>>

Singspielstück #17: Karaoke Wrap

Pademelons, I know you have been anticipating this particular *Stück* with all the animal enthusiasm a small marsupial can muster. It shall be the seventeenth and final theatrical episode of words and action, song and speech, pain and joy, all concocted in/by Harry's hyperactive wetware. Wetware striving to engage with something/anything since the demise of the Big Top had left it bereft and idle.

As we endure for the last time those odious bucket seats, so unaccommodating to marsupial tailbones, we ponder the studio setting before us. It has the same ample extent as in the previous production, but its props and their arrangement are unlike those of any *Stück* we have previously enjoyed, whether beneath proscenium arch, on turntable stage, or in studio. We see a charred wasteland: bent and blistered structural members, gnarled and shredded sheet steel, scorched wooden pallets, &etc. Twisted circuit boards – once hopeful bulletin boards and the like – languish in ash-strewn puddles of congealed metal. If one can believe the backdrop, representing a slice of the industrial landscape to which the former Big Top had belonged for the best part of two decades, one must conclude the sad ruin making up the foreground is at the mercy of the open sky. The open *night* sky, complete with full moon.

However when we look closely, we see the components of this ruin are not real at all but are, in the manner of theatrical props, tangled, rough-hewn, jagged, and conjoined set pieces, out of polystyrene, papier-mache, and the like, variously painted black and silver. They are designed to resemble the real thing, in this case the remnants of premises reduced to ashes by fire. But thought has also been given to their potential for assembly/disassembly, in a jiffy, at the will of the floor manager, in some future theatrical space.

Lighted candles occupy strategic positions throughout the derelict set, lending a friendly feel to the otherwise gruesome scene. These candles are 'pretending' to provide illumination, but we all know the real lighting comes from around and above.

Cameras roll. Mikes do what mikes do. Both agents have live action to record.

Five black business suits and five white business suits prowl grim-faced through this mock-up of a torched terrain, giving an occasional poke to a low-lying prop with the toe of an expensive brogue. The black suits are not happy about the presence of the white suits. And vice versa. The black suits wear conventional off-the-rack affairs accessorized by blue neckties, black leather footwear, and yellow hardhats. The white suits wear tight fitting slacks and matching jackets with super-slim lapels, finished off with gaudy bow ties and sleek dress shoes in pastel colours. They do not wear hard hats.

All the black suits are men. They are armed with clipboards and pens. Each of them wields hardware of one sort or another, e.g. one has a metal detector, another a builder's tape measure, another a digital camera, etc.

Though trying hard to appear androgenous, two of the white suits are recognizably male and two female. One would be obliged to speculate on the gender of the fifth. All five are armed with computer tablets and swishing fingers. And a stash of luggage tags, with which they busy themselves tagging the props.

Obviously the Sandalwood push is in town. We recognize Godfrey as one of the white suits of male gender. He carries with him the equipment mentioned above, equipment *de rigueur* for the white suits, except in lieu of luggage tags he clutches a swag of sealed white envelopes.

From the right, other actors appear: Harry, Sticks, Timmy, Matt, Sonia, Elena, and Izzie. Yes, Izzie. Izzie is on set.

They play their contemporary selves, dressed according to their tendency should they venture out in public: Harry and Sonia wear jeans, Izzie his amber cravat, Matt his blue bow tie, Elena her short skirt and top in peach hues, and Sticks her blouse and long skirt in rainbow colours. The twelve-year-old Timmy is in his school clobber, expurgated of items he and his peers dub nerdish. Cap, necktie, and anything bearing school colours or emblems are uncool.

If you count, pademelons, you will find this puts seventeen people on set. We know the significance Harry has invested in this number, but it does make the venue uncomfortably crowded.

These most recent arrivals on set, principal players as opposed to rent-a-crowd, are of course familiar to us, almost family one might say, though we do not necessarily talk happy families here. They bring with them the wherewithal for a celebratory wrap and, in particular, an overabundance of magnums of champagne and the determination to put it away. Their conversation is animated, indicating they have already had their first drink or three for the day, though we would hope not Timmy. Since they have a tendency to all talk at once, it is difficult for us in the audience to discern coherent conversation. Instead we resign ourselves to a flurry of disconnected and mostly inane snippets, confusion to our ears. Snippets such as: '… fat chance there, boyo …', '… yodel till the cows come home …', '… some would say he's on the spectrum …', '… worry the b'Jesus out of those turkeys …', &etc. But this is nothing more than white noise.

As they take up position in the make-believe rubble – spreading themselves uniformly throughout its terrain, talking and laughing incessantly, popping the magnums as they socialize, pouring the liberated spume into glasses, enduring and ignoring the suits who prowl silently amongst them – we, the audience, become aware of piped music, pre-recorded on Izzie's synthesizer. A melody pretty enough but rather innocuous, in unhurried 4/4 time and major key.

After the brief introductory phrase of this melody *sans* vocals, Izzie produces from thin air a hand-held mike. In the manner of master of ceremonies – an unlikely role, one might have thought, for this tetchy muso – he adds a lip-synced vocal line to the melody, which it will transpire is to serve as a musical bridge to the main event:

Izzie:

You have my consent,
should karaoke be your bent,
to yodel to your heart's content,
then pass the mike that I have lent you.

He passes the mike to Harry. Harry rewards him by topping up his glass.

Shazam!

The music changes from dominant to tonic key. The innocuous bridging melody has run its course. The main event, in the form of stanzas, is about to begin. The melodic basis of these stanzas could scarcely be described as 'innocuous'. It exudes soul, warmth, beauty, uplift, and optimism. Even nostalgia. Harry, who doubtless composed it, clearly intends it will capture the hearts of all whose ears are available to shepherd its passage to the mind.

Harry, alacrity and alcohol his companions, takes the first stanza. He rests his glass of bubbly and a depleted magnum on a convenient charred beam, then lip-syncs into the mike:

Harry:

Where things go from here's for Delphi to declare
Scrutinize the crystal ball. The goat's entrails lay bare.
What the future holds
when cryptic time unfolds
is fitful rise and fateful fall.
So reads the writing on the wall.

The other actors, *sans* the suited folk, cheer and raise their glasses by way of toast. More champagne flows, calling for more cheers and toasts, and yet more champagne. We conclude, pademelons, the tetragenarian Harry has, in the course of a single stanza of his seductive music, given us an encapsulation of his unique take on life, his effort duly appreciated within his circle on set. Pademelons, do you also feel the urge to clap, cheer, and whistle like a wolf?

The suited folk are less appreciative. Absorbed in whatever it is they regard as their mission, two of the black suits proceed with a topographic survey of the scene. One of them, his eye to a theodolite rigged up on a tripod, signals to Harry by means of a brisk hand wave that he should step aside. Which, taken aback, Harry does ...

... to be presented with a white envelope by white-suited Godfrey. Harry opens it to find an A4-size pink slip inside. He scans it, grins, then folds it into a paper aeroplane, and launches it skywards in a fatal trajectory.

Harry hands the mike to Sticks. She takes up the challenge to project *her* worldview through the medium of the stanza allotted to her:

Sticks:

Don't go asking what the world can give to you.
Ask instead how you can give this precious earth its due.
Let your instinct serve
to harness native verve
to services all humankind
will thank you for with heart and mind.

There is a riot of cheers and toasts. Her effort, despite its mawkish message, is much appreciated. The bubbly continues to flow freely, Harry attending to Sticks' glass.

But an officious black suit, wielding a tape measure, is quick to indicate to her she is in his way. Stepping aside, she is confronted by Godfrey with a white envelope for her. She opens it, peruses the pink slip inside, laughs, and spikes it on a nearby charred jag.

Sticks passes the mike back to Izzie. The music morphs back to the dominant key. The melodic line, its heart suitably attenuated, becomes that of the bridging melody.

Izzie uses the moment to encourage others to bare their cognitive all, i.e. to expose to the world the full monty of their respective mindsets:

Izzie:

Give the world your whole.
Accept catharsis as your goal.
Contribute with your crooning soul.
The stream of song must never falter.

Izzie passes the mike to Sonia. The key passes from dominant to tonic. The unassuming bridging melody is replaced by the *force majeure* of the next stanza.

Sonia, mike in one hand, glass of champers in the other, accepts the invitation to give lip-synced voice to *her* full monty.

Sonia:

Serendipity plus exercise of will,
is the secret formula, the way it's done, the drill.
Sweet revenge, we're told's,
a platter best served cold.
My swingeing blades shall seek to snip.
I'll field your tuck with my deft nip.

Nobody knows how to read Sonia's cryptic stanza. Some might perceive a veiled threat. Perhaps *most* might. This doesn't dampen the exuberant mood of the wrap, which has an impetus all its own. Cheers and toasts prevail. Champagne flows.

Sonia, her face impassive behind an alcoholic flush, pushes aside an importunate black suit, who is taking photographs of the debris. An importunate white suit, Godfrey, presents her with the white envelope. She scans the pink slip inside, crumples it into a ball, and flicks it in his face.

She passes the mike to Matt, who proceeds with his stanza. Because he also has had a tad too much to drink, his lip-sync is less than perfect in its execution, but his message is unmistakable:

Matt:

In memorium, please let me voice my say.
My departed mate still haunts my tortured heart today.
Chancing our malignant earth,
he lost the game for what it's worth.
His coming out, when done and said,
condemned me to an empty bed.

The gist of Matt's message might seem more appropriate to a wake than a wrap. But is not a wake a wrap of sorts? Or a wrap a wake of sorts? Cheers and toasts do not abate. Nor is any less champagne thrown back.

Matt falls backwards over a black suit crawling on all fours behind him, intent on a forensic examination of debris with brush, pan, and magnifying glass. When Matt picks himself up and smooths himself down, Godfrey is there to hand him the white envelope. Scanning the pink slip inside, he laughs, folds it, and tears it studiously so as to produce a string of small pink figures holding hands. He surprises Godfrey by making him a present of his artistry.

Izzie takes the mike from Matt. The melody passes from tonic to dominant. Izzie proceeds once more to add his vocals to the bridging melody. For him, too, alcohol is playing havoc with his lip-sync:

Izzie:

Flaunt your show and tell.
Contrive with vigour to expel
vibrations from your voice canal,
so others realize what you're selling.

Izzie passes the mike to Timmy. The melody passes from dominant to tonic. Stanzas are in play:

Timmy:

Never let your luck go gallivanting by.
Luck's a whiff of oxygen. Without it, you will die.
Roulette, blackjack, craps,
and such sirenic traps,
are deities plain folk would serve,
which tribute these great gods deserve.

Wild cheers greet this astute contribution from young Timmy, whose lip-synced delivery is notable for its sobriety.

Timmy backs into a black suit who is waving a metal detector from side to side. Realizing he has trodden on the man's toe and intending to apologize, Timmy turns to face his victim. Instead, he finds Godfrey in his sights with the inevitable white envelope. After scanning the pink slip inside, he laughs, lights it in an adjacent candle, and lets the burning paper waft to the floor.

Timmy passes the mike to Elena.

She, it turns out, has been entrusted with the coda. In deference to musical parlance, this is how the final stanza may best be described. It is a mutation of the regular melodic line, designed to bring the music to a fitting conclusion, so it will not be left hanging in an awkward harmonic space.

Elena, alumna of the school of hard knocks, knows how to hold her liquor. She delivers the vocal line in near perfect lip-sync:

Elena:

Grasp brute destiny and never let it go.
Hold to it tenaciously in face of friend or foe.
Don't accept defeat.
Contest each warring street.
Intelligence must vigil keep for hostile ebb and hostile flow.
Intelligence must vigil keep for hostile ebb and flow.

Elena returns the mike to Izzie.

The cheers and toasts are uproarious, a reflection of the popularity Elena has gleaned for herself, especially after she was generally perceived to have played a significant role in the rout of the criminal gangs.

A black suit, oversized pedometer on his wrist, paces the floor with measured strides. He collides with Elena, who turns to find Godfrey in her face, eager to deliver his white envelope. Upon reading the pink slip with deliberation, Elena feels obliged to comment.

Chto takóe éta dyermó?[57] she asks.

To Godfrey's surprise, she kisses the pink slip with extravagant irony and stows it down the front of her blouse, patting things down afterwards.

Glasses having been topped up, all participants in the wrap are moved to mimic in unison the last lines of Elena's stanza. In particular, they feel obliged to parody the ingenuous manner in which she has contrived to fracture syntax. Their spontaneous alcohol-fuelled outburst is unaccompanied, in full-throated *a cappella*. For the occasion, lip-sync has been given the bum's rush:

All (*sans* suits):

Intelligence must vigil keep for hostile ebb and hostile flow.
Intelligence must vigil keep for hostile ebb and flow.

The air is full of champagne spume. The party-goers are shaking up their magnums, then releasing the frothy streams under pressure, directing them at each other. It is what might happen on the winners' podium at the conclusion of a rally for purblind petrolheads. An abundance of enthusiasm and hilarity grips those celebrating, but the suits, caught in the crossfire, are less inclined to appreciate the jape.

The enmity between black suits and white suits has, for the duration of the *Stück* so far, resembled the slow simmer of

---

57 *Chto takóe éta dyermó?*: What is this shit?

bolognaise sauce on a kitchen stove. Now the ruddy brew boils over. Drenched in spume, and feeling the ignominy, one of the white suits – Godfrey in point of fact – tries to carry off one of the tagged props, an unwieldy conjunction, in papier-mache and the like, of mock beam, fake sheet iron, and faux encrust of charcoal. A black suit, also wearing copious amounts of spume, trips him up. Godfrey's tablet, and the remainder of his white envelopes, take wing. Godfrey and prop crash to the floor.

Scrambling to his feet Godfrey, affronted, challenges the black suit.

Who the eff do you dark-suited dudes think you are? asks Godfrey.

The black suit replies with scorn.

We are insurance assessors, he says, empowered to process the claim for fire damage lodged by our policy holder, a claim made in what the law obliges us to presume, but not necessarily to conclude, is good faith.

White indignation meets black indignation, and morphs into a mocking laugh.

These are theatrical props, turkey, says Godfrey. You've crashed the wrong frigging party. There's been no actual fire here.

And who do *you* white-suited weirdos think *you* are?

We are theatrical underwriters, says the weirdo, empowered to wind up this project. We are invested with the right to take full possession of all technical gear, props, and personnel, and to redirect them or return them to source as deemed appropriate.

Then take the effing stuff.

The black suit stands the contentious prop on its end. It teeters for a moment like a wobbly domino. Then, with deliberation, the black suit nudges it in the direction of Godfrey, who sidesteps. The domino crashes to the studio floor with the sort of dull thud a heavily upholstered stick of furniture might make.

Mayhem breaks out.

The white suits are at the throats of the black suits. The black suits are at the throats of the white suits. Faces become bloodied and bruised. Shins, kneecaps, and more suffer trauma. Clipboards, tablets, magnums, props, and camera equipment become airborne. Tripod, theodolite, metal detector, tape measure, and much else find use as weapons. Suits, the garments as opposed to those wearing them, are ripped off torsoes, then shredded and trampled. Suits, those wearing them as opposed to the garments, stand shivering in their smalls.

It is the turn of the party-goers to get caught in crossfire. Owing to their inebriated state, they do not react with the urgency and mindfulness needed to affect a successful retreat from the mayhem. Their helplessness in the chaos brings to mind a windsock in a gale.

Harry is floored by a stray UFO, not one of extraterrestrial origin, and ends up on knees and elbows trying to protect his bloodied head from further blows. Matt and Sticks crawl off the tangled set on all fours, like wild pigs through a thicket of mangrove roots. Chivalrous Timmy helps Sonia and Elena stagger out on feet *sans* the requisite number of shoes.

Izzie remains behind in the melee, relishing the opportunity to demonstrate to the suited yodellers some of the skills he picked up in the US marines.

The set becomes shrouded in darkness, except for the feeble light of the flickering candles. This does not deter the warriors from their honourable missions. The violence may be barely visible, but it has all the audible hallmarks of battle enjoined with vigour.

We decide the better part of valour is discretion. Our exit is unobserved as indeed was our presence throughout.

< <

It was the year of twin scourges: isis and ebola. The year a flight out of Kuala Lumpur traded its tropospheric embrace for that of the Indian ocean.

Worse was to come.

The third Sunday in the eighth month was a day fit for rueing. Those tooled for another age, and with a penchant for grandeur, might have rendered it in full, as 'The Seventeenth Day of August, in the Year of Our Lord 2014'.

In the wee hours of this day, the red steer charged through the factory floor – colloquially known as the Big Top – of Integrated Electronic Imagery, reducing it to a pile of sodden ash and twisted steel. Harry remembered the date because it invoked, among other things, the accursed number seventeen, a number constantly stalking him.

Some weeks after the fateful day, when the traumatized matter inside his skull had come to terms with the passing of a significant phase of his life, the news reached Harry that, against all odds, his insurance claim had been successful. Consequently, the disaster had not adversely affected his personal wealth. His bottom line was secure. The black ink, though late and loath to flow off the nib of the pen, had blotted out the red.

Some said Harry's misfortune and the subsequent insurance windfall had come at an opportune time. The market for electronic bulletin boards had been getting increasingly competitive for some time owing to the assault on it by serious Asian interests. The writing had been on the wall for Integrated Electronic Imagery. Harry had, apparently, done a Mr Polly.

… if one were intent on drawing a parallel between Wells' fey novel and the events befalling Harry more than a century later, one would tend to be drawn to a predictable yet profound conclusion, viz. fiction can sometimes be more potent than truth, especially when it has a mind to morph into truth …

Harry and Sticks made sure their contingent of techies received generous severance payouts over and above their accumulated entitlements. This was not a good time to be looking for a job.

The great Oz mining boom, driver of the cargo cult, had tanked, though nobody was going to be the first to say so. Despite these adverse circumstances Sticks, using her acquired contacts in the non-extractive trades, drummed up a placement for Ramon before she returned to her unfinished business in Malaysia.

So where did this leave Harry?

His contact with Sticks was intermittent, confined to the layovers between episodes of her Asian adventurism. Contact with his son was equally intermittent. These days Timmy spent more and more time with his indulgent grandmother in Bee Street, free from prying parental eyes. Lack of human contact was an issue for Harry, but something else of equal import was missing from his life. For the first time in twenty odd years, Harry was without work responsibilities to crowd his hours. He was in retirement prematurely, and not sure how to handle it.

Day after day he felt the emptiness of his existence close in, as a wolf might on prey whose cover was blown. The interior of his home – frigidly modernist – as impersonal as any 21st century public atrium – as clinical as any padded cell – its svelte surfaces regarding him disdainfully from all sides – seemed hostile to him, especially as much of the time he was its sole occupant. Emoh Ruo was an environment of his and Sticks' own choosing, yet he felt estranged from it.

He found himself dragging his body, weary with boredom, to the other side of town, where he would sit for hours over a cup of coffee in the more empathetic quarters of *La Spag*.

Whereas previously he had been a habitué, now he became entrenched. At his lonely table, night upon night, his bent elbows bookending his steaming brew, the sights and sounds of human activity abroad, he sought solace. Yet even here, solace often avoided him. He was easy prey to the ghosts of his past, ghosts finding his unaccompanied sojourns at *La Spag* an opportunity to torment him.

First ghost was his mother's original sin, her lie bequeathed to him via the benign medium of lullaby. Then followed the concatenation of disasters of which Sonia was root cause. In tandem with these treacheries came his ignominious involvement in the faith of the clap-happy crowd, his abject days as an outcast at university, his slow realization of Matt's unrequited love for him, his uninvited lust for Elena, the advent of the criminal gangs, his many faux deaths, the very real death meted out by accident to one Mark Larker, the final conflagration, &etc.

These traumas may have been in his face, but his triumphs were more reticent, so much so he found it necessary to invoke them. With pride and pleasure he contemplated his bold display of juvenile gamesmanship summoned up in Main Street, his ability to rustle up a ditty at the drop of a hat, his successes in the alternative economy at Porridge realized by way of the cherry bob, the fillip to his self-esteem achieved in the service of Nigel Unthank, the legal battle for the right to intellectual property he won, the technical and commercial success of Integrated Electronic Imagery, the give-and-take cut-and-thrust dynamics of his cherished relationship with Sticks, the birth of his son, the street cred he gleaned following the rout of the criminal gangs, &etc.

He found himself thinking of these events, the traumas and the triumphs, in theatrical terms, made up of scenarios, song, music, dialogue, choreography, and so forth which, in combination, amounted to *Singspielstücke* playing out in his head. He dreamed them up variously under proscenium arch, in the round, and on camera in a studio setting. He even dreamed up events not involving him directly, events in the lives of parties such as Sticks, Elena, and Matt. And of my earthbound personification, Mark Larker.

Pademelons, I know what question hovers on your furry lips. You are about to ask what it was inclined Harry towards theatrical venturism at this time in his life, when by all accounts he had never before felt the irresistible siren call, dormant we are told in all of us, thralling every practicing thespian.

We shall need to track back a tad in time in order to address this question.

<

During one of his lonely drives to *La Spag*, Harry found himself caught up once more in gridlock, Sleek Street's gift that kept on giving. Seeking escape from it, he pulled over at premises that had flashed past his side view on many occasions past and which now promised temporary diversion.

The premises stood out from the sleazy apartment blocks dominating the street. Out front, an ancient melaleuca tree of prodigious size presided over the paddock of organic debris it had shed. The apartment blocks, by contrast, presided over paddocks of crumbling green-painted concrete, once shed as slurry by a mixing machine.

Tired weatherboards told of the age and derelict state of this iconoclastic structure. Duel Janus masks in wooden silhouette told of its former function. It was not easy to imagine it having any viable present-day function.

Harry walked to the solid front door out of antique hardwood, pitted by years of weather. It was locked. Half way along the eastern wall of the building was a high window with a drainpipe alongside. Harry shinnied up and, gripping the sills tenaciously, peered in.

In imagination, and through grimy glass, he saw a palace of sorts, albeit dusty and cobwebbed. Late sunlight, streaming in through an identical window on the opposite wall, revealed a stage with proscenium arch and, facing it, multiple rows of spring-back seats in royal green. Fond childhood memories resurfaced, of a pantomime perhaps, to which his mother would have taken him, not here certainly, but in one of those glittering pleasure palaces in the CBD of the city. For an instant, he imagined he saw, on this moribund stage in Sleek Street, mummers and players plying their craft, and imagined he heard the laughter of a rapt audience responding to them.

Imagined he saw? *Imagined* he heard? Harry would swear he *actually* saw and heard. For him, it was a prescient epiphany.

He lost his grip, and crashed to the hard earth.

>

During his theatrical thought experiments, Harry sat still and silent over coffee, staring into space for hours on end as if catatonic, a lonely recluse at his single table. This worried Bruno, who felt obliged to approach him.

Things alright at home, Harry? he asked.

Uh?

At home. Things alright?

Yes, thank you, Bruno. Things are fine.

You like a grappa with the coffee?

Thank you. But no.

Following this embarrassing tangle with Bruno, Harry always brought a laptop with him. He would open the device up, tickle the keyboard, and in every respect appear to be using it. But nothing was ever written onto its hard disk. It was all pretence. The only activity bearing fruit was the hyperactivity inside his head.

Contemplating his *Stücke* as they made their pilgrimage one by one from the murky depths of his mind to its more cognitively friendly surface, Harry began to anticipate a completed work of thespian artistry, capable of stunning a world hungry for such entertainment, but intended never to be streamed to them.

On a less grandiose plane, thought Harry, it was harmless fun, serving a much-needed cathartic function, an ideal undertaking for a person like himself who was at the loosest of ends. When it was done, he alone would be privy to it, as befitted material of a nature so sensitive and personal. To others it would be as if classified '**ACCESS DENIED**', imprinted only on his, Harry McMinn's, neuronal network.

Little did Harry realize I – Mulki Larka as some choose to call me – the imago whose emergence from the chrysalis was consequent on Mark Larker's untimely death – eking out an eternal stint of omniscient enterprise – in a world outside of time where pademelons play – and hence at a loose end as was Harry – would have access to and moreover would jump at the opportunity to – colonize these *Stücke* for the purposes of my own in-house conception – thereby co-opting the unwitting Harry as my second unit.

If Harry *had* realized, he would have been justified in musing along the lines of, Who the b'Jesus *is* this piratical interloper purporting to inhabit a world beyond the grave?

>

When Harry wound up the theatrical venture he had secretly enacted in his head, there were seventeen *Stücke* in total. They covered his immutable past, up to the brink of his ephemeral present, necessarily stopping short of his unknowable future.

There's the rub. The future may not have been Harry's to know, but it was/is/ever shall be *mine* to know, unconstrained as I am by considerations of time shackling residents of the mortal world. I have the option to take the narrative into the future, rounding things off the way a well-honed work of art should be, for the sake of aesthetics and critical acclaim.

Harry was *compelled* to conclude his story on – another auspicious date – the seventeenth of April 2016. By way of contrast, I am *not* so compelled. But I *am* disinclined to proceed.

Disinclined? Yes ...

... I have mixed feelings, pademelons, about making this excursion into the limitless forecourt of time. My obligation to you is over and I feel to take things further would be to trample on the graves of others.

Nevertheless ...

... though it sits at odds with my better nature, I shall bite the bullet. I shall cobble together an epilogue which, when taken in conjunction with the main body of my presentation, should satisfy aesthetic considerations and perhaps even invite critical acclaim.

As for Harry? We see him puncture the air with his right index finger, to which gesture Bruno responds by organizing another coffee for him.

>

An Epilogue to My Presentation of the Life and Many Deaths of Harry A McMinn Told with Some Reservations by Me, Narrator, to You, Pademelons, Captive as You Are with Me in This Timeless Realm.

My epilogue needs a context. Let me provide it. In the months following the demise of his business interests, Harry A McMinn, at a loose end, completed seventeen *Singspielstücke* in his head. This brought Harry's account of his past life (and many deaths) to a point in time coincident with the then present moment in his mortal affairs. Hard up against the implacable future, he could progress no faster with his theatrics than at the real-time rate of one day's happenings per calendar day. He had necessarily to wait for his future to happen, a future ordained to proceed for him at the speed of growing grass, before he could re-enact it.

But, as I have already made clear, I am in no such way constrained.

Accordingly, I shall dwell on a select bracket of future events shaping Harry's destiny. Events I have an exclusive privilege to see. I do so for the purpose of winding up my presentation to you in accordance with aesthetic criteria. Be warned, pademelons. Aesthetics shall guide not only my choice of happenings to recount, but also the order in which I choose to recount them. Chronology shall not be a consideration for me. If it's chronology you crave, you must consult the sun, moon, and stars.

~

Matt was found by joggers early one morning hanging by his neck from the rafter of a public toilet block on the other side of town from where he was known to work and hang out. Please excuse the unfortunate pun.

Matt was dressed for the occasion in his usual immaculate manner, which included – no prize for guessing – a blue bow tie, only apparent when the noose was removed from his neck.

There were no suspicious circumstances. I marked his passing as he once marked mine and, in doing so, found myself in much the same company round *his* casket.

Did I grieve? you ask. By way of reply, pademelons, I ask *you*, For what? The unfortunate event left him no less accessible to me. No less accessible and no more. Totally inaccessible. So what had changed for me? For what should I mourn if I had lost nothing? For what should I rejoice if I had gained nothing?

However, I *did* share his anguish and his ignominy. The profound anguish that must have driven the poor boy to such extremity, flayed raw some vulnerable feature of my supernal susceptibility. And the squalid ignominy he must have felt as he swung was as much mine as his.

The noose I was unable to share with him.

~

'I kissed her lips, I missed her lips, and found to my surprise/ she was nothing but a pirate ship rigged up in a disguise.' These are lines from the pen of a popular songwriter, circa 1950.

Ramon's naked and mutilated corpse was found in a pool of blood, human blood mixed with dragon's blood, in the Sheridans' greenhouse beneath *Dracaena draco*. He had been stabbed multiple times with pruning shears. Forensics concluded his penis had been severed with the same implement. So had a number of major appendages of the alien plant so much cherished by Mr Sheridan.

The police had been alerted to the homicide by Sonia, who was subsequently arrested. She pleaded guilty by reason of temporary insanity.

Ramon's grieving parents arrived from Argentina, and stayed for the inquest. An unlikely bond was forged between the two pairs of distraught parents, Ramon's and Sonia's. As part of the process of their reconciliation to the unfathomable realities confronting them, they attended mass together, consoling themselves afterwards with a few rubbers of four-handed canasta. After all, the game had its origins in South America.

The good news was *Dracaena draco* made a full recovery over a period of years. As a relieved Mr Sheridan reflected philosophically, time heals all. Mrs Sheridan was much less complaisant. She reflected ruefully that her prayers on Sonia's behalf would have fallen short of saving her daughter's soul even when directed, as they had been, to the Heavenly Host *en masse*.

She made no concurrent intercession on behalf of her husband. She was content with her conviction his soul would and should be dragooned by celestial powers to plumb the depths of hell.

~

Timothy McMinn was able to embark on his career of choice. On the one hand, he considered himself fortunate, and on the other, he considered it his due. He arrived at this golden moment through a convoluted process.

Timmy had been frequenting casinos, necessarily understating his age, for some years prior. His *modus operandi* was to count cards at blackjack tables. Hereditary capabilities meant he was very good at this. He could count successfully even when as many as eight decks were shuffled together.

He became a legend. In no time at all, he was on the black list of every casino in Oz.

But soon after this setback, at the tender age of seventeen, he was approached by the head honcho of a major chain of casinos. By repute, this man was packer[58] of a mean financial punch. He invited Timmy to 'take the floor' as 'scrutineer', to watch over tables for signs of 'incursions', including card counting, designed to target gaming profits.

Nothing avoided Timmy's eyes.

Before long, he found himself scrutinizing the high rollers' tables.

Harry was terrified on Timmy's behalf, aware of the dangers the inevitable corrupt practices could represent for his son. Timmy told his father to go take a powder.

~

Sticks was on a learning curve.

She had discovered that countless micro-economies based on the notorious palm-derived oil thrived in Malaysia. But their activities were no real threat to remnant rainforest. The constituents of these micro-economies were former subsistence farmers who, having struck gold so to speak, were thriving as a consequence. Their small allotments, which formerly grew food for local consumption, now supported a cash crop for export. Certainly, this represented a distortion of the agricultural paradigm, one inimical (perhaps) for communities down the track,

---

58 'packer': intended as an oblique reference to James D Packer, Australian entrepreneur, billionaire, and dabbler in the operational aspects of gaming ventures.

but Sticks decided such a problem lay outside her brief: protecting the natural environment.

Moreover, these small communities, suddenly and unexpectedly finding themselves in the way of good fortune, were like Wild West towns. She was like the ingenuous *hombre*, come all the way from the big smoke, tethering his mount outside the saloon, then venturing inside to partake of a strawberry milkshake. It would have been a serious, possibly fatal, mistake on her part should she stand out in such a community, much less set herself in direct opposition to it. Anyway, such was Baharudin's view, and she was readily persuaded of it.

Consequently, she decided to focus her attack on the multi-nationals busy acquiring, invariably by corrupt means, tracts of thousands of hectares of land cobbled together from individual farming allotments, with a substantial admixture of virgin rainforest. Physical danger was still inherent in this global play, but because her movements and those of the multi-nationals would from the outset attract media scrutiny, her murder – should such an unthinkable act be perpetrated – would be less likely and could never be anonymous. It was not going to happen that (say) her throat was cut by a lone vigilante farmer, her body flung into a disused well, her remains never found much less identified, and all of this without anybody bothering to ask questions.

Instead, should her death in criminal circumstances come about, it would be broadcast to the wide world. Her cause would be writ large and she would be a martyr. Such an outcome, she concluded, was preferable to an anonymous and unheralded death. As a martyr, she would lose the battle, but would strike a blow in the righteous war.

Sticks, as you would be aware, was not inclined to philosophical speculation. So the irony of her position would not have occurred to her: the irony of – in life – preferring a certain mode of despatch, from which – in death – she would be incapable of deriving comfort.

... such is the paradox of martyrdom. The paradox may, of course, be resolved by postulating an afterlife. We, pademelons, must embrace this postulate. Otherwise we jeopardize our very existence ...

By the galloping goitre of my gormless granny, let's get back to Sticks.

This brave eco-warrior, putting aside all terminal scenarios and their hypothetical outcomes, made the wise decision to opt for her first preference: to stay alive in pursuit of her cause.

~

Baharudin became the new Sultan of K. No surprises there.

~

One day, out of the blue, Izzie turned up at Harry's digs. Harry, with nothing more constructive to do, was immersed in, and (predictably) deriving comfort from, Cervantes' illustrious *magnum opus*. Greetings between the two friends – who had been out of touch for many years – were effusive.

They compared notes over cool beers. Harry had little to report beyond his enforced idleness. Izzie, by contrast, had found a group of likeminded musos and, with them, was touring the country doing gigs for the benefit of outback yodellers with spare shekels. By such means, he and his fellow musos had managed to make recalcitrant ends meet.

It was not only news of himself Izzie brought to Harry. He brought news of Elena no less. He and she had been in touch via electronic media since the demise of Harry's business enterprise.

Where is she? asked Harry.

Search me, dude, said Izzie. But she wants to see *you*.

Why me?

That's the question *I* asked her.

So one evening Harry, his dress more swanky than his usual practice would have had it, appeared at *La Spag*, greeting Bruno and Roberto with a friendly wave as his eyes sought out the table at which Elena was waiting. And found it.

Elena rose. She was wearing a close cousin of the two-piece outfit habitually worn years earlier for Baharudin. She knew what worked for her, and it was no longer ethnic blouses.

After the obligatory exchange of embraces, Harry and Elena sat. Elena, her business-like manner a foil for her prodigious beauty, wasted no time getting to the point.

I have good idea for project, she said.

She paused, took a breath.

I'm listening, said Harry.

I need person like you who has knowledge of ropes.

You need a boy scout.

No, Harry. I need skilled person like you, who can pull levers when required.

Not ropes any more. Now it's levers.

Giulietta, arriving with Harry's coffee, put it down, and left discreetly, her eyes lowered.

Is Sal involved? asked Harry

Sal is old man. These days, he is only *tryápochka*[59]. From him, I have taken my freedom. I am my own agent.

Is it legal?

Elena responded with belligerence.

Is *not* illegal to be free! she said.

I mean your proposal to me. Is *it* legal?

Konyéshna. Of course. It is most legal. Do you suggest otherwise?

No, no. I'm sorry. Tell me about it.

Elena proceeded. She told of her idea and of the help, not merely technical but pecuniary, she sought from Harry. As, by degrees, she fleshed out details for his benefit, Harry's eyes widened and he leaned forward in his seat. From the outset he could see her idea had merit. Then, as she progressed further, he

---

59 *tryápochka*: softie.

saw it as ground-breaking, and could not help becoming more and more amazed by what he was hearing. At the finish of her spiel, he was sold. It was an offer too good to refuse. He did not refuse.

Pademelons, excuse me if I choose not to divulge the details to you. My presentation is all but over. What we have here is the start of Harry's brand new life, a second life eminently suitable as a presentation in its own right. Call it a sequel if you will. Perhaps you might name it 'Pademelons Play On' or something along those lines. But I am out of it. It is a sequel upon which one of *you* may choose to embark. It would be unconscionable of me to introduce a spoiler at its moment of conception. The unwritten house rules do not condone such behaviour.

All I shall say is, when Elena had concluded her winning proposal to Harry, Harry was moved to such a degree of enthusiasm she felt obliged to caution him.

Ostorózhno![60] You know there is risk, she said.

Just to breathe is risky.

Elena winked.

Not to breathe is more risky, she said.

Harry relaxed his body, slumped back in his seat, exhaled noisily.

Somebody once remarked, he said, you'd be running the country soon enough.

Who said that?

Matt, I believe.

Then we must honour him by all necessary means.

What means do you mean?

Elena flashed Harry a sly look, and reached across the table to touch his hand.

Don't get hopes up, pal.

Mandated by the conversational drift, silence took over at this point. Elena broke it.

Making Matt's prophecy come true, she said. That's what I'm talking about.

---

60 *Ostorózhno!*: Be careful!

~

I was convinced I had covered all bases in this epilogue to my presentation. Then I remembered Ronnie Dash. How *could* I have overlooked him? He, alone of my protagonists, was not pressed by events to overhaul his life's directions. He was more than content to continue pursuing dalliances with virginal god-bothering damsels. Despite this, or perhaps contingent on it, he was content also to feed his addiction to the services of compliant escorts. Additionally, he continued to enjoy dilettantish adventures into territory usually considered the preserve of salaried scientists. And, of course, he persisted with his predilection for mutilating the lyrics of many a much-loved song.

Pademelons. To conclude my inimitable presentation, I offer you a further, and likely final, sample of such wilful mutilation. Raise *your* glasses to Ronnie as he raises *his* voice to you:

> I'm looking over
> my dead dog, Rover,
> his feet in the air, all four.
> First foot is pleasure.
> The second is pain.
> Third's the old derro[61]
> who pees in the lane.
> Fourth in contention,
> I need not mention's,
> the arsehole we all abhor.
> I'm looking over
> my dead dog, Rover,
> who ain't gonna bark no more.

■

---

61 derro: Australian slang meaning 'derelict person'.

About the Author

The author's main paper qualification is a PhD in photonuclear physics, i.e. nuclear reactions induced by photons, from the University of Melbourne. He has necessarily written a number of scientific papers in this field.

In the 1970s, he wrote a review paper on the subject of Global Atmospheric Consequences of the Combustion of Fossil Fuels, which (as might be imagined) was ground breaking at the time.

His literary accomplishments are a short story published in the Australian literary journal Tabloid Story in the 1970s, and a screenplay funded by Film Victoria in the 1980s but never produced. Where Pademelons Play is his first novel.

www.ingramcontent.com/pod-product-compliance
Lightning Source LLC
Chambersburg PA
CBHW020643110726
47901CB00001B/24